GENTLE
GREAVES

Ernest Raymond

GENTLE
GREAVES

Saturday Review Press

New York

Library of Congress Catalog Card Number: 72-79035

ISBN 0-8415-0173-4

Saturday Review Press
230 Park Avenue
New York, New York 10017

PRINTED IN THE UNITED STATES OF AMERICA

SECOND PRINTING

FOR *Diana Raymond*
and with it
all my love

Every character in this tale is wholly imaginary. It attempts no portrait of any person, public or private, living or dead

CONTENTS

EX UMBRIS

EX UMBRIS

EX UMBRIS

THE HOUSE at the corner of Coburg Square had stood fractured and splintered and derelict since that day in 1940 when the bomb fell in Osgrave Road. The bomb struck the camber of the road at four minutes to eight on a cloudy November night. For some minutes past an enemy aeroplane, its low monotonous song heard easily in the clouds, had been moving in circles, or so it seemed, above this quarter of the Royal Borough of Kensington. Untroubled, apparently, by the maddened and frustrated barking of half the guns of London, it had sung its song ; and whenever for a moment, this monstrous orchestration stopped, the gentle song was still there, trailing after the aeroplane as it weaved its circles in its high, inhuman places.

To those in the corner house, and indeed in all the houses of the square it seemed as if their private chimney stacks pointed straight to the centre of these circles ; but when the first bomb dropped, it fell at a considerable distance away. That was comforting, but the second whistled down a little nearer, as if the aeroplane, singing happily at its work, were aiming truer ; the third shook the whole structure of the world in a neighbouring square ; and the fourth hit the camber of Osgrave Road. And Osgrave Road runs from Warwick Road to the corner of the square, by the side of this house.

Every light in the house went out. The walls cracked, the ceilings fell, the front door blew out on to the steps, and the windows leapt to the pavements, where they added their tinkling treble chord to the last bass arpeggios of the bomb. Four minutes later, a timepiece in one of the darkened rooms, now open to the night, struck eight idiotically.

An old gentleman of seventy-seven, its owner, lived in the house at the time in a ground-floor maisonette, he having announced to the square, and to the uttermost circle of his acquaintance that no enemy should drive him from it ; that he might (in the language of Elizabeth) have the body of a weak and feeble old man, but that he had the heart of an Englishman, and thought foul scorn that any prince of Europe —and still less any paperhanger from Braunau—should drive him from his realm. But the enemy did drive him forth : the bomb sent him out, feet first and protesting blasphemously, on the stretcher of an ambulance. He had been sitting erect in his deep chair, rejoicing, exulting, in the guns of his beloved London, and in their mighty and multitudinous defiance ; he had risen to meet the bomb like a gentleman ; and a heavy fragment of the ceiling had struck him down where he stood. The ambulance carried him to the hospital, where a few days later he died, proud that, if he had to die, it had been by enemy action ' like our boys.'

And the house stood empty. Nightly thereafter the lightning of the gun-flashes illuminated its bare and broken rooms, and the drum-fire kept its sashes quivering. In the daytime it was visited only by the dust and the wind and a few of the dead leaves from the garden in the square. The leaves lost themselves in its large rooms ; and so at times, did the wind. Men came and nailed black tarred-paper to the unglazed windows, but the passing seasons rent this sober covering so that it hung about the house like the rags of an outcast.

For more than five years the house remained as blind and insensitive to the marching events as it was to summer sun or winter gale, to the brilliance of noonday or the deep dark of night. It apprehended nothing of the armies assembling in London or of their departure and invasion of the continents ; it felt nothing when the flying bombs shot desperately into the Earls Court and Kensington streets as the continent of Europe fell ; it put out no flags on Victory Night, except the old black rags in its windows, which, to be sure, fluttered a little in the peace-charmed air.

The four houses on its left (there were none on its right, since it was the corner house) were in similar case ; for, after all, it was only one of ten thousand houses struck blind and dumb in those violent years. Like it, and like Man's reason for a time, they were left to fust unused, their concrete fallen in chunks, their stucco pealing and pendent, and the black rags flapping in their windows.

It was a tall and pompous house, No. 1 Coburg Square, and one of fifty such that stood around the London garden. Five stories high, if you include the basement, it was built of white mansion brick, with stucco architraves about the windows ; and it had a balustraded parapet along the sky, and a balustraded balcony above the Corinthian portico, beneath which eight stone steps descended with dignity (or did heretofore) to the area railings and the pavement. The long rectangular garden behind met the long rectangular garden of a house in Warwick Road.

This back garden was on a level with the pavement in front, so, if you have the picture aright, you will see that, besides the area in front there was a well at the back, and the tall houses stood, as it were, ankle deep in a concrete tank between pavement and garden.

Fifteen houses in the square were blasted and left lifeless by the bombs ; but all the rest were inhabited. These had long ceased, however, to be occupied as single homes, well staffed with servants ; they were now converted into maisonettes, flatlets, service rooms, or boarding houses. A few of the maisonettes were the homes of the well-to-do ; but for the most part the poor, or, at any rate, the unprosperous, had inherited the Corinthian columns, the balustrades, and the big lofty rooms. But this meant that the inhabited houses were full of life ; indeed throughout the years of war Coburg Square was an assembly of quick and dead houses, the former quick with the life of children, the latter a happy row of targets for the same children, since if a window pane is gashed, or its paper substitute is rent, it is legitimate to extend the lesions. The children even penetrated into some of the lifeless houses, like the dust and the mice which had gone before them ; but they made no entry into No. 1, because its lower windows were boarded up and its broad front door secured by a rusting padlock.

The children of 1940 grew from ten and eleven to fifteen and sixteen, and the house remained the same. They did not know, as it looked blindly down upon them, that it had been bought at the war's close by a new owner. They did not see, on a winter afternoon, two people, both hatless, standing before the house and gazing up at it. The one was an elderly man, tall and slender, with a straight-featured, clean-shaven face, and hair of the whitest silk. He wore a well-cut grey overcoat and carried a well-rolled umbrella, now at the trail, now in both hands behind his back. Had the children watched him, they might have noticed that he walked with a barely perceptible limp, as if his left foot were in a shoe and his right in a slipper. This would have interested them. The other figure was that of a young woman, thirty perhaps, nearly as tall as he but less slight, and of rather masculine features and habit, with her green tweed suit, high-collared shirt, thick stockings and low-heeled brogue shoes. She might have been his daughter, niece, secretary or young wife.

As they looked up at the tattered windows the man breathed a half-humorous sigh. ' Well, well, well . . .'

' But will it ever be any good again ? ' asked the young woman. ' Can anyone really live in it again ? '

' Of course,' he affirmed. ' Why not ? Its heart is sound.'
And again he gazed up at it and murmured, ' Well, well well . . .'

There was no doubt that the man was looking longer at it
than the young woman, as if his interest were deeper. While
she turned to look at the garden in the midst of the square, he
didn't seem able to take his eyes from the house. He stared and
stared at the first floor window. ' That was the playroom,' he
said ; but she didn't hear him. He walked up the front steps,
lifted the padlock on the door and peered through the coloured
panes. ' No good,' he announced. ' A pity, because I should
like to have seen the stairs.' For a while he looked down into
the area and especially at the door of the coal cellar under the
pavement. And he smiled somewhat wistfully again. Then he
came down the steps and turned the corner into Osgrave Road
and looked at the high garden wall. It was a long grey wall
with shards of inhospitable glass on its coping, to protect the
privacy of the garden. He tried the door in the wall, but it
was locked. He stepped on to the roadway and stared up at
the high back of the house—stared as if time were nothing.
Perhaps, now and again, a face of long ago appeared for him
at a window.

The girl joined him on the road and asked him what he was
thinking of.

' Of many things that I've always remembered,' he said,
' and quite a few that I had forgotten.'

And he smiled to himself rather sadly, nodded his head, and
murmured, ' Well . . . there it is, Roberta, my dear . . .'

Then back to the corner of the square, and he was gazing at
the garden in its midst.

' Fancy that being the garden,' he said.

No railings were round it now ; only the stone base which
had supported them, and the border of privets which the children
had parted and torn. Nearly all the grass was worn away,
and the grey earth humped itself over the roof of an underground
air-raid shelter. In the far corner was an Emergency Water
Tank of the National Fire Service, now drained and rusty.
November hazed the garden, and the lofty trees and the low
shrubs were bare ; but he looked at their London-black skeletons,
turning his eyes from one to another, as if he could give a name
to each and dress them in their summer leaves : chestnut and
poplar ; willow and plane ; lilac, laburnum, and thorn. He
stared for a very long time at an iron seat, listing and rusty,
under the bones of the lilac tree.

At last, since one cannot stand and dream for ever, he said,
' Well . . . there it all is. . . . Come along, Roberta.' And

the two visitors walked away together, he with his umbrella
held in both hands behind his back, and his right foot slightly
dragging, she with her fingers slipped into his arm.

§

Then the spring of 1946, all silver and golden light, broke
like a salute of trumpets over the square ; and the trees and
shrubs became what he had seen : they became domes and
globes of gentle verdure.   The sunlight twinkled in the fanning
leaves of the poplar and lay in chequered patches, like fallen
leaves of light, beneath the sober and unwinking plane.   Blue
shadows bestrewed themselves on the trodden earth, and the
willow, above its own blue shadow, hung out its first yellow
tresses, which quickly flushed into green.
   And as the life ran with all this zest up the trees, an escalade
of steel scaffolding ran up the face of No. 1 ; and ladders and
ropes ran up the scaffolding ; and builders and painters ran
up the—no, let me not lie—builders and painters went leisurely
up the ladders or up the staircase of the now opened house.
They went in obedience to a notice nailed to the front door :
' DANGEROUS STRUCTURES,' it said.   ' To the Owner
and Occupier of the structure known as 1, Coburg Square in
the Royal Borough of Kensington in the County of London.
It having been made known and represented to the London
County Council that the said structure is in a dangerous state
. . . the said council does by this notice require you forthwith
to take down repair or otherwise secure portions of front wall
where cracked sunken loose defective insufficiently supported by
rotten bressummer or otherwise insecure——'
   But the rest was torn away.
   Within the house the builders and joiners removed the party
walls which had converted it into maisonettes ; and the house
was single and whole again.   Outside, the painters painted the
stucco a cream-white and the window frames a decent black,
and the broad front door a fresh and glistening green ; and
the house was brightly alive again.   The only trace of its recent
decrepitude was a baluster missing, like a lost front tooth, from
the parapet under the sky.
   The children watched the work daily, for there was excitement
in the square at this rejuvenation and embellishment of No. 1.
Stories ran from door to door and from area gate to area gate.
The adults told one another that the new owner was Sir Theodore Allan Mourne ; that he was a book publisher and therefore

a man of wealth ; and that he was going to occupy the house himself, now that the war was over, and the young men home, and he could retire from an active part in his business ; but why, they asked, did he come to this house, why spend all that money on such an old-fashioned place, why come to Coburg Square which had never, even in its best days, been a really fashionable quarter and was certainly not fashionable now ? The children flew much higher with their stories ; they visited the stratosphere. Mightily impressed with the fact that he was a " Sir," they told each other that he was a hugely famous man, that he had been knighted by the King, that he was spending thousands on the house, and that he was probably a millionaire.

They stood around in ever increasing numbers on the day when the famous man's furniture was moved in. Some of it was large enough, or handsome enough, or curious enough, to compel their silent wonder. There was a long mahogany side-board table with scrolled legs, each leg topped by a grotesque mask. There was an enormous mahogany dining-table which went into the house in three parts : two semicircular and one oblong. There was a mahogany writing desk with a top like a skating rink. And there were bookshelves, bookshelves, book-shelves, in units so many that it passed the wit of children to number them.

And now they noticed for the first time a tall slender man with white silken hair ; dressed in a grey suit, and carrying an umbrella at the trail. He had suddenly appeared from nowhere, and they noticed him because he was noticing them : he was standing by the pantechnicon and looking down upon them with a pleased smile. And since the removal men began to ask his instructions, and he to give them orders in his quiet voice, they whispered to one another that this was He. And they stared at a millionaire. Perceiving that he dragged ever so slightly his right foot, they debated whether or not he was lame. With him was a tall woman with a much louder voice who issued commands too, and ran in and out of the house. They could not think of this brisk, loud-voiced, managing person as either young enough to be anyone's daughter or old enough to be the wife of a man with white hair, so they did not know at all who she was. They were surprised when the white-haired man called her ' Roberta darling,' and when she slipped her hand into his arm, as he went, with a last smile at the children, into the house.

But in a very few days all the women in the square knew who she was. They had heard that she was his adopted daughter and that the new inhabitants of No. 1 were Sir Theodore, this adopted daughter, a manservant who had been with him since the first world war and still referred to him as The Major, and this manservant's wife, Mrs. Bradford, who did the cooking. There were no other resident servants, and the adopted daughter did much of the housework herself. Evidently they were not all that rich after all. Mrs. Bradford was the women's chief informer. ' Yes, Miss Roberta's mother died when she was born, poor mite,' Mrs. Bradford would say ; she was a long, grey woman, three inches taller than her husband ; but she had a kind, motherly heart, even if she looked like a retired grenadier. ' Her granny looked after the wee thing while her father was at the war—the first war, you see, not this last one. He was killed in the Battle of the Somme, and then she didn't have nobody, poor chick. He was a doctor, her real father ; and she was called Roberta after him. Yes, Dr. Robert Drury, his name was, or Captain Robert Drury, when he was killed ; and of course she was Roberta Drury to begin with, but she goes by the name of her adopted father now—Roberta Allan Mourne. Yes Allan Mourne's a surname : a kind'a double surname. They're a good family, you see. Well, the granny was an old lady, and she died soon after the Major and Mr. Bradford got back from the army. The Major had his mother and sister and his old father living with him then ; and he adopted Miss Roberta straight away, because she was his god-daughter, and he and Miss Connie, his sister, and Miss Roberta's mother had been like one family when they were children. He and Miss Connie and Miss Roberta's mother were cousins, but more like brother and sisters, as far as I can make out. I went myself with him to fetch the poor little mite from her granny's home. Five years old, she was then ; and a sweet little thing. It was one of the best things he ever done for himself, I always say, when he adopted Miss Roberta, because she's all he's got now. Mr. Hugh, his only son, was killed quite early in the war—*his* war, you see. He was an air-gunner in one of them big bombers, and crashed somewhere in Germany ; and the Major's never been quite the same since. You know how it is. Miss Roberta's been a real comfort to him, I'm sure, and he's loved her quite as much as if she was his own daughter.'

In reply the women maintained that they weren't at all surprised to hear she wasn't his daughter. She wasn't really a bit like him, they said, except in being tall ; not half as good-looking, if you asked them ; all right as far as she went, but ordinary ; not distinguished-looking like him. Probably the doctor, her real father, was a less gentleman-like type, less refined altogether—was that it ?

'Yes, you're just about right there,' said Mrs. Bradford with knowing nods. 'If you ask me the Major's been a better father to her than ever her real father would'a been. From all I can make out Doctor Drury was no better than he ought'a been. It's an awful thing to say but I've a fancy his death in the war was a good riddance. He bullied his wife when she was alive, and married another when she was only six months dead, and as like as not he'd 'a bullied his child too, when he come home. I don't think there was much good to Doctor Robert Drury. But there you are : I don't really know : it's only what I've heard.'

§

The tall, hatless, white-haired figure of Sir Theodore was an object of curiosity to the women for many days. They would watch him from their windows as he set out in the morning with a shopping basket on his left arm and the rolled umbrella in his right hand, carried at the trail. If it was a day of heavy shopping, he would drag behind him a wheeled shopping basket and return into the quiet square, the vessel heaped to the brim with loaves, lettuces, onions, spring greens, kitchen powders and soaps ; for there were no deliveries from the shops in those stripped and naked days. Sometimes in Earls Court Road they would see him standing in a queue outside the green-grocer's or the fishmonger's and reading *The Times* through his looped pince-nez as he waited his turn to buy. They observed him because his small white head, uncovered, was always above the heads of the chattering women.

One Saturday afternoon when the children were at play in the ruined garden he came across the road to the border of privets and stood watching them. May with its full-grown sunlight was in the garden, and it had burnished the leaves and died the trodden earth to the tint of putty. The trees were loud with spring birds, but not so loud as this lean play-ground with the shouting of children at their cricket. For a while he watched them with a smile, standing behind the privet ; then came through the ragged hedge and stood like a spectator on the field. The ball bounced his way and he picked it up and tossed it back to the bowler. This was enough : he was now one of the bowler's team, fielding or catching the ball in his turn. Nay, I will say he was now the captain because he was instructing the children in certain rules of the game, of which hitherto they had not been cognizant. 'At least that was the rule when I was a boy,' he would say with a twinkle ; and the polite children hid the fact that they found it difficult to imagine this quiet, white-haired man as a boy. But he was amusing. If he muffed his catch and dropped the ball, he addressed himself as 'Butterfingers.' If he failed to stop his ball and it ran past him, he turned and ran after it ; and they laughed loudly because it was so funny to see him running like one of them. One delighted little girl, chasing the ball at his side, fell with a crash ; and he picked her up, exclaiming, ' Oh, my darling ! ' just as if she were his own child.

But after about half-an-hour of this, his susceptibility to abstraction increased, so that his misses were more frequent, to the vast entertainment of the children ; and at last, having achieved a successful catch and earned some applause, he asked them, ' Will you forgive me if I go now ? ' and those whom he could not see smiled at such courtesy. They suffered him to go, but with protests and lamentations ; and he walked towards the privets—but paused to gaze for a long spell at the crazy iron seat under the lilac.

Then, his hands clasping each other behind his back, he passed through the privets and out of the square.

Immediately one of the boys, a leader of men, thrust the ball into his pocket, cried ' Come on ! ' in a mysterious whisper, and led those who would follow him after Sir Theodore. He liked to pretend that the new owner of No. 1 was a Mystery, with a Secret Occupation somewhere ; and that now they were stalking him to his lair. Three other children joined him in this Red Indian game : two boys and a girl ; and they crept after Sir Theodore, fifty yards behind, on tiptoe.

They followed him along Warwick Road, past its sad, discoloured houses. He crossed Old Brompton Road ; and they came after. On the far side of the road, beyond the traffic, stretched the procession of grey arches which was the sombre wall of Brompton Cemetery. Through the arches you could see the old tombs and headstones and monuments in a lake of wild grasses, and the white cow-parsley and golden ragwort that grew tall and flourished among the dead. In the centre of the wall stood the massive Roman gateway which you might liken to the gatehouse of a prison or to a triumphal arch, according to the faith which is in you. Sir Theodore passed through the gates. The children, their voices hushed by those heavy gates, crept after him and saw his lonely figure walking up the broad avenue between the limes. It was easy to keep him in view now, because the avenue ran straight as a processional way to the domed chapel in the far-off and shimmering gaze.

The avenue of limes was also an avenue of tombs. Mausoleums, sculptured angels, high-based urns, countless tall crosses, in white marble, grey stone or red granite, faced that processional route from their stations behind the limes. Many of the angels had stood at this duty so long that their full-bosomed bodies were draped in creepers as well as in stone. Some of them pointed upward as Sir Theodore passed by.

It was very quiet in the deep of the cemetery; so quiet that the senses of even London children were set free to hear the call of a chaffinch, the chirping of the sparrows, and the clipping of a gardener's shears; and to smell the scent of cut flowers and the honeyed fragrance dropping from the sun-drenched limes. It was the silence of a hundred thousand sleepers.

' From Shadows and Fancies to the Truth.' The children had not observed this inscription over the door of a mausoleum; but Sir Theodore had glanced at it, as he always did, because it crowned the last bedchamber of an old actor and his wife, who had been greatly celebrated in his youth. ' From Shadows and Fancies to the Truth . . .' *Ex umbris et imaginibus in veritatem.*

In veritatem? Perhaps. Only perhaps.

For a quarter of a mile he walked up the avenue, musing on the proud and opulent epoch that lay buried around him. Far in front, hand in hand, a young couple strolled along, pausing sometimes to heed an inscription; and he thought of the thick, curtaining mist that lay between them and the old century in which these actors, officers, Q.C.'s, stout merchants and fine ladies had worked and wantoned and sinned. It was a mist through which they could see so little, but he could pass through it and visit that world again because he had lived in it as a child.

Suddenly his meditations were startled by a distant roar. It was a roar in unison from many thousand throats. Hitherto there had been but an undulating murmur in the direction whence it came, but now, abruptly, it had leapt into an immense hurrah that filled that corner of the sky. Ah, yes—he remembered; over against the far end of the cemetery was the Chelsea Football Ground; and this was a Saturday afternoon. So near were the quick and the dead, the clamour of to-day and the silence of yesterday.

He turned from the path on to the grass; and, some way behind, the children halted. He walked between the graves to one in the third row, a white grave with a plain marble cross ; and here, unaware of his young watchers, he stood at the grave's foot, looking first upon the inscription, and then upon the earth beneath.

In Loving Memory
of
KINGSLEY ALLAN MOURNE
Major General
Queen's Royal Worcester Regiment
Born Nov. 2nd 1834   Died Jan. 31st 1922

At last he left this grave and threaded his way between the white rows to a portion of the cemetery nearer the football ground.   Somewhat less expensive, less fashionable, this corner of the city ; and the grass, unscythed, swept up to the graves with its wild flowers and swirled around them.   But the graves themselves were well tended and trimmed, not old enough yet to be forgotten.   Here in the heart of this rank and seeding earth he stopped at the foot of a grave with a plain but neat headstone.   And he looked down at its inscription and at the cut turf—long indeed at the turf, before lifting his eyes to the inscription again.

GENTLE MARY GREAVES
Wife of Robert MacShennan Drury
———
April 20th, 1915
———

And this is what he was saying within himself, this is what he was trying to realise and possess as he said it, his eyes upon the turf : ' You are here, Gentle.   You are not five feet from me.   I am close to you again—as close as I can get now.   For thirty years the earth under the rain has been settling down upon you.   It is bright sunlight to-day, but the sunlight cannot reach you ; and I am standing in it still.   Are you there, Gentle ? '   He tried to believe that her spirit must be very close to him, but he felt nothing near him, nothing approaching his shoulder ; only the sweet sadness within him, like a hand gently holding his heart.   He heard nothing, except another sudden roar from the football ground.   ' Never any more, I suppose, Gentle dear.   That, I must believe, is the truth.   I'm afraid I've only a little hope of a hereafter.   *In veritatem*, perhaps, but, more likely, into the dark.   This is as close as I can get to you now, and as close, maybe, as I shall ever get.'   He stepped an inch closer. ' Well, one accepts . . .'

But one does not accept. His next words belied the statement. 'Shall I ever find you again? It is impossible that I
should not. Never find you again—oh, no! If you can hear
me anywhere, my dear, I love you still.' One can say such
things when no one listens but oneself. 'I love you as I always
did, and as I shall forever. If there is any meaning in the
universe, God bless you and keep you for me.'

Well, one could not stay here for ever, though it was hard
to turn away. He turned and walked through other graves
back towards the broad straight avenue and the way home.

Meanwhile the children had been standing around the first
grave he had visited, telling themselves that this Kingsley Allan
Mourne, a Major-General, must have been his father; they
had waited there while he stood, as in a dream or trance, before
the further grave; and one of the girls, embarrassed by the
long wait, had begun to giggle. But now they saw him leaving
it, and as soon as it was safe they hurried towards its headstone,
leaping over the corners of the graves. They stood where he
had stood and read the inscription, but could guess nothing
from it. Only the name pleased them : 'Gentle Mary Greaves.'
It pleased them with its music; it rang in their heads, so that
they chanted it like a song, as they returned along the avenue
behind the distant figure of Sir Theodore. 'Gentle Mary
Greaves one day . . .' The words put a rhythm into their
feet, and they danced sometimes as they sang them together.
'Gentle Mary Greaves one day . . . Went about gathering
nuts in May . . .'

§

Behind the first-floor windows of the house, while the square
was quiet because the children were at school and the women
at the shops, Sir Theodore sat writing. He sat writing in his
study at the great mahogany desk with a top like a skating
rink. And these were the words he had written so far.

'To-day is the 20th June, 1946, and I have been in this house
nearly two months now. Or I should say I have been back
in it nearly two months, because I have lived in it before. Here,
half a century ago, my childhood was spent with my father and
mother, and my sister, Constance; and if I think of one place
more than another as home, it is this. I left it when I was
seventeen, and then it was Gentle's home for a few years, and
I used to come and see her here. Because of my childhood,
because of my father—yes, chiefly, I think, because of him—
and because of Gentle, no house in the world has the same

place in my memory I wonder how often, in the fifty years during which I have been away from it, I have dreamed that I was a child in its rooms again with Con or Gentle or my father. Seldom have I been able, when I found myself in Earls Court or Brompton, to resist an urge to come and look at it, and to wonder who was in its rooms now ; and some dozen years ago the idea came upon me that when I retired from business I might come and live here again. At first I treated this notion as an idle fancy, but in 1940 a bomb fell and changed the fancy into a mastering whim. The house had been converted into three maisonettes then but the tenants of two of them had fled from the nightly air-raids and only the ground floor was occupied by the old man who owned the house and scorned to fly. He died from the effects of the bomb ; the house came on the market ; and the whim became the complete master of my will. I bought it.

'I was nearly sixty then, and I told myself that when my boy came home from the war—or rather, if God was good, and he came home—I would retire at sixty-five and live quietly in the old place, doing only a little reading and advising for the firm. It did not please God to let the boy come back to me ; but I was tired, so the task which I had designed for him I laid in other hands, and came here to rest. I obeyed the ancient call—the call that comes to all of us from places we have known as children : 'Come you back ; come you back and look on us again.' Why not obey it? Why not indulge the whim when one was nearing one's span and soon would not be able to enjoy the quaint savours of life any more ?

'But directly I was in the house every room, every door, every staircase flight—day after day—stirred a new memory that had been asleep for fifty years ; now one wall and now another would slip a memory into my hand as I passed ; and since one is always lonely in retirement, and one's time is empty, I decided to amuse myself trying to re-create all the things that had been, and that had such magic for me now, by writing them down. I foresaw an extraordinary happiness in thus re-creating the past ; and indeed it is proving as happy an employment as I have known for years. It has been extraordinary to stand in the rooms and let the present fade from them and the past come into them again. I declare that once or twice the past has seemed so real that I have felt like a ghostly and unseen spectator from the future standing among people who were still alive, and watching their games, their tears, their love making, and at times their shame. It has been strange to stand at the window and look out upon the garden in the square as it is now, a sacrifice to the King's enemies, and then to come away from the window and walk in it as it used to be, among the children at play on its enclosed and quiet lawns.

' I do not yet know for whom I am writing these pages. Sometimes I think I am writing them for my own pleasure and no one else's ; sometimes I think that, when they are complete, I shall give them to Roberta to read. They would tell her things which she has a right to know and which so far I have been far too shy to tell her, face to face. They would tell her everything about Gentle, her mother. But I wonder. If I tell the full truth as I want to, and as I must if I am not to lose all wish to write, dare I show it to her ? I do not know. Not yet. I shall write on, and perhaps as I write the answer to this question will become clear to me.

' Can it be fifty-seven years ago since that May afternoon when Con and I first ran up the steps of this house ? . . .'

§

Fifteen months afterwards, in the fall of 1947, the word ran about the square : ' He is dying ! ' Each person asked the next : ' Have you heard ? Old Sir Theodore Allan Mourne is dying.' They had heard it, those who possessed this exciting information, from Mrs. Bradford, or her husband, or the milk roundsman. Soon all knew it and looked with interest at the doctor's car before the door, the nurses coming and going, and the light in the windows of the second-floor room where he lay. And as one day followed another they gathered further information from Mrs. Bradford at her area gate or in the queues before the shops. ' Yes, he's going,' she said, with a sad shake of her head and a moistening of the eyes. ' He was taken suddenly bad in his study. He was standing by his desk when it come upon him—an awful pain like a screw twisting up his heart, he said. He couldn't move. I was passing his door and heard him call Miss Roberta—but so low that I wasn't sure I'd heard aright. " Roberta ! Roberta ! "—just like that. Just a whisper. I went in and saw him standing there with his hand clenched tight and pressing against his heart. And he was panting. I couldn't get him to move, and I thought at first he was kind'a paralysed. But he got a little better and Miss Roberta and I helped him up to his bed. We got the doctor to him, and the doctor insisted he must have a nurse night and day. They keep him absolutely still, but Nurse Mayer says it's only a matter of time. Of hours, she says.

She's a nice creature. Yes, he's passing on . . . and he was the best master ever. Mr. Bradford is taking it very badly. They were more like two friends than a master and servant, having been in the war together, if you see what I mean. Miss Roberta won't believe that he's dying. I mean she *can't* believe it—he's been more like a father to her than ever her real father would'a been. No, she don't believe it, but '—and again Mrs. Bradford shook her head sadly—' *he* knows. You can see it in his eyes.'

Yes, he knew. Lying within that house, behind those second-floor windows, he recalled again and again—what else could be of such interest ?—the onset of his agony and the instant knowledge that came with it : ' This is death. This is It.' It was a moment of the strangest quality, blending anguish, terror, wonder, interest and a great hope. The doctor might attempt some comfort, saying : ' There's always a chance. I know plenty of men of your age who've recovered from this and are playing as good a game of golf as ever,' but Sir Theodore could only smile, for he had known from the first moment of the seizure that he was going to die. And on the second evening, the doctor having gone, and Roberta having taken the day nurse's place, he turned his eyes towards her and thought, ' If I am to say anything to her, I must say it soon. At any moment it may be too late. Shall I say it or not ? ' And after a while he said ' Roberta.'

She came to the bedside. ' Yes, darling ? '

' I don't quite know what to do. I'm hesitating.'

' About what, my dear ? '

' There is something—there are many things—I have been too cowardly so far to tell you—or perhaps too wise. I don't know.'

' What are they ? ' She laid her fingers in affection upon the back of his hand where it rested upon the coverlet. ' Tell me.'

With his other hand he gathered up hers. ' If I've been too weak morally to tell you before, I'm too weak physically now. It's a very long story. But, Roberta——'

' You're going to get well again——'

' But, in case I don't . . . in case I don't. . . . Roberta, do you know what I've been doing sometimes—often—when I've been shut up in my room ? '

' No.'

' I've been writing the long, full story of many things that happened in the past. And I wrote as far as I shall ever write some three or four weeks ago. And not once when I was writing did I know for certain whether I was going to show it to you or anyone else.   I don't even know now.'

As he said this the privacy of the room, and of their talk together, seemed enhanced by the shrill voices of the children in the garden and the long sighs of the traffic in Earls Court and Brompton Roads, which were low and subdued like the sighs of a lapping sea.   Something heavy grumbled along Warwick Road, so that the house shuddered and the windows quivered ;   but its passage was a remote affair ;   it was as nothing.

' Why don't you want to show it to me ? '

' Because there are things in it that might hurt you . . a little.'

' I can bear them.'

' Would you like to read it ? '

' Yes.   Yes, of course I would.'

' There's much in it about your mother. . . . About Gentle, your mother.'

' Oh, *is* there ?   *And* my father ? '

' Yes.   Yes, indeed.   A lot about your father.'

' Oh, let me read it.   *Please.*'

' I suppose the fact that I've told you all this means that you must know the rest.'   He paused for a moment more and then told her where the manuscript was to be found—in a drawer of his great desk.   ' Go and read it, and, darling, don't come back till you have finished it.   I'm afraid you'll find in it much to forgive.   Whether or not you ever show it to anyone else is for you to say.   The secrets are yours.   There now.   Go and read it.   My boats are burnt.   But don't—don't come back till you have read it all.'

Roberta smiled, touched his hand again with the tips of her fingers, and went.   And when he was sure she must be reading the long script, he lay, as it were reading it with her ;   for he knew how it went, page by page, scene by scene.   A slight sweat broke upon his brow, and his fingers played upon the coverlet in some anxiety, some fear, as he surmised that she was now at such-and-such a scene.   And each time the hand rose in a gesture of acceptance.

But Roberta, who had found the heaped manuscript and taken it up to her room above his, was reading it, rapt by every page.   How was it possible that she should put down these pages which spoke about her mother as a child and her Aunt Constance as a child and Sir Theodore as a child—in this very house—in this very room ?   She read on and on.   The night fell about her, the voices in the streets died, the murmur of surrounding traffic ceased for long spells; and she undressed and, getting into bed, read with the lamp at her side and her arm on the pillow.

Till midnight and after the people in the square saw the light behind her windows, high up and dull gold in the indigo dark. Then the square slept, but the light was still there for any to see who might wake and come to a window. A man and his wife, returning from a dance at three o'clock, saw it and wondered what it meant. Had old Sir Theodore died? A policeman on his rounds mused upon it at four o'clock when the night was nearing its end. And up there, at that time, Roberta's heart was beating wildly as she read, for she saw, she guessed, the revelation that was coming.

It was the first twilight of morning, and the birds were astir, when she read the last words. She closed the pages slowly, her eyes alight, her breast lifting, because a happiness at her heart was greater, for the moment, than her anxiety. Her seizure of happiness had been an experience not wholly unlike the sudden physical pain which had gripped the heart of Sir Theodore three days before. Rising, she carried her joy to the window and looked out at the dawn. The birds in the branches were singing cheerfully now, each reading his ancient score on the new-lit page of the sky. Their songs gave a voice to her joy. Certain lifelong disappointments, of which she had never spoken, were healed this morning; and, could she have seen herself, she would have observed a new carriage of her head and shoulders as if she had drunk deep of summer air and sunshine. London lay before her, asleep and unheeding; and she could not hold back from it the childish words which had sprung to her lips. 'Oh, I am happy. . . . Oh, Mother, Mother, I never knew. . . . And my father, my father . . . why did I never know?'

The lively memory of all she had read drove her from the room. Wrapping her dressing gown around her, she went down the stairs of the silent house, now pale with morning. She walked into her father's study and gazed at it; into the drawing room and looked from the window at the side door in the garden wall; down the last flight of stairs, considering them; and into the hall where she looked long at the small door which led into the garden. Its upper half was still a frosted window, in a framework of red and orange panes.

Constrained to share her happiness and her interest, she ran up the stairs again and very quietly opened a little way the door of Sir Theodore's room. Peeping in, she saw by the brightening daylight that he was awake and that his eyes had turned towards the sound. His hands were still upon the coverlet, as if they had not moved since she left him ten hours before. The night nurse sat in a deep chair, her hands upon her lap, waiting for her release.

' Oh, nurse, may I speak to my father alone . . . please ? '

' Why, certainly, dear,' said the nurse and went from the room.

Instantly Roberta ran to the bedside, knelt there, picked up one of his hands and exclaimed, ' Oh, I'm so happy.'

' Happy ? '

' Yes, everything that I've read has made me happier than I've ever been. Oh, the more I think of it, the happier I am. It is so. Truly, truly.'

' That is good.'

She bent her head and pressed her lips hard upon the back of his hand, as if this were the only way to say something that could not be said aloud.

In gratitude, and in humorous imitation, he carried her hand to his own lips. ' And you forgive us all ? ' he asked.

' My dear, I understand everything that happened. I understand it perfectly.'

' And nothing hurt you too much ? '

' Only my darling mother's death. I wish I had known her. I love her so now. I think she was lovely.'

' So did I.'

' Some people said such different things about her. I've always understood that Grandmama Greaves used to suggest that she'd died because she didn't want to live any longer.'

' Grandmama Greaves was a fool.'

' She used to say that she'd died of a broken heart. That made her seem a rather weak and ineffectual person who abandoned life too easily.'

' Gentle didn't abandon life. It was taken from her.'

' Oh no, you mustn't say that. You've made it all so perfectly clear. . . . And he——' she paused before speaking the name—' Robert—Grandmama Greaves always implied that he was just a drunkard and a bully.'

He stared at her, rather as if he were staring at the man to whom she referred ; then said quietly, like one who pronounces a verdict, ' He wasn't bad.'

' No—not bad at all. You've made it so clear.'

' Your grandmother Greaves never forgave him for marrying again so soon. She didn't know the reason why.'

' No, of course not. Oh, I wish I had known all this years and years ago. Do you think I shall meet her one day ? '

' Who ? '

' Mother.'

At this he smiled. ' That's almost the very question I was going to ask you. I've been lying here wondering and wondering, just as I have wondered, off and on, for thirty years. What do you really think, Roberta ? I am old and was brought up in a sentimental age. You are terribly severe and sane. Do you think there's any hope we shall see again the people we've loved ? I'm afraid I can't say I believe it. I hope ; that's all. And it's only a poor little undersized hope, cast out much of the time—a frail thing. And yet—do you know, Roberta, I've had a happy life on the whole, and yet I've always been ready to die because of that frail hope. It has made death quite exciting. What is your answer ? What do you think is the truth ? '

' My dear, I can only say the same as you. I don't believe ; I only hope.'

' Well, I shall know very soon now. Very soon.'

They talked thus together for an hour, and later again that day ; and were as happy as might be, for, thanks to the doctor's drugs, the patient was without pain. It was, in truth, one of the happiest days they had known, since there is no happiness quite like that which rises from a new mutual understanding and affection. And this, as Sir Theodore had said, was good ; because it was his last day in the world. In the evening, about five o'clock the same driving pain in the breast, the same terror of the coming nothingness, the same tiny but brilliant wonder, lifted him up in the bed before her eyes ; and he cried ' Roberta ' in a voice that was no more than a gasp ; and she ran to him, and he took her hand in fumbling fingers, while she gently laid him back upon the pillow. Now, holding her hand in a convulsive grasp and looking towards her face, he tried to smile as she laid her hand on his forehead and said ' Darling ' ; he pressed her hand more than once in affection and farewell ; and so passed from her to the void—or to the answer.

§

For some time she stood looking down upon the calm face while the nurse sat in her chair, and together they waited for the doctor. Occasionally she raised her eyes and gazed through the window, without sight, at the tree-tops and the sky. Occasionally she walked back and forth, with her fingers interlocked and twisting behind her. But mostly she stood at the bedside contemplating the dead face, which looked so much younger now, and thinking how different were her knowledge and her thoughts from those of the nurse. That which she had read was all about her ; it was in her and around her ; hardly to be laid aside for more than a few seconds ; ever returning, scene after scene, to possess her again.

BOOK I

THE CHILDREN

CHAPTER I

CAN IT be fifty-seven years ago (so began the tale which she had read through the night) when Con and I first ran up the steps of this house, driven by an excitement that almost lifted us from the ground. The pantechnicon stood backed against the kerb; some pieces of our furniture, a chest of drawers and a washstand stood, awkward and embarrassed, on the public roadway; three men were piloting a sofa into the hall with some difficulty; and we two ran towards them, eager to explore our new enormous house. Behind us, unvisited by our excitement, and even a little tired and depressed, came Mother, Uncle Humphrey, and Lettice our old servant. My Father, General Allan Mourne, was already there, standing like a tall statue on the steps, directing the field of operations with his malacca cane as a general should, and enjoying every moment of the battle. He at least was almost as inspired as we by the glory of the hour.

'Welcome, Mr. Doric,' he said to me; and 'Welcome, Tricks,' to Con. 'I pray you enter. It is only a small home but the best I can do for you. I am but a poor man, and would not have you expect the moon. No, ladies first, Doric : Tut, tut ; the lady first.'

Uncle Humphrey walked past him and into the house with a vagueness of manner, an abstraction, an unconsciousness of the world about him, that was more assumed than real ; he wanted to appear unconscious of the four-wheeler in which we had come, and of the cabman on its box waiting to be paid. His eyes tranced (most deliberately) in a dream, and roving remotely over the doorway and ceiling of the new house, he passed into the hall and out of the danger zone. Father's eyes followed him into the hall and up the stairs with a perfect understanding, and even a delighted appreciation, of the performance. I was quite near him in the hall, but he called out loud enough to be heard by that figure ascending heavenward, 'Mr. Doric, I take it that, as a gentleman, you have paid for the fly. As a gentleman in charge of the ladies, you will certainly have discharged this duty. What is that? What did you say? You expected your Uncle Humphrey to pay him? Don't be absurd, child. Your Uncle Humphrey is a philosopher and has higher things to think of. Come at once and pay this most excellent man.'

Rejoicing in the game, as I always did when Father was organizing the play, I went down the steps with him to the four-wheeler's side.

'How much?' inquired my father of the cabman aloft.

'Three bob,' the cabman assured him.

'Three bob!' My father repeated it in astonishment. He was so astonished that he, too, used the abominable word 'bob,' which normally would have stunned him with its horror and left him for a few seconds as one dead. 'Nonsense, driver: eighteen pence: I am not a fool.'

'Three bob, with all them people, guv'nor. One gent, two ladies, two nippers—all in one cab.'

'Three bob—that is to say, shillings—for less than a mile? It is outrageous; let me perish.'

'I had to wait a long time, guv'nor.'

Father considered this point. 'Yes, that may well be. I can imagine it. Yes, you certainly scored a point there. Mr. Doric and I spend the greater part of our lives waiting for the ladies. Very well then. There you are, Doric: give the gentleman this and say "Thank you" to him for his great kindness in bringing you to this house. Ask him to add to his kindness by keeping the small balance.'

I held up a half-crown and a shilling to the cabman, who stooped, took it, and said, 'Ta, sonny,' touching his hat with his whip. Then he flicked his hangdog old horse with the whip and drove away.

Father took my hand. 'Now come in and see all that is to be seen. Come and give me your advice and help which I very badly need. This house needs an artist's eye, which you can certainly provide. You have, I always consider, a most remarkable eye.'

'Oh, yes!' In my impatience I dragged him back towards the house. 'Come along, General.'

When I was with my father, my humour took its colour from his; and it had been my pleasure to call him 'General' ever since I'd heard his cronies at his United Services Club so addressing him.

' Gently, gently ! ' he begged, as I pulled him along. ' I am old . . . old. . . . All in good time. But you must certainly see the furniture properly bestowed. We must have it exactly where you wish it, because this is *your* house, and it will be your home long after I am dead.'

A quick alarm pierced my heart, and marred for a second the sunlight, and the fun, of the afternoon. A great threat seemed to come close, and my heart pleaded ' *Oh no ! No ! *'

' It'll be ages before you're dead,' I said, to make the world secure again. ' Absolute ages.'

' No, no,' he asserted confidently. ' I am old . . . very old . . . and terribly battered by life. My system will not stand it much longer. The end must be soon ; and when it comes, I doubt if I shall repine.'

He was so obviously ' being funny ' that I refused to be further alarmed and skipped at his side. ' You'll almost certainly live another twenty years,' I suggested.

' Twenty ? My God ! Twenty more such years ? '

' Yes, twenty at least,' I insisted without mercy.

' All right then,' he consented sadly. ' So be it. If I have to sustain the battle, I will. I shan't desert my post till the Cease Fire is sounded. But twenty—twenty years ! '

' Yes, twenty.'

' Have it as you will. I will do my best to obey. Whatever Mr. Doric commands, must always be done.'

And on this understanding, hand in hand, we went back into the house—he to his General Headquarters in the hall, I into the uncurtained whiteness of the rooms and their smell of scrubbed floors and new paint.

I suppose my father really was as fine a figure as I think him now. People who remember him tell me that he was, and that I could hardly exaggerate his fine presence ; but all people are apt to say big things of the dead. He was fifty-six at this time, and tall and lean and straight, as a soldier should be. His nose was large and well-shaped, and his long moustaches were grey for the most part but chestnut under the nostrils. These moustaches did not turn downwards in ogee curves, but extended outward in a horizontal line to two sharp points, like the yard-arms on a mast. The points, I hasten to say, lest his sleep is disturbed, were not waxed, but protruded in their own strength, as if the grey hairs were of steel. He would have scorned to wax them. ' I am not a colour-sergeant,' he would have protested. ' A general officer may twist his moustache ends—I do myself, on occasions—but wax them, no. *Nom d'un nom,* no ! ' Dark thick eyebrows, splashed with white and pointing upwards, seemed to accompany the stiff moustaches like two junior aides-de-camp whose swords were unsheathed. Beneath them were two caverned eyes, brown, bright, and full of mischief—except when they were full of rage, which happened sometimes with Mother, or with a cabman, though never—never once in all my life—with me. Then they glistened with steely pin-points ; but far more often they danced—I had almost written *bubbled*—with suppressed laughter. When the eyes laughed, the eyebrows seemed to join in, coming close together to share the fun. So, too, when the eyes blazed with wrath, the eyebrows had a share in it, standing sternly together and stiffening their grip on their swords.

It was he who had invented for me the name Doric. ' In a weak moment,' he would expound, ' I consented to his being called Theodore—a ridiculous desire of Madam's. But it was slowly borne in upon me that people, the vast majority of whom lack all sensitiveness, would come to call him Teddy ; and as this was inconceivable in a child of mine we arrived together, he and I, at Doric which you will allow to be a pleasant abbreviation of the name Theodoric. We agreed that Teddy had to be outflanked somehow.'

On this famous afternoon he wore a suit of heavy grey cheviot tweed, square cut ; a high white collar ; and a broad black cravat illuminated by a large pearl pin. In his hand he held his thick malacca cane with the gold band (which he had bought in Singapore off a Chinaman) and used it like a lecturer's pointer to direct the removal men and their burdens up the stairs or into the rooms. So did the Emperor with his baton point the way to his Old Guard at Waterloo. If the men were in two minds about an Order, he marched ahead of the furniture with his cane on his shoulder like a sword at the slope.

Father addressed these sweating and struggling men with an extreme courtesy. To all servants or working men and women he spoke with this courtesy and insisted that I, as a gentleman, should do the same. ' Without these cannot a city be inhabited,' he would say, for, as I shall show you, he loved the Bible and Bunyan and Shakespeare, and was forever employing those of their lines or phrases which had raised in him a rich delight. ' They shall not be sought for in public counsel, Doric, but they maintain the state of the world. Always remember that, and be as polite as you are grateful.' Having heard the foreman call one of the men George and another Fred, he referred thereafter to these two as Mr. George and Mr. Fred. ' I am sorry, Mr. Foreman, but my wife tells me that Mr. George and Mr. Fred, in their last journey, put that sideboard against the wrong wall. Would you be so very good as to ask them to move it ? '

' Certainly, sir. That's all right, sir.'

' Thank you. It is exceedingly good of you. The fault was mine. I directed them to the wrong wall, and my wife is heartbroken about it.'

' Oh, well, we can't have that, sir. Can't have the lady upset. 'Op in Fred, and shift it where the lady wants it.'

' Righto, Bill. Soon see to that.'

' Thank you, Mr. Fred. I am obliged.'

' And Mr. Mourne, sir,' began the foreman, having my father at hand for questioning, ' did you wish that there cupboard——'

' God forbid that I should be unnecessarily punctilious, Foreman, but, as a matter of accuracy, my correct title is not Mister but General. However, let that be. It's of no consequence. God forbid that I should interrupt what you were going to say.'

' He's General Allan Mourne,' I explained.

' Blimey, so he is, sonny. Yes, I knew that, sir, only I forgot. I knew you was General Mourne.'

Father closed his eyes in some distress at being called Mourne instead of by our full surname, Allan Mourne, but he forbore to continue his corrections. It was of the essence of good breeding not to embarrass or discomfort anybody ; and especially was this true of the poor. His left hand waved an invisible something away. ' It is of very small consequence. Let it rest. There is nothing particularly admirable about a general. You were saying ? '

' I was saying, did you want that there little cupboard in the parlour ? '

Again my father closed his eyes, while the pain of hearing his drawing room called a parlour swept over him. When he was recovered, he said with a sigh, ' Yes. Drawing room, Foreman. By which I mean the back room on the first floor.' And he moved away from an area where he was subject to such stings and barbs.

Not perceiving that I was still at hand, the foreman mumbled to Mr. Fred, ' Comic old codger, isn't he ? ' and the foundation of my world shook. ' Old,' yes—I always thought of Father as grey-moustached and old ; ' comic,' well, yes—the idea was all right, since he was easily the most entertaining person in the world, though the word itself seemed a shade disrespectful of one who was a gentleman ; but ' codger ! ' I was glad for Father's sake that I alone had heard that word. I felt as if I had stopped on my own breast an arrow sharper than any which had gone before.

The furniture from our tiny house at Walham Green looked wistfully small and cheap in the large rooms ; and this palpable incongruity, this evidence of a recent narrowness in our style of living, disappointed and depressed my father. The small-ness of the carpet in the drawing room, the narrowness of the stair carpet roll, the slightness of some bamboo chairs put him to shame before the foreman and his mates, those representative in our midst of the world that measures a man by his money. It was a weight of humiliation that, after a while, he found he could not bear. ' Yes, leave it there,' he told George who was carrying a meagre little side-table into the drawing room. ' The furniture from my house in the country will come to-morrow, and I shall know better then where to put things.' My hand shot to my mouth, for we had no house in the country. ' Put nothing against that far wall. I shall want to put my Chippendale bookcase there, and it is a monstrous piece of furniture. Una—where is your mother, Doric ?—Una, are you there ? ' he shouted down the stairs. ' Una, your counsel and advice, please.'

' Yes, Kingsley.'

' I think we'd better put the Hyderabad carpet in the drawing room, don't you ? '

' What carpet ? '

' *Nom de Dieu, nom de Dieu*, the huge Hyderabad that I brought from India. Then the Jaipur carpet can go in the dining room, can't it ?—if it's not too large. Is that all right ? *Caramba !*—the woman's gone. I don't know where the big tallboys are going, do you, Doric, unless we put them on the landing ? ' And his left eye winked at me under its thick spiked eyebrow.

§

Old-fashioned indeed, to my mind's eye, seem the figures that were moving in this house that day—and at the time I imagined our modes of dress to be everlasting !—myself in a blue sailor suit ; Con with her brown fringe on her forehead and her hair curling round her shoulders ; Mother, who was thirty-three then and not yet stout, in a long dark dress that fitted close to her corseted figure, and had a row of buttons from the high collar to a point below her waist ; and Uncle Humphrey in his dark serge with his black spade beard and black felt hat that was neither bowler nor topper but something between the two. How well I remember his hat that day. For much of the afternoon it stood on a table in the front room, out of the dust and danger on the stairs, but he kept replacing it on his head for fear of taking cold when he went out on the pavement to look for his furniture.

Then there was Lettice. Lettice, our servant, must have been a little less than fifty, but we always thought of her as old. She was a short woman, very roomy about the hips and breast, and slightly rounded in the back from her forty years of household tasks. She wore small steel spectacles low down on a pug nose and threw her head back to look at you through them. To mention her is to see the width of her rump as she bent over dustpan and brush, and to hear the creaking of her stays as she came erect again. Quite often she talked and muttered to herself as she worked. This afternoon she muttered a deal as she carried scuttles of coal and firewood up the staircase, because she was even more worried by the size of the house than Mother was ; which is to say she was exceedingly worried. Once I heard her telling the staircase wall in a favourite phrase that she ' was but yewman.' ' These stairs. Oh, these stairs. I don't know how one'll cope with them. One is but yewman, all said and done.'

Mother heard that phrase and, terrified lest she gave notice before this overloaded moving-day was done, came hurrying out of a first-floor room with comfort and conciliation.

' That's all right, Lettice. The master has promised that you shall have help. He says we shall have at least a housemaid and a scullery maid and perhaps a woman in to help. Don't trouble about that scuttle now.'

But Lettice didn't want to be relieved of her worry. She held on to her heavy scuttle, which was its black and concrete form. ' I *must* trouble about it, ma'am. The bedrooms are like ice, being that big. And I wouldn't say they didn't feel damp to me. If I don't get some fires going, we shall catch our deaths.'

' Yes, yes, but they can wait, Lettice, they can wait.'

Lettice set down the scuttle behind her and stood above it like a bulky statue of Patience on the stairs. ' Didn't those fires ought to be lit, or didn't they ought not ? ' She waited for an answer, looking at Mother. ' They ought, didn't they ? '

' Yes, yes, I quite think they should, but look here, then, let me help you. Let me take that. There *are* a lot of stairs.'

' No, you've got all you can do, Ma'am.' She snatched at the scuttle and continued her laboured climb. ' That's no work for a lady. That's my business. But how one's going to warm

this house and keep it clean with all these stairs, I just don't
know. A week or two of it, and one'll be worn out. You don't
want to have me on your hands. You won't like it if you have
me on your hands.'

' But I've *told* you you're going to have help,' protested Mother,
beating her toe on the boards.

' Well, I'll be glad when it comes, I must say. I'm willing
to do all I can, but there's a limit to what yewman flesh and
blood can do. That I shall always say.'

At that moment my father, his malacca cane swinging from
his fingers like a pendulum, was leading the principal wardrobe
up the stairs. His progress, because more enthusiastic, was
faster than Lettice's, and he caught up with her and heard her
plaint. Immediately he stooped and took the scuttle from her
hand. ' Allow me,' he begged, with the courtesy due to one
of those who maintained the state of the world.

" Oh, no, sir ! *You* can't : *you* mustn't carry a scuttle.'

' Of course I can carry a scuttle. You are tired. We can't
have you worn out. Without Lettice we are lost, aren't we,
Una ? Miss Lettice is the most important person in the house,
Mr. Foreman.'

' Yes, sir ? '

' Without her the city cannot be builded. We're all very
clear about that. It is she who sustains us all. Doric, come
and light the fires. Lettice is tired, and you would wish to help
a lady who is tired. As you hear, and as she says so rightly,
she is but yewman. Take you my stick. I take the scuttle.'

I was overjoyed to light the fires with him, though surprised,
and much impressed, by his condescension in stooping to so
lowly a task. We had great fun, lighting fires in all the rooms,
including Lettice's, over whose grate Father expended the largest
supply of creative imagination and energy. ' She is our servant,
Doric, and therefore we must serve her. He that is great
among you, let him be as your servant. Always remember that.'
Then, her fire blazing, and ourselves well lit with a sense of
rectitude, we came down the stairs and on the lowest flight
met Uncle Humphrey's writing table and deep armchair coming
up, with Uncle Humphrey following anxiously behind. If
Father went ahead of his furniture, Uncle Humphrey came
behind his ; and this I conceive to be a symbol of something.
Father was of the restless kind who go ahead in the world,
dragging their circumstances after them ; Uncle Humphrey,
less energetic—somewhat weighed down, indeed, by inertia—
was of the kind who sink easily into disciples of their circumstances. Or, again, we may say that Father's eyes were cast

into the future, while Uncle Humphrey's surveyed the present over-anxiously.   Father led his wardrobe like an advancing host ; Uncle Humphrey came behind his writing desk and his deep chair lovingly, like a shepherd guiding his lambs into their fold.

It is clearly time that Uncle Humphrey was explained.   What is he doing on our stairs ?   Why go his writing desk and his deep easy chair, and Uncle Humphrey himself, like an irrelevant thread in the bright pattern my father was weaving ?

§

Uncle Humphrey was a bachelor brother of my father, three years younger than he, half a foot shorter, and as much inclined to fat as Father to spareness.   He had full and rosy cheeks, though their flesh didn't look healthy, and a square black beard that seemed to partner the square felt hat.   By profession he was a barrister, but not by practice ; for when he was about forty-five he had inherited a matter of some £300 a year from a woman friend in circumstances which it would be better, perhaps, not to probe ; and he had thereupon retired from a tedious and unprofitable occupation to give his days to a great work—or to say that he was so doing.   This great work was a book on philosophy, which he declared was his major interest, and we gathered from his description of it that, when it was complete, it would stand without shame by the great systems of Spinoza, Hegel, Schopenhauer, and Spencer.

In the first years of Father's retirement from the Army, and before he had piled directorship upon directorship in that rich era of company promoting, we had been poor enough, and obliged to confine our aspirations within the small narrow house at Walham Green.   But now that the directorships had more than trebled his income, he had been able to move us all into a house worthier, as he did not hesitate to say, of his rank.

It was then that he suggested that Uncle Humphrey should come and live with us ; giving two reasons—one, that though we were much less poor now, we were by no means wealthy, and Old Humphrey's contribution as a paying guest, and his bits and pieces of furniture, would help in the upkeep and equipment of the new, big house ; and two, that he was fond of Old Humphrey who, as his only brother, had been his play-mate in their Worcestershire home ' in those innocent years, Una, my dear, when we joined our little hands in love and roamed the daisied fields together.'   The suggestion suited

Uncle Humphrey, who would have got nowhere else, for twenty-five shillings a week, such comfort and companionship, and such a good address ; it pleased my mother less, and Lettice not at all ; but what my father wanted came to pass in our house.

So Uncle Humphrey came for a few months to the little house at Walham Green before moving with us into the new big one. He brought a few pieces of furniture with him, the most significant of which were his fine writing desk and his splendidly upholstered easy chair. The writing desk represented his dream ; the easy chair the reality. He wanted to think of himself as a writer, but now in his fifty-fourth year he had achieved nothing but a few brief, constipated articles which struggling journals had printed without payment (and which he had stuck, one and all, in a press-cutting album) ; a slim paper-bound book of poems for whose ' publication ' he had paid thirty pounds to a vanity publisher ; and an anthology of quotations which had been put into print by the same firm on similar terms. But this was before he had discovered Philosophy and the superiority of his mind. This superiority was revealed to him by his interest in, and his apparent ability to understand, Philosophy. And thenceforward he was disabled by the superiority. Why write, except for oneself, and for the few who were his peers ? Why talk much when none that he met had the minds to understand him ? Easy to explain to people now why his work had never been, and never would be, acceptable to the multitude. One day perhaps his qualities would be recognized and a high place accorded him. ' I shall dine late,' he said with Landor ; ' but the dining-room will be well-lighted, the guests few and select.'

Nevertheless, with or without a public for the present, a professional author he accounted himself to be ; and on the strength of the two paper-bound volumes, he got himself elected a member of the Authors' Society. He was one of the first members of the Authors' Club, when it was founded in 1891, and got a pleasure from writing on its notepaper and from leaving the paper-bound volumes on its tables for other members to see. He believed himself to be a final authority on good writing and was shocked and wounded if any layman disputed a pronouncement of his on syntax or style. But even if in addition to his desire to be a scholarly writer, and his interest in the technique of writing, he had had any ideas to write about, it seemed unlikely that he would have had the will-power or the stamina to complete a book. An hour at his writing desk, and he found an excuse for ' further research ' in the easy chair ; an hour striding the carpet in a Laocoon wrestle with sentences, and his legs began to 'feel tight about the calves,' and he decided that he must continue the labour in the easy chair with his feet upon a stool. But at fifty-three one does not compose a book with one's feet upon a stool ; one composes oneself and sleeps.

His desire to write an important work was strong, but his fear for his bodily health was stronger. Ever since he had entered the fifties and seen sixty as the next milestone he had been unable to shake off the idea that his natural forces were fast abating : that his eyes, ears, teeth, joints or stomach (according to which was aching at the time) would fail him ever more quickly now. As regards the stomach, the loss of course was figurative, since, in respect of its contour there was a regrettable advance. He feared, in brief, that he was falling to pieces, bit by bit ; and it was now a steady aim of his life to arrest or diminish this time-erosion by careful policies of self-protection and rest. For instance, he had been careful, when his woman friend and benefactress died, to be sorry but not to grieve overmuch, lest the nervous disturbance should be a drain on his strength ; and he was careful now not to work too hard lest the mental strain and conflict should induce a fatigue that amounted to a poison in the blood stream ; not to climb too many stairs lest he stimulated a dubious vein in his leg or put a strain upon his heart ; and not to abridge those periods of rest in which both heart and legs could recuperate. To-day he had been careful to go up the stairs as little as possible until his own furniture came out of the van ; and this was easy because his own pieces were the only ones in which he took any interest. The room to which he must shepherd them was the front room on the third floor ; which may seem a strange choice in one who so disliked climbing, but he had chosen it because, as he said, he needed silence for his work and at any lower stage the family would ' press on him too much.' When Father and I met him coming up behind his writing desk and chair he was ascending for the third time and was fatigued ; and Uncle Humphrey, if fatigued, liked others to know it.

' I suppose it's going to be all right,' he sighed as he met Father.

' What's going to be all right ? ' demanded Father, not quite liking the sigh.

' All these stairs.'

' Stairs ? What's wrong with them ? It's a most handsome staircase. Twice as wide as the one we had in Walham Green. The banister rail is solid mahogany.'

' There are three flights of stairs up to my room.'

'Obviously since it's on the third floor. I can't see how you'd reach it in less. And what's the matter with three flights ? They'll get down some of your fat.'

'I'm not happy about them.'

Father's heavy, pointed eyebrows met. 'Well, it's a bit late to grumble now. You were enthusiastic about the house when we first discussed it. It wasn't ten minutes before you'd had " 1 Coburg Square " printed on your cards.'

'I didn't realize then that the stairs were so steep. I'm wondering what effect they'll have on my heart.'

The irritation smouldering inside my father burst into a conflagration : Lettice had complained of his beautiful new house ; Mother had appeared to sympathize with her ; and now Humphrey was sighing like a furnace. The gleams of the conflagration lit in Father's eyes. 'Well, *sacré nom d'un nom*, get out of the house ! ' he shouted. 'Nobody need live here who'd rather not. London is a large place. There are good chambers to be had in Jermyn Street and the Albany. Let me summon a hansom for you if you would wish to go there. A pleasure to assist you in any way, I'm sure.' His voice rang up the staircase shaft and into the empty rooms; always when a fury seized him he addressed his opponent in a voice better adapted to barrack square or battlefield. His voice gonged through the house, sounding a general alarm. Con hurried from one room on the first floor to lean over the banister and study the drama ; Mother came from the other room to consider it ; the foreman and his men laid down their burdens in the hall to stand still and gaze up at it. And Father, indifferent to them all, continued : 'If you don't want the expense of a hansom there are plenty of trains, I understand from Earls Court District Railway Station. I won't detain you in this house a minute longer than you wish. Don't imagine it.'

'I only made a remark,' Uncle Humphrey protested. 'I have to be careful, as you know.'

'Well, if you'd rather be careful elsewhere, please say so at once. I offered you a share in my house, but I never guaranteed you a nursing home. And I can't undertake to build you a lift. I shall have expenses enough without that. There are plenty of first class nursing homes in the neighbourhood of Wimpole Street and Devonshire Place. And there are about twenty hospitals in the Fulham and Brompton Roads. Come on, Mr. Fred, bring that up.'

The tone of this last command suggested that *he*, at any rate, was going to move into the house, even though the rest of the world moved out of it.

Controlling his resentment, Uncle Humphrey followed his desk up the stairs quickly. He left the field to Father, first because he didn't want to imperil his residence at this good address, and, secondly, because an emotional upheaval might be bad for him. Only, as he passed Mother, did he emit a low protest. 'If he speaks to me in that fashion, Una, I don't answer him. He's best left alone in that sort of mood. Shouting at me as if I were one of his niggers in India ! And before the furniture men ! What does he think I am ? Some subahdar major in a regiment of sepoys ? ' And, having justified himself thus, he carried his sad eyes towards his lonely asylum upstairs.

Meanwhile Father, mounting the stairs behind Mr. Fred, turned to me. ' *You* like the house, don't you, Doric ? '

I was only eight, but this appeal to me for comfort in his disappointment cut through to my heart. I remember the sudden pang, and the outflow of pity, as I write now. ' Not half ! ' I was in a passion to assert. ' I think it's ripping. Absolutely ripping.'

' And, Tricks, *you* like it, don't you ? ' he inquired of the face over the banisters.

' Oh yes, papa. Frightfully.'

' It's a nice house for parties, isn't it ? You'll be able to have all your little friends here, and play your little games.'

' Oh, can we, papa ? *When ?* '

' Whenever you like ; and don't let your Uncle Humphrey try to stop you. There's not a better house in London for " Hide and Seek," or better flights of stairs anywhere for a toboggan. And you've got your own playroom. *That's* going to be your playroom. To-morrow I'm going to buy you a lot of nice furniture for it.'

' Oh, when ? Can we come too ? '

I remember being surprised that Con could be only interested in the parties and the playroom when he was so obviously hurt. She must be disappointing him too, I thought ; and I felt compelled to reassure him again. ' I think it's a lovely house, papa '—I was in no mood to be funny and call him General. ' I think it's corking. Absolutely corking.'

He nodded in vague approval of my assertion and proceeded up the stairs, announcing to all who cared to hear, ' Mr. Doric and I always agree. Thank Heaven I have one friend in the world.'

§

The next inspiring event on this famous day was the sight of Aunt Henrietta and Gentle at the other corner of the square.

Con and I were always excited when Gentle was coming to the house. She was the chief of our friends ; by which I do not so much mean that we loved her for her own sake as that we desired her company for ours. When one is grown up, two may be company and three none, but when one is eight or nine, three is a company compared with which two is almost solitude. At least, so it was with us.

'Here they are ! Here's Aunt Henrietta and Gentle.' It was Con who shouted this from the window of the first-floor front room, which was to be our playroom. It is the window at which I am looking now.

I ran to it. There they were, coming along the pavement. There was Aunt Henrietta, tall as a maypole, almost as thin and quite as well bedecked, in a tight-fitting and beribboned dress, with mutton sleeves, and a heavily trimmed hat that protruded from her high coiffure like the exalted canopy above a bishop's throne. And as the back of the bishop's canopy is flush with the high back of his throne, so the back of her hat was flush with her elongated back—except, as I recall now, for two streamers which it let down below her shoulder blades. She carried a fluffy parasol whose thin stick among the flounces seemed to associate well with her long thin limbs among the sleeves and ribbons.

And there at her side, holding her hand, walked Gentle ; long-legged too, but with a natural, not an elongated, slimness. Her hair was fair at this age, and hung in two long plaits down her back ; her eyebrows were darker than her hair ; and her eyes brown. My impression is that on this sunny afternoon she wore some pale, yoked frock, tied with a sash some way below her natural waist. It was inaccurate to say that she walked by her mother's side ; she skipped there and *chassé*'d there, and sometimes, for variety, slid.

'Good Angels ! . . . *Sacré nom d'un nom !* . . .' These exclamations, deeply informed with despair, had come from a voice high above me at the window. Father was at my side, contemplating the figure of his sister-in-law. It always diverted him to utter shocking things about Mother's elder sister ; and to-day, while pretending to utter them to himself, he was well satisfied that Con and I should hear them. 'The extraordinary woman. . . . Just look at that now ! . . . Did you ever see anything so extraordinarily like a camel—and a camel consumed with earnestness ? What on earth was God about when He designed our Henrietta ? She's surely one of His mistakes.'

Con looked up at him shocked. 'God can't do anything wrong,' she pronounced.

' Is that so ? Well, it may be that there is a case for women of that shape, but it hasn't been revealed to me yet. In your own good time, you will doubtless declare it unto me.'

' God can make a door open and shut at the same time,' explained Con ; which didn't seem to have much to do with anything.

' Consumed with earnestness ' was an accurate description of our Aunt Henrietta at all times. The earnestness seemed to fill her long body from the long head to the long feet. Like a jet from a hose it poured over you and damped you, as she directed her long nose and fixed her long stare on your face, before uttering the most obvious comments as if they were words of a portentous significance. The intense, large-eyed stare seemed much too weighty and sustained a prelude to the inadequate remarks that followed it. Normally there was no laughter in the large eyes ; only this beetling seriousness ; but occasionally she was greatly amused at some story which you would have imagined could draw from an adult only a faint smile, and then she gave the joke a laughter that was six times what it was worth. You watched amazed. Rarely, however, did she know when Father was jesting. To most of his flippancies she would respond with an overwhelming seriousness, turning gaiety, at a breath, into gravity ; and the strain of keeping up with this seriousness was more than he could support. He would escape from her, murmuring, as Bunyan said of Mr. Talkative, ' I find her more comely at a distance than at hand.' His title for her was the Intense Inane.

Five years older than Mother, she had married rather late in life Brian Greaves, a senior clerk in the firm of Boulton and Mills, produce brokers, who bought and sold food in all parts of the world ; and Gentle was their only child. Gentle was the maiden name of Brian's mother ; and Henrietta had seized upon it as ' such a lovely name for a girl,' and caused the baby to be christened Gentle after one granny and Mary after another. As a child Gentle always pretended to hate the name, but really she loved it—a name no one else had ever owned before. If I wanted to infuriate her I would alter it to Jenny, and then in her spitting anger she was anything but gentle and would hurl at me ' Theodore, Theodore,' and ' Teddy, Teddy,' knowing that I liked only my father's name for me, Doric.

They were near our house now, and Con ran down the stairs to meet them, and I raced after her. We arrived at the top of our steps just as Gentle, breaking from her mother, arrived at the pavement below them.

Suddenly shy, her hands behind her back, she said, ' Hullo.'

It was a habit of hers, at eight years old, to stand with her hands behind her back. ' Hallo, Con.'

' Hallo,' said Con, suddenly shy too.

' Good afternoon. Oh, good afternoon,' I shouted, in a humour for foolery. ' Good afternoon, the Greaveses.'

' Is this your new house ? '

Unfortunately I saw nothing fatuous in this question and missed my chance of satire. I only said ' Yes,' proudly.

' Coo-er ! ' exclaimed Gentle.

' Have you come to see us ? ' asked Con, in a question equally fatuous.

' Yes, I simply *forced* Mamma to bring me along as soon as school was over. I just *had* to. D'you think Uncle Kingsley and Auntie Una'll mind our coming ? '

' The General and Mrs. Allan Mourne will be more than pleased,' I assured her.

' *What* did you say ? ' A laugh began to widen her large mouth.

' I said General and Mrs. Allan Mourne would be highly gratified.'

' Help ! ' said Gentle.

' Come in and see it all,' invited Con, taking no notice of me. ' It's lovely.' Con's momentary catalepsy was at an end ; her life had flowed back into her, as she stood beside me on the top step. And Con's natural life was one of complacence, self-satisfaction, superior information, and general bossiness. ' Come along,' she repeated in her self-possessed way ; and with her most competent air, she picked up Gentle's hand and led her into the house. Gentle, though led by her, and a year younger, was the taller of the two. Like many bossy little girls, Con was rather short for her age and round and compact. I, younger than Gentle by a month, was also taller than Con. Visitors, much to my pique, used to remark on the difference between us two : my legs long and weedy, Con's round and plump ; my face lean and pale, hers soft and pink ; my hair fair and lank, hers dark brown and so plentiful and pliable that Mother was forever damping and curling it and crimping it with irons.

Con dragged Gentle into room after room explaining everything all the time ; and in each room Gentle said ' Coo-er ! ' presumably because of its size, since there was precious little furniture in most of them. On the stairs we met Father leading the removal men down to the hall again, after some campaign which he had brought to a successful issue on an upper landing. He looked at Gentle's high-flushed cheeks, gleaming brown eyes, and two fair plaits, and greeted her, ' Hallo, Spring Sunlight.'

'Hallo, Uncle Kingsley,' answered Gentle brightly; whereat all ideas of anything else to say departed from her. So she asked, 'Is this your new house?'

'Well, we've made a lamentable error if it isn't,' said Father. 'We've moved a lot of furniture in. Do you, Doric, escort the lady over the house and show her all she desires to see. I must go. I have further business with these gentlemen downstairs.'

'Certainly, General,' I agreed; and as we went up the stairs, I said, 'I suppose you realise, Miss Greaves, that this is my house.'

'It isn't!' snapped Con, swinging her face round.

'Oh yes, it is. The General said so.'

'He didn't!'

'Yes, he did. He said it when we came in.'

'Why should it be yours more than mine?'

'Because you're a female. Houses can't belong to females.'

'As a matter of fact it doesn't belong to either of you,' insisted Gentle. 'It belongs to Uncle Kingsley.'

'No, it doesn't,' Con denied.

'*Course* it does.'

'It doesn't,' repeated Con.

'Well, who does it belong to?'

'It belongs to God.'

This was so profound in its implications that Gentle and I were temporarily silenced; and Con was left to continue. 'Everything belongs to God. Everything that you possess is only a sacred trust from God. Mr. Peterson said so last Sunday.'

I was now recovered, and ready to pursue this thesis with the fierce, unflinching logic of a child. My toys, I asked: did they belong to God? Yes, said Con. My clockwork engine? Yes. My underpants? Yes. They were simply a trust from God, and on the Day of Judgment I should be required to give an account of my stewardship.

I think there was never anyone less disturbed by the Higher Criticism than Con.

'This is going to be our playroom,' she explained, for we were now on the first landing and she was well in command of the expedition again. Taking Gentle by the hand, she led her into this room where I am writing now. 'Papa says you can come whenever you like and play with us here.'

'Good-ee!'

As I sit here writing, I can almost see those three children coming in at the door: Con leading Gentle by the hand, Doric following behind. Strange little creatures they seem,

hardly connected with the man who holds this pen. There
they stand, as they take possession of the house on a summer
day of 1890—believing all things, hoping all things, enduring all
things.

They pass from the room and go on up to the top of the
house to the very cistern cupboard under the roof. They
even, at an inspired suggestion from Gentle, try to mount on
to the roof, but without success.

When we had solemnly visited every room we came down
the many stairs, jumping the last three steps of each flight.
On the lowest flight I, to show off, jumped four steps and wished
I hadn't ; for the tiles of the hall jarred my legs. Con and
Gentle, both wanting to equal my achievement, poised themselves on the edge of the fourth step, and I watched, interested
to see them suffer as I had done ; but like a would-be high
diver who thinks better of it, they both said 'No' and
ignominiously came down again ; and I was disappointed of
my entertainment.

At the further end of the hall was a door leading to the garden.
Its upper half was a glass window framed with red and orange
panes. The sun of late afternoon was a powerful light behind
these coloured panes, and Gentle's eyes were caught by the
brilliance. The light seemed to leap from the panes to her eyes
and become a light of inspiration. 'Shall we *escape?*' she
whispered to Con.

'Oh yes !' said Con. 'Where ? '

'I know. Come on. Come on, Con.'

Con and I ran after her to the door, but directly she and
Con were through it, Gentle, in a sudden desire to tease and
hurt, pushed me back, saying, 'No, only Con and me. Not
you. We don't want Doric, do we, Con ? It's a Secret.'

'Oh, let me come too,' I pleaded.

'No.' She was emphatic. She banged the door in my face.
In an uprush of misery—the misery of unexpected and complete
loneliness—I pulled at the door to open it again, but both of them
held it shut on the other side.

'Let me come too.'

'No.'

'I *will* come.' The misery was now a passion. That door
is still there with its orange and red panes, and I look at it
sometimes and wonder that a child could suffer so deeply about
so little. I pulled and pulled, but it was a tug-of-war in which
their united weight beat me. Suddenly, however, they let go
and ran down the steps into the garden. I opened the door
and wandered wretchedly after them. They had disappeared

through the garden's side door. I followed them through it, but they were nowhere in Osgrave Road. I walked round the corner of the house and saw them skulking in the garden of the square. I went into the garden, as if asserting my right to be with them, and they danced mischievously away from me like two Morgan le Fays or Fair Maids of Ireland, leading me on. Some spell drove me after them, while my lips trembled.

Con saw the unsteady lips and jeered, ' Cry-baby ! '

' I'm *not* crying,' I shouted.

' Oh yes, you are, you fibber.'

' Fancy a boy crying at his age,' scoffed Gentle, glad to share in the tormenting.

' You shut your face. You cry often enough,' I retorted, still following them. ' And you're older than I am.'

' Boys don't cry after they're eight.'

' They do. There's a boy at our school, and he's ten, and he cries sometimes. Ten and a *half*.'

Gentle, facing me at five yards distance, walked backwards mocking me. ' Doric's not a boy. He's a cry-baby. He's a milksop. He's a saw . . . ny,' she sang. ' A saw . . . saw . . . sawny.'

The song stirred such pain and wrath that I clenched my fist, crooked my elbows, and padded towards her, with my scranny legs bent at the knee like those of an attacking ape. She laughed. ' Coo ! Look at him now, Con, look at him. Did you ever see anything so funny ? '

' Don't laugh at me.'

' I'll laugh if I want to.'

' You won't laugh at *me*.'

' Oh, won't I ? You can't stop me, skinny old Doric.'

' Can't I ? '

Suddenly hot with the lust to hurt, I ran towards her ; she ran away laughing, but not so quickly as I. I got my arm round her neck, and with my teeth biting on each other, twisted her till she was down on the ground. There I got her on to her back, spread her arms as if for crucifixion, and knelt on them. I remember the excitement, the zest, the exaltation in the throat, as I got her in my power.

Did my temper fly from me more readily than from other children in those days ? I think not ; but Gentle's certainly did. Gentle's boiling point was exceedingly low. You had but to put a match to Gentle, and she boiled ; so you can be sure that she was steaming now, with everything savage in her rising to the surface like scum. In her eyes was the very lustre of hate. As she struggled, her amber-yellow hair broke from its

braids and hung like a bacchante's wisps.   The turf of the lawn
had been watered that morning, and the damp was assaulting
her back and her behind—so perhaps I ought to have said that
some of the heat which I had applied to her was cold.   Her fury
gave her strength to throw me off.   I got up and retreated before
her ; she ran at me, gripped me and kicked me on the knee ;
and I threw her down again and ran further.

'I hate Doric,' she cried, throwing the wisps out of her eyes.
'I hate him more than anyone else in the world.   I wish
somebody'd kill him.'

'Mamma'll give him a whipping,' Con promised.

Terror leapt like a rider on to my heart and drove it at a
gallop.   I tried to strike that rider from his seat.   'She won't,'
I said, ' Papa's here.'

'She'll whip you when he's gone.   She'll *thrash* you.'

'She won't,' I repeated.

'I hope she does,' declared Gentle.   'I hope she whips him
till he's dead.'

'She won't. . . . Papa's here.'

'I'm wet to my skin.   I can feel it all over my skin.   And
I think I've broken my knee.'   She had rolled down her black
stocking on her long, schoolboy leg and was looking at a point
beneath her knee-cap.   'D'you think a bone *ought* to stick
out like that ? '

'It looks funny,' Con agreed.

'It hurts, too.   Quite a lot.   And look at my dress.   Look
at it.'

'We must show it to your mamma.   Coo, it's all green,
Come on.'   And Con took Gentle by the hand to exhibit her
to Aunt Henrietta.   Gentle, after wiping her eyes on the hem
of her skirt, followed, eager to be shown.

I walked before them so as to get to the house first.   Too
proud to run in their sight, I did not quicken my step till I was
beyond the railings.   Once through the front door, I ran up
the stairs to where I heard my father's voice.   He was on the
first landing, leading Aunt Henrietta and Mother on a conducted tour of the new home.   I came beside him and put my
hand in his.   Touched, but unaware that I had come for
sanctuary, he gripped it firmly and announced, ' This is the
real Master of the House.   It is Mr. Doric's home, and I merely
act as his agent.   Just at present, sir, I've been showing the house
to your good aunt.   I hope you approve——'

But then Con came up the stairs, leading the exhibit.   Mother
saw the significant approach.   Gentle, impressed by Con's
interest and pity, was now pitying herself and crying.   ' Oh

dear !' exclaimed Mother. ' Oh, Con, whatever's happened ? '
Father, turning, let slip his favourite imprecation, ' *Sacré nom
d'un nom !* ' (which I always heard as ' Sackray gnawed a
gnaw.')

Con stood still and explained. ' Doric *went* for Gentle.'

Mother tut-tutted behind her teeth, but stood helpless. Had
Father not been there, she would have promptly slapped me
on both cheeks and then dragged me into the nearest room to
enjoy the luxury of applying a stick. But my hand was safe
in my father's.

Aunt Henrietta went down on one knee and drew Gentle
against her breast. And as the waters gushed when the
patriarch smote the rock, so her condolences poured over the
weeping Gentle. ' What's the matter, my babe ? Oh, never
mind, my pretty one. Doric didn't mean to hurt you. He's
much too nice. There then : that's all right, my wee girlie.
Everything's quite all right. Girlies of eight don't cry.' And
I stood listening ; astonished that Aunt Henrietta's talk should
have such little correspondence with reality. I had certainly
meant to hurt Gentle ; I wasn't nice ; the situation wasn't
' all right ' yet ; and I'd never met a girlie of eight who didn't
sooner or later cry. Why even Con, the uncritical, was perturbed by Aunt Henrietta's refusal to accept reality. ' He took
and *hurled* her down,' she explained.

' No, no.' Father could not suffer this to pass. ' Not Mr.
Doric. That's not possible. Doric is a gentleman and would
never overthrow a lady.'

' He hurled her down and knelt on top of her,' persisted Con.

' She——' I began indignantly.

' Hush.' Father's great hand pressed mine till it hurt.
' Hush, Doric. Gentle, it's no good asking Doric what you did
to anger him because he'd never tell tales on anyone, or try
to get anyone into trouble ; he often says he'd rather die first.
He said to me only yesterday that he desired to be the Soul of
Chivalry. But you, Gentle, are the Soul of Honour and would
be the first to tell us what happened.' None of this was any
nearer the harsh truth than Aunt Henrietta's effusive affirma-
tions, but I was able to perceive its difference of quality.
Father's exceedingly unreal statements were designed as humour
and therefore not offered for belief; Aunt Henrietta's were
serious and therefore silly. ' You wouldn't wish Doric to get
all the blame if it's not all his fault. When pain and anguish
wring the brow, a ministering angel thou.'

' She's wet from top to bottom,' interposed Con. ' *And*
green in places.'

Gentle, not displeased, at being the Soul of Honour and a ministering angel, decided to confess to a minimum of guilt. ' I only laughed a little,' she submitted.

' I feel it must have been a little more than that.'

' No, it wasn't,' Con maintained.

' And yet he hurled you down and stamped on you ? Did he hurt you ? '

' Her knee looks a very funny shape at one point,' said Con.

And Gentle agreed that she was injured in parts.

' Strange. Very strange. Because he's usually a Model of Courtesy. What's that, Doric? What did you say ? ' I had not spoken. ' Oh yes, certainly ; I quite agree with you. He says he's shocked and beyond measure distressed at what he's done, and will know no peace till he's made you a public apology. What's that ? ' He bent over me again. ' Oh, yes, you're right. That's the point exactly. He says he realizes a man should always be gentle with a woman because he's so much bigger and stronger. He also says it's dreadful—" unpardonable " was his word—to have been unkind to a guest in his own house.'

' It was in the garden,' amended Con.

' Oh, shut up ! ' Her interruptions, irritating him, overturned for a second his high Corinthian style. ' Yes, Doric, you are quite right to take that view of the matter. I knew you would feel like that. Come, then, and say you're sorry.' Holding my hand firm, he led me to Gentle who was still within the arms of the kneeling Henrietta.

There was a conflict in me between my desire to be all that my father said, and my still throbbing dislike of Gentle ; but the pressure of his hand won. ' I'm sorry,' I said, without fervour.

' And you will wish to kiss her, I take it ? '

There was nothing I could have wished less ; and I strained back from the obscene ordeal.

' No ! ' cried Gentle, and stamped, and buried her face in her mother's breast out of danger.

' Go on, Doric,' said Father. ' That doesn't mean anything. They all do that.'

I laid a token kiss on her light brown hair, recoiling from the dry smell of it.

' Fine.' Father released my hand. ' Well, that's all over. We all love each other again. Now, Gentle, do you run down to the excellent Lettice and ask her to dry you. She has fires all over the house. And come on, Henrietta. Doric has much to show you. This is to be the children's playroom. Come in.

This is Mr. Fred, who's kindly helping us to move in. Yes, I bought the house mainly for the children, since my life is nearly over. This is Doric and Tricks's house, and I am but a lodger whose tenancy will be brief.'

Aunt Henrietta fixed her gaze on him. 'Oh, you're just being absurd,' she announced, after thought. She announced it somewhat archly, as if to let him understand that she could detect humour when it was about. 'What a nice room ! Oh, I do think you're lucky, Con and Doric. We had nothing like this when we were children, did we, Una ? *Won't* you be happy here ! And now what next ? The drawing-room . . . oh, what a room ! You'll be able to make this a perfectly lovely room. All this makes our little home seem very small. Oh, I do think it's nice when you're able to afford to have nothing but beauty around you. So good for the children. I always think children should be brought up in an atmosphere of beauty, if it's possible. And you *ought* to have a home like this, you know, Kingsley. It's only right : Walham Green was never right for you.'

'Why ? ' he demanded, scenting flattery, and not unwilling to hear it.

'Well, you know—I mean—you understand—your rank ! ' She was looking at him a little roguishly. 'Brian and I don't pretend to be anybody—just people in business. We don't aspire to anything like this. I make no secret of the fact that Boulton and Mills are tradesmen ; tradesmen in a large way, of course, but still, tradesmen. I always say we're just grocers, buying and selling food.' And she laughed coyly at this exceedingly humorous statement. 'But you—you are different —you have a position to maintain.'

Father liked flattery as well as the next man, but not if it was cumbered with an embarrassing humility ; and he promptly said, ' I'm sure Brian's work in the world is infinitely superior to mine. Despatching food about the world to feed the hungry millions—it's a noble occupation. Me—I am nothing. I am but a hired assassin.'

Not at once, but after poring upon this statement, Aunt Henrietta rebuked him, ' Oh, now you're teasing ! He's making fun of me, Una, isn't he ? You mustn't be naughty. What, upstairs now ? Oh yes, *please*. I want to see everything. This is your room and Una's, is it ? How nice ! *You* will probably sleep in the dressing room ? Oh, well, it's nice to sleep alone sometimes. I know ; Brian likes to, occasionally. Men do. Isn't it a lovely home, Con darling ? Aren't you going to be proud of it ? Your mamma and I never had

anything like this ; we were always poor. Now do we see the
guest room ? May I open the door ? Oh, very nice. So
sunny. I don't think Papa ever had more than four hundred
a year, or he would have given us everything. I'm sure, I
think it's so wonderful that we all want our children to have
better than we did. It makes one believe in Human Nature.
Where do we go next ? I like to think that Human Nature
gets better and better. It must be so dreadful to believe——'

'No, that's the water-closet,' said Father. 'The Throne
Room.'

'Oh ! ' Henrietta walked quickly away and was quite
discountenanced for a minute. Her chatter limped and stalled
as we climbed the next flight ; and Father delighted to stir
up her discomfort by mentioning that there was a similar
establishment for the maids downstairs. Approaching Lettice's
room, he said to me, ' Doric, do you run down and ask the
excellent Lettice if she has any objection to our going into her
room ! ' and as I obeyed I heard Henrietta telling Mother how
she always said to Brian that Kingsley had the manners of an
Old Grandee. When I returned I saw Father and Mother
walking behind the beetling and peering Henrietta and heard
him whisper to Mother, ' It's a mistake to be too eager if you
have a long nose ; it makes you look so like a pecking hen.'
They had not delayed long in Lettice's room since it was only
the maid's ; and they were now about to enter the front room
on the third floor, Uncle Humphrey's self-chosen retreat. He
was in the room, arranging and re-arranging his furniture.
We'd heard him for the last half-hour pulling the desk this way
and the great easy chair that way, and dragging the high bookshelves along the floor, regardless of any pain in his heart or
his calves.

Father flung open the door. ' Our Philosopher's Chamber,'
he announced, with a wave that swept it all. ' It is here that
the great work will be written. Here very great thoughts will
be thought. But in the name of thunder, Humphrey, what
are you doing ? '

' I am getting it right,' said Uncle Humphrey, not moving
from his stance at the end of the room. ' I am gradually getting
it right. Good afternoon, Henrietta. By degrees I'm getting
it right. I have what I call an irritable eye—by which I mean
an eye that can't stand a piece of furniture, or an ornament,
so much as a hair's breadth out of its right relation to the other
pieces or to the room as a whole. A room is a picture, you see ;
and I always say that just as the perfection of a sentence depends
on the right placing of every word, every syllable, every comma,

so the beauty of a room depends on the furniture and ornaments being at exactly the right angles and heights. A hair's breadth out, and the whole pattern is wrong. My eye can detect the slightest error, and is offended by it. It's like a musician's ear in that. It's like my ear for a sentence. I don't claim many things, but I do claim a perfect eye. It's imperious in its demands, but I wouldn't be without it, even though it takes a lot of lifting and shifting before the hair's-breadth accuracy is achieved.'

He was standing with legs apart and head on one side, as he pondered on the angle of the easy chair. It dissatisfied him and he went and turned it five degrees ; then came back to his original position to consider it again, his legs apart and his head on one side.

' Well, I'm sure it looks very nice to me,' said Henrietta. ' I can't pretend to have an eye like you, but——'

' Oh no, it's not right yet. Far from it. Nothing comes exactly right till you've laboured and laboured on it. Occasionally a sentence leaps into the mind, perfect from the start ; but rarely, very rarely. Only a writer understands that. That vase, for example.'

He hurried to the chimneypiece and moved a Venetian vase an inch nearer the marble clock. ' There! You see ? All the difference.'

' Well, I'm sure it's going to be lovely when you've finished with it,' said Henrietta, not liking to admit, before an artist, that she could see no difference at all. ' If you'll be able to write anywhere, it'll be here. It must be so important to a writer that his surroundings should be congenial. What a lot of books ! Have you really read all those ? You must be clever. Brian should see this. I can never get him to read anything really good. And will the great masterpiece be out soon ? '

' Oh no. No,' he affirmed at once, not wishing her to think the work he was engaged upon could be written with ease or speed. ' Certainly not. Not for a long time yet.'

' Why ? How long ? '

' Ten years, perhaps,' he suggested, to drive the lesson home.

' Oh, my goodness ! Will it really be as long as that ? Ten years ! But he's teasing me, Kingsley. I know he is.'

' Not at all,' said Uncle Humphrey, something sulkily. ' Not at all. I'm not writing a child's story-book.'

' But ten years ! Ten years is just teasing, isn't it ? All men are such teases, aren't they, Una ? Well, thank you, Humphrey. Good-bye. I shall expect the great work in '—and at the door she nodded roguishly—' about five years.'

' She can expect what she bloody well likes,' muttered Uncle
Humphrey to Father ; who had lingered behind to express by
a grimace and a spread of the hands, his utter ennui and despair.
' The woman's an idiot. Take her away. Take her from me.
Keep her away. Good God, Kingsley ! How are you feeling
after an hour of *her* ? '

' Pinnacled dim in the Intense Inane,' answered Father.

§

It is late afternoon as I write, and about the hour when the
last of the furniture was aboard the house, and Gentle, Con and
I, at Gentle's eager suggestion, were at the window of this room,
waiting to see the pantechnicon rumble away. It is very quiet
this evening because Roberta is out, and Bradford and Mrs.
Bradford are resting in their room far below ; and I can almost
imagine that I hear again the boots of the men on the bare
treads of the stairs, and Mother and Lettice talking in a distant
room, and Uncle Humphrey dragging his desk to a new tentative
site, since his eye has not yet given him the true æsthetic thrill.
I hear Father talking courteously but rather loud (as he did to
the simpler classes) while like a good host he followed the
furniture men down to the door.

In the hall he tipped them. There was a note of surprised
gratification in their thank-you's ; and I suspected that he had
tipped them all the more handsomely because his brother, wife,
and servant had complained about the house.

The men appeared on the pavement beneath us and tossed
their sacking and ropes into the pantechnicon, now as empty as
a parish hall. They shut its doors, disposed themselves on its
tail-board, and were carried by their stout horses out of our lives
for ever. Gentle waved to them as they went ; we copied her
forthwith ; and they waved very heartily back.

Then it was time for Henrietta and Gentle to return to their
smaller and narrower house in Redcliffe Street, just across the
rattling highway, Old Brompton Road. And a little later it
was time for us to go to bed. There was excitement in being
put to bed by Lettice in a large, strange room at the top of the
house, which was only half furnished and smelt of paint. Lettice
was always friendly and gentle with us when she saw us into
bed ; perhaps because children are more lovable when they
are going to bed ; more pardonable when they are in their
under-garments or naked ; and more pitiable when silence and

darkness are about to close upon them, though the rest of the world is awake.

'Don't be a nuisance to old Lettice now,' she begged us to-night, standing with her fists on her broad hips and watching us over her steel spectacles and snub nose as we danced and cavorted about the wide invitation of the great bare floor. 'Give over now and get into your nightgowns and into bed. Old Lettice can't stay here all the evening; she has plenty to do downstairs.'

'How old are you, Lettice?' asked Con, stopping her dance and standing immediately before her, a plump little girl in combinations. 'How old, really?'

'Don't ask silly questions. How old, indeed! Gracious to glory, what's that to do with you? You aren't a Miss Inquisitive, are you? Oh, no!'

'How old?' pursued Con, putting her head and her curled hair on one side in a pretty, beseeching way.

'You heard what I said. Give over all that nonsense and get into bed.'

As this rhymed, I sang it several times, dancing to its measure about the room.

'How old?' demanded Con, beating an impatient toe.

'All right, all right, miss, I heard you first off. I'm as old as my tongue and not quite as old as my teeth. There now!'

'Would you be fifty?'

'No, I wouldn't. Get along with you. Nor forty either. Get into your beds, both of you; or you'll catch your deaths.'

'Somewhere between forty and fifty?'

'If you like. Here, Master Doric: here's your nightgown; stop havering around and get into it for mercy's sake, or you'll be taking cold and your mother'll have you on her hands. That's right; no, the other arm, Clumsy. Drat the boy; don't you know your right arm from your left? Now Miss Con. Quickly does it! She don't want you on her hands just now, you may be quite sure. There you are: two beauties; into your beds you get, and snuggle down.'

We jumped into the beds and did what she called 'snuggling down'; while she lit a night-light and put it into the washstand basin so that it shouldn't set the great house on fire. Then she tucked us up, kissed us goodnight, and creaked through the door and down the stairs.

We were alone in the big room. Our two beds, side by side, seemed much smaller in its broad open spaces and a long way from the fire which still fidgeted and grunted and cracked its joints in the grate. Had it not been for Father's footsteps as he walked up and down the creaking stairs and in and out of the uncarpeted rooms, feeding his pride in his new home, and for his voice calling Mother to hear one suggestion or another for its beautification; and had it not been for Uncle Humphrey's sighs, across the passage, after he'd shifted a cupboard again in response to a new inspiration, and was still unsatisfied, I doubt not but that we should have been a little afraid.

Perhaps it was this faint, unconfessed fear which reminded Con, and impelled her to remind me apace, that we hadn't said our prayers. She got out of her bed with admirable promptness and knelt by its side with her face in her hands; and as I was not wholly averse to-night from falling to prayers, I copied her and knelt by the side of mine. My only distress was that, when I was satisfied I had prayed enough, she was evidently a long way from the same confidence, and I didn't quite like to slip back into my warm, lazy bed while she was still hard at work. But I did this at last with an impatient, ' Oh, Sackray gnawed a gnaw!' because my knees were hurting and Con, her face still deep in her hands, showed no sign of putting an early term to her worship. She was, as she told me afterwards, repeating to God all the children's hymns she could remember—' I love to hear the story ' and ' There's a Friend for little children ' and ' We are but little children weak, Nor born in any high estate ' —a hymn to which my father took some exception, since, as he said, we were the children of a general and that was high enough estate for anybody.

A remarkable difference between Con and myself was this, that she liked and copied Mother's religiosity and churchgoing, while I, though not daring to say so, was in some doubt about the quality of Mother's religion and warmly disliked the church-going. Con *liked* going to Church twice or thrice on Sunday; I could not understand it then; and I'm afraid I still do not. As early as seven years old, observing that Father's interest in churchgoing was best represented by the cipher nought, and that, as I knew in my secret and voiceless soul, my own interest would have required a minus sign, I used to wonder if there was a sex difference in this perplexing matter. Con loved a visit to Morning Service in her best frock and with her hair prettily curled on her shoulders; I dreaded the long session in my stiff Eton suit, with a prayer book in my hand whose pages must be kept moving, and a petrifying eye, as of Medusa, ready to turn upon me (either Mother's or Con's) if I shuffled on my seat or fingered the pew. If you will credit it, Con loved learning her catechism or her collect, and spouting it at high speed to Lettice or Mother. Still more she loved to ' hear ' me say my catechism or collect. She accepted and instructed me in every superstition of Mother's or Lettice's ; for example, that nothing, not even a prayer book, must rest upon a bible ; that any one taking God's name in vain might be struck dead, and that the end of the world might be upon us at any hour, yea, even as she was speaking.

The curtains were drawn, the nightlight in the wash-basin threw an unsteady aureola on the ceiling, the fire stuttered and purred, and the atmosphere of the twilit room, now that Con had finished her orisons, was definitely religious ; so we were soon in the pit of a theological discussion. I had said in an anxious moment that I thought I heard someone in the room, and she, lifting her head from the pillow, listened carefully and at length pronounced that there was no one in it except God. I asked if she really believed that God was in it, and she replied, Of course ; He was everywhere. Straightway my unsparing logic insisted on driving this idea to its extremes ; even then I had some innate understanding of, and pleasure in, a *reductio ad absurdum*. Well, was He in the wardrobe, I demanded. Yes, said Con firmly. I looked at the closed door of the wardrobe. Was He in the small top drawer of the dressing table ? Yes, she asserted, but a trifle less firmly. My eyes travelled round the fire-flushed room and rested on the pedestal cupboard between our beds. The question demanded to be asked, and I asked it : was He in the pedestal cupboard, along with the vessel that sat hidden there ? Of course, declared Con, angrily now, because she felt the ground was being cut from beneath her. Well, was He—but no, even I halted this side of the next obvious question, lest I were struck dead for its indecency. I turned away from the pedestal cupboard and its divine content. Too many complications and difficulties lay in the heart of it.

We were now quiet, and Con was soon asleep, and the last thing I remember, before that day went into the dark and haunted past, was the sound of Father's voice in converse with Mother on the landing below. It was raised in happiness because of his delight in his new home.

' I may have failed you emotionally,' he was saying, as he followed her into the back room and out again, ' I may have failed you spiritually, I may have failed you in a thousand ways, but at least you will grant me that I have provided you with a handsome home. You *do* like it, don't you ? Good. I'm glad. I have little doubt that I am detestable in many ways, but the fact remains that nothing has given me quite such pleasure as making this nice home for you. *And* for poor old Humphrey— he's completely happy, shoving his desk around. It's a home worthy of you, Una, because you're a damned good-looking woman, and at last you have a frame that fits you. And me too. Me too. That fool, Henrietta, said so, and though, coming from her, its effect was slightly emetic, she did but speak the truth, I must confess. At last I have a house instead of a hutch ; a home in which I can stretch myself to my full height, and breathe. At last I can be comfortable. I'm fifty-six, I'd have you remember, and at that great age one is entitled to a little largeness of living, a little comfort, before the end comes.' This was a text such as his soul loved, and he elaborated it, as he went behind her down the stairs. 'My sun is setting fast—I know that only too well—and it has always been my ambition to die in a house of some size and distinction. Mind that new paint. One cannot die in Walham Green. Here I can wither away with some feeling of fitness. We must get some magnificent carpets for the hall and the stairs ; I'm not in love with those black and white tiles. " I have warmed both hands at the fire of life. It sinks and I am ready to depart." ' Fitting words for a voice that was fading as it descended into the deeps ; and I should have heard no more, had I not caught my own name. One always hears one's own name. I raised my head.

'And what pleases me most of all, perhaps,' Father was saying, ' is that we have now a home worthy of Mr. Doric.'

Somehow I knew that my mother had stopped on the stairs. ' *And* of Con,' she insisted.

' Of Tricks too. Of course,' he allowed. ' Tricks is a charming child. A thought too pious for an old heathen like me, but an excellent child in her fat way. You must allow that I've provided you with two delightful children—sickly disappointment though I am.'

That was all I heard. They went on together, leaving a silence on the stairs ; and on my side of the silence I fell asleep.

CHAPTER II

THAT CHILD upon whom I am looking back, Doric Allan Mourne, was, I see, a happy, fearless, and impudent child in the presence of his father ; and an insecure, timid, furtive, and dishonest one in the presence of his mother. Odd that the same child, opposite one parent, could be in his composition something fairly good, while, opposite the other, he was a blend of unwholesome things.

What happiness it was when Con and I, breakfast over, escorted Father along Warwick Road to the green bus which would carry him to his occupations in the City. And what entertainment. In his frock coat, and top hat, he looked tall as a tower ; and we danced along on either side of him, seeming, I imagine, lesss than half his height. In one hand he carried his malacca cane and his kid gloves ; in the other his post-breakfast cigar. But I wouldn't have you picture him as a dandy. ' To look like an animated figure out of a tailor's show-card is the ambition of a shop-boy,' he used to say to me ; and he shut his eyes as if *in articulo mortis* the first time he saw that I had signed my name to a letter with an arabesque of flourishes. ' Oh, vulgar, vulgar ! ' he sighed, as in a last judgment on a world he could bear no more. ' Precisely, Doric, why should your name be more bedecked with ornament than the name of the person you are addressing ? That I should have lived to see this thing ! '

Some men, it is said, cannot pass a wayside cat without approaching it and stroking it, and certainly Father, on our walk to the bus, could not pass a baby in its perambulator without approaching it for some social exchanges. He would examine its fat, pink face under the hood, bow to it, and say ' Good morning, sir ' ; and after nodding to himself in appreciation, would turn to the mother or the nursemaid and compliment her. ' Yes . . . very fine . . . very fine indeed.' And because he was thus fascinated by children (at least as a beautiful idea) we did not pass a company of children playing cricket against a wall without his pausing to enjoy a few moments of the game to proclaim, ' Well bowled, sir ! . . . This is the demon bowler, Doric. . . . Good ! A boundary. A most palpable boundary.' Nor did we pass a street-singer carolling down the middle of the wide Warwick Road, or the pavement artist reclining against the dwarf wall in Kensington Road, but Father promptly stood still, his hand went into his trouser pocket, and it emerged with coppers which he thrust into my eager fingers with the instruction, ' Go you and deliver them to the gentleman, Doric. I expect he's a rogue, but I cannot see that his occupation is any more scoundrelly than the one I am going to now, and I have a suspicion his profits are less. We are all sinners making money out of the gullibility of our neighbours. Besides, in so far as he is an artist, you, Doric, would wish to be his patron. Go you and thank him for his efforts to create for us a little beauty.'

I see now that he urged my willing feet towards street-singer or pavement artist because he wanted to furnish us on these walks, not only with entertainment, but also with edification. He desired with all his heart that we should be good, that we should be better than he, and he laboured each morning on the pavements to this end. Once I remember Con was about to stamp on a sleepy wasp, and he dashed his hand forward and stopped her, exclaiming, ' Oh no, Tricks, no. " I would not enter on my list of friends The man who needlessly sets foot upon a worm " ' ; which quotation inspired him with a memory of Wordsworth, and he spouted to her, ' " One lesson, shepherd, let us two divide, Never to blend our pleasure or our pride With sorrow of the meanest thing that feels." ' After which he turned to the wasp and said, ' " Go, poor devil. Get thee gone. Why should Tricks hurt thee ? This world is surely wide enough to hold both Tricks and thee." '

Often when he produced the coppers for the beggars the sight of them would stir a covetousness in Con, and she would begin to pester him shamelessly for some pennies for herself. And he would shake his head and say, ' My fairest child, I have no coppers to give thee. Besides, what can you want with pennies ? You are well fed—I might even say you are fat with good feeding ; you are well clothed ; and your schooling is excellent ' ; but she, not listening to this purely formal and rhetorical resistance would strengthen her request by putting her arm around his waist and her head against his elbow ; and he, touched, would lay his arm along her shoulder, and say, ' Ah Tricks, Tricks ! Well have I named you Tricks. " Con " is certainly the short for " Confidence Trickster." ' Then perhaps I, feeling left out, would slip my hand into his ; and he, understanding, would press it very hard and hold it tight all the rest of the way. And he would surrender, saying, ' Mr. Doric is the gentleman and must treat the ladies. There is nothing that he likes better than to buy a trifle of butter-scotch for his sister. . . . Well, well, I will see if I can find a couple of coins. There, there— take it. Take all I've got. I am but a poor man, and to-morrow we will starve.'

And so we came to the bus, and he entered it, bending his tall head, and sat within it, waving a hand as it bore him away.

§

He was gone, and for me the threat was down upon the world. I walked home with Con, not miserably, but not happily, because I was wondering whether during the day the threat would fall. In the event it was possibly quite a jolly day, with Mother almost as vivacious with me as with Con ; but I know there was never a day in which I didn't long anxiously for my father's return. From about five o'clock I would stand at the window of this room, the play-room, and watch the square for his appearance. There was a large wastepaper-basket under the window, blocking access to it, and in my desire to get as close to the window as possible, I would step into the basket and stand in it like an ornamental fir in a tub.   After what seemed hours I would see him turn the corner, and the day was free again.   Or I might be away from the window when I heard his key turning in the front door ; and at the sound my heart sprang like a deer on the mountains with delight.   The clicking of his latchkey was the sweetest sound of my childhood.   I would race from the play-room and run helter-skelter down the stairs to meet him.   Sometimes if I hadn't heard the key there was no such happy rush, and he would call up the lifeless stairs, ' Believe it or not, this is General Allan Mourne entering his home.   Where's everybody ? Universal gaiety, please ' ; and Con and I, hearing his voice, would cataract down the stairs to welcome him.   I recall an evening when I ran down and flung myself at him, and he was so touched by this dog-like greeting that he said to Mother in the dining room, ' That young Doric has absolutely wound himself round my heart.'   I wasn't meant to hear this, but I did, and the words remain with me to this day, blinding me to his sins.

Because his presence in the house was my safety, Sunday was a happy day ; and this despite the church parades under Mother's command, which he excused himself from attending. There was an occasion when, Mother being unwell, *he* took us to church, and then the day was without flaw, for even church-going was fun.   Surprised by, and greatly pleased with, the access of nobility which had inspired him to take this church parade, he was in the highest spirits, and the quotations from Bunyan, the Bible, and Shakespeare leapt with a wonderful felicity to his lips.   ' Once more unto the breach, General. . . . Stiffen the sinews, summon up the blood. . . . Come, Tricks ; come, Doric ; let us to the Steeplehouse.'   There was something of genius, I must always think, in his joyous and ready use of splendid or picturesque phrases, whether from sacred or profane literature, and in his sense of the ludicrous as he applied them.   He studied the Bible, not, I fear, as his book of Standing Orders, but as a mass of beauty, parts of which would touch him to tears as, compelled by beauty, he read them aloud.   In the same way he loved Bunyan, not for his puritanism which made no appeal to Father, but for his superb manipulation of homely words, his monosyllabic pungency, and his sly, salted humour. No ; though ; I think I miss the target ; I should have said, not that he loved Bunyan and the Bible rather for their vigour and beauty than for what they enjoined him to do, but that he loved the injunctions too, in theory, and only regretted that their practice was too difficult for him. I remember him saying to Mother once, ' Fiddlesticks, my dear Una ! I find it quite possible to love the beauty of holiness, even though I'm given over to all manner of filthiness.'

' Come on, Tricks. What are you waiting for ? I am more than ready to sit under the ministry of your holy Mr. Peterson. Hie we to the Steeplehouse. "There was a man dwelt by a churchyard wall." Come on, Doric—I will accompany you, though of all the Saints I am the most unworthy. Good-bye, Una, my dear. Not at all ; why should you thank me ? It is my honourable task to bring them up in the fear and nurture of the Lord and to the praise of His holy name. I remember the padre saying that when we were married. Or something like it. Excellent phrases ; excellent phrases all. I protest I am going to enjoy this. Come on, children.' He was plainly enthusiastic about a new and untried experience.

In the church he rose and sat and bent forward in conformity with the congregation, but did not add his voice to prayer or hymn until he suddenly recognized a hymn of his youth whose famous and irresistible air, *Alleluia dulce carmen*, he'd sung on many a church parade ; and he let, it go with a roar,

> ' Praise, my soul, the King of Heaven,
> To His feet thy tribute bring,
> Ransomed, Healed, Restored, Forgiven . . .'

so that I was startled and slightly ashamed ; and Con giggled.

The sermon appealed to him too, and at its more beautiful parts he blew his large nose on his cream silk handkerchief scented with eau-de-Cologne ; for he was a ready weeper. 'At the foot of the Cross,' said Mr. Peterson solemnly, ' there were three women and only one man. Oh, the fidelity of women ! ' And Father, having meditated on this, blew his nose loudly. ' We worship the mother of our Lord,' continued the preacher, ' not because she was divine ; that is the error of the Papists. We worship her because she was at the scaffold's foot till He died and needed her no more.' I looked at Father. His lips were tight-set and quivering as he controlled the storm of tears within.

He wept at the beauty of it all, but he did not go a second time.

He took us to church once ; not twice. Next Sunday, Mother being still advised to keep the house, we besought him to come, dragging at him in his chair, but he protested, ' No, no. Explain to them, Una, that my sins are of too bloody a colour.' And as he said this he looked from under his forked eyebrows at Mother, hoping that the old tinker's words had shaken her. ' Go you along, children, and sing your hymns. Con was in magnificent form the other day with her " Come unto me, ye weary." Pass me those cigars, Doric, and then take her ; take her along ; and do you both pray for your old father, who, as your mother will surely tell you, is a vessel given over to corruption, wickedness and lies. Thump up my cushion, Tricks. A match, and the *Observer* news-sheet, please ; and good-bye to you all.'

§

I am too old now to bear malice against a mother who died long ago, and I shall try only to describe her exactly as she was : a comely, vivacious, stupid, unscrupulous, and at times, alas, cruel woman. To the outer world she gave of her vivacity, and was well liked by women who resembled her, and by the men whom she sought to attract ; to Father she was sometimes good but more often sour, and not without provocation; to Con she gave all the affection that her selfishness would allow ; upon me, as the years went by, she directed an increasing dislike which issued often in cruelty.

Father had married her when he was forty-six and she a slender and beautiful girl of twenty-three, and it had wanted but a year to ripen their disappointment in each other. Discontent sat upon her lips when she was not among friends ; a brooding gloom would plunge my father, now and then, into a silence as of the dead—but only now and then, for his up-surging humour would bring him buoyantly to the surface again. They maintained a fair partnership in the long periods between their quarrels. He would discourse merrily with her when he needed someone to share his dreams, or an adult receptacle, as well as two juvenile ones, for his humorous output. Uncle Humphrey was another valuable audience, but he was too often dwelling in a chambered solitude upstairs. Well aware of her bitterness against him, Father would cut out and pin upon her mantelpiece suitable headlines from his news-papers, such as ' Ninety per cent. of Marriages a Failure, says Judge,' or ' Wife Murders Husband and Goes Free. Justifiable Homicide ' ; and Mother would tut-tut at them and pull them

down, for though she had humour, it came off a different shelf
from Father's. I need hardly say she thought it a higher shelf.
He was always very courteous to her, except in moments of
rage when he cared not at all what he said to anyone—or,
rather, when he preferred what he said to be as wounding as
possible—and he was never more courteous than in the days
of estrangement after a tumultuous row. 'Stately' was too
small a word for his courtesy then ; it was imperial ; it wore
the purple and the bays, and spoke with the dignity of kings.

At thirty-three Mother was still quite slender and her neat
features and soft skin were little spoiled ; only her expression had
hardened. Her small eyes seemed to me sometimes as hard
as the heads of her hatpins, and her once lovely mouth as tight
as a strained bow. She might laugh and be merry with her
gossips, or with the man (or maybe two men) whom she was
attracting at the time, but, as I think of her now, in her tight-
waisted dress, with its collar as stiffly whaleboned as its bodice,
it seems a fitting attire for one encased in disappointment and
self-pity.

Flirt as she might, she sought the largest assuagement for her
'emotional starvation' (a phrase of Father's for *his* hapless
state) in her churchgoing and religious exercises ; Father sought
it almost exclusively in other feminine company ; and to judge
from the ratio of gaiety to bitterness in him and in her, his
blend of medicine was the more effective. He sought it also
in me, and was as vocal about this anointment for his wounds
as he was silent about the other. Just as she believed everything
in her religion that it was comfortable to believe, so he invested
me with virtues that I didn't possess, and made his mythology
out of them. 'Doric is generous to a fault,' he would say—a
new idea to me, and one that impressed me very much, so that
I actually set about the job of making it a little less untrue ;
and a difficult job it was.

Because he so obviously preferred me above Con, and because
Con was born before the earth parted under their feet, and I
after the crack had widened, and because when I was born
my father was wandering far afield and out of view, and up
to heaven knew what games, Mother developed a hostility to
me and, by a process of self-suggestion, confirmed and enlarged
it throughout the years. She was eager for opportunities to
quarrel with me, and when an opportunity presented itself,
went like a lover to the punishment. To light up with wrath
at an offence of mine was a joy to her. She had discovered the
fine tang and stimulation of a flaming row, and the two people
from whom she could get this strong satisfaction were Father

and myself. She had learned that to ' let oneself go,' to drink deep of the wine-cup of indignation when it was red, and to let it intoxicate the veins and the brains, was as good an orgy as another. Sometimes her storm was a real *tour de force*, a brilliant affair which she had created out of almost nothing. But with me alone could she get the secret and carnal delight of wielding a cane. I should lie if I hid the fact that she got a zest, an exhilaration, an exaltation, out of spreading me upon a bed and thrashing me. In part, perhaps, it was because I was the whipping-boy for her husband.

To justify this punishment she had to make out that I was worse than I was—though, to be sure, I was hypocritical and sullen and mendacious enough with her ; and she soon persuaded herself, being a woman unburdened with any power of self-criticism, that she didn't like me at all. After a time she rather preened herself on this, as if it were striking and original. ' It's no good pretending to something I can't feel, Henrietta dear,' she would say proudly. ' Heaven knows I've tried to feel affection for him, but I can't. He's not a nice child. He's altogether too like his father. I wish I *could* like him ; it's a great sorrow to me that I can't. I know this must sound strange in a mother, but I'm trying to tell you the truth, not what you'd expect me to say.'

At times I got the impression that she had to force herself to dislike her own child ; a temporary gentleness towards me would appear ; but it would not fit comfortably into her complex of emotions, and she was relieved when she could get back to the dislike.

I must forgive her all because she was stupid. She was stupid because she was able without difficulty to be thus selfish, unscrupulous, vindictive and cruel, and at the same time to speak all the set words of current morality and all the high sentiments of religion. She was stupid because her religion was sincere. The same phenomenon showed itself, though less markedly, in Con ; and I think I have hinted already that at an early age this dichotomy began to perplex me intellectually and offend me æsthetically. I was a hypocrite myself and knew it ; these two did not know it, or seemed not to. I used to wonder if men could see their own hypocrisy and stayed away from church accordingly but women were untroubled by the sight ; and I must say that, after sixty years, the same wonder will visit me still.

§

In the first weeks after our arrival at Coburg Square Father spent much of his time, when board meetings and business luncheons were over, browsing in West End shops and selecting articles of furniture for his new home. The furniture from Walham Green was only fit for a signalman's cottage, he said, and he could not, would not, live like a signalman. So hardly a day passed but some unannounced piece of furniture, huge or small, stepped out from a van on to the pavement before our door. We never knew what was coming next, or where to put it when it came. Mother, hurrying to the window to see the latest arrival, would tut-tut and ask. ' Oh, whatever is it this time ? ' The size and costliness of some of the pieces frightened her, who had never, from her childhood, been used to large and easy spending. For the dining-room came a table large enough for one of Father's board meetings ; for the stairs a broad and deep pile carpet of red and blue ; for the drawing-room a white Indian carpet, well suited to the Taj Mahal, a Steinway grand piano, a lacquered cabinet, and some smaller things like Japanese fans and photogravure prints of Rosetti and Burne-Jones pictures, which were just becoming modish.

And on a June afternoon I returned from school with my satchel slung, and my mind somewhere in the satchel by the side of a drawing which both my mistresses, Miss Greenway and Miss Eltham, had praised somewhat ecstatically. I was eager to show the drawing to Mother and Con. Running up our steps, I pulled the bell ; it clanged in the basement, and I heard Lettice dragging herself up the steep kitchen stairs.

She opened the door and peered at me over her steel spectacles. ' Oh, it's you, Master Doric ; it's you, is it ? Well, I declare ! Gracious to glory ! I'd only just sat down. The girl's out for her afternoon. I'd just sat down and dropped off to sleep, and your bell didn't half give me a turn. I do think they might let you come in by the area door when I'm all alone. It's not so very much to arst."

' I can't very well come in by the area door,' I submitted, surprised, and slightly hurt, that she should have suggested such an indignity.

' There's no such word as " can't ",' she said.

' Oh yes, there is ! ' I cried with triumph. ' You've just used it.'

' Clever, aren't you ? There'll be no holding you one of

these days, you're that clever. Now run along and let me have my little sit down.'

' Is Mamma in ? '

' No, she's still out. She went out above an hour ago.'

' Where's she gone ? '

' Never you mind. I don't know. I expected her back before this.'

' Is Miss Con in ? '

' No, she went out along of your mamma.'

' Oh ! ' It was a disappointment, so impatient had I been to display my sketch ; but I only expressed the disappointment with a ' Well, well, well,' and an imitation of her expletives. ' They're both out, are they, Lettice ? Well, I declare ! Gracious to glory ! '

' Now, none of your sauce,' she protested, but not unkindly. ' You make too free sometimes, you know. " Well, well, well," indeed ! What's the good of a well without water ? And " you declare " ! Hark at him. He declares ! Now run along into the dining-room, and they'll be back any minute to their tea.'

I did not go into the dining-room, whose door was forbiddingly closed. As Lettice went back into her kitchen shaft, I saw the broad rich carpet leading up the stairs to the drawing-room. Mother, fearful of the drawing-room's white carpet, and the delicate tables and chairs that stood in such peril upon it, and the unscratched piano, had forbidden us on any account to enter the room. Each time a new treasure arrived for the room, she saw it into its place, glanced anxiously around the shining chamber, and then firmly shut its door.

But that stair carpet, wide and soft, ran up the treads before me like an invitation. Its soft texture and its lively colours beckoned me with the mischievous witchery of a woman. ' Remember the piano ? ' it said. ' And the golden clock, and the brass coal-scuttle like a fireman's helmet, and the bulrushes in the tall Chinese vases, and the peacock's feathers and Japanese fans on the mantelpiece ? Come. I lead you to a cave like Aladdin's. These riches are your father's and yours. The house is empty ; come and see them again.'

I went quickly and quietly up the stairs, and the soft carpet abetted me all the way. There at the top was the door of the enchanted room. The forbidden territory cried to be visited, and I opened the door soundlessly and tip-toed in. After gazing in admiration for a few seconds I stepped towards the golden clock on the white marble mantelpiece. And at my third step the floor creaked beneath me.

I stopped and stood still ; but my heart had stopped and stood still before I could ; and now it was pounding. I had heard a movement in the dining room below, and a voice. Mother was at home after all, and Con was down there with her. Lettice, at rest in her kitchen, and perhaps asleep, had not heard their return.

Downstairs the dining room door opened. Mother was in the passage. She was at the foot of the stairs, listening. I stood in the midst of the white carpet, unable to move, scarcely breathing. Now her feet were on the stairs, and there was a purpose and resolve in her step. She had quaffed the red wine of indignation, and now it was coursing in her blood-stream and dancing in her brain. I could no more move than a bird transfixed by the eyes of a serpent.

She walked into the room, and the light of her purpose gleamed in her eyes. Had I been older I would have seen the lust shining there too.

' Did I not say you were not to come in here ? '

No answer. The victim is silent while it is slain by the basilisk's eyes.

' Did I or did I not ? Answer me ? *Will* you answer ? Did I not forbid you to come in here ? '

' Yes.'

' And you've deliberately disobeyed me ? '

How could I deny it ?

' Very good.' That ' very good ' expressed more than she understood. ' You shall learn to obey.' And she took me by the wrist and led me from the room. Down the soft, treacherous stair carpet we went ; and terror armed me with words and strength. ' Oh, no, mamma,' I pleaded, and struggled and dragged myself back. But her fingers were a steel clamp about my wrist, an eager lustful embrace, and we went on down.

' You disobeyed me.' One must justify oneself when one lusts to be cruel.

' I didn't touch anything.'

' That doesn't matter. I forbade you to go into the room and you went in. You shall learn to obey.'

Con, finger at mouth, was at the staircase foot, watching our descent with more interest in the coming execution than pity for the criminal. From the hat-stand Mother snatched my father's supple Wanghee cane.

' Oh no, mamma ! '

' I shall teach you to obey.' Her voice was like the serpent's hiss, and she led me along the passage to the dining room. Con watched us go.

In the dining room Mother forced me on to the fine new table, face downwards, and slashed me again and again with the cane. I screamed and struggled, and she desisted, lest my screaming should shock Lettice in the kitchen or alarm the neighbours beyond the wall.

'The expense of spirit in a waste of shame . . .' Mother had now to fight her shame. 'Do you think I *enjoy* whipping you?' she demanded. 'I hate it. But one day you will realize that I did it for your good. I don't have to whip Con. Stop that squawling. *Stop* it, I tell you! I didn't hurt you all that much. *Will* you stop? Oh, my God!' French windows opened on to a glass veranda, and she thrust me, moaning and sobbing, through them. She could not stand my moaning. 'Come in when you've stopped whimpering,' she said and slammed the windows to. I was shut out in a little bower of flowers. My fingers tight together, and twisting in misery, I stood on the tiles between the windows that had rejected me and the boxes of gay geraniums, marguerites, and lobelia. Down towards my head, as if wishing to feel it, hung the pink geraniums from their wire baskets. At their feet, in their damp and shaded earth, the ferns uncurled and crook'd their fronds. To this day the warm earthy smell of a glasshouse builds that veranda around me.

I stamped on the tiles. I said to the flowers, 'I hate her, I hate her; I hate everyone. I hate God.' Remembering Con's assertion that if you took God's name in vain, He would strike you dead, I said deliberately, 'Damn God! Damn God!' partly in a mutiny against Him and His world, and partly in a sincere readiness for annihilation. But nothing came down upon me through the glass roof; and I stood in all the stillness of a world gay with flowers but empty of God. And as if the shelf with its flowers were an altar, I continued my Black Mass before it. Defying everyone, visible and invisible, temporal and eternal, I said aloud: 'I do not believe in God the Father Almighty, Maker of Heaven and earth; nor in Jesus Christ His only Son our Lord. . . . And I do not believe in the Holy Ghost, the holy Catholic Church, the Communion of Saints, the Forgiveness of sins, the Resurrection of the body, and the life everlasting. Amen.'

And I was rejoiced and uplifted by my daring and my superiority to Mother and Con. *Sursum corda.*

CHAPTER III

BETWEEN OUR taking possession of this house and my being
sent to Draycote School I seem to see in my backward vision
a long six years of play. To the adults in the house these
years, I doubt not, went hurrying by, depressingly evanescent ;
to us children they seemed a continuing stillness, not unrelated,
it may be, to the mystics' Everlasting Now. The years passed
over the house, and all that we knew of them was their change
of face and temper as spring succeeded winter, and summer
consumed the spring. Now we were playing in the square's
garden, in the warm, golden afternoons of July ; now among
the same trees in the first red blush of autumn ; now in the
early September dusks ; and now it was deep midwinter and we
sat at the playroom table with our puzzles or our playing cards
spread beneath the wavering candlelight or about the orange
halo of the lamp.

It seems to me that there were always three of us at play ;
but it could not have been so. It is just that I recall more
easily the times when Gentle was with us. Mother and Henrietta
were two sisters who loved to talk together for hours and hours,
and so Henrietta came often to our home from Redcliffe Street
across the highway, bringing Gentle with her. And there we
would all be : Mother and Henrietta talking and talking in
the drawing-room, Lettice and the servants in the depths below,
Uncle Humphrey high above on the third story like Paul caught
up into the third heaven ; and we children at our games in
the high, hollow house, or out in the square's garden on some
day of azure and amber, running with loud shouts over the
shadowed or the burnished grass.

In the first half of these years Gentle was our leader. Her
creative vitality was more usurping and irrepressible than
Con's, who, like many plump little girls was a happy but stolid
and ' accepting ' child. Gentle's inventiveness (like her
temper) came much more quickly to the boil ; my inventiveness later equalled hers, but at this time, though she was only
a month or so older than I, she was far maturer ; and so she
became naturally our captain, and we the subalterns—in fact,
not in theory, for neither of us would have conceded to her
this honourable title. Again, Gentle's reverence for holy
things was as weak as Con's was powerful, and this gave her
a great advantage in the invention of what she called ' Holy
Games.' Con joined in these, rather than be left out, but her

performance was somewhat hampered by her doubts and fear of the Lord.

Let me further interpret. Henrietta in her intense, her over-intense, desire to mould Gentle into a holy and beautiful character would deluge her with moral and elevating talks and a power of earnest instruction ; and Gentle, unconsciously creating her own protection, had turned herself into a kind of radio set which automatically switched itself off directly the edifying talks began. She received nothing from the ether, even though the programme was still being relayed. If the talks had any effect on Gentle it was to sow in her the first seeds of a desire to be the opposite of most things her mother stood for. In these early days, however, Gentle's resistance to all this pursuing earnestness expressed itself only in a drive to turn every solemn experience to which she was subjected into a new game. She was not ten years old when Henrietta, intent upon her sanctification, took her to a Confirmation Service, and then to a First Communion of the newly confirmed (which Henrietta would declare, with her great eyes staring at you, was ' one of the most moving and beautiful sights in the world ') and Gentle was certainly interested in these ceremonies, but only in such a way that she must repeat them in our playroom next time she was at our house. Robed in a white nightgown for an episcopal rochet, and in a red curtain for an academic hood, she confirmed us in this room, laying a hand on each of our heads as we knelt side by side before her, and saying, ' Defend, O Lord, this thy child . . . and this thy child.' And when we were thus initiated she (I write it in some dismay) administered the sacrament to us at an altar rail composed of two chairs and a curtain rod.

As earnest a devotee of Culture as of Religion, Henrietta dragged Gentle to art galleries and picture shows whenever the opportunity offered ; and once again the chief fruit of this sedulous tillage was a sudden desire in Gentle to have an exhibition of her own works and ours, with a charge for admission and a catalogue at a price. Driven by the tremendous pressure of this idea, she steamed round to us early one morning, shunted us speedily into the playroom, and there opened all her valves, so that the place was soon loud and hissing with her plans. It was a day in the Christmas holidays ; we had it all to ourselves ; and we devoted five or six hours, under her restless direction, to preparing the pictures, hand-printing the tickets of admission, and writing out six copies of the catalogue ; ' 1. *Venice by Night*. Gentle Greaves. 2. *Still Life*. Constance Allan Mourne. 3. *In Darkest Africa*. Theodore Allan Mourne . . .'

The charge for admission was a penny for those who cared to

pay, with relief from this impost for those who didn't. Likewise
the price of the catalogue was a penny, and the same relief was
attached to it. 'Henrietta doesn't frightfully approve of my
taking money from anyone,' Gentle explained. Ever since she'd
heard me calling Father 'The General' she'd referred to her
mother as Henrietta and to her father as Brian. 'But she can't
mind if it's only Una and Humphrey, can she? And, oh—
anyhow—nobody need pay if they'd rather not. Call them up.'
Straightway we summoned them all : Mother, Uncle Humphrey,
Lettice and the two new maids ; and I must say they all played
their parts most loyally. Mother praised my pictures as readily
and merrily as Con's or Gentle's ; Lettice studied each picture
over and through her spectacles, and forced up her praises well ;
and Uncle Humphrey came out particularly strong, insisting
that he must pay for all the 'ladies,' which term included the
servants. He produced a sixpence, but drew the line at paying
for more than one catalogue. 'They can read mine,' he said.

It had been fully five o'clock when the gallery was opened to
the public, and the public was just withdrawing with many
protestations of pleasure, when a key clicked in the hall door.
Father was home. We raced to the banisters and screamed to
him to come up. 'Come to the Art Exhibition !' It was not
in Father to disappoint three children, however exhausted he
might be with the day's labour, and he came up instantly in
his heavy overcoat with the astrakhan collar, and holding his
silk hat, which lent an agreeable air of fashion to our show.
And he paid cheerfully for admission and catalogue, and even
inquired if there were not other charges to be met. And he
stood in the centre of the floor and swept his eyes around the
pictures ; then turned and looked whimsically upon the artists ;
and I can still see the great tenderness in his eyes as we stood
before him, staring up at his face. Not one picture did he pass
by, but went to each, all the artists following ; and before each
he consulted his catalogue, and nodded his head, and stood
before it, walking back a few steps and putting his head on one
side to consider its effects better.

'Yes. Very fine. Very fine indeed. Such draughtsmanship!
Such colour tones ! And such a sense of design—of pattern !
What is it ? A coffin ?—oh, I beg your pardon : *Coburg Square,
Kensington.* Yes, of course, of course. And *this* one : will you
only look at this one ? *Portrait of a Girl.* What a speaking likeness, to be sure ! Who is it ? Con ?—no, Gentle—I beg your
pardon—Gentle, of course—a remarkable likeness—and the work
of Theodore Allan Mourne. Very fine. This really is a most
important exhibition. And here : what have we here ? Now

we really are in the presence of genius. Whose work is it ? Let me see. " Gentle Greaves." A lady, I imagine. Well, she certainly has a great future before her. And this by Constance Allan Mourne. The Himalayas, is it—my old friends, the Himalayas ? *Not* the Himalayas ?—oh, I'm sorry—no, *Storm in the Atlantic*. Obviously a storm in the Atlantic. It couldn't be anything else.' He stopped and turned round upon us. ' Are these excellent pictures for sale ? '

' Oh, yes, yes ! ' Gentle got in with her answer first.

' Then I shall most assuredly buy some. Let me think : I need about three. I shall take this very striking picture . . . and this one . . . and—let me consult the catalogue—yes, this.' Oddly enough, he had chosen one picture by each exhibitor. ' Now who is the Curator ? '

' Pardon ? ' said Gentle.

He shut his eyes in an agony at this expression, which was one of his abominations ; and when he was recovered from it, he paraphrased, ' Who is the Person in Authority, the Lord High Chief, the Boss, the General Cock of the Walk ? '

' I am, I am, I am ! ' cried Gentle, leaping up and down. ' I suggested it.'

' You are, are you. I see.'

He drew his little gold sovereign-case from his waistcoat pocket, where it was attached to his watch-chain ; and pressed from it a sovereign.

' Then perhaps you will be so good as to divide this among the three artists whose remarkable pictures I have purchased. I thank you. Good evening.'

Gentle looked at the gold coin in her hand. ' Coo-*lummy !* A pound ! A *pound !* Oh, I do think Uncle Kingsley's the loveliest person in the world. *A pound !* Coo ! ' And she tore from the room to show it to Mother, Lettice, and the maids.

§

Now it was spring and we were out of the house—out in the street bouncing a tennis ball against the side of the house. The game was to clap our hands once between each catch,fand we took it in turns to see what score of catches we could achieve in these difficult circumstances. Gentle, long, supple, alert, and as concentrated upon the ball as if her life stayed or fell with it, would count up to sixty and seventy and eighty. ' Sixty-one,' she would say breathlessly, ' sixty-two, sixty-three—Gosh, I'm good !—sixty-four, sixty-five. . . .' When at last the ball defeated her, she would toss back her two corn-sheaf plaits with

their yellow bows, leap on to a window sill, and sit there sideways, her hands folded on her lap, her feet crossed, and her
long legs swinging. She must have been older now, eleven or
twelve, for she had learned the pleasure of being generous and
would say ' Oh, hard luck ' when Con failed in the forties, and
' Oh, hard luck ' again (though relieved) when I just failed to
reach her score.

I remember—how clearly !—when Gentle greeted the spring
by an adventure which left her partly outside the house and
partly in it. We had been looking through the playroom
window to see if the day was now dry enough for a game outside, and Gentle of a sudden noticed the long stripes which the
rain had left upon the panes. We must clean the windows, she
immediately decided ; we must sit on the sills and wash them
like the housemaids opposite.

In perfect co-operation we all three ran for basin and flannels
and brought them to a window. ' My turn first,' Gentle claimed.
' It was my idea ' ; and, pushing up the sash, she swung herself
out on to the cold sill and sat there. She looked down the front
of the house, past the breakfast room and kitchen windows to
the paved area, and declared that she wasn't afraid at all.
' There's nothing in it. Absolutely nothing.'

Indeed she was so pleased with her fearlessness and with her
work on the windows that she bragged, ' I shouldn't mind
cleaning the window of the room above. There's nothing in it.'
We dared her to do this, and she promised ' All right ' ; and we
all ran upstairs to the room above, which was Father's bedroom.

Here we opened a window, and Gentle, the performer, looked
out. It was plain from her silence that, up here, she was less
happy about the enterprise, but, too proud to retreat, too vain
to brook our jeers, she pushed the sash up higher and—doubtless
suffering—worked herself on to the sill and pulled down the
upper sash on to her thighs.

But at this point the Devil, ever desiring mischief, whispered
to her to look down. ' Look down, my dear ; just once. Look
down and see how high you sit, and how far below you is the
dull, unadventurous world.' She looked down, saw the great
cliff of the house below her, and was instantly undone. ' Oh,
oh, oh ! ' she cried, and gripped the top of the sash. ' Hold my
legs, hold my legs.' We promptly held them, one each, and
she screamed ' Don't let go.'

For a minute I did drop her left leg (which was my share)
and tried to lift the sash, but she bawled ' NO ! ' and gripped
it as if it were her last frail hope of life. ' Don't be a fool. Leave
it. Hold my legs ! Hold my LEGS ! '

I resumed hold of her leg, and there we were, fixed apparently for all time, Con and I in the house, she outside (or largely outside), we holding her legs, which we mustn't let go, and she holding the sash, which mustn't be moved.

How this dilemma would have been resolved I cannot say, if the clamour hadn't disturbed the studies of Uncle Humphrey in the room above, where he was reclining in his easy chair and reading Pollock's *Spinoza, His Life and Philosophy*. His window shot up, and his rosy cheeks and spade beard shot out. He looked down the face of the house and saw Gentle sticking out below. For a second or two he only looked at her and said nothing : Gentle, sitting on the high sill with the window dragged down before her and her two yellow plaits hanging down behind her, sat in no known system of philosophy. Not perhaps the wisest of men, for all that his studies were of philosophy, he merely asked, when he did speak : ' What are you doing ? '

But Gentle, speechless with terror, could only throw up at him the last hopeless glance of the perishing.

' Get in at once,' said he ; and added the least wise remark of all. ' You may fall.'

' Oh, oh, oh ! ' wailed Gentle.

' Gracious ' and ' 'Tst, 'tst ' muttered Uncle Humphrey ; and he came down the stairs into Father's room and saw us holding the other ends of Gentle.

' What on earth are you all doing ? ' he asked. ' Stop that at once.'

' We can't stop, or she says she'll fall.'

' Don't stop ! Don't stop ! ' screamed Gentle.

' That's all rubbish. Make her come in at once.'

' But how ? ' asked I, and ' She won't,' Con affirmed.

' She's got to. How can I get on with my work ? I never heard such a noise. What d'you mean : " she won't " ? '

' She won't let us touch the window,' I explained. ' If we try to, she holds it tight and yells to us not to.'

' But don't be silly. Are you all going to stay there for ever ? '

' I don't know.'

Uncle Humphrey put an arm round Gentle's indoor thighs and gathered up the mass of them as a sailor gathers up his kit bag to embark upon the liberty boat. ' Now you're quite safe,' he called. ' I've got you tight. If you go, I go. Lift the window, Doric.'

' Oh, must he ? '

' Yes.'

' Oh . . . oh . . .'

' Go on, Doric. We can't leave her out for ever. It'll get the house a bad name.'

I raised the sash bit by bit, and Gentle gasped ' Oh ! ' at each instalment. When it was high enough, Uncle Humphrey gave her a hand, and, all danger past, she hopped to the floor as happily as if it were now her turn with the ball.

' Gosh ! ' she said with a brilliant smile. ' That was a thrill.'

And Uncle Humphrey hurried from the room lest his health should be depleted by any similar strains.

§

On Mother's visiting cards, in the left-hand corner, were the words, ' Last Thursday.' They indicated that Mother's At Home day was on the last Thursday of the month ; but Father maintained that they were an ingenious method of preventing any stupid women from coming at all, since, on consulting Mother's card, they would conclude that it was now too late, since the At Home day was last Thursday. On Mother's At Home day she and her drawing-room were dressed for company. The room was garnished with new cut flowers ; a lace-bordered cloth and dainty tea things covered an occasional table ; and a three-decker wicker-work cake-stand stood patiently by the sofa, with rolled bread and butter on its top story, hot buttered cakes on its middle story, and one big chocolate cake, or an asterisk of pink and brown fancy cakes, on its ground floor. And from about three o'clock Mother sat on the sofa in her best afternoon gown, waiting for the visitors' bell to ring. Sometimes several ladies came from the streets around ; sometimes only Henrietta. Henrietta nearly always came ; and if no one else appeared, she and mother enjoyed a happy afternoon on the sofa together, talking, talking.

In the long gallery of my childhood this picture recurs again and again : Mother and Henrietta closeted in the drawing-room, both on the sofa, Mother face forward, Henrietta sideways ; Mother talking, Henrietta in the more earnest moments bending towards her ; Mother still slight and shapely, Henrietta (in Father's phrase) ' improperly long '—an elongated edition of her younger sister. If Uncle Humphrey was right when he said that a sentence depended for its beauty on the elimination of every unnecessary syllable, then Mother was a well-phrased sentence, and Henrietta was the same statement six words too long.

Mother was a big talker at any time ; with the sympathetic

Henrietta she was a huge one. Generally she was enlarging on someone's sins; a servant's, or Father's, or mine ; but it was early plain to me that, on the whole, she was indifferent to what she talked about so long as she talked ; I discerned this because she would change the subject—any subject—at a breath. Henrietta was an intense listener and would say beautiful and consoling things when my malpractices, or Father's, were under review. She idealized everything in her talk : Gentle, Brian, Miss Laventer, of Gentle's school, and the Vicar of St. Margaret's, Bolton Square, 'who really was a saint.' (He was nothing of the sort.) In due time she took to idealizing—that is, making a great thing of—my father's wickedness and mine. It was this habit, and that drawing-room door shut on them both, which developed in me the shameful habit of eavesdropping. I could not see it without feeling sure they were talking about me, and I would halt in the dark passage, guilty and ashamed, to catch what Mother was saying.

But this was only when it was winter and dark, and we children were in the house. On bright summer days we three, for Gentle came always with her mother, were in the square's garden at play. Gentle had learned, Heaven knows where, certainly not from Henrietta, how to do a hand-stand and turn a cart-wheel and she was so pleased with these skills that we never knew, as we turned round to find her, which way up she would be. For Hide and Seek the iron seat under the lilac tree was always ' Home.' The one who was ' He ' would conscientiously face it till the ' Coo-ey ! ' sounded from the shrubs and then rush out and chase the hiders back to it. I remember once when I was ' He ' and Gentle, two yards from this ' Home,' was screaming to the sky because she heard me but three feet behind her, I pushed her with both hands so violently, to convince her of her capture, that she crashed against the seat and one of her legs (or so she furiously affirmed) was ' bashed open and all messy with blood.' She rolled down her stocking to examine the limb, and, yes, the skin on its knee was cracked and bloody. ' I think I'm going to be sick,' she said. Con, who had come up, was much interested in this prospect, and, looking up into Gentle's face, increased the chances of disaster by declaring that she looked awful. I had to admit to myself that she had turned very white, but I thought that, for all our sakes, the matter had better be kept on the humorous plane, and, since my humour at this time was to use shattering big words, I said, ' I cannot express how grieved I am, and how extensively I apologize.' And when she retorted, ' Oh, *you* shut up, you complete and filthy idiot,' I only stated, ' I do not propose to be criticized much,' and continued kindly, ' If I may offer a word of advice, I should lie down for a few minutes and think of nothing.'

' Yes.'   This appealed to Con.   ' Lie down absolutely straight. Nothing may happen then.'

Gentle, who really was in danger of an eruption, lay full-length on the seat, her eyes shut, her lips parted, and her bare knee bleeding ; and I stood at her side and looked down upon my handiwork.   Con stood by me waiting to see if she would be sick.

But it was May, and the scent of the lilac, drawn to the warm earth, fell about Gentle and delicately soothed and comforted her.   It is at any time a mild and healing unction for a body that is disturbed or a soul that is inflamed.   Her sickness settled, her temper sank ; and she sniffed at the sweet, laden air.

' Coo ! ' she cried ; and the syllable was a whole lyric in its intent.   ' Isn't the smell of the lilac lovely ? '

' Are you all right ? ' asked Con.   ' Do you think you could play again ? '

' No,' said Gentle, ' I'm going to lie here and smell.'

I rise from my desk and go to the window.   The square is very different from what it was on that day.   Then the houses were still young ; they were well-dressed in a costume of cream paint embroidered with window-box geraniums ; and in the pride of their youth, and their smart attire, they supposed they would always keep their present importance.   The Corinthian columns, the plush curtains, the holland blinds, demurely lowered, seemed to know that they lived in the Royal Borough of Kensington.   Trim servant maids came to the doors or the area gates in their pink cotton frocks, and as the afternoon wore on to ' calling time ' reappeared in long black frocks and neat white caps and aprons.   When the lady of a house came down her steps she wore the badge of her caste, which was a veil drawn tightly under her chin, and drew over her fingers the long, tight gloves with an air, well satisfied with her place in Society, and unaware that she was doomed.

I am not suggesting that ours was a square of the first fashion, but simply that it was a very polite enclosure.   It was a reservation, so to say, for ladies and gentlemen and their children. There were one or two moneyed tradesmen in it who lowered its tone a little, and, in our house, we were not yet sure that the doctor at No. 23, though he was fetched daily from his door by a victoria or a brougham, and went forth in silk hat and frock coat, was quite the equal of my father, who was an officer.   But for our peace of mind we decided that the tradesmen did not dilute the good wine too much, and we accepted the doctor as one of ourselves and an example of the Changing Times.

Such was our square when Gentle lay under the lilac tree. And now? Now the houses, fifty years older, look tired and gaunt, and the cream paint of some of them is leprous ; now there are three or four bell-pushes to each front door, and as many different curtains in the windows as there are flats in the house ; now there are two perambulators under the Corinthian columns of No. 23, four empty milk bottles on the threshold of No. 39, and it is the ' lady in the basement ' who comes up to the area gate of No. 31.

But do not mistake me. I am not suggesting that our Coburg Square is now a slum. Just as it never reached the top of fashion so it has never sunk below the foothills. There are still professional people among the tenants, and even an old admiral and his wife ; but they are all taxed and poor ; and their life has been compressed into a few of the large rooms. I am the only one with a whole house to myself.

It is the garden which has sunk to the marsh levels and is now an open and abandoned waste, with none so poor to do it reverence. I shut my eyes, and, like one of the old transformation scenes at Drury Lane, the garden as it was rises from the dust and litter. The railings rise and surround it again, and each rail has a head like a spear. Within the rails the trees are much smaller than now : the chestnut half its present size, the poplar a slender feminine thing, the acacia a sapling. The grass is a green pile carpet patterned with beds of flowers.

I open my eyes, and only the torn and broken privets surround the waste. Where was trim turf there is now a trodden and putty-coloured dust or a wilderness of rosebay, white clover and red sorrel. Difficult to believe that that poplar, tall as a steeple, with all its fluttered leaves glistening like sequins, is the same poplar, and that silent and sombre plane is *our* plane. We paid a guinea a year for the upkeep of the garden, and it is extraordinary, as I watch, to see it fenced no more, and strangers walking without shame across that ancient and secluded privacy. It is they who have trodden our turf to putty. There, rising from the dry earth, is Gentle's lilac tree, the first as you break the privets, and on a May day it still smells sweet and blossoms in the dust.

And here comes Roberta, returning from Earls Court Road and the shops, her easy stride like a youth's on a walking tour. She brings, not only her purchases in her basket, but strange thoughts for one watcher as she swings past the lilac tree.

§

Once a shower came down upon us in the garden, and we scampered indoors and up to the playroom. Mother was out ; the servants were at rest in the basement ; and the house was silent except for intermittent rumblings along an upper floor. We went to the door and listened to these mysterious sounds ; a rumble and then footsteps ; a pause and then footsteps and a rumbling again. Their meaning was quickly understood by us : Uncle Humphrey was rearranging his furniture and studying it in new positions. We could hear him singing gently to himself as he did so. He sang frequently up there, and always his songs were sad, elegaic airs that matched well with his sad, St. Bernard eyes. The noises and singing stopped, and as we waited and listened, he began to come downstairs.

We stepped back into the play-room ; he passed and went down to the hall. We ran to the window. The shower was over, the sun was about again, and people were returning into the streets to shake hands with it. We saw Uncle Humphrey come down our steps into the light, his buttoned jacket straining over his paunch, and his umbrella hanging by its crook on his arm. It was an unfortunate moment he had chosen for his appearance on the pavement, because two Salvation Army girls with collecting boxes had just arrived in the square, and one of them, rattling her box, immediately approached the shrinking Uncle Humphrey. As a snail's horns withdraw from an approaching finger ; as the leaf of the sensitive plant folds together with irritability at the touch of a moth, so Uncle Humphrey contracted at the touch of that jangling box ; but he hadn't the heart, or the courage, to reject it entirely, and he appeased the unwelcome thing with a coin ; after which he walked on, re-arranging his coat on his stomach and his umbrella on his arm, as if the unexpected assault had disordered him.

' Isn't he a pet ? ' said Gentle. ' But what does he really *do*, up there in his room all day ? '

' He writes a book,' said Con.

' But he's been doing that for three years. You can't take three years writing a book.'

This sounded sensible, and we didn't know how to confute it ; but Gentle swung round with a proposal alight in her eyes.

' Let's go and *see* what he gets up to up there. Let's go and explore.'

' Oh, *yes* ! ' muttered Con, her finger shooting to her mouth.

' Girls, girls ! ' I objected. ' Would that be strictly honourable ? Consider, I beg of you.'

But Gentle only inquired of Con if I wasn't peculiarly loathsome with my everlasting efforts to be funny ; and led the
expedition up the stairs.   She muttered ' Sh ! Sh ! ' each time a
stair creaked ; and each time she did this Con stifled a giggle.
I began to feel that we really were stalking a mystery in the
house.   Here we were on the third landing, and there was
Uncle Humphrey's door, brusquely shut.   Our guilt halted us
before it, and we looked at each other as if asking whether it
was to be opened, and, if so, by whom.   I was in a mood to
display my boldness, and I went forward and turned the handle
though not without a shaking heart.   Acting the sleuth, I
tip-toed into the room, and the girls followed me.

We stood still and surveyed the place.   At an angle with
the window stood the large desk, its papers and books scattered
upon it because of its late up-ending and removal.   At an
angle with the fireplace was the long, deep, easy chair with
some books lying open at its feet—books which, presumably,
he had laid down abruptly when the current arrangement of
his furniture offended his irritable eye and compelled him to
rise and act.

I tip-toed towards the books on the desk, as if they held the
solution of the riddle ;   I looked at their titles, and the girls
looked with me :   Mansel's *Prolegomena Logica*, Hegel's *Philosophy of History*, and Bain's *Composition and Rhetoric*, which was
open at *Part First.   Intellectual Elements of Style.*

' Crikey ! ' whispered Gentle.   ' He must be clever.'

But this afternoon he must have retired early from these
studies, to judge by the impress, deep and broad, in his easy
chair, and by the books lying open at its feet.   With the long
careful steps of a stalker I crept towards these books and picked
up the largest of them.   It was the first volume of *Every Man
His Own Doctor* and it was open either at the article *Fat* or at
the article *Fatigue*.   With the utmost satisfaction I read parts
of these articles to the girls, for here were rich and succulent
words that rejoiced the palate.   ' Obesity is often alimentary
in origin.   The patient eats too much or takes too little exercise,
or generally both——'

' No wonder he started shifting his furniture about and then
went for a walk—if he was reading that,' said Gentle.

' Obesity is often alimentary in origin,' I repeated, because
I had so enjoyed the sentence.   ' Fat is stored in the lax folds
of the peritoneum.   It really is, dear girls.   Fatigue, on the
other hand, is a symptom of overstrain and warns us to protect
ourselves from further harm by resting.   Sometimes it produces
a state of hypersensitiveness and unrest. . . . Golly ! '   I

replaced this book, and picked up one of the other books lying open on the floor. It was a sixpenny paper-backed novel by Charles Garvice, and its title was *Just a Girl*. Gentle shrieked when I handed it to her ; so did Con, as she looked at it ; and I protested, ' Girls, girls ! Your voices are overloud. Don't *shout*. It goes *through* me. Furthermore it's no behaviour for delicately nurtured females.' I picked up the other open book—another sixpenny novel. It's title was *Her Heart's Desire*.

' Well ! ' murmured Gentle, as I passed it to her.

In a bookshelf within reach of his chair was a packed row of these sixpenny paper-backs, and I scanned their titles and read them out : *A Coronet of Shame, A Girl of Spirit, Where Love Leads . . .*

' Gosh ! ' whispered Gentle, the mystery sparkling in her eyes.

We had crept up the stairs to disinter the mystery of Uncle Humphrey's room and his activities therein. There was no mystery, of course, except the mystery that is every human being. Simple as we were, we did not see far into that, but I feel now that, without knowing it, we did on this occasion, come upon the materials for an assessment of Uncle Humphrey ; we did, as it were, come upon some of his essence. This is what I surmise had happened on that afternoon. First he had wearied of philosophical study. Some abstruse and tormenting passage had started in him a doubt of his intellectual superiority, and without this superiority he was unhappy indeed, he was undone, because it was the fantasy by which he lived. The idea had come to him that he was not as great as Spinoza and Hegel, and he couldn't bear it. If he was of just ordinary ability, then he would write no great work, and there would be no world-fame for him after death—a suggestion to which he could never listen because he couldn't live in the same world with it. Depressed, sad, he took refuge in his chair and a sixpenny romance. These romances could always bathe him in a sweet melancholy because they recalled to him the two or three broken romances of his youth, of which he was very proud. Uncle Humphrey always liked to hint at good, even tragic, reasons why he had never married. His elegiac songs were an expression of his quiet happiness in the recollection of them. I am sure that he was happier remembering the collapse of a love-idyll than he would have been if its promise had been fulfilled. He preferred to love the women he had lost than to live with any of them.

And even as I set that down, I ask myself, Who am I to smile at him for that ?

After a while, I think, some wisp of thought from outside, or some incident in his story-book, put the disturbing question

to him, Was he getting too fat, or, maybe, Was he too fatigued ?
The question drove him to his medical book and to the article,
Fat—or the article, *Fatigue,* as the case may be.   He was nearing
sixty at this time, and more than ever apprehensive of an early
break-up.   Many symptoms of this he detected, or suspected,
each day—a failing memory, a slackening in his perceptions, a
slowing of his walk, an aching in his joints—and he was resting
a lot just now so that his faculties should not wear out too soon.
He went to bed early and slept late, hoping that, since he had
the chance of doing this, and other men hadn't, he might last
a little longer than they.   ' Old Humphrey,' Father used to
say, ' is so busy keeping alive that he hasn't time to live.'
   Possibly the phrase ' hypersensitiveness and unrest ' in the
Fatigue article caused him to look up at his furniture, and he
could not deny that the present position of his desk in relation
to the window irritated him.   His eyes were drawn to this
unsatisfactory composition again and again, and at last he got
up to change the vexing angle, worrying, as he heaved the
desk about, whether this hypersensitiveness to the spatial
relations of his furniture, and his inability to leave it long in
one place, was really due, not to his irritable eye, which was
an admirable thing, but to mental fatigue, which was not.
Lest this should be the truth he gathered up his hat and left
his room to take a little quiet exercise in the health-giving air.
   How long we children would have remained in his room,
stalking around the margin of his secrets, I do not know, but
suddenly we heard the front door open and close, and we fled
soft-footed down the stairs, like trespassing cats which the house
dog has frightened.   In the play-room we realized that it was
raining again, and Uncle Humphrey had come briskly home.

CHAPTER IV

UNCLE HUMPHREY was not the only mystery in the house.
There was another, and it was much more exciting, because
it was real and not a make-believe.   It hung around our mother
and a Mr. Payton, and Gentle had little part in the probing
of it, because this was pursued at night.   I do not understand
why the probing of it affected me differently from Con ; but
it did so ; to her it was a thrilling game and nothing more ;
to me it was a game that was somehow oppressive, as if played
in a still and thundery air.

My eyes were acuter than Con's, but, even so, how simple, incomplete, and inaccurate were my vision and conception of the adults around me. My real mother, in her full character, I never saw till I was a man ; my real father, with all his sins about him, I can even now see only with an effort, because of the love I bore him. Like the moon each parent presented only one face as they moved in their orbits around me, and I saw nothing of the moon's other side with its ' silent silver lights, and darks undreamed of.'

For me my father was entirely good, and in him was no fault at all ; I gave him the uncritical devotion of a dog ; my mother was compact of unpleasant qualities, and in her I saw, and wanted to see, little that was good : she was violent in temper, cruel to me while gay with others, astoundingly unscrupulous in the use of money and slander, and a stupid woman because, along with all this, she was able to go to church.

Such were the lit faces of these two moons when I turned to consider my father and mother.

And the truth, the real round truth of them ? Father—but even yet, though I, too, am an old man now, my father's hand seems to be laid gently on mine, to arrest it, as I try to write the truth about him. But I tell him I must write it, and his hand lifts, and I write on. He really loved us two children, but he was as selfish as other men and liked to enjoy all that was gratifying in children—their fun, their affection, and their leaping delight at his bounties—while evading all that was exasperating in them. He was out of the house most of the day, and only played with us when in the humour. There were times (though we were blind to them) when he ran from our ' pressure ' as incontinently as Uncle Humphrey. He did not easily sacrifice one of his pleasures to our needs or desires. On nights when he was going forth to some big dinner, he would come up to our bedroom in all the panoply of evening dress, and looking, as even Mother would say, more splendid than a king ; and he would crush down and shoot out his opera hat twenty times for our amusement, before kissing us good-night ; but on other evenings he would leave the house very quietly and rather shamefacedly, without a word of good-bye to us in play-room or bedroom. I would hear the hall door shut, and my heart would sink and die. On such evenings Mother was very silent and rather sour ; and if, all uncomprehending, we plied her with questions, she would snap, ' Oh, don't *worry* me ! Don't *pester* me.' Though he could never hurt a child or even lift his voice to one, he could be merciless to his wife, or to other men, if they had enraged him,

shouting them out of his presence, regardless of bystanders in
the street or other persons in the house.

Oh, yes, he could be merciless. Once at a big dinner, when
a great lord was receiving the guests in the ante-room, the
toastmaster announced 'General Allan Mourne'—and the
great lord offered Father only three fingers. Father, after
meditating more and more darkly upon this, went round to
the entrance again, and when the toastmaster asked his name,
said sweetly, ' General Allan Mourne ' to the surprise of the
toastmaster, who felt sure that he'd shouted that name before.
However, he had no course but to shout it again, a little impatiently : ' General Allan Mourne ! ' Again the great lord
offered Father his three fingers ; Father looked at them and
then brushed them aside, saying loud enough for all the bystanders to hear, ' I am quite ready to shake your whole hand,
sir. I see no reason for thinking you my inferior. But if you
feel so, very good ' ; and he walked away and enjoyed, so he
told us, an excellent banquet ; which was more than the great
lord did.

In a sentence, Father loved us, and he loved a few women,
but he loved himself more. I see it all now. And yet—and yet,
ever since he died, even in my fifties and my sixties, I have
had two recurring dreams, the one that I was a child again
and walking happily at his side, the other that I was my natural
age but that he was still alive and we were talking together ;
and I have awoken from the dream and wished that I could
sleep again and get back to it.

Mother I saw more clearly, because I was not blinded by
love and had no need of her as a rock of refuge without cutting
edge or slippery foothold. I saw in her all those sins which I
have listed above ; I saw also the high vivacity which alter-
nated with her self-pitying glooms and made her so many
women friends ; what I never saw, nor dreamed of, was the
tenderness and sweetness, the caresses, blandishments and
coquetries, with which she could capture and for a while
enchain a man. It did not occur to me that a woman who
could be so hard and repellent to one person could be a soft
and fascinating companion to another. Besides, I thought of
her as middle-aged and finished with love.

Hence the bewildering mystery of Mr. Payton. The quality
that troubled me in this was not any ' immorality,' of which
I would have had no understanding, but the deceitfulness
which was at its heart, and its air of treachery to my father.

§

Mr. Andrew Payton began to appear at our house when I was about eleven and Con twelve. With his lithe and elegant figure, his hair parted in the middle, and his chop-whiskers joined across his face by a soft moustache, he had a remarkable resemblance to Mr. A. J. Balfour, then Leader of the Opposition in the House. Proud of this likeness, he cultivated it, wearing a long frock coat and holding its lapels with both hands in the Balfourian style. A bachelor like his model, he lived not too expensively in a Knightsbridge hotel, and had plenty of money to entertain his men friends or to remunerate a mistress.

But if Mr. Andrew Payton resembled Mr. Balfour in appearance, he certainly didn't resemble him in character. He was too much the crude, self-satisfied Philistine for that ; bragging in loud talk-you-down tones that he never opened a book, unless it was his profit-and-loss ledger, from one year's end to another. It would have been impossible to imagine our Mr. Payton as a member of the ' Souls,' or as writing *A Defence of Philosophic Doubt*, or as standing on a platform with his hands on his lapels and lecturing an earnest audience on *Theism and Humanism* and on *Criticism and Beauty*.

By trade he was a furniture dealer, a fact which, when Mother first told it us, we found somewhat upsetting. The pillars of our temple shook a little, and they were not adequately under-pinned when Mother explained, ' He's in the business in a very large way. A shop ? Nonsense ; of course not ; don't let me ever hear you say that again. It's quite different from that. He has galleries—large galleries in Knightsbridge. The Payton Galleries are one of the most famous shops—I mean galleries—in London.'

Mr. Payton would arrive at lunch time (Father was never at home for lunch) or at odd times in the afternoon (Father was rarely home before five.) An extremely hearty person, he would greet us as we came in from school, ' Hallo, Con, my love, how are the studies ? And what do you call this ? Puppy fat ? And this, eh ? Some good solid stuff here. Gammon and fiddlesticks ! You don't mind being pinched. Hallo, young fly-by-night, and how's the world treating you ? You don't put on much flesh, do you ? And why does he look so pale, Una ? Is he working too hard, or do they tan him twice a week at that school ? What do you call this, Young Sack o' Bones ? A chest ? Go on with you ! What you want is some of this——' and again he pinched Con's fat, round behind. 'You could swap a little over, you two. But come here, young son-of-a-gun. Listen. Just between you and your old Uncle Andrew—your Ma isn't listening—how are the finances? Pretty low, eh? Bankrupt, eh? And your pretty sister the same? Well, we can't have that. I mean to say, that'll never do,' and he would press a shilling into my palm, and one into Con's, who, on guessing the drift of his whisper, had drawn near.

Naturally we approved at first of Mr. Payton, and saw nothing out of the ordinary in his visits. Mystery only descended upon his graceful, frock-coated figure when Mother, under the impression that we were still babies, incapable of questioning the facts around us, enjoined us that we were never to mention Mr. Payton to Father. On our asking, 'Why not?' she retorted, 'Because I don't want you to. That's enough'; and when she saw from our eyes that it wasn't enough, she added, 'Because Papa doesn't like him. He wouldn't like it if he heard he came here.'

'Why doesn't General Allan Mourne like him?' I asked, inopportunely humorous. And I remember that, as I asked it, I doubted, from the insincere tone of Mother's voice, whether Father had ever seen him. 'He seems to me a good man.'

'Oh, I don't know,' Mother affirmed, her defences overthrown and disorganized. 'Why does anyone not like anyone?'

'Do you like him?' asked Con.

'Yes, of course I do; but he's just a friend. One must have one's own friends, whether other people like them or not. But there's no sense in upsetting other people unnecessarily, and you're never to say a word about Mr. Payton to your father. See? Promise?'

We promised, since we could do no other; and Mother supposed that the matter was now at an end. But it was not. The mystery increased—indeed for me the world ceased to make sense—when the careless Mr. Payton, in our presence, addressed Mother as 'My lovely one,' and 'Child', and even pinched her bottom as he'd pinched Con's.

Child! Con's curiosity was now thoroughly and delightfully aroused, and she took the lead in a game of 'Detectives'—a game in which, as I have said, my pleasure was oddly mixed with discomfort and fear. We watched the advents of Mr. Payton and spied upon every activity of his or of Mother's that was strange. We noticed that sometimes he didn't pull the front-door bell, but let Mother open to him quietly, Uncle Humphrey being closeted upstairs, and the servants downstairs and only we children within earshot in the playroom. We noticed that on an occasion when ' the Master wouldn't be in to dinner,' Lettice and the only other servant we had at the time were both given an ' evening out,' and Father, in all his full-dress regalia, would hardly have gone from the house and the square before Mr. Payton arrived.   Often now, of an afternoon, Mother would go from the house, after an hour of elaborate dressing, and if we demanded where she was going, she would either prevaricate or be intolerant of all questioning.   I see her now, leaving the house—we knew not whither—in a small hat and black-spotted veil, and carrying a long-handled umbrella, decorated with a black bow.   Later, when it was deep winter and dark, and Father was out and the servants at rest in the kitchen we would see Mr. Payton entering by the side gate in the garden wall, which must have been left on the latch for him, and coming into the house by that small garden door with the many-coloured panes.

One night, Father being out, the servants below, and our-selves sent to bed at an unusual hour, we guessed that he was coming.   And scarcely had Mother kissed us good-night and left us but Con, in her nightdress, was at the window of her room, watching the garden, and I, in my nightshirt, had left my adjoining room and was standing near her door to keep *cavé* and listen for the front-door bell.

' Sister Anne, Sister Anne,' I inquired, ' do you see anyone coming ? '

' *Yes !* Doric, Doric ! ' She danced with triumph. ' Here he is.   He's there.'

I rushed to her window.   It was now spring and not so dark but that we could see a figure crossing the garden from the side door.

In a trice we were out in the passage, holding our breaths and directing our ears down the staircase well.   Neither Mother nor visitor was speaking, but they were coming up the first stairs to the drawing-room.   The drawing-room door shut on them quietly.   Had not the lock turned ?

So !   A quick council in Con's bedroom, and we were creeping down the stairs in our bare feet.   One flight only, and we were on the landing above the drawing-room, leaning over the banisters and listening.   No sound in the drawing room ;   no voices ;   only after a while the grunt of a sofa's back or the creak of a floor board.   A few steps further down, and the door of the mysterious room was in view.   No light showed from under it.   And within the room there were only such movements as sleepers might make in the night.   A sigh—a pant—a sound like a kiss—and then a chair or sofa moved along the floor, and Mother laughed low, and a man's voice spoke.

We flew up the stairs, one behind the other, like a brace of wild ducks rising from water.

§

The quiet visits of Mr. Payton, and the unxeplained exoduses of Mother, must have continued for some months, because it was full summer when the fire crept along the fuse and the dangerous mixture exploded.

An afternoon in July Con, Gentle and I were loitering in the square's garden, baulked for want of a new game, till Gentle, visited by inspiration, whispered, ' Let us escape.' She whispered it because it involved disobedience : we had been bidden keep to the gardens.

' Oh, yes,' we both agreed, because Mother, well-dressed and silent, had gone from the house, and escape would be easy. Slipping from our square, we hurried into the broad safety of Warwick Road, sped through the traffic of Old Brompton Road—or Richmond Road, as we knew it then—and crept along the gloomy grey-brick arcade which was the wall of the Westminster and West London Cemetery. Yes, that was what we called Brompton Cemetery fifty years ago.

Its heavy and dark arched gateway, open to the long, sunlit vista of trees and carriageway and tombs, begged us to enter. ' Come,' it said softly—does a cemetery gate speak other than softly ? ' Come in quickly. Who is there to see you ? The entrance is free. Come . . . quickly.'

We walked through the arch ; the clangour and din of the traffic fell behind us ; and we were in a Sunday silence. There was no sound anywhere except the soft sighing of the wind in the lime trees that bordered the avenue, and ever and anon the scared flutter of a bird. Awed into silence ourselves, and a little ashamed, we walked along with our thoughts unspoken, crossing the long shadows that striped the carriageway, as the sun fell to the west. I remember that for my part I was considering the contrast between the narrow ribbon of well-tended graves on either side of the avenue and the wide spaces of the untended ; between the graves of those who were still remembered and the graves of those who had none to recall them. Scarlet geranium, yellow calceolaria, and blue lobelia adorned the green turf above the loved and remembered ; only the gold of hawkbit and ragwort, and the royal purple of knapweed and spear thistle, honoured the vast acres of the forgotten.

Still silent, we walked on and on between these sepulchres and pavilions of the dead ; on and on beneath the scented limes, since no one raised a voice to suggest that we did anything else. Only the grey, domed chapel, looming before us at the avenue's end, caused us to retard our steps and turn away to the left. We were walking now by one of the two imposing semi-circular colonnades that embrace the area before the domed chapel as the colonnades embrace the piazza before St. Peter's, Rome. We were off the main roadway and hidden by the clustering tombs, and not a soul was near to watch us or chide. And we came upon a broad flight of steps leading down to an arched portal beneath the colonnade. The double doors of the portal appeared to be of black iron, and their ornate pattern was pierced with slits less wide than the finger of a man.

Those slits, like the great gateway of the cemetery, summoned us. ' Come and look within,' they said. ' No one is near. Come and see what we imprison or protect ; ' and we descended the broad steps somewhat fearfully, for they had a deserted look and took us down beneath the level of the ground. Thick ivy muffled their enclosing walls ; wild willow herb and self-sown ferns sprang from the cracks or interstices of the treads ; and in the bottom space a drift of old leaves leaned against the silent doors. Peering through the vertical slits in the doors, we saw dimly a vaulted gallery or tunnel with rotting and rusting coffins lying side by side, and one above another, on successive shelves of slate.

It was a catacomb under the colonnade.

Then Gentle, with a happy gasp, saw that a heavy key had been left in the lock of the double doors. She turned it, pushed nervously, and one door gaped. We stepped in. We stepped into an air colder than that of a cellar and smelling of damp stone, rotting wood, and dry mould. Left and right of us the coffins on their shelves stretched into the vaulted darkness, for there was no light save that which came through the aperture and the slits of the doors.

' Phew, but this makes my blood run cold ! ' said I ; and Con declared that if ever a place was haunted, it must be this, where corpses lay side by side, and head to foot, in a dark curving tunnel of which no end could be seen. Surely one at least of the dead rose from his unquiet sleep at midnight and paced by the coffins.

' I wouldn't like to walk in there,' said Gentle, keeping in the small halation round the doors and gazing into that complete and ultimate darkness.

' I shouldn't mind,' I bragged.

' Oh, yes, you would. Swankpot ! '

' I shouldn't.' And to show off, I walked a little way into the black midnight of that tunnel. Once invisible, I stopped and stayed quiet, not wanting to go further, but hoping they would think I had done so. The triumph, however, was not with me. There came a giggling behind me ; Gentle's voice hissed, ' Come on, Con ' ; the door clanged to ; the key turned ; and feet ran away up the steps outside.

They had locked me in and gone. I was immurred with the dead. In a panic that almost stopped my heart and impressed me into their army I rushed to the doors. The vertical slits were just wide enough to admit the fingers of a child, and I thrust mine through and shook and shook the doors. But they did not yield. Neither Gentle nor Con was in sight ; I saw only the broad stairway leading up to a sanctuary of white tombs and an apse of blue, untroubled sky.

In sixty-five years of life I have had no worse moment than this. Mad thoughts of being left alone in my prison with all that ghastly company while darkness came down, and only night and the dead occupied the vast cemetery, grappled at my breath with stifling fingers. I held on to the bars and gazed out at the daylight as if that alone were my life. A few terrible seconds, and Gentle's eyes peeped round a granite pier at the top of the stairs. She saw me ; her face shot back ; and her voice, deliberately loud, called, ' Shall we go home now, Con ? '

' Yes, let's,' shouted Con from the opposite side of the stairs. ' It's time for tea.'

' Come on, then.'

A passion of hate joined my terror and I knew that the minute I got out I should strike at them both. But I did not speak, because I had no voice. I just held the bars with both hands so tight that my arms trembled.

Gentle peeped again. She saw me gazing through the slits like an ape in a cage, and in a sudden invincible pity she rushed down the stairs and turned the key. Then, with a shriek of mock alarm, since I was now free, she raced up the stairs again.

That was the first time I saw Gentle's pity. It had driven, almost hurled, her down the stairs, because the sight of me gazing through the slits was not to be borne. Many times before I might have observed this pity, had I not been a child, or had the displays of it touched me closer. I had seen her snivelling when Henrietta, on a wet afternoon at her home, read us very soulfully the pathetic little tale, *Misunderstood* ; I had seen her run from the room with her tears on another such occasion, when Henrietta came to the tragic close of *A Dog of Flanders*. Gentle might ridicule, resist, and almost despise her mother, but I had seen her, if Henrietta was plainly hurt (which happened quite often), run and throw her arms around her in a strangling embrace and lay a cheek against hers. But none of these episodes had been of much interest to me. They were but the usual behaviour of girls. Why, even Con, though she had no tears for little Humphrey in *Misunderstood*, or for the dog of Flanders, could oblige Father with a similar strangling embrace.

And to-day, though the pity came doubling down to me, I saw it only, as it were, through a slit, darkly, and was less interested in it than in my hate. I wasn't going to let it divest me of my revenge. Pushing the door open I raced after both girls up the steps and along the path between the tombs. Con, unhandicapped by an inexpedient spasm of pity, had got away to a better start than Gentle, and was in front of her. Gentle's legs were long swift schoolboy limbs, but not so long, nor her body so light, as mine, and I came up with her and caught her arm and, swinging her round, hammered her with my fist as I would have a boy. The life in me heightened as I felt her soft arm in my fingers and her breast resisting my blows, and heard her maddened cries.

A low blow near her heart doubled her up, and she gasped. I was afraid, and stepped away.

Con, watching from a distance, suspected a disaster and ran up. She looked at the bent and groaning Gentle and asked one of her senseless questions. ' Has he hurt you ? '

' Yes . . .' But she had hardly breath to utter it.

' I haven't.'

' Where has he hurt you ? '

' Everywhere,' said Gentle, in a generous estimate of her lesions.

' I haven't.'

' Yes, you have,' gasped Gentle, ' you filthy little blot.'

' Golly ! ' murmured Con, wide-eyed.

' And it was I who let him out. I felt terribly sorry for him and went and let him out—I was good—and he comes and half murders me. He's a cad. An unutterable cad.'

' I'm not.'

' I've got an awful pain here. It's my heart, I think. I can't breathe properly. I can't . . . truly.'

'There's no such word as " can't ",' I offered, with untimely humour.

'I *can't*, I tell you! Con, I can't. I'm not sure that I'm not dying.'

' Golly ! '

As I was not sure either, I remained on one side, watching anxiously, but masking my anxiety with an unsuccessful grin.

' He'll be hung if you die.' By this assurance Con achieved two desirable things : she soothed Gentle with the promise of some posthumous compensation, and she struck out at me.

' I hope he is,' said Gentle.

' He will be.'

But I was not allowing Gentle her posthumous triumph. ' Oh no, I won't.'

' 'Course you will ! '

' Oh no, I won't. You aren't hung till you're a lot older than me.'

' Well, you'll be put in prison for the rest of your life.'

' No, I shan't.' But this time it was a mere unhappy denial, with no sure facts to sustain it.

The point was made irrelevant by Gentle coming erect again.

' Better ? ' inquired Con.

' Yes.'

' Goody.'

' But it still hurts,' Gentle added, lest sympathy were withdrawn too soon.

' We'd better get you home so that you can lie down. We shall have to tell Mamma in case it's serious. You may have to see a doctor. Come on.'

They walked on together, nurse and patient. I, disgraced and unwanted, walked a little quicker than they towards the gates. I was very unhappy, and not a little afraid, but by this age, thanks to Mother's oppression and Con's insensibility, I had learned to keep most of my heartaches in a taut control, imprisoning them behind a silence. In silence I walked ahead of the girls up the sun-striped avenue, not unconscious of the disharmony between the brightness and fine colour of the day and the greyness of my thoughts. Turning my head to look at the tombs, I half envied all these sleepers their quiet beds, where sorrow and fear could touch them no more. I sauntered out of the great gateway which had welcomed us so mischievously, and along Warwick and Osgrave Roads to our house, now harbouring a menace, at the corner of the square. Entering the house I climbed as far as I could from everybody, to my bedroom at the top, where I stood by the window, which looked only upon the blank side-wall of the next house.

I was waiting for Mother to return. Con, I knew, would tell her of my crime. Gentle would let her ; for in Gentle's head, somewhere beneath her amber-gold hair and behind her brilliant brown eyes, she possessed a microscope for the contemplation of her wrongs, and this was a powerful instrument indeed, magnifying an injury, when she thoroughly examined it, many a hundred times till it was a horrible thing, a crawling thing, a thing that actually grew fruitful and multiplied like the seed of Abraham under her very eye. It was inconceivable that she hadn't put my ungrateful assault under this microscope and seen it for the unnatural and revolting thing it was ; so that pity was scorched from her heart, and she would let Con say what she liked, and even endorse it. Mother would listen to the story, and then hurry up the stairs, glad of the chance to drag me away for a thrashing.

In my hands I held a long string—part of an elaborate system of twine and staples and eyelet screws by which, from my pillow, I could haul up the distant blind and let in the new day—and I absent-mindedly undid knot after knot among those I had made at its end. And I don't know how it was, but suddenly, untying these knots, I unravelled one tangled thread in the skein of my life. I knew what I was going to do when Mother came up. Excitement displaced much, though not all, of my fear. And when I heard her enter the house, and Gentle and Con speaking with her, my heart beat violently, but at the thought of what I was going to do, not of what was going to be done to me.

I stood quite still, imagining her pulling off her gloves and blowing into them, as she listened to the girls ; then drawing off her veil and folding it up. And here was the sough of her skirt and petticoats as she hastened up the stairs to a pleasure that was justified. So hastens a lecher to a room above.

She was in the room ; and I had turned to meet her.

' What have you done to Gentle ? '

' Nothing.'

' Don't tell lies. She was good to you, because she saw you were unhappy, and all you could do was to strike her brutally.'

' She did something to me first. She locked me in.'

' You struck her again and again in a way that might have hurt her. She's a girl, and you might have hurt her. You're a wicked little boy, and you shall know what it is to be hurt. Come here.'

I drew back.

' You heard what I said ! Come here.'

And she seized me by the arm, exactly as I had seized Gentle. I dragged my arm away.

'Let me alone,' I said.

Her temper leaped at this defiance—how she loved to flame into temper !—and she tried to seize me again. I struck at her with my fists : and she, maddened by this inconceivable act, closed with me and swung a stinging slap on my cheek. It nearly stunned me, but intuition told me that I must win this issue—I must win !—or it'd be years before I could open the battle again. So, accepting her madwoman blows, no matter how they hurt, I hammered and hammered on her breast—I can still feel the painful impact on her boned corsets—and shouted for all the world to hear, ' Let me alone. I'm not afraid of *you*.'

And as I said the words—or, rather, as they shouted themselves—I knew they were true. And I knew that she knew it too, and that she was frightened by the fearless devil she had raised. Her hand was slapping no more : it dared not. I had broken prison and was free. Grey walls were behind me, and I stood exulting in a sunlight. Mother who yesterday was someone to fear, was now little or nothing. She was powerless, and power was high in me, like wine.

I pushed her away with both hands, and we stood staring at each other. She, too, was perceiving that a crisis had come—and gone.

' Get away,' I said almost contemptuously ; my fists clenched, ready to defend the outpost I had won.

' You dare talk like that to me ? '

'Yes, I do. I'm not afraid of *you*. Get away.' I took a step towards her, and she retreated a step. This was victory : Mother retreating before me.

' Keep away.' Her fear compelled the words. ' Don't come near me. You're dangerous.'

' So are you.'

' You're a bad, bad little boy.'

' So are you. You do bad things.'

' What do you mean ? '

' You do lots of things that you're ashamed of.'

' *I* do things that I'm ashamed of ? '

' Yes, you don't want Papa to know when you whip me. You don't do it when he's here. You've never once done it when he's in the house. You don't want him to know when Mr. Payton comes.'

She was staring at me, confounded ; and my fighting instinct told me to drive on, because an enemy confused is an enemy undone. ' I shall tell him every time you touch me, and every time Mr. Payton comes to the house.'

' You'll do nothing of the sort,' was all she could say.

' I will. I will if I want to.' Already some pity for a woman completely outwitted and defenceless was stirring in me ; but every gun that lay at my side, loaded, must be fired off before I showed mercy. ' You do heaps of deceitful things and then go to church. It's stupid.'

' Stupid ? '

' Yes. It makes me sick.'

Mother, a dull woman, could only gape at the miracle of a child's growth.

' Papa doesn't go to church.'

' There's a lot about your father that you don't know. He does deceitful things ' —

' —but he doesn't go to church at the same time, like you and Con do,' I panted.

' I don't want to discuss your father. I only want you to know that you'd hurt him if you told him about Mr. Payton. You don't want to hurt him, do you ? '

I didn't answer.

' You mustn't say a word about Mr. Payton to your father. Understand that. . . . You won't, will you ? '

The enemy suing for terms ! It was pitiable, and I was moved to some magnanimity. ' I will unless you let me alone.'

' You mean that ? '

' Yes. But it jolly well depends on your letting me alone,' I explained that she might feel my power.

' Well . . . I'm relying on you. . . . Understand that. I'm relying on you . . . I . . .' But she had no more words, and turned and went. Never did a challenger, with lance broken and discomfited mien, make a more lamentable exit from the lists.

§

The exact means by which Father discovered all about Mr. Payton I shall never know. It is enough perhaps to say that there is no concealing from one shrewd partner in a home the stealthy intrigues of the other. The jealous partner will sooner or later suspect ; and once he suspects, he will have to know ; and unless he is a man of the most austere conscience (which is no description of Father) he will spy and trail and trapan in order to know. Soon another detective besides Con and me was on the prowl ; but he was working alone. Once, about midnight, stricken awake by the fear that I heard a burglar downstairs, I carried a pounding heart into the passage and peered over the banisters. The alarm in my heart was a considerable visitation because, however impudent I might be with

Father, however triumphant now over Mother, I still suffered these shameful night-fears when alone, and they did not fall from me till I was a tall lad of sixteen. There was a fan of light moving on the first landing. It swung and contracted and extended. Someone was examining the drawing-room with a lamp or candle in his hand. I went down a little way, fascinated like a moth by that moving light. Mother was in bed and asleep ; I could hear her heavy breathing. Mr. Payton had long ago gone. Who was in the drawing-room ? I could not move for fear. Then the man in the room coughed, and I recognized Father's cough. He was in there with his bedtime candle, scrutinizing the room. Instantly a black sky, lit with an evil gleam, rolled away from me and left a great calm. I slipped happily upstairs again.

I had never known Father so little lively as in these days, nor so frequently sunk in one of his brooding silences. His jesting with us was forced and feigned, but the silences were deep and real.

Somewhere out of our sight he made his suspicions sure. Did Uncle Humphrey tell him anything ? I have only to ask myself that question to shake my head in disbelief. Uncle Humphrey never played the informer. But what was he, Uncle Humphrey, doing all this time on his secret side of the moon ?

On some evenings he went to his new club, the Authors', but more often he felt unequal to this effort. He had realized, too, that there were not many there who wanted to hear him talk about himself, and he was never at ease doing the other thing, since he got no pleasure from hearing other men talk about themselves. So he stayed in his upstairs room with only his thoughts for companions—and they were the best companions because they dealt only with the one subject that interested him, Humphrey Allan Mourne and his dreams.

There were evenings however when, aching from a semi-recumbent attitude, he wandered about the house, and up and down it, a lonely spirit, and often at such times he must have seen that drawing-room door and known that Mother and Mr. Payton were within. I make no doubt he was as interested as Con. I remember hearing him once go downstairs in the darkness and listen, just as we children did. He was down there listening for quite a long time, and then Mr. Payton's footsteps sent him leaping like an ibex up the steep stairs without any thought for the condition of his heart and his varicose veins.

But he did not take Father aside and tell him the tale. I am sure he did not. For many reasons. In the first place because, though wholly self-centred, he had a good heart and was really fond of mother who made him so comfortable, and of Father with whom he shared so many childhood memories, and of us children. Indeed, he liked everybody, and was pleased to be kind to people so long as he didn't have to deny himself for them. What's more, he liked people, not only from good nature but from set purpose, because he'd read somewhere that it was bad for one's health to harbour emotions of hate. In the second place he perceived that a quarrel between his brother and sister-in-law might break up their home and scatter his little portion of comfort to the inhospitable winds. If the elm tree fell what of the rook's nest on the tree-top ? And even if things did not come to this pass there would be days of alarm for him lest they should, and he would fain avoid this mental stress. In the third place, since it was in his interest not to speak, he recalled his own broken love affairs (with the usual pleasure) and decided that it was not in him who had suffered to lay the axe to anyone else's happiness. I suspect that he was shocked at first by his sister-in-law's behaviour, and then remembered on a sudden, and conveniently, that he was no orthodox, conventional man but a philosopher who believed in freedom.

So, like us, he watched and wondered and was interested, but said not a word to anyone of the things he saw.

In any game of concealment and cozenage Mother and Father were unfairly matched : he was far the subtler player. One morning at breakfast he explained at length and in detail, being a fluent liar when the occasion required it, how he would have to attend in the afternoon a board meeting of the British South African Development Company and in the evening a dinner of the Governors of Ampthill's Charity, and how the board meeting, a damnable nuisance anyway, would be a deucedly long affair, probably not finishing till six o'clock, so he'd be obliged to dress for the dinner at his club, and we mustn't expect him back till midnight or later. These matters enunciated in a melancholy style, he went upstairs, put his dress clothes in a bag, came down and went from the house. He went without a word to us children, either because he was in no mood to be merry, or because he felt that our innocence went ill with his plots and his bitterness.

I have often wondered, did he in his determination to know the truth have his agent in the square, watching the house, or did he stand and watch it himself ; did he lie in wait at some corner, an old man of sixty, hurt and heavy in heart, since Payton was twenty years younger than he. Sometimes I have passed one of the corners of the square and imagined his tall, sad figure standing there, with his malacca cane held in both hands behind his back, and peering round, now and again, at the fine white house which yesterday he had so loved.

Or was the house not watched at all ; did he perhaps gamble that day and win the bet ?

It was soon evening, and Con and I were in our adjoining bedrooms on the third floor, a low gas-jet burning in the passage for our comfort. We were not at Con's window in our nightshifts, watching for Mr. Payton, because we were used to his visits now, and the interest of that game was spent. For a time I conducted a shouted conversation with her through our open doors, and at last, receiving no reply, knew that she slept. The house was now silent except for the muted antiphon of Mother's voice and Mr. Payton's in the shut drawing-room two floors down. He was in a lively mood and laughed loudly once or twice ; Mother laughed too, but softly ; only once was her laugh uplifted and shrill. Then there was a spell of complete silence.

It was so protracted that it mystified me. Many times I raised my head from my pillow to learn if they were speaking yet, and at length I became possessed by the fixed idea that I shouldn't be able to fall asleep till that unaccountable silence ended. I lay waiting for a voice to release me, my senses alert. And in the silence came a sound, quite unmistakable because so dear : the turning of Father's key in the lock. The front door closed ; his malacca cane touched the base of the hat-stand ; his bag touched the tiles of the floor. He coughed, but even I knew a warning cough when I heard it. ' Una,' he called up the stairs. And again ' Una.'

Of course there was no answer. Not a sound ; not a breath.

' Una, my dear, where are you ? ' There was a studied cheerfulness in his voice—how sinister, even to me ! ' Children in bed ? '

Still no answer to his call.

' Is everyone dead ? Good gracious, good gracious ! Where are we all ? Una, my dear.' Now he was coming up the stairs with a tread that was meant to be heard, and humming to himself as he came.

Though I loved him, my sympathy for the two trapped in the drawing-room was enough to stop and weaken my heart. My knuckles went to my teeth as he came near their closed and silent door. But he passed it ; he came up the two next flights, treading heavily. He was leaving a way of escape for Mr. Payton. He looked into my room and met my wide-open eyes. ' What ? Not asleep, Doric ? It's nearly nine o'clock. Good gracious, good gracious ! This'll never do. Tricks asleep ? '

' I think so.'

But he had not heard me. He was only pretending to be merry. He was standing sideways in the gas-lit doorway and his ear was given, not to me, but to a floor downstairs. And he and I—he in the doorway, I in the bed—heard the intruder go. We heard his step on the stairs, no matter how soft, and the click of the front door, no matter how gentle.

That door had no sooner clicked than Father left me and broke unceremoniously into Uncle Humphrey's room next door, from the window of which he could view the square. No one's susceptibilities were allowed to stand in Father's path when he was driving towards a goal of his own.

' Hallo, Humphrey, old man.'

' Hallo, Kingsley. I thought you were out for the night. How comes it——'

' Just a minute, old son.'

He went, as I could guess, to the window. Having seen what he wanted to see, he said, ' Yes ' and left Uncle Humphrey's presence as quickly as he had entered into it. He presumed that Uncle Humphrey knew what he was about, and that in this affair they were brothers.

Now his steps, and very firm they sounded, were going down to the drawing-room floor.

I sprang from my bed and ran to my doorway. Here there was a brief but most embarrassing meeting between Uncle Humphrey and me, he having just leapt from his chair and arrived at *his* door. Our eyes met for a second, and he at once withdrew from my sight. But I knew that he was still standing near his door and listening as intently as I. It was cold, and I began to shiver in my nightshirt, but I could not drag myself away from my listening post.

Down below, on the drawing-room landing, Father's voice had begun : not very loud as yet, but uttering the first notes of a thunder that might, or might not, swell and shake the house. ' Your visitor went quickly.'

I didn't hear Mother's answer—if there was one.

' He was pressed for time, I take it ? '

Some words from Mother, but I doubt if Father heard them any more than I (or Uncle Humphrey) did, for he proceeded immediately, ' He went like a shot from a gun—only rather more quietly. Or, to put it with complete frankness, he ran from my house like a low, sneaking rat.'

Here I think that Mother, her temper rising too, and with it her relish for an uncontrolled and flaming row, asked, a danger lamp lighting up in her eyes, if he'd been trying to trap her.

'Trap? Good heavens, no! Trap? I'm not, I think, in the habit of trapping people. I merely felt rather unwell after a long and tedious meeting and decided I couldn't face an over-rich dinner, so I had a quiet meal at my club and came home.'

Yes, Father could lie with the skill of a De Rougemont or a Münchausen when he wanted to.

'And now, if you please, what was he doing here?' Not being answered, he roared in such a voice as long ago he had used to some subaltern, or some sweeper, '*What was he doing here?*'

'Who?'

'Payton. The furniture man.'

'How do you know it was he?'

'The architect did not design this house to have a blank wall in front. He thoughtfully put in some things called windows. Their glass is not opaque, and from almost any one of them you can get an excellent view of the street. I watched the fellow in his retreat; and I may say that he executed that always difficult manœuvre with considerable speed and dexterity. I should think he's half way to Hyde Park by now. Perhaps you will kindly answer me. What was he doing here?'

No doubt Mother said he was her friend, and she was entitled to her friends.

Father's voice rose again. 'Don't insult me by treating me like a fool. A man who comes only when your husband's away is not merely a friend. I take it the man is your lover, and I hope he pays you well.'

Now, if you like, Mother's voice rose to the level of his. 'How dare you say such a thing to me? How dare you?'

'For the simple reason that I want an answer. That, I think, is the usual reason for asking a question. Answer me.' And again in the voice that he'd used on the Indian plains he roared, '*Answer me!*'

'He is not my lover, as you are pleased to put it, but who are you to talk to me? Do you think I don't know the things that *you* do? And very ridiculous they are in a man of your age. I suppose you are not aware that people laugh at you.'

This must have wounded him deep and near the heart, but he was not the man to show by wince or word when his armour was pierced and the blood drawn. 'Leave me out of this. I have never set up to be a saint, but so far as was possible I have tried to look after you and give you a good home——'

'I will not leave you out of it. Why should I leave you

out of it?' Mother, delighting in a paroxysm, was now shouting like a maniac. 'If it's right for you it's right for me. The position is the same. The same for both of us, I tell you! If you take your freedom I intend to take mine. Who are *you?* Who are you?'

'It is not the same. It is by no means the same. You may think it's very unfair that it's not the same, but that's not my fault: I didn't organize the universe. Do you think any husband's going to risk having someone else's child fathered on him? And has it never occurred to you that it's of some importance that children should know for certain who their father is—and that the world should have no doubts? Nor that, if you have greater obligations in this matter than I, I have sterner obligations in other matters? Great God in Heaven, am I the only person in Earls Court and Brompton who uses his brains? Either you give me your sworn oath that you'll never see this man again or I go. I go at once— to-night—and this home ends. And if I go, I go for ever. Then if you like, the position will be somewhat the same, and your upholsterer—or ironmonger, or whatever he is—will be able to acknowledge and pay for his own brats. Are you going to give me this undertaking?'

'Most certainly not. I'm giving no undertakings. Ever.'

'Very well, then. I go. I have loved this house—loved it more than I can say—but I will never come near it again. That's no threat, but the truth. This is the end. I will pack a few things to-night, and go in the morning. I want to say good-bye to my children, and they are asleep now. We must make some arrangement by which they can come and see me sometimes, because at least I love them. I don't know whether I shall see you in the morning. If not, good-bye.'

And as if this were the end he turned and walked quickly up the stairs. But, blinded by his anger and, I am sure, by a great inward pain, he missed a step about halfway up and fell. He fell upon his face. I was just running back to my bed when I heard the fall. It was not a heavy fall, but it was followed by a groan. With a good excuse now I ran out again, just as Uncle Humphrey who, like me, had been hurrying back to his innocent chair, appeared on the landing too. We could face each other without shame now.

'What was that?' I asked.

'I think your father has hurt himself. I was sitting reading my book when I heard a fall.'

We went down and saw Father prone upon the stairs, forcing himself up on an elbow, while the other pressed his abdomen.

Mother was bending over him and asking, ' What is it ? What is it, Kingsley ? Are you hurt ? '

' Yes . . . yes . . . I am sorry. I am sorry to give you this trouble.' He tried to rise, but the effort forced a groan. ' God . . . God . . .'

' Oh, my *dear !* ' Mother laid a comforting hand upon his shoulder ; and in that moment the moon turned for me a little and I had a glimpse of her sweeter side. ' Let me help you.'

' Thank you. . . . I am grateful. . . . I don't want to give any trouble but I seem to have hurt myself . . . rather.'

' Where is the pain ? '

' Here,' He pressed on his abdomen. ' I fell on my stomach, but not badly. . . . I don't understand. And here, too.' He shot a hand to the tip of his shoulder. ' It'll be all right in a minute perhaps. Hallo, Humphrey, old man. I'm perfectly sober. But this is no way for a gentleman to come home, is it ? I slipped and . . . give Una a hand, old boy. Hallo, Doric, what are you doing here ? ' He looked at up me, and I saw his face was white as a veined marble. A fear like a sword in the hand of Death went through my heart. ' Look at your old father tumbling about. Stupid, isn't he ? But it's nothing. Sorry if I woke you up. Run back to bed or you'll catch cold.'

I did not move but stood above them, waiting. Mother put a hand under his armpit and asked, ' Can you get up, dear ? '

' I must. I must try. Thank you, Humphrey. I seem to be a proper casualty this time . . . a stretcher case. *Douce-ment, doucement.* Thank you. It's very kind of you. *Sacré !* . . . It's exceedingly kind.'

Somehow they lifted him up, though his legs seemed limp as a jelly and his face, with its brows straining together, its teeth set, and the sweat bedewing its forehead was the very portrait of a man in the hands of the Tormentor. Uncle Humphrey's brows were also knit, and his lips set, and his eyes unhappy ; and I guessed that he was worried by the strain that Father's weight was putting upon his heart and by the damage that all this alarm and shock must be doing to him, but ready to sacrifice himself in duty to his brother.

' Run up, Doric, and light the gas in your father's room,' said Mother.

' Yes, thank you, Doric. . . . It is good of you.'

I ran up and lit the room and then waited on the landing for them to come.

They came, dragging and supporting Father's almost helpless

body like a long, ponderous sack. Uncle Humphrey must have feared that this would initiate the end for him, but he nobly gave his all. When they got him into the room, Father fell back upon the bed. They did not attempt to undress him, frightened by his pallor and his short quick breaths which appeared to lift only the upper part of his chest and leave the stomach still. He asked for water ; Mother ran for it ; and he drank thirstily.

'We must get the doctor at once,' she said.

'I'll go,' said Uncle Humphrey, by this time proud of his self-sacrifice.

'It's very kind of you,' Father breathed. 'Very kind. And now, Doric, go to bed. This is nothing. Yes . . . your mother is being very good to me.' Putting out a hand, he picked up mine and pressed it. 'Go to sleep. Everything will be all right in the morning.'

I went. I got into bed, but not to sleep ; to lie there, listening. I heard Uncle Humphrey return with the doctor ; I heard many voices round and about my father's bed ; I heard a carriage drive up, and, drawn from my bed by curiosity and fear, I ran to the window of Uncle Humphrey's room. The carriage down there was an ambulance, its lamps golden in the night. The ambulance men came upstairs. Peering over the banisters, I saw them carrying Father out on a stretcher, with Mother in her hat and coat following behind. Father said, 'Good-bye, Humphrey, old man ; get back to your books ; write us a good one,' and the front door closed behind him. I went back to my bed and sobbed for a long hour upon the pillow.

CHAPTER V

IN A turning off the busy and clangorous Fulham Road, not far from the Hospital for Consumption and the Royal Cancer Hospital, stood the Hospital of Our Lady of Mercy and Good Counsel, like a smaller sister of these great institutions, and one who had taken the veil and the vows. Founded by two English ladies, who had gone for this purpose as postulants to the first House of Mercy in Dublin and returned as professed sisters, it occupied a large grey-brick house, which had once been a private mansion in its own spacious and timbered garden. To this central block new wings and a convent had been added, the latest wing being in red brick and white stone, like the blocks of flats which at this date were rising from all the waste-grounds of West London. The hospital had beds for some hundred patients, and its Constitution stated, 'Although the patients are under the care of Sisters of Mercy, all are received irrespective of creed, the sole test being their need of help and treatment.' The good sisters honoured this rule, but, like most Catholic houses, they had a tenderness towards class distinctions and provided a few private-rooms for people of rank and substance. To this quiet asylum, and to a room worthy of his rank, they carried my father that night.

Mother, worried as she was by this new, sudden menace to her home, had yet an unconscious pleasure in the dramatic story she could tell us at breakfast in the morning. 'Dr. Willowson said I must get him to hospital without a minute's delay,' she explained, putting sugar into her coffee, 'as there was certainly a hæmorrhage somewhere. He said they'd have to operate on him at once to find out what was the matter. I understand they'll operate to-day. They may be doing it now.'

Hiding my anxiety, which was a white emptiness at my heart, I asked, 'Is he going to be all right?'

'I don't know,' Mother answered, stirring the cup. 'How can I know? We shan't know anything till after the operation. We must hope so. For God's sake don't fiddle with that fork. We must hope for the best.'

'But he won't *die*, will he?' asked Con, using the word I had not dared to speak aloud lest to utter it were to create it as a fact—lest, by being spoken, the word became flesh and dwelt among us.

'Of course not.' It was Uncle Humphrey who had spoken. 'You don't kill yourself by a fall upstairs. You may injure some part, but you don't kill yourself.' But I saw that he was asserting this because he needed to believe it; to imagine that this accident might overturn the house and scatter his comfortable top room would be a grievous worry, and he was anxious not to worry, for his health's sake.

It was Saturday, and a holiday, and I wandered with my unspoken fear up and down the stairs and in and out of the rooms. I took a spear-thrust of pain when I saw Father's coat and stick in the hat-stand. And, passing the hat-stand, I heard Lettice talking to our charwoman as she helped her turn out the breakfast room. I knew she was speaking of Father and I stood still by the hat-stand to listen, pretending to examine the stale, yellow visiting cards on the tray. 'Oh, it's serious,' she was saying. 'It's serious all right. They don't run you off to hospital like that for nothing. He was gone when I come back at ten o'clock, and the mistress gone with him. It gave me a turn, I don't mind telling you, when I heard all about it. It gave me a real nasty turn, I give you my word. The mistress told me when she come back that he'd just slipped on the stairs, but I shouldn't be surprised but what he'd been in one of his tantrums. I shouldn't wonder but what they'd had a real set-to. He can get very hot sometimes, and then we all hear from him. He storms and stamps about the place like a—but there!—I couldn't tell you the real truth of what happened last night, not if you crowned me with gold. Can you lend me a hand with this here : it's heavy ; and after this room, if you don't mind, Mrs. Barton, we'll just set the dining-room to rights. There may have been Words. They're having Words a lot lately, and I think I know what about, but it's not my business, I always say, to pry into my master and mistress's affairs. All I know is, he's always been a perfect gentleman to me. To tell the truth, I've always preferred him to her. I should be sorry if anything was to happen to him ; very sorry. I'm not so set on operations, myself—not at any time, and least of all at his time of life. I suppose they know what they're doing, but it always seems to me like Tempting Providence.'

In the afternoon, it being Saturday, Gentle arrived, wide-eyed with curiosity and alarm ; and in the chastened atmosphere of the playroom she reported to us a tremendous solicitude on the part of Henrietta. ' She's flapping all over the place. I heard her say to Mrs. Alston, " It's *very* serious " ; and when I asked her how bad it was, she said it wouldn't do to make light of it at all. She said that even if the injury wasn't serious, you might get pneumonia or something after a fall like that. It isn't as bad as all that, is it, Con—is it, Doric ? ' Gentle looked with a real anxiety from one to the other. ' She's just being terribly intense about it, isn't she ? '

' Yes,' I said, in the low voice of one who isn't as sure of his assertion as he could wish to be.

But Con, still untroubled by my superstition, immediately said, ' Does she mean he may die ? '

Her brown eyes wider than ever, Gentle looked into Con's eyes and answered. ' She *says* he may. Oh, my beloved Uncle Kingsley—he mustn't ! He mustn't. I love him. I always have. I think I love him better than anyone else in the world. I don't care *what* Henrietta says—or Brian either ; *I* think he's sweet.'

I allowed three seconds to pass, that there might be nothing remarkable in my going, and then went from the room. Slowly

I climbed the stairs, sometimes stopping on a tread as if I hadn't the will-power to go further. Reaching my bedroom, I shut the door on myself, ashamed of what I was about to do. Then I knelt by the bed and, pressing my face into my hands, and my hands into the cold quilt, prayed, ' Oh God, please, please make him get all right. Forgive me for having said I don't believe in you——' and here, to make amends, I raised my eyes towards the ceiling and repeated ' I believe in God the Father Almighty, Maker of Heaven and Earth——' and so on, to the end. Then sank my head again, and continued in prayer.

Even though I had thrust my mother's whip aside, even though I spoke, as a rule, in the lordliest language, I still suffered from the palpable dislike and hostility of my mother, and needed —desperately needed—my father for a refuge and compensation ; and my prayer, therefore, was more on my behalf than on his. I could see this—see it enough to ask God to forgive it. I remembered that when, in my growing arrogance, I disputed with Con the efficacy of prayer, she would retort angrily, ' But the Bible *says* so ! The Bible says, " The effectual fervent prayer of a righteous man availeth much," ' as if this, instead of begging the question, disposed of it. She was very silly, sometimes, but her text was a comfort to me now. Only I saw that I must try to be righteous if I wanted God to grant my petitions. I determined to be so—at least until the question was decided ; and I rose from my knees, almost pleased with the difficult exercises before me.

All that day and the next I went about doing righteous things, but not without indulging occasionally a day-dream of what I would do if God failed me and let Father die. First I thought I would run away from this now-desolate house, and then that I would commit suicide. I wandered into the bathroom and, opening the medicine cupboard, looked at a little bottle labelled ' Antipyrine.' It contained a pile of white tablets that Mother would take for her ' splitting headaches,' which, it used to appear to us, were almost diurnal in their impact. Often I'd heard her say that Antipyrine was bad for the heart and too many of those tablets would probably kill you. Should Father die in that hospital, I would lie down on my bed behind a closed door and, taking every one of the tablets, go after him.

§

Whether or not the prayer of a temporarily righteous child availed anything, the issue was a happy one. Later that day we learned that Father's fall had ruptured his spleen which, enlarged by malaria in India, was frail enough to sustain damage from a trivial blow ; but it was a small rupture with slow bleeding, and the doctors said they had good hopes of a quick recovery. Dr. Willowson even went so far as to tell Mother that there was but little cause now for anxiety ; and she, in a kind humour, and much relieved, I'm sure, despite their quarrels, came up into the play-room and said, ' It's going to be all right, children. Isn't that splendid news ? ' And I, as was only fair, only decent, went up to my bedroom to say my thank-you to God.

After about four days we were allowed to visit Father ; and we set off with Mother to the hospital off the Fulham Road. There it was, the large grey mansion standing among its stout old trees with a huge gilt cross over its portico and a notice board in its garden saying.

Hospital of Our Lady of Mercy and Good Counsel
Founded 1861
Under the care of
The Sisters of Mercy

Entering a bare, tiled hall, we saw in a niche immediately facing us a painted statue, half life-size, of the Good Shepherd with a finger pointing upward and a lamb at His feet. Over the arch above Him were the words, ' In this Hospital I reign.' Beautiful, said Mother. We went up a wide staircase and passed an ancient nun in her black robes coming down. She stood and bowed to us as we went by ; for we were the guests of her house. On the first landing, in a niche similar to the one below stood a statue of the Madonna, crowned, and with her child in her arms. A vase of bluebells and white hyacinths honoured the hem of her robe. Through a room of the old mansion, now converted into a passage, we entered one of the new wings, and there on the wall, facing us, was a statue of the Sacred Heart with a hand extended as if to welcome and direct us on. We now found ourselves in a long corridor with a row of windows on one side and a row of closed doors on the other. Bare except for a few tables and trolleys, it seemed to hold but one thing, a clean, pungent smell as of ether and lysol.

Mother touched a bell on a table and straightway a nursing nun, a large woman looking all the larger for her bunched white robes and flying white cap, came sailing along the corridor, like a well-rigged ship, with a smile at the prow. The smile enlarged into the very symbol of benevolence as she saw us children. Putting about and sailing ahead of Mother, she escorted her into one of the rooms, after throwing back to us a friendly nod and a signal to wait. We waited by an open window, looking down upon a sunken garden where battalions of tulips stood on parade down the centre of a flagged pathway. Somewhere beyond the old trees a gardener was mowing the grass, and the music of his unseen wheels seemed one with the fragrance in the air. My eye, wandering back into the corridor, alighted upon a stone plaque fixed to the wall, and I went at once to study it. I read :

The Lord and Lady Guesthope Wing

_____

In accordance with the wishes of the late Lord and Lady Guesthope the west wing of this hospital is always to be called The Lord and Lady Guesthope Wing and the Catholic inmates and the nuns in charge thereof shall once every day recite the Our Father and Hail Mary and also at least one day in each week for all time say the Litany of the Holy Name for the repose of the souls of Lord and Lady Guesthope.

As I finished reading, I heard again the sound of the lawn mower, like the wheels of Time made audible in the silence of Eternity.

Now the sister, with a smile that embraced us both, and all other children, rich and poor, black and white, summoned us into the room, a high, narrow chamber with a small crucifix on the chimney-piece and a large picture of the Sacred Heart hanging above it. The metal bed strangely high stood against the opposite wall ; and Father lay on it, propped up with pillows. His face was still very pale, and his big brown powerful hands looked unusually white as they rested on the counterpane, but there was a twinkle in his eyes to greet us.

'Well, children,' he said. 'This is clearly the end.'

'It's clearly nothing of the sort,' snapped the sister. 'What a thing to say to them. Poor lambs ! Don't you believe him, my dears. He's doing very well indeed and you'll have him back in a very few weeks.'

'Blarney, Doric,' explained Father. 'That's just their blarney. This most excellent hospital has its roots in Ireland, where they never tell you the truth but only what they think you would wish to hear. I should know because, as I've told this kind sister, the Mournes have the blood of the Irish kings in their veins. She merely said that to comfort me. She said it to keep me from despairing and hastening the end.'

' I know,' I agreed ; ' I quite understand ' ; and to jolly him up, I inquired, ' But how are you really feeling, General ? '

' *General !* ' screamed the sister. ' General indeed ! Mercy on us all, what an extraordinary child ! '

' He is something of a humorist, sister. Doric, this is Sister Mary Evangelist, an angel from Heaven. This is Mr. Doric, sister, and this is Tricks. They're not much ; but they're all I've got : my sole earthly joys—one rather fat and one rather thin. You'll like the fat one. She's holy too.'

We shook her hand and said How-do-you-do, and Sister Mary Evangelist played upon us a veritable beam of benediction. She even passed her hand over Con's head, who was short and small.

The presentation completed, Father, who had watched it with his own brand of benediction, returned to the main and exceedingly important subject. ' Yes, beyond question the end. Life was good while it lasted, but *tout passe, tout casse.* . . . I do not complain. If it is allowed to me, children, I shall look down from Heaven and bless you both.'

' It's not the end,' remonstrated the sister. ' I never heard such nonsense. General, you are awful. And Heaven ! Who are you to be sure of going to Heaven ? We're so little sure of it that we're going to patch you up and give you twenty more years in which to repent.'

' But, sister, consider my great age.'

' Your age ? What on earth is sixty ? '

' Is that all I am ? *Nom de dieu,* I feel ninety. I've been so beaten and battered by the storms of life.'

' Stuff and nonsense ! Reverend Mother is nearly eighty.'

' But she'd been serene and good all her life. Una, it is very pleasant and refreshing, after the brutalities of the world, to find myself in this quiet haven where everyone is good and sweet— or nearly everyone. I'm not sure about Sister Mary Lucrece. Look, Tricks, at my holy room. And have you seen the statues ? There's a saint in every corner, and I feel almost in heaven already.'

' Is this the Sacred Heart ? ' asked Con, looking up at the picture over the chimney-piece.

' Of course it is. That is the Sacred Heart. I know all about it now. My daughter is but a heretic, I fear, sister, but a holy one. You must take her in hand. Nothing can exceed Sister's kindness to me, Una.' The quarrel between Father and Mother was still in being because they'd had no adequate opportunity to unravel it, but he was grateful to her for her help, and treating her with his usual post-bellum courtesy. ' She

tells me all about her holy religion, and she's given me this little
prayer book. It's all there : the Our Father and the Hail Mary
and Night Prayers. The night prayers I found particularly
helpful in my bodily anguish. And where's that little book
about the Mother Foundress ? Here it is. Listen, Tricks.' He
felt for his spectacles on the side-table, mounted them on his
nose, found the page in the book, and began to read to us.
' " Soon every alley in Dublin knew Mother Mary and saw her
quiet ministrations to the most derelict and degraded "—that's
me—" ministrations offered with all courtesy, for she knew that
charity must come with a gentle face in order to be welcomed."
Did you hear that, Doric ? Always remember that " To her
sisters she would say that they must show a great reverence to
the sick and lowly because Christ had graciously permitted their
assistance of Him in the persons of His suffering poor." ' At
words of such beauty Father blinked wet eyes, swallowed
heavily, removed the spectacles, and felt for his handkerchief.
' Isn't that rather lovely ? I tell you the goodness of these dear
ladies is almost more than I can bear.'

' Mother Mary was a saint,' said Sister Mary Evangelist.
' We are not. We are only sinners like the rest.'

' No, no, sister. I cannot hear that. Sister Mary Lucrece,
perhaps . . .'

' But it is so. And in any case I can't stay here to argue. I
must go, because I have other patients who are really ill. Good-
bye, General.'

A smile for Mother, a particularly warm-hearted smile for us,
and the door shut on her. Directly it clicked, Con asked of
Father with great interest, ' Is she making you good ? '

' I don't know. I rather fancy so. My deepest sentiments
are certainly touched. I love them all, with their sweet faces.
They are saints, all of them—except one who's an infernal
woman——'

' Who's she ? ' demanded Con.

' The cat's mother, child. A certain Sister Mary Lucrece,
and may she perish everlastingly. I suspect that the abominable
woman has the impudence to disapprove of me and to show it
by a certain brusqueness ; and by all the gods above, I may be
progressing a little in sanctity but I haven't got to the point
where I accept reproofs from a fool of a woman with humility.
I'm nowhere near it in fact ; and, quite frankly, I detest the
woman. But the others—they can do what they like with me.
They have only to come near me to convert me. After they've
gone I lie here and think of my sins until they amount to such a
volume that I change over and try to recall my good deeds

instead. And what pleases me, Con, is that I've been able to remember quite a few.'

'But that's " spiritual pride," ' objected Con.

'Dear me, is it ? Oh dear, dear ! Then am I of all men the most miserable ; and where shall I go for comfort ? '

I have often thought that Father's nonsense-humour required a male mind to enjoy it ; I loved it and copied it, but Mother apparently had little appreciation of it and half despised it ; and now, as if she had not been listening, she interrupted, ' Henrietta wants to come and see you.'

This scattered his peace and sanctity like a bomb. ' *Gott im Himmel*, no ! She mustn't be allowed to. It would put me back weeks. It might even rupture my spleen again. She must be diverted—she must be circumvented. Or, if she must come, for God's sake let her be well diluted. Let you come too, and Gentle, and the children, and even old Humphrey. Not Henrietta neat.'

'Why, don't you like her ? ' asked Con, impishly.

'Like ? My child, I'm fascinated by my horror of her.'

'Hush, Kingsley. She's the children's aunt.'

'But it's so : God forgive me, I cannot abide the woman. She would destroy in five minutes all the religion these excellent women have implanted in me. Do you know, Doric : if I had my life over again, I should like to be a monk and devote myself to the poor. I should like to be the opposite of everything I've been : to live in a cell and wear a coarse frock and go among the poor in the alleys of Dublin. The idea makes such an appeal to me that I begin to suspect I'm a monk *manqué*. I mean, Una : my deep feeling for the Catholic ceremonies and liturgy must have *some* explanation. The words cause me a singular delight, especially when they're in Latin. " *Ave Maria, gratia plena* . . ." ' but unfortunately forgetting the rest of the words that so delighted him, he changed to : ' " *Credo in Deum Patrem Omnipotentem* . . ." ' but this too perished in a mist of oblivion. ' Why, just the name, Sister Mary Evangelist, is so pleasant on my palate that I say it to myself over and over again. I think I ought to have founded an Order. I chose a name for it last night : The Brothers of Kindness and Good Counsel. They would teach the world that all that matters is kindness—kindness that nothing can beat back, neither hostility nor hate nor ill-usage. Someone once saw that this alone would save the world. Yes, *Credo in Jesum Christum, Dominum nostrum*. . . . Well, well, I bequeath the task to you, Doric.'

It was not written that I should found a monastic order, but this little seed, dropped by my father at his bedside, did send an unexpected sprig above ground, many years later. It was only a tiny seed, lightly tossed ; but of small beginnings who shall bound the issue ?

§

In three weeks Father was allowed to get up for a few hours and walk about. He was greatly relieved by the permission. Bored by his narrow room—bored, it must be confessed, by the Sacred Heart—he would put on his Indian dressing-gown, of blue silk heavily embroidered with gold, and wander along the corridors or stand at one of their windows and consider the quiet life in the garden : the patients seated under the trees, the nuns entering the convent, and the old gardeners sweeping the blossom from the paths or the worm-casts from the shadowed and sun-shot lawns.

Gentle had not yet visited him, and she was almost burned up by her desire to do so. She wanted also to see the nuns and the statues and the interesting convalescents in the garden. And one Saturday—ever escaping from oversight and control, ever demanding an ' adventure '—she whispered low, with a huge mischief prancing in her eyes ; ' Let's go. Shall we ? Let's go and see darling Uncle Kingsley. Yes, come on ! Don't be swines : you've seen him and I haven't. And he must be dying to see me. Come on : be sports.' It was a bright day, and without a word to anyone we went. We hurried down Redcliffe Gardens to Fulham Road and the hospital. To the burly porter in his cubicle I said ' General Allan Mourne ' like an Open Sesame, and he allowed us to pass, though casting a dubious eye on Gentle who chose that moment to lose her grip on a giggle. Proud of our knowledge, we led her through the old mansion and into the new wing and the clean, medical smell ; and there, the one figure in the long white corridor, stood Father, looking strangely tall and pitiably thin, in his handsome blue and gold dressing gown. Spectacles on nose, he was staring up at the plaque which commemorated the bounty of Lord and Lady Guesthope. Hearing steps, he turned and saw us—three of us, for here was Gentle in a blouse of tussore silk and a cream skirt, with her two amber pigtails tied by two yellow bows.

' Hallo, Two Yellow Bows,' he greeted her. ' Good day to you.'

' Hallo, Uncle Kingsley.' Gentle, at twelve, had just begun to detect admiration and like it ; and she let her eyes sparkle for him. ' I've come to see you.'

' That is kind.'

'We escaped. It was my idea. You won't split on us, will you?'

'I think it is exceedingly kind. It is true religion. " I was sick and in prison——" '

'I've been aching to come and see you in hospital. Isn't it a jolly place? I love it. I wish I could be ill and come here : I've never been in hospital. What's that on the wall you're reading?'

'It's a holy plaque.' He looked up at it again and began reciting, ' " The Catholic inmates of this wing, and the nuns in charge thereof——" '

'Can we see the nuns?'

'*Doucement, doucement*, child! Allow me to finish. "The nuns in charge thereof shall once every day recite the Our Father and the Hail Mary and also at least one day in each week for all time say the Litany of the Holy Name for the repose of the souls of Lord and Lady Guesthope." '

'Gosh! Do they do it?'

'Certainly they do. How could they have the heart not to? Why, I do myself.'

'Coo! You don't!'

'I do. I say the Our Father and the Hail Mary. I tried the Litany of the Holy Name, but there's rather too much of it, between ourselves. It—to put it quite frankly—it goes on for ever. But it would be worth doing if you could manage it, because there's seven years' indulgence for those who say it devoutly, and I've been calculating that if I said it daily for twelve years that would make about four thousand times ; and seven years' indulgence for each time would equal twenty-eight thousand years, which would surely cover even my sins. But there it is : I am lazy. I say only the Hail Mary. I trust you say your Hail Mary.'

'I couldn't. I don't know it.'

'You don't! Good gracious, child. You don't know your Hail Mary! But this is lamentable.'

'Of course I don't.'

'You do, Doric, I trust? What, not you? Well, I never! You do, Con, for certain? Not even Con? Dear, dear. I am shocked beyond measure. Not even the *Ave Maria*. "*Ave Maria, gratia plena*——" ' but, as before, he was stumped at this point, and continued the lovely words in English. And when he had said them, or some of them, he announced, ' Now we'll all go and see a gentleman friend of mine.'

'Oh, yes!' Gentle agreed most readily. 'Who is it?'

'It's Mr. Terence.'

' But what is he ?   Is he ill like you ? ' pursued Gentle, putting
her hand into his and skipping along at his side.

' He's a distinguished private patient and occupies the next
room to mine.   He's just had his tonsils removed.'

' But I thought only kids had their tonsils out.'

' Not at all.   That's by no means the case,' said he.

' Is he old then ?   Is he as old as you ? '

' Alas, no.   Few are as old as that.   In point of fact Mr.
Terence is what I should call fairly young.'

' How old ? '

' Four and a half.'

Gentle expressed some disappointment.   ' Lummy ! '

' But he's a charming child, none the less ; and I'm sure he'll
be pleased to see some other children—not but what he finds me
entertaining enough.   I go and visit him several times a day
because he's as bored with his bed as I am.   I have an arrangement with him by which he hammers on the wall when his boredom has become insufferable.   He hammers quite frequently.
I honestly think we comfort each other a little.   He tells me all
about his parents, and I tell him all about you children, which,
oddly enough, interests him.   He's taught me various crafts,
such as building, modelling and drawing, and, in short, I've
been greatly enlarged by the association.   I've taught him one or
two games with my Patience pack, but I'm not quite sure that the
holy sisters approve of my cards.   Here we are.   No. 7.   Mount
guard all of you for a moment while I go in.   There's an appalling woman called Sister Mary Lucrece, of whom I'm terrified.
And there's the Reverend Mother Prioress too, of whom I've
the proper fear.   Good afternoon, Mr. Terence.'

' Hallo,' said a child's voice within.

' I've brought a gentleman and two ladies to visit you.   The
visitors simply pour in to see you.   You're clearly the most
popular person in the hospital.   Come on, children.'

We trooped in and saw a flaxen, peachy, but pale little boy,
sitting up in bed and a toy farm on the bed-table over his knees.

' This is—where are you, child ?—this is Miss Gentle Greaves.'

' Are you her Daddy ? '

' Unfortunately not.   Because she's easily the nicest child I
know.'

' I wish I *was* his daughter like Con,' said Gentle.

Father closed his eyes at this grammatical solecism, and when
the pain was overpast, opened them again and proceeded, though
with less liveliness, because so shaken : ' This is Con.   And this
is Doric. . . . Mr. Terence McClure, a very fierce Irishman.
. . . Now what about a quiet game of Animal Snap ? '

' Oh, yes ! ' shouted Terence.

' Very good.' Father sat on the foot of the bed, and we gathered about the bed-table. Animal Snap, you will certainly know, is played in the following fashion. Each player chooses to be an animal—a lion, a dog, an owl, a hyena—and when one player sees that the card he has turned up is the same as one just turned up by another player, he must not cry ' Snap ! ' but emit the unpleasant noice peculiar to the other player's animal —a roar for a lion, say, a bark for a dog, a hoot for an owl, or a maniac laugh for a hyena. A kindly provision allows that if a third party perceives the sameness of the cards before either of their possessors, he may make both noises—the roar, say, and the maniac laugh, and snap up both packs. Now, as the spirit of competition is high among children, and as Father's hawk-eye was quicker than any of ours, there were times this afternoon when all five of us were roaring and quacking and loosing maniac laughs together, Terence shrieking with delight and fear, when we snapped up the cards. Such a vociferation may have been heard in the lion house at the Zoo, and occasionally in Bedlam, but never before, I think, in this House of Mercy and Good Counsel. Even Father, who contributed some fine animal impersonations, was driven at times to say, ' *Doucement, doucement,*' and ' *Piano, piano* . . . please ! '

In the midst of one such uproar Sister Mary Evangelist burst in. ' General, General, General ! ' she screamed. ' What on earth's all this ? Stop it, stop it ! It's Pandemonium.'

' *Nom d'un tonnerre* ! ' murmured Father, dropping his hands to his lap in dismay. ' I was afraid it was Reverend Mother. Doric . . . Sister Mary Evengelist. Gentle . . . Sister Mary Evangelist. Con . . .'

' Never mind introductions. What are you doing ? I never heard such a noise.'

' Mr. Terence has visitors.'

' So I see.'

' These are my children, whom you've met. And this is Gentle, easily the nicest niece I've got.'

' He hasn't got another niece,' complained Gentle, ' so that doesn't mean a thing.'

' Never mind that. Never mind nieces. I'm talking about noises, not nieces. We can't have a noise like this in hospital, General. It's enough to wake the dead.'

' I don't mind that, so long as it doesn't arouse Sister Mary Lucrece.'

' You're the worst of the lot, General.'

' I ? I've done nothing but try to establish a little order.'

'You can hear it all over the wing.'

'I know, I know. Children will shout so. It goes *through* me.'

'You? You encourage them. If you go on like this, I shall have to send both you and Terence down to the Children's Ward. Besides, this is too exciting for both of you. Don't you realize that you've both just recovered from operations?'

'I do. I thought that was what we were celebrating. But, if you insist, dear lady. . . . I am a man under authority. . . .'

'You may play a little longer, if you keep quiet. Now good-bye, and be good.'

'There you are, children,' said Father, when she was gone. '*Lusisti satis . . . Tempus abire* . . . or, in other words, I have played enough, and it is time for me to go.'

'Oh, no,' cried Terence. 'Just a little longer. She said you could go on.'

'One game more then. But whisper—please whisper your roars and your hoots. The good sister was right : we must always think of other people and be kind. Especially when they are sick and ill. Always remember that, Mr. Terence. And now lead, sir. . . . You, Gentle. *Snap*!' We were all softly roaring again.

CHAPTER VI

WHEN FATHER came home from the hospital he was very thin, and his fine suits of heavy serge hung loosely on his shoulders and lean limbs. His long face too was leaner and (as I can only describe it) more ascetic, more spiritual. He himself noticed this new spirituality and was pleased with it. His decision to leave home, announced just before his fall, was either conveniently forgotten or explicitly withdrawn. He disliked the idea of leaving a house and children both of which he loved ; Mother disliked the prospect of a broken home and comparative poverty ; so they were Christian and forgiving with each other, since it suited them both ; and Mr. Payton was seen no more in Coburg Square. Moreover, Father was grateful to Mother for her goodness to him in his illness, and genuinely softened by the influence of the nuns. I heard him saying so to Uncle Humphrey one day as he followed him from one room to another and down the stairs. 'I'm very much better physically, old boy, but what's much more remarkable than my physical convalescence is my spiritual convalescence. In that respect I'm a different man :

nobler in every way. In fact, I don't quite know what's going to happen to me, I'm so filled with a lively sense of my sins and with aspirations after the beauty of holiness. Where do we go now : down to the drawing-room ? They laid sore at me with their goodness, those beautiful nuns, and fairly captured my heart. My conscience is in a most tender state, old man, and smarts at a touch, like John Bunyan's. I begin to see that one's closing years should be one's noblest, and that, if that's so, I'd best take a hand with them at once. Sixty is a great age. And what about you, old son ? Hadn't you better begin too ? ' That there were grains of truth in these flippancies I am sure : Father really did want to be a nobler man for a week or two after his return from the hospital.

For me the year following his return was a happy year, and the only completely happy one that I was to know for a long time. It always astonishes me to remember the sudden develop-ment of my character round about my twelfth year. From the moment I thrust my mother's tyranny aside something was liberated in me, and I began to transcend the girls in self-assertion and leadership, as I outstripped them in height. Now, more often than not, I was captain of the band, and they, without being aware of it, accepted the change. The shadow of my mother partly withdrawn, Father's flattery warming me, I put out an abundance of new and rather showy blooms like an hydrangea plant in the July sun. My dazzling big words were now the most elaborate flowers : I would speak of Mother as ' The Infuriate Woman ' or ' The Stormy Sister ' ; of Aunt Henrietta as ' That Intense and Interminable Matron ' or ' That Infatuate Female ' ; and of Mother and Henrietta, closeted for a chat, as ' The Loquacity Mongers ' or ' The Comedy Duo.' To all females, however, when talking to them, my courtesy was of a rotundity and stateliness that exceeded Father's, even when he was in one of his periods of constraint after an up-roarious quarrel. I inspired most of our games now, because my ideas were at least as prolific as Gentle's and usually more ludicrous and exciting.

Consider the game of ' Dr. Allan Mourne ' : I must still think it a happy creation. A wet winter day ; a cheerless view from the playroom window ; grey and heavy-hearted clouds moving along beneath a blanket of white ; rain-drops visiting the pane —what are we to do ? The doctor's brougham goes forth from No. 23, and I have it : I shall be Dr. Allan Mourne, and one of the girls my patient, and the other the nurse. Gentle of course wants to be the doctor, but I explain that there's no such thing as a female doctor, and she has to agree. ' Oh, all right,

I'll be the patient,' she consents, not averse from the rôle. ' I'll give in and be the patient. Gosh, I'm nice sometimes.' And we put Gentle to bed up in Con's room ; Con stays by her as a nurse (in a becoming cap made out of a table napkin) ; I go from the house with a bag, but return at once and rattle the knocker ; the nurse admits me, and I ascend the stairs with a heavy, masculine tread. I enter the sick room and am not disturbed by the silly giggling of the patient. ' And how is our little patient to-day ? ' I ask. Gentle says that she's pretty mouldy. ' Dear, dear, we can't have that,' I say ; and my homemade stethoscope comes out of my bag, and I sound most of the upper part of Gentle, who protests with inapposite laughter that it tickles. Here I can tell, of that small stranger who was myself, that this stethoscope examination of Gentle, now a soft-bosomed child, and not my sister, created in me a slight stimulation which I didn't understand but certainly enjoyed. ' Nothing very serious there, as far as I can see, young lady. How are our bowels ? ' This provoked a shocked laugh from the patient, who, nevertheless, humoured my indecency to the extent of saying they were fine. ' Well, nurse, we shall have to keep her in bed for a month ; and meantime I'll send you some medicine. I'll dispense it myself.' And down in the bathroom I mixed a disgusting concoction in a bottle : pink carbolic tooth-powder, water, a solution of primrose soap, and a tincture of brilliantine.

Once Gentle twisted her knee in a game (there was always something wrong with Gentle's knee) and Dr. Allan Mourne was immediately called (at his own instance). He and the nurse examined the leg and, diagnosing a compound fracture, bound it in splints from ankle to thigh, and carried her on an improvised stretcher up to bed. It was a difficult journey—up the stairs.

From the doctor's dispensary it was but a side-step to the dentist's surgery. Again I was the dentist, since there could be no such thing as a female dentist. Gentle, not without enthusiasm, consented to be the sufferer in the chair. She sat and groaned on a rocking chair between a small tripod table (from the drawing-room) and a tall dumb-waiter (from the dining-room). On the table was a basin and a tumbler ; on the dumb-waiter a bradawl, a gimlet, compasses, pincers, dividers, and other dental instruments. With these, one after another, I poked about the pink and white cathedral of Gentle's mouth—' Wide open, please '—and only paused to say, ' Now rinse ' ; which by this time she certainly needed to do. ' Towel, please, nurse,' I said to Con ; and be sure that by this time I needed the towel.

This was the winter of the Dreyfus Affair, and the world-wide controversy often blazed up and sparked in our Coburg Square rooms. Father was an ardent Dreyfusard ; Mother believed Captain Dreyfus guilty, chiefly because she disliked Jews ; Uncle Humphrey averred that ' none of their hands were clean.' For my part I have never been more fascinated by a tale than when Father told us, one evening after tea, how Captain Dreyfus, though almost certainly innocent, had been found guilty of disclosing national secrets to the German enemy and condemned to degradation and perpetual imprisonment ; how they had degraded him on the parade ground before the assembled soldiers, ripping the gold lace and red bands from his uniform, snapping his sword before him, throwing it on the ground, and then, with their swords drawn, marching him round the square that every eye might see his shame. Father could draw the utmost from a story that caught at his heart-strings. ' His strange dignity, Doric, so silent, so unprotesting, so proud, was something that no one who saw it ever forgot. Even his enemies allowed that this was so. Though there was not a button or a badge on his uniform, and his sword lay in pieces behind him, he marched between the drawn swords with his head erect, his weak eyes staring in front of him through his pince-nez, and his hands at the seams of his trousers, as a soldier should. " He nothing common did, nor mean Upon that memorable . . ." but enough . . . enough. . . .' Father could not proceed for tears. He was feeling for the large silk handkerchief that he might blow his nose and dab both eyes.

Sure, I was Father's best listener. The tale so moistened my eyes and swelled my heart that I had to tell it at the first opportunity to Gentle ; and I must have told it well (but not so well as Father) for Gentle insisted that she must be degraded and marched around. So we degraded her in the square's garden and marched her around it—her head very high—before the assembled shrubs ; then conducted her, with our swords still drawn and her head still high, to our coal-cellar under the pavement for perpetual imprisonment. Her pity for the disgraced officer with his weak eyes and his pince-nez—it was the pince-nez that finished her off—was so poignant, and so enduring, that for some time after this she declared she would devote her life, when she grew up, to proving his innocence ; but in this business Colonel Picquart and Emile Zola were ahead of her.

Is it noteworthy or not that in these games Gentle was always happy to be a victim, and I to have her in my power ? I cannot say ; I only know that I got a curious faint pleasure from being her dentist, tormentor, jailer or executioner (we beheaded her once on the lavatory seat), and drew no such pleasure from Con.

§

Soon I must leave these pleasant playgrounds of childhood, but not without mention of those games I played quite alone ; because these dramatized a new, secret, almost passionate aspiration after greatness and achievement—but not, be it noted, an achievement that would be seen only of my Father in Heaven, but one that the whole world would acclaim, and all future time. Father had often told me of General Gordon's death on the Residency steps at Khartoum ; and I, standing alone on our landing at the top of the stairs, fought the Mahdi's followers with my swinging sword to the last—fought them on my feet, on my knee, on my back—and died. Nansen, at this time, attempting to reach the Pole with his vessel, the *Fram*, stirred the world by reaching a point 86° N., the furthest north of any man ; and I at the window of No. 1, quite alone, drove the house on and on, through the pack-ice to the Pole. Mr. Gladstone, now eighty-five, was in the last year of his premiership ; and Father, who admired him while Mother detested him, would dilate on the grander occasions of his life and quote his more eloquent passages ; I, having heard him out, would hurry upstairs to the playroom, close its door, and standing at its table, deliver an oration that shook the conscience of the House and caused several strong Members to weep. Cycling for ladies had just become, not merely tolerable, but the fashion, the craze ; and Mother, in her amiable times when she was happy to please, would lend me the new safety model on which she cycled in Hyde Park. I rode it round and round the square, pedalling at the fastest possible speed, my breast on the handle-bars ; but I was not taking part (at least, not as a rule) in one of the famous cycle races at the Wheeler's Club ; I was on a machine with wings and flying over the roofs of Kensington and Brompton and Earls Court. I was the first man in history to fly.

Yes, in those days you had only to leave me alone with my dreams, and I went swaggering down all future time.

§

And then the shadow of Mother began to fall again. Father, now as vigorous as ever, came home one evening and announced that we must make the most of him while we had him because in a few days he would be going. Strange that he never knew

how he could founder my heart with words like these. He
never knew because I never told a soul or showed a sign. Going
where, we demanded in chorus. To India, children, India.
The Empire Co-operative Society, one of the first and most
prosperous of the co-operative stores, was sending him and two
other directors to establish branches in Bombay, Calcutta and
Madras, and agencies in Delhi, Patna, Benares and Lahore.
Though as pleased and excited as a youth with this commission
he pretended that he was only leaving the comfort of his home
at the call of duty. ' They asked for volunteers for the place of
danger, and I offered myself at once. I could do no other since
I alone knew my India well.'

On Mother's asking what was the danger, he affected to be
shocked at her ignorance and hurt at her lack of anxiety. Were
there not savages there by the million? And lions and tigers
and rhinoceroses? And elephants? Why, you could hardly
move for elephants. And curries. The curries alone were
enough to incinerate a much younger stomach than his. ' You'll
be lucky if I return unscathed—always supposing you have
any wish for my return.' He took me with him to buy his
heavy ulster for the liner's deck and his tropical kit for the
hot plains. ' I have great faith in Mr. Doric's taste for dress.
His eye is the eye of an artist.' He brought home one evening
a picture and a plan of the P. and O. liner *Allahabad*, which
would take him away, and a booklet filled with pictures of life
on board and views of Port Said, the Suez Canal and the
Harbour of Bombay. And at the last he took us to see him
off. We went over the ship and saw his stateroom and the
saloon where he would dine, and I made my jokes, ' Marry,
but it's a spacious galleon,' while my heart was as heavy as
the trunks on the cranes. We came down the gangway and
stood on the quay ; and I saw him by the rail wiping his eyes
and blowing his nose, or gulping back the tears as he used the
handkerchief to wave. The *Allahabad*, drawing away, diminished
from a tall hull-side to a single whole ; and I waved and roared
' Don't eat too much curry ' and ' Mind the lions,' though my
hope of happiness was going into the haze with the ship.

§

We returned to Coburg Square, and now the shadow was
really upon me. It was not that I was whipped, for I was now
thirteen ; not that I didn't enjoy noisy games with Con and
Gentle, for my disposition was to be lively when possible ; but

that the absence of any love for me in the house weighed upon my heart and head like a lack of ozone in the air. There were two lonely figures wandering about the rooms now, myself and Uncle Humphrey. Mother's dislike and shunning of me increased as I grew towards fourteen. There were two causes of this increase. One was my ever-stronger defiance : if, not daring to hit me, she vented her violent temper by shouted abuse, I shouted back at her anything that came into my head, the ruder the better. The other was the fact that, between thirteen and fourteen, I who had always been thin and lank, shot up into a most unlovely weed, meagre, droop-shouldered, necky and pale. Hurt by the sight of such an unprepossessing child, she kept her eyes away from me and directed them upon Con, now a mature and shapely, if short and plump, young person of nearly fifteen. The result was that, while Con walked in curled hair and elegant laces, my white, hollowed face was capped with uncut hair, whose fringe was always in my eyes ; my bony frame was hung with suits that were crumpled, out-grown and stained ; and my skinny ankles were barely covered by the socks which had collapsed over my shoes. I shall never forget my humiliation when my headmaster wrote to Mother, complaining of the condition in which I attended school ; and she, frightened, abused me for the slovenliness which had brought this shame upon her.

Sometimes I would hear her discussing me with Henrietta behind the closed door of the drawing-room, and then I would stand on the dark landing and listen, body still, breath held. Very wrong, no doubt, to eavesdrop thus, but I must suspect that he who, passing a door and catching his name, does not halt to hear a little more, is on the way, not to his playroom but to sanctity. From my dark place I could picture them there in the sunny room : Mother, rather stout now, sitting at one end of the long Chesterfield, and Henrietta, as long and thin as ever, sitting sideways at the other end and leaning forward like a wind-blown telegraph pole, her intense sympathy being the wind that enforced this slope. I could see Henrietta's fixed and earnest gaze as she listened, her nods as she under-stood, and her touch on Mother's knee, as she encouraged or consoled.

Mother was speaking. ' He really is the most extraordinary child. There are times when I'm afraid of him. I rebuke him for something, and he shouts at me like a raving lunatic.'

Henrietta : ' History repeats itself, my dear. Like father, like son.'

Mother, not listening to anyone but herself : ' And he goes

about like a tramp. It makes one so ashamed. I tell him he looks more like an errand boy than a lady's child. His school complained of his appearance the other day ; but what can I do ? I can't be for ever brushing his clothes. I can't take him and wash him every day.'

' It may be partly physical. Perhaps he's not well. I'm sure he looks as pale as a sheet sometimes. Brian says that fourteen is a curious age in a boy.'

' He's as well as I am. Just lazy, that's all. I think it's time he was sent to a boarding school where there are men to take him in hand and knock him into shape.'

' You mustn't worry too much, Una, my love.' Here I suspected a touch on her knee. .' You've one dear child in Con. She shows you plenty of affection. Brian thinks her the sweetest child. Don't cry. I always say that sometimes a mother's love must be content to travel downwards—you give your love to them and they give it to their children. Love them and ask nothing. The love is not lost. It travels down and down. Brian says we can't hope to——'

' But I don't love him,' objected Mother, after a trumpet blast on her nose : ' I cannot feel any love for him at all, and I'm not going to pretend to something I don't possess.' Once again I heard her pride in this unusual and original attitude and the bold statement of it. ' I can find nothing to like in him : he's sly and self-centred and lazy and rude. Sometimes I wonder what'll become of him, he has so much the look of a wastrel. And yet he has ability. He can draw wonderfully when he likes and he reads the most astonishing books. He's as clever as they make them in some ways. Perhaps he's going to be one of those unpleasant sorts of geniuses.'

' Hardly a genius, I think,' laughed Henrietta, who would have said the same if her sister's child had been the young Michelangelo or the young Will Shakespeare.

It was true that in my loneliness I had begun to read. That was a pregnant hour when I began to read : the reading began as an escape from a grey and loveless world and led to a craving for knowledge and wisdom. It led in the end to the perception, and the enthusiastic embrace, of my purpose in life.

Captain Marryat was the first of the good friends who took me by the hand and led me away. I walked with *Peter Simple, Midshipman Easy* and *Masterman Ready*—and how I loved them ! When the Captain had showed me all he had to show (and magnificent stuff it was), he handed me over to Fennimore Cooper, who led me deep into the forest where the Mohicans were, but left me much sooner than the Captain—left me to be picked up by Sir Walter who led me off to the Holy Land and the Border and I know not where. But the good knight became a little tedious in his later itineraries, and I left him for a hearty, laughing, cheering, weeping, sobbing giant ; the best company in the world, who took my hand with the words, ' Night is generally my time for walking ' (*Old Curiosity Shop*, line 1), and in this great company, why, all the past was a sleep, and life began. With him I laughed and laughed, unheard of Mother and Con and the servants ; with him I wept. Together we wept, abundantly. We lifted up our voices and lamented over Little Nell and Poor Joe and Paul Dombey—was I not a shamefully neglected child myself ? I say we watered their graves with our tears. On the giant's personal recommendation (*David Copperfield*, chapter IV) I introduced myself to Smollet, Fielding, Goldsmith and Le Sage. Somewhere in the train of these gentlemen I found George Eliot, and though I could only digest two of his novels (I supposed him to be another gentle-man) I owe to one of them my first love. Peter Simple and Midshipman Easy were my first brothers, but Maggie Tulliver was my first love. My tears as she sank beneath the flood waters of the Floss, locked in Tom's arms, would have made an appreciable contribution to the flood.

It was now that I began to assemble my ' Golden Calf Library.' As other boys collected butterflies or stamps, I collected books— but only such as were bound in full calf or half calf and had golden tooling on their spines. I searched for and found these on the shelves of the second-hand bookshops in Kensington High Street and Old Brompton Road. Of course I bought them for the gold on their covers rather than the gold in their contents, but it happened that among my purchases were two volumes of Boswell at a shilling a volume, and I not only bought this handsome pair but read them right through. And it was again a red-letter, or, shall I say, a full-calf and gilt-edged day, when I entered upon Boswell, for he directed me to Addison, Burke, and Steele.

But perhaps the most unexpected signpost on this climbing road of mine was Henrietta. To her I owe my introduction to poetry. Delivering the set speech for a woman of culture, she would declare that she was ' passionately fond of poetry,' and since it was a fashion at this time to laud the beauty of Fitz-gerald's *Omar Kháyyám* and to leave the poem about the drawing room in a fancy costume of limp leather, Henrietta bought a ' sweet little copy ' of it, read it, and promptly jetted her ad-miration into the air like an oil-gusher or an Iceland hot-spring. Was it not exquisite she asked of everybody, in her deep, unlaughing tones, and she would clasp her hands in front of her breast and quote :

'Alas, that Spring should vanish with the Rose,
That Youth's sweet-scented Manuscript should close.'

I have no better instance of her foolishness than this, that she thought the beauty of a poem was a matter of words and rhymes alone and that its vision and content were of small import ; for had she understood old Kháyyám at all, she must have seen that he sang of all the things that should shock her pious, strait-laced and sentimental soul. She never perceived that all the values of her time must be shaking on their seats if the new world could tolerate this ancient poet's elevation of the wine cup above any cup that religion offered, and his hedonism, sensuality, despair and fatalism. So far from perceiving this she gave the book to Gentle and begged, urged, her to read it. And Gentle showed it to us, saying, ' Look what I've got to read so that I may become an intelligent girl. It's a poem, and Henrietta's gone all gushy and goo-ey about it. I've tried to read it, but I can't make head or tail of it ; can you ? Some-times I'm afraid I'm not bright. Oh, but I am, really. I must be.' I took it from her, while she and Con were chatting their heads off, read, there in the playroom,

' Awake ! for Morning in the Bowl of Night
Has flung the Stone that puts the Stars to Flight ' ;

and awoke to the wine-cup of poetry.

§

But I was still far from seeking in my books the real good, Vision and Knowledge, when I heard the tremendous words, screamed by Con, ' Father's coming home ! ' He was on the way home. The long year, like the long childhood days when, between breakfast and dinner, he was away from the house, was coming to a close : it was, so to say, teatime and soon his key would turn in the lock.

And he arrived, his luggage heavy with gifts for us all : a silk-embroidered shawl and a silver-handled fan for Mother ; a girdle of brocaded silk and a gold, enamelled bracelet for Con ; a set of ivory chessmen and a sheathed dagger with a damascened blade for me ; a sari of silk and brocade and a necklace of gilt rings for Gentle ; and elephant-and-rider in cast brass for Uncle Humphrey ; a prayer carpet for Henrietta ;

and temple hangings, silver dishes, lacquered vases, swords, shields and talwars for the house. He was touched by the jubilation with which we welcomed him, and our entrancement with the gifts ; and we were all very happy for some days. I breathed the grateful air of health after sickness, peace after pain.

But the peace of his presence was short-lived. On the other and unseen side of his life, the midnight side of the moon, there lay a knowledge and a dream that he dared not tell. These were not the only gifts that he had brought ; he had brought one for himself, and one that, to him, was the most valuable of all. In India he had formed an attachment with a lady, a Mrs. Sinclair Skene, the widow of a major in the Indian Medical Service ; and as Paris returned from Lacedaemon with Helen in his dark-prowed galley, so Father sailed homeward from India with the lady in the liner. He was sixty-two at this date and had never been more remarkable looking, with his skin as coffee-brown as an Eurasian's, his thick, spurred eyebrows standing grey on the brown, and his dark, deep-set eyes sparkling with humour beneath them. But he was desperately conscious of having entered upon his last lap before seventy, his ' last decade,' as he called it, and he wanted one more chance of romance, one more venture into the magical world of loving and being loved, one more draught of the exquisite cup before Life's liquor in the cup was dry. He longed for a woman to soothe and comfort him—just once more, before his humour, and his sense of fitness, bade him desist, lest the people laughed. I never saw Mrs. Sinclair Skene, but I have been told that she had much beauty and much grace and charm, and that she really loved him as she had loved no other—and, well, there it was : his hunger for the love that she could give him was stronger than his love of his house and children. The love could only be enjoyed in chambers of his own, unwatched and unhampered by wife and family, and very soon after he had come back to us —when he felt a coldness and bitterness in his wife, when he learned that she still traduced him to Henrietta and the neighbours, when he suspected that Mr. Payton had a successor, when he saw that we were growing older and could spare a father—he began to brood upon schemes by which his liberation could be achieved. And very soon his decision was come to : he would leave the house and live elsewhere ; and now he was all set to pick a quarrel that would justify his marching out, even as the dictators of our day pick a quarrel as an excuse for marching in.

He was not happy in what he was about to do. Once when, after his habit, and in some context that I forget, he was explaining to us all that he was the chief of sinners, Uncle Humphrey asked what had happened to that fine purpose of repentance and amendment which had blossomed so promisingly after his stay with the Sisters of Mercy, and he lamented, ' Ah, yes, but it came too late, old boy. Too late, too late. I had hopes then of becoming something rather fine, but nothing came of them. As the incomparable Mr. Bunyan said, I have overstood the time of mercy. I thought I should catch salvation, but I fished for nothing. How that boy could handle his words ! No, there was nothing in that pool for me. I must accept it, that we are castaways, you and I.'

So he would joke, but his conscience was fretting him, and because of this he was more than usually gentle and kind with us children. I would see him watching us for long minutes, with sorrow in his eyes. He was really sorry to be doing wrong again. In the last days before the end he would sometimes shut his book abruptly, lift himself out of his deep chair, and come up to the playroom to see what we were going. And, standing there, he would smile down upon us with the love and the sorrow in his eyes. One such evening he found Con, who was now much given to her dress, stitching a white garment as she sat in the rocking chair ; and he asked, ' What's that you are making : a shroud ? If it's mine, I beg you make it fit, for I shall occupy it a long time.' And he sat himself down on a hard upright chair by the table.

It was a day that could still claim the name, October, but was really one of winter's first pioneers, so dark and brown that we'd had the gas alight at breakfast and again at tea. And now, after tea, all the dim colours of the day had sunk to a dull monochrome of dusky tan. Even the gas globes on the wall seemed depressed by the brown twilight, and Con had put an oil lamp on the table that she might see her close stitching better. I was pencilling, within the spread halo of this lamp, some illustrations for a sequence of comic verses which I had lately composed and pen-printed (with borders, flowers, swelled rules, and vignettes) in a small leather-bound book for my library.

' And I think you'd better hurry up with it,' continued Father, ' because I shall need it soon.'

' Don't be absurd,' said Con, who, at fifteen, was entering upon the impudence of young womanhood. ' You won't need it for a hundred years yet.'

' Therein I beg to differ. I am sixty-two, and my life has been lived—all but a few dreary years at the end of it, which were best not protracted.' It was the more absurd because he looked so splendid sitting there, tall and upright and unbowed, his cigar between his strong brown teeth censing the lamp-lit air, and his deep eyes trying to look melancholy but ever twinkling in the light. ' It's all very sad. One's power begins to fade just as one's mind begins to see. Just as I'm beginning to perceive that in wisdom I'm still quite immature, this senile inertia takes hold of me, and I can do nothing about making myself better. For all practical purposes I am already walking about in my shroud, for, after sixty, what is one's body but a shroud ? '

' But you said the very opposite the other day,' Con reminded him. ' You said you'd never felt so fit in your life.'

' Did I ? '

' Yes, you said you felt about twenty-one.'

' Is that so ? Did I, Doric ? '

' Yes, you did,' I endorsed. ' You said you thought you were marvellous for sixty-two.'

' Impossible ! '

' You did. There's no getting out of it, General.'

' Well, well : " Do I contradict myself? Yes, I contradict myself. I am large. I contain multitudes." '

' Crums ! ' exclaimed Con. ' What conceit ! '

' Walt Whitman, my dear. An American poet. You're but an ignorant child, and read nothing. What is this book that the boy's been reading ? ' He picked up the golden calf volume of Tom Hood upon whose punning poems I had modelled my own. ' Tom Hood. He reads Tom Hood, does he ? ' And to show that he too was well read in Tom Hood, he laid down the book and spouted the only lines he could remember of that poet—spouted them with much feeling, and with a genuine break in his voice at the last :

> ' Alas for the rarity
> Of Christian charity
> Under the sun. . . .

> ' Cross her hands humbly,
> As if praying dumbly,
> Over her breast.
> Owning her weakness
> Her evil behaviour
> And leaving with meekness
> Her sins to her Saviour.

' I must go. I must really go. I only came to see what you were up to, and if I could still feel affection for you.' He put the cigar between his lips and rose. ' If either of you would like to play a game of bezique with me, you'll find my remains in the easy chair in the breakfast room.'

' Oh, don't go, don't go yet,' Con besought him, charmingly. ' Stay with us, please, *please*. Oh, yes, *please*. It's jolly.'

' Jolly ? ' Father removed the cigar.

' Yes, stay here and go on being jolly.'

' *Jolly ?* ' He considered this description of his present mood. He sank back in to the chair to consider it. He put back the cigar as if it would help him to ponder it. ' Jolly ? Well, sometimes, perhaps . . . yes, sometimes . . . but grief is my element. I may laugh now and then, and try to amuse you two children because you are young, but the bases of my life are melancholy. Do you know what an iceberg is, child ? '

' Of course I do. Who doesn't ? '

' Well, I am very like an iceberg in that the part which you see, floating lazily around, may occasionally smile in the sun, but the lower part is sunk in darkness and solitude. I was always like that, and I get more so as I grow older. A very little wisdom, and one knows that every thought one can think, even the most amusing, is encompassed by a vast ocean of sadness.'

Con told him that this was all piffle, and when he had recovered from the word, when his eyelids were lifted again, he assured her, ' It is true, child. Only too true. Consider the iceberg, and be wise. My gaiety as opposed to my melancholy is as one to three—if it stands even as high as that. I am made aware of this by the fact that I cannot hear of someone who has just died without a kind of peace descending upon me. And I notice the same sudden access of consolation and calm every time I pass the mortuary over against the Chest Hospital in the Fulham Road.'

' Golly, you do say awful things,' Con rebuked him, still plying her needle. ' D'you know what Henrietta said——'

' *Who* said ? '

' Auntie Henrietta.'

' Henrietta, indeed ! Such disrespect. Speak of your excellent aunt properly.'

' Auntie Henrietta said it was shocking, some of the things you said in front of us children.'

' She said *what* ? ' He pulled the cigar out of his mouth in horror.

' Yes, she said it to Mother. She said you didn't seem to mind in the least what you said in front of us, and she thought it was a pity because we were delicate plants who might be damaged irreparably.'

'The foul and foolish woman! My talk is an education for you both. Many people have said my talk was as good as a education. And *she*—doesn't she know that hers is a debauchment? God, but I've had small comfort of that woman in my life, and now she's trying to set my children against me. *You* like my talk, don't you?' He was serious now, and this was an appeal for appreciation so pitiful that we hastened to give it to him. I leapt to his aid. 'Ra'*ther*!' I said.

'*You* know when I'm only trying to be funny?'

'Of course,' I comforted him.

'You do, Tricks, too?'

'Naturally,' she said.

'And you enjoy it a little . . . sometimes?'

'Yes,' we both declared.

'Good. That is good.' The one thing he could not bear was that his children should not admire him. 'I only say funny things to amuse you. These terrible people who cannot detect a joke when its put plumb beneath their eyes! Every day in these benighted parts I meet someone who doesn't perceive that what I've just said was intended to have an ironical or nonsensical twist. There are times when I wonder if I'm the only person in Earls Court and Brompton who can deal in the finer shades of humour. You're sure you don't take her seriously?'

'Good crikey, no,' Con reaffirmed, really anxious to comfort him.

'Not even for one doubting moment?'

'Of course not.' And throwing the needlework aside, she rose and put her arms around him. 'We know our Henrietta.'

'That's right.' He cheered up, and when the embrace was over, put back the cigar. 'Fine. Then I bind her lies and slanders on me as an ornament. Bunyan. I don't want to say a word against her—it's quite wrong to depreciate parents before their children, or aunties before their nephews and nieces—so I will only say that this world is mostly fools but there are few as idiotic as she.'

'On that point, General,' said I, continuing my sketch, 'we shall not disagree.'

§

The enabling quarrel, the row which Father desired so that he might load up his baggage and go, was most unwisely provoked by Mother. She made the tactical error of offering a battle just when the foe, behind his breastworks, was all ready for it—guns trained, crews in position, and ammunition up. She opened with one gun, and he replied with fifty. Then, before she could recover from her surprise, he charged with his whole force and captured the field. Your present war-correspondent was expelled from the scene before the engagement opened and can therefore only conjecture the first shots ; but on hearing the uproar of battle, he returned quickly to the dining-room door and can report the rest.

It was seven in the evening, and Father's key turned in the lock. I ran to meet him from the breakfast room where I was doing my homework and together we entered the dining-room where the long table was laid for dinner. At the far end, by the marble chimney-piece, stood my mother, her back to the table and door, and her face to the fire. Her fast-rounding figure was clad in a close-fitting bodice with Bishop's sleeves, and a billowing bell skirt ; the bodice was buttoned down the back ; and if ever a tight back proclaimed that a complaint was about to be broached, hers did then.

'Well,' began Father in good humour, 'good evening, People. How are we all ? ' 'People' was Mother, for he'd lost the power of saying 'Una' or 'my dear.'

'Run away, Doric,' said Mother, turning round. 'I want to speak to your father.'

Wondering, I glanced at her and walked out. The door shut behind me. She had come from her place by the fire and shut it. My eavesdropping habit did not at once take command, and I returned to the breakfast room and the Latin Prose book ; but when I heard Father's voice, louder than Mother's, say, 'All right, I will go '—terrible words—I ran into the hall to listen by the door. I imagine that Mother, having heard of Mrs. Sinclair Skene, had charged him with the affair, and said something like 'Things cannot go on in this fashion. One or other of us must go ' ; and to her astonishment he had replied promptly and without anger, 'All right. I will go.' She had opened an exit door an inch or two, and, before she knew what was happening, he had dashed through it to the place where he wanted to be.

'I will go in a few days. To leave you all will just about kill me, but it can't be helped ; it is simpler if I go. Simpler in every way. I have loved this house, but I will give it up. You are fond of the house, too, I think, and I do not want to disturb you and the children. All I ask is that the children may come and see me.' He made it sound as if he were being most considerate and generous. You would have thought that he was proposing a self-sacrifice. Mother's wit, unready

for this high-minded mood, was bereft for the moment of con-
secutive thought, as of words ; and he went on, ' I am deeply
sorry that things should have come to this, but we must accept
the facts as they are. We must do what is best for us both.
For my part, let me say frankly that I'm not prepared to do
without a little love in the few years that are left to me. I need
affection and cannot live without it. I need someone who'll
give me a little solace and comfort when I'm tired and worn
out with business cares—someone who'll lift my thoughts to
higher things. I believe I should have been a different man
if ever I'd had this. I just cannot breathe an atmosphere of
hostility and disapproval. No doubt I've brought the hostility
on myself—I will admit it, if you like, though there are always
two sides to these questions—but whether it's justified or not,
it's more than I can bear. It—it suffocates me. I meet it
when I enter the home ; I feel it around me in every room.
I may laugh and try to be funny with you and the children,
but my life has really been abjectly miserable for years now.
You are correctly informed about this woman—I confess it—
she has felt able to give me her love—she seems to have found
something in me to love——' at this point he was very near to
tears—' her love, if I may say so, is great indeed, and I do not
propose to turn away from it. I repeat, I am very, very sorry
to have failed you, and will allow that most of the blame for
the failure is mine. How soon would you wish me to go ? '

But Mother's poor little single gun was silenced. Its crew
lay dead at their stations, their eyes staring, their mouths gaping.

So Father proceeded. ' If you think it best I should go at
once, I will go. I wish to consider you in every way. The
last thing I wish to do is to be completely selfish. I will go
to-morrow if you like, but perhaps——'

Now I heard Mother's voice : ' Are you meaning this ? '

' Certainly. Were you not meaning it ? You said one or
other of us must go.'

' Yes . . . yes . . . but it's too serious a business to be
decided as quickly as this.'

' I don't agree. If it's to be done at all, it's best done quickly.'

' But this is ridiculous.' Mother's voice was easily heard
now for she was speaking loud and angrily. I heard her foot
beating. ' Don't be ridiculous. Where will you go to ? '

' I don't know. Anywhere. There's no difficulty about
that. Some hovel. Some insanitary hutment. I am an old
soldier, and, if need be, can bring my requirements down to the
barest—a table, a chair, my books. I'm not at all worried
about that.' Indeed he wasn't, for he'd already secured an

option on an admirable suite—sitting room, bedroom, and full
service—in Pall Mall, nearly opposite his Club. ' I will find
some small *pied-à-terre*, no doubt about that.'
  ' And you will live there alone ? '
  ' I shall live there alone. You may believe it or not, but I
shall live there alone. Only I shall be free to live my life in
my own way without the necessity of having to choose between
being deceitful and being watched and disapproved of—and at
the same time giving pain. I don't like deceit. I'm not
naturally deceitful. All lies I hate. And I don't like giving
pain. It will be better for you all if I go than if I stay. You and
the children like this house—to which I came with such hopes—
and I want you to stay in it. You won't be able to live in quite
such good style, but old Humphrey's contribution will help—
indeed he might well begin to pay some more—and all that's
in my power I will do. I will make a list of the few things I
shall want to take with me—and all the rest shall remain with
you. That is all, I think. Are we to have any dinner to-night ?
It is half past seven.' For him the brief engagement was over.
' I should like to have the meal and be done with it, as I've
brought back some important papers——'
  ' Yes, but. . . .' Hopelessly defeated, Mother could do
nothing but break down in tears. I heard a creak and guessed
that she had flung herself into one of the easy chairs by the fire
and was sobbing on its arm.
  ' Don't . . . don't do that.' Father's voice was kind, and
I think he went up and touched her gently. ' It will be better
so. And I will do everything possible for you . . . everything.'
  ' Oh, go away ! ' she cried—nay, screamed, hammering her
fist on the chair's arm and enthusiastically abandoning herself
to a voluptuous frenzy. ' Go away. Don't come near me.
You are wicked. Wicked.'
  This put Father back precisely where he'd been ten seconds
before. He did not like being called wicked. The intolerable
indictment straightway turned his sweetness sour. That she
should meet his gentleness like this was injustice enough to
kindle all the firewood in him. ' Oh, Christ and Corpo di
Dio ! ' he exclaimed. ' Oh, Hell and Sacramento ! . . . if
that's the way you're going to behave, we may as well suspend
all rational talk. I can't waste my time like this : I've work
to do. Doric——' the door opened abruptly, and he didn't
seem disturbed to see me standing immediately behind it.
Wrath proscribed all thought. ' Doric, do you go to the kitchen
and say I desire my kind regards to the maids, and would they
send up some dinner.'

Ashamed at being caught, I hurried down the basement stairs, that my presence by the door should not cause him to excogitate upon it. But when I returned from my mission, climbing the stairs somewhat slowly, he was still pacing by the door, hands gripped behind him ; and it was evident that he was still thinking of other things, for he saw me and said, 'Desire the servant girl to bring up the soup. Oh, you've been, have you ; and it's not ready ? Very well. Be you so good as to fetch my hat and coat, and I'll see if I can get a crust of bread at an eating house.'

Realizing that this was not meant to be obeyed, I glanced into the room and saw Mother lying overthrown, Bishop's sleeves and all, in the easy chair, her arms along its arm, her head on her hands, sobbing. The clinking of a tray below whipped her to her feet, and she stood with her fingers on the mantelpiece and her face to the fire.

§

It was a day of dull, speechless misery when he went. A sick despair was like a solid pressure in my breast ; and he, as I could see, watching him all the time, was suffering too. 'To leave you all will just about kill me,' he had said in a grand exaggeration ; but it was proving less of an exaggeration than he had known at the time. He was torn by what he was doing, and full of doubt : his self-love was hard put to it to overcome and leave behind his pleasure in us children ; his desire for the woman who awaited him had to strain on the rope to drag him from a home upon whose comfort and adornment he had spent so much love. He wasn't sure that he hadn't sentenced himself to a lonely exile, and the idea cloaked him with gloom. There were no jests this morning ; in fact, he hardly spoke. He wandered about the house alone, and once or twice came to the outside of the playroom where we children were, and hung about near us, silently. I stole a quick glance at him there and saw that his eyes were awash and the tears glistening on his cheeks.

Oh, God, our human blundering.

Towards lunch time he went up to his bedroom, and I heard him packing his cabin trunk, portmanteaux and gladstone bag, silent all the time ; not singing or whistling as he so often did ; and never coming to the stair-top to call out a comic remark for our amusement. There was no one near him up there, for Uncle Humphrey had gone early from the house, probably in

terror of some unhappy scenes and their drain upon his con-
serves of vigour.

At lunch he came and sat in his usual place at the breakfast
room table—at the foot, with Con on his left, me on his right,
and Mother at the top. Do I remember every item of that
meal ?—aye, and ever shall : the way we all sat down to what
seemed an everyday meal, almost a nursery affair, and was
really a final meal, a sacrament of pain and farewell ; the way
Father and Mother tried to talk naturally but fell often into
silence ; the utter and incongruous ordinariness of the courses—
steak and kidney pie with potatoes and cabbage, junket and
cream with stewed plums ; and the way the talk failed entirely
at last, leaving only a silence.

' Would you like some more ? ' Mother asked him, her spoon
poised over the junket.

' No, thank you. Not any more . . . I thank you.'

Not any more . . . I thank you. The relevance of it !
The first relevant thing that had happened.

' Well, I'll go . . . I'll go and see to the trunks.' And he
went from the room without a word, glad to escape, longing to
get it over quickly. But all the trunks were packed, and he
stood alone in that upstairs room, doing nothing. Mother
went up to ask if she could help, and I, at the playroom door,
heard him say, ' I must go quickly. I cannot stand this.
Where is that fly ? Why doesn't it come ? '

' It's not time yet,' said Mother. ' You didn't order it till
three.'

' Till three. . . . Lord, Lord. . . .'

At about ten to three he brought down his own bags, one
after another, as if ashamed to ask anyone's help. Having
dumped them on the steps outside, he stood by the breakfast
room window alone, watching for the cab and sometimes
drawing out his heavy gold repeater from his vest pocket.

The four wheeler clopped and jingled up to the kerb, and he
carried his lighter bags down to it, for something to do. He
couldn't bear to ask me to help him.

Con and I stood on the step, watching. Fitly enough, the
January sky was a grey-white basin covering the world and
holding a blue-grey mist within its sides and rim. The trees
in the square were all stripped except for a few rusty leaves on
the elm and a single yellow laggard on the sycamore. A rank
of worn laurels and the framework of privet were the only green
things in the deserted garden. Never once did the sunlight
break through to touch with poetry the ancient sadness of the
world.

' Well . . .' sighed Father, hesitating on the step. But none of us had anything to say, standing there in the still afternoon, and looking down upon the cab.

The driver had planned to go by Cromwell Road and Piccadilly to Pall Mall ; and thus the cab with its sleek horse was facing the same way as the old cab with the lean horse which had brought us six years before from Walham Green.

Time faces only one way, and its chariot was at the door.

It was Mother who found the courage to speak. ' Well, good-bye,' she said. There was a dignity about her fattening figure such as I had never seen before ; and I admired and pitied her.

Father's eyes had filled. ' Good-bye. I am sorry it has come to this.'

' It can't be helped. I hope you will be happy.'

' I will do all I can for you. I don't like hurting people, believe me I don't.'

' It can't be helped.'

They had forgotten us children, standing by. Father, old-fashioned in his courtesy, had a wonderful bow which he made to any woman, young or old, mistress or servant ; and now, consciously or unconsciously, he offered such a bow to Mother ; almost as if he were saluting someone of a higher quality than he. Then he bent over Con and kissed her. ' Good-bye Tricks, my dear.'

' Good-bye.'

' Good-bye, old man.' He kissed my forehead and patted my back ; I could not say a word ; I could not say good-bye. ' Come and see me often. I'll take you to theatres . . .' but his voice broke and he turned away.

There was no comfort for me in the invitation. The thought of visiting him once a month was a feather in the scale against the knowledge that he would never come home at eventime again—never turn his key in the lock—never any more.

' Yes,' said Con ; and flung her arms around him.

' Yes,' I managed to say.

A helpless shrug, and he went down the steps to the cab. He waved to the driver to go, and, sitting in the cab, looked out once, smiled, and lifted a hand ; then sank back from sight. The cab, clopping and jingling, carried its broad back round the railings of the garden and out of the square.

BOOK II

THE SCHOOL

CHAPTER I

ANY TIME you travel north from King's Cross, you may
look from the train window at Draycote School, for its level
playing field marches for a few hundred yards with the railway,
and at the far side of the field its red buildings stand with their
backs to the green expanse and their eyes on the Hitchin road
and the woody hills beyond. The main block is a tall red
barrack with a clock tower in the middle, a chapel at one end,
and the Headmaster's house at the other. From the hinder
parts of this block three wings extend at right angles, and the
two asphalt playgrounds which they embrace are given their
fourth side, and turned into quadrangles by a chain of low
one-storey buildings.

Draycote School, a community of two hundred boys, all
boarders, claims to be a public school, and I do not see how
we can dispute the claim, since no one in England has yet
decided what a public school is. It is one of several Church
of England schools founded in the latter half of last century by
good Bishop Horsley ' to provide a public school education,
and a training in the religious principles of the Church of
England, within the means of parents of moderate income.'
So the Statutes say, not thinking it necessary to add that the
schools of the Horsley Foundation were a counter-attack by
the evangelical Party in the Church of England against the
advances of the Oxford Movement, with an eye directed
apprehensively towards the schools of the Woodard Foundation.

To this school I came at the beginning of one summer term
when I was just fifteen. Mother had done nothing about
taking me away from my private school in Kensington while
Father was in India, though I grew older than any boy there ;
Father had been careless in the matter, too. And if it is a
matter for blame that I was finally sent to Draycote, then they
must share this blame between them. Father, obliged to support two homes now, and anxious to hold on to the fine house

in Coburg Square, could not afford to send me to one of the big public schools; he loved me, but he loved his desires and his state in the world a little more. Mother, somewhat afraid of me at fifteen, and wishing to have my critical eyes removed from any visitors she might invite to the house, persuaded Father in an interview that I ought to go to a boarding school, where there would be men and bigger boys to lick me into shape, more especially now that I had no father at home. It was not good for me, she said, to be kept at home among a parcel of women. I should become soft. Men would handle me with more understanding and greater firmness. I think that, without knowing it, she wanted me to suffer at a boarding school.

And Father consented that I should go to this place called Draycote which Mother advocated so warmly. She was enthusiastic about it because the second curate at our church, having been a junior master there for a term or two, had recommended it to Henrietta and to her as 'a good school and cheap, under a headmaster, the Rev. Joseph Harlen, who's simply wonderful with boys'; and Henrietta and Mother accepted the words of a clergyman with a reverence almost as uncritical as that given by Catholic ladies to the counsel of their directors. It didn't occur to them that the curate, a pleasant enough fellow, was just gratifying a fugitive fancy to do a good turn to, and be liked by, his late employer, the Rev. Joseph Harlen.

And so on a late April day I arrived with Mother at this reverend headmaster's house, to find, with a sick self-consciousness, that I was much the oldest and the tallest of the eleven new boys. They were all under fourteen, and I felt like a detached campanile moving among them; for I was as lanky and undeveloped as an overgrown lad of sixteen. I deliberately stooped, as I stood with them in Mr. Harlen's drawing-room, that I might suppress thereby an inch or so of my stature. After we'd been presented to Mr. Harlen we were sent away to take our tea in the long, echoing desert of the dining-hall, while our parents ate and sipped theirs with a genteel grace in the company of one another and the headmaster; and here I bowed over my place at the trestle table and sat low on my bench, because the boys were already finding my height a topic for titters.

The afternoon would have held nothing but hidden unhappiness and fears, like the first afternoon of a prisoner in Wormwood Scrubs, if an astonishing thing had not befallen me in the headmaster's drawing-room, within a minute of my entry among the other new boys and their mothers. I had fallen in love. My eyes had alighted on one of the new boys who was standing by his rotund and fur-covered mother, like a lamb by its unshorn ewe, as she chatted vivaciously with Mr. Harlen ; and from that moment they had hardly left him. They were held by him ; for he possessed the fatal gift of beauty. About thirteen and a half, he had fair hair, large blue eyes, small features, oval face, and a slight childish figure ; and I loved him. This was the first time in my life that I surrendered at the sight of beauty, and exulted in my surrender. And now I was sinking my shoulders and bowing over the table that he at least might not deride me but might even admire me. And when we'd had our tea and were loitering in the desolate hall, wondering what to do next, I hung near him for a time and then faltered up to speak to him—so flits the bee to the bloom. As I came near he watched me with bewildered eyes ; and to allay his doubts I put out a shy and awkward smile. That smile was the white flag I carried towards him, to sue for friendship.

' Hallo,' I greeted him. ' I say : what's your name ? '

' Gotley,' he answered, his eyes turned up to mine but still unwon.

' Yes, but *what* Gotley—Herbert Gotley, Joshua Gotley, Jehoshophat Gotley ? ' I demanded, trying to be funny in that forlorn and comfortless atmosphere.

' Felix Gotley.'

' Well, that's a nice name. And where do you come from ? '

' Devonport.'

' A perfectly good place.' Oh, I was very humorous and condescending, as became a boy eighteen months older than he. ' All ships and sailors, isn't it ? And do you live anywhere near the docks ? '

' Oh yes. My father keeps an hotel there, almost beside the dockyard gates : Gotley's Private Hotel.'

I was deeply shocked. It was the first shock that my love had to take. My love had rushed out blindly to one whose father was an hotel-keeper. Why, manifestly he wasn't even ashamed of the hotel, but proud of it, since he had mentioned it thus early. I smiled in a kindly way that he might suppose me, not shaken, but pleased ; but really I was wondering at what manner of school I had arrived. Evidently it was not limited to ' the sons of gentlemen.' But he was beautiful, and my longing to love him proved stronger than my dismay. I swallowed the hotel quickly, and once it was safely swallowed, tried to forget all about it. Too considerate to put him at a disadvantage by saying ' My father's a general,' I merely told him my name and, to keep the conversation going, for it stood quite still at this point, added shyly, ashamed of my demonstrativeness, 'I wonder which house we shall be put into. I say : it would be rather jolly if we got into the same house.'

'Yes, I suppose it would be,' he said ; and I was hurt that he should be only polite about it, and not enthusiastic.

'Yes . . . it would.'

I couldn't think of another word to say ; nor could Gotley ; and we stood silently facing each other till I ended the mutual embarrassment by giving him a debilitated grin and drifting away.

I went with an ache at my heart ; but it was the ache of a bruised, not a dying, love. To ease it I told myself that he was much younger than I and probably even more uneasy : like me he was using all his energy to hide his fears and had little left for talk.

For an hour or so we were left to amuse ourselves, or to suffer, in that bare hall and then Mr. Harlen himself appeared at a door and bade us come and say good-bye to our parents. In his drawing-room Mother gave me a formal kiss, and the plump Mrs. Gotley enveloped her lamb in her fur-clad arms and kissed him with a twisting mouth ; but the tears in her eyes put none into his.

As it chanced he and I were placed in the same house, and I chose to see in this a sign that Fate desired our friendship. There being no 'prep' that night, all of us younger boys went early to bed ; and as Gotley and I were escorted up the stairs to our house dormitory, I whispered, 'I vote we try to get beds side by side ; shall we ? ' and he said, 'Yes, if you like ' ; and again I was disappointed. I learned on those stairs the ancient truth that almost every love affair is conducted by *un qui baise et un qui tourne la joue.*

The two hundred boys, you must understand, were all congregated under one roof, and fed in one hall, but they were divided into four 'Houses' (were we not a public school ?) according to the dormitories in which they slept : there was North House, Central House and South House, each in its wing, and School House in the main block. Thus herded into separate pens, the boys learned, as I soon knew, to exalt their own house and sneer and jeer at the others. These others might join them as allies on a Saturday afternoon when the School played another school, but, as soon as this war was over, the Houses fell apart again and despised and quarrelled with and spat at their former allies, like other sub-divisions of mankind.

Our house, Gotley's and mine, was the School House, and that night, in a dormitory on the top floor, we, with two other new boys, were initiated into its membership by the ceremony of Crowning. To assist at this mystery, since it was as fascinating as a public execution, even some of the senior members came strolling into the dormitory. The dormitory had a row of fifteen black iron beds under each of its two longer walls, and a third row, head to head and foot to foot, down the middle of the bare, boarded floor. There were no curtains to the tall, narrow windows; the walls were whitewashed; and the only colour in the room, apart from any that sun or moon or gas lamp might throw, was the bright red of the blankets on the beds. Under the gas lamps to-night we new boys were pushed and crowded by a cheering mob towards the midmost bed of all, and there a loud-voiced boy, aided by others, expounded the rite and mystery of Crowning. We must each mount the bed and sing a song, after which, if the songs were approved, the company would consent to crown us with a chamber pot. One of the boys fetched this crown from under the bed and brandished it before us, even lifting it high in our honour pretending to drink a toast from it.

To sing them a song! I have never been so harried by nervousness as in the few minutes before my turn came to sing. I cannot remember at all what the two boys who preceded me sang, because all the time my brain was ransacking the past for some song that I could sing without being laughed at. And the minutes ran by, and no song could I recall that seemed the least suitable. I thought of 'My pretty Jane, my dearest Jane, oh never look so shy,' which Brian Greaves, Gentle's father, used to sing, but I couldn't believe that this would meet the occasion. I remembered 'If with all your hearts you truly seek me' from the *Elijah*, but dismissed this, too, as inappropriate. Oh in what song was I word-perfect and time-perfect? Again I heard Brian singing in fine voice, by his ebony piano, 'From the desert I come to thee on my arab shod with fire . . . I love thee, I love thee, with a love that shall not die'; but regretfully I rejected this. Only at the last, two seconds before I mounted the bed, did I remember a song from *The Geisha* which Gentle had been singing and whistling for the last year; and with its words in my mouth (and my heart there, too) I got my overlong figure on to the springy and insecure platform and delivered them in my still unbroken treble to the gaping boys: 'A goldfish swam in a big glass bowl As dear little goldfish do . . .'

It was a success, my song; a success in the sense that the laughter and the swaying bodies beat about my figure on its eminence like the wind and the waves about a lighthouse.

I heard one boy comment, ' Law-lummy, It's like Nelson's Monument singing a song ' ; and I saw Gotley laughing with the rest. When I stepped down, the ironic applause, accompanied by stamping, jostling, yelling and cat-howling was more violent and prolonged than any we'd had so far.

' Now young Gotley.'

' Now young Gotley. Last item, and let it be a good 'un.'

' Shove him up.'

' Push him up : what's his bottom for ? '

But Gotley, for all his girlish face, jumped unaided on to that bed with no apparent trace of shyness or shame. He was well prepared with a song—one which, maybe, he'd heard in the taproom of his father's hotel—and he sang it with an enviable ease and aplomb.

> I have learned a comical ditty
> From some of my friends in the city.
>   Though the verses are short
>   I think that you ought
> To admit that the chorus is pretty.
>
> It's Folderolol, folderolol, folderolol-dero-lady . . .
>
> There was an old Man in a boat. . . .

Each verse was a familiar limerick with this easy chorus trailing after it and soon all the boys were uproariously joining in. If they didn't know the limerick, they were well acquainted with the chorus by now, and yelled it to Heaven. They liked the song so well that when he had given them four verses, they clamoured for more ; and Gotley, his girl's face flushed and pleased, answered, ' I'm sorry, but I don't know any more unless they're smutty.'

It shocked me like a blow on the breast. Not that I was unaccustomed to smut, because there'd been plenty of it flying about at my Kensington school, but that the mention of it came so ill from the character I'd dreamed of as Gotley's.

' Come on then ! Give us the smut.'

' Spit it out, kid.'

' Let it rip, me lad.'

The prospect was welcomed with cheers, and Gotley, now beyond question the success of the evening, sang for them in his pure, passionless, choir-boy voice a series of exceedingly dirty rhymes, the boys hurling themselves about with delight, or standing and sniggering, as each last line closed in a new ribaldry. They made him go on and on with the limericks till at last, his eyes wide as a child's, he insisted, ' I don't know any more,   Honest, I don't.'

' Oh yes, yes ! ' they clamoured.   ' Come on ! '

But no ;   he only shook his pretty head.

A pity, a disappointment—till one big boy jumped on to the bed and sang to the same tune a dirtier limerick than any yet, and, one by one, others followed him with similar contributions ; while the audience showed their appreciation of these efforts by greeting each new obscenity with boisterous laughter and the full-throated chorus, ' Folderolol, folderolol, folderolol— dero—lady.'

Then the crowning began.   Each new boy was compelled to kneel by the bed ;   the pot was placed upside down over his brows, where it looked rather like the Imperial Crown of Austria ;   and all the boys laid their hands upon it, just as the bishops at the altar steps lay their hands on a priest when they are making him a bishop like themselves.   It was a painful business, as I learned when my turn came, because some of the consecrating brethren, the wags, turned their two fists into drumsticks and beat a heavy tattoo on the pot.

When it was all over, I took into the dark beneath the bed-clothes the memory of my ridiculous and derided song, and lay with it a long time, unable to sleep.

§

It was Felix Gotley who first inflicted upon me that be-wildering check, that sad balking, which a woman will some-times inflict upon her lover when he perceives that the physical beauty of his idol is not matched by any mental beauty, and that the softness and delicacy of her features are one of nature's lies, concealing a hardness and coarseness within. All the same I persisted in my love.   In my longing to love someone I blinded myself to his coarse fibre as I did to the failings of my father.

He did not know that I was his lover, but he was content with me as a friend.   For a couple of terms we made the usual schoolboy partnership of two.   We sat in different classrooms, he in a lower form than I ;   but in playtime we met and walked together.   We strolled the green plain of the cricket field, his arm in mine, or my arm along his shoulder, and his about my waist.   This physical touch meant nothing to him ;   it merely implied that we were ' chums ' ;   but it was joy to me.   Getting as far from the school buildings and our schoolmates as we could, we would sit on the wooden fence by the railway and watch the trains go by. Or we would break bounds and, escaping into the farmlands, sit in some hollow tree, smoke cigarettes or sticks of cinnamon or the touchwood of the tree. Or we would lie on the grass, under the sun, and exchange our fantasies for the future or our philosophies of life. Often I bragged to him now about my father, General Allan Mourne, exaggerating his travels, his military adventures, his power in the City to-day, and, most often, his height and size. Somehow my father's height was a source of strength and sustenance to me when the days of dejection and loneliness compassed me round. Gotley was not in the least humiliated by my father's distinctions but bragged in his turn (though without affection) of his own father's prosperous state, his high position in Devonport, his quick sharpness in business, and his sheer physical strength—all of which seemed to him equivalent distinctions with my father's. The other boys, seeing us always together, made fun of our partnership, calling it The Firm of Allan Mourne and Gotley ; and their mockery was music in my ears.

He could be a jolly companion, and we got up to plenty of mischief together ; but he could betray a sullen vindictiveness at times. He would aim this vindictiveness at me if I had offended him, but most often it was revealed in this chatter about his father. His father, I quickly deduced, was a hard-drinking, hot-necked, punishing man, and Gotley's relation to him was much like mine to my mother, the only difference being that while I, thanks to the books I had read, was learning to contemn and pity my mother's cheap vindictiveness, Gotley believed firmly in reproducing his father's. He was not within a hundred miles of perceiving that the vindictive blow, so far from being a strong man's act, is a weak and puerile thing. He was unvisited by any glimmer of the beauty in altruism or of the unutilitarian purpose in art. He let loose a gale of high-pitched laughter when I in an expansive moment disclosed that ' though of course I no longer believed any religious stuff, one part of me was quite keen on founding a sort of monastic order, to be called ' The Brothers of Kindness and Good Counsel ' ; and he showed not the dimmest response when I tried to convert him to the worship of poems which Father used to quote or which I had discovered for myself. His values were the money-making values of his father. ' I don't mind what I turn my hand to when I grow up,' he would say, ' so long as it makes me a fortune quickly.' His manhood woke much earlier in him than in me, and then his mind and his talk ran on sex—but I don't assert this to his discredit ; because all the other boys in our dormitory were the same, and a little later I stood in the same place myself and differed from them only in being less open, more ashamed and secretive, about this strange new tide in my thoughts.

For me this was a Greek friendship, though I had never heard of such a thing. I was in love with him, and the love had a passionate quality. When he walked with another boy and made it clear he didn't want me, I suffered the true anguish of jealousy. Away from him, in classroom or at home for the holidays, I created dream-pictures of sharing a house with him always, or of taking him into my home when he was destitute, or of crossing the world to his assistance when he lay dying. It shames me to write that one evening in chapel, dreaming of him, I caught the words of the choir, ' The Lord comfort him when he lieth sick upon his bed : make thou all his bed in his sickness ' ; and as the voices sang on, and the organ outrolled its music, I let the chapel fade away and watched myself comforting Gotley upon his sick bed and remaining at his side till the crisis of his fever was passed. In similar dreams I have run to the police court and paid his bail, I have stormed with a regiment of bravoes the prison in which he was held, and like Sidney Carton, one of my heroes, I have changed places with him in his condemned cell and gone to the scaffold in his stead.

Two terms and two weeks this one-way Greek communion lasted, and all the time I tried to believe him worthy of my love ; but in the end his dull response to my affection, his insensibility to what I conceived to be rare thoughts and fine enthusiasms, defeated the love so that it turned from the field and went home. One repulse too many will destroy the morale of an army, and the day came when, discomfited by a new obtuseness, I suddenly abandoned all effort to conquer such a difficult terrain and all desire to possess it. In that moment I stepped out of my love as a man steps out of sodden and clinging garments ; and extraordinary was the relief when I stood naked in the cold, clean air again and felt strong, hale, new-braced and free. I rejoiced in the strength which had snapped the bands about me. It was an exultation to see Gotley as he was, instead of as I had painted him in my soft-hazed and Greuze-like portrait. It was an exultation to see him as worse than he was. Gotley ? Pfaw !

How could I have been such a mug ? God send that no one ever knew some of the thoughts I had indulged in these last few months at Draycote. Gotley ! A crude intelligence, a dull vision, a poor creature in every way. The love of such as I would be given to someone finer than he. It was wonderful. I had not known that you could cure yourself of a love in a moment, by one strong effort of the will. And indeed I have not been able to do it since.

CHAPTER II

ONCE WHEN Gotley and I broke bounds and escaped into the village of Wincombe we were caught and given a caning by Mr. Harlen.

The Rev. Joseph Harlen was a small stubby man with black stubbly eyebrows and a black stubbly moustache. Only on Sundays did he wear the black suit and round collar of a clergyman ; on all other days he wore a slack, grey-serge suit and a turned-down collar : it is possible that the bristly uncompromising moustache, the slack, unpriestly suit, and the collar turned down deliberately like an Emperor's thumb, were designed to stress his evangelical character and defy the Oxford Movement, with an especial reference to the schools of the Woodard Foundation. He was a bachelor, and Henrietta had expressed the view of other sentimental persons when she affirmed that ' all his love was given to his school, and he was married to that.' It was true that he loved boys : he loved them as a species, and the good-looking ones as individuals ; and it was this deep interest which had brought him to his present position. He stood now where his nature had carried him. He was as happy as a man can be in his occupation and work. The school with its Dining and Lecture Halls, its Laboratory and classrooms and playing field, its two hundred boys and ten masters, was his big plaything. He enjoyed being in a position of absolute authority. He enjoyed sitting in the centre of the high table in the Dining Hall. He enjoyed taking the chapel services and preaching sermons in which he touched delicately on the problems of adolescence. He enjoyed listening to a boy's difficulties in the privacy of his study. He enjoyed appealing to a boy's better nature after he had thrashed him—in truth I do not know which part of this double bill he enjoyed the more.

I think I enclose his character between its two extremes, the best and the worst, when I say that he sincerely loved boys as an idea, and that he enjoyed caning them when he could feel morally justified in doing so. In two booklets which he published with the Society for Christian Education, *The Boy of Public School Age* and *The Schoolboy's Religion*, there are some sentences which reveal more (or less) than he intended. Here is one : 'What an adolescent boy needs above all is love : chide him, rebuke him, punish him, if need be, flog him, but love him.' And here another : 'Some of my happiest and most sacred relations with a boy have been after I have had occasion to flog him.' It is unlikely, I think, that a man who could pen such sentences had any power to stand outside himself and examine the forces which were driving him. Satisfied that it was his moral duty to cane a boy he would have denied, as certainly as my mother would have done, that the business contained any element of pleasure—denied it with the vehemence of one who isn't sure that he's speaking the truth.

We nicknamed him 'Joey,' and it is not to be denied that we liked and admired him. Hearing on all sides that he was 'wonderful with boys,' and being uncritical sheep, we came to believe that this was the truth and that we had a great affection for him. That he caned often and well we deemed natural in a headmaster and therefore neutral in the account—neither to his debit or to his credit. It was powerless against the universal suggestion that he was wonderful with boys.

A caning by Mr. Harlen was a ritual as solemn as a sacrament. I know : I've partaken of the sacrament. It was performed in an anteroom that intervened between the corridor of the school and his study in his private house. The ceremony decided upon in the study—regretfully (or so he told himself)—he drew on his gown as a Master of Arts. Then he and the boy walked from the study to this anteroom as might a conducted prisoner from the place of trial to the place of execution. In the anteroom the headmaster drew a cane from a cupboard and touched a bell to summon the school porter. Till the porter appeared the executioner and victim waited in silence, the former holding the well-gripped cane at his side. The porter, 'Ginger' Tufnell, a stout old soldier with a bald round head and a fierce apricot moustache, arrived through the school door. Not a word said Mr. Harlen to him ; no word was necessary ; the master, the boy, the cane, and the silence showed the porter what was required of him. Silence was the noblest music for such a solemnity.

'Bend over,' the porter commanded in a low voice.

The boy obeyed. The porter turned back the boy's jacket and then held him in this bent-over posture by placing an arm under his stomach and a flat palm on his back. Having clamped him thus, he remained impassive—as indifferent to the experiences of his prisoner as a pillory or the twin stanchions of a guillotine.   The headmaster measured the correct distance by laying his cane against the target area, and then slashed at it six times in succession.   After the sixth stroke he turned away ; and the porter unclasped his prisoner and smoothed his own sleeves.   It was over ; and to the end they had invested a dignified celebration with silence.

The porter, as uncritical as any of us boys, saw nothing indecent in the ceremony ; it was normal and therefore right. Nor did Mr. Harlen, though his intelligence was university-trained, find anything in it to disturb him ; not even a degradation of his servant's manhood.

§

When I put out the light that rested on Gotley, there was little but darkness for me in Draycote School.   The valley I trod now was gloomy indeed.   Of course now and again I crossed a sunny patch, because a boy of fifteen, however moody, will have times when he is gay.   But for the larger part of my four terms at Draycote I walked by the waters of Marah, and my dearest friend was Melancholy.

What caused the melancholy ?   Well, in the first place my thoughts of home were grey thoughts.   Father was gone, and despite his promise we did not often meet ; all through the holidays the conflict between Mother and myself, now that Father was no longer there to damp it down, smouldered and crackled, or burst into a blaze.   I could see well enough that she wished me back at school and resented all that she had to do for me.   Con and Gentle were being very silly just now, and I no longer cared for their company.   They were enjoying, greatly enjoying, a religious craze, under the able direction of Con who had converted Gentle to the beauty of a certain curate and of his High Church faith ; and I, a professed atheist, and very proud of it, must argue and argue with them, demonstrating that in the face of Science it had become impossible for an intelligent man to accept the Christian dogmas.   Con rebutted my arguments by asserting that I was only trying to be clever (which was true enough, but seemed inadequate as a rebuttal) and Gentle said, ' Oh, Crikey, I can't think what's come over Doric these days.   He used to be quite a decent child, and now he stinks.'

' It's you that stinks,' I retorted ; which for an avowed

rationalist was weak, so I improved it by the proposition that neither of them wanted to listen to my arguments because they were afraid of the truth. ' You won't think because you don't want to. God, am I the only person in Earls Court, Brompton, the Royal Borough of Kensington, and West London generally, who uses his brains ? '

In addition to this gaudy flower of religion they had put forth a bright and full-blown interest in several other young men besides the curate ; and they would walk about the streets where these jewels might be glimpsed, and giggle together if they passed one of them. Fiercely logical as ever, I would submit, ' Permit me to suggest, if I may make so bold, that this vanity and this worldliness sit ill with your protestations of religion ; ' and Gentle would turn on me and snap, ' Oh, you shut up. Gosh, Con, isn't he dire ? I used to like him once—not frightfully but quite a little—and now I just dislike him rather terribly.' To which I would retort, ' No acidity now ! I speak only for your good. And I would have you know it's unwise to talk to me like that because I have a haughty stomach. Go seek your swains, if that's your idea of happiness. Gather ye rosebuds while ye may.'

Gentle's pursuit of the young men seemed more absurd than Con's, for while Con, nearly seventeen, was a tight and complete little woman, like a small cob mare, Gentle was still a loose-limbed, wild-pated foal of a girl with heated cheeks, red hands, and silly, swinging, yellow pigtails, and it passed my comprehension that she imagined anyone could love her.

But though I might banter and burlesque them I was really very miserable—I who had been their leader and was now an outcast. It was as if Father's back was turned to me ; Con's and Gentle's too ; and Mother's eyes only turned my way to wish me out of the house ; and these four persons were all I had. The despondency was so real that I have sometimes climbed to my room at the top of the house and there, hidden from the world, flung myself upon my bed in a luxury of un-explained weeping, while the words murmured themselves, ' Father, come back.'

§

Such was my home in the background. At school there were more weights to be hung on my melancholy. The boys made fun of my gangling figure, calling me ' a walking clothes line with boots on the end,' and shouting after me the ever tedious jest, ' Is it cold up there ? ' Because of my lonely slouching, and my silent moodiness they had invented for me the nick-name, ' Weary.' One gorilla of a boy was a persistent menace and spring of fear. Square-set, thick-limbed, and strong as the gorilla I have named him, he would walk after me in quadrangle and cloister, with his following of smaller chimpanzees, baiting me and shouting the news, ' Old Weary's a funk,' because I was so obviously walking away in a white-faced fear of him. Though many inches taller than he, I couldn't have survived ten seconds of a fight with him ; and, ashamed of this and of my palpable fear, I would escape, when he was about, into the empty changing room, the deserted gymnasium, or the reeking but peaceful lavatories.

By the time my second summer came, and my sixteenth birth-day was passed, I had persuaded myself into a dark hate of the school. Proud of my perceptions, which I held to be as superior to those of the other boys as they were to those of Con and Gentle, I told myself, imagining that I'd discovered something new, that, because it was an institution, it was without a heart and insensible, sacrificing its inmates to the need, not of making a profit, but of avoiding a loss. Everything that I looked on attested this : the bare, inky classrooms, the bleak dining hall with its trestle tables, the dormitories with their bare floors and black iron beds, and the worn green field with its lurching fence along the railroad—there was no softness, sweetness, or beauty anywhere, and I was weary of it—weary of it. How well on the mark they were when they dubbed me ' Weary.'

And I was always hungry. There was hardly a day during my four terms at Draycote when a hollowness within didn't nag and worry me. This clamour for food crept around all my thoughts and built my dreams at night. Let me not suggest that Mr. Harlen consciously underfed us ; but he was a short, tough, well-fleshed little man, and he'd forgotten in his middle years what it was like to be a boy and growing. No villain, but a clergyman who wanted to believe that he was good, he must have satisfied himself that our victuals were enough. For some time past he had been his own bursar, having persuaded the governors, after the failure of the previous bursar to balance the school's account, that he could find opening for economies and yet make the school pay. Doubtless this was proving a difficult task, with only two hundred boys, none of whom paid highly, and some of whom he had accepted on reduced terms, partly out of a real desire to help them, but mainly because he wanted to keep up his numbers.

For breakfast we had tea, porridge, bread and butter, and jam. Some boys had an ' egg order.' That is to say, their parents having paid for this ' extra ,' they were given in the course of the meal an egg and a spoon   Servants carried round the eggs and spoons in baskets and dumped them on the plates of these privileged boys, while the rest of us watched the distribution enviously.   For dinner we had two slices of cheap meat with potatoes and greens, and a disc of jam roll or a wedge of suet pudding.   ' Good, plain, wholesome food,' said Mr. Harlen to the parents ; and so perhaps it was ; but there wasn't enough of it.   For tea we had stewed tea, and bread and butter and jam again ; and that was all except for those who had a ' meat order.'   To these marked cattle the servants brought a cold sausage or a couple of slices of salami.   There was no supper, but such boys as had a ' milk order ' went to the dining hall at seven and received from the steward a tumbler of milk.

I had none of these orders, and in this I was only one of the majority.   My mother, to whom Father had given a round sum to cover all my school expenses, was as anxious as Mr. Harlen to show a small profit on the year's working, for she had none too much money these days.

I didn't starve, but my body was so restive in its demand for food that it drove me, like a two-legged herbivore, into the pastures and cornfields in search of something to pull up and eat.   I chewed grass, I ate the young ears of wheat, and on one occasion pulled up a portly mangold and drove my teeth into it, but it so offended my mouth with its violent, sharp sweetness that I spat it out and returned to the wheat.

But chiefly I remember those summer fields of long ago for the solace their beauty gave to my mind ; not for any meagre comfort their raw fruits lent to my body.   It was very lovely in the country, that summer of my seventeenth year.   Breaking bounds alone, I would walk through oatfields of fawn and ivory, watching the breeze bow them with a silken ruffle ; and on through barley fields, happy for a while because their acres of ash-green feathers were brightening and darkening as they sighed in the wind.   I came to cottage gardens and sipped a little healing from their roses and marigolds, their canterbury bells, tall hollyhocks, and sweet peas.   Sometimes I climbed a hill, purple with thyme, and—I don't know how it was, but my deep despondency would be joined by a nameless and blissful glow, like a light from the greatness that would one day be mine.   I walked with despair, and yet was capable of all things. What had been a creative gaiety when I played with Con and Gentle became now, for want of a friendly audience, these exquisite dreams of greatness.   The greatness that was coming to me had no name as yet, but always it contained one thing :

a triumph over Mother and Henrietta, Con and Gentle, and all
the boys of Draycote School.   On the hill I loved best there was
a crown of beeches, and I would lie on my back beneath them,
one knee drawn up, the other slung over it, and my arms spread
wide.   And I would listen to the thrush singing, ' Cherrydew,
Cherrydew,' and the great tit chirruping, ' Teacher ! Meet
yer ! ' and the chaffinch shouting (what other word for his gay,
repeated assertion ?) ' I'll bring your pretty love to meet you
here.'   Through the tracery of the beeches I watched the downy
clouds heaping together in a pale turquoise sky ; and they and
the whole sky were friends to my greatness.   My powers were as
wide as the sky.

§

High indeed among the clouds were these dreams ; for down
on the real earth, even as I lay there, wearing my greatness,
the calamity was waiting that would bring these schooldays,
and all my schooldays, to an abrupt and shocking close.

How far the hunger in my stomach helped the dreams I
cannot say, but I think it was the prime agitator which raised
up all my spiritual hungers and hates to mutiny and created the
catastrophe.

CHAPTER III

A JULY evening after tea, when the summer term had no more
than three weeks to run, I was dawdling alone and moodily by
the school's kitchen garden.   Beyond the high gable-end of the
dining hall there extended a long low annexe which housed the
kitchens, stores, steward's office, and some attic rooms above ;
and behind this building, and beyond it as far as the railway,
stretched the kitchen garden, railed off from the playing field,
and sternly forbidden to the boys.   To be caught in the kitchen
garden, plucking currants or uprooting carrots, was to be certain
of the porter's sombre embrace and the kiss of Mr. Harlen's
cane.   But one may at least look at the earth's fat fruits when
one is hungry, and I strolled on by the railing, considering
which vegetables would be good to pull up and chew, supposing
no one was behind the windows of that long kitchen annexe.
My eye passed from the rows of coarse, crowding beans to the
lines of crisp lettuces and thence to a green fleece of feathery

carrot tops ; and my mouth watered ; and my hunger became as a clawing hand, dragging at stomach and breast.

It was a warm evening, and windows were open all over the face of the school.   The kitchens were quiet.   Was there anyone there, now that the servants' day was done ; anyone at all ? I walked past the open windows of the annexe to see.   The first I came to was that of the steward's office.   Its lower sash was pushed right up, and I had a naked view of the room.   It was a narrow, colour-washed room with an office desk against the wall, between window and door.   On the sloping lid of this desk a ledger and a box file lay open.   On the level ledge above the lid stood a stack of invoices and a black and gilt cash-box. On the wall immediately above the desk, like the retable above an altar, there ran a narrow shelf ; and on this shelf, smart and erect as a platoon of paraded soldiers, stood two lines of piled coins.   And as soldiers are paraded according to their heights, shortest on the right, tallest on the left, so these coins were arranged according to their value, coppers on the right, silver in the middle, and gold sovereigns on the left.   The failing sun poured down upon these neat, erect little piles so that the metal of their round bellies and flat heads glistened in the light— clearly the Devil, perched high in the wings of the world, was turning this spotlight upon them ; would he not convert the finest thing in the universe, God's good sun, into a means of evil ?

I had never seen money displaying itself like this before ; and instantly a craving for one or two of those silver coins leapt up from my stomach.   Just as my mouth had watered at the sight of lettuce so my fingers craved the feel of one or two of those round, milled coins.   Not the gold ; the recoil from taking gold was too violent.   Say two of the half-crowns, for that would make the good round sum of five shillings.   Not more.   I looked at a pile of half-crowns.   There was magic in their milled edges : to handle them would be a balm for many pains.   For the moment everything I wanted seemed to have concentrated itself in these silver coins : comfort, security, importance, power. The quantity of money on the shelf made the taking of two half-crowns seem a small thing ; the gold made the silver of little account.   The little piles were beyond the reach of any hand from outside, but my eye turned to the door of the room. Like an evening light against a thundery sky my perceptions seemed to be throwing everything into sharp relief, and I saw, not only that the door was closed, but that its key was on this side and that therefore it couldn't be locked.   In imagination, too, since this was his room, I saw the steward : a little narrow man in a blue suit with a drooping moustache and a club foot ; and in the next instant I recorded the fact that nowhere in the building was there the sound of a club foot stumping.

All these thoughts had swept through my mind in the time it took me to pass across the window. And as I strolled on, the picture of the room stayed on my memory like a sharply defined photograph snapped by a flashlight camera. And my mind became the scene of a debate between two persons : a familiar person and a stranger ; my normal self, Theodore Allan Mourne, and a rebel without a name.

'Gosh,' said the first, 'couldn't I do with two of those half-crowns ! I'd have one huge feed at the tuck shop and spread the rest over the remaining three weeks of the term.'

'Well, why not take a couple ? ' asked the stranger. 'Yesterday you took those apples from that orchard. What difference is there between taking apples from an orchard and money from a room ? '

'I don't know, but there *is* a difference. One's just fun and the other's a crime.'

'But why ? That doesn't make sense. That won't bear thinking on for a second. That's just thinking like one of the sheep. You pride yourself on your intelligence, but there's nothing very intelligent in that. Think for yourself : precisely now, what is the difference between taking a fruit shaped like a sphere and a piece of metal shaped like a disc ? '

'Well . . . I don't know . . . you may be right . . . but I know this, that I'd be ashamed to death if anyone saw me taking money or heard that I'd done so.'

'All right then : you're just a coward who daren't defy the world. Now we know. You'll never be able to stand alone in a splendid indifference to the opinions of the world.'

'I don't admit that I'm a coward. I'm just not certain yet that you're right. I don't believe it's right to steal apples ; I only think it's fun ; and if it's a bit wrong to take twopence-worth of apples it'd be a lot more wrong to take five shillings in money.'

'How would you do it ? '

'I'd go into the Dining Hall and pretend I'd dropped something there at tea-time. If no one was about I'd slip into the corridor that passes the steward's room, and if anyone found me, I'd pretend I was just larking around. If there was no one there, and not a sound, I'd dash into the room, snatch a couple of coins, and dash out again.'

'There is no one there. You noticed that there was not a sound anywhere. Listen. There's not a sound now. They've all gone because Tea's over.   Can you hear the Steward's club foot ?   No.   It'd be as safe as houses to stroll along that corridor.'

' Oh yes, it'd be easy enough, but there it is : I don't like the thought of stealing money.'

' But is it stealing ?   Wait.   Listen.   I don't reckon it *is* stealing.   Old Joey Harlen owes it to you.   He's paid to give you enough to eat, and if he doesn't, you're entitled to have some of the money back.   Good heavens, five bob's a drop in the ocean compared with what he owes you after half starving you for a year.   It'd be an act of spirit to get some of it back. Why should you go about racked with hunger ?   Yes, why ? You weren't afraid to rebel against your mother.'

The scales, so far tilted against action, had suddenly balanced. A hair's weight, and they would tip down on the other side. Did I cast about for the hair's weight ?   I think so.   In my loneliness of late I had read under the trees, or tried to read, Ruskin, Arnold, Mill and Morris, and despised the other boys for not doing the same.   I had also read the biographies of some of these, for they were among my heroes.   But not these Lives only ;   my course of reading included the biography of one Dick Delaney, the Gentleman Burglar ;   and this enthralling work had alienated some of my admiration from the detectives —what were they but the blind, slavish tools of an unjust society ? —and given it to the free, bold laughing outlaws.   I will not say that this was the hair's weight.   I only know that as I saw the door of the Dining Hall and softly tried its handle I saw also the Gentleman Burglar and caught some such whisper as ' Open ? Then why not do a burglary for the fun of it ? '   In addition to my craving for food and my sour rebellion against life there was an element of adventure and emulation in the pile that tipped the scale.

The Quad was empty—empty as a prison yard after the convicts had gone to their cells.   The boys were in the Reading Room, or around the Fives Courts where two House matches were in progress, or in the playing fields enjoying the last bene- diction of the sun.   I opened the door and slipped in.   The long Dining Hall was as empty as a church on a bright week-day evening :   only the dust-motes thronged the sunbeams that slanted from the lofty windows.   The long trestle tables still wore the coarse, stained cloths which we had left an hour before, but now they were laid with the mugs, plates, and spoons for breakfast.   By the hanging skirts of these cloths the long, back- less benches stood like dogs come obediently to heel.   Those breakfast mugs, those empty benches, and the cloistered silence suggested that a day's work was done and that all the servants of this refectory had gone home. There in the corner was the door that led to the kitchens and the steward's room. It stood ajar.

I walked as quietly, but at the same time with as innocent an air as I could assume, towards it. Glancing through, I saw the white corridor on to which kitchens and steward's room opened. That third door must be the steward's room. Go on, go on ; if you're seen you can say that you were 'just exploring' and take the consequences. I sauntered along it, my step as slow and soft as my heart was fast and loud. In my heart I still believed that theft was sin, and yet I was ready to commit it, just as, all too often, I was ready to yield to other cravings of my body when their power had risen in an overwhelming tide. The steward's door. Silence. I touched the handle. If anyone saw me I would laugh and, using a phrase of Gentle's, declare that I was 'on a voyage of discovery.' The door opened before me. Four steps, and the half-crowns would be mine. I took those steps. With the half-crowns in my hand—but gripped there guiltily, nervously, for my heart was in tumultuous protest—I slipped out through the door and shut it behind me. The snap of its shutting was louder than I liked.

Rapidly I walked back towards the Dining Hall, but before I reached it a very tall young man in shirt sleeves came through its door, humming rapidly to himself and carrying a pink evening paper. It was Rob Andrews, one of the two young men who, with two girls, waited on us at meals. Astonished to see a pupil in these parts, he hesitated—then stopped and blocked my way.

'What you doin' in 'ere ? ' he shot at me. ' You know you boys are not allowed in 'ere ! What'you been up to, eh ? '

'Nothing,' I stuttered. ' I . . .'

But there was terror in my eyes, and he saw it. He stared at it. ' What is it ? What is it now ? '

' I was only just exploring.'

' Explorin' ? Come off it. What you putting' in yer pocket ? What did you put in yer pocket then, eh ? You been pinchin' somethin', 'ave yer ? '

'No . . . I haven't . . . I was just on a voyage of discovery. I——'

' A *what* ? Nark it, son. Anyone can see yer lyin'. Why, you've gawn white. And you've got somethin' in yer 'and. Show me yer 'and.'

I drew my hand from my pocket and spread it before him, empty.

' Yes, that's easy. Whatever you got you left in yer pocket.'

' What's the matter, Rob ? ' The other young waiter, by name Sladden, but known to us as Jumbo because of his huge belly and rump and his fat, plum-blue cheeks and chins, had now come in after Andrews. ' What the hell's the row ? '

' There's a lad in 'ere and I fancy he's been nobblin' somethin'—don't know what.   I sor 'im put it in his pocket—sor 'im distinctly.'

' Well, make him show you what's in his pocket.'

' Show us what's in yer pocket,' commanded Rob.

I stood unmoving, save that all my limbs trembled.

' What's in it ? '

' There's nothing in it.'

' Well, pull it out and let's see.'

' There's only things in it that belong to me.'

' All right, let's see 'em.   Come on.'

' I'm not going to.'

' Oh, aren't you ? '   Like all youthful, or undeveloped people like my mother, Rob Andrews was set alight by defiance.   He seized my hand, heaved it up above my head, and commanded Sladden, ' Empty his pocket, Slad. *That* one.   No, it's no good struggling, mate.   I'm stronger than you.   You may be a long 'un, but I 'appen to be six-foot-two. . . . Hold still.'

Sladden thrust his fat hand into my trouser pocket and pulled out a dirty handkerchief and my locker key.   As the handkerchief came out the two half-crowns clinked to the floor, bowled drunkenly along the boards and lay down to rest.

' Yo-*ho* ! . . . *H'mmm !* '   Rod nodded his head very significantly.   ' Money ! '   He was on a more exciting trail than he'd imagined.   ' Two 'alf-dollars !   Any more of 'em, Slad ?   No. Well, where did you get 'em, eh ?   Was it them you put in your pocket ? '

' No. . . .'

' But they must'a been, me lad.   They was on top of your handkerchief.   Could he've got 'em in 'ere, Slad ? '

' Only from Mr. Weekes's room.   But Mr. Weekes was there when we left.   Just a minute, Bob.'   Sladden walked to the door of the steward's room and knocked on it.   No one answering, he opened it and looked in.   ' Oh,' he muttered, and there was as much understanding in the sound as in Rob's ' Yo-*ho* ! ' ' Oh, that's it, is it ?   Come here, Rob.   What do you say to this ? '

Pushing me before him, Rob came to the door.

' Will you take a look at those piles of half-dollars,' invited Sladden.

' Half-dollars !   Yes. *Gee !* '

' Yes, but look at them.'

' What about 'em, mate ? '

' Look.'

Rob looked, and was not illuminated.

' That pile in the middle is only six,' Sladden explained. ' All the others are eight, making up a quid. What do you say to that ? '

' Well, what do I say ? '

' Seems to me there's two missing from that middle one. Why the hell should Mr. Weekes make that middle one only six ? The end one p'raps ; but not a middle one.'

Rob turned to me. ' D'you take those two half-dollars from in 'ere ? Did yer now ? Come on. Mr. Weekes'll know.'

I was dumb. To lie was useless ; to confess impossible. And my wits were knocked awry by the idiocy, the blind incompetence, of what I had done. Rob stared at my white face and commented ' Good . . . *gawd !* '

' He'd have done better to have snaffled a whole pile,' suggested Sladden. ' Then we mightn't have noticed anything. You clever ones are never quite so clever as you think.'

' We'd better get Mr. Weekes, Slad. Where is he ? '

' I don't know. He can't be far. P'raps he's up in his room.'

' Well, you stay 'ere with the young devil while I find him.' Rob, as the discoverer of the crime, was determined to have the pleasure of telling Mr. Weekes ; and he went leaping up the stairs at the end of the passage. So leaps the agile antelope up a hill when suddenly surcharged with the joy of life.

Meantime, down in the passage Jumbo Sladden improved the waiting minute for me. ' You're a young fool, you are. You've done for yourself now. This'll mean a public hiding and expulsion, if I know Mr. Harlen. We had a boy once before who was caught rifling the boys' pockets in the Changing Room, and Mr. Harlen had him up before the whole school and gave him a hiding—yes, in the Lecture Hall it was. His name was Heaseman. Next morning he was gone, and that was the last we ever heard of young Mr. Heaseman. And *he* only took coppers. Lor' love us, I wouldn't be in your shoes. And I reckon you can consider yourself lucky in getting off with a public hiding and an expulsion. D'you realize that if you was a working lad, you might get prison for this. And in the old days they'd have hung you.'

His objurgations were stopped by the sound of Mr. Weekes's voice and by the quick iambic thump of his club foot on the stairs. As he came nearer, I caught what he was saying. Conscious that he was in fault for having left his door unlocked, he was offering loud, wordy, and repetitive explanations. ' I wasn't gone above two minutes,' he kept saying—and this was a lie because there'd been five minutes at least between my sight of the money and my invasion of his room. 'Not above two minutes. I had to find these old invoices because I'd no use for Giffard's account as it stood ; and you'd 'a' thought it safe to leave a room for two minutes—especially when everybody was out of the place. There was not a soul in the place till you chaps come back. But no—not two minutes gone, and some-one's in. My God, it's a lesson to me. Never again. It's a mercy you and Sladden were due back when you were, or he'd 'a' got away with it. I think you chaps have done well. I do really. . . . It was largely the money for the wages of you chaps,' he added, as if to strengthen their alliance. 'But would you believe it : only a couple'a minutes ? '

Now he came stumping round the staircase bend, dragging his heavy boot after him. Behind came the tall Rob, as satis-fied as a junior policeman who's been able to report to his inspector a smart arrest.

'Now then, what's this ? ' demanded Weekes, when close enough to me. 'Andrews tells me you've taken money from my room ? '

I had been thinking as I waited ; and I had seen that the only way out of my pit of despair was by an appeal to mercy. I asked him to throw me this rope. 'I'm sorry, Steward. I don't know what came over me ; I don't really. I saw the money from the window and before I knew what I was doing, I'd taken it. Please don't tell the Head. Please don't.'

'Oh, you confess, do you ? '

'Yes, I don't know what came over me. I'm sorry. Don't tell Mr. Harlen.'

'Certainly I'm going to tell Mr. Harlen.' His pity, if any, was not so strong as his appetite for excitement. To ask him to drop the curtains on this play before its best scene was to ask of him more than his spiritual muscles could achieve. 'It's too late to start being sorry now. You're only sorry because Andrews and Sladden have caught you. I reckon that's right, don't you, Andrews ? It's too late now : you're coming along for a chat with the Headmaster, my boy. This sort'a thing's going to be nipped in the bud. Better come along too, Andrews, as you found him.'

'Yes, Mr. Weekes,' said Rob, flattered and delighted by the invitation.

'Well, get your coat on. You can't come to Mr. Harlen like that.'

'Right you are, Mr. Weekes.' Rob ran to the kitchen for his coat.

'Now then, march!' Weekes pushed me in the back, as
Rob reappeared, dragging on the jacket.

'Please,' I begged again.

'Nonsense. No whining. Lead on, Andrews.'

'Should I come too, Mr. Weekes?' asked Sladden who
wanted to be in at the death.

'Yes, if you like. Yes, come along.'

'Please . . . oh, please. . . .' I dragged back like a child.

'Stop that and come along.' He gripped my cuff like a
policeman. 'Come with me.'

I twisted it free. 'You needn't pull me,' I said. If I had
to die I'd go to the scaffold with some dignity.

We walked up the length of the Dining Hall and out of a
door at the far end into the school corridor. First went the tall
Andrews; then the limping Weekes and myself, taller than he;
then the corpulent Sladden, round and red as a Dutch cheese,
and waddling because of his weight; four of us; three greatly
interested, and therefore pleased; one an automaton whose
limbs walked while his brain stood still. Along the corridor we
went to the door which led into the anteroom of the Headmaster's
house. What is this memory? I see Gentle in the part of
Dreyfus being marched out of the garden, between the drawn
swords of Con and myself, to her imprisonment in the cellar.
Her head is high. But Dreyfus was innocent—innocent. How
be proud, how lift one's head, when guilty? Con . . . Gentle
. . . Mother . . . *Father!* Shamed, branded, before them all!
Branded before Mother and Henrietta! Oh, happy days in
the garden before this death.

Into the anteroom we go—it was the room where the solemn
beatings were staged; it held a table, a bench and some untidy
bookshelves; little more. Yonder was the cupboard where the
cane rested; opposite it the baize door of Mr. Harlen's study.

Weekes stumped to this door and tapped on it. 'Come in.'
Mr. Harlen's voice. Weekes went in and pushed the door to;
but it didn't latch; instead the latch tapped against the lock,
and tapped again, as a light draught played with the door.
Andrews and Sladden remained with me. Andrews looked
along the titles of some books that were on a level with his eyes;
Sladden picked his teeth with the nail of his little finger and
examined its finds before chewing them. I stood by the bench
with my limbs quivering.

'Hadn't been gone above two minutes. . . .' I could hear
Weekes repeating his wordy explanations. '. . . safe when the
place was empty . . . none of my staff I can't trust. . . . He
admits having done it. Couldn't very well do anything else

because the money was in his hand . . . admit I was wrong not to turn my key . . . admit it frankly.'

A chair creaked as Mr. Harlen leapt out of it. He was coming straight to me, with quick steps. He believed himself shocked, but in reality he was pleased—pleased with the drama, and with his power, and with the prospect of an execution.

Here he was before me. Though I had been more than a year in the school I'd never before seen his face in such detail, because now my eyes were strained to it, like the eyes of a leveret on the polecat that will kill it. I saw the tough sprouting of his black eyebrows and moustache, the strong lashes to his normally kind eyes, the slight flattening at the tip of his short nose as if it had been pressed on when putty-soft, and the dent in his square chin. I perceived also how short he was, and that I was far taller than he.

Since it was six o'clock of a warm evening, and his day's work was done, he wore over his dark suit an old striped blazer, stained and frayed; and he held his pipe in his hand. The old college blazer smelt of tobacco; and his breath of tobacco and whisky.

'What's this, what's this, Allan Mourne? Is this true? Is it true, man? *You* breaking into the steward's office and stealing money! Mr. Weekes says that you admit to it. But this is terrible—too terrible. What have you to say?'

But if I had been dumb before Rob Andrews, how should I be other than dumb before the Headmaster?

'Say something. Speak, man, speak. This is serious—serious beyond measure. I suppose you know what it means. There's only one punishment for this sort of thing. It means expulsion. I'm having no thieves in my school. When boys of your age take to stealing they need to be brought up very sharply indeed . . . for their own sakes. If I catch a boy stealing I make a public example of him without hesitation. I don't care who he is. Both he and his schoolfellows shall be made to realise the enormity of his offence. I don't care who he is.'

Not only was I staring into his face but also into his character. It was as if the agony of the last few minutes had forced up my apprehensions as the unnatural warmth of a hot-house forces out a fruit. I saw that he was justifying the sternest punishment to himself as much as to me; and I saw that he had been impressed on my arrival by the fact that my father was a general and, as he supposed, a man of wealth.

'I don't care who he is. I've had this kind of thing once or twice before—only once or twice, I'm glad to say, because my

boys are good boys—and each time my action's been the same.
You remember young Heaseman, don't you, Weekes?'

'Yes, sir,' said Weekes, glad to provide a helpful remark for
his employer.

And Rob Andrews nodded in corroboration, wishing to be in
favour too.

'I blame myself for leaving that door unlocked,' added
Weekes, who had impressed himself with his own frankness.
'I certainly do.'

Mr. Harlen did not heed him. He continued addressing me.

'I don't like having to do it. I don't like being compelled
to cane a boy at any time, and still less in public. It is repellent
to me in the extreme . . . in the extreme. But I have two
hundred boys to consider—honest, clean-living boys—and there
are two things to which I show no mercy at all : immorality
and dishonesty. I act at once before that kind of thing spreads.
Are you listening? Do you understand?' He hammered a
fist on the table. 'Don't just stand there gaping. This is
serious. Say something. You don't deny it, I suppose?'

I shook my head, unable to speak.

'Well, can't you explain how you came to do such a thing?'

Again I shook my head ; and my lips, as if out of my control,
pressed themselves tight together.

'Well, if you won't speak, you won't speak. Have you
thought what this'll mean to your parents? Your father an
officer and a gentleman, a man of the highest honour, and
now he has a thief for a son. He's not a young man, as I understand ; and you've brought this disgrace upon him. What'll
he say? What'll he *say*? You've disgraced his name for ever.'

Now my teeth shot over my lower lip and bit on it. I could
have cried to him to stop, but there was no voice in my throat.

'I'd spare him if I could, but unfortunately it's out of the
question. I shall have to write to him to come and take you
away, because this means your expulsion—have no doubt about
that. Besides he ought to know all. I should be failing in my
duty if I didn't tell him all. Young Heaseman's father, Weekes,
told me that he endorsed everything I'd done ; if anything he
was even more angry with his boy than I was.'

'Yes, sir.'

'You can go now, Andrews and Sladden—no, wait ; you
may be useful in a minute. I can't think what's come over
you, Allan Mourne ; you're a mystery to me. When you first
came I expected great things of you : a boy from a good home ;
the son of a distinguished father—you were just the sort of lad
I wanted in my school. When I first saw you I thought you

were a fine type : intelligent above the average, and gentler and more considerate than most. I liked the look of you ; I tell you that now. But you've turned out lazy and sullen and difficult. You make no response whatever to the influences of this school. Other boys—boys without your advantages—have responded in the most remarkable way to all my efforts to make fine men of them. For some time I've been watching you and wondering about you, but I never expected this. And there's no excuse for it. None.'

He walked up and down the length of the room. Weekes, Andrews and Sladden stood watching.

'Well. . . .' He stopped and sighed. 'There's no use in talking to you any more. It's too late now.' Pleased with this as a dramatic ' line,' he repeated it in another form. ' The end has come. I will deal with you to-morrow. To-night and to-morrow you will spend in solitary confinement. I can grant you no further contact with your schoolfellows. The next day, or the day after, you will leave this school for ever. Now come with me. And you, Andrews, come too. That'll do, Weekes and Sladden. Thank you.'

He led the way from the room and along the corridor ; I followed with a hand at the lapel of my coat ; Andrews sauntered behind me, closing my retreat like a detective especially chosen for his height. Boys in the corridor, who had been getting their books for First Preparation, turned to watch us as we passed, and I heard them halt behind us and mutter and whisper. We went up two flights of stairs to the Infirmary at the top of the South Wing. At the Infirmary door Mr. Harlen dismissed Andrews, motioned me into the room and, locking the door on me, went to find the Matron.

§

The Infirmary was a clean, bare, bright room with six red-blanketed beds, like a small hospital ward. Its two windows looked down upon the South Quad and the Lecture Hall in the Centre Wing. ' It was in the Lecture Hall . . .' Sladden had said, speaking of young Heaseman. I spent that night and all the next day in this locked ward—twenty-four hours of a despair too dull, too dead, too dumb, to take the name of anguish. The Matron brought me my food ; it was the same food as the other boys were having—no bread and water diet—but I could swallow it only with difficulty. I could drink water and plenty of it ; that was all. Mrs. Wanstead, the Matron, was a woman no less kind, but no wiser, and therefore no more compassionate, than most. Left early a widow, she had a boy at the school, Paddy Wanstead, and gave her services as payment for his education; but always with the sense that, if Paddy's father had lived, her position would have been very different. She was tender with the sick, hearty with the hale, and neither of these things with the disgraced. Just as many a wife is but a mirror reflecting the back view of her husband's opinions, so Mrs. Wanstead reproduced the attitude of her bachelor principal, Mr. Harlen. When she brought me a meal she either spoke in a cold tone or avoided speech altogether, that I might feel her disgust.

Between her visits I stood or sat or walked in that room, stupefied by the thought that my life was ruined. Sixty more years of it, and all of them shadowed! At sixteen I had no perception that time would pass quickly and this incident be forgotten ; no knowledge that many another boy had left school under a shadow and lived to make a distinguished career. At sixteen expulsion meant being branded for ever. Mother . . . Henrietta . . . Brian Greaves . . . all those whom, because they spoke harsh things of me, I had wanted to impress! I had handed the day to them. The victory was theirs. And Father ! Would Mr. Harlen write to him rather than to Mother ? He'd said he would, and I believed he would, because he seemed fascinated by him. ' Father, come back,' I had implored, and in this character he would come back—but leave it, leave it ; some thoughts are so unbearable that they can only be denied an entry or run from at sight.

Could I use another name in the long years before me ? But it was the name of Theodore Allan Mourne that I had wanted to make deathless, and now already it was dead. Like Wolsey I said that day a long farewell to all my greatness ; and this was not a farewell to something before it came, but to something that had been ; because the greatness had existed in my dreams. I had borne my honours thick upon me as I lay in the sunlight under the trees.

Escape ? Escape and run away from the sight of all who knew me ? I played with this idea. But the door was locked ; the windows were high ; and they were overlooked by the windows of the Centre Wing on the other side of the Quad. Moreover the Quad was seldom empty. In between school hours the boys stood in a noisy crowd, staring up at the Infirmary windows. I heard their loud voices. ' Old Weary's up there, waiting to be expelled.' ' He'll get a leathering first. Old Heaseman did.' ' Will he really ? ' ' Not half he won't ! And if Joey's in good form, Old Weary won't be able to sit down for a week.' ' It'll probably be done before the whole school. Old

Heaseman's was.' ' Will it ? Good egg ! Good biz ! ' Doubtless the bazaar rumour of my disgrace, started by Rob Andrews,
and confirmed by those boys who had seen me led away, had
buzzed in every head before lights were out last night.   Once
I looked from my window and saw the thronging boys below,
but as my face appeared, a murmur swept over them and their
faces swung upwards, like grass-heads touched by a puff of
wind. ' There he is ! There he is ! ' I withdrew, and did
not show myself again.

Could I die ? Was there anything lethal in that cupboard
by the door. No ; no tablets of antiphyrine or aspirin ; no
blue bottles labelled ' poison ' ; only some torn books, ragged
magazines, and cracked games.   It was the silence of First
Period now ; and I went to the window again and looked
down upon the empty Quad. Dare I throw myself down ? It
would be good for Mr. Harlen to see me lying dead upon the
asphalt. But I hadn't the courage to suffer that awful crash ;
and turned away. I tried holding my breath in the hope that
it would stop my heart ; but learned this could not be done ;
one breathed again before one burst. I let the held breath go ;
and I was still alive ; still in the world where the terror waited.

' I will deal with you to-morrow.' To-morrow was now to-
day. Any moment they might come for me. They might be
on the stairs now. ' It was in the Lecture Hall. . . .' I feared
the pain, but I feared even more the public humiliation : exposed
before two hundred boys and the masters as a thief. ' Look,
all of you, upon a thief.' When I tried to forget these thoughts
by idling with one of the cupboard games, ' Snakes and Ladders,'
I found myself ever throwing the dice with the thought, ' If I
can throw a six everything will be all right. Somehow everything will be all right.' And I threw my sixes, and knew it was
but a game. In the cupboard there was a shard of broken
mirror, once used perhaps by a bored patient to flash the sun
into the Lecture Hall opposite ; I looked into it and saw that
my face was less white than green. I saw also that it seemed to
have changed from that of a boy to that of a hollow-eyed young
man ; and I remembered that I was very tall ; and this made
the thought of a public whipping the more humiliating.

I told the time by the school bell. Now it was First Period,
and the school was hushed ; now it was Break, and the mob
was in the Quad again, speculating in a hundred loud voices ;
now it was Dinner, and silence occupied the Quad ; afternoon,
and the sun was visible in the west ; tea-time, and the light
was changing, and the shadow of the Lecture Hall lay aslant
on the asphalt.

Bell for First Prep., and the day was nearly done; was there then to be no public execution after all? Second Prep., and a great quiet, while the sun's light failed, and the day began to shut—oh, then it is not to be——

But look: the lamps had gone up in the Lecture Hall. All the six tall windows were alight. Why? And now the sound of many feet and many voices; see, all the boys were being herded from the Prep. rooms towards the Lecture Hall. Behind the herds like shepherds came the two young masters on duty, in their caps and gowns.

Standing there, erect, though a knee was trembling, I turned my face from the window to the door. Steps approached; the door handle turning; the porter, Ginger Tufnell, in the doorway.

'You've got to come along to the Lecture Hall,' he said.

'What for?'

'The Headmaster wants you.'

'What for?'

I think there was a rough pity in the man, under his brown uniform, for he said only, 'How should I know? He hasn't told me. He's just sent me to fetch you; that's all. Come along now; there's a good boy.'

I said no more: when one is tall one cannot speak to a servant about being whipped. I followed him down the many stairs to the door into the Quad, and I learned that it is no easier to go down steps to a scaffold than up them: all the way I was nothing but a huge heart throbbing. We went across the Quad towards the six lighted windows, and I was aware of little but that my heart was throwing itself about like an idiot in a padded cell. The porter opened the Lecture Hall door and stood aside for me to pass in; he the footman, I the guest.

I blinked in the bright illumination of the room like one who steps from the dusk of the wings on to a flood-lit stage. The whole school was congregated before me; and since the rows of desks were not enough to seat two hundred boys, many were standing at the back and along the walls. Heads swung or craned, and there was a rustling of bodies, as I halted near the door; but not a boy uttered a sound, though they were as excited as children at a play when the curtain moves. I cast a quick, compulsive glance in one direction and saw Gotley watching me with a fixed, unfeeling stare.

The only masters there, besides Mr. Harlen, were the two young masters on duty. Mr. Unwin, the senior of them, sat at the desk on the platform; Mr. Sawley, a very young man, stood in the central gangway with his hands behind him under his gown. Mr. Harlen stood on the floor between the platform and the door ; and his hands were also behind his back because he was holding his cane behind his gown.

He turned towards me. 'All right. Stay there. Close the door, Tufnell.'

'It is shut, sir.'

'Oh yes, I se . . . . Very good then.' He stepped up on to the platform. Mr. Unwin rose to give him his seat at the desk, but Mr. Harlen declined it with a deprecating palm, saying, 'That's all right, Unwin,' and stood by the desk's side. Mr. Unwin dropped his eyes on the desk and left them there.

Mr. Harlen fingered a pencil on the desk. This was the same pause as he used in the pulpit before announcing his text ; and it certainly produced a tense and expectant silence. The boys concentrated their eyes on him, while he fixed his on the pencil. Mr. Harlen has been many years dead, and it may be that in some wiser world, where the lights shine brighter, he sees now—without condemning himself, for we are all, until wisdom comes, the playthings of motives that lie beneath our sight—that he was not displeased with his leading rôle in this solemn last-scene of a tragedy.

He lifted his face, as he was wont to do above his pulpit lectern, when he adjudged the stillness meet for his opening words ; and the ceiling lights illuminated it.

'Well, boys,' he began, 'I find it hard to speak. You are probably aware by now why I have had to assemble you here this evening. All I can say is that such an occasion as this is one of the unhappiest a headmaster can know. Only twice before in my twelve years as headmaster of Draycote School, have I had a similar experience ; I pray I may never have it again. One of your number has been caught stealing money from the steward's room. He was found with the money in his hand, and does not deny that he took it.' Now his right hand, index finger extended, flung itself towards me. 'This is the boy, Theodore Allan Mourne.' He paused to think out his next words, or for effect, or both ; then shook his head, despairingly. 'I do not understand it. It defeats me. He is a boy who has had every advantage that a good home and kind parents could give him. At home he has never known what it is to want, and at school he has had every good influence brought to bear upon him. He has moved only among decent, honest, clean-living boys—for I'm sure there's not a better set of lads anywhere than you boys before me, whom I'm proud to have as my pupils. Well, boys, his crime leaves me with but one course. That he cannot remain among you will be obvious to you all. Drayoote School does not tolerate thieves in its midst. To certain things—and you will know what other things I am thinking of—it is not safe to show clemency. Not, alas, for a moment. Yesterday I wrote to his father, General Allan Mourne, and only an hour or two ago I received a telegram from him saying that he would come himself and take him away to-morrow.'

He paused, that the boys might feel the drama of this telegram, and its justification of his actions. When he was satisfied that the pause had been long enough, he spoke again, and now his voice began to rise, like a preacher's whose words are firing him.

'But that is not enough. His offence has been against the community, and he will expiate it before you all. That's my invariable rule on such occasions. In the army, as you may know, when a defaulter has gravely offended against the honour of the regiment, the whole battalion is paraded that they may hear the nature of the offence and be associated with its punishment and repudiation. His father, a general in the army, will tell him that this is so. It is a thoroughly salutary tradition, and we practice it in this school. By a public punishment now this boy shall learn, and you, I hope, will be confirmed in, the high canons of our small society—which are, after all, merely the canons of the civilised world in which you must one day take your places. Let us trust that this sharp lesson may yet be the saving of him. I pray so.'

With that he came down the three steps from the platform. 'Tufnell,' he said to the porter, and nodded his head once.

But before the porter could clamp me in his arms I gave the headmaster one look of white steel-eyed hate. The whole school saw it ; and I meant them to see it. I turned to the porter and gave him a faint smile of contempt, slightly tossing my head. Then I swung round with my back to the boys that Harlen and Tufnell, both of them, might get on with it. But before I swung round, and was arranged for punishment, I saw the young Mr. Sawley, who'd been watching from his stance in the middle of the room, turn away that he might see no more. I have never met or heard of him since that night, but because he turned away, I think of him always, young though he was, as a man taller and more adult than his Head.

My white, steely look may have disturbed Mr. Harlen. The thrashing he administered was severe—it is likely that he was thrashing his doubt as well as me—but it was not unbearable. The pain did not force me (as sometimes happened when Mr. Harlen flogged) to abandon all effort to stand and, throwing my legs away from the tortured buttocks, to leave my weight on the porter's arm.

After the sixth cut he said to Tufnell, ' That will do. Take him away ' ; and to me, ' Now you can go. Never disgrace your school or your parents again.' His tone and expression suggested that he was removing a repellent substance far from him with the toe of his boot.

But I did not go at once. I stood quite still ; gave him one more look, twin brother of the former one ; dilated my nostrils in contempt of him before the whole school ; then turned and went.

§

Out in the dusk I muttered for Tufnell's hearing, ' There's plenty of time.'

' What did you say ? ' he asked.

' I said, There's plenty of time.' These theatrical words were meant—I think, but I don't know—to threaten Mr. Harlen with some nameless revenge one day. One day, one day. . . . My teeth were close as I uttered them. I felt amazingly older than I had been twenty-four hours ago. Yesterday I was a child, begging, ' Please, oh *please* ' ; this evening I was a man, and the world was my enemy. If it wanted a fight, it could have it ; and I would use every weapon I could find. There was always crime for a man who didn't choose to bare his back humbly to the whips of the world. ' I can wait,' I assured Tufnell, hardly knowing what I meant.

' Now you be quiet,' he urged. ' You only got what you deserved.'

' Yes, and so perhaps will you one day.'

' What yer mean ? '

' I wonder how often *you've* pinched things. And he, too.'

Tufnell halted in the midst of the Quad. ' D'you want to go back to the Head ? '

I halted, too, and stood before him. ' Yes, if you like. Yes, I think I do. Shall we go now ? ' Had we gone back, had he taken me at my word, I think I'd have struck Harlen and fought with him, as I had fought with Mother.

But Tufnell, his thinking deranged by this unforeseen answer, could only retort weakly, ' A little more, and you will ' ; and walk on.

' As you wish,' I said grandly ; though the grandeur was spoiled when I added, ten seconds after, the schoolboy boast, ' I'm not afraid of that s——.'

' You think yourself mighty clever, don't you ? '

' No, I don't,' I denied, childishly near to tears. ' But I'll be clever enough to get my own back on him one of these days. I'll ruin him.' And to stress my defiance I added ' Bloody Hell ! ' and ' Damn ! ' These two oaths were as two chords bringing a fine *forte* passage to a powerful close.

' Now nuff'a that,' he said. ' We don't want any of them sort of words. I wonder at you. If you was a man, you'd take your punishment without whining——'

' I'm not whining——'

'——you'd say " I've dug my own bloody—my own grave, no one else dug it for me, and now I got to lie in it." It's hard, I admit.'

' I'm not going to lie in any grave.'

' Well, now, that's better. Try to make the best of it. You're still young and strong.'

The tears sprang at these kindly words, and I turned my face from him.

At the top of the stairs the Matron came to the door of her room.

' Good evening, Matron,' I greeted her. ' A fine evening, isn't it ? '

' What's that ? What did you say ? '

' I said " Good evening." Any objection to my saying good evening ? It's considered polite, isn't it ? '

' Don't take any notice of him, madam,' Tufnell advised. ' He's had a tanning, and doesn't like it.'

' Oh, I see. Well, I think he's a very rude boy.'

' That's the first time I've heard that it's rude to say good evening.'

' He'll get over it,' said Tufnell, and his words sounded again his note of pity.

' Oh no, I shan't ! ' I promised them both. ' Mr. Harlen hasn't heard the last of me yet. Not by a long chalk. You'll see.'

' Don't you listen to him, madam. He's just sore. Now you go back there, and don't be silly.' He guided me into the Infirmary.

' Good night, Matron,' I called. ' Sleep well.'

' I wonder at you, I do really,' said the porter. ' Talking to Mrs. Wanstead like that ! '

' Good-bye, Mr. Tufnell. I take it I shan't have the pleasure of seeing you any more. Thank you for all your help in the Lecture Hall just now. I don't know how we'd have got on without you. And give my love to your employer in case I don't see him again. Not for some time, at any rate.'

' You'll come to no good if you go on like this,' said he.

' I don't want to come to any good,' I shouted, as he locked the door on me.

CHAPTER IV

AT ABOUT half past two the following day, between dinner and afternoon school, I heard the key turning in the lock and, jumping up, saw the Matron in the doorway.

' Your father's here,' she said. ' You're to come down to Mr. Harlen's study.'

' All right.' I followed her with a dull acceptance. I had dreaded my father's eyes more than the massed eyes of the boys, and his anger more than the headmaster's cane, but my bitterness and despair had blent into an anæsthetic, and now I could feel but little.

The Matron led me through the anteroom into the study. Here Mr. Harlen was standing with his back to the fireplace ; and Father was standing sideways to him and staring at the door. His height seemed to cut yet more inches from the headmaster so that he seemed smaller than he had ever been. I looked at Father's face and saw that it was nearly as white as (I have no doubt) mine was at this meeting. One hand held his silk hat to his fawn waistcoat ; the other pressed his gold-mounted malacca cane into the carpet ; and both, I saw, were trembling.

' His things are packed ? ' Mr. Harlen asked of the matron.

' Yes, they have been packed some time. They are downstairs.'

My father bowed. ' I thank you, madam.'

' Thank you, Matron,' echoed Mr. Harlen. ' The General's cab is still there. Will you very kindly see them put on it ? '

' If you will be so good . . .' Father bowed to her again. ' I beg they may be put upon it at once. I am much obliged to you.'

' That is all, Matron. You needn't stay.'

The Matron retreated, shutting the door. We three stood alone in what was plainly a charged and dangerous atmosphere.

Mr. Harlen turned to me. ' Here is your father. He has come to fetch you.'

' Most certainly I have come to fetch him,' said Father.

' Well, as you have heard, General, his things are all packed, and he can go with you now.'

'Oh no.' Never was a firmer negative. 'Oh no. Not yet. Not at once. I intend to repeat before him some of the things I've already said to you.'

'I don't think that is in the least necessary.'

'I think it is very necessary. Doric, you did this thing, I suppose? You took this money?'

'It was found in his hand,' Mr. Harlen reminded us.

'Will you let the boy speak! You don't deny, Doric, that you took these miserable half-crowns?'

I shook my head. It was not possible to say, 'Yes, I took them' to my father.

'Have you ever done anything like this before?'

'What—how do you mean?'

He jigged his knee impatiently. 'God, isn't what I'm saying plain?' He lifted his voice. 'Have you ever taken money before?'

'No.'

'Why did you do it this time?'

I returned no answer.

He drubbed his foot on the carpet. '*Answer me!* Why?'

'I think chiefly because I was terribly hungry and wanted to buy some grub.'

'That is nonsense,' interposed Harlen. 'That is absolute nonsense. The boys here are well fed.'

'Let him speak. Hungry?' The word had plainly bewildered him. 'You say you were hungry? Have you often been hungry here?'

'Always.'

'I never heard such rubbish——' began the Head.

'*Always hungry?*'

'Yes. A lot of us are. Ask any of them.'

'But good God in Heaven, child, why in the world have you never told me this, or your mother? What in the world do you think your father's for?'

'I told Mother, but I don't think she believed me.'

'It is nonsense,' repeated the Head. 'There's no school in England where the boys are better fed. I see to it myself.'

'I prefer to believe him. All right then. You are hungry. You see some money lying around, and you yield to a sudden temptation to snatch a couple of coins. You deserve punishment—stern punishment, perhaps—but not the dastardly treatment you've received at this man's hands.' His eyes flamed, his eyebrows, knitting together, seemed to be of sprung steel wire, as he flung out the word 'dastardly.' 'I have just informed him, before you came in, that I consider it *dastardly*.'

Mr. Harlen left the fireplace for the door. ' Really, sir, this sort of thing is not going on. I think it would be better if you and your son were to go.'

' You may think so. I do not. You have branded my boy before all your school as a thief. As someone too degraded to associate with other boys. This boy here is my *son*—you don't seem to realize it. My *son*. He and I don't suffer this sort of thing without saying a word. He yields to a moment of temptation, and you exhibit him in public as an untouchable. Great God above, have *you* never yielded to temptation? There are other temptations besides stealing—and if it comes to that, did you never steal anything when you were a boy? My son is not a thief. He's no more a thief than you're a liar because you told a few lies, I'll be bound, in your childhood. Understand that. He—he commits a small crime, and you not only expel him, as you're perfectly entitled to do, though it's a grossly savage sentence, but you also thrash him in public. Well my sense of justice, if not yours, says that no man—and still less a child—should have two brutal punishments for one offence— just because you want to show off before your wretched boys——'

' I've had this happen before, and the boy's father endorsed everything I'd done. Draycote School, let me tell you——'

' Well, I'm sorry for the boy then, and still more sorry for the father. I'm always sorry for the blind. And that he agreed with everything you'd done proves exactly nothing, except that there are two blind people in the world. Oh yes, I mean what I say, and I'm going to say it, and no one's going to stop me. I intend this boy to hear it. I say that your treatment of him was damnably cruel, and that cruelty to a child is infinitely worse than stealing two half-crowns—a point you would do well to consider, sir. You take and thrash him before his comrades——'

' It was entirely necessary as an example to the others. Draycote School——'

' Oh, of course, if you believe in human sacrifice——'

' Human sacrifice rubbish! I did it for his good. And right well he needed a sharp lesson. I don't mind telling you, he's been going from bad to worse. He's becoming a hopeless boy.'

' Hopeless? My son hopeless? Any lad hopeless just because in a weak moment he's stolen something? Come, Doric; this man is right; we'd better get you out of here quickly. Would to God you'd taken something sooner, and I could then have learned a little earlier that you were in the hands of a fool. I begin to see, sir, that you are a much greater danger to your pupils than ever my son could be.' And then, after a moment's silence, my father, his lips shaking, said a remarkable thing. He was an old-fashioned Whig, which meant that he believed more in toleration and understanding and less in the ' strong hand ' than the Tories of his day, but he was also a military man who'd been in his time a strict and impatient disciplinarian, and I suspect that he would have been incapable of this moment of vision with anybody but me. It was his love that gave him light. ' For myself,' he said, ' I should have thought it obvious that when a child steals for the first time it needs, not punishment but love.' I think he too was impressed by this statement, and for a second con- sidered it would be a good line on which to make his exit, because he thereupon laid a finger on my elbow and said, ' Come, my boy, let us get out into the air '—but at the same moment he thought of further effective words, and turned to utter them to Mr. Harlen. ' A boy trips up—he trips up badly, I allow—and all you can think of to do is to hold him up to obloquy and then drive him out like a leper. You try to ruin his career for him. You try to ruin his faith in himself. Well, let me tell you, sir, that you will do neither. You will not damage his career to the tune of one halfpenny. *I* shall see to that. I shall see to it more than ever now. I trust you will live long enough, sir, to see him in the fine position he will occupy in the world. And you will not injure his faith in himself. Between us, he and I will see to that. I say to you here and now, Doric : *I* used to pick and steal sometimes when I was a boy. I'm not proud of it, but I know that I grew up to be a man with a sense of honour—though, unlike our friend here, I'm only too conscious that I often fail badly to be all that I'd like to be. I'm sure, my boy, that I'm a far greater sinner than you—and with less excuse, because I'm not young like you.' Dear Father : the usual tears were near his eyes and he was clearly pleased, in the presence of a pharisee, to play the publican and speak of his sins. ' But this gentleman is a padre and of course does not sin. He's a Christian Minister and therefore one who doesn't believe in forgiveness and mercy. Come along. The excellent matron said, I believe, that your trunks would be conveyed to the fly. Do you go now and find your hat and coat——'

' His hat and coat will have been taken to the cab,' said Mr. Harlen in a tone as low and level as a sword-blade.

' Oh, they have, have they ? Excellent. I cannot thank you enough, sir. Then lead on, Doric.'

His hand at my elbow guided me towards the door into the anteroom, but Mr. Harlen, taking a step towards us, pointed to the door opposite, which led into his house. ' You'd better go this way.'

' Why ? '

' Because that other door leads into the school, and you'll have to pass the boys. You had better go out through my house.'

Father stood in thought for a moment ; then said, ' No, sir. Not at all, sir. We will go the way we came. We're not leaving by any back door. Come this way, Doric.'

' Oh, but, Father——' I begged.

' Come ! ' he commanded impatiently. ' And to you, sir—a very good afternoon.'

His left hand held the silk hat against his breast, and as we passed into the school corridor from the anteroom, he transferred the malacca cane to this hand as well, and deliberately laid his other arm along my shoulder. And as we walked along between the boys in the corridor who stopped in their tracks to see us pass, he talked loudly and lovingly of anything that came into his head. With the malacca cane (and the top hat that accompanied it) he pointed at everything on which his eye alighted. ' Those are the classrooms, are they, Doric ? And that door there, where would that lead to ? The Dining Hall ? Well, I never ! Now who's this a picture of? It's a padre of some sort. The Founder ?—Oh, I see—well, a handsome old buck, isn't he ? What's behind that door, besides an infernal noise ? The Quad ? Very good, let us walk that way. I shall like to see the lads at their games. I take it we can walk round the buildings to the front of the school, where the fly is waiting.'

Placing his hat on his head, he deliberately put his arm into mine ; and together we walked down the steps into the Quad. The boys were playing a noisy game of Touch Wood on its asphalt, but our appearance stopped the game and evoked a universal silence. Apparently unconscious of this stoppage, Father, his arm in mine, affectionately, proudly, walked me across the Quad, pointing at doors and windows with his cane. ' Well now, what's that, old chap ? The Lecture Hall. And that ? The Gymnasium. The place seems tolerably well equipped. And this leads into the playing field, does it ? I saw boys playing there when I drove in. I think we'll have a look at them before we go.'

On the broad green plain one group of boys was playing French Cricket ; another stood in a ring to play Catch with

two balls ; while in the far field some of the older boys, candidates for the Eleven, were being given Fielding Practice by the
groundsman.

There was a high grass bank by the chapel, and here my
father stood with me and, in view of them all, in view of the
whole world, laid his arm along my shoulder while he pretended
to watch the games. Sometimes he swung his cane as if he
hadn't a care in his head, and sometimes he exclaimed, as if
much interested, ' Oh, well caught, sir ! . . . Well fielded !
Very fine indeed.' Then he said to me, ' Come, let us go and
watch these youngsters over here. We march out in good order,
I think, Doric. Colours intact. This is French Cricket, isn't
it ? It certainly looks like it. Oh, well held, sir. Next man
in. Yes, you're fairly out, sir. Better luck next time. " Alas,
regardless of their doom, the little victims play ". Well, Doric
we mustn't keep that fly waiting for ever ' ; and we went round
the chapel and on to the front drive. The fly, an ancient open
landau, stood before the front steps, my trunk and white tuck-
box on the seat by the driver. Off stage now, Father said,
' I suppose all your things are there, but if not, what the hell
does it matter? Jump in. I trust we haven't kept you waiting
too long, Mr. Cabman. The station, please ; and thank you.
. . . Well, here we go, Doric. There'll be about an hour before
our train, but we'll have some refreshment while we wait.
There's an excellent tea-shop near the station ; I noticed it as
I came, and thought it would do. You can have whatever you
like. I used to like éclairs and meringues when I was a boy.'
The cab, behind its cow-hocked horse, was crunching and
jingling over the drive, and as it passed through the gates of
Draycote School on to the green-banked country road, he
touched my hand with the tips of his fingers and said, ' Good.
We're quit of that place for ever. . . . Well out of it, I'm sure.
Now we can begin to do great things.'

CHAPTER V

AT HOME—what would it be like at home ? How would
Mother, Con, Uncle Humphrey, Lettice, and the maids receive
me ? Father had scarcely brought me to the door before I saw
that Mother, Con, and Uncle Humphrey knew all about my
disgrace, but not Lettice and the maids. As I entered the hall
Con said nothing but stared at me as at an object of unusual,

not to say fascinating, interest. When I came into the dining room, Uncle Humphrey took one look at me, and fled upstairs from a worrying situation. Mother made no allusion to the reason for my return, but her grim and protracted silence was heavy with unspoken words.

I construed the shape of things in the next few days. Father had instructed Mother to tell the truth to no one, but to give out that he'd heard I was unhappy at school and had removed me at once ; and this tale suited her very well with strangers and servants, since my expulsion was her shame as well as mine, but of course she'd told Con before the interdict fell, and she had neither the scruples nor the strength of character, after it, to refrain from discussing so sensational a matter with her sister. She couldn't forego enacting a deep despair before Henrietta, having the wound stroked and soothed and softly poulticed by that intense, inane, but emollient woman. The first time Henrietta came to the house and sat herself with Mother in the drawing-room, my pungent interest, my complete certainty that they were talking about me, drove me to the closed door that I might hear their actual words. And it seemed that my certainty was a true clairaudience. Mother was saying, ' I just can't make it out how I came to have a child like him. What does one *do*, Henrietta, what does one *do*, if in spite of all one's efforts a child persists in turning out badly ? That a child of mine should steal. I'm the complete failure—I am, I am ; really.' Here a snuffle. ' His father tries to make light of it, but to me it's too terrible . . . too *awful !* If he's turning out as he is, it's largely because his father always spoils him. That I shall say to the end.' And oh, I could almost hear Henrietta nodding. I could almost hear her touch Mother's knee as she told her not to cry. And soon I caught her words, ' It is terrible for you, I know, I know. What could have possessed him ? A gentleman's son ! It's inexplicable. I know I went absolutely stone-cold when you told me. And when I told Brian he turned white for a minute—he did really—quite white. . . . He's absolutely heartbroken about it. Oh, no, of course, I won't tell another soul, my dear. Is it likely ? I realise what it means to you. I wouldn't breathe a word to anyone, for your sake. Don't be too unhappy. You're not a failure. Think of Con. There's a very dear child. There's one you can always be proud of.'

Not once did Con speak of it to me, or make any mention of the school, but I suspected that her view was the same as the others, and that her silence contained her shock. It may be I did her an injustice, but in my quivering sensitiveness I fancied that, without being quite conscious of it, she was not displeased at my fall since the further I sank in the estimation of Mother and Henrietta, the higher she rose.

Then Mother, Henrietta, Brian, and Con all knew : one nagging question remained, did Gentle know ; Gentle, my other playmate ? Henrietta, I surmised, had taken too tragic a view of the disaster to speak of it to her daughter ; but what of Con ? Could Con, any more than Mother, keep the dark and thrilling tale from her chief confidante ?

How could I learn whether Gentle knew ? To ask was impossible, because I couldn't speak of my disgrace to anyone ; for years no word of it would form upon my lips. Could I tell from Gentle's manner ? On the Saturday, eight days after my return, she was coming to spend the afternoon, and I awaited her arrival with a sickly discomfort and fear.

She came running into the house with a liveliness that was overacted. She gave me one quick, fascinated look, rather like Con's, swinging her eyes away directly she thought I'd seen the look. And by that look, and by the way she said nothing about my early return from school but talked instead, and somewhat too gaily, about our plans for the afternoon, I knew that she knew.

But I couldn't catch from her looks or her words what she was feeling about my disgrace. Indeed she hardly looked at me once again ; she seemed afraid to look. And her gaiety remained a little forced. There was no reading the thoughts behind that nervous brightness. July, that year, went out in a blaze of heat ; and this was a day of bright blue in the heavens and spun gold in the trees, and she suddenly cried, ' Gosh, I know ! We'll go for a row on the Serpentine. Oh, yes, let's ! ' Con agreeing with an equal fervour, Gentle turned to me and asked, ' Coming too, Doric ? ' It was a most pointed invitation, but a slightly embarrassed one.

' Yes, if you like,' I said. They were only two girls, but all boys of my own age were tainted with the poisoned memory, and I needed companionship. ' Yes, I'll come.'

' Good-ee ! ' said Gentle—but did this mean anything ? Was it any more than an habitual phrase. ' Cheers ! Doric'll do the rowing while Con and I loll in the stern and try to look rather attractive. Come on, beloveds.' I was just feeling a dim pleasure that I should be included in the term ' beloveds ' when she corrected it, as if she'd made a mistake, into ' Come on, chaps. Don't stand there wasting time. The sun may go in. Gosh, how tiresome people are.'

Her reaction to my disgrace hadn't been the only target for

my eyes and thoughts all this time. Gentle, rushing into the house, had brought me a great surprise. Five weeks older than I, she was now nearly sixteen and a half, and she was—yes, there was no blinking or dodging the astonishing fact—she was rather beautiful. In three short months—or so it appeared to me that day—she had changed from a long-legged child, whose femininity was chiefly revealed by her two long plaits, into a most shapely young woman. Three months ago she had been a young hermaphrodite, with far more of Hermes in her slight body and swift, winged feet than of the round-hipped Aphrodite ; now the young Hermes had flown from her breast and limbs and left only the young Aphrodite there.

Of course this transformation in Gentle hadn't really been as miraculously swift as this. It was just that until now I'd had no eyes for any ripening in Gentle's sapling body ; at fifteen I had been blind ; at sixteen I could see. And it may be that the sight of my eyes had been quickened by the darkness through which I had come ; to be hurled into ignominy is, perhaps, to be made susceptible to light and beauty, and hungry for it.

This was the Gentle I was looking at, staring at, now. Her hair in its plaits, once a pale amber, was now a dark brassy gold ; her skin was a mocha-cream, which interesting tint seemed to enhance the brilliant brownness of her eyes ; her nose was firm and straight ; her mouth was much too large, but made amends for this error by the largeness and fullness of her lips ; her chin was like the point of a small pale brown egg. She was many inches taller than Con but all her lankiness had dropped from her like a last childish vesture. When she first came into the house she had flung herself on to a chair, drawing her black-stockinged legs up under her, and I'd immediately noticed the soft pressure of her breasts on her bodice and the smooth roundness of her flanks in the sheath of her skirt.

I remember that she was wearing that day a frock of some old-rose colour with a ruching round the shoulders, and a large Leghorn hat with a pink rose on it somewhere and two green velvet ribbons streaming behind.

Her young beauty hurt. It hurt because I wondered in the aftermath of despair whether any such beauty was ever for me. It stirred some thoughts that were secret and shameful. Understand that there was no trace of love in these thoughts, for Gentle was no more than a playfellow ; but they created around her an exhilaration that was somehow independent of Gentle. She had ceased, as it were, to be Gentle Greaves, the next thing to a sister, and had become a representative of abstract girlhood. I imagined her with all her clothes wafted away, and the picture cut my breath ; I imagined myself possessing such a young feminine body, and my heart seemed to dissolve in air ; I saw in a vision the perfect girl whom I would love, and whose love, mingling with mine, would compose the sure balm for every wound ; and I began to feel a craving for this unknown girl like that which I had felt, a few days since, for the comfort of those silver coins.

§

I too was well dressed to-day ; and this because Father, shocked at my appearance in the headmaster's study in frayed and greasy clothes, anxious to rebuke Mother for letting me go about like that, uneasy in his own conscience, and planning in his wisdom to rebuild my self-confidence, had taken me to his Empire Co-operative Stores and there indulged in an orgy of expenditure on clothes. So on this hot July day, as we set out for the park, I was in white flannels, blue blazer and boater hat, all new ; and the awareness of these good clothes was certainly a faint antidote to despondency.

After walking the shocking length of Earls Court Road, Gentle said ' Phew ! ' and suggested taking a bus since it was still ' miles ' to High Street, Kensington. It was in fact about half a mile. The bus appeared. Until recently Henrietta had been quite unreconciled to the idea of a ' young gentlewoman ' riding on a bus, but long and intense discussions with Brian and others had persuaded her in the end that, whether she liked it or not, these were ' the days of Democracy and she mustn't be a silly old-fashoined old fogey any longer.' Gentle endorsed this view of her mother's obligations enthusiastically, and so was free to lead us with leaping steps to the top of the bus and to the front seats on either side of the driver's perch.

' You sit there, Con.' Gentle pointed to the right hand seat. ' And Doric, come and sit by me.' She had said this with the same studied naturalness, and still not looking my way. Was it only her nervousness that had forced the words ? ' No, you take the corner seat, Doric. I insist on sitting by the driver.'

' I will not be spoken to imperiously,' I said, trying to be humorous as of old. ' Nor pushed impatiently. If I sit in the corner, it is to oblige.'

But she couldn't answer me in this fashion—couldn't toss back this very light ball—and instead she seated herself beside the driver, examined his round beard and low-crowned felt hat, and inquired of us both in a whisper whether he wasn't ' sweet.'

'Divine,' said Con.

'Heartrending,' Gentle agreed and, always acting on the immediate impulse, leaned forward to establish an acquaintance with him.

'Good afternoon,' she began.

'Afternoon, miss.' His eyes hardly left his horses. 'Pleased to meet you.'

'We're going for a row on the Serpentine.'

'Well now, are you? And I'm going for a row along Knightsbridge and Piccadilly.'

'Don't you get bored with it sometimes?'

'I've known myself get a trifle bored with it—yes; that's right, miss.'

'I'd rather be us than you this afternoon.'

'Well now, would you? I'm not so sure as I would.'

'Why's that?'

'Well, the coppers are picking up people out of the Serpentine every day.'

'Are they?'

'Yerse—not a day passes but someone's lying on the bottom, waiting to be dragged up. And whenever they empty it, they find heaps of 'em lying around.'

'Help! Heavens! But if it comes to that, people are being run over in Piccadilly every day.'

'Not bus-drivers aren't, ha, ha. They do the running over.' He seemed to think this very funny. 'It's a sight safer up here than in one of them Serpentine boats. I was in one of 'em once, and I didn't really feel there was enough between me and the next world. What's more, they topple over if you forget yourself for a tick, and then where are you? If you fall off a bus and hit the road, the people at least know where you are. No trouble for the ambulance men or the p'leece at all. But on that there Serpentine, Gaw-lummy, they got to empty the whole can to get to you. And you're dead long before that.'

'But I can swim. I can swim quite well.'

'Not in them clothes, miss. Your petticoats and all'd have you down in no time. Not a chanh'st.'

'My cousin here'd come and save me.'

'Oh, no, he wouldn't. His boots'd have him down. Not a chahn'st. Just more trouble for the p'leece. After they've found you, they got to look for 'im.'

So much wit determined Gentle that we must stay with him as far as Hyde Park Corner and the park gates there. Here we said friendly good-byes; and he said, 'Don't get drowned

now. Your various men 'ud be quite upset if you was ' ; and
Gentle, jumping down the steps, summed him up again as ' An
exquisite creature. Heartrendingly sweet.'

§

Other summer days have faded ; they are imprecise in
memory, or altogether lost ; but this one has remained with
all its details distinct. It has never dimmed because I have
dwelt upon it all my life, and so can see it still, as clearly as the
afternoon of yesterday.

We walked into the park ; into a warm silence under the
trees. Above us the sky was a world of blue, except where the
morning breeze, like a forgetful servant, had swept the clouds
into a corner and left them there. The giant elms stood in
lakes of shadow, and the grass around the shadows spread away
into heaving prairies of sun-flooded green. In the distance the
low rounded hills quivered behind a heat-haze that rose like
the visible breath of a world alive.

' Where's this old Serpentine ? ' demanded Gentle.

I pointed to some drifts of mist which lay about the ground
and clung around the tree-trunks so that the young trees appeared
to be stepping, like women, out of their fallen draperies. ' Just
there behind the Dell . . . if it hasn't moved since we were
last here,' I added, still striving to be funny and unashamed.

' Well, do come on,' she urged, pretending not to notice my
over-strained efforts. ' I'm impatient. I want to get on to the
water. I feel just as I do at the seaside, when it's horribly hot
and I'm going down to bathe.'

And half a pace ahead of us, avoiding all sight of me, she led
us on, between the trees. We didn't speak again. The influence
of the trees seemed to keep us from speaking. The old sturdy
ones, chestnuts and elms, were as motionless and silent as old,
musing men ; the younger, light-hearted ones, the slim ashes
and acacias, whispered among themselves ; and their whispering directed our thoughts to the sun-warmed breath on our
cheeks.

And so we came to the long silver water. It lay stippled and
sparkling under the high sun, and sage-green and smooth by
the banks, where it mirrored the trees. A breeze from its
surface ran to meet us with its welcome ; and we hurried to the
boathouse and hired a rowing boat. I, as the man, took the
stroke oar ; Gentle insisted on taking the oar behind me ; but
she soon abandoned it to Con and clambered over me to the

stern seat where, curling her legs under her, she sat gracefully and steered, in the main, disgracefully.

And Con and I rowed in silence ; nor did Gentle say a word as she gazed over the water. Here and there an outrigged skiff, sculled by a townsman in shirt-sleeves, who was snatching an hour of primitive happiness, moved on the tinselled lake with no more sound than a boat on a cinema screen. No bird-song dropped from the trees into the far-spread silence ; only at intervals, and from the lake's side, came the harsh cry of a water fowl. Along the brinks sat the anglers, and no one was more silent than they. Beyond the waterside path old gentle-men dozed on green chairs, and tired tramps lay asleep on the pied grass, in sunlight or in shade.

I was silent, partly because of the summer day, partly because of the grievous memory which sat always with me, and partly because I was looking at Gentle. She had rolled up the bishop-sleeve of her old-rose dress that she might trail her hand through the water; and I was noticing how round and smooth was her arm, clasped by the silver snake bracelet which Father had brought her from India. Once again that round arm and her round knees were stirring the breathless fantasies in my brain.

Under the bridge we rowed, and on to the Long Water, which was even more silent since it was less visited. The trees crowded down to it, rather than the people. We rowed into the stillness of shadowed and virgin water, and two grey geese followed us. We rested on our oars near an overhanging willow and gave ourselves to dreaming. Drinking deep of Gentle's impersonal beauty, for she was turned away from me now, with her elbow on the seat's back, her chin in her palm, and her eyes on the smoke-blue distances, I wondered what immense, self-centred hopes, hardly to be slaked, but not yet wrecked like mine, were lodging in that breast so lately ripened. To be sixteen, as I knew—or had known—was to have all the desire and élan of the universe crowding into one's breast.

'We've had our hour,' said Con at last.

'Oh, no,' begged Gentle ; 'no ! It's so lovely. I'm happy.'

'We must be getting back if we're to be in time for tea.'

'Who wants tea ? Hang tea.'

'She was dreaming of some wonderful future,' I said.

'That's exactly what I was doing.' For the first time her eyes were fixed on mine, and opened wide. 'How did you know ?'

'Pure magic,' I explained, keeping up the desperate facetiousness. 'I can do you a thought-reading act any day.'

'Well, that was rather clever of you, I think.'

' What was the future ? '

She smiled once, uncomfortably ; then quickly avoided my face again, and gazed out at the far blue distances beyond the trees. ' I was thinking that it would be rather fun to be married to—or, rather, I just *had* married something quite nice.'

' Who ? ' asked Con.

' I don't know at all. I couldn't see his face. But I think he was about fifteen years older than me, and terribly attractive and immensely clever—only he needed me to spur him on.'

' Which you did,' I provided, beginning to cut the water with my oar.

' Oh, yes ; and it was thanks to me, I think, that he arrived quite soon at the very top of his profession.'

' Which was ? ' demanded Con.

' I haven't the slightest idea. Something quite distinguished. The wedding was an extremely swell do at St. Margaret's, Westminster, with heaps of bridesmaids and a congregation packed to the doors, and a crowd waiting outside. It was a lovely summer day, and we drove off with everybody cheering and the police opening a way for us, and, of course, all the bells clashing out.'

' And then ? ' I prompted.

' Oh, well, we loved each other an awful lot—right up to the end—and we travelled together all over the world, and we had a house in the country—not large, but with a tennis lawn and lots of horses—where we entertained all the most celebrated and interesting people of the day. I was rather famous as a hostess. And we had a nice little set of chambers in Pall Mall, rather like darling Uncle Kingsley's.'

' Any children ? '

' Oh, yes. . . . Yes, I think we had one or two quite nice children—but I hadn't come to that yet. As a matter of fact, I was back at the wedding when Con said something about tea and spoiled it all.'

' Well, we won't speak any more,' I said. ' We'll just wait here till you've had your first baby and then go home to tea.'

' Doric ! ' rebuked Con.

' Oh, but I think that was rather funny,' Gentle allowed. Had she said this to take my part ? For a few seconds I believed so, for she deliberately added, ' I always think Doric's rather witty—sometimes,' but then, as if embarrassed by this admission, she said hastily, ' Oh well, we must go home if we must, I suppose. All nice things come to an end.'

I dipped my blade again. 'Yes, home to tea.' And we paddled back to the boathouse.

We walked homeward along a path of ashen-blue asphalt that ran straight as a taut ribbon to the Queen's Gate. The sun had fallen, and the trees along the path striped its hard ribbon with their shadows. They were mostly chestnuts and planes ; and, as they stood in that lowered sun, the lop-eared chestnuts were full of darkness, and the spreading planes were full of light. We wandered on between them without speaking. Near the Queen's Gate we turned on to a path that wound between high shrubberies and flower beds, with garden seats standing about it, each a murmurous haunt of nursemaids, this summer eve. Fat babies tottered across the path from the nurse's knees ; older children bowled their hoops along it ; and plump dogs went on visits from railing to railing. The flowers were paraded in regimented squares behind the railings : phlox and begonias and petunias and one poor company of blown and tattered roses.

Some of these beds made a very brave show ; and Gentle and I stopped to consider an array of Galilee pelargoniums, while Con walked on, looking at the other beds, till she was full thirty yards in front of us. Then Gentle and I left our gazing and walked after her side by side. And suddenly, unexpectedly, now that Con was far away and could not see, Gentle put her hand into mine. Her fingers closed nervously upon mine ; she spoke no word ; but if ever the touch of fingers said, ' I am with you,' it was Gentle's then.

My heart seemed to stop. A gratitude that was speechless swelled and overflowed so that my arm, which was our channel of communication, trembled. Somewhere over the Kensington roofs at that moment a clock should have struck for a new hour begun ; because Gentle, putting her hand into mine, had put herself into my heart.

A love for her poured out from me. I did not suppose that she loved me, or that her hand laid in mine had been more than the gift of her pity, but I knew that it was love which was making me press her hand with so tight a grip. She pressed mine in friendly acknowledgment ; and I kept hers as we walked because I could not let it go. For a little way we went on together hand in hand past the eyes of the nursemaids and the old resting men. Glancing down at her face, as it chanced to look up at mine, I saw a smile in her eyes and on her large full-lipped mouth, and I asked myself, Would I like to kiss her and my heart stormed its answer.

§

I had to loose her hand as we came near to Con ; and I remember nothing of what happened on the rest of our way home, except that the tide of life in me, which had been very far out, was flooding home again, higher than ever before.

CHAPTER VI

TEA WAS laid in the breakfast room when we got back ; and the girls, led by Con, ran up to the bathroom on the second floor to wash their hands, soiled and roughened by the oars. I climbed to the dim landing by the playroom and waited for them there. There was no thought in me of going to wash my own hands. My mind was possessed with thoughts too rare and agitating to allow of any room for so dull and homely a notion. It was not a little thing to be loving for the first time. And not a little thing to have resolved that in a few moments I would ask Gentle to kiss me. Like a bear in its pit I paced the dusky landing, waiting for them to come down.

Once before at a Christmas dance in our parish hall I had asked a girl to kiss me. She wore a white accordion-pleated frock ; was not very pretty ; and I did not much want to do it ; but other boys had boasted of such achievements, and I forced myself to copy them. I took her out into a narrow yard, overlooked by housebacks, and said, ' Now I'm going to kiss you ' ; but she said, ' Oh no, you're not ; I'm not that sort of girl ' ; and this so abashed me that my cheeks burned and I said, ' Oh, I see. Well shall we go back ? '

But to-day I was older, seven months in calendar time, vastly more in maturity, and desire was a pressure within me that hammered at my heart and vibrated in my limbs.

Con came down first, as I knew she would ; and I moved out of her sight into the playroom. She went skipping down the last stairs, and I returned to my ambush in the twilight of the landing.

Now Gentle had slammed the bathroom door behind her ; now she was at the top of the stairs, shouting, ' Gosh, I'm clean ! Let no one suggest I'm not gorgeously clean ' ; now she was running down the stairs to where, unseen at first, I waited. As she arrived I put out a hand, caught hers, lifted my finger as if a game were afoot, and drew her into the shadowy recess between staircase and wall. She came with me, smiling but surprised.

In the greater darkness of the recess I said, ' Gentle, let me kiss you.'

Unoffended, though surprised, she just laughed. ' Why ? '

' Because I want to. I want to terribly. Let me.'

There was only a look of ridicule in her eyes.

' Please, Gentle. . . . I want to so terribly.'

' All right then,' she said, still half playing ; but as I gathered her waist (which I had so longed to do) the ancient and ever-lasting fear of a young girl caused her to turn her head quickly and save her lips from my invasion. I kissed the averted cheek, and, gently forcing up her face against that old resistance, pressed all my love and gratitude upon her mouth. At the touch of her lips—the first I'd ever felt against my own—the desire in me became a wild rapture and I pressed my mouth on hers till the pressure must have been pain.

In anger a little, but more in surprise, she struggled to get out of my hold, and for a minute we were like the two children who'd so often fought together before. She escaped me, since I would not hurt her ; and when she was free, said, ' Don't be silly, Doric dear. What's the sense of doing it like that ? ' for her body was not alive to passion as yet, and she did not see why a kiss should be more than a soft touch on cheek or lips. But passion was well awake in me and I said, hardly knowing what I said, ' Oh Gentle, I love you. I've fallen in love with you. I have really. I fell in love with you the minute you put your hand in mine. And I think you're so beautiful. I've been thinking it ever since I first saw you to-day.'

All her anger was gone ; it had yielded place to great liking—and certainly to a great interest. As she stared up at me, with a half smile, her only comment was ludicrously inadequate. She muttered her usual, ' *Gosh !* '

My own words, though as unoriginal as love itself, were at least abreast of the moment, and of the high tide in my heart, for I drew her to me again and repeated, ' You're utterly lovely, and when you gave me your hand, I knew you were utterly sweet. And I began to love you with all my heart and soul.'

' I'm not lovely, and I'm not sweet,' she protested. ' I only wish I was.'

' You're almost sweeter than I can bear.'

She rebuked me for such foolishness with a smiling frown and an ' Oh Doric, you *are* being absurd, but you're rather a darling ; rather heartrending, I think ' ; and then fell silent, staring at me and at the mystery.

I dared not ask her if she could love me, because it seemed too impossible, so I just begged, ' Are you glad I've fallen in love with you ? '

' I don't know.' She arched her brows. ' I must think it over. It's so *funny*.'

' It must be nice to be loved,' I pleaded.

' Yes, I think it is, rather. I think—yes, I think I'm pleased. I've often thought I'd like to have someone in love with me—lots of girls at school have—but I never thought it'd be you. It's so extraordinary. It's—it's just incredible. Oh, well——' and she laid a hand on the lapel of my coat more affectionately than ever before—' come to tea. They'll wonder what's up. And, oh Doric, for heaven's sake don't tell them what happened just now.'

' Of course not.'

I walked down the stairs behind her, studying the graceful figure that had been, but now, in my arms, and alight with the exultation, hardly to be matched in kind again, which comes from a young man's first kiss.

§

We could not advance the extraordinary business any more that evening, because we could not escape from Con. We played card games on the playroom table, and Table Croquet on the large dining-room table ; and very badly I played my part, for these childish pastimes, belonging to a careless yesterday which had perished an hour ago, were of small interest to me to-night. And Gentle, I saw, was playing with an over-acted gusto, her flippancies too frequent and her laughs insincere, because she was thinking of another matter most of the time. The games a doubtful success, Con read us *The Prisoner of Zenda*, of which she was much enamoured just then ; and there were times, I am sure, when Gentle and I missed large tracts of the tale.

So did that Saturday die, with a threefold farewell on the steps, two of us acting an innocence we did not feel. Gentle gone, I could only wander about the house with my memory of what had happened. I was foolish enough to stand and gaze at the dark place on the landing where I had kissed her. Alone there, I tried to recall every word she had used and every expression on her face. ' Yes, I think I'm pleased ' : that seemed the best thing she had said ; and she had laid her hand affectionately on my coat. Could this mean, then, that she was going to love me—she who was beautiful ? How was it possible that she could raise any love for me—I who'd been laughed at by the other boys for my long and weedy frame, I whose pale, bony face was anything but beautiful, I who'd just committed a nasty little crime and been cast out from my school with contempt, I of whom her mother and my mother spoke the harshest things? I couldn't imagine myself giving my love to anyone who had no bodily beauty; were girls, when they loved, untroubled by this need for visual beauty? And was Gentle indifferent to my crime and disgrace? Or had her reprobation of it been completely dissolved in her pity? If so, had Harlen's stern punishment given me Gentle?

I walked into the drawing-room and looked at my face in the gold-pillared mirror on the white marble mantelpiece. It was very different from the haggard face I had seen in the broken shard of mirror, when locked in the Draycote Infirmary. The pallor had given place to some colour, the eyes had renewed their brightness and were capable of a sparkling laughter like my father's (or so I thought after some experiments) and the whole face appeared a year or two older, with the set features of a young man rather than the late-forming features of a boy; but it was still a lean face, a little sunken at the cheeks, and I could not see in it anything that Gentle could love. Surely her beauty entitled her to something better than that.

I did not expect to see her again till the following Saturday when her school term would be over, and we could all enjoy the long free days together; but the very next afternoon, our Sunday dinner over, she appeared at the door, stuttering and blushing, and equipped with the excuse that she wanted to know more about our Saturday plans. She came for a minute up to the playroom, insisting all the time, 'Can't stop, can't stop. I must go, I must go,' but when Con went down the stairs with her, she abruptly broke from Con and rushed back, shouting that she'd left something behind; she dashed in, slipped a letter into my hand, and dashed out, escaping at once from the house, patently ashamed. I rushed to the window and saw that she was running from the square so as to escape from my eyes.

I tore at the envelope and read, 'Darling Doric——' yes, the word was 'darling'—' I've thought over all you said and I know that I'm just dreadfully happy about it. I'm sure I love you too and I just wanted to tell you so, that's all, it's such ages till Saturday. I'm sorry if I was huffy when you kissed me but I didn't know then what it was to be in love. I'd love you to kiss me again. Gosh I'm pleased about it aren't you but just what are we going to do about it. We can't tell Henrietta, she'd have a thousand fits or Brian who'd pass out and I don't feel I want Con to know somehow not just yet. I vote we keep it our secret I think you're sweet. Absolutely tons of love, From Your devoted and very dear Gentle Mary Greaves.'

'I didn't know then what it was to be in love.' Now (in a favourite phrase of my father's culled from his beloved Bunyan) now was I got on high. And 'I'd love you to kiss me again.' It was so out of measure amazing that I might hardly bear up under it. All the next days I walked with this sentence a ferment in my veins—no, not walked—paced, strode, wandered, stood still, and strode again—strode the rooms, the landings, the garden, and the road, and sometimes stood quite still to savour the words more perfectly. She had given her love to me whom yesterday all despised—and she was beautiful. That was what left me humbled and amazed. A thousand times a day, and always with a brief ecstasy, I considered the astounding contrast : yesterday Infirmary and Lecture Hall ; to-day Gentle's assurance, 'I'd love you to kiss me again.' My gratitude and my love were the same thing ; they amounted to a tenderness that could barely be borne.

There is no doubt that this summer of Harlen and Gentle, this quick succession of storm and sun, wrought a ripening in me that would normally have taken years. It was as though I advanced in a few weeks from sixteen to eighteen. Gentle's willingly given love, like the generous and uncensuring sun, raised in me thoughts that were beyond the scope of a normal sixteen-year-old boy : profound ponderings on the mystery of the isolation of all human souls ; on the wonder of the approach of two such souls to one another, in a longing to blend ; and on the tragedy of that impotent longing, since, love notwithstanding, they could never lose the whole of their isolation and merge in one another completely. Impressed by the quality of these thoughts, I told myself, 'I believe I've only just come alive. I'm fully alive at last. One only comes fully awake and alive when one loves.' And I pitied the boy who yesterday had been unawake, and all his poor noisy schoolfellows at Draycote who were still unawake.

Monday . . . Tuesday . . . Wednesday . . . the days that lay between me and Gentle were slipping slowly behind ; three of the five had gone and two only lay before me ; I was over the top of the hill. Wednesday evening ; and I was sitting in the playroom, trying to read, but returning always to the one thought, when—unbelievable ! a sudden halt to all thought ! —I heard Gentle's voice at the front door. She was talking to Con. The bell must have rung in the basement, and Con must have hurried to the door, while I in my drugged abstraction heard nothing. Only Gentle's voice had suddenly rebuilt the house around me. In a second I was on the landing, catapulted there by curiosity and delight ; and to my bewildered joy, for I could still hardly believe in her love, I heard her say, talking with all the speed of one who is suppressing a sense of guilt, ' I just can't do it, Con. It's the most filthy bit of Prep. I've ever been given. No one should be allowed to set us such unspeakable stuff. And who was Virgil anyway ? Oh, thank God I shall have done with school this time next year. I thought it might be intelligible to Doric ; boys for some strange reason are so much better at Latin. D'you think he'd tell me what at least some of it means ? Where is he ? He's got to help me. I'm in grave trouble.'

The exquisite, the heart-breakingly lovely creature ! She had invented this excuse to come and see me sooner. Then she really did love me ; she longed for me as much, or almost as much, as I longed for her. Oh, the astounding, incredible contrast : yesterday the bottom of despair ; to-day *this*.

' He's upstairs in the playroom, reading.'

Not so ; not so, Con ; he's upstairs on the dark landing, waiting, his heart hammering its impatience, his throat a dry thirst for her.

' I'll just nip up and ask him, shall I ? I won't be a sec.'

I slipped back into the playroom to wait for her. She ran in and, casting aside the useless Latin book when she saw my arms spread out to welcome her, ran into them. That moment I was as much her goal as she was mine.

We did not speak ; no words could compass what the long kiss could say. Once she explained in a whisper, ' I wanted to come. I'm loving you so ' ; and I dared not answer, because if I had spoken, I should have cried. I only held her tighter and kissed her passionately, in the way she had rejected before ; and this time I felt that she was kissing me with something of my delight ; not with all of it, and far more innocently, for she had yet to learn the meaning of the sap that was rising in her. Still, there it was : Gentle, who was beautiful, had come to the brink of desire in my arms and none other's. As I felt this fact against my breast Harlen's study and Draycote Lecture Hall lost substance and faded ; they became poor, unimportant things ; and all the universe chimed together.

BOOK III

I SPIN MY TRIUMPH AND MY GREAT DEFEAT

CHAPTER I

OF COURSE the little secret idyll which Gentle and I staged during the next year was largely a game, a continuation of the games we had played as children, on the stairs or in the street. Or perhaps it would be truer to say that it was largely a game for Gentle and less so for me. Gentle with her immense affectionateness was very fond of me and she enjoyed my adoration of her. She liked hanging with both hands on to my arm as we walked, and listening to my talk, which, she was pleased to say ' was ever so much cleverer and wittier than anyone else's and made her feel bright and intelligent.' She was happy in the game. For me, too, it had the elements of a happy game, but at base it was serious. My love, because it had sprung from a tilth of pain, had a root that was tougher than hers and much stronger than is usual in a lad of seventeen. My love was my master-thought, and its grip was increased by the dread lest hers, being less, should one day fail.

Perhaps the love of both of us was saved from weariness by the obstacles that hemmed it round. For a year or more it was an affair of snatched meetings in London's open places, or snatched kisses in our house. Henrietta would have been shocked into an hysteria, and Brian hardly less disapproving, if they'd known she was meeting any male creature unchaperoned ; and though my love for her, because it was real, was reverent and protective, they'd have imagined me more likely than most to endanger her innocence. So we had to meet far away from their eyes, and it was not often we could manage this.

We managed it perhaps a dozen times in as many months. The only green and open places near our homes were Kensington Gardens and the great cemetery with its lime-tree avenues among the tombs; and it was the Gardens that saw most of

our smiling encounters. I see us walking the glades beneath
the florid and dissipated face of old October, either blown along
by his rude and bantering breath or kicking our way, like two
children, through the gold leaves he'd scattered on the paths.
She is hanging on my arm with both of hers and sometimes
leaning against me. I am no longer the lank, untidy, stooping
youth from Draycote School, but an erect, well-dressed, merry-
eyed lad, with this burden of beauty and love on my arm. Or
it is winter, and we are walking together, happy but silent, she
leaning against me for warmth, between the old trees cataleptic
with frost. Once, and only once, I see us treading in the same
places over hushed and winking snow. Next it is spring, and
the trees are almost as full of small, brown birds of as small,
green buds, and the lusty young sun is throwing heliotrope
shadows on the ambered paths ; and the spring leaps in Gentle
too, so that she skips and dances at my side.

But we were not always walking arm in arm ; alas, no ;
there were times when estrangement walked between us all the
way home, and we left a yard or more between our arms that
we might walk in comfort. In these months I was discovering
in Gentle (in this wonderful, largely unknown country which
I'd so strangely conquered) many delightful tracts but some
very thorny ones as well ; and more than one laceration did
I take in these entangled places : lacerations which ached for
long minutes because I couldn't bear not to be loving her.
Among the delightful things was her way of looking up at me
with a fund of love in her eyes. All her life Gentle, when
talking with you, would look up into your face as if for the
present you were all that mattered in the world or (when you
did the talking) as if she were less listening to you than loving
you, till at last you had to abandon your fluent enthusiasms
and take and hug her. At least that was what I always had
to do. She never knew it, but the movements of her face were
beautiful. When she was full of a skipping zest and laughter
her eyes would fold up mischievously, or a sidelong and private
smile would just move the corners of her over-large mouth.
And what she could do with a pair of eyebrows, whether arching
them in astonishment or knitting them in rebuke—well, if there's
such a thing as damnable unconscious, unscrupulous coquetry,
this was it. But most attractive of all were her gestures of pity.
Convinced that I was ' pathetic ' and therefore ' sweet '—' Oh,
why is everyone so pathetic ? ' was a favourite cry of hers—she
would stare at me, decide that I looked sad and rush at me
with her strangling embrace. Her language then was an animal
language : no words said, but her lips touching my cheek

without further movement, or her own cheek laid firmly against mine, or her head administered like a comforting poultice to my shoulder. It was clear that she much enjoyed these methods of alleviation and restoration.

With such unwitting coquetry did she throw lassoes about my love ; but she could throw other things as well ; barbed things. Her warm blood might produce affectionateness, sympathy, and an impish defiance of her parents ; but it produced also wraths, resentments, and cruel, wounding words. If her beauty was but skin deep, so likewise was all this tractability and resilience ; I would go further and say it measured but half that depth : a prick and you were through to the angry blood beneath. A prick and you received a jet-propelled, streamlined wrath.

Once, and most unfortunately, when she and I were in the playroom, she chanced upon two booklets that I'd bought immediately after I'd fallen in love with her, *Strength and Beauty in the Male* (Health Publications Ltd.) and *Strength and How to Obtain It* (Eugene Sandow) ; and she let forth a scream of laughter and, rushing to the stair-top, shouted ' Con, Con ! He's going to be strong and beautiful. Doric's doing a beauty course. Strength and beauty in the male.'

Instantly all my humour deserted me, for the old wound was touched ; I turned sour and silent. My cheeks went the whole way from a burning red to a cold white. As I intended, she soon perceived my tight-lipped silence and inquired, lifting her brows, ' Whatever's the matter, my sweet ? '

Glad of the opportunity, I pricked her with a needle-sharp word : ' I see no occasion to laugh like an idiot. It sounds like a half-educated factory girl outside a pub. I've no particular desire to be made your butt.'

No sooner spoken than I caught the full blast ; the words came at me like a stinging dust in the wind : it was I that was the idiot, I that was utterly without humour ; I was just filthily vain and as touchy as a girl ; nobody was going to call her an idiot and a factory girl ; and if I thought she was only half educated, she'd quickly relieve me of her company ; there were plenty of others who liked her and thought well of her ; and, Gosh, there were times when I was awful—times when she would like to murder me !

' Oh dry up,' I shouted ; and she assured me she wasn't drying up for anybody.

Hardly a word did I speak to her that evening ; and very few said she to me ; but her chatter with Con, so far from having dried up, was most striking in its volume and sprightliness ; and ' striking ' is the word, for with it she was striking at me.

Thinking only of her, while pretending not to ; glancing at her, while feigning no interest, I told myself, with some truth, that she wasn't really hurt by the quarrel but enjoying it ; whereas I—I was wounded unto death.

'Good-bye, Doric,' she shouted, when she was leaving the house.

'Good-bye,' I murmured, hardly to be heard, and wilfully despairing. (Good-bye, summer, good-bye, good-bye.)

On another occasion, a hot September afternoon, she met me at the King's Arms Gate of the Gardens with an indignation against her parents that was as high as the midday sun ; and her first words were, 'Hallo, Doric, my precious. Look : I can't see why people go on living.' She was then seventeen.

'Can't you ? I can see one or two excellent reasons why they should.' And I looked her up and down.

'I'm not at all sure that I can. It may be all right for you, but the world's just a wash-out for women.'

'Granted ; but what has suddenly brought this truth home to you.'

'Everything.'

'As much as that ? Tell me all about it, my exquisite.'

And out everything came, as we walked along, linked together. For a week or two past, I must explain, she had been aflame with the idea that she wanted to go to Lady Margaret Hall, Oxford, instead of to 'a silly finishing school at Brussels.' It was a new and most surprising (and quite temporary) notion, for nothing in her schooldays, or in her talks about her future, had revealed any craving for the higher education ; it was, in fact, due solely to her affection for an older girl, Helen Dukes, who was going up to Oxford next Michaelmas term. She'd just been advocating the idea to her parents with some heat, said Gentle, and Brian had turned it down flat. He offered her music lessons instead ! He'd said a university career was quite unnecessary for her, because she'd never have to earn her own living ; he'd said he was doing frightfully well with his old tinned foods, and she could always live at home with her parents until such time as she got married. 'That's the way he talks : " until such time as you get married." ' And it was all rubbish. Who wanted to stick at home and be nice to the kind of creatures Brian and Henrietta knew ? At Oxford she'd meet hundreds of interesting people and hear wonderful talk ; it was the loveliest city in the world—everybody said so ; she'd see me often, which would be lovely (I was then at a Kensington crammer's, being coached for Oxford) ; she'd probably play tennis for her college, and swim for it ; and it was a perfectly wonderful plan. She didn't *want* to be absolutely dependent on Brian. There was a book, *The Economic Tragedy of Women*, that Helen Dukes was going to lend her. ' I'm longing to read it. I haven't read it yet, Doric, but I agree with every word of it.' She was delighted with her agreement.

' You do ? '

' Certainly I do. Of course I do.'

' Why ? '

' Because I'm a woman, and because I think I'm very much to be pitied.'

' Pitied ! *Pitied*, she says, when she's been given eyes and a nose and a figure that most girls would give their souls for.'

' Yes, pitied ; and don't just grin and try to look superior and clever. I don't want to be grinned at.' She pulled on my arm in pretended anger. ' You don't seem to understand that just now I'm feeling most frightfully sorry for me.'

' So ? '

' Certainly so. I don't think it's right I should suffer so much.'

I picked up her fingers and saying ' Come with me, child,' led her to an empty seat in the Broad Walk ; and there, with the sun's warmth, and the sun's bright glances through the trees, to inspire us, we talked of the many and splendid things she wanted in life. The same warm, leaping blood that produced the loves and wraths produced also wants that were boundless. When we tried to get them into shape, there under the trees, they seemed to solidify into a desire to be married, to be a great hostess to famous people, to travel all over the world, and to have, say, four children, three boys and one girl. Now, since I was necessarily referring all this to myself and wasn't at all sure that I could fit in with these demands, or that she was supposing I could, I began to be much less happy than she in the fervent recital. And when she added that her love had got to be a 'grand passion,' and her lover must have a huge manly breast on which she could cry when she felt as she did to-day, and I was still unsure that it was my breast she was thinking of, then, indeed, I was really unhappy. I turned my own microscope on to her statements and her manner and found them of a shape so unpleasant that I went silent and gazed, with tight lips, down a long vista between the trees.

As usual she saw the tight lips and inquired what was the matter.

' Oh, nothing . . .' I said, ' nothing.'

' But there *is* something. You've gone all unhappy.'

I unsheathed a blade and stabbed her. ' It's not a very

happy thing to realize that one loves someone passionately who only half loves one in return—if, in truth, she loves one at all.'

' What on earth and under God's good heaven are you talking about ? '

' You talk about a grand passion and marrying a rich man. I thought you were going to marry me. I happen to love you, you see.'

' I love you too.'

' Oh no, you don't. When you talk of marrying, you're not thinking of me.'

As she didn't immediately declare she was, I demanded, almost longing for the mortal blow, ' Are you ? *Are you* ? '

Only came a silence that, for me, was like a slow death.

' Do speak. Do speak,' I begged. ' I'm suffering.'

And she said, ' I wish you were a little older.'

I sprang from the seat and walked away from her.

She came after me, and I heard her voice a foot's distance from my ear, ' Don't be silly, Doric. You *are* being stupid.'

' Tell me,' I commanded, without turning round. ' Are you going to marry me one day or not ? '

' Yes, I think so.'

' *Think !* Oh, my God, *think !* . . . That seems to settle it. . . . Well. . . . Good-bye.'

' Oh, you're impossible,' she cried ; but still her steps came after me. ' I never knew anyone so idiotically sensitive as you. You fire up at the least little thing.'

' *Little ?* It doesn't happen to be little to me. It happens to be death to me.'

And thus we walked on, northward towards Bayswater, she a yard behind me, and that yard filled with silence. I looked westward at the railings and the grass ; she eastward at the path and the trees. On I strolled, with my hands clasped behind my back as I used to see Father stroll when he was miserable. I came to an embowered seat near the Inverness Gate and threw myself on to it ; not once looking towards Gentle, though I felt her loitering near and loved her with an anguish that was both despairing and poignantly sweet.

And at last that loitering figure flung itself at my side, and the strangling arms were about me.

' Don't be unhappy,' she whispered. ' I can't bear it when I see you unhappy. I know that I love you when I see you like that. I do, I do.'

Not disposed to forgive her at once, I just endured the embrace like some large patient dog.

She laid her cheek against mine. ' I'm sorry if I hurt you,

Doric darling. I'm filthy sometimes. I've been in a horrid mood all day, hating everybody and wanting to hurt them. I get like that sometimes. I shall grow out of it. I shall really. I shall grow into something quite nice.'

But I wasn't sure that I was going to be charmed by lightly humorous words, and continued to bite my lip and stare in front of me.

Then I felt her head sinking on my shoulder ; so I put my arm around her, but slowly, that she might not suppose she was easy to forgive.

She held her lips against my cheek without kissing it. 'I'm being loving and nice now, aren't I ? ' she requested.

Still not speaking, I grabbed her like a hungry animal, forced up her face, and kissed her harshly and long and voraciously.

'That's right,' she encouraged, her eyes full of tears, when I'd set her mouth free. 'I do love you. . . . And, oh dear, I do love crying sometimes.'

'You beloved and silly child,' I teased her ; loving to call her 'child,' because of the hateful five weeks by which she was older than I.

'I'm forgiven, aren't I ? Yes, of course I am.'

'No,' I said, 'but I adore you.'

'You've just got to be patient with me sometimes,' she advised, forcing herself against my side in a quite deliberate effort, for once in a way, to be impudent and charming. 'You must remember that I'm still young and rather wild.'

'I must remember that you're adorable.'

'No ; I can be repulsive quite often, I know. I *meant* you to be hurt when I said I wished you were older. Gosh, I'm horrible sometimes. Why don't you shake me or beat me or something ? '

As she said this, my heart leapt with desire, and I knew that something in me would enjoy shaking and beating her, and then hugging her when I'd done enough. I felt afraid of the vehement and lustful thing that leapt in me then.

And meanwhile Gentle, unaware of this thought, and lively and happy again, was suggesting, 'But I did make the first advance, didn't I ? Gosh, that showed a fine spirit. There are times when, in spite of all, I quite approve of myself.'

§

And then we left this house of our childhood, and it became Gentle's house.

On a dingy February eve, as I returned from my crammer's,

Con met me at the door with a whispered ' Hush ! Father's here. He's in the breakfast room, shut in with Mother.' I looked at the breakfast room door and murmured, ' For the love of mercy, woman, what impends ? ' We learnt what impended the minute he had gone. He went without a word to us, as though unhappy or, perhaps, ashamed. And hardly had the door closed behind him than we heard Mother's now fat and heavy figure hastening up the stairs with its dead weight of news. She cast it down before us in the playroom.

' We've got to go. He's turned us out. We can stay no more in this house which you've loved. He says we've got to go. He says he can't afford it any longer. Such nonsense ! And if he can't afford it, we know why, we know very well why. We've got to get out of here into something quite small— *I* don't know where. Anywhere. We're just turned adrift.' Her lips came together and quivered and twisted, as she worked up the melodrama and held back the tears which it extracted, and which she was so enjoying. ' *I* don't know where we'll go. And this at a time when Con ought to be meeting people and having them to the house ! He's giving the house—*our* house— to Uncle Brian of all people, and Gentle'll have everything that my child ought to have had. Never mind, never mind, my dear, we'll go somewhere. We'll find somewhere to go. We'll find somewhere to lay our heads.' And she touched Con's hands with her fingers, as if they were the fingers of a mother who would never desert her.

I was shaken by the news but unimpressed by the scene. Since for ten years Mother had complained about the house— its size, its stairs, its basement, and the impossibility of finding servants to do its work—I discounted nine-tenths of her words, and all of her tears. From her wordy, repetitive, and lachrymose Jeremiad, which continued most of that day, and much of the next, I built my own picture of what had occurred.

Father had come that evening to explain in person why he could no longer give her an allowance large enough to maintain a big home. His explanations were copious and cogent ; and I've no doubt that some were true, some a degree or two off the truth, and a few of them (I fear) elaborate and plenary lies. His expenses were unbearably heavy, he said—but he didn't detail these expenses ; and he didn't make any mention of Mrs. Sinclair Skene ; on the contrary, he implied that he was living in the simplest style—almost on the poverty line. He'd lost a large sum in an unfortunate investment, he further explained, but without disclosing the nature of the investment, though he was very willing to ' blame himself entirely for his foolishness.' He reminded her that he'd be sending me to Oxford in the autumn ; that this would cost him at least £300 a year ; and that he mightn't be able to meet this new expenditure out of income, but would have to sell ' some of his small capital.' And finally there was the war. (The Boer war, as he spoke, was not five months old ; the shadow of its early disasters was still over the land and a god-send to him, who needed all the excuses he could gather.)   The war, he explained, had been detrimental to every company in which he was concerned, and he couldn't yet say how far their losses would affect him ; but affect him seriously they must.   Brian Greaves was ready and eager to take the house off his hands, and really in the circumstances, such dark and disturbing circumstances, this was too good an offer to decline.

Ah well, my eyes were as open now to my father's frailties as to my mother's, and I saw quite plainly that he was preparing to stint Mother and Con for his own sake and for mine.   His love for me, and his unforgotten anger against Harlen, who'd dared humiliate a child he loved, ensured that he'd honour to the uttermost his promises to me.   To Oxford I should go, but some of the cost must be stripped away from Mother and Con.

It was no great surprise that Brian Greaves would take the house.   He'd been doing exceedingly well in the firm of Boulton and Mills and was now a partner.   His self-esteem had been swelling during the years, and he'd long coveted a fine house like ours and been a little ashamed of his narrower home in Redcliffe Street.   And now his firm, since it dealt with food, was prospering and expanding in the warm air of war ; and Brian's income and aspirations were expanding with it.   He had a position to maintain, he said ; he must dress his window with a far greater show of success, and have a home in which he could entertain and impress his customers and the big men of the business world.   In short, Brian at fifty-two was exactly where Father had been at fifty-six, when he came with joy to this house, bringing his sheaves with him.

§

A day or two of melodrama and high pathos, and then Mother was quite pleased with the prospect of a move.   For some years she'd been watching the blocks of red-brick flats rising among the high, grey stucco houses, and envying those wives whose rooms were all on one floor instead of strung up and down a staircase ; whose lives were lived horizontally instead of perpendicularly, as she would say—for she could joke sometimes. And now she set her heart on finding such a flat, 'a cosy little place that Lettice and I and Con can nip round and keep clean in no time.'

Lettice agreed, saying that it wouldn't upset her very much to have none of them rackety girls around, so long as the place wasn't all that large. She'd never been so set on this big house, she said, though of course the Master had liked it, and it had been nice for the children, but they were getting that big now that Mother wouldn't be having them on her hands much longer. If the next place wasn't all that large——

'It's not going to be a bit larger than I can help, Lettice,' declared Mother, enthusiastic now. 'Oh, I think we're all going to be very comfortable together. I'm quite looking forward to it.'

Indeed there were only two people who were gravely perturbed by the move. One was Henrietta who in her long and intense colloquies with Mother would say, 'It's so terribly big, Una dear, this house of yours. I don't know how I'm ever going to manage it. But if he wants it, he must have it. He knows best what he needs for his work, and it's my duty to help him in every way. I must do my duty. A wife's place is at her husband's side. He is My Man, and I hope I shall always do my duty by him.'

The other was Uncle Humphrey. Father in his schemes hadn't given a moment's thought to Uncle Humphrey in his chamber upstairs ; verily I believe he'd forgotten his existence. Nor had Mother remembered him when first she lifted her voice in a lamentation ; not for a moment had she considered him as a factor in the difficult sum before her. But there he was—upstairs ; and when on the second night after Father's visit he sat at our dinner table and heard Mother's continuing plaints and incipient plans he looked startled and promptly withdrew into himself, behind his sad eyes, as a man turns into his private tent for thought. And upstairs in his room that night he came awake to the fact that while he'd been living up here in (as it were) the eternal stillness, the temporal world had been going on around him—not to say underneath him. He awoke to the fact that the ship was sinking under his feet, and crew and passengers had forgotten all about him in his cabin and were taking to the boats. And the more he considered this fact in his cabin, the more, as can be imagined, his alarm increased. It increased with such celerity that it drove him down the stairs to the breakfast room, where we were all seated by the fire. He had come to secure his place in a boat. And his eyes above his square beard were sadder than ever as he appeared at our door in the magenta dressing-gown and blue felt slippers which he wore of an evening for his comfort's sake.

' Hallo, Uncle ! ' said Con, greeting him with surprise, because a visit from him was unusual at this hour.

But he had eyes only for Mother. ' Una, dear, I shall still be able to live with you when you move, shall I not ? '

She looked at him. She looked at him as at a new point which certainly no one had considered ; and for a while she had no answer to give him, for her brain was easily paralysed.

' Will there be a room for me if you move into a flat ? ' he pleaded, his eyes like a dog's who begs to be taken for a walk with the rest.

' Oh yes,' Con cried, her bowels of compassion stirred, and no responsibility resting on her shoulders. ' Uncle Humphrey must come too.'

' It needn't be a large room,' pursued Uncle Humphrey. ' I quite understand that it can't be a large room.'

' But that would mean that we should want five bedrooms,' said Mother, who was coming to grips with the sum. ' I hoped to get something quite small. My idea was to keep down the housework.'

' I could help with the housework,' offered Uncle Humphrey.

' But a five-bedroomed flat would be expensive, wouldn't it ? '

' I could pay a little more,' said Uncle Humphrey, desperately advancing his offer.

Now, Mother had become more and more of a money-digger since Father went, taking the money-bags with him ; she would fix her hungry little eyes on any glimpse of a profit, however small ; and tonight, as Uncle Humphrey said this, I saw in those little eyes that he'd produced something like a trump card. He saw it too and hastily added, ' I could afford a little,' emphasizing the ' little,' but her ideas were larger than his.

I watched the quick calculations behind those two little windows, Mother's eyes ; if Uncle Humphrey paid only what he paid now there'd be a good profit, since the upkeep of a flat would be much less than the upkeep of this house ; and probably she could make a case, now that he'd committed himself, for charging him ' just a little more—things are so difficult in these days.' Yes, the sum was coming right.

' Oh yes, I think we must try and get Uncle Humphrey in, don't you, Con ? ' she said. ' It wouldn't be fair to turn him adrift after all these years. Even if we have to put ourselves out a bit we must find a place for Uncle Humphrey. I'm not going to be inconsiderate, as some people are, and think of nobody else.'

The relief in his sad eyes was like a light.

' Thank you, Una dear. It's a relief, I must say. I'm the sort that grows attached to places. I always feel rather lost if I can't get to my usual chair at the club or my usual table in a restaurant or the same pew in church.' I swept the last ten years for any memory of Uncle Humphrey going to church, but the effort produced nothing. ' And after ten years I've got used to you all. I should be most unhappy to leave the dear children.' I tried to think of any time in the ten years when he hadn't fled from us children lest our noise frayed his nerves ; and again without success. ' The whole base for my work would be disturbed if I had to make a new home among strangers ; and I'm just at a most important part—a part that deals with Spinoza. And I was hoping to discuss other parts with Doric, now that he's becoming so intelligent. You're really sure you can find a little room for me ? It needn't be very large.'

' Well, we shall certainly try,' said Mother ; and Con endorsed, ' Yes, Uncle Humphrey must come too. Oh, I think it's all going to be rather fun.'

So, fairly happy again, slightly more comfortable in his dressing-gown and slippers, but not to be wholly free from fret till the flat had been found, and he'd been shown his room, Uncle Humphrey went slowly up the stairs again.

Of course I see now that in any case he'd have accompanied Mother to her new home. To Mother, now that Father was gone, he was not only a source of profit but a habit. He was a habit like a husband. He was a companion at meals who listened only occasionally to her chatter, like a husband ; he was a man in the house whose absurdities she could publish to Henrietta and her other gossips ; indeed he was better than a husband because between him and her there were no strained relations, no chafing fetters, and no need for jealousy. And to him she was as good as a wife ; she was someone to mend his clothes, to listen to the records of his pains, and to medicine, massage, and plaster him, as required. To be sure, save that they didn't share a bed, I do not see in what way they differed from a husband and wife very tolerably married.

§

Uncle Humphrey was now nearly sixty-three ; it was ten years since he'd built his nest high up in our house and given himself to the hatching of a great book on Philosophy ; he had strained and pressed and fidgeted, and rested and strained again ; but still there was no book. There were notes and synopses and scenarios, and some complete chapters ; there were five box files of which he was very proud ; but no book. Whether any part of him was uneasy at this swift running-by of the years I do not know ; but he would disclaim any such unease to me, and comfort himself, by pointing out that Kant had given nine years to the production of his three *Critiques* and Carlyle fourteen to his *Frederick the Great* and even Gray some ten to the perfecting of his brief *Elegy.* ' It's not a work that can be scamped,' he would tell me, though his eyes as he said it were more sad than assured. ' Don't forget I have to survey the whole field of Philosophy since Thales, and that's two thousand five hundred years. You can't distil the wisdom of twenty-five centuries in twenty-five months. You have to read and read. And think a lot too. Sometimes I do little else but think. And I take immense pains with the writing, as you know. The one thing I can't stand is inaccurate and slovenly English.' Uncle Humphrey was a man firmly persuaded that he understood correct English better, and cared for it more, than ninety-nine out of a hundred writers ; I have met others such, including business men. ' I'm absolutely determined that its style shall be perfect ; I'd rather not write it at all than write it quickly and carelessly. Let the popular writers do that. This isn't going to be a light and popular work by any means. I couldn't write a small and popular book if you asked me to.' And he seemed quite angry at the thought that anyone should ask him to.

Mother found a flat in Addismore Road among the smaller homes, red-brick, of a newer London. It was not the mansion-flat of her dreams, for one will never find that at the end of any road, but it was on the first floor of a clean, new, red-and-white block, and had seven good rooms ; and its neighbourhood, though disconcertingly close to the poor streets of Hammersmith, was polite. On the other side of Addison Bridge, there is a sudden change of scale and tone in the houses and the streets and the style of living therein ; there are many such points of sharp change in the ground-plan of nineteenth-century London. And we, in this year 1900, moved off the old Victorian map of London on to the lately built-up waste grounds ; hard on Time's heel, we passed from stucco to red-brick, from house to flat, from amplitude and pretension to a shrunken but still genteel life. Not without sadness we walked down the white steps of No. 1 Coburg Square to the four-wheeler that would take us on this journey : Mother, Con, Lettice, and I—and Uncle Humphrey followed humbly behind. In his high-crowned hat, and with a portfolio of irreplaceable manuscripts under his arm, he stood upon the pavement while the women crowded into the cab ; and when I'd stowed them and their bags on the seats, he asked nervously, ' There isn't room for me, is there ? ' I put him in, with some gentle shoving ; laid his life-work, or the core of it, on his knees ; slammed the door, and myself walked along Warwick Road, thinking of Father, and over Addison Bridge to our new and narrower home.

§

And Gentle went into the old house ; and the upper room that was once Uncle Humphrey's became her bedroom and boudoir. We were both eighteen now ; she was done with her schooling ; and I was just about to go up to Oxford. She had come back from her finishing school in Brussels very ready to resume our secret idyll ; but our move to Addismore Mansions, our crossing of Addison Bridge, had snapped the easy meetings between the two families, and she and I found it more difficult than ever to be alone and snatch a kiss. The West London Railway, in its wide and coal-black hollow under Addison Bridge, roared between us. We would slip out sometimes and meet at a street corner, but there was no place in the populous and many win-dowed roads where we could embrace as we wanted to do ; we were too young and ashamed, too much the children of Kensing-ton and Earls Court, to enfold and hold each other under a lamp-post or against a dreary London wall.

It was I who first mentioned the side-gate into her garden through which Mr. Payton used to come to his assignations with Mother ; but her eyes kindled with mischief, as I hinted that it was there to be used. She put up a proper pretence of shock and chided me severely for the hint ; but when she had dis-charged this duty, and I had argued impenitently, ' But child : consider ; have a heart ; soon I shall be gone to Oxford and you won't see me for months and months,' she promised, partly for the lark and the daring of it, to signal to me from a high back-window some evening when Brian and Henrietta were at ' one of his old dinners ' and the maids were resting in the front kitchen. I promptly recommended the window from which Con and I used to watch the guilty entrances of Mr. Payton ; and she agreed, since I was obviously an expert in this field.

And one October evening, Oxford not four days away, when the moon was just bestirring itself on its couch below the sky, I loitered on the pavements near her garden wall, watching the high window that had once been Con's. Should it come alight, and its holland blind travel half-way up, this would be Gentle's message, ' I am coming, my sweet ; ' should the blind go the whole way up, it would be her invitation, ' Come ; all is clear.' My heart, enlarged and agitated, beat on its confining doors as I waited ; and not once nor twice but twenty times my lips varied the lyrical summons of Tennyson's hero, whose hunger and love, 1 will swear, were no more than mine, ' Come to your window, Gentle ; I am here at the gate alone. . . . Come, oh, come . . . come quickly.'

Look, the light was there, a saffron glow on the night's dull blue ; the blind was whispering up like a curtain on a play ; it had gone as far as it might so that only its lace fringe hung below the window-top ; and I could see Gentle's figure in the daring and risky light before, half-frightened, she fled from its contact and denied all part and lot with it.

I turned the handle of the garden gate and slipped like Mr. Payton of old across the grass and up to the narrow door whose red and orange panes were now a luminous pattern because of the lamp in the hall. Soon Gentle's shadow was behind it and she was opening it to me. I slipped in. She picked up my fingers without a word and ran me on tip-toe up the familiar stairs to her white bedroom, once Uncle Humphrey's brown work-room and the scene of his brown studies. So different it was now !—the same four walls, but its paper a pale old-rose (her favourite colour) and all its furniture white : white book-shelves ; white desk ; white wardrobe ; and, besides the bed, a white *chaise-longue*. Brian had made her a beautiful room because, as he liked to say, she'd ' done him a kindness by becoming, to his never-ending surprise, an almost beautiful daughter.'

She shut and locked the door. The servants were far below ; we high up here ; and we came together in a long embrace. Gentle, breaking it to inquire with arched eyebrows, ' Is it all very bold ? ' Then we lay in each other's arms on the *chaise-longue*, quite silent, save for our intermittent and slow kisses.

But wait—sounds—someone coming up the stairs ! Gentle mumbled ' Help ! ' and jumped up and stood listening. The steps came nearer, and she laid her hand on her middle and whispered, ' Be still, my stomach ' ; the steps were on the stairs below our door, and she murmured, ' God of visions, plead for me ' ; but they passed on ; it was only one of the maids visiting her room in the attics above. Gentle drooped her shoulders forward, and hung her arms as if exhausted, and sighed, ' Oh, Heaven, Heaven, have pity on me. I shall certainly die if I have to go through that again. . . . Oh, Doric, my lovely one, I aged years and years in that minute. And lost pounds.'

The maid returned to the kitchen ; the house was now quieter than ever ; and we lay back again on the *chaise-longue.* Here in my arms she began to tease me with talk of a swinish Belgian fellow who'd loved her in Brussels, till at last I implored, ' Don't, please don't ' ; because what was a game for her had become a storm of pain and jealousy for me. ' Did you let him touch you ? ' I demanded. ' You didn't let him touch you, did you ? ' and she said, ' No, it was nothing, silly. I was only teasing you ' ; and laid her consoling lips for a long time on my cheek. ' You are mine, aren't you ' ; I insisted, ' mine only ? '   And she answered in a voice hardly to be heard, and with eyes that laughed, ' Yes . . . my pet . . . yours . . . yours. . . .' Then I could only hold her in an embrace that was almost cruel, and exultingly cruel, while my lips pressed her brow, her eyelids and her hair, and my heart cried that I must die if ever I lost her.

CHAPTER II

IT WAS in my third term at Magdalen, Oxford, and the term was not ten days old, when there broke upon me, with all the suddenness and clarity that attends a revelation, the knowledge of my purpose in life. Where better could this sudden illumination have come to me than in that haunted and aspiring city ; and what was my number, I wonder, in the endless roll of young men whom she has endowed with a vision and summoned to urgent tasks of exposition, interpretation, proselytizing and prophecy.

The day was a Saturday, in the second week of the Summer term, and I was sitting in my room in the Cloisters of Magdalen. The little room was clouded and pungent with tobacco smoke because I was pulling and sucking at my encrusted pipe, as was almost compulsory in an undergraduate and especially in a first-year man. My books were all around me, including the Golden Calf Library which I had brought in its entirety two terms before to impress the other freshmen. In my hand, as I lay back in my one deep wicker chair, was a tattered green volume, a study of the *philosophes* from Diderot to Condorcet ; for the school that I was reading was History. And out of that old borrowed book the word of the Lord came to me (so I have always liked to conceive it) as to Amos the herdsman and Ezekiel the priest.

I had begun the book, the Lord knows, with little ardour, but now it was holding me in an ever-tightening grip ; so much so that my pipe went out, the smoke-cloud slipped out from the room, and all the sounds beyond my window ceased to be. I heard no more the footfalls and voices in the quads, the low liquid syllables of the pigeons on the eaves, or the jangling of cycle bells in the High. The entangled chimes in the towers clanged the quarters, or the hour itself, but not for me. My interest was now so potent that I was leaning forward over the book to read on. I was reading of that fine brotherhood of writers who in the mid-eighteenth century, opened their campaign to unseat and expel the world's current rulers, Superstition and Ignorance and Oppression, and set upon their thrones, Reason and Knowledge and Humanity and Full Liberty for the Mind. I read of their loathing for despotism and cruelty, their faith in the potential greatness of Man and their boundless hopes for his future ; and, being nineteen, I threw the whole of my loyalty at their feet, like a man casting all he has. I read how they strove with their writings, whether serious or lively, earnest or ribald, to let slip the dogs of war against Bigotry and Bondage and Credulity everywhere. Wonderful was their belief that if you loosed into the world enough knowledge and vision the old tyrannies must tumble, undersapped from below. I leapt to the idea that ignorance was but the sour unripeness of a man and that the sunlight of full knowledge would plump that green fruit till it was as full and sweet as nature wanted it to be. If I could have found words for the ardour that was plumping my heart then, they would have been, ' These are my people. This is my church.'

I read of Diderot and his Encyclopædia which was to be ' an instrument of universal education ' and ' produce a rational interlude in the long night of Man's enslavement.' I read of d'Alembert and d'Holbach, of Turgot and Condillac and Voltaire ; but with the deepest love of all I read of Condorcet. Condorcet, that spring morning, became my master ; what Christ and Francis and Ignatius de Loyola have been to many, he was to me. I read of his young fervent spirit, his splendidly keen intelligence, his warm and generous emotions, and his lifelong devotion to the human good. It jumped the tears to my eyes to read how, even when he was hiding from the shadow of the guillotine, he wrote his *Outline of the Progress of the Human Spirit*. And the tears sprang forth when I read how, hiding in the house of Madame Vernet, he told her he must quit her kindly shelter, lest he jeopardized her life, and she answered, ' *Monsieur, la Convention a le droit de mettre hors la loi ; elle n'a pas le pouvoir de mettre hors de l'humanité : vous resterez.*'

Vous resterez—yes, yes—they might drag him out, as they did, on bleeding feet to die in his prison, but—*vous resterez.*

Soon the delighted passion in my heart was so great that I could read no more. I got up and paced the little room. Next to my love for Gentle, I have known nothing like this joy in the possession of a loyalty that could claim all my devotion for ever. But what could I do to be like my heroes ; to live as far as possible the life of a Condorcet ? I had none of their gifts ; no restless creative fount like Diderot's, no surge of dazzling wit like Voltaire's, no natural nobility like Condorcet's. I had all their vision and enthusiasm, but little else except very normal abilities and a small gift of humorous invention acquired from Father. Think ; let me think ; what exactly was the faith ? It was this : bring enlightenment to Everyman, and there is no known limit to the fineness he may achieve. And what was the task ? To scatter all over the world the means of intelligence and vision ; to publish to every class of man—

To publish ! *Publish !* The word was like a bell. It had all the suddenness of a summons in the middle of the day. I would be a publisher. Somehow or other I would be a publisher. My task would be to assemble and direct about the world the liberating books which abler men had fashioned. I glanced at my Golden Calf Library and all my other volumes : one day the bookshelves of the world would hold *my* books with *my* imprint on their spines. The resolve was as final as the idea had been sudden. Round it flowed the waters of a dozen meeting streams : my love of books as ornaments ; my love of Literature, which was Father's gift ; my desire to be famous and a power, which, always strong, had been stiffened to steel by Mother's and Henrietta's dispraise and Harlen's cane ; my need to be rebelliously different from them—agnostic where they were religious, radical where they were Tory, internationalist where they were jingoist, and understanding and forgiving where they were vindictive ; my need of *some* religion, so long as it was not theirs ; and lastly, and somewhat incongruously with all these, my desire to be good and great, like Condorcet.

It did not worry me that there was nothing new in my vision and my plan ; that both had come, in the generations after the *philosophes*, to an apostolic succession of other men—men like Godwin and Shelley and Bentham, Matthew Arnold and Morris and Morley and Dent. Any vision suddenly seen and experienced and *known* seems new, just as every morning is new, though it has happened a million times before. If the figures of these others appeared in my mind at all, I fortified myself with the thought that I was ' one more come to the fight.'

Soon the vision and the desire were not only in my heart but in my feet as well ; and they drove me out of that small, immuring room—out through the cloisters and over the little Cherwell bridge to the water meadows and the Water Walks of Magdalen. Here the warm sun of early May kept splendid company with my inward glow. The lawns and the leas were a deepened green after the April rains, and where the sun fell on them they were not green but gold. Among the trees and by the lagging water a silence hung, as if the warmth had created it. The silence and the scents seemed the same thing.

Hands behind my back, in Father's style, I walked round and round the meadow beneath the aisled trees. At one point the scent of the limes swept me back over the years to the Cemetery where I'd walked with Gentle and Con ; and I saw again its urns and broken columns and limitless parade of tombs ; but I was in no mood to-day to dwell upon the vanity of human dreams. Never were day and scene in sweeter and more perfect tune with the basking thoughts within : above me the beeches and chestnuts were opening their buds ; beside my feet the ivied banks were sprinkled with daffodils and blue grape hyacinths ; before me stood all the grouped buildings of Magdalen—Chapel, Hall, Cloisters, and Bell Tower—at once the gate and the essence of Oxford, which is England's dream by the river that it is Learning maketh Man.

And as I looked, a new love of England, infinitely more poignant than any I'd known before, came upon me and joined my new love of those magnificent eighteenth-century dreamers, and of all their kind, never to be sundered from it. I looked at the gabled and crenellated walls married so peaceably to the foliage around them ; I saw the tower outvying the poplars by the bridge ; I heard the rooks speaking in the great elms of the deer park, and my love of England soared up into a longing that she, my very dear country, should lead the world, not in military conquest and acquisition, but in enlightenment and fine and bountiful giving. And I felt a buoyant and glorying confidence, far more certain than the irrational glories which used to exalt me in the fields around my school, that these two loves, now allied together, would fill me as well as any religion with power to strive and toil in the task I had chosen.

§

Ever since I'd come up to Oxford Father had taken to visiting me two or three times a term on a Sunday. Lonely in his handsome Pall Mall suite, and bored with Sunday in London, just as he'd been lonely in his hospital bedroom and bored with the Sacred Heart, he would wander out of London and down to my city of Oxford, as he'd wandered out of his hospital room and into that of the four-year-old Terence next door. Sometimes, I must confess, the note announcing his arrival would sink my heart because I'd wanted to spend the day with a friend, or a book ; but of course I hid my disappointment from him and acted a joyful welcome on the station platform. And here on this Saturday, though I'd been up but a week, was his note saying that he'd arrive to-morrow because he ' wanted to see Oxford in the spring, and some wild flowers, and smell a cow-pat or two.' But this time I was glad of his coming, for I was filled with the warm wine of my new inspiration and eager that he should drink of it too.

I hurried to the station to meet him, at noon next day, and saw him step out of a compartment fifty yards from me. But instead of seeking my head above the others on the platform and waving to it with the malacca cane, he turned towards the carriage and offered his hand to the gloved hand of a lady. And the lady jumped in a child's fashion to the platform. She was wearing a large straw hat, a blue summer dress with a bell-flounced skirt, and her brass-brown and braided hair rolled in a chignon at the nape. It was—I ran up to make sure—yes, it was Gentle.

She announced the fact in case there was doubt. ' Here's Gentle,' she said.

And Father without a smile introduced us. ' Doric . . . Miss Greaves.'

' Well ! . . . ' I exclaimed, in delighted astonishment.

Her eyes danced. ' I absolutely insisted on his bringing me too. Of course ! You know how I've always wanted to see Oxford. I made Henrietta's life a misery and Brian's too, until they said I could come. There was much unpleasantness in the home until I got my way. They seem to think I'm still a kid, and Oxford a most dangerous and corrupting place.'

' No, no,' Father amended. ' The facts are simpler than that, Doric. It is just that your excellent auntie approves of neither you nor me.'

' Which is absurd,' declared Gentle with a pout. ' He's been absolutely sweet to me all the way, Doric : putting me into cabs, buying me newspapers, and dusting the seats for me. I've simply loved being treated like that.'

' Merely the tribute of an old man to beauty,' said Father.

' I don't believe it. I believe he'd have been just as sweet to me if I'd been old and ugly.'

' I know he would,' I agreed.

' But not with such ease,' said Father. ' Certainly not with such ease and naturalness. The one was a pleasure, the other would have been a duty. Thus are we made. I take it, Doric, that you've observed, in the midst of your studies, that your little playmate has turned into something very beautiful.'

' Yes, I'd noticed something of the sort happening, Father.'

' You're both being very silly,' she protested, much pleased.

' We shall be losing her soon, I fear.' Father shook his head sadly, as we walked towards the ticket collector. ' The young sawneys will be lining up for her with their silly mouths agape.'

The words were like a sword-thrust, and their pain for a second put out the sun. It was a double pain : among those rivals would there be one stronger than I ; and wasn't there a danger in Father's inability to conceive of Gentle and me as lovers ?

' What do we show her first ? ' he went on, unaware of the hurt. ' Your college, I think. Yes, she must certainly see Doric's college. Come along, Beautiful.'

I was exhilarated to show my college to her, and her to my college, because I'd boasted to my fellow undergraduates about a beautiful lover at home and looked forward to telling them to-morrow, ' Yes, that was she,' and watching them whistle with admiration.

' Oh yes, yes ; come along,' cried Gentle, her hand in Father's arm.

I put them into a cab, dusted the seat for her since that was what she liked, got in opposite them, and waited, watching her face and signalling to Father not to speak, till the High Street with all its glories should burst upon her. We bowled over Carfax, and there was the High : gables and tower of Brasenose, spire and Italian porch of St. Mary's, pediments and cupola of Queen's, and, down by the river the bell tower of Magdalen ; and all of them standing chequered and mottled in the daffodil sunlight of a May noon. She gripped my hand like one troubled and bewitched, and gasped, ' Oh . . . oh, Doric ! . . . '

We descended at the gate of Magdalen and from this point I had little occasion or opportunity to speak, for Father with a vast and voluble enthusiasm, and all the pride of a new proprietor, made himself into her guide and instructor. He it was who led us into Chapel and Cloisters and Hall, indicating this feature and the next with his malacca cane, telling its story or stressing its qualities, and not suffering her to miss a single object of interest or beauty. Behind this erudite and ardent conductor we passed out of the cloisters into the flowered gardens and on to the little stone bridge across the Cher, taking the very steps that I had trodden yesterday when the power of the Lord was upon me.

Gentle lingered by the bridge, not wanting to take her eyes from the charmed lawns and the shadowed grass and the grace-ful-stepping deer. Father and I walked on between the ivied brinks and under the aisled trees ; and I began to unload upon him all the splendid thoughts which so charged and packed my heart here yesterday.

He listened, smiled, nodded, and declared that he must have been very different from me at my age, because he could remem-ber telling two loving parents and his brother Humphrey that his one firm resolution was to leave the world no better than he found it. ' And I must say, Doric, that if I die to-morrow, this will be the one ambition that I have clearly achieved. But there ! I mustn't discourage you. Keep your dreams. Keep your dreams ; and I hope that when *you* come to die the world may seem just a little better . . . just a little. . . . Be a pub-lisher by all means and publish elevating books, if you believe the world is educable. I suppose one does believe it really, because if one didn't, one would have little heart for anything but to lie down and die. It may be I can help you a little. I know several publishers. There's Old Thingummy-bob, of Sands and Hume, a first-rate house. I meet him often at the Reform and have dined with him and his brother at the Garrick —*you* know, what's his name ?—Old Hammy.'

' Hammy ? '

' Yes, Hamilton Hume, of Sands and Hume, a funny old cockatoo—the elder brother of Angus Hume, the actor. Angus is one of the pillars of the Garrick. He used to be a padre in some Scotch church or other, but he was such a success in the pulpit that he discovered he could sell his gifts at a greater profit as an actor, and now the profaner he becomes, the more righteous his elder brother, Old Hammy, gets. We'll fix up a meeting with Old Hammy. He's worth seeing and studying, even if nothing comes of it—a most extraordinary old buzzard—'

The conversation was broken here by Gentle's running up with the irrelevant question, ' Anyone been saying I was nice ? '

' Certainly not,' Father answered. ' We were . discussing serious affairs. Besides, there's no more need for us to say that than to say that the sun's shining.'

For which she squeezed his arm in gratitude. ' Thank you, Uncle darling,' she said.

Having made our circuit of the Meadows, we went up the High and along the Turl to the Broad, I and Father rejoicing to use these terms of familiarity. Not that I had much chance to speak, for Father was still the guide and instructor, fervent, fluent and often wrong. Making great play with the malacca cane, he pointed out to Gentle the colleges, the streets, the famous shops, and each interesting architectural feature as it came in view.

'Teddy Hall, my dear . . . Queen's . . . All Soul's . . . and this is the Turl . . . this is Lincoln, and you should peep in at the devil over the gateway . . . Exeter . . . Jesus, chiefly made up of Welshmen : they say that if you stand here and shout " Morgan " a face looks out of every window. Just try it, my dear. You won't ? All right, then : come on into the Broad. The Turl, you know, was once a narrow opening in the city wall. I take it you were well aware of that. That is something everybody knows. I'll show you a bit of the old wall in a minute. Look, there's the Sheldonian, where Doric'll take a very fine degree. There's Trinity ; and there's Balliol. Believe it or not, your Uncle Humphrey nearly went to Balliol. Perhaps it's just as well that he didn't. Now come here : do you see that little cross let into the middle of the road ? That's where Ridley and Latimer were burned just outside the city wall. That really is. Ridley and Latimer.' And being Father he stood there on the pavement, leaned on his stick and gloves, gazed at the sacred spot, and quoted most feelingly, ' " Play the man, Master Ridley. We shall this day light such a candle as, by God's grace, I trust shall never be put out." ' Tears shook his voice and he had to gulp them back before he could continue, ' What words ! . . . " Light a candle . . . Never be put out. . . ." Surely we should stand and uncover, Doric ? You don't feel so ? All right then, but when I come to be burned, may I say something as fine as that. Now let me show her the Randolph Hotel where we had lunch last time. This way— along the Corn.'

§

Over our lunch at the Mitre we debated what to do with the bright afternoon. And Father perceived, all too easily, that Gentle and I would like to go off together, unhindered by a third person who was old ; and when we avowed, with shows of indignation, that this was not so, Gentle saying, ' Oh but you came to see him ! Now I've spoiled your day, and I wish I'd never come,' he only smiled, because he could see that these were but the insincere words with which we covered our selfishness. He understood and shook his head. ' No, run away and play. Youth to youth. I will stay here and rest a little. I am a tired old man and will sit and think of the End. " Contemplate, when the sun goes down, Thy death with deep reflection. . . ." I may even sleep.'

We continued our protests, but it was no good ; Father was incapable of marring the happiness of anyone who was young.

So, glad to escape, though feeling a little guilty, we ran from the Mitre and down the High. I had but one desire ; to get Gentle out of the populous city and into a quiet place where we could kiss ; and when I suggested that we walked out into the country, and she said ' Oh yes ! ' and skipped in agreement, I knew that, like me, she wanted to be embraced more than to see the storied stones of Oxford. It was wonderful to know this.

Over Magdalen Bridge we went, and out along the Iffley Road. Four years more and it will be half a century since we walked together that day along the Iffley Road. The suburban fields were not built over then as now, and it was only a little while before we were walking between hedgerows, Gentle hanging on to me after her fashion, with both hands clasped over my arm. The banks of the hedgerows were so bright with speedwell and stitchwort, and the ditches so lively with the tossed sprays of ladysmock, that the same joy got into our veins and compelled us to lighten the empty road with some flowers of song. The sun might be high in a sky of porcelain blue, but we sang softly, ' In the twi-twi-twilight, Out in the beautiful twilight, They all go out for a walk, walk, walk . . .' and when we had done with this, we fell to chanting even more softly because of its pathos, ' Three fishers went sailing away to the west, Away to the west as the sun went down. . . .'

Between songs I dilated, with all the desperate earnestness of nineteen, on my great new plan, and she listened to the cascading words, looking up at me from her place on my arm. But from the fund of affection in her eyes I suspected, as always with Gentle, that she was less listening to the talk than loving the talker. She cried, ' Oh *yes*, Doric ! Let's do it. Yes, *yes !* ' but it was more love for me than love for the idea. Her love would always be for the individual rather than for the general. She said so in her own way. ' Oh dear,' she sighed, ' I'm afraid you're nicer than me. I only dream of wonderful things happening to me, not really of helping the world at all. I never have a Call to Service. Is it that men are different, or that I'm not really a nice type ? . . . Oh, but I shall improve. People either get nastier or nicer as they get older, and I'm sure I belong to the latter class. I mean, I was a horrid child.' And when I did not at once deny this, she pulled on my arm impatiently. ' Say I wasn't. Say I was rather sweet. Gosh, you are slow ! '

And so we went on, putting forth our plans and hopes, beneath the young May sun, and between the fields newly harrowed and seeded, or just powdered with the green of young wheat; and we, I suppose, were much the same as they.

Yonder was a stream, marked by yellow-budding willows and silver, shimmering grass; and we left the road to walk by the water. It brought us to a low, round hill with a crown of beeches on its summit and a shawl of sunlight on its shoulder. Joining hands, we climbed to the beeches, and there on the brittle brown mould and among the long lavender shadows we lay down and embraced.

And as I kissed and kissed her, contrasting this lad on the hill, so exquisitely happy, with the lonely boy who'd lain on the hills by his school, I felt of a sudden that she was wanting my lips and my body as much as I was wanting hers. Her instincts were mounting to a desire and a pleasure that I am sure were incomprehensible to her. She pressed herself upon me with an ardour that was almost frightening.

Child of my generation as I was, with a conscience puritan-trained, I knew that my pleasure was being shaken by a slight shock. I felt bewildered and confused. I wanted her ardent, but I wanted her modest too; I wanted the incompatibles; and I was relieved, but not wholly, when she broke from the embrace and, turning her face aside, said with amused, arched eyebrows, ' I'm not sure that I'm behaving quite nicely. What on earth would Henrietta say? She'd die.' Disturbed and distrustful, a jealous lover, I ran the brown mould through my fingers and then asked her if there were any others who loved her and wanted to kiss her.

' Oh well . . .' she answered, looking down and beginning to play, like me, with the rusty leaves.

That awful pain and fear which had stabbed me on the station struck deep at me again.

' Are there any? '

' Oh, yes,' she said, and was not displeased, perhaps to admit it. ' But they're just silly.'

' Silly? '

' Yes, of course. They're just silly kids. They're not clever and witty and full of thrilling ideas like you.'

' Good-looking? '

' Oh, good-looking enough, I suppose—some of them.'

' And you don't really like them at all? '

' I like them, Doric darling, but I don't love them.' And she turned to me with that small, private smile of hers which would hardly move her wide, full-lipped mouth. ' How could I love them when I love you ? '

Whereat I seized her, and she gave herself to me again, with the same warm, quickening passion.

Then we remembered Father and she asked me, between kisses, what I supposed he was doing now. ' Oh, sitting alone in the Mitre,' I suggested, ' or walking up and down the High. And oh, I've just remembered that he wanted to see some wild flowers and smell some cow-pats.' She leapt to her feet, crying, ' Don't ! I can't bear it ! He mustn't be unhappy. Let's go back at once and comfort him. He's so sweet and he came especially to see you and the wild flowers. Oh, what pigs we are ! My darling, *darling* Uncle Kingsley.'

I rose into a sitting position, leaning back upon my arms ; and immediately it seemed that a large map of England lay spread below me : the meadows a blue green, with the slow cows at pasture ; the ploughed fields brown and fawn and lit by the sun ; and woods like an anchored fleet : line upon line of them, old brown for the most part, but patched in places with the new, living green.

And I remembered my new love of England, and this led me into more and more talk of my great schemes for the improvement of England and its elevation above all countries, as, hand in hand, we ran down the hill. I had Gentle really excited about the publishing venture by the time we reached the road and were walking back between the hedgerows. It *was* a wonderful idea, she said, and she was absolutely thrilled by it ; but what was her part going to be in it. ' Isn't there something a bright girl can do ? ' She would be my partner, I said, dragging her arm against my side ; and when we'd made ourselves into the finest publishing house in England, she would have to act as hostess to some of the most famous men of the day—statesmen and travellers, scientists and philosophers and poets. Had she ever heard of John Murray's drawing room in Albemarle Street, where some of the greatest men in the world had gathered as the guests of their publisher—Byron and Canning and Scott, Livingstone, and Borrow and Darwin ? And I'd have to go to America and Australia to sell my book rights and acquire others and interview more celebrities—and of course she would come with me, always.

' Oh, Doric, Doric—my angel—do you think it'll happen ? '

I glanced down the long road before me and stated my creed. ' I believe anything can be made to happen, if you want it enough.'

' Gee, I hope it does. Oh, Doric ! '

So, with our eyes on the visionary gleams, we walked back towards Oxford, Gentle swinging into a rhythmic stride as she hung on to my arm ; and I have often remembered in later days that all the time, as we painted our dreams to each other, I was hearing in the distance the boxwood note of the cuckoo.

CHAPTER III

THAT DAY, while Gentle was with me in Oxford, our love-affair was discovered, with a tremendous and staggering shock, by Henrietta at home. Some of the details of this exposure, and of the uproar that ensued, I learned from an immediate and indignant letter of Gentle's ; the rest she told me years afterwards, when I was older and no longer ashamed to speak of my school and my disgrace there.

Henrietta, talking with a silly and gossipy housemaid, as she helped her clear away the Sunday dinner, chanced to mention that Miss Gentle was in Oxford where she would see her cousin ; and the girl, either inquisitively or mischievously, said, ' Yes, that's the one she's partial to, isn't it ? ' Henrietta, startled and standing quite still, demanded what she meant ; and the girl answered, Oh, she'd seen us together in the house and in the street, and she'd always supposed I was the young gentleman that Miss Gentle got the letters from. Letters ? *Letters ?* Yes, mum, Miss Gentle got letters sometimes, but she did hope she wasn't saying anything she oughtn't.

Telling herself it was her duty as a mother, Henrietta went straight up to Gentle's white bedchamber, and there in an un-tidy drawer, under her huddled and disarranged clothes, found a mob of my letters, some with envelopes, some without. They were the letters I'd written to her when she was in Brussels, or delivered at her door during the vacs, with an air of indifference or induced a friend to deliver in the same place, and with a like air, in term time. They were packed with love and tomfoolery and illustrated on every page with tiny, spidery sketches. Some of their foolery was good enough, I think ; much of it was heavy and laboured ; but the sketches, I will maintain, were excellent. Caricatures and comic cartoons were something I could do really well. But the comedy in pictures or letterpress had no time to impinge upon Henrietta ; it was drowned in her horror ; and whatever may happen when other things drown, this poor casualty never once came up to breathe. That Henrietta endured a deep distress, an increasing despair, up in that room which had once been Uncle Humphrey's, I cannot doubt ; for she'd always convinced herself that her own daughter was nicer, nobler, and more innocent than the ordinary breed of daughters, and she would speak of her to Mother as 'an unspoiled English girl'—the inference being that the girls of all other nations were somewhat dilapidated.

When Gentle returned that Sunday evening, delivered at her door with the utmost courtesy by Father, she was at once haled up to the old playroom, which was now Brian's study ; and may I again remind you that it was this very room in which I sit and write these words.

On that day, forty-six years ago, as Gentle entered by yonder door, it must have looked rather like a Charge Room at a police station, for Brian seated at his writing desk, might well have been the station sergeant, and Henrietta, padding unhappily up and down, the tall policeman who'd just brought in the prisoner. There were some differences, however, from the usual ceremonies in a Charge Room. Gentle did not stand apprehensively before the desk but padded up and down like her mother, only on the opposite side of the room and in the opposite direction, she marching to the window as Henrietta marched to the wall, and *vice versa* after the about-turn. Nor did she speak ingratiatingly, or even respectfully, to the police, but spat bitterness and flashed fury. In the words of her letter to me, she was 'absolutely livid '; and I've no doubt that her inner microscope was magnifying her wrongs at its highest power. Nor did she receive a ' caution ' and avoid incriminating admissions ; on the contrary she wilfully, defiantly, and joyfully affirmed that she was not only guilty of the charge, but far more guilty than they knew.

How long had it been going on, Brian asked.

' Three years,' said Gentle, ' and we're more or less engaged.'

Henrietta shrieked. She would never, never consent, she said, shuttling up and down ; I was not a nice boy ; I had been expelled from my school ; I stole money——

' Only once in his life, and when he was hungry,' interrupted Gentle, shuttling in the opposite direction, ' and they were absolutely brutal to him, *I* shall always think. And anyhow he's different now. He has the most wonderful ideas about his future in life.'

' I shall be very surprised if that boy does anything with his life,' snorted Henrietta, swinging round by the window. ' He did nothing but loaf and be lazy at school. He was idle and good for nothing.   And so, unless I'm much mistaken, he always will be.'

' Well, anyhow,' said Gentle, swinging round by the wall, ' he's above opening people's drawers and reading their letters.'

This, said Henrietta, stamping her foot, was her duty as a mother. ' You don't understand. You're just a young, innocent girl. He's not a nice boy. He's a very dangerous boy. Your auntie Una says he's rude and ungrateful and sometimes violent. And completely irreligious—almost blasphemous, sometimes, in the things he says.   I don't like to have to say it to you but he takes altogether too much after his father.'

' Uncle Kingsley's utterly and absolutely adorable.   I love him.   He's a pet.   An absolute pet.   He's divine.'

' You're only a slip of a girl, completely innocent—what can you know of things?   He's not a good man ; not at all a good man.   Oh, dear ! . . . dear ! . . . Sometimes, if you *must* know, I can't help wondering whether Doric isn't a little mad. Why, do you know what he said to me once, when I rebuked him for being rude to dear Una ?   I've never forgotten it.   He turned on me with a deathly white face and said, " My dear auntie, I regard your comments as in equal parts intense and inane."   Those were his exact words :   " intense and inane "— I'm sure of it.   Well, the boy must be mad.   No boy who's sane'd talk to his auntie like that.'

' Intolerably rude,' agreed Brian ; but did not his tone faintly and unconsciously suggest that there was a difference between saying a thing was rude and saying it was untrue ?

' A most dangerous boy.   Oh, what are we to do, Brian ?   I felt all along that it was wrong to let her go with Kingsley.   I *said* so.'

Brian pointed out that the visit to Oxford was hardly the point at issue ; whatever had happened, had happened long before that.   But Henrietta, not wanting to be disarmed by Reason, that cold quality which damped down the heart and fire of every drama, took evasive action and diverged into tears.   Dabbing her eyes and her long nose, she proclaimed loudly, ' I always hoped she'd marry a good man and have little children.'

Gentle represented that it was equally possible to have little children by a bad man.

' Tut, tut,' muttered Brian, upset by the tears and by this dangerous approach to indecency ; and his fingers said the same two syllables on his desk.

Had Gentle and I been left alone in Oxford, Henrietta inquired through the tears ; and Gentle said, Oh yes, we'd walked miles and miles and miles together into the country, and it was all absolutely lovely.

' Did '—Henrietta could hardly bring herself to ask it—' did you let him kiss you ? '

' Why, of course,' said Gentle, with eyebrows lifted in aston-ishment at the question. ' Hundreds and hundreds of times, and I loved every minute of it. We kissed on top of a hill, and most of the way home. I like kissing. I like it a lot.'

' Oh . . .' Henrietta turned to Brian. ' Oh, won't you forbid her even to see him alone again ? That's the only thing to do. She must never, never see him alone.'

Brian, disliking the hysteria, urged her not to make too heavy weather of it. ' It's just a silly boy-and-girl affair. Too stupid. Gentle can't marry anyone for years yet without my consent, and I certainly shan't consent to her marrying Doric. I agree with you that he's completely undesirable. And anyway it'll probably be ten years before he's in a position to marry anyone— if he ever is. I can't see *that* boy ever making much of his life. This will pass. And in the meantime, Gentle, there's to be no nonsensical talk about being engaged. Just you remember that, if necessary, I can remove you right out of his neighbourhood ; and I will. Now let that be the end. All this will pass.'

' It will not pass,' said Gentle at the door, grandly, and determined to toss down the last word.

As I write I look at the door through which she went.

§

' After this unholy row,' her letter concluded, ' Henrietta took me aside and talked to me earnestly and intensely and kindly ; and this was worse than when she went on at me. It was impossible to lose my temper when she was trying to be sweet, so I could only be impatient inside ; altogether a head-achy and frustrating business because I rather enjoy losing my temper ; in fact, I love it. I must stop here because it's horribly late, and I want to get the whole appalling affair off to you. Bye for now, my blessing, my sweet. Your always adoring and adorable Gentle.'

§

I read Gentle's letter in the porter's lodge at Magdalen. At first I smarted with wrath and bruises, but then there came back to me the grim, unspoken, iron-lipped resolve that had kept me working well ever since I came up to Oxford. They should see ; they should learn ; something was coming to them that would confound and stupefy them. The pressure that had driven me was superheated now, the heat raised by the combustion of many elements—my great new ambition with all its motives, selfish and unselfish; my firm desire to gratify my father who'd believed in me; and, best fuel of all, this hidden determination to rout Mother, Henrietta, Brian and Harlen. I thrust Gentle's letter into my breast pocket and stepped out into the High.

> Into the street the piper stepped
> Smiling first a little smile.

But never any more—never to anyone—not even to Gentle —did I speak of the road I was treading or of the city of shining towers I saw before me.

I read for my Schools as few could have been reading in the twenty colleges around me; and if I was lonely in my rooms I was happy and whole, because I was doing every minute of the day what I wanted to do. I see myself in those years at Oxford as a tall, shy, retiring figure; not unpopular because I could make a joke with the best, and because, having retired into my cloister with a dream, I was quite unaggressive; but certainly not popular. I was so shy that, though in company I assumed an air of ease and merriment, I was always aware of a wish to escape into the night, and of relief when at last I was alone; and even then I would walk homeward across the quads or along the cloisters, rehearsing all that I had said, lest haply it had made me, not liked, but laughed at—not admired but despised. And if I remembered a statement that was silly or boastful, my teeth chattered as I walked. The craving for approbation caused many a boast to slip my tight control, so that I very often suffered this sick and exaggerated shame. I made no mark as an athlete or as a figure in the clubs or the Union. My chequered school career had given me no opportunities of becoming good at cricket or football; and only an increasingly powerful game of tennis saved me from being called a bounder by the Rugger and the Rowing Push; and only a few unkind but best-selling *bons-mots* ensured that I was not wholly ignored by the wits. My recreation was always to walk alone in the wet meadows, or among the shadows and sunlight by the river, or up to the tall, attenuated beeches beneath whose high canopy Gentle and I had lain on the leaves and mast. I would gaze at the brown leaves which had been our bed.

Never in my life have I been an easy mixer with other men; never since Draycote; and I was even less easy at Oxford than I have become since. Not only did my unspoken ambition wrap me in something like a Trappist's robe; there was also a

fear that walked with me along the medieval streets, past the
groups of men gossiping in grey Gothic entries, and into lecture
rooms, or into the J.C.R. when the freshmen came. It was the
fear of seeing a boy from Draycote School. There had been
little difficulty in getting me into Magdalen. Father, knowing
one of the Fellows, had told him the truth about Draycote ; and
Magdalen, a large college, had been willing to accept me, as it
had accepted other lads who'd left their schools under a cloud,
offering them their second chance. Father would have been
perfectly ready to lie about me, but had decided, after thought,
that the truth was less risky. Fortunately no one at Magdalen
had ever heard of Draycote. Why, most of the men had hardly
heard of Haileybury, Cheltenham, Wellington and Uppingham.
There was no reason why they should, since they came from
Eton, Winchester, Harrow and such, or had been ' privately
educated '—like myself. And fortunately Draycote was a
cheap school that sent few boys to the universities ; in all my
time at Oxford I heard of only two who were there : one at
Keble, miles away, and the other at Univ. across the road.
Once I saw a man looking after me, as I cycled up the High
with my gown round my neck like a muffler ; and I wondered
if he was the man from Univ. But nothing happened ; my
enemies in the outer world did not find me ; the mine that I
had feared beneath my feet was not there to explode.
     And grimly, secretly, I read on.

§

     In the Long Vac, Father, pleased to think he had influence
and could help me, took me to see Mr. Hamilton Hume, ' Old
Hammy,' the publisher. Together we walked up Gower Street
to the famous house which for nearly a hundred years had been
the home of Sands and Hume. As I drew near it, my eyes
sought the graceful door with its fluted pilasters and semi-
circular fanlight, and on the steps and space before it. What
famous men had trodden those steps and stood before that door !
Painted on the wall beside the door you could still see the single
name ' Mr. Sands,' as if there had been but one Mr. Sands of
any importance in London. On the door itself a neat brass
plate announced ' Sands and Hume, Ltd., Publishers.'
     As Father and I stood before the threshold, where the great
men had stood, I looked up at the three tall windows of the first-
floor room and said, ' That's the famous room, I suppose,' for,
like Mr. Murray's drawing-room in Albemarle Street, the front

room of old Daniel Sands, and of Sands and Hume after him, had entertained many of the greatest persons of the century just dead.

The door was opened by a thin, spectacled, elderly woman, and Father asked her, ' Mr. Hamilton Hume ? ' in the way one does, though knowing quite well that this is the right door and that the householder is within.

' Yes,' said the woman ; but was otherwise unhelpful.

' He is expecting me.   General Allan Mourne.'

The name made no impression on the woman.   ' I'm afraid he's engaged at the moment.   Yes.'

' He said three o'clock,' Father submitted.   ' It's just three, I think.   General Allan Mourne.'

' I am afraid he's engaged with an American gentleman for the present, and will be some time.   Yes.   But will you step this way ? '

Father followed her in silence, and I knew that he didn't quite like the idea that his host was too busy to see him at once ; it decided too easily who conferred the honour, Mr. Hamilton Hume by receiving General Allan Mourne, or General Allan Mourne by calling on Mr. Hamilton Hume.

The woman led us along the narrow, dark passage to a small square waiting-room that appeared to have been built on to the back of the house.   It was sparely and sparsely furnished with half a dozen leather-seated chairs and a small square table.

' Take a seat, will you ; and I'll tell Mr. Hume you're here.'

Father bowed, but did not take a seat.   He stood very erect and very still, holding his top hat, gloves and cane against his breast.   The posture affirmed to all that he wasn't accustomed to being asked to wait in a kennel at the back ; and it added as a corollary that, so far from sitting himself, he wouldn't even seat his hat or his gloves on the table.

I, young, shy, and humble, was not above looking at the pictures which hung all round the walls.   All except one were portraits of the famous persons who had published with the firm, and many of the more recent ones were autographed under some flattering tribute to Hamilton Hume.   But it was the odd picture that interested me most : a coloured drawing of Old Fleet Street with men in tight nankeen trousers, high cravats and tall beaver hats, and women in poke bonnets and long, embroidered shawls, passing a double-breasted shop-front whose fascia proclaimed it the shop of ' Daniel Sands, Bookseller and Stationer.'

' Look at this,' I said.   ' The old original shop.'

But Father would no more look at a picture in the kennel than he would sit on one of its chairs.   He stood where the woman had placed him, his toe beating the floor, his lips bolted together, his spiked eyebrows coming towards each other and retreating, like two wire-haired terriers in the preliminaries to a fight.   He consented at length to lay his hat, cane, and gloves on the table, on top of Mr. Hume's Spring List and School Catalogue ; and now his hands were behind his back, resting one over the other on his rump, and the upper one wagging to and fro like an impatient tail.   Behind the tight lips couched a tigerish silence.

He caught my amused eyes, and demanded, drumming his boot again, ' What does he think we are ?   The men about the gas ?   The window cleaner and his mate ? '

I grinned. ' I say, Father, you won't insult him, will you ? No, please don't.'

' For your sake I will not. . . .   At least I hope not. . . . But, two minutes more, and I am going.   Two minutes at the outside.   The airs these fellows give themselves !   May they be damned.'

He walked a step or two, this way and that and back again, but still declined to be diverted by the pictures on the walls or the lists on the table.   He pulled out his gold watch and consulted it.

' *Santa carissima !* . . . *Nom d'un nom d'nom !*   In the name of the devil, what does he think I am ?   A commercial gent with a bag of samples ? '

' Well, that's just about what you are at the moment, isn't it,' I suggested.

' I ?   Me ?   How so ?   Fiddlesticks ! '

' Haven't you come to try and sell him a rather dubious commodity ? '

' Nothing of the sort.   I've come to offer him someone who'll be an ornament to his business.   *I* shan't be the beneficiary ; *he* will.   And if something doesn't happen in two more minutes, I shall just withdraw the offer.'

But the next two minutes were as empty as the two which had gone before ; and I could feel that his figure beside me was filling like a balloon with gas, and filling so fast that it couldn't much longer be held to the ground ; soon it would blow through the door and out into the air, as if a wind had caught it.   More-over, I thought, the gas was not the new helium, but the older-fashioned hydrogen and dangerously inflammable.

' God,' he breathed, and it was like a tiny jet of the gas escap-ing, ' there's been nothing like it since the Earl of Chesterfield kept Dr. Johnson waiting at his door.   The pompous fool thought he was God Almighty and Sam Johnson a beggarly scribbler : and now he's chiefly famous for having kept Dr. Johnson waiting. I haven't the least doubt that Old Hammy's sole claim to fame will be that he once kept the young Mr. Doric Allan Mourne kicking his heels in an outhouse.'

'I wish I thought so too.'

'It is beyond question. I haven't the least doubt about it.'

At that moment a table bell was struck in a room above and gave forth a single ting.

'Come, Doric,' said Father. 'He has rung for the boot-boy.' And he picked up hat, cane, and gloves that no one might suppose he had ever laid them down.

Steps, and there came upon us an exceedingly well-dressed young man in a wide-winged collar and a white waistcoat-slip, his manners as polite and crisp as his attire. 'The Chief is ready to see you, sir.'

For a second I was alarmed lest that 'ready to see you' should act as a match to the gas, but either for my sake, or because the 'sir' had screened the flame, Father only bowed stiffly, and there was no explosion.

We followed the young man up the narrow stairs and into the famous front room. And because of the room's great interest my mind, like a camera, caught its details before focusing on its one occupant, Old Hammy himself. It was a long room, and one wall was entirely filled by a book-case almost as large as old Daniel Sands's shop-front in Fleet Street. On a narrower wall hung a life-sized picture of the same Daniel Sands large enough to hang in the vestibule of the National Gallery ; it showed him in nankeen trousers, brown frock coat and high Regency cravat, as if he'd come upstairs from the little picture in the waiting-room, swelling to life-size as he came. Obliquely on the deep red carpet stood a magnificent writing desk with cornice and carved bracket feet ; and before it, and beneath the three tall windows, stood a handsome family of Chippendale chairs with riband backs and cabriole legs.

'General Allan Mourne, sir,' announced the polite young man, and retired.

Old Hammy had risen from his chair behind the desk. 'Ah, General ! Sorry to keep you waiting, but an American Professor arrived who's doing an enormous book on the last days of John Clare and he wanted all the information we could give him. I've placed him upstairs with a file of autograph letters and a pile of relevant volumes. And this is the young man you were speaking of, is it ? Bless me, he's almost as tall as you are, General.'

Mr. Hume himself was as tall as Father, and perhaps five years younger, but he might well have belonged to a generation twenty years older ; for he wore grey side-whiskers so soft and thin that they seemed never to have known the razor ; an open Gladstone collar to give play to his full chaps and large dewlap ; silver framed spectacles with the smallest oval lenses I had ever seen ; and a loose black frock coat, and grey trousers as thick and roomy as a shepherd's on Sunday.

' Sit down, General, sit down. And sit you down, young sir.'

Father consented to sit down in this place and even to ask pleasantly, ' This is the famous front room, is it ? '

' Yes, sir, this is it. These walls have seen Leigh Hunt, Lamb, Wordsworth, Coleridge, and dozens like them. Cobden probably sat in that very chair. Look at that old fireplace. The story goes that Tom Hood flung the manuscript of his *Tylney Hall* into the fire there with a splendidly tragic gesture because old Daniel Sands didn't care for it. It was published by someone else, however, because Tom had a spare copy at home. A cigar ? You'll find these very good, I'm told.' He offered the box to Father, but not to me, a boy. ' I neither smoke nor drink myself. This is my one vice.' And he pulled a snuff-box from a vest pocket and gave each nostril a pinch : the wide nostrils were brown with the stuff. His action seemed to match perfectly with the old-fashioned whiskers and frock coat. Back with a snap went the snuff-box into the vest pocket, and he asked, ' Well, my dear General, what can I do for you ? '

Again I saw that Father didn't much like this way of phrasing it: it made him no more than a suppliant, and it showed that his eloquent description of my aims and hopes had been largely forgotten. ' I think I told you that he had a strong desire to become a publisher when he comes down from Oxford.'

' Has he now ? A publisher ? Just that ? ' Old Hammy looked at me as at an amusing child ; as though Father had said I wanted to be a prime minister or a field marshal. ' And does he realize that, as far as I can see, every third young man at the university has the same idea ? Good lord, not a day passes but we hear of some young man who wants to be a publisher. He likes books, you see, and so decides to be a publisher. And when he says " publisher," bless your heart, he means that he wants to start right away at the top, because, after all, there can't be much to learn in the simple business of publishing. It's just a day in an office, perhaps. Well, let me tell you, my dear General, that it's nothing of the kind—nothing of the sort. Publishing is just about the most exacting mistress you can find in a month's search. And I'm not at all sure that a career at

Oxford is any help to a young would-be publisher. I'm inclined to suspect it's more of a hindrance than a help. It's apt to give him ideas.'

'And are they not useful in publishing?' asked Father.

Old Hammy waved this aside with a big, fat hand. 'I meant ideas as to his value and usefulness. He thinks that his only right place is at the top of the ladder, and there's no need for him to climb it rung by rung. And the plain fact is, General, that it's a good three years before a young man's much use in a publishing house. Before that we have to teach him everything, and, to put it bluntly, he's more nuisance than he's worth.'

'I see.' Father nodded twice as he said it, and closed his lips tight over his cigar ; and it was plain to me that he didn't see at all. He was finding it very difficult to see that the daily labours for three years of a well-educated and eager young man could take more from a firm than they brought to it. 'I see.'

Having temporarily clapped this extinguisher on to Father, Old Hammy turned to me. 'Now let's consider your case, my dear boy. You have been well-educated. Your school was——'

'He was privately educated,' Father interposed, coming instantly to life, and lying efficiently. 'He went to a prep. school at Kensington—an excellent school—and after that he was privately educated. His mother's desire was that he should go to Winchester or Charterhouse—Charterhouse, wasn't it, Doric ? —but I was always anxious that he should do well at Oxford, and I'd heard of a most excellent tutor in Kensington, and it's always seemed to me that a lad's going to make far greater progress if he has individual attention from a tutor than if he's just one of a crowd of unruly boys. I've none of this conventional belief in the rough-and-tumble of a great school. They claim that he makes many friends there, but no boy ever kept touch with a school friend after a year. And if he's going to Oxford, he can make his friends there. So I concentrated on Oxford.'

Now, my honour was no tenderer than that of most other youths of nineteen, but it couldn't support this ; and the reason, I sincerely hold, was that the vision which I had seen by the water meadows had an aura of sacredness such as my father could not perceive, and I didn't want to walk towards it over a bridge falsely built. So I began, 'There was that school, Father——'

'Certainly there was,' he agreed before my untimely honesty could do any damage. 'Most certainly there was. And it was the utter failure of that school which convinced me I was right. Yes, I took him away after a term or two—five terms, was it ?

All right : five terms—because he was learning nothing there. Absolutely nothing. Just as I was saying ! And I wanted him to do well at Oxford—as he *is* doing—*very* well, I'm told. Your tutors, Doric——'

' Yes, yes.' Old Hammy, accustomed to do the talking in this room, and in his present chair, drove in between us. ' Yes, yes. I've not the least doubt he's intelligent, but, if you'll forgive me, my dear General, so are very many young men. It's only the few who are fools. I've no doubt, my dear boy, that you know all about Plato and Virgil, but what—and this is the point !—what do you know about packing, paper-making, printing, type-setting, block-making, moulds, stereos, book-binding, book-travelling, book-selling—eh ? '

Father, very stiff and straight, his lips pressed up, was clearly thinking that his son knew nothing of such tradesman-like activities, but he suppressed the thought for my sake.

' To be a good publisher,' continued Old Hammy, ' you need immense technical knowledge and business ability. What do you know, for instance, of the Continental book market or translation rights ? What do you know of the Law of Copy-right and the Law of Libel ? What do you know of Typography ? Of format ? Of type faces ? '

' Of what ? ' inquired Father, from the side of his cigar.

' Type faces, my dear sir.'

' Oh, I see,' said Father ; and didn't see ; but wasn't going to admit it.

' Yes, type faces, my dear boy. Have you ever heard of Baskerville, Bodoni, Fournier, Bembo, Garamond ? '

Father, keeping silence, frowned, as one who was being bombarded by shrapnel but declined to bow his head beneath the bullets ; and I said, ' I quite realize that I shall have everything to learn, sir,' not because I was really modest, but because I thought an assumption of modesty would be the best line with this bewhiskered old bashaw. ' Still, I imagine that—— '

' " Everything to learn " is right, my dear boy.' Old Hammy wasn't interested in my imaginings. He wanted to maintain his barrage : let him discuss a topic on which he considered himself a specialist, and his method was a non-stop drumfire that spread death upon all interruptions. The barrage, and the my-dear-boys that punctuated it, gave me his character as he talked : a strong brew of absolutism, self-esteem, and over-bearance sweetened by a good teaspoonful of benevolence. ' My father, just like yours, wanted to get me a job with Daniel Sands the Second, and I began in the packing-room at five shillings a week. I went on to the trade counter where the booksellers' collectors kept me at it for nine hours a day ; then to our old Sales Department at Blackfriars, where I was no more than a looker-out of titles ; then from one department to another, Production, Editorial, Foreign Rights, Illustration and Design, Counting House '—Father blinked at this further fall of shrapnel—' and in each place I learned to know that I knew nothing.   Then I went on the road, travelling London first, and after that the provinces.   Why, my dear boy, even now, at sixty-two, I'm in here by nine o'clock and seldom leave before five, and then, let me tell you, my real work begins—reading manuscripts night after night, night after night, all the year round.'

The bombardment appeared to have ceased ; and Father announced its complete failure with the words, ' All the same, I may be partial, but I still think the firm will be lucky that gets young Doric.'

' I can give you a good glass of sherry,' sighed Old Hammy, almost as if he thought it easier to give a military man sherry than an insight into the difficulties of publishing.   ' Would you care for one ? '

' Thank you,' said Father.

And, without rising, our host produced from a cupboard in his big desk a decanter and glasses, both of the finest cut glass. He filled a glass for Father, and I wondered if I was going to get one.   I did ; but with a ' There you are, my boy,' uttered in the tone of a parent giving an especial treat to a child.   For his own refreshment he applied another pinch of snuff to his nostrils.   Sniff, sniff, and snap went the box.

' Now what exactly would be your aim ? ' he asked me after he'd sunk the box into his pocket.   ' To rise to the top in some good publishing house ?   But there are only one or two managerial positions, even in the greatest houses, and they don't carry large salaries because there are no large profits in publishing.   Or is it your desire to learn the trade '—Father winced at this word—' and then set up on your own ?   But that's a very dubious business ; very hazardous ; risky in the extreme.' He shook his head over it, sadly.   ' There are far too many publishers already—the competition is ruining the business— and yet I can think of a dozen new ones who've sprung up in the last twenty years.'   The temptation to load his gun with new publishers and fire them off at us was too great.   ' There's Fisher Unwin, Elkin Matthews, John Lane, Dent, Methuen, Hodder, Hutchinson, Heinemann.   Well, at this rate there's no big money to be made by anyone. . . .   No, very little money, I assure you,' he repeated, pushing back his handsome Chippendale chair.

'Most of the publishers I meet at the Reform and the Garrick seem to do themselves pretty well,' Father submitted.

Old Hammy nodded, but with lips firmly closed by a demurrer —or by several demurrers. 'You can make a living at it,' he conceded. 'But certainly no fortune.'

'But from what young Doric has told me I gather that he's not going into it for what he can get out of it so much as for what he can give.'

'Well, that's the right attitude,' Old Hammy allowed, as if this was the first thing he'd heard in my favour.

'If he makes a fair living, he'll be satisfied. That's so, isn't it, Doric ? '

'Yes, Father.'

'Anyone who thinks he's going to make a fortune at it has everything to learn,' continued Old Hammy. Like a farmer, he preferred to speak of the threats to his crops rather than of any small bounty that the seasons might bring. 'People get very wrong ideas. You may have a big seller now and again, but it has to carry a dozen doubtful sellers on its back. Because, you see, book after book that you publish either loses money for you or locks up your capital for twenty or thirty years. And unless you have several big sellers—which rarely happens— the margin of profit on the books that are selling just isn't enough to carry many such losers or slow starters. And you've no guarantee that any book isn't going to be a failure. It depends on the public mood, which can quite easily change over-night. It's a sad, sad business, sometimes. And, as far as I can see, the prospects of publishers—never very good—are steadily getting worse. Our expenses go up and up every year. What people won't give a moment's thought to is this : that the ratio of over- heads to turnover has always been infinitely higher if you're producing books than if you're producing soap or candles or shoe-buckles ; it always has been, and it's enlarging every day. So is the cost of distribution and advertising. So are author's royalties. Since the Society of Authors arrived upon the scene, and the literary agents—but I'd best not speak of *them*—the power, believe me, has passed from the publisher to the author. Authors can simply ask what they want now.'

'Indeed ! ' said Father, as one who would say ' Shocking ! '

'Yes.' Old Hammy appreciated the sympathy. ' To-day it's the author who gets the advantage from any substantial success his book may have. But nowadays it's few books that make any money for anyone. The free libraries have seen to that. They've discouraged everybody from buying books, and it's more than probable that half the books they circulate have never been paid for at all. They're merely discarded review copies bought cheap. Yes, as someone has well said, " Anybody can write a book ; it's easy ; it requires only pen, ink, and paper. But it needs genius to sell one. . . ." Very true. . . . Believe me, very true.'

' It's wonderful you can even make a living,' said Father, and sipped the admirable sherry.

Old Hammy nodded and shrugged. ' Oh, one makes a living,' he admitted again. ' I wouldn't like to suggest that one can't make a living at it. I wouldn't for the world wish to discourage your boy—entirely.'

This was really the whole of the interview, and when we'd finished the sherry we went somewhat chastened and subdued —Father first and I following—down the melancholy stairs and out of the house.

When we were out in Gower Street Father remained silent for a considerable stretch of that long, quiet road ; and I who could so often read his feelings knew that he was worried lest Old Hammy had damaged my dream and disheartened me. And at last he asked, turning to me with a half-twinkle in his eye, ' Are you going on with this job ? '

' Yes,' I said.

' What ? Even with the workhouse looming over you ? '

' Even so. One day you'll see me sitting in a room just like that. I'm absolutely confident of it. You'll see.'

' Then you didn't swallow all the old Brahmin said ? I noticed you weren't speaking much.'

' The opportunities for my speaking were somewhat infrequent.' This I said in my best undergraduate manner ; and Father laughed, ' How true ' ; but it wasn't the whole truth, or even the larger part of it. The larger part of it was that my tongue had been weighted down by my shyness and diffidence in the presence of a business chief. ' I was thinking a lot,' I assured Father. ' I was thinking that, even if it was all true, I was going on. I'm going on no matter how big the difficulties, or how poor my chances. You bet your life I am.'

' Of course you are. Naturally. I fully concur. Did I ever tell you this story ? I once asked an old sergeant of mine what he'd do if he and his platoon were surrounded by an enemy in fifty times his strength, and they were calling upon him to surrender ; and do you know what he instantly answered ? '

' No. What ? '

' " Why, fix bayonets and charge, sir." '

CHAPTER IV

IN THE summer term of 1902, a year after Gentle's visit to Oxford, her family moved from the old house to Holm St. Martin, in the Sussex weald. And I, pleased to feel important and a martyr, chose to believe that they'd carried her away because of me ; but it was not so—or it was so only in part. Brian's ambitions were the prime cause of that move ; not my love for Gentle.

Brian's position, income, pretensions and, correspondingly, his paunch, had waxed fat in the three profitable years of war ; and now at fifty-five he claimed the right to some relaxation from his labours—a home in the country (if possible, with oak beams), a garden, a golf club, and some fishing. In the fashion of the new century he would travel up from the country to his office five days a week.

And in Holm St. Martin he found a quaint house and was as delighted with it as he had been three years before, with No. 1, Coburg Square, and, fifty years before, with a toy farm and animals. It was an old, restored place, timber-framed, with a steep roof and tall, moulded brick chimney stacks and the date 1596 carved above its door. The Chapter Mill it was called because the old water-mill in the grounds had belonged, once upon a time, to a monastery that used to stand in the meadows across the stream. Built later than the water-mill, it stood on a slope and gazed down at the slow but sleepless Bent stream, and the still panel of the mill pond above the wheel and mill-race. This slope, once a pasture, was now a well-furnished landscape garden between the timbered front of the house and the narrow twists of the Bent. Indoors the house had all the oak beams that the most romantic city merchant could crave ; and Brian was very proud of the fact that he could crack his bald head at six different places in his big Lounge Hall.

To this pretty place they carried Gentle ; and the world might call it the Chapter Mill, but she called it Stratford-on-Avon.

' I'm afraid we're terribly well off now,' she said to me when we met for a farewell. ' It's going to be rather lovely in some ways : Brian says I can learn to ride, and have all the dogs I want, and that we shall have our own tennis court and croquet lawn, and that he's certainly going to get a dog-cart which I can drive, and may even get a motor-car, though darling Henrietta's terrified of the things. It seems to me that I'm going to be a pretty good example of the Idle and Useless Young Person, but it'll be rather fun—and, beloved, will you only listen to this : he's bought himself a grey bowler hat and a shepherd's-plaid suit, rather like a rat-catcher's, to walk about his estate in, on Saturdays, and he's growing a beard, a marvellous red and gold one, like the sun in its strength.   I got into an awful row with Mummy for calling him Jerusalem the Golden.   He *is* rather a lamb sometimes—but oh, my pet, you *will* be able to come and see us quite often, won't you ?   You *will* ?   Promise !   You see, I love you.   Oh, why can't you come, too ? '

' I'm not only coming to see you,' I averred proudly.   ' When the time comes, I'm coming to fetch you.'

To this she replied nothing, but smiled with very bright and encouraging eyes and squeezed my hand.   And so we parted at a London street corner by the old square.   A few days later I went back to my lonely Oxford room and worked harder . . . harder. . . .

The summer term slipped beneath my feet as I sat there and worked, and it seemed but a few days (as when Jacob worked for Rachel) before the Long Vac sent me home from Oxford to our flat by the Hammersmith Road.   Home again, I would wander alone to the old square and loiter on its pavements, looking at the house in its south-west corner.   They were gone, and it stood empty : sightless the window of the playroom ; sightless the windows of Gentle's white boudoir where we had lain together ; sightless the high window at the back from which she had signalled me to come to her.   Drawn towards the square whenever I was in the streets nearby, I went many times that summer and gazed first at the house and its windows and then at the trees and turf of the central garden.

And so back to Oxford for my last year ;   back with my hidden hope ;   back for a year of grim and unremitting work while other men played.   They played in their college fields, those who would have to compete with me in the History Schools ;   they punted along the Cher ;   they hunted with the Bicester ;   they read their papers to societies and clubs, spoke at the Union, and wined and dined ;   and I worked.   I worked as I shaved in the morning ;   I worked as I walked alone in the bright afternoons ;   I worked, committing dates and sentences to memory, or reading an antique history, as I strolled along the towpath to Iffley and Bagley Wood, or between streams in Mesopotamia ;   I worked in the same way as I cycled alone to Abingdon or Woodstock or Islip ;   quite alone I guided my punt into some green cavern beneath a drooping ash and, tying the painter to a bough, lay down on the cushions with my thick,

stuffed notebooks and my stark resolve. I worked at night
after Hall, clapt in my room with the door shut—worked in
my wicker chair or at my table till my eyes throbbed and
watered behind the spectacles that I must now use for close
study ; and then laid down the book, doffed the spectacles
and gazed at illustrious futures in the glowing hollows of the
fire.

And never a word of what I was doing did I say to anyone
at home ; hardly a word to my friends in Oxford ; and to no
one at all did I hint at the target upon which my sights were
set. And because of this reserve, because I was so shy and withdrawn all my time at Oxford, no one ever fancied me for a
First. By some, I believe, I was backed for a Second. But
I knew what I was at, and as June came in all her loveliness
to the pinnacled city, and the time for Schools drew near, a
huge, tumultuous hope possessed me ; and the last few days
before the final Question I gave to one tremendous but well-
controlled recapitulation. I trained for my seat in the Examination Schools more resolutely than any of the huge sweater'd
galley-slaves for their sliding-seats on the Isis.

But when the day came to go to the Schools in my subfusc
suit, white tie, and gown, I was a vehicle of dread rather than
of assurance, because the issue meant so much. My breast,
as I went to my table, held only fear and hope—and the hope
was but a poor, caged, fluttering sparrow.

Day after day, however, the papers revived my confidence
till, like the grain of mustard seed, it was a mighty plant, and
many birds of fine plumage lodged in its branches. Few were
the questions I couldn't answer with a niagara of words—and
huge, high-sounding words at that. I wrote and wrote and
wrote ; and while other candidates looked more and more
depressed, and paler and paler, and talked despair in the street,
I nursed in my bosom a great, quaking hope. It was not that
I was abler than they ; my ease and fluency were just the teem-
ing fruit of much sedulous husbandry upon a faithful and fertile
memory.

The vigil of the last day I read far into the night ; and in the
morning, at the door of the Examination Schools, I strengthened
my tired body with some gulps of whisky and hurried to my
place, wishing the papers would come before I forgot what I'd
learned last night. And when I saw the papers I knew that
I had them in my power and could beat them to the ropes and
to their knees. This last inquisition over, and only the Viva
before me in a few weeks' time, I came down the stairs of the
Examination Schools, seeing all the time Mother and Henrietta

and Brian and Harlen.   I stepped into the sunny street like the Pied Piper, smiling to myself a little smile.

Before I went down from Oxford I arranged with the porter at Magdalen to telegraph the result to me as soon as the lists were displayed in the Schools across the road.   I could know only approximately the date of their publication, and in the days after my Viva, I kept to the flat, afraid to wander from it lest I missed the telegram, and each morning I opened *The Times* with a secret terror lest the porter had failed me, and I should see the lists there.

At last a double knock drew me like a taut elastic to the door ;   Con came running and skipping, as she always did when that manner of knock announced a telegram ;   and Uncle Humphrey's beard and face peeped round the jamb of his bedroom door at the end of the long passage.

' It's all right ;   it's for me,' I said, taking the brown envelope from a heedless and cold-blooded boy.   ' I was expecting it.'

' Oh, hang ! ' said Con, disappointed, but waiting to learn more.

I broke the envelope in a sick, breathless agony.   The porter, an old hand at this task, and proud of his Latin, had sent the exact words from the lists :   ' Classis Prima T Allan Mourne Magd My Respectful Congratulations.'

A *First !*

Oh, Gentle. . . .   Oh, Father. . . .

And praise be to Mother, Henrietta, Brian, and Harlen for the power they had lodged in me.

§

I heard Con's voice :   ' What is it ?   What is it, Doric ? '

' Wait,' I said, and with the telegram in my hand walked along the straight passage of the flat to the dining-room where Mother was sitting.   Con came after me, skipping.   And the rest of Uncle Humphrey, overcome by curiosity, followed his beard and eyes round the door of his room and came towards us.

Mother sat at the dining table turning the handle of her sewing machine.   She stopped the wheel as Con and I entered and Uncle Humphrey halted in the doorway.   ' What was it ? ' she asked.

I waved the telegram on high.   ' This, you people, is the result of my Finals.'

' Oh, what—what is it ?   Quick ! ' commanded Con.

' No undue excitement, please.   Is everyone here ?   Answer

your names, please : Uncle Humphrey, Mother, Con—where's
Lettice ?—— '

' Oh, don't be silly,' interrupted Con. ' We want to know.
Quick, quick ! '

' I've got a First.'

They gaped.

' I trust you heard what I said. A First. A First in Modern
History.'

' Oh, *Doric !* ' Con, twenty-two now, had long changed from
a disapproving elder sister into one who was rather fond of, and
took some pleasure in, her tall brother. ' Doric, how *marvellous !* '

' Isn't that rather wonderful ? ' asked Mother, seeking elucida-
tion.

' It's certainly good,' I allowed modestly. ' Much better than
I dared hope.'

Uncle Humphrey said, ' It's very good indeed,' as one who
was himself a scholar and should know.

' " Good ! " What are you people talking about ? ' cried
Con. ' Mother, it's terrific. I've always heard of people with
Firsts—Mr. Brewer—you remember, the curate at St. Mark's—
was a First in Something—but I never expected to have one in
the family. Oh, I must go out and tell everyone. Who can I
write to at once—— '

' It's very fine indeed,' came from Uncle Humphrey's voice
in the doorway ; and it came a little sadly, so that I suspected
a conflict in him. Some jealousy that another member of the
family than he, and one so much younger, should attain to
academic distinction was fighting a small battle with the thought
that this was something he could brag about to friends at the
Authors' Club. ' I do congratulate you, Doric. Most sincerely.
It couldn't be better.'

' Of course it couldn't,' protested Con. ' What can be better
than a First ? Oh, who can I sit down and write to at once ?
Can't we wire to someone ? The Greaveses—surely they ought
to be told. They're the Family.'

Mother didn't quite know what her part should be now. It
was years since we'd said any words of affection to each other,
or exchanged a kiss. The days of our violent combats might be
over, but our relations were hardly more than correct. There
was always a difficult barrier between us. Therefore it must
have cost her an effort to do what she did now ; but she made
the effort. She did not fail in this moment as a mother. Rising
from behind the sewing machine, a stout woman half a head
shorter than me, she nervously drew down my face and laid a
single kiss, not without shame, on the side of my forehead.

The action was so unexpected that the tears jumped into my eyes (I was very like Father) and I at once turned and kissed her cheek. 'I am so pleased about it,' she said ; and her eyes filled too, her closed lips trembled and she wiped her eyes and blew her nose as she sank back on to her chair, because her own action, and my kiss, had rocked her sentimental heart.

Mother's eyes always swam at anything the least sentimental.

I do not remember that we ever had the courage to kiss each other again, except formally at my wedding, and lamentably as she lay dying ; but in this moment I forgave her all, and she, I think, forgave me much.

It was a strange victory over Mother, and much sweeter than anything I had foreseen.

'It's very good indeed,' said Uncle Humphrey, and retired along the passage to his room. Some time later he went out ; and I still believe that he went to tell the members of the Authors' Club.

§

Having enlightened the family, and left them exulting, I had but one idea—to go out and find Father. I ran from the flat and the street and over Addison Bridge into Kensington Road, my intention being to leap on to a Piccadilly bus ; but as I waited impatiently to cross between the traffic I looked up the long highway and saw to my astonishment, walking with his back towards me, a tall figure in a top hat and morning coat, with his gloves and cane held behind him. Father surely ? The figure turned about and walked slowly in my direction without seeing me. Yes, it was he ; it was Father walking back and forth in some doubt, and halting between two opinions. He halted at the top of Warwick Road, which he and we had once known so well when we used to escort him to his bus in the mornings.

And then, suddenly, I guessed why he stood hesitating there. For some reason he had wanted to come and see us all in the flat, but now that he was near it, his resolution had faltered. Shy of Mother and shy of Con, he was doubting—with his hands behind his back and his eyes on vacancy—whether he wouldn't abandon the enterprise and go home again. He knew that Mother and Con, because they shared their religion, were unrelenting in their judgment of him. That Con had joined Mother in her high and scornful attitude towards his behaviour was one of his larger sorrows, as I knew. ' I think I was no coward in the Crimea, Doric,' he would say glumly, ' and I was held to have deported myself with some gallantry at the Rawalpindi affair, but I confess to a slight dread of meeting those two religious women. I'm a sinner, I suppose, but I hate to feel like one. And they make me feel, I am now convinced, even worse than I am.' So there he stood this afternoon, at a place where he'd once been happy with his children, an old man of seventy, excellently accoutred in silk hat, fawn waistcoat, grey cravat, and pearl pin, with a cigar at his lips, and feeling like a boy who'd run angrily out of a room and was now shy of coming in again.

' Father, Father,' I shouted, and his face turned. ' Hi, General . . . General Allan Mourne. . . .'

He saw me, waved the malacca cane triumphantly like a climber who'd just conquered the Matterhorn, and hurried towards me. His lips called something, but I could not hear it ; his words were cast beneath the wheels of the traffic and the hooves of the horses.

At last I caught them. ' Have you heard ? Have you heard ? ' he was shouting. ' *I* have. Your result ? '

' Yes, I've just had a telegram.'

' It says the same as mine, I hope ? ' Anxiety sprang into his face. ' A First ? '

' Yes.'

' Well. . . .' And we stood on the pavement, and stared at each other smiling.

' Well . . .' he repeated. ' Think of that ! I was just coming to tell you. Thought you mightn't know yet. I was coming to the flat to tell you, saintly women or not. I set off immediately I heard, but '—and here he shrugged—' *que voulez vous*, some slight alarm overcame me at this point, I confess—still, I should have got there in the end. There are times when one must face anything. I was just about to fix bayonets and charge.'

' And *I* was just coming to tell *you*. But how on earth did you hear ? '

' That admirable man, Lacon, sent me a wire.' Lacon was the Fellow of Magdalen whom he had once known well. ' Extraordinarily decent of him. Why, I haven't seen the man for three or four years—not since I discussed with him your admission to Magdalen. I think it exceedingly kind of him. God, Doric, I bet they're glad they took you now. I told him you'd be a distinction to the college, and the fellow only smiled at the stupidity of parents—but was I right ? Allow me to ask you : was I right ? And, I say, Doric, what about that little fool, Harlen ? He's bound to know, isn't he ? He'll see it in *The*

Times to-morrow. " 'Theodore Allan Mourne " there can't be any mistake. I suppose the idiot reads *The Times*. How can we make sure, without loss of dignity, that the miserable little man sees it ? D'you remember I told him the time'd come when—that he'd live to see you taking a finer position in the world than any other of his low-grade pupils.' With his knuckle he dashed a tear from his right eye, and with the same knuckle brushed both sides of his steely yard-arm moustache, that the world of Kensington might suppose it was for this purpose his hand had gone to his face. 'D'you think the little fool's still alive ? I hope so : after all it was only six years ago, and what was he then : forty-five ? I sincerely trust that God has pre-served him. *Nom de dieu*, this is a very excellent day. What are you going to do now ? Coming to tea at my club ? I was going to the club, after I'd seen you, to brag a little, here and there—to this old gaffer and that. They ought to know. Would you care to come too ? '

' Well, no, Father ; thanks awfully. I was going somewhere else this evening.' Yes, I was going to jump on the first train for Holm St. Martin, find Gentle somehow, and tell her. ' But what about your coming into the flat for a little ? '

Father turned his eyes towards the red tops of Addismore Mansions, and away again. ' Well, perhaps not now that I've met you, my boy. . . . I wouldn't wish to disturb the Lady of the House. She's at home, is she ? '

' Yes. And Con.'

' And Con too . . . well, I don't think there's any point in my disturbing their activities just now. They're probably getting ready to go to church, or to a Polynesian missionary gathering at the vicarage. Sure you won't come with me instead ? '

' Sorry, Father, I really can't. I—I have an engagement.'

' All right. Perhaps it's as well. I'd rather be alone when I brag ; I shall do it better. I've already told Simpson, the new man who's looking after me, and he was very pleased. I shall also tell a certain lady whom I meet at dinner this evening : I always brag most horribly when left alone with a receptive woman. But look, Doric, I must do something to mark the occasion, mustn't I ? Yes, surely. I must give you—are you walking this way—? Good—I must give you some small present, and one to Con, and one to your kind mother. We can forget Uncle Humphrey, I think. Look : I'm but a poor man, but say a hundred, and you're to buy something very fine out of it for Con and your kind mother—a new dress, or a new hat, or a hymn book. Your mother's pleased, I should think. Yes, a hundred—yes, yes, no nonsense, no argument—I am but a poor man, and times are hard, but I can afford that. I don't get a First every day.'

§

A road that was little more than a cart-track ran by the side of the Bent to the grounds of the Chapter Mill. I sat on the wooden fence that ran with the road, my back to the little stream, my thoughts with Gentle in the unseen house. How was I to let her know I was here? I didn't want to enter the house, first because I wasn't liked there, and secondly because I didn't want Henrietta and Brian to think I was surprised, excited, or impressed by what I had done. I tried sending a telepathic summons to Gentle, *willing* her to come forth, but the old leafy road absorbed it as it absorbed the lenient air, and answered me nothing.

The light of early evening was over the meadows before me, and this is always a strange and lovely light, but to-day it was as I had never known it before, because it was bright with the glow in my own mind. The meadows were lit with the day's victory, and with my dreams of the things to be.

While I was wondering what to do, I heard steps in the cart-road and saw Beecher, one of the young raspberry-faced house-maids (Brian, ever since he became a country gentleman, had called his servants by their surnames) returning from Holm St. Martin to the house. She saw me on the fence and recognized me, so, obliged to act at once, I dismounted from my seat and went and asked her to tell Miss Gentle I was in the lane. The look in my eyes, a mischievous one, invited her not to tell the master and mistress, and the look in hers, nearly as mischievous, told me I could trust her.

Two minutes later Gentle came at a rush from her garden gate, waving a telegram above her head. It was more than six months since I had seen her, and I had forgotten she was so tall and beautiful with her autumn-gold hair and mocha-cream skin—or perhaps she had never been so beautiful as now when she was twenty-one, and all the health of the country was in her eyes. I know that as she came towards me this unexpected beauty stabbed me with adoration and fear : she was five weeks older than I ; it would be years before I could marry her ; how could I hope that anything so lovely and so marketable would be kept for me? I could have wished some of that beauty away from her. On any other evening, when the light of victory was not on the fields, this fear must have sunk my heart, but to-day I was able to recover from its blow, because of the high confidence that was in me. And, to increase my confidence, she flung herself into my arms, unaware of her value, like a child.

'Doric, my own. . . . Let me kiss you instantly . . . oh, I'm so happy; it's so wonderful . . . we got the telegram an hour ago, and I've been dancing ever since. Gosh, I wish I were clever like you! What I really think is that I'm incredibly clever in some things and incredibly foolish in others.'

'Telegram, exquisite thing? What do you mean? Who sent it? I sent no telegram and you've never been so lovely.'

'Con sent it. Here it is. She sent it to us all, but I pinched it.'

'Bless her. It was nice of her to be so excited, but I'm not sure I'm glad she sent it.'

'Why ever not?'

'I don't want to appear to gloat.'

'Don't be an ass. Of course gloat. Wouldn't I gloat if I'd done anything like that? Oh, I wish I was clever. I'm sure I must be somehow, in a way that doesn't show in exams.'

'So Brian and Henrietta know?'

'Most certainly they know.'

'What did they say? What did Henrietta say?'

'Henrietta? She stared.'

'Stared? Child, make your meaning clear, and don't look so beautiful. What precisely did our Henrietta do?'

'She stared at us all rather as if the earth had quaked. And while Brian was reading the telegram, she said, "I don't quite understand. Is it very good?" And Brian, who's never been so down on you as she has, said, "It's a remarkable achievement. Make no mistake about it."'

'Thank you, Brian. And what did Henrietta say then?'

'She said, "He must have his father's brains. His father was always clever and made a success of anything he turned his hand to"; and Brian nodded, and Gentle just stood around and said hardly anything, because they don't like to hear the child going on about you.'

For this I kissed her and when this interruption was over, though she was still in my arms, she began, 'And then Henrietta went all sentimental and said——' but here abruptly she stopped and murmured, 'Oh . . .' as if rebuking herself; and looked away.

'She said what?' I demanded.

'Oh, never mind. It was nothing. It was silly.'

'But I've got to know now, you most beautiful of all creatures. You've raised my curiosity.'

She kept her eyes adrift, and I gripped her arm viciously and shook her (such bullying of Gentle always delighted me) and commanded her to obey forthwith. 'Woman, will you speak? Obey me at once. What was it?'

Tossing her head as though she tossed a nuisance from her eyes, she fingered my coat's lapel and said, 'Oh, she alluded to that silly business at that dreadful school.' This was the first time that Gentle had mentioned Draycote, and my heart shrank at her words. 'As I say, she went all intense and said something about—well, you know what our darling Henrietta is: she does so love an enormous plunge into intensity—about your having wiped something off a slate.'

I could not speak of this; I said nothing; and Gentle left the subject quickly. 'My darling, I shall have to be getting back soon. They don't know I'm with you.'

'Do they still worry about me and you?'

'*No!*' Her eyes danced in front of mine. 'They think I've got over that.'

'And you haven't?'

'Of course not. What am I doing here in your arms? What am I kissing you for in this unseemly way? It's like a kitchen maid on a Sunday night in a lane.'

'You may forget me. I never seem to see you now. If you do, I shall die.'

'I shan't forget you.'

'Darling . . . darling . . . my own too beautiful love . . . wait for me . . . *please.*'

She didn't answer this, but pressed her lips on mine as if they were sealing something.

§

Father had been lunching with a Liberal Member at the Reform, and these two were now taking their coffee in the Library. It was only three days after our meeting at Addison Bridge, and Father was still making opportunities to say to his friends, 'I had a very nice piece of news the other day. My boy at Oxford got a First.' He had said it over the lunch table to the Liberal Member, and now, sitting against one wall of the long Library, he suddenly saw Old Hamilton Hume's large frame seated against the other wall, and straightway crossed over to those soft whiskers to say it to them. His opportunity came easily here because, as he sat for a minute by Old Hammy's side, the publisher inquired, 'And how's the tall son you brought to see me ? '

' Oh, he ? ' answered Father, as though I was the last person he'd been thinking of. ' I had a very nice piece of news about him the other day. He got a First at Oxford.'

' *Did* he ? Really ? ' Father, whose eyes beneath the wiry grey eyebrows were as acute as any judge's on his bench, saw that Old Hammy was wondering if he'd make a mistake in being so dubious and discouraging with me a year before ; he was considering whether I mightn't be a more profitable title for his list than he'd imagined. ' A First ? Well, that's splendid. And what's he going to do now ? '

' He's thinking of trying for a fellowship at All Souls, and I've no doubt he can easily get it,' said Father ; all of which was a ready and full-blown lie ; the handsome flower having sprung from no larger a seed than a remark of mine that it would now be possible for me to sit for a History fellowship with a view to becoming a tutor in some college which had a vacancy. But he felt safe in this luxuriant exaggeration because Old Hammy had graduated at Glasgow and presumably knew little about Oxford. ' There's little he can't do now,' he went on, putting a cigar like a pipe of peace between his lips. ' He ought to be able to make himself a fine career at Oxford.'

' And he seemed such a quiet lad ! ' said the surprised publisher.

' He's quiet,' agreed Father, pulling at the match flame through the cigar, ' but very able. Immensely able.'

' One of these dark horses ? '

' Exactly.' He nodded over the flame and tossed the match away.

' Too shy, I suppose, to display his real quality ? '

' Precisely.'

' And he's given up all idea of publishing ? '

' That I don't know. He hasn't told me. But I suspect he learnt his lesson from you that there's really nothing in it.'

' Oh, I wouldn't go as far as that,' Old Hammy objected, applying a meditative pinch of snuff to this nostril and that. ' He might make a niche for himself.'

' He'll need to make a living,' said Father. ' I am but a poor man——'

' He can make a living at publishing.'

' He can, can he ? It is really possible to be a publisher and live like a gentleman ? '

' Oh, yes.' Hammy willingly conceded that it was possible.

' With ability and luck, yes. Look here, General : if he's still interested, do let him come and see me again. I *mean* this. I might be quite ready to give him a start. My partner and I, like you, are getting a bit long in the tooth '—Father pressed his lips on the cigar ; he liked saying this sort of thing about himself, but didn't at all like hearing it from others—' and we could do with a young man in the firm who understands the ideas of the new generation and knows the coming men.'

' Oh, he knows everybody at Oxford,' said Father, largely. ' He was immensely popular with everyone there—fellows and dons and students alike ' ; and again this was an ample lie, since there could seldom have been a student at Oxford as silent and secret as I, and as shy of the great and the brilliant. ' They think the world of him up there. Yes. I feel sure of that.'

' Well, I fancy he might do quite well. He had a good appearance and manner, I remember, and that's in his favour. Quite seriously, General : send him along to me for a talk.'

Delighted with his diplomacy, and impatient to get at me, Father hurried from his host and the club, posted up St. James's Street, mounted a bus in Piccadilly, bought a ticket for Addison Bridge—but, as the bus left Kensington Gardens behind, and the red chimney stacks of Addismore Mansions loomed in the mist, he lost all courage and descended from a vehicle that was bringing him into such dangerous parts. He walked slowly back along Kensington Road till he came to a post office where he telegraphed to me an urgent invitation to dine with him that evening at the United Services Club.

And the first thing he said to me, when I walked up to him in the club was, ' I've got you into Sands and Hume's. I saw Old Henrik Ibsen and his whiskers at the Reform this afternoon—— ' and there and then he told me all the above story. ' He's ready to offer you a job, I'm sure ; but listen, Doric : I shouldn't go and see him for a day or two. We don't want to appear too eager. He needn't think we're disposed to be patronized by him. Didn't he leave us on his doorstep like old Sam Johnson ? No, let him wait. Let him wait a bit and cool down his high-cocolorum opinion of himself.'

So Father might advise, but my excitement and hopes drove me to write to Old Hammy before the next day died ; and two afternoons later I was sitting again in the famous front room at Gower Street. I was sitting in the Chippendale chair that Father had occupied (and Cobden before him) on one side of Old Hammy's vast stackyard of a desk, and Old Hammy was sitting on his own side, comforting his large nostrils with gifts of snuff, and looking, in truth, very like Ibsen, with his soft grey whiskers, full; flaccid cheek-folds, and tiny, thin-framed spectacles.

He offered me almost at once a small position in Sands and Hume's, but with the melancholy manner of a Christian apologist defending a difficult clause in the Creed. My salary at first wouldn't be more than a hundred a year—no house in England would offer a young learner more—but in any other profession I should have to serve my articles for four or five years, would I not, and probably be asked to pay a premium ; at the bar I shouldn't be earning anything for years ; in the army I shouldn't be able to keep myself—of course I might earn a little more as a schoolmaster or a don, but certainly no more as a young minister. ' You have no idea of going into the ministry, I suppose ? '

' Oh, no,' I assured him ; and forbore to give any irreligious reasons for this assurance, because, what with his whiskers and his broadcloth, he looked so like an elder or a deacon in a Scottish kirk. ' Oh, no, sir.'

' But what was that your father said about a fellowship at All Souls ? '

' About *what* ? '

' Your father said you thought of trying for a fellowship at All Souls.'

'Oh, well . . . yes . . . yes . , . yes, I did mention something like that as a possibility. . . . Yes, I did.'

' With a view to becoming a tutor ? '

' Yes. . . . a History tutor.'

He pursed up his lips, nodded three times, and decided that he must add one or two more grains of encouragement to the dish he was mixing for me. Of course my salary would rise a little as I proved myself. To four pounds a week, perhaps, or even five . . . in time. And I might be given a small financial interest in any good books I brought to the firm—a *small* interest, he quickly emphasized. I must know many able young men at the university who might be the writers of the future. What the firm wanted was someone who would be fertile in ideas for new books, and perhaps in new ideas for publicising them.

As I had no doubt, at twenty-one, that I should be fertile in ideas, I didn't hesitate to let him think that I could be of some help to him in these fields ; and we parted on the understanding that I would let him know my decision as soon as I could.

I went out from that famous doorway into Gower Street carrying a battle in my head. I turned northward in the long, empty road, to avoid the din and the distractions of New Oxford Street. Falling naturally into my father's habit of meditating with my hands behind my back, I walked very slowly, and head down, up the long half-mile of pavement towards the Euston Road.

There were really but two choices facing each other on the battlefield : the pleasant academic life among the gardens and cloisters of Oxford, and the blind adventure up the bare slopes towards the precipices and mists of publishing. And all the guns spoke in favour of the former. A tutorship, though it would bring me no wealth would offer considerably more than a stool in Sands & Hume's. I could earn £250 a year, perhaps, with rooms and keep, and I could almost certainly add to this by coaching in the vacs. Mother and Con were loud in favour of the Oxford life, Con saying, ' It'd sound so well. I'd love to be able to say, " My brother's a don at Oriel ".' Uncle Humphrey was in favour of it, too, probably for the same reason as Con's. Henrietta and Brian would surely be less hostile to me if I sat in so dignified a place as Oxford, though they would never like the idea of my marriage to Gentle. Gentle herself had always felt drawn towards Oxford and might jump with enthusiasm at the picture of herself as a don's wife ; in the field of publishing it would be five years at least before I could marry, and ten before I could give Gentle a position of any substance and distinction. In five years she would be twenty-six ; in ten, thirty-one.

Indeed there was nothing in favour of the venturesome road except my vision in the water meadows of Magdalen.

But that vision was unbeatable. Only Gentle could come near enough to shake it, and she had said, in the lane near her home, that she would wait for me. I would trust her. Like the vision—nay, even more than the vision—love, it seemed to me then, was unbeatable.

I had turned back as I walked and weighed these issues, and was now approaching the house of Sands and Hume again. As I came to it, I stopped and looked at the doorway, and up at the three tall windows of the front room, and down again at the name, ' Mr. Sands,' on the wall. And seven seconds later I came away with my decision in my breast. After all, I had carried the first line of defences in two years ; and however far my capital city might be, however many entrenchments might ring it round, I would drive on towards it. The decision sat firmly on my lips and was a joy in my feet, as I walked with a quick step home.

CHAPTER V

AFTER THE high, bracing upland comes the plain, where the light is shadowed and the air begins to press. I had not been many weeks at my table in Sands & Hume's before I knew that I was feeling and fighting a disappointment in my job.

Daily I climbed up the narrow stairs of the Gower Street house to the top back-room, which was really nothing but half a room and one window, since the original double windowed room had been partitioned into two. In this nearer half, spare and bare, I sat with Edwyn Fellowes, an assistant editor, each of us at a small writing table ; on the far side of the partition, alone in his glory, and with his knees under a very large writing table, sat Mr. Gretton, the Chief Editor ; and we three were the whole of the Editorial Department. Under the tuition of Edwyn Fellowes, whom we all knew as Wyn, I learned to be an editor. I recorded the passage of each manuscript : its arrival, its departure to an outside reader, the name of that reader, its return with his report, and the name of the partner or the Chief Reader, who was considering it now. Once a manuscript was accepted, I prepared it, page by page, for the printers, combing it, as I did so, for any words that could be construed as libellous or interpreted as obscene. I learned the terror of libel that sits all day in a publishing office and gets into bed with the publisher at night. And I learned that in our house, at any rate, the smallest hint of profanity or indecency outraged the puritanism of the Chief, Old Hammy. When the galley proofs came from the printers, I studied them in the office, forwarded them to the author and, on their return from him, read them again and sent them to Production for paging. Back from the printers came the page proofs, and after I had read these (now weary of the book) I stamped and initialled them and passed them for press. And if I was not thus ' seeing a book through the press ' I was writing letters to authors, querying such and such points, or begging the removal of imprudent words, and taking them downstairs to the Chief to sign. And all this time Father was walking about his club, telling the generals and admirals, ' My boy is now a publisher,' while I was calling myself ' a mere office hack and one of the lowest forms of life.'

Wyn Fellowes was a plump, blond, genial companion of thirty-four. He might be twelve years older than I, but this difference was completely erased by the effect that in high spirits, mischief, and clownery he was no more than eighteen.

Save for arithmetical measurement I was, if anything, the older
of the two ; and I was certainly the quieter. Wyn was a man
(or shall I say, youth ?) of no culture except the superb culture
of goodwill, kindness, and ever-ready good cheer. The son of
Old Fellowes, who had risen, during fifty-one years with the firm,
from boy-messenger to the charge of the Trade Counter, he
would declare gaily, ' I'm neither a gentleman nor educated.
I know nothing at all about books, but everything there is to
know about a book.' And this was true enough : endowed
with a memory as perfect as a machine, and with an aptitude
and love for mathematical and mechanical detail, he could
instantly detect in a manuscript any ambiguity, discrepancy,
anachronism, grammatical slip, or danger of identification
(which might mean libel) ; he knew by heart all the Clarendon
Press *Rules for Compositors and Readers* and could answer without
opening that *vade mecum* any question about vowel ligatures,
foreign plurals, customary abbreviations, capitalization, or word
division ; he had the eye of a hawk, or a satyr, for possibilities
of obscene interpretation and danced, whenever he found one,
an antic hay. In short, he was the perfect mechanical screen
through which to put a book and free it from grit, and other
dubious matter. So high was his reputation for this kind of
work that he was called into consultation on a couple of points
by Mr. Howard Collins, who was preparing at this time his
Authors' and Printers' Dictionary ; with the result that, once that
valuable work was published, Wyn kept it for the rest of his life
on his desk, and in his head, and in his heart.

I never tired of hearing, as we worked in that littered room,
Wyn's passing observations on Old Hammy and Publishing
generally ; though I could see that, in his love of paradox and
extravagant statement, he was less than fair to both. ' Yes . . '
he would say, suddenly laying down his pencil and deciding
that a time had come to talk about the Chief. ' Yes, young
Theodore Allan Mourne, he's a good and Christian old fossil,
but he wants his way. And he wants his profit. He believes
like anything in God Almighty and Jesus Christ—oh, granted,
granted—but he also believes like anything in a good bargain.
Perfectly honourable, mind you, scrupulously honourable and
pure-minded, but he'll take just as much from his authors as
the mugs will let him have.' Likely enough, at this point,
enamoured of his subject, he got up and paced the bare boards.
' Ah, yes, a cautious old devil who secures himself at every
point ; and I don't blame him. Don't think, for a moment,
that I'm blaming him. Not at all, sir. But I wish he'd realize
that Mr. Wyn Fellowes, his capable sub-editor, can read him

like a callow young writer's first manuscript. Mr. Fellowes can see exactly where page sixty doesn't quite tally with page five. Fr'instance, he makes the deuce of a song about publishing learned and uneconomic works that won't pay their cost in fifty years ; and there's no doubt the old catamaran does do so ; but it's not only from a sense of duty that he does it, but also because it draws other good writers to his imprint—so they're not really as unprofitable as he makes out. He says it's purely public spirit that makes him do it, and I daresay he believes it ; but *I* know that it's largely publicity.' Or he would leave his desk and stride the little room for a sudden discourse on publishing. ' Theodore. Are you awake ? Yes ? Well, a mighty lot of gammon and guff the old goat talks about publishing. Publishing, I can assure you—and I've been twenty years in the trade—is ninety per cent. arithmetic—ninety per cent. a matter of casting off, costing, knowing the weights of papers and how they'll bulk, and type faces and how they'll page, and so on—and this is true of any blasted book, whether it's a twenty-guinea work of high scholarship or a five-shilling juvenile. So all that's really needed is a boss to choose the books, a cove to design their lay-out, and a few arithmetical machines like me to do the rest. That being so, my young Innocence, there's no future in it for you and me, unless we can become bosses ; and we can never become bosses in this outfit because it's exclusively a family affair. So, cheer up, and don't expect anything, and be happy.'

Old Hammy's attitude to his new assistant was a mixture of benevolence and severity. The business of the day over, he would meet me on the stairs and say, ' Well, young Theo ? Settling down all right ? Good. When are you coming to see us again ? Come and have dinner on Thursday, if you can bear with a couple of old people.' In business hours, however, he seemed to delight in pointing out my errors of judgment, punctuation, or syntax ; he evidently believed that a young man was best chiselled into shape by much correction and chastening. ' I can't pass this, Mr. Allan Mourne,' he would object. ' Will you write it again, please ? One mistake is one mistake too many. Mistakes cost money.' It was the difference in the attitude of a colonel, off parade and on, towards a subaltern who chanced to be his general's son. ' Smarten up, Mr. Allan Mourne, please.' . . . ' Well, young Theo, how are you liking the regiment ? ' When my hidden sensitiveness was not hurt or my hidden vanity riled by him, I used him as a perpetual source of amusement. Much entertainment I extracted out of his attitude to authors ; it belonged to the sixties, when he began publishing.

He might say—and did say a score of times—' My relations with
my authors have always been of the happiest ; ' but his basic
feeling towards them was that they were a dangerous race and
a threat to publishing. They were a nuisance in a score of
ways—wanting an impossible share of the profit on their works,
wanting to come and talk about their books at all hours, wanting
to know how their books were selling, banding themselves into a
Society to defend their exactions and hinder and hamper their
publishers at every turn, and employing agents (but of these he
could hardly bring himself to speak) who encouraged them in
extortion and distrust and poisoned the hitherto ' happy relations.'

Never was he able to feel that authors, who were not tradesmen, had the right to draw off money from his firm in the same
ratio as printers, binders, and booksellers ; and his resentment
against them for their unreasonable claims came to a head when
he wanted to publish a translation and there were two of the
robbers to pay. Never could he quite free himself from the
notion that authors should have some other means of livelihood
and not expect to live solely on the book trade, like printers and
binders and booksellers.

These small but ever-fermenting resentments forced him to
say of all authors, though he liked and was good to many of them,
that they were vain and acquisitive and to maintain that most
of them couldn't write. It was his stable conviction that there
was hardly an author who couldn't learn much from him about
English composition, punctuation, the construction of a story,
and the inventing of titles. Affronted and inflamed if any author
tried to teach him *his* business, he was yet ready at all times to
teach his authors theirs ; and he was little patient with them if
they queried his improvements of their punctuation or prose ;
for his was plenary knowledge that excluded all taint of error.
And if they were galled and incensed by his well-meant tuition,
he lamented, when they were gone, that not even actors could
equal authors for conceit.

I was often restive in the house of Sands and Hume ; but two
causes held me to my seat there and battened down my temper.
One was my visionary city in the far-off haze ; I knew that
whatever the idiosyncracies of its Chief, and they were the froth
rather than the real brew of the man, Sands and Hume was a
fine and famous house in which to learn my craft. And the other
was just this, that I dared not fail. My First Class had not
cured me of my need for success, nor stilled my aching desire
for a wide renown. Henrietta and Brian were still there, at
Holm St. Martin ; and Harlen was still there, in the past.

§

And soon my disenchantment was shouldered aside by a far greater anxiety ; and there was room in my heart for nothing but this new dread.

I had been with Sands and Hume about eight months, and in all that time had seen nothing of Gentle.   Like men in uniform, each much the same as the last, the days had filed by—filed by in their sections of seven, week tramping after week—and all too soon this great company of them had passed.   Eight months and no sight of Gentle !   Was she out of my orbit for good ? Henrietta, I suspected in my secret and too sensitive way, had become only the more afraid of me because of that First Class ; she feared lest it should revive Gentle's interest in me, though, as she would argue, it had proved no more than that I was fairly able—not that I was a nice boy or any the less my father's son.   Neither Henrietta nor Brian encouraged me to visit Holm St. Martin, and when they met me in London they were polite, but cold.

At first I had written long, jocose letters to Gentle, all illustrated with my little spidery sketches, chapter-headings and vignettes, and received the merriest replies ; but the time came when I wrote one which she did not answer ; and then I wrote no more.   Oh, no ; she should answer me before I wrote again. And the dull, uniform weeks marched by ; a lovely April broke over London and dressed it in fresh green ; May came and dappled the green with pink and white, lilac and gold ; and at last, the gracious spring air in her blood, perhaps, and the blossoms, too, Gentle wrote.   But not a word in her gossipy letter showed that she understood the pain, the day-long heartaches, which her silence had caused me.   She did, however, say on about the fifth page that the country round Holm St. Martin was ' quite heart-breakingly beautiful just now,' and that I simply must see it ; and couldn't I get away from my old office next Saturday when Henrietta and Brian would be in town, and come down to Gentle and enjoy it all alone with her ?   It was such ages and ages and ages since we'd seen each other.   ' Oh, yes, Doric, my pet ; this isn't an invitation ; it's a command from Gentle. *Come !* '

And I went down to her that Saturday in May, but with a small grievance upon me that was like an abscess which only a quarrel could lance.   I waited at the gate of the cart-road that led to the Chapter Mill ; and she came running towards me between the hedges and the trees just as she had done that evening when I hurried to her with the tale of my success. And, as on that day, I was wounded and made greatly afraid by her beauty ; it came towards me like a thrown spear ; tall and straight, and with the sun touching her uncovered hair, she was like a young yellow tulip ; and for a moment all my resentment was displaced by a rush of love and desire, so that my heart cried out, ' Oh, Gentle, Gentle. . . .'

And of course she flung herself into my embrace and suffered my many kisses, with her head thrown back and her eyes closed. And she kissed me as fervently, and when from sheer breathlessness I had to stay my kissing, she would not end the sweet contact but left her large mouth lingering on mine.

' Come,' she said at last, picking up my fingers. ' Come and let's walk and be terribly happy.'

This, and that deep fund of love in her eyes whenever I caught her gazing up at me made me very happy for a little in the sun, as we walked off along the country roads, she hanging as usual on my arm with both her hands and sometimes leaning her head against my shoulder.

But the soreness was still there beneath the happiness, ready to ache at a touch ; and soon her gay talk was beating upon it. I saw, as I listened, that her social triumphs in the fine houses of Holm St. Martin and in all the parts around had equipped her with a new vanity ; I who was so tempted to brag myself knew bragging when I heard it, no matter how she might cover it with the trappings of modesty. She was being driven to tell me about a certain Mrs. Galliday, a wealthy woman with a mansion and park, who'd more or less adopted her, telling everyone that she'd ' fallen in love with Gentle Greaves,' and was now taking her to dances and balls and parties all over the county and in London, too. Gentle, late of Redcliffe Street, must speak about Lord Milland's ball in Grosvenor Place to which this Mrs. Galliday was taking her next week, and how she ' intended to look rather nice at it ' ; and about the local lords and landowners with whom she'd dined or danced or played tennis ; and about their lordling sons or titled daughters whom she was careful to call, for my instruction, by their Christian names. Jim, I gathered, was Lord Delvin's heir ; Tristy was the Honourable Tristram Webbe, the younger son of Lord Behring ; and Urse was Lady Ursula Crowther, a half-sister of the Duke of Shelton.

Oh, I knew, as I listened that I should have been tempted to a like braggartry, but this did not enable me to forgive her. Others I could have forgiven, but not Gentle.

And at last, dancing and skipping at my side, happy in her

many successes, she mentioned Max. I suspected that she'd been shy of mentioning him before.

' And who is Max ? ' I demanded somewhat impatiently.

' The gentleman's name is Max Drury,' she answered with a new, rather angry note. ' Robert MacShennan Drury. And, for short, Max.'

' And is he a duke ? '

' He is not. He's a doctor, and a dear. He's old Dr. Thurkle's new partner, and he arrived here soon after the Greaveses.'

' Is he old, too ? '

' No.   Thirty-ish.'

' I see.   Very pleasant.'

' You're right.   He is.'   And, not quite liking my tone, she deliberately prattled on about Jim and Tristy and Max, pleased to hint at their admiration, and their flirtatiousness. And I withdrew into a hurt and stern-lipped silence, behind which I armed myself for battle. One question tormented me, even as I tempered my weapons to strike, and this was, Did they dare to kiss her ; but I didn't ask it, partly because I wanted her to notice my silence, but mostly because I couldn't have borne the answer, Yes.

We were walking along the high ridge-road that spans a segment of the Weald between Holm St. Martin and Chadbury. It was just such a day as that on which we walked together in Oxfordshire lanes, but I was nearly as heavy-hearted now as I was happy then. The wood sorrel and the violets peeped in the hedgebanks ; the butterflies, white and red, wantoned along the quickset hawthorns ; the Weald lay beneath us, a pattern of shining green and rich umbered browns ; the sky was a clean blue emptiness draped with flakes and fischus of cloud ; and all these things mocked me and tried to tease the tears into my throat.

And while I stared glumly before me, down the long road, I saw a vehicle and its dust-cloud racing towards us. So extraordinary was its speed that we knew it at once for a motor-car. Lately the speed limit had been raised to twenty miles an hour, but this vehicle was coming at thirty or more. I had hardly descried it before it was close enough to be seen in detail : an open carriage on big bicycle wheels, with a high-perched seat for two, and a kind of tin trunk in front to enclose its works. Its driver was a young man in a black suit and starched white collar, his dark hair as exposed to the wind as the high, hoodless car in which he sat. He saw Gentle, waved a wild greeting, and stopped the car with a jerk that shot him forward in his seat and hurled an angry blasphemy from between his shut teeth, ' Mary Christ and Holy Mother o' God ! '

He jumped down from the high seat, leaving his anger there, and I saw him for what he was : a tall and splendidly male young man with big limbs and a chest as deep and thick-walled as a safe. Though I was even taller than he, I felt slight in his presence. A strange aura of animal vigour seemed to exude from his massive breast as he stood before us. His hair, dark, stiff and dry, capped a large, high-coloured face ; but if his hair didn't shine, his brown eyes did : they shone with a mental activity as high as his muscular development. 'Hallo, my Gentle,' he said. And by the light in his eyes I saw, with a pang of jealousy, that not only was he much handsomer than I, but his social manner was as easy and free as mine was constrained and shy. And he was ten years older than Gentle, while I was five weeks younger.

'Max, Max, my *dear* ! ' protested Gentle. ' Do be careful. Gosh, you are an ass. You'll kill yourself with that contraption one day.'

' Not a bit of it, my darling. She's a beauty and travels like holy smoke.'

' Smoke's the word. Doric, this is Dr. Drury. Robert MacShennan Drury, universally known as Max. He's more than half an Irishman, which accounts for what you've just seen.' I knew she was glad, after my sullenness, that I should be seeing Max and his motor-car. ' And this is Doric, Max . . . my cousin, but we were almost brought up together, so we're more like brother and sister.' Was she excusing my presence to him ?

' Oh, yes ? ' He looked at me as I had looked at him. And he seemed as untroubled by my friendship with Gentle, as I was terrified of his. ' How do you do ? '

' How do you do ? ' I said. And neither of us answered the other's question because neither of us cared to know.

He turned from me to Gentle. ' Lamb, you look lovely.'

' Well, never mind that, Maxy. Just precisely what do you think you're doing ? Visiting the sick ? '

' Confound it, it's Saturday, isn't it ? I'm trying out Esmeralda : she's a darling. I can get thirty miles out of her easily ; I was doing more than thirty just now. That was why my stop wasn't all that could be wished.'

' It looked more like sixty. That's the second motor he's had in two years, Doric. He must always have the latest thing. The last one generally came home behind a horse.'

' Yes, she was a tiresome and temperamental little hussy, God rest her soul. But this one's a darling.' For politeness' sake he turned to me. ' D'you drive one of these things ? '

' Gracious, no. I'm not a millionaire.'

' Holy Heavens, nor am I.'

' Doric's a publisher,' explained Gentle, ' and a very good one.'

' Well, that sounds opulent enough.'

' It certainly does,' I agreed, ' but it doesn't happen to be true. I'm merely the least important clerk in a publishing office.'

' Don't you believe him, Max. He's really rather brilliant.' Gentle was now showing me off to him. ' He got a terrific degree at Oxford, a First Class.'

' And that doesn't mean as much as it sounds,' I pointed out. ' And, anyhow, it was a fluke.'

' A First Class ! Jesus, it was as much as I could do to squeeze through my exam. I was the world's worst student at Bart's, and now I'm the best doctor in Sussex.' And he loosed a great laugh that shattered the calm between Weald and sky. ' I say, Gentle : where are you off to ? I'll take you there in no time.'

' We were going to tea at Chadbury Farm.'

' Well, jump in, beautiful ; and you jump in, too, brother. She'll only seat two, but we can crowd up together and be neighbourly. It won't take her two minutes to get to Chadbury, so I'll take you for a sail round the harbour first. Jump up.'

Gentle looked at me as if she'd like to go, but, seeing a disappointment in my face, she filled at once with pity. ' No, no, Max ; not now. Doric and I have heaps of things to talk over.'

' All right. O.K. Whatever you wish.' There was no trace of jealousy or fear in him. ' But look here, lovely : I'm taking you to-morrow. Your Mamma won't mind ; I can always talk her round. And she knows you're safe with me.'

' Safe in that thing ? '

' Sure to God. Safe as St. Patrick. And I'll show you what she can really do. And Gentle, darling, are you not coming to Cecilia Lupton's tennis party next Saturday, because if you're not, I'm not.'

' Oh, yes, I'm coming. Pooh, Max, that contraption of yours does stink.'

' Yes, she does, doesn't she, God forgive her. But I don't trouble about that. The fœtor's behind, and it's fairly fresh in front where I sit.'

Left on the outskirts of this conversation, I felt compelled to speak. So I quoted, trying to be clever, ' " From the barge a strange invisible perfume hits the sense . . ." '

'Eh?' inquired Max. 'What's that?'

'Enobarbus,' I explained. 'Enobarbus in *Anthony and Cleopatra*.'

'Don't know the lad. Sorry.' And he turned back to Gentle. 'I say, Gents, what d'you think of this. Look.' From the high seat of the car he drew a motoring cap, peaked like a yachtsman's, and put it on. 'D'you think I can wear it? What'll Old Man Thurkle say? D'you think he'll say that it'll let the practice down?'

'Didn't I say that Maxy must always have the latest thing, Doric? Any new invention, or any new fashion——' but, looking at me, she saw my impatience to get her away, since I was the odd-man-out in all this; and her quick pity leapt again. She gathered up my fingers. 'Look, Max, we must really be going now, Doric and I. It'll take us all our time if we're going to walk. Besides, we want to see you start up and go off.'

This invitation to show his skill was something Max couldn't resist. 'All right,' he said. 'Good-bye, both of you, and God forgive you. So long, Gentle, sweetheart, I'll be round at the Mill to-morrow. Now then, let's see.'

He produced a pair of motor 'goggles'; affixed them, grinning (while Gentle said, 'Told you so! Must have everything that everybody else has'); pushed them up on to his brow, showing that they were for decoration rather than use; and went to the starting-handle. He swung it sharply—swung it once, and again, and again. As he stretched his arm to do this I noticed the thick black hairs on his wrist, and the power of the whole arm. The engine did not start; he swung and swung, and it did not start; and there came a look on his heated face so tight-lipped and hard that I knew at once he'd be a ruthless opponent in a quarrel. That ugly look pleased me, because I hoped that if he often showed it to Gentle, he'd lose some of his charm for her. He was barely parting his teeth as he muttered, 'God and all His saints,' and swung the handle viciously again.

The engine started. Instantly the black look dropped from his face, and he climbed up to his high throne, let in his clutch and drove away, forcing up the car's speed to impress us, and waving his arm in an exaggerated arc, as he and his dust-cloud diminished into the distances of that sun-bleached and tapering road.

§

He was gone, and we walked on in silence—and slightly apart. I was grateful to Gentle for her moments of pity, but the gratitude was quickly buried beneath the resentments I had brought with me and those which the day was adding. When I spoke it was to hurt.

'What the hell right had he to call you " sweetheart " ? ' I asked.

'Oh, don't be silly,' she remonstrated. 'Max calls everyone that—all the factory girls, and all the old biddies whom he attends when they're ill ; and they love it.'

'He seems a charming type.'

'I think he is.'

'All the same I shouldn't care to quarrel with him.'

'Why ? '

'Because he looks as if he'd kill anybody he quarrelled with. I suspect he can be quite a lot of a bully.'

'Rubbish ! You're——' she was going to say 'jealous,' but tossed her head instead. 'Why do you say that ? '

'I can see it in his face. There's a temper there that'd be pretty murderous if you really provoked it.'

'It seems to me we've all got tempers. I know I have.'

'You certainly have, my sweet, but I don't think you're proud of it ; whereas I'm pretty sure that your beloved Max is quite proud of his. He's the type that believes in two blows for a blow, and glories in the belief. He thinks it " strong " instead of puerile and weak and something that adult minds have grown out of.'

'Oh, don't *preach*, Doric ! . . . At any rate Max doesn't lecture me.'

'No ? Well, I've no doubt he's an improvement on me.'

'Oh, lord, lord . . . ' she sighed. 'Look, there's a red-backed shrike—the first I've seen this year.'

'Why did he say about some damned party that if you were not going, he wouldn't ? '

'Oh, Gosh, Gosh, Gosh, he'll probably say that to six more girls before the day's out, and to several grandmothers, too. He'd go if I were there or not. He loves tennis. He's one of the most wonderful players anywhere around.'

'Anything else he's wonderful at ? Let's hear some more. Tell me, I beg of you.'

'He's certainly wonderful at games. Absolutely wonderful.' It was Gentle now who was out to hurt. 'He played Rugger for Bart's—they say he was the best forward in the Fifteen—and now he plays cricket for Holm St. Martin ; and the people just stand round and yell, when he really starts smiting.'

' A real popular lad, in fact ? '

' Just so.   And one of his uncles is a bishop, and another a judge,' she added brightly, if illogically.

' Oh, well. . . .'   My lip was within my teeth, for I was very nearly crying, but must not let her see this.   My heart seemed to have changed into a rising lump of tears.   ' Oh, well. . . there it is . . . let it be.'

' What do you mean by that ? '

' Oh, never mind, never mind.'

She looked up at me, and the pain in my face went to her heart.   She put her hand into my arm and drew it against her side.   ' What is it, Doric ? '

' Gentle, is he '—I could hardly ask the question—' is he in love with you ? '

' No ! ' she cried emphatically.   ' He just likes me as he likes everybody.'

I remained silent and unhealed, because unconvinced ; silent for so long that Gentle pressed my arm and begged, ' Don't be unhappy, Doric.   I can't bear to see you unhappy.'

And then—just then, when I should have been appeased and almost happy again—the big quarrel came.   Point blank I asked her, ' Gentle, when are you going to marry me ? '

She didn't answer at once ;   and that hurt me.   When she did speak, she meant her words to be merry, but they only lacerated my too vulnerable sensitiveness, my preposterous pride.   She asked, ' How long'll it be before you earn a lot of money ? '

' Ten years,' I said, eager to hit her and force her to hit. ' Ten years, at least.'

And she said, ' Crikey ! ' and that silly, simple word fell upon me as the final blow.   I unlinked her arm.   I widened the space between us.

She looked up again.   And again she demanded, ' What's the matter ?   What is it ? '

' Oh, nothing,' I assured her.   ' I'm quite happy.'

' But you've gone all silent again ? '

' Have I ?   Well, I was just wondering, why Crikey ?   There's no need for Crikey.   I merely said it'd be ten years before I make any money.   No one need wait for that happy day who'd rather not.'

' Oh, my God—oh, Doric, you are difficult.'

' I'm going on,' I said, pretending not to have heard this, and addressing my eyes to the blue vapours at the end of the tapering road. ' I'm going on with the job I've chosen, and I don't care if I don't make any money at it for years and years. If one person won't wait for me, someone else will, I dare say. Someone who believes in me. Someone who wants to help me. I shall win in the end. I did all I wanted to do at Oxford, and I shall do what I want to do in the world. And I shan't want anyone near me who doesn't believe in me.'

These words made a desert of that golden day. Wrath dropped upon Gentle's brow and eyes like the vizor of an iron helmet. ' I don't know what you mean,' she murmured ; ' or what you're suggesting ' ; and, this said, we walked on through the wayside loveliness, hardly speaking. We had tea in the green garden of the farm, sitting opposite each other at an iron table, and hardly speaking. Once or twice I tried to recover from the depth of self-pity and anger into which I had deliberately plunged myself, but I could not. We walked back to the station at Holm St. Martin with our arms unlinked and no words said. At the station there was a cold kiss ; and when Gentle looked up at me after it, there was none of that fund of love in the upward gazing eyes—or was there ? Was there a mass of tears behind those speechless eyes ? From my train window I saw her walking home very slowly with her head drooping.

' How long before you earn a lot of money ? ' I took this sentence home with me in the train. It beat to the clangour of the wheels. ' How long before you earn a lot of money ? Ten years, ten years, ten years. In ten years she'll be thirty-two. In ten years I may be earning three hundred pounds . . . with Father's allowance of a hundred, I shall have . . . but what girl with lordly friends will marry on that ? I don't care ; I don't care ; I'm going on. You're not the only thing I love, Gentle. But I'd have starved for her. I'd have waited ten years for her—ten years, twenty years, thirty years ; ten years, twenty years, thirty years ; I love her, you see, I love her. She's the loveliest thing in the world. And she loves me, but not enough . . . not enough . . . not enough. . . .'

And, as the train beat on, the disappointment enlarged my love beyond anything it had ever been, by filling it with pain ; so that all the rest of the way, as I stared out of the window at the sweet spring landscapes I was saying, ' Gentle . . . Gentle . . . Gentle . . .'

§

One night of the next week, when the sky had hung out all its best stars, and the highroads of London were growing quiet because it was after ten o'clock, a crowd loitered and swayed, shifted and swelled, on a pavement of Grosvenor Place ; drawn there by a glow streaming from a high portico, and by a striped awning and a strip of red carpet that, between them almost enclosed the glow. A snake of carriages and hansom cabs was creeping towards the foot of the red carpet and then heading away from it.

Standing, shifting, and peering, on either side of this covered way, it was an exceedingly diverse crowd : there were some young working lads with their girls ; some laughing and loafing youths from the districts around Vauxhall Bridge Road ; a few heavy mothers in men's caps or bareheaded from the same streets ; a single tall soldier in a tight-waisted scarlet tunic and pill-box cap with his arm about a girl half his size ; some lean, loud urchins who ought to have been in bed ; one or two decently dressed men, in top hats or billycocks, pausing on their way home ; and two women, with hard features, feathered hats, and draggled skirts, who looked to have drifted up from their night market in the shadows of Victoria Station. And I stood behind them all—well behind—with my hand about my chin that my face might not be recognized.

I had been waiting there for a weary hour—waiting to see one person step from a carriage, but, as a watched pot never boils, so she seemed never to come. Once, in some desperation, I worked myself forward so as to cross the carpet and look up into the house. The doorway framed a brilliant picture. A powdered flunkey in knee-breeches stood in the hall ; two bare-shouldered women were ascending the stairs and lifting their coloured skirts from their shoes as they went ; two men in full evening dress followed them, drawing on white gloves. I saw and smelt the massed flowers at the base of the stairs, and heard the strings and a drum behind an interweaving of many voices in the ball-room above.

I passed through the light, like some moth in summer, and went back into the darkness on the hem of the crowd. The carriages—one was an electric brougham—delivered their occupants on to the carpet ; the hansoms came slurring up and deposited the elaborate young bachelors ; the crowd stirred and whispered when a face familiar in political cartoons issued from a carriage ; and they attempted a cheer when they recognized the monocle and keen nose of the most popular politician of the day. Two officers in full-dress uniform, coming from or going later to some levee, stepped down from a hansom, and the same humorists sang, ' It's the soldiers of the Queen, my lad, Who've been, my lad, Who've seen, my lad . . .' When a girl of peculiar beauty alighted on to the carpet, the lewder lads whistled at her and smacked their lips and emitted the sound of luscious kissing ; and they tossed up facetious remarks when a couple appeared on the balcony above the portico and looked down upon us.   One couple even braved the crowd and strolled along the pavement to get the cool air ; and all the heads turned to watch them, while a voice shouted, ' Enjoying yourself, mate ? ' and another asked, ' Is the King coming ? '

And the minutes dragged on, and I hesitated on the point of abandoning my quest, but ever stayed to see one more carriage arrive.

And at last a late carriage came spanking up, its footman jumped down and opened its door, and out of it stepped Gentle —Gentle in a dress of coral satin and a white cloak, with a coral rose in her brass-brown hair.   No girl had looked lovelier than she, as she stood for a moment, stage-lit in the darkness ; and the lads whistled at her and cat-called and exchanged their ribaldries with one another.

' Coo-blimey, Fred, here's a fruity piece.'

' My eye ! '

' I say, 'ah'd yer like that in yer bed to-night ?   Jest fer once, eh ? '

' Dow'n't—*dow'n't* make me mah'th water.'

' Is that all she done ? '

' 'S'truth, some boy's going to 'ave a good time some day.'

' Probably 'ad it.   She's married, I'll lay yer.'

' Caw, some chaps 'ave all the luck.'

They did not know the awful, the unspeakable, stabs their words were giving to one standing behind.   Were these the first thrusts of a sword that must stay in my heart for years ?

Gentle stood facing the carriage while her companion alighted —a thin but stately woman with silver hair, in a black velvet gown, green wrap, and a dog-collar of pearls.   So that was the Mrs. Galliday who had ' fallen in love ' with Gentle Greaves, and was taking her to Lord Milland's ball.

I watched Gentle go up the steps into the lit house ; I lingered there a little longer, listening to the violins and the voices, my eyes travelling to the balcony in the hope—or dread—that Gentle might appear there with some offensively beautified young man.   But of course she did not, and I walked away, my jaw thrown forward in a tearless despair which I almost enjoyed, because it was what I had come to find.

CHAPTER VI

I DID not see Gentle for many weeks after this because I could not humble myself to plead for her kindness. I did not write. Nor did she write to me, for though her sensitiveness did not burn as easily as mine, her pride could rear its head as quickly as my pride, and as high.

It was August, and three months after that unhappy day in the country, when I again heard something of her. Then, and it was another Saturday, I came home from the office in the afternoon, to hear from Lettice, ' Your Aunty Henrietta's in the drawing-room with the mistress and Miss Con.'

' Oh, the hell ! ' I said.

' Now then, Master Doric ! ' she rebuked, but only pretending displeasure.

' What's she come for ? '

' That's none of my business, but I did overhear her say that she and Mr. Greaves had come up for some dinner and were staying at a hotel.'

' Tell me not that Brian's in there, too.'

' Brian ! Brian, indeed ! That's no way to speak of your uncle. Whoever heard ! No, there's only your aunty.'

' And where's my Uncle Humphrey ? '

' He's gawn,' said Lettice.

' What ? Dead ? '

' No ! Of course not. And just give over trying to be saucy. He went out directly your aunty come.'

I grinned at her ; and she half-smiled at me, over the steel spectacles. ' In short, he ran,' I said. ' Wise old bird.'

' Now, Master Doric, you've no call to say that sort'a thing. He may have had very good reasons for going.'

' The Chief Reason is sitting in the drawing-room, Lettice dear.'

' Oh, you go along with you. I've got the tea to make.'

' Can I have tea with you in the kitchen ? '

' Certainly not. Gracious to glory, whatever next ? You go in and be nice and civil-spoken to your aunty.'

As a matter of fact I was well pleased to go into Henrietta, because I had come home with that in my hands which it would be good for her to see. Old Hammy and the Chief Editor were both on holiday, and I had been given complete responsibility for the editing of a famous judge's autobiography. Of this commission Wyn Fellowes had said, ' His Whiskers must have a higher opinion of you than I have, young Theodore. Why, you haven't been under my instruction for a year yet, and it's usually three before one's entrusted with the complete job. Law love us, you're still only a baby ; my editing was super-vised by the bosses for at least three years, and I'm a natural, born editor. I was a better editor after two months than you are after ten.'

Pleased with the trust, and playing at being a publishing Chief, I had brought the typescript home ' to read during the week-end ' ; and now here was Henrietta to see me in my hour of importance. I must always act before Henrietta, so I carried the typescript, and my fountain pen, into the drawing-room, intending to provide the three women there with the picture of a publisher correcting and punctuating a judge's prose.

Ours was a crowded little drawing-room in the flat because it held the large furniture from Coburg Square ; and the grand piano seemed to occupy half of it. As I entered I saw Mother and Henrietta sitting on the long sofa between piano and chimney-piece, the lean elder sister, as usual, bending towards and as it were over, the younger and stout one. Con sat on the edge of a deep chair opposite them. Here were my audi-ence, my public, and I came upon them with my typescript under my arm.

It was almost impossible for Henrietta to say things which were not unwittingly offensive to me, and she began, ' Well, how are you, Doric ?   Still at the publisher's ? '

' Yes,' I answered with a somewhat bitter smile.   ' Why not ? '

' And you still like it ? '

' Of course I do, aunt. It's my chosen profession. One's always pretty happy if one's doing the thing one wants to do.'

' Well, I'm so glad you're happy in it. That's satisfactory, isn't it, Una ? ' She said it—or so I imagined in my quick vulnerability—as if it were rather surprising that things should be turning out satisfactorily with me.

' And what's that ? ' demanded Con, looking at my parcel.

' That,' I said, trying to sound as modest as I felt vain, ' is an autobiography for which I've had to take over complete responsibility in the absence of the Chief. It's Sir Philip Soane's —actually : Mr. Justice Soane's.'

' Oh, is it ? ' exclaimed Henrietta. ' A real book that's going to be published. A judge's ? Oh, do let me see, do let me see ! ' And, clasping her hands before her, she jigged up and down on the sofa like a schoolgirl, and looked extremely ridicu-lous. ' He's *very* famous, isn't he ? Oh, please—I must see it ! '

I showed her the typescript, on which there were already a

few of my corrections, thank God. And with much girlish
excitement she looked at these esoteric symbols of the proof-
reader's mystery and asked what they meant. I sipped a
considerable pleasure from telling her that ' c. & s.c.' meant
large and small capitals and ' clar ' meant ' change to bold
type ' and ' rom ' meant ' change to roman.' Even more I
enjoyed expounding the ' bastard title ' and seeing her shiver.

' Well now, isn't that all interesting ? ' she said when she had
readjusted her thoughts, which this phrase had shaken. ' And
to think that you're doing work like that ! '

I wondered what age she thought I was.

It wasn't interesting to Mother and Con, who'd seen similar
instructive performances by me before ; and Mother changed
the subject as I carried the typescript to a seat by the window
and continued my act there. ' You haven't told us anything
about Gentle yet,' she said.

I uncapped my pen and pretended to make a correction on a
page, but really I was listening, only listening.

Henrietta did not answer at once, and I glanced up from
under my brows, to see that she was looking very mischievously,
very knowingly, at Mother.

' I think she's very happy, Una. There's every reason why
she should be.'

' Why ? How's that ? '

' Because . . . I think . . . I think . . .'—Henrietta was halting
for effect—' I think the Right Man has come.'

Again, but with a hand that quaked, I made a mark on my
page. I did not imagine that she'd said this especially for me
to hear, first, because she'd almost forgotten my presence, and,
secondly, because she liked to believe that the ' silly flirtation '
between Gentle and me was a thing long dead. She might well
believe this because I never spoke of it, and Gentle never spoke
of it.

' You mean she's in love ? ' pursued Mother.

Henrietta nodded happily. ' I think so. . . . I think so. . . .'

And Con cried, ' Oh, this is exciting ! ' and jigged up and
down on her chair as Henrietta had done on the sofa. ' Who
is he ? Do tell us.'

' He's our doctor's young partner, dear. Of course nothing
decisive's happened yet, but there's no doubt he's madly in
love with her. I've never seen anyone so much in love. He's
absolutely heart-broken when she can't go out with him.'
Henrietta must always speak in superlatives.

' Oh, do tell us more . . . please, please,' cried the excited
Con. ' What's he like ? Is he good-looking ? '

' *I* think he's very good-looking ; and so does Gentle. You know what Gentle is : she always calls him " The Vision." " The Vision "—it's so silly ! '

' Is he dark or fair ? '

' Dark. Very dark. And a splendidly built young man : nearly as tall as Doric, but broad in proportion.'

(Damn her !)

' And does she really like him ? ' asked Mother.

Henrietta put on her archness again. ' I think . . . I think she likes him the best of all. But we daren't say this, or she flares up. *We* like him. Brian thinks he's suitable in every way. One of his uncle's a bishop, and another a judge.'

' Really ? ' exclaimed Mother, delighted.

' Yes, and he's quite well off himself, with an income inherited from his father. Tobacco, I think. He's perfectly well able to marry.'

' Gentle ought to marry fairly soon,' suggested Mother. ' She's twenty-three next birthday. How old is he ? '

' Thirty-one. Nearly ten years older than she. Which is so much better, I think.'

' Ever so much better—— What's that ? Did you say something, Doric ? '

' No. There's a mistake in the manuscript here—that's all.'

' Thirty-one's a nice age, Henrietta.'

' Yes, but you'd never think he was much more than twenty by the way he behaves. Really, he behaves as if he were still a medical student,' protested Henrietta with a rich appreciation of this behaviour. ' He just doesn't mind what he says to any-one. Do you know : the first time he saw Gentle he came straight up and sat down beside her and, without being intro-duced, said, " Who are you, you most attractive girl ? I love you." What a way to speak to a girl the first time you see her ! Wasn't it naughty ? But he's half Irish, you see. And now he *will* call me " Auntie " or " Mums " or " Ma " ! ' She giggled coyly. ' He's the most terrible tease, I'm afraid. He's always very respectful to Brian, calling him " Sir," but behind his back he will refer to him as " Pa." I must say I can't help laughing. It's so comical. He's like that with everyone. The people are absolutely devoted to him. To tell the truth, they prefer him to old Dr. Thurkle. They say he can't come into their rooms without making them feel better.'

' He sounds a Dream,' said Con. ' Has he asked her to marry him yet ? '

' Oh, yes. Yes, dear. More than once. I persuaded her to

tell me that. I said it was our duty to know, and our only desire was her happiness.'

' And what did she say to him ? '

' That I don't quite know. You know how secretive Gentle can be, telling us absolutely nothing. She didn't accept him, but she can't have refused him outright because they still go about together. He takes her out whenever he can in his lovely motor-car. I let her go with him—do you think I'm wrong, Una ? Brian doesn't altogether like it, but I tell him she can only be young once, and it's such a beautiful sight, two young people coming together ! Oh, I *do* think two young lovers are the loveliest sight in the world.' Apparently it was beautiful enough to lift a tear to her eye, for she brushed one away. ' The car only seats two,' she explained, when her way was clear again. ' I'm an old fool, I suppose, but, really, Una dear, I'm enjoying Gentle's little love-story almost as much as if it were my own. It's so true, isn't it, that we live again in our children ? I think I shall be glad if she marries him—yes, I think I shall. A doctor's is a wonderful life—always doing good—and a doctor's wife should be a beautiful life, too, almost like a clergyman's——'

' Oh, damn ! ' I muttered, suddenly rising. ' There's something missing in this manuscript. I shall have to go. I shall have to go back to the office. Excuse me, Aunt ; I'm so sorry ; but it's important.'

And I got myself out of the room.

§

Like a driven animal, I went from the house and leapt into an Underground train for Victoria ; at Victoria Station I paced a platform like a captive animal fretting at the constriction of its bars. The train for Holm St. Martin came slowly in, and I threw myself into a corner seat like a limp bag. It was the 4.45 for the sea, on an August Saturday, and the holiday-makers crowded in after me, parents and children, hot and noisy and excited, all travelling to their pleasure, and one among them to his likely doom.

Why, why, I asked of the seared August fields as they swept by, why was she yielding to this fellow, why (as I seemed to know, ahead of the event) would she give herself to him ? He was breezy and boisterous, and good laughing company ; he was well-favoured in his large, muscular way ; he had a fair position and some money ; but surely these things were not

enough.   Unless I misread him, he was without culture, and
without one strong unselfish ideal ; surely I had more of these,
if only a little, to offer to Gentle.   Was it something else that
attracted and held her—something that it was utter terror, real
anguish, to think of, as I stared, wide-eyed, from the window.
' There is a desire in her blood as there is in a man's—did I not
feel it in that first embrace, and again on the hilltop at Oxford ?
Women want what men want—we're fools to think they don't
—and she can't wait for me.'   I tossed my head to hurl the
thought away.   But it returned in the form, ' Why should she
wait—how should she wait for years—if there's the same desire
in her blood and limbs as in any youth's ? '

Holm St. Martin.   The name on the station boards drove an
ache between my eyes.   I broke from the train and walked the
long mile to the Chapter Mill.   It was yet only six o'clock, but
the country lay beneath a strange summer darkness, as if the
light were running too quickly out of the vat of the sky.   I do
not think I projected this stormy twilight upon the landscape,
from the misery in my brain : it just was so.   Beneath a low,
slate sky the farm-steadings and the insulated woods stood out
with a sharp clarity ; and so did the shocked wheat on the
arable, and the piebald oxen lying down in the pastures.   The
downs along the south were unusually clear in outline and
seemed to have come much closer.   The tree-tops quivered
apprehensively in an unfelt wind.

Through that darkened and yet heightened landscape I came
to the main door of the old Mill house.   It was agape, and
I stepped into the wide, beamed living-room or ' lounge.'   This
was empty, but I heard voices in the little drawing-room at the
back, which looked out upon the flagged court and the climbing
terraces of the garden.   The casements alike of lounge and
drawing-room were open to the garden, so I was able to stand
quite still in the midst of the lounge and hear all that the voices
were saying.   And the first sentence from Gentle, and Max's
first huge laugh, told me that they were sitting in there alone.
Were not Brian and Henrietta away ?

The old habit, gift of a punished and suspicious childhood,
took instant command of me : I stood there with a turned and
straining ear, intently listening.   Not without shame, not without despising myself, but I *had* to know.   I listened and listened.
Four hundred years old, perhaps, that room with its drooping
beams and old oak chests and dressers ; and no doubt it had held
pains as great as, or much greater than mine, many times before
—though how does one take the measure of pain ?   Gentle was
giving to him some of the arch and impudent drolleries with

which she used to charm me, hanging on my arm, till I had to take and kiss the lips that spoke so. Max was greeting them with his too-loud but appreciative laugh. And all the time something in that closed room was knocking, knocking—a muffled, rhythmic beat. And all the time (as I remember now) down in the garden below I could hear the mill-pool water rushing over the dam.

'Oh, Mrs. Hillman's sweet. Gosh, Maxy, I wish I were as sweet as she.'

'You're not too bad, ducky.' And again the great laugh, followed by the muted beat . . . beat. . . .

'Oh, yes, I am. The more I think of it, the more I fear that I'm an exceedingly un-nice person, really.'

'No, no. Come, come. I wouldn't go as far as that.'

'But it's rather true, Maxy. I've got masses of faults—masses of them—though I can't for the moment think of any.'

'I'll tell you, shall I ?' Beat . . . beat. . . .

'No, you won't. I'll tell *you*. Let me see . . . no, as far as I can see, I've only one fault—a vile temper.'

'I'll tell you another, my dear—far more serious than that.'

'All right, but tell me first—honestly—have I as kind a face as Mrs. Hillman, with as kind a smile ?'

'I wouldn't say so. No.'

'Oh, yes, you would, Maxy. . . . Wouldn't you ?'

'It depends.'

'Oh, no, it doesn't. It doesn't depend. Don't say it depends.'

'Yes, it does, sweetheart. I'll explain : when your very large but attractive mouth is partly open, it's easily the sweetest thing in Holm St. Martin ; when it's tight shut, it bodes the devil for everybody.'

'Oh, does it ? Yes, I suppose it does. But you wouldn't suggest that I've got a hard face . . . not like Mrs. Alden . . . that horrible, fat and odious woman.'

'Sometimes.'

'Oh, *no*, Maxy ! '

'Oh, yes, exquisite.'

'Oh, dear, dear, whatever am I to do ? '

'Give me your hand. That's what you've got to do. Now I'll tell you the worst fault of all.'

'Yes ? '

'Your beauty is quite disgusting and whether you know it or not you use it—lips, eyes, nose, brows—for the overthrowing and the maddening of us all. Come here.'

'No, Maxy, don't. Not now.'

'Yes, now. Of course. It's your fault for being so lovely. Come.'

I could have stopped that kiss—and its torment for me—by a cough or a call, ' Is anyone in ? ' but I waited, fascinated, driven to know all and endure it.

And there was silence in that room, while my left hand clenched on my right wrist ; a long, full silence, till Gentle said, ' No . . . don't be silly. . . . You're hurting . . . there's no sense in biting.'

' Oh, isn't there ? ' And he loosed the great laugh. ' Come here, Beauty ; no nonsense ; I command it—— Damn ! Is there someone in the house ? I thought I heard someone. Oh, hell, why just now ? '

' Is there ? '

This forced me to move. One pities and will save the face even of an enemy, so I called out cheerfully, ' Anyone at home ? ' and paused and called again, ' Gentle, are you there ? ' to give them time to get back to their chairs. The knocking began again.

Two or three seconds while Gentle rearranged her hair ; and then she opened the door of the drawing-room and stood looking at me. She was in white tennis clothes.

' *Doric !* Where in Heaven's name have you sprung from ? Well, this is lovely. Come in. Max, here's my dear Doric.'

I followed her and saw Max leaning forward from a deep cretonne-covered chair and beating his tennis racket on the floor. He also was in tennis clothes ; and his face and neck were burned to a sandstone red beneath the dark, glistening hair.

' Who ? ' He looked up, but, soured by the interruption, did not rise.

' Doric Allan Mourne. All the way from London.'

My heart might be perishing, but nobody was going to see it die ; so I explained merrily, ' Sorry to burst in on you like this but I had to go and see an old Judge in Brighton about his old book. I've just finished with him, and I thought I'd jump off the train and see how the Greaveses were faring. You've been playing tennis, I see, while I work.'

' Yes, Max very kindly brought me home from the Hillman's. You know Max, don't you ? You met once before.'

' Did we ? Oh, yes, I think I remember.'

' Gosh, you look tired, Doric. You're pale.'

' Overwork, that's all. Never felt better in my life. The Chief and my boss are both on holiday. That's why I'm on this job. Well, Gentle, sweetheart, how about giving this evening to me ? ' The ' sweetheart' was the last desperate appeal of a drowning man.

Max had risen. Anger pressed upon his mouth, giving it an uglier set than any he had attributed to Gentle's : I was not addressing him, and for the first time he was suspecting me as a rival. I saw again that the heady wine of heartiness in him could flatten and sour quickly, when his temper would be dark indeed. As I continued my small chatter with Gentle I felt that he was scanning me with some scorn. He was measuring me against himself and deciding that he was unafraid. At last the swelling anger impelled him both to go (after all, he'd had his kisses and drunk deep of them) and to show me his power over Gentle.

' Well, I'm going. I've a lot to do, Gentle, sweetheart ; I've got to get out of these clothes, and it's going to rain like hell in a minute. But I'm coming for you to-morrow. Let there be no nonsense about that. I'm coming with the little old barge and we'll go and have a look at the sea.'

' Bless you, Maxy. That'll be angelic.'

' Well, so long, then. I expect you and your visitor want to talk.'

' Visitor ! ' I scoffed. ' That's a good word, Gentle, isn't it ? Why, Gentle and I have known each other for twenty years.'

' Well, your long-lost brother—whatever he is. Good-bye, my sweet. Good evening—er—Mr.—I've forgotten your name again.'

' It's of no great importance. Good evening, Dr. Drury.'

We escorted him to the threshold, and he went with a wave to Gentle, and the words ' To-morrow's mine,' into the premature dusk.

Gentle waved, too. ' Bye for now. Get home before it rains.' And then, obviously anxious, she returned ahead of me into the lounge, and there, acting a fine unconcern, said, ' Well, Doric, this is the loveliest surprise. Fancy your—but what's the matter ? You're shaking. . . . Doric ! . . .'

' Gentle,' I began, fronting her in that beamed and antique room, among its blackened ' period ' chairs, ' listen. I've something to say to you, and I can't wait. Henrietta came to tea with us to-day and told us all about this fellow proposing to you.'

' Oh, Gosh, Mother's dire sometimes.' She dropped uncomfortably to the edge of an old carved Jacobean chair. ' Doric, it's——'

' No, let me speak. I know you let him kiss you. He makes violent love to you, doesn't he, whenever he can. Well, I want to say this. Gentle, I love you as I love no one and nothing else in the world. I have loved you ever since that day you slipped your hand into mine—do you remember? That was six years ago, and my love hasn't got less; it's only got deeper and deeper. That is just true, Gentle. It's so much my life now that I feel part of you. I want to be part of you always; I want to give my whole life to you and, if possible, the whole of eternity. I think you've grown very beautiful and I suppose that in some ways I'm not good enough for you—though that doesn't make sense in my heart, because I seem to know that we're already one. In a year or two—perhaps three years—I may have just enough to marry you and be poor with you. Last time I saw you, you asked how soon I should make a lot of money. Well, the answer is, I see no hope of it for years. I'm quite determined to build my own publishing house some day—I'm not going to desert the vision that came to me once—I don't think I ever could—but even when I've set up on my own I shan't make much money for a long time. So there it is, darling: I shall be poor for many years. You understand?'

'Yes.'

'All right then. What I have to say is quite simple. Rich or poor, you have everything of me—absolutely everything—always; what have I got of you?'

She gazed up at me, silent.

'Please say something. I must know, my dear one; I must know.'

'Doric, I do love you—of course I do—but——'

'There are no buts in my love. There are none, and never will be.'

'Let me say what I was going to say. I've thought and thought about this for months past. I've lain awake all through the night sometimes, wanting to be loyal to you——'

'Is it so difficult?'

'No, but, you see, I'm all confused. A part of me seems to love you in a different way from anyone else——'

'A part of you!... Seems!...'

'Oh, don't make it more difficult for me. Don't be too terribly touchy. I do like Max, and it's quite true he's asked me to marry him; he's asked me many times, and it was simply because of you that I told him I couldn't answer at once.'

'You couldn't answer at once!...'

'No, don't scoff at me. Don't, Doric. Please be reasonable. I'm only twenty-two, and I still can't quite understand myself yet. I often don't know what I really think or what I really feel. And Mummy's no help. She wants me to marry Max.'

'I couldn't have answered No to the whole world. As long as you're alive I shall always be able to say No. For me you are one thing, and the world is something else. Something outside me, and unimportant. Isn't it the same for you ? '

' I—I don't know, Doric.'

' You don't know ! . . . Six years, and you don't know. I think that's my answer. You love him ; that's plain ; you loved me, and now you love him too ; and you're quite a lot confused——'

' I like him——'

' Please don't go on—don't—don't.' Both hands were on my temples, and my head bent. ' He and I are equal in the balance. Oh, my God, my God ! ' My heart went down to death and above its grave a fire of bitterness arose that burnt up any dignity I had shown so far. And the suspicion which had bedevilled my hour in the train shot up the tallest and wildest flame in that fire. ' You're confused. I'll enlighten your confusion for you. His kisses in the car were rather wonderful, weren't they ? To be hugged by a bear like that is good. Once treated to it one craves it again. " Don't be silly—you're hurting "—oh, I heard that much—and then silence, because it's paradise, it's ecstasy, to be kissed like that. It's so wonderful that the sooner you're in his bed——'

Gentle rose. If she'd sat down on that old carved chair like a bewildered child, she rose from it a woman, her shoulders squared, her breast uplifted, and her eyes burning. ' If anything could have killed my love for you, Doric——'

' No, child. That little tale won't pass. It's quite another thing that's killed your love for me. Quite an ordinary thing. I see it all. I am far away and out of sight, and even if I were not, my kisses are stale by now. I'm like the customary husband whom it's nice to have about, and feel some affection for, but it's no grand passion such as a girl should have, at least once in her life, and you're wondering if you can't do something better, all things considered, with this '—I shot an open hand in the direction he'd taken—' this most handsome and exciting person, this " Vision " as you're pleased to call him. He's handsome, he's exciting—I'm not—or I am no longer ; I came too soon— much too soon—he's rich, he's got money in tobacco, he's prob- ably got lots of other women after him—what more could a girl want ? The fact that he's also, unless I read him all wrong, a rather crude and ignorant bully—— '

Her fists were now clenched and shaking at her side. ' Will you go, please ? I ask you to, because I don't trust myself. If you say more to me in this fashion, I may behave as vilely as you.'

' Unity, identity,' I said, looking up and down at that firm- limbed feminine body to which outraged pride was lending so splendid a shape ; at that large, rich mouth now closed with hate as Max said it could be ; at those large brown eyes, now furious, which had been the answer from the world without to all the emptinesses of my soul and body. ' Oh, my God . . . I could have sworn my sense of unity with you had some meaning —I could swear it even now. It must have some meaning somewhere. No, perhaps it has not. It seems it has none. Life befools us with lying dreams. One day I shall accept that. I thought of you as someone with a tremendous fount of love and a great gift of pity. I still think it somehow—and it's not there. Where is the Gentle that I loved ? I don't know. I don't know. Perhaps one day I shall find her again—she was so lovely. That she never existed is a thing too difficult to believe. One day, perhaps, I can believe it. Give me time. It's very difficult : it's like learning too suddenly that the religion by which one lived is all a lie. . . . The love I believed in is something shallow and cheap and selfish. Well, marry this man. I should think that in that respect he's a match for you.'

She flung herself now on an old panelled box-chair and her arms along its side-arm, and her head on her wrist ; and I wonder, as I write, how often that heavy chair, three hundred years old and one of Brian's treasures, had received the like distress. ' Go. Go away from me. You've said things I shall never, never forgive you. I did love you ; I loved you with all my heart. But I don't now, and never shall again. I hate you.'

So like the child who used to fight with me in the garden of the old square !

' Oh, I'm going,' I said. ' Have no doubt of that. I don't enter into competition with anyone, and certainly not with the great prize ox you've found now. I don't offer my love in competition with his ; it's worth something better than that. I withdraw, and you needn't be confused any more. Tell him you're free so far as I am concerned. Tell him to-morrow somewhere by the sea. Good-bye, my dear. I'm not coming back. I had a hope your love would be strong enough to suffer poverty with me . . . if it isn't . . . well, go your ways. I am loyal to my vision. I don't come back unless by any chance you send for me.'

She laughed harshly, and as if ashamed of her childish outburst in the chair, rose and stood in all her hot and high-crested pride again. ' *I* send for you ! That's not very likely. If you wait for that, you'll wait a long time. It is not I who'll go on my knees to anyone. You can do what you like. I don't care if I never see you again.'

' So ? Well, that's the way the world wags. Thank you for

telling me. It's best to know. Now I can look out for someone else to love me and work with me. Good-bye, Gentle dear.'

And I went into the clouded summer evening ; into the scent of wet herbage and rinsed earth and the sound of the mill-water rushing over the dam. It was raining now, only slightly, but steadily ; and the air was like a cold palm on one's brow. I walked quickly towards the gate, asking myself, 'What have I done ? What have I done ? ' Suddenly I heard her steps running after me as far as the doorstone, driven, I suppose, by the old pity ; I do not know to this day but that she cried out, ' Doric ! ' for the old, mad, iron pride in me held my head immovable, and, as I walked on, I heard her steps turn and the door close. Once out of her sight, I dropped my high front and staggered along by the hedge of the cart-road ; but I could not stay erect, and at the first field-gate I hurried through to the kindly cover of a screen of hawthorn. There I threw myself face-forward upon the grass, gripping the wet tufts with my nails as a sufferer grips his pillow and murmuring, heedless of the rain, ' Gentle, my lovely one.'

§

My buried diffidence and my towering pride were the same thing, I take it. The whole was like a tall flagstaff whose base was sunk in the shameful pit which Harlen had dug for it but whose top flew a majestic standard for the eyes of the world. Yes, Harlen's rod, like a wand, had created both my desperate love for Gentle and my armed and fighting pride ; and now the pride was fighting the love—or, rather, it had thrown it into a dungeon whence nothing could escape but its cries.

' My love is withdrawn. It will never ask anything of her again. I have written my last letter to Gentle, unless she writes and asks me to come to her. I cringe to no one.' Knitting such fine sentences, I would wander, after my day's work, to Coburg Square and roam about outside the old house, looking up at the playroom and Gentle's bedroom, and the high windows at the back which used to light up with her invitation. Standing at gaze on the opposite pavement, careless of passers-by who turned to look at me, I played with the idea of knocking on the door, telling the strangers within that I had lived years ago in the house, and asking leave to look into its rooms again. If they welcomed me with a smile, I would look at the painted glass door into the garden and, climbing the stairs, visit the playroom and the drawing-room and that bedroom which was Uncle

Humphrey's once, and then Gentle's—and is now Roberta's. Sometimes the window of Gentle's bedchamber, and the single thought to which it led, would drive me from the square, since one cannot suffer and stand still, and I would play with thoughts of suicide, or even murder. Die? No, that would leave her to him. Kill Max and Gentle both; then die myself. . . .

There were months of this daily despair; and yet I will not say but that, in some strange way, I was happy in my tent of misery. Say what I might, I still believed she must be mine. Like a condemned prisoner I had to believe that the appeal against sentence would succeed. 'It cannot be—it cannot be that she isn't mine. This sense of unity—it can't have no meaning. I deny that it has none. Something must come of it in the end.' And for comfort I hugged her words, 'A part of me seems to love you in a different way from anyone else.' She had said that.

In our small upper room I would discuss with Wyn Fellowes, when we ought to have been busy on our manuscripts, an academic question, 'Was the lover's feeling of unity always an illusion?' and he from his table would plump merrily for 'Yes,' and I, deserting my papers and striding the boards, would argue frantically for 'No.' And one evening, desperately seeking a different answer, I thought of Uncle Humphrey. Neither Con nor Mother would be any good to me—each would give a purely sentimental or 'religious' answer—but Uncle Humphrey posed as a philosopher and perhaps could argue dispassionately—if his own emotions were not concerned.

It was a late November day, with a cloud of pale mist lying on the roads, and cold-breathing winter seated in the cloud; and when I entered Uncle Humphrey's little room at the end of the flat I found him reclining on his heavily upholstered chair, with a shawl round his shoulders and his legs on a stool. The gas stove was glowing behind his legs, except in two places where the asbestos was broken and it showed only an unhealthy yellow flame. He had no book in his hand, but my eye saw on the leeward side of his chair the sixpenny paper novel which he had consigned to the floor directly he heard my knock.

Uncle Humphrey was sixty-eight now; his beard was no longer a black spade but a grey brush, and the flesh around it was fat and pendulous and pulpy. Hope of help from this constipated source drooped in me as he turned his sad St. Bernard eyes on mine.

'Busy?' I asked, sitting down upon his bed.

'No. No, not just at the moment. I was resting a little. After some rather exacting study.'

' I've just come from a long argument with a friend, and I've decided that you must solve the problem for us.'

' I'll try to, Doric,' He was pleased to be the consulting specialist. ' What is the difficulty ? '

' Well, he's terribly in love, this chap,' I began ; and then outlined the problem ; this overwhelming sense of identity with the beloved—was it illusory or was there anything of reality in it ?

Uncle Humphrey brought the points of his fingers together above his breast, as a philosopher should. ' My dear boy,' he said, ' you couldn't have come to anyone better than me. It's a subject to which I've given much thought. I've had reason to. I had that feeling once about a woman, but it came to nothing in this world.' And his sad St. Bernard eyes became even sadder.

So I'd been a fool to think he could escape from himself and argue objectively ! Well, never mind. Let me hear what he had to say. He was obviously going to enjoy talking about himself, exhibiting his knowledge, and decorating the exposition with fine ornamental names. Let him be happy.

' I suffered a lot at that time, Doric, and I had to think and think about it, if I was to find a *modus vivendi* without her.'

' Find a what ? '

' A *modus vivendi*.'

' Oh, I see. Well what did you find ? '

' Yes, what ? To answer that satisfactorily I should have to give you a resumé of my whole Philosophical System.'

' Go on then, Uncle.' I stooped and picked up a strand of wool from his bedside rug, that I might twist and trifle with it as he talked.

Absent-mindedly copying me, he lowered his hand and picked up the book he had been reading, but, remembering what it was, dropped it back again, out of view. ' I suppose that if I'm a follower of anyone, it's Epicurus ; though I like to think I'm no one's disciple. My system is eclectic and synthetic and thus, I hope, original. Still, my final conclusions have much in harmony with the best in Epicurus and his school. My descent— if I'm descended from anybody——'

' And not like Melchizedek.'

' Not like who ? '

' Melchizedek—the chap in the Bible who was without father and without mother.'

' No. . . . Yes. . . . Perhaps. . . . Well, as I was saying, my descent, if any, is through Pyrrho and the Sceptics to the Stoics—Seneca, Epictetus, Marcus Aurelius '—here came the

Great Names—'with their characteristic doctrine of apathy—
" apathy " not meaning indolence or inertia, of course '—he
rose a couple of inches from his cushions as if to show that
' inertia ' was no word to apply to him—' not inertia certainly,
but freedom from passion, superiority to passion, a grandeur of
mind *above* passion—and so through the Stoics, through apathy,
to the pleasant garden of Epicurus. To Epicurus, but not to
mere hedonism, mind you—oh no—that's just a vulgar view of
Epicurus. Epicureanism is certainly not that. It's always been
a creed for the highly intelligent, and the most civilized, in the
best sense of the word.' I gathered that I was listening to, and
looking at, one of the highly intelligent and most civilized in the
best sense of the word. ' It proclaims, not crude pleasure, but
serenity and peace of mind. So far from advocating the pursuit
of pleasure it demands of its adherents a prudence in the pursuit
of pleasure. They are to allow themselves no such indulgence
in pleasure as will issue in pain. And that includes, most
patently, the pleasure of loving.'

A pain began to close upon my heart because the unwanted
answer was coming.

' Epicurus was supremely wise when he said that all pleasure
which begins in painful desires and ends in painful satieties was
best eschewed in favour of serene and quiet contents. Love is
certainly such a pleasure and the only wisdom is to partake but
moderately of the rich dish—to love another creature only so
well that her loss cannot hurt.'

I saw Gentle and cried my protest. ' Oh, no, no, NO ! '

Uncle Humphrey presented towards me a fat, deprecating and
silencing palm. ' I'm not saying that I agree. Only that he
was very wise. I try to follow him now because I have suffered
enough, but I didn't do so in my youth. I was unwise enough
to love very unwisely then.'

' And you had this sense of unity ? '

' Certainly. Of course.' It was not in Uncle Humphrey to
admit that, as a lover, he'd been less than the best. ' Of course.'

Still looking down upon my broken strand of wool, I asked,
' And there was nothing in it ? It meant nothing ? '

' Oh, I wouldn't like to say that. It may have some meaning
in some other world. Epicurus held that the soul died with the
body, but I prefer Kant who believed in immortality. Not that
I can say with Kant, ' I believe.' I believe in nothing ; I only
hope a little. I doubt if you can realize how profound is my
scepticism. I am sceptical of everything, including the sceptics.
I don't think you'll find a first-rate modern mind, Doric, that
isn't profoundly sceptical. There is nothing that we can know

for certain—no, nothing.   And there is very little that we dare hope.   Very little.'

In these latter days of war, when I have taken upon me the shopping for Roberta, and the greengrocers have seemed to rejoice in the scarcity of lemons and potatoes, I have often thought of Uncle Humphrey romanticizing his youthful love, but rejoicing in the shortage of knowledge and hope.

'I must say I find Peter Abailard'—deliberately he pronounced the familiar name in this learned way—'very sympathetic, with his faith in doubt as the chief instrument of philosophic thought—I have made a great study of Abailard.   And Bacon.   " Patience to doubt, slowness to assert "—those were Bacon's words.   Yes, after Abailard the great humanists are my best inspiration with their conception of Man in his strength and beauty as the proper measure of all things and a more profitable study than God.'

I looked up from my wool to consider Uncle Humphrey as he lay there among his cushions, content with his strength and beauty.

'Descartes also proclaimed doubting as a virtue.   We must doubt everything that can be doubted, he said ;   and I agree. Oh, it was a wonderful moment in my youth when, like Kant, I awoke from my youthful slumbers and began to doubt.   Even if it led straight into loneliness.   Have you ever thought of the loneliness of the really great minds, the loneliness of those who can *see* ?   Socrates, Plato, Krishna, Christ, Buddha, Lao-Tse. . . . Still, there is something bracing in an absolute loneliness '—and he braced himself a little in his chair.   ' There is something uplifting in it.   Well, where have we got to now ? '

I, too, had begun to wonder.

' I am saying that mine is a synthetic philosophy, a synthesis of the prudence of the Epicureans, the—er—what else ?—the apathy of the Stoics, the doubt of Abailard, and the refusal to decide of Bacon—is that it ?   I think so.   If I may so put it '—and here he spread out both of his fat palms—' I hold doubt in one hand and trust in the other, and do not presume to judge between them.'

' But how does all this apply to my first question ?   What do you really believe about this extraordinary conviction of unity when one loves ? '

He shrugged.   ' How can one know ?   I decide nothing.'

It seemed a tremendous preparation to establish the statement, ' I don't know ; ' an immense pedestal for so small a statue—or, to be more accurate, for no statue at all.

' All I know is that I have a profound pity for all young people in their tragic ignorance ; a deep pity for those whose romances are broken and an even deeper pity for those whose romances are momentarily fulfilled. For the hour of fulfilment holds the first moment of decay.'

I would not accept this : I must have my belief or die. ' But some have lived all their lives together and preserved this sense of unity to the end ? '

' A few perhaps. But they're as scarce and as gifted as genius or saints.'

' Well, one can make up one's mind to be a saint.'

' Yes . . . yes . . . but one wearies . . . sooner or later one wearies. The odds are very long against love's survival after marriage. That's why I pity all young lovers. Take, for instance, poor little Gentle. What's going to happen to her ? '

' *Gentle ?* '

' Yes. Haven't you heard ? She's engaged.'

Show nothing. Play with your strand of wool. This must be endured alone.

' I didn't know this. I hadn't heard.'

' Yes, Henrietta wrote this morning. She is engaged to some young doctor.'

' Well, well ! This—this is exciting. ·I must go—I must go and hear more about it from Mother and Con. Do you mind if I go ? '

§

Once Gentle with her kiss had put a shattered world together for me. Now she had undone the miracle and made a waste of it once more.

CHAPTER VII

SO ON a June day, Roberta, Gentle was married to Robert MacShennan Drury. (Why did I write ' Roberta ' then ? Perhaps it has only just been revealed to me that I am really writing this story for you, Roberta ; perhaps, on the other hand, you will never see it. The truth may be too hard for you to bear.)

We were all at the wedding. My pride, riding me with curb and bearing rein, drove me to the festival. I believed—I had to believe—that a part of her reason for marrying was to punish me, and I did not purpose that she should see how the whip hurt. 'Oh, yes, I shall go. She shall not see a wince on my face ; only a smile. She shall think me healed of my love.' I had sent them my present, breathing thereon a private sigh ; and it was as handsome a one as I could buy : a full-calf set of the English Poets. To it I attached only a card, 'With best wishes from Doric.' In return I received a grateful letter—'It was so sweet of you, Doric ; they are quite lovely '—but the letter did not mention the name of Max, and I suspected, because I needed to, a hidden strain in the happy words.

The old grey church of Holm St. Martin is not small, but it was crowded that day. From tower door to chancel arch it was a mosaic of people in bright clothes. At first I sat myself with Mother and Uncle Humphrey and Lettice (yes, Lettice in her best and wiping an eye) in the front seats reserved for the bride's family and friends. Behind us and the groom's guests sat all the women of Holm St. Martin, whispering and watching and turning their heads, so popular was Max, their young doctor, and Gentle of the Chapter Mill. Away by the door Con waited among the bridesmaids, five girls in sea-blue, of whom by natural right, she was the chief.

Uncle Humphrey at my side supported a grey woollen muffler swaddled about his neck, because he was suffering from a sore throat (or thought he was) and had afflicted himself and us all for two nights with fears that he wouldn't be able to come. The day was entirely given over to the sun but he had brought, besides the muffler, his heavy and loose umbrella for safety. And all the time, as he sat in that church open to the golden air, he was staging for mother and Lettice and me all the effects proper to a sore throat : inhaling deep, pained breaths or short, sad, sniffling ones ; feeling the affected site and stroking it ; corrugating his brows and looking round for draughts ; coughing, swallowing and nose-blowing ; and after a rest sighing and siffling again, to draw our attention when he feared we'd forgotten his pain.

I looked often behind me, and just before noon saw Father come diffidently in. No, I am *not* partial : he was certainly the finest figure there with his notable height, and a new silk hat held against his new fawn waistcoat and an orchid in his lapel for Gentle's sake, and the gold-mounted cane dangling from his grey-gloved fingers. His entry was diffident and embarrassed, in the first place because, though he was little meek or wanting in confidence outside a church's walls, he had much humility and disquietude within them, never quite knowing what was toward ; and in the second place because Mother and Henrietta and Con must be somewhere about, and their neighbourhood always made him feel like a naughty boy who had yet to be forgiven. Indeed the thought of their attendance had nearly kept him away, but he decided (so he told me afterwards) to do his devoir by Gentle. The enemy was strongly placed, he said, but, for his dear Gentle's sake, there was nothing to do but fix bayonets and charge. So he fixed his orchid and came.

A young ' friend of the groom,' splendid in spats and white carnation, surmising at once that this was some very eminent guest, invited him to come forward to a high place, but Father waved him aside with a courteous hand and the dangling cane, and sat himself down in the hindmost seat of all beside the verger and the hymn books. I allowed myself two seconds of doubt and then left my place and went and sat beside him. This I did partly for his sake, and partly because I felt I could bear the hour better at his side.

His malaise within these solemn walls, and his ignorance of the deportment which they imposed, caused him to talk to me nervously and too often, and a little too loud.

' I say, Doric,' he began.   ' Where's the M.O. ? '

' Where's who ? ' I whispered.

' The M.O. fellow. The doctor chap she's marrying. I want to see what he's like. Devil take it, he's my nephew now, isn't he? Where's the best man put him?' He stood up, saw Max standing in his front pew, considered him for a long while, and sat down again, this time on a straying hymn-book, which he quietly cursed in a commanding style and returned to its ranks. ' Big fellow, isn't he, and a good looking lad in his way. A hearty, happy-go-lucky type, I should think ; I don't wonder that she likes him. But who's the best man ? What? Another M.O.? Oh yes, I see. He looks a weedy little devil. It's the very deuce being the best man, Doric, and having to see that the bridegroom doesn't come to church without the ring or leave it without his hat—or without the bride.'

' Tsh, Father ! Softly, please ! '

' Yes, but I know ; I had to do it once, fifty years ago. Every bridegroom tries to leave his wedding without his hat, and it's as much as the best man can do to force it on him. Good God, there's old Humphrey. And what's he making those filthy noises for ? He really ought to get rid of that frock-coat. He could get a few potted ferns for it.'

' Ssh, Father ! '

' Have the goodness to stop saying " Ssh ! " Everybody else is chattering. Where's our Con ? I want to see our Tricks, all

dressed up. At the door ? Why didn't the stop me when I
came in. Is she ashamed of me ? '

' She'd be a damned fool if she were.'

' Hush, Doric. This is holy church. Profane not the
steeplehouse with your villainous words. Who's the padre
peeping round the corner ? A bishop, and Max's uncle ?
Good God ! . . . Oh, *'cre nom d'un nom,* here's Henrietta.'

Though she had certainly not intended it, Henrietta's entry
drew and held the eyes of all. The church's central alley was
empty and waiting now, and Henrietta, preceded by the
groomsman, sailed up its whole length to her front place,
wearing a large black hat with plumes and a long black dress
with a white lace jabot and a cape, and carrying a bouquet of
roses which Max had sent her. Silently the congregation
watched this royal progress.

' What on earth's she dressed like Charles II for ? ' muttered
Father who had stood up again to consider her passage. ' And
why's she carrying a bouquet ? People'll think she's the bride.
I suppose she's weeping—I can't see ; but they always do,
and Henrietta certainly will. Ah, here *is* the bride.'

Gentle—Gentle sheathed in ivory satin and clouded in her
white veil ; one golden bracelet on her long white sleeve—
Gentle on Brian's arm, with her five bridesmaids following in
their foamy sea-blue dresses and bearing nosegays of pink
roses—one heard above the organ's triumphant swell the
pleased, admiring sigh of the rising people ; one felt the outrush of sheer tenderness—love mixed with pity—from the
older people towards this younger one ; one felt the generous
hope in many hearts that she might do better than they had
done and be happier than they had been.

' God bless her,' breathed Father with much feeling, as,
taller than all, he·watched her as far as the chancel steps. And
from a starched cuff he drew his huge silk handkerchief and
touched one eye and both nostrils. ' Ah, God be good to her.'

And I saw him bend his head and tightly close his eyes, and
knew that he, though a sinner, was determined to pray.

Many others, I am sure, asked of God at that moment that
he would be good to her ; and I tried to say Amen. Like
Macbeth, I tried to say Amen, but I could not. Alone in that
church I could not pray for Gentle and Max. Standing, and
able, like Father, to see above all others, I watched Gentle
remove her left hand glove and give it, together with her sheaf
of lilies, to Con behind her ; I looked at Max, ready to take
her hand, and cried ever louder in my heart, Damn him, *damn*
him, DAMN him !

Few words I heard, or cared to hear, till the Bishop, with his face turned towards Gentle, raised his voice as he said, ' forsaking all other, keep thee only unto him, so long as ye both shall live.'

' Forsaking ' . . . Yes. . . .

' I will,' said Gentle in a voice which all the silent people heard, though it was a shaken and whispering voice like a schoolgirl's.

Then through a great silence, and spoken in that same shaken and halting voice, came the words, ' I, Gentle Mary, take thee, Robert, to my wedded husband, to have and to hold . . .' and, even worse in their power to tear the heart to pieces, those in Max's deep, clear, confident tones ' . . . with my body I thee worship . . .'

After that I heard nothing : there were prayers up there, a psalm, a hymn, a mumbled address by the Bishop to the young couple, more prayers, and then it was over : Gentle on Max's arm was passing into the vestry, and some members of the two families were being shepherded there, too. Mother looked round for me to follow her, but I did not move ; nor Father. He was shy of Mother, I was shy of Gentle, and we remained together at the back among the people who were not even guests.

A long and, as it seemed, unending wait, while the people chattered and the organ meandered, and then a stirring of all heads like wheat in the wind, a universal rising, a loud greeting from the organ, and Mrs. Max Drury was coming down the nave on the arm of her husband, with the principal guests behind her and the others preparing to join the procession. Father and I fell behind the last.

We passed out into the sunlight to find a crowd of excited people about the path and to hear the full jubilation of the bells. Of late a large factory àrea had affixed itself to the east of Holm St. Martin, and to-day all the factory women, and many of the male hands, had hurried in their dinner hour to join the townspeople and the cottagers in the churchyard, and see their popular young doctor come out with his bride. So popular was he that the men immediately raised a great roar and kept it high, the women willingly adding their shrill cheers and the girls sustaining theirs till their faces were ripe for bursting.

This cheering in the sunlight, and the happy voices of the young girls, and the independent clamour of the bells above, which were opening their throats and vociferating goodwill in their own way—all this was too much for the matronly women and dragged up the tears to their eyes. ' God bless you, sir,' they cried ; 'God bless you both' ; 'Good luck, dearie' ; 'Be 'appy' ; and one said 'God bless you, *miss*,' to a roar of laughter.

'It's ever so moving, ain't it ? ' I heard, as I went by.

'Yes, that's right ; it gets you in the throat, some'ow.'

'And don't she look lovely ? '

'I'm shore I 'ope they're 'appy. The young doc deserves to be, I'm shore.'

'And Miss Gentle, too : she's sweet.'

And a man's voice : ' Ah well, 'ope it keeps fine for 'em.'

Always so ; always this overwhelming goodwill to a young couple ; this wish for them to be happy though the experience of most may belie the hope ; this watching and loving of them as they go by, because they are the symbols of the eternal dream, the eternal fairy-tale which so seldom comes true ; always this manifestation of the good heart of humanity.

All were for Gentle and Max that day in the sunny church-yard, save only I. I did not wish them happiness. I don't know what I wished. I remember only that as I walked past the graves, new and old, I envied their sleepers who had done with pain.

§

Like other guests Father and I decided to walk the pleasant mile to the Chapter Mill. And in the High Street, following the example of others, we stood to look at the house which was Brian's gift to Gentle and Max. It was a long-fronted, two-storied house, old and gracious, with its flat façade rising directly from the pavement, and its doorstep treading on it. To the townspeople it was known as the Rent House, because at one time it paid a rent to the Crown of sixpence a year ; but to most strangers and visitors it was ' the black and white house,' because its plastered face was painted a dead white, and its tall windows and door a glossy black.

'The right house for a doctor,' said Father. 'Well placed in the High Street and yet beyond question the residence of a gentleman.'

'Yes,' I said.

'I'll wager its little mistress will be proud of it.'

'Yes.'

I was looking at it as at one of my enemies. It had ranked itself against me, I thought, because Brian had offered it to Gentle if she married Max, and thenceforward it had played its part as a pander and helped to seduce her love. I seemed to know all her emotions as I stood there. She had been violently angry with me and at the same time impatient with me for taking her wild words too seriously ; she had a passionate need to punish me ; she was ever ready for a daring ' adventure ' ; and now, in her hot imprudence—her mind compact with dreams and her body, alas, with desires—she had set out upon this hazardous and irreversible course. I looked at the sitting-room windows and at the door and the step ; but, as a man on a mountain bridge can hardly look at the chasm below, so I took but one quick, awful look at the bedrooms above.

' Well, God's blessing on her home,' said Father. ' May she have much happiness there. Come along, Doric.'

We walked on between the hedgerows whose ditches, I remember, were crammed with cow-parsley and meadow-sweet, their banks starred with herb robert and speedwell and bush-vetch, and their ragged tops strung with wild rose. Strange that wild flowers could wound so deep.

At the Chapter Mill we entered the wide, beamed lounge (where, last time I was here, I had spoken so madly to Gentle and driven her into Max's arms) and saw Brian and Henrietta. side by side, shaking the hands of their guests. The butler, flurried by the presence of people, shouted only ' General Allan Mourne,' not mentioning me ; and Henrietta gushed, ' Kingsley ! How *very* nice to see you. *And* Doric.'

' A very lovely wedding,' said Father.

' Yes, it *was* nice, wasn't it ? Such a beautiful service, our wedding service, I always think. So terribly moving. I couldn't help crying a little. Just a little ! Very silly of me, I'm afraid. Very naughty.'

' Nothing of the sort, my dear,' Father insisted. ' I was in a thoroughly damp state myself. What else could we do ? We love our Gentle.'

' How nice of you, Kingsley. Isn't that nice of him, Brian ? '

' It certainly is.'

' You had a perfect day for it,' I offered, since I must say something.

' Yes, perfect, wasn't it ? ' And she turned again to Father, as if she were happier talking to him. ' I've always hoped my Gentle would be married in May or June. A young bride should be married in May or June, don't you think ? It's so fitting.'

' I only know she looked more beautiful than the June day,' said Father. ' That's all.'

' Oh, I'm so glad you think so. We had a terrible time with

her, didn't we, Brian ?   I had her in tears all last night and this morning.'

'She seemed to have taken fright at the last moment,' explained Brian.

'They always do that,' Father comforted them. 'There's nothing in that.'

'I know, I know,' agreed Henrietta, the tears now in her own eyes. 'Still, it's rather sweet to think that at the last moment she didn't want to leave her old mother.'

'Exactly. . . . Yes . . . well, we mustn't keep you.' And as, somewhat hastily, Father guided me away from them, he murmured, 'The woman's a fool. A mother like that's enough to make Gentle marry the first hedger-and-ditcher who asked her.'

We passed on to the garden doors where Gentle and Max were receiving the congratulations of the guests. Gentle saw me behind Father, and a terror sprang in her eyes. She instantly concealed it, crying out, 'Uncle Kingsley ! Max, here's my Uncle Kingsley !'

Father bent his body, lifted her hand, and kissed it. So bends the humblest subject over the hand of his queen. I am convinced he kissed her fingers in a moment of real worship for Gentle as the symbol of youth's hopes and dreams. His whole heart was on his lips just then.

'The loveliest bride I've ever seen,' he said, when he was erect before her again. 'This is my very dearest niece, I'd have you know, Mr. Max. There is nothing in England quite like her.'

'I guess I know that, General,' said Max, with his loud laugh.

'And this is my very dearest uncle, Max, whom I love next best to you.' Only a merry, careless utterance, not meant to hurt me. 'Incidentally, he's got no other niece, but he really did mean something when he said that. He meant that if he hád a hundred other nieces he'd like me a lot better than them—the horrible things. And thank you, Uncle darling, for your quite incredible present. I don't think I've ever seen real pearls before.'

'It was nothing,' demurred Father. 'A mere nothing.'

'Congratulations, Gentle,' I said.

Her face coloured a little, but she carried the discomfort bravely. 'Thank you so much, Doric dear. . . . Max, you remember my cousin, don't you ?'

'Oh yes, rather !' he agreed, heartily. 'So glad you were able to come along.'

'Many congratulations,' I repeated, putting out my hand.

'Thanks, old boy.' And he crushed my fingers with his thick hand and all the force of a Rugby forward.

'You had a lovely service, didn't you?'

'Yes, quite a good show, old thing, wasn't it?'

'We think the Rent House delightful.'

'Not a bad little crib.'

'Well, come along, we mustn't monopolize them,' interrupted Father. 'They are the hero and heroine of the day; we are nothing. Nothing.'

And so we left them, passing through the doors into the garden. The garden, falling to the mill-stream, made a many-hued picture of festival, with its big marquee on the lawn, the tables and chairs outspread upon the grass, and the women in their cloudy draperies and the men in their dove-grey top-hats moving slowly among the flower beds, while the waiters in white coats carried drinks to the old people seated in the shade of the trees.

I kept with Father, and since he, like me, was shy of meeting certain persons on the grass, I think we were a comfort to each other. We saw Uncle Humphrey seated quite alone with his woollen muffler spread over his shoulders like a shawl; and by a common instinct we went to him as a refuge. On seeing us he began to inhale pained breaths, put a deep infestivity into his eyes, and stroke the site of his sore throat. There was a welcome in the sad eyes for two confidants; and he told us all about the throat. It was very wearying, he said; very tiring; and he feared that as soon as the speeches were over he'd have to go home. 'It seems quite a nice young man she's got,' he added. 'I hope it'll be all right.'

A sudden attempt at cheering showed us that the bride and groom were going into the marquee, followed by Brian with Max's mother on his arm, Judge Drury, Max's uncle, with Henrietta, and the little best man with Con. The rest of us crowded after these, and we saw the long buffet table dressed with cold entrées and sweets and fruits beneath bouquets of white flowers, and the hired servants behind it, handing drinks and trays to the gentlemen. Max, I observed, was now at the counter and plying himself with draughts of 'dutch courage,' since he would soon have to make a speech.

Both for something to do and as a demonstration before Gentle of my perfect composure I served round sandwiches and drinks to the ladies, though my hand that held the trays never ceased to tremble.

Now it was time for the speeches, and His Honour Judge Drury, who'd been a county cricketer before he was a county court judge, scored a boundary with his opening sentence.

'Ladies and gentlemen,' he began, 'you may remember that Lady Mary Wortley Montagu once expressed the view that she was reconciled to being a woman because it meant she could never be married to one;' and when the laughs at this sally were over, went on, 'but I imagine our Max's feelings to-day are slightly different——'

'You bet!' roared Max; and his friends laughed and applauded him.

This pleasant opening led the Judge easily into some happy and elegant phrases about Gentle's charm, which were dutifully clapped, and so to his peroration, sincerely felt, and probably true of everybody in the tent except one: 'All our hearts and hopes are with you, Gentle and Max, in this hour. Not a heart here but is filled with the prayer, " God be with you both".'

'Hear, *hear!* ' called Father, and flicked a tear from each cheek.

Max, having to respond, drank another draught of courage amid the laughter and cheers and jeers of his friends, many of whom had been his fellow-students at Bart's and some of whom, to judge from their size, his colleagues in the Rugger Fifteen.

'Shut up, you fools,' he commanded, wiping his mouth, 'and let me get this over. This is the moment I've been dreading for weeks. It's ruined for me what might have been quite a pleasant and interesting day. While you folks have been enjoying yourselves, I've been wondering what in the name of Holm St. Martin and Papa and Mamma Greaves I was going to say. I don't mind confessing to my good uncle, the Bish, that I was worrying about it during the service, and it was then that I understood for the first time why in the prayer book the Solemnization of Matrimony is immediately followed by the Visitation of the Sick.'

This won him a laugh and a prompt interjection by the Bishop, 'It ought to be followed by the Publick Baptism of Infants'; which much increased the high good-humour.

'Thank you, sir,' said Max to his uncle, 'I'll do what I can about that'; and there was laughter again, and perhaps some slight shock to Henrietta, who, however, took comfort in the thought that doctors were always rather frank in these matters— and sweetly smiled.

'In despair of finding anything in my head suitable to say,' continued Max, 'I took down the Encyclopædia at our hospital and looked up any information it might provide on Women.

And you can believe it or not, ladies and gentlemen, but not even that mighty work, the Encyclopædia Britannica, felt equal to dealing with so difficult and incomprehensible a subject. All I could find, after articles on Wolverhampton and the common Wombat, were a few paragraphs on The Law Relating to Women, the last of which referred me in despair—I assure you this is true, folks—to the articles on Adultery, Bigamy, Divorce and Settlement.'

This provoked unroarious laughter. It was a hit better than the judge's ; it was a six over the pavilion.

'He's *so* comical sometimes,' whispered Henrietta, ' but always rather naughty,' and she smiled sweetly and pretended not to be shocked.

Pleased with this success, his eyes bright, Max raised his hand for silence and went on, ' Next I took down a Dictionary of Quotations, but the quotations about women were all so dreadfully rude that I put the book back in some alarm. They didn't seem to have any bearing on this woman I've married '— loud laughter—' whom I quite like, but perhaps I shall find out later that they were true after all.'

If it's right to begin a speech with laughter and end it with tears, then Max did his task well, for he passed now to a very simple statement of his love for Gentle, his gratitude to Life, and to her mother and father, for the gift of her, and his earnest desire not to fail her as a husband.

There were murmurs of appreciation, and some wet eyes, as he said these things in a dropping voice ; and a tremendous outburst of applause when, somewhat shaken by his own words, he came to his close, and turned his face from the people.

§

His speech over and everywhere praised, Max gave himself up to enjoyment. He drank largely of the champagne, he went forth with a bottle in each hand to induce others to drink, he joked loudly with his friends from Bart's, loosing the great laugh, dragging them by their arms ' to the tent where the bubbly was ' ; and leaving Gentle to look after herself. Once when I was in the marquee, getting some claret cup for Mother's refreshment and Uncle Humphrey's healing, I saw him come in arm-in-arm with two of the Bart's forwards. He dragged them towards the counter where Gentle was standing with Con and another of her bridesmaids.

' Come on, old boy,' he was shouting. ' Come on, Stinks.

No, you've got to come, Corky. You too, Boney. You can only marry me once.'

'Yes, but careful, Maxy,' said the one called Stinks. 'I don't think he ought to have any more, d'you, Corky? If he consulted me, I should prescribe *nux vomica*. Or a stomach pump. Dammit, he's got to get that shocking old bassinette of his to Salisbury, and we don't want Gentle smashed up on her wedding day.'

'It's not a shocking old bassinette. It's a new Daimler, my present to me and Gentle. And, anyhow, don't talk about bassinettes at this point. It's worrying. Come and drink.'

'Maxy, don't,' begged Gentle; and I thought she was a little ashamed—so soon had she become a wife! 'You'll never be able to drive.'

'Don't you believe it, my pet. That little Daimler's a peach and the easiest little filly in the world to manage. And listen, young lady, I love you dearly but I don't intend to be disciplined. It wasn't me who said 'obey' to the Bish, was it, Corky? I haven't got to obey anybody.'

'That's what *you* think,' laughed Corky.

'That's what I *know*, old cock. No one's going to bully me. You're the sweetest girl I've ever met, Gentle pet—at least I *think* so, but you aren't going to bully young Max, so come and have a drink with my dear old Stinks and Corky. They're good lads, though you mightn't think it to look at 'em. All the same, take my advice and never lend 'em any money. And as for old Boney, bar that man altogether. It's safer. Tell you what: go and get some of your nice girls for 'em. They haven't been properly catered for in that line. She's collected some very fruity little morsels for the party, Stinks. Almost makes me wish I was a bachelor again.'

I went from the tent to carry the drinks to my people, and when I had delivered them, I wandered back with the tray. I saw Gentle coming out of the tent alone, and at the sight of me she veered off in another direction, pretending not to have noticed me. All day she had avoided me thus, going anywhere except where I was; and I was glad of this, because I liked to believe that she was afraid of me and of her cast-out love.

Longing to escape soon, I strolled down the sloping lawns to the flower beds and walked along them, reviewing the blue delphiniums, the red sweet-williams, the rosy thrift, and the purple scabious; but they reminded me of the flower beds of Kensington Gardens, where Gentle with shy, seeking fingers had first taught me to love, and I left them and sauntered on to the wooden bridge that lay across the mill-stream. Here I leaned against its rail and looked down on the narrow water slowly slipping beneath the green sunshades of alder and elm. It was brown in the shadows and bestrewn with floating light. A few birds whispered and fidgeted among the leaves, but their little sounds were overlaid by the roar of the fall behind me. I lost myself in thought for a little, and then suddenly turned my face towards the lawns again, certain that I should see Gentle looking at me. It was so : she was standing apart and watching me ; and in that instant of mutual knowledge, I felt her passionate pity—the same which had run to me when I was locked in the cemetery catacombs, and touched my hand after I was expelled from school. Promptly I straightened myself, thrust my hands into my pockets, and strolled back into the garden, acting an untroubled content ; for I did not want her pity.

Some time after this, after I'd played before her eyes my serene and happy rôle, after she'd left the throng to go and change her dress, I slipped from the garden into the empty fields. I had hoped to sustain my pride to the last and wave them away in Max's car ; but I had to spare myself this. In the excitement and buffoonery around the car, amid the scattering of rice and confetti, she would have no chance to miss me ; and when it was over I would come back again and pretend I'd been there. It was now three o'clock. They would be at Salisbury by six. They would dine together in the White Hart Hotel, honouring the hour with wine, and then . . . then, as the night stole across England, I must give myself to the Tormentor.

§

Prothalamium. It was the last grey of dusk, and the night with its torment for me would soon possess the roads. I hurried down Warwick Road, that old highway of our childhood, and Finborough Road, which ran by the cemetery, for this was the straight route to the river. As in a seaport town there is a natural goal for the lonely walker, and it is the sea, so in a riverside city he will be drawn to the river. By these straight roads I should come to Chelsea Reach and the long embankments.

I passed by lighted taverns, loud with many voices, and into each I went in and drank whisky, hoping to get drunk before the night. But I learned that mental pain will produce its own anti-toxin to alcohol's poison ; and the whiskys did nothing for me but wash for a while the sour stain from my mouth ; they did not touch my power to suffer. My only comfort, if it deserved the name, was to smoke cigarette after cigarette ; and I bought a hundred to see me through the night.

Here were the lights of Chelsea Reach, and a fresh sea-smell from the river. I went to the river wall and saw that the tide was low and that the stranded barges lay on their beams in the shadows and sheens of the mud. It was almost dark now, and the lamps of the farther bank drove their shivering stakes of silver and yellow light into the mid-channel stream.

A clock struck nine o'clock. Nine. Perhaps even now he was having his joy of her and, even more unbearable, she was delighting in him. The anguish of it craved its end, and I considered a death in the water, but no, I could not snap the last link with Gentle : I must be in the same world with her. Besides, the iron pride would not permit that I conceded the victory to her ; it was now like an iron pillar in a concrete bed, which no flood could unseat or bend.

' Broken for me.' My self-pity found a poor moment of peace in saying this to the mud. ' I do not want her now. I should not want her now even if he were to die.'

One must keep moving when a torment is at its worst, and I drifted on between the parapet and the plane trees, gazing numbly at the lighted buses as they moved soundlessly over Battersea Bridge like targets in a shooting gallery. Little traffic broke the silence of the embankment road, but such as passed me by mingled the traffic of two centuries : the old slow, jingling vehicles of my childhood's century were easily overtaken, or insolently passed, by the motors of the new century, swift and smooth and exulting. There seemed to be no one but myself walking on the pavement : only on the infrequent seats among the plane trees the lovers sat entwined. Lovers entwined !

I wandered on by the bridges, as far as the embankments would take me—five miles—and back to Chelsea pier—ten ; then turned again. It was after midnight now and even the lovers had gone, and I staggered to a seat and, laying my arm along its back sat there with chin down and mouth agape. I suppose I dozed, for a clock struck two, and the continuous sighing breath, which had been audible all these hours, was apprehended by me for the first time—because it had stopped. London's breath was silent in sleep. ' She is asleep too . . . in his arms.'

' God give her happiness.' I said this once—or it said itself— and instantly I saw that I'd got a small healing from it ; so I said it again and again. ' Yes, it was the only way to bear it ; the only way to endure. If one could shake off one's own desires and lift up one's love so that it sought a happiness in her happiness, one could endure—just endure. But how hold one's love on that height ? Holding myself there, like a man on a brink, I repeated a hundred times, ' God give her happiness. I love her and care only for her happiness. I never want to hate anyone any more.'

And these last words, with their strange but immense appeal to the deeps of one, and with the light of truth that so strangely invested them, reminded me of the revelation (as I liked to think it) which had enlightened me in the Water Meadows of Magdalen ; but to-night my joy in that vision, that Call, was not the exuberant thing it had been then ; it was a weary and strain-ing thing. None the less I clung to it, because it was medicine and comfort, releasing me for a little from myself. I was going to do my best, throughout my life, to bring to the world the ancient vision of the seers : that man became adult and strong only when he grew out of his easy, self-centred hates, out of his animal delight in retaliation and reprisal, out of his primitive lust for revenge and zest in punishment. All advance in vision everywhere had brought men to the worship of unselfishness and gentleness and forgiveness and to the dethroning of all wrathful retribution in favour of correction by love.

' God give me strength never to hurt anyone as I have been hurt.'

In the spirit of these thoughts I tried to believe that my love for Gentle was unselfish now. ' I am happy if you are happy, Gentle. Sleep well . . . only don't wake, don't wake to give yourself to him . . . unless you . . . oh yes, be happy ; that's all I want.'

At some time I must have dozed again, because I dreamed that I was a schoolboy whom Mother had just punished and that, as I sat alone in some room in the old house, Gentle—not a child but a woman as I'd seen her some hours ago—came to me and stretched out a hand and said, ' Don't tremble so ; oh, don't, my darling.' And I awoke to find that this hadn't really hap-pened, and I was sitting on an iron seat in the cold of early morning and looking at the river on which the light of a new day rested.

BOOK IV

THE HOUSE OF ALLAN MOURNE

CHAPTER I

WELL, ONE adjusts : one adjusts to an amputated limb, and likewise to an amputated love. One goes on one's way. But the old wound aches when the wind finds it ; and for many years I liked these shoots of the old pain so little that I ran from the risk of them. My next years, the years between Gentle's wedding and the first of the German wars, were nine years of flight : flight from all knowledge of Gentle, from the sound of her name, and from the thought of her in Max's arms.

There was a flight of the body and a flight of the spirit. In my body I would hurry to the solitude of my bedroom and my books, because there I was in no danger of hearing Mother or Con—or Henrietta on a visit—speak of Gentle and Max in the Rent House at Holm St. Martin. Now more than ever when I took a walk I wanted to walk alone. Alone I would wander in the London streets, looking at the houses where my heroes, the makers of books, had lived (and where there was forgetfulness of Gentle). I went on pilgrimages to Thackeray's home in Kensington, Dickens' in Doughty Street, William Morris's on Hammersmith Mall. Hampstead saw me standing and staring at Keats' house in its garden ; the Vale of Health at the site of Leigh Hunt's cottage ; and Highgate Grove at the house which had been the last home of Coleridge. Always I could stand and gaze at thresholds which had known the feet of famous men ; and always as I loitered there I was dreaming of great things for myself. But sometimes, so perverse is an old but unspent passion, if I heard that Gentle was staying at her favourite hotel in Earls Court, I would make for those familiar parts and walk quickly past its windows in the hope and dread of getting a glimpse of her and suffering a lancinating pain.

The flight of the spirit was on to the higher slopes of Selflessness. I had learned by the river that there was no enduring the thought of her ' possession ' by Max unless I could want less for myself : if I escaped into my dream of helping to educate

the world, the pain sank ; if I turned back into selfishness it
was torment again. But it was very difficult to stay on those
upland places and I used a dozen private and rather shameful
methods of holding myself in the right course. I kept a visiting
card in a vest pocket on which I had written very neatly several
guiding lines, such as ' Joy in Large Giving,' ' Joyous Striving
but not Disabling Conflict,' ' The Right, irrespective of Happiness or Pain, Praise or Blame ; ' and I would take them out and
read them again as I walked along. At table for the sake of
practice, I would deliberately give the potato that had attracted
me to Mother or Con ; and if Lettice was out I would go and help
these women wash up, because I didn't want to in the least. In
the street I would give a coin to every musical mendicant I
passed, though it irritated me much to have to stop and search
my pocket.

And all the time another and opposite motive drove me : a
yearning for success and fame so that I could teach Gentle
something (I don't quite know what). The best in me might
condemn all vindictive punishment, but there was a masterful
need to punish Gentle. Gentle was now with Mother and
Henrietta and Harlen, goading me on to success ; and Gentle
was stronger than them all. Both motives, incongruous though
they were, kept my eyes on my goal. As a great publisher I
could do great good—and be great, for the instruction of Mother,
Henrietta, Harlen and Gentle.

Let me put it like this : my chariot was drawn by two ill-
matched horses, both of whom were out of the same mare though
by different sires. One was an exceedingly powerful beast, by
Egotism out of Humiliation, and the other was a lean and
struggling colt, by Vision out of that same brood-mare. This
second animal was as awkward as most young colts and often fell
down in the traces, but there were times when he was well filled
with corn and pulled even better than his partner. This was
not frequent, though : I should call him a horse of fair promise
but in a different class from his mate, whose strength was as the
strength of ten.

He was the one I loved, however, and I would try to fatten
him up with certain noble opinions which I had on other
visiting cards in the other vest pocket. I have these visiting
cards still—why not ? Their guidance is still good—and on
their yellow faces I read in faded ink : ' To promote the increase
of knowledge to the best of my ability in the conviction that there
is no alleviation for the sufferings of mankind except veracity of
thought and action. T. H. Huxley ; ' and ' That there should
one Man die ignorant who had capacity for knowledge, this I

call a tragedy, were it to happen more than twenty times a minute, as by some computations it does.   T. Carlyle ; ' and ' It is better to light a candle than to curse the darkness.'

So there was I in these years before the German axe fell, a shy, awkward, wandering, solitary young man, preoccupied with a hidden memory and an unspoken dream ; and never perceiving that, while I was hugging my melancholy like a loved possession (since it was Gentle's gift) and dreaming of lighting my new lamps of civilization, others were making ready to put out those that now burned.   I read, sceptical of its significance, that Admiral von Tirpitz was building a huge and heavy-armoured German Fleet ; and I heard, but little heeded, the flying tales : that Count Bulow, the German Chancellor, was in the mood to force a quick war upon France ; that Count Schlieffen, the German Chief of Staff, had a plan for the rapid overthrow of France by the sudden over-running of Belgium.   One day, as I walked along Oxford Street to my office at Sands and Hume's, and even as I was reading one of my visiting cards lest I backslid from grace, I felt a stir in the street, looked up, and saw German soldiers in spiked helmets slow-marching along the gutter.   Over their Prussian uniforms they carried sandwich boards announcing that Mr. William Le Queux's story of the Invasion of England would appear as a serial in the *Daily Mail*.   I turned to laugh at these scrubby and ill-kempt warriors (who were all over military age) and walked on.

I did not see in those days, but I see very clearly now, as I look back upon that young stranger, how much he resembled my father.   Both in appearance and in character I reproduced much of him, though on a smaller scale.   I was taller than most, yet shorter and slighter than he.   My face was like his, though, with its smaller bones, it was far less striking ; I wore my hair brushed up over the ears as he did (our faces were narrow and needed this correction) ; and, copying him, I dressed my figure in the best garments and swung a gold-mounted cane as I walked the streets. Like him I carried a stable melancholy beneath cloaks of solemn foolery or mischievous fun.   Like him I loved to parade sardonic despairs.   Like him I could lie when the occasion really demanded it, but I certainly lacked his fluency in this art and his fount of invention.   The only thing in which I surpassed him was in my passionate hatred of self-righteous punishment.   He enjoyed being gentle with some people but could be merciless towards others : I in the centre and heart of me wanted clemency for all—except Gentle.

§

During those years there was one refuge in which I took shelter from solitude and was happy ; and it was the home of Wyn Fellowes, my cheery and frolicsome colleague at Sands and Hume's. This was a cosy little red house, one of a long uniform row, in a quiet road off Wandsworth Common. Here in its small rooms, Wyn lived and made merry with his wife Lucy, a little round woman, blonde like himself, and his two excitable children, Michael, aged ten, and Sheila, aged nine ; and here I was a welcome and indeed a loved guest on almost every Sunday of the year.

The small rooms were furnished with little better taste than you would find in a working-class home ; after all, Wyn was the son of a working man, and Lucy was but the daughter of a small hosier in Bradford. But if the suites in dining-room and ' parlour ' were cheap stuff from Balham High Road, and the superabundant pictures were shining oleographs and stock steel engravings, the human quality that irradiated the rooms was a dear and precious thing. It might seem strange that in the home of a highly-skilled publisher's editor there were no books except the few that would be found in any other house in that street— Dickens, Tennyson, Marie Corelli, Anthony Hope, and some odd volumes of Hall Caine—but we have heard Wyn's statement, ' I know nothing about books but everything about a book. Personally I hate books ; ' and we know that he had little to learn from books, or from Abou Ben Adhem, about loving his fellowmen. May his tribe increase.

Wyn and Lucy, having risen in the world, were well-content with their present position and therefore always at ease and merry. I, in their house, was admired and loved and therefore free from shyness, pretension, and strain. Looked up to, but not without laughter, as a ' scholar ' and an ' aristocrat ', but loved for my own sake, I was as comfortable in one of their cheap easy chairs as in an old coat and slippers. After a Sunday afternoon walk on Wandsworth or Clapham Common, Wyn and I would rush into the house to chase and tickle the children, who would run with delighted shrieks from the attack ; and Lucy would cry, ' Mercy, mercy ! Quiet, *please* ! You set them off, Wyn ; and Mr. Allan Mourne, you're as bad ; you encourage him. Rampaging about the house like that ! ' to which I replied, ' I don't quite like " Mr. Allan Mourne," thank you. My name is Theodore ' ; but she could never quite bring herself to call me by my Christian name. It was very different with Wyn, to whom I was always ' Young Theodore ', and at tea or supper he usually made it his business to give a report to his wife about this young man's progress with the firm.

' He's going on very nicely, thank you, Lucy ; and pass the vinegar ; and Michael, for the love of Mike, don't talk with your mouth full.　Your uncle Theodore comes from a high-class home and isn't accustomed to sights like that.'

' He's completely accustomed to it,' I interrupted.　' He always ate like that himself.'

' That's nonsense, and don't you believe it, young Michael. Nor you, Spots '—Sheila was a spotty child.　' He's the son of a blooming general—General Allan Mourne, I'd have you know —and general's children eat nicely.　Yes, the lad's doing very well, Lucy my own.　I happen to know that Old Gretton told the Chief, " This boy's pretty good.　He's got brains," and Old Hammy, though not quite liking it, said, " Oh, well, bring him up to five pound a week."　They gave him a period in the Trade Department with my old man, and another in Production with Old Ted Williams, and that means they're bringing him on.　But, best of all, Old Hammy, as you remember, gave him some Reading to do, at ten bob a time, and now the lad's picked a blooming winner, a damn silly novel about God.　He recommended it strongly, and hell ! the damned book's begun to sell like the devil.'

' Hush, Wyn.　The children ! '

' Hell ! the damned book's begun to sell like the devil,' said Michael promptly.

And Sheila repeated the bad words and giggled.

' You are dreadful, Wyn.　You set them off.　And Mr. Allan Mourne, you're as bad.　You only laugh at them.'

' Not at all.'　I waved the aspersion aside.

' Michael, behave yourself ; Spots, be good,' ordered Wyn. ' And the sure way, Lady Fellowes, to stand well with Old Hammy is to pick him a winner.　Gaw-blimey, if the lad goes on like this he'll be a junior partner in forty years' time.　But there was one place where he was a real out-and-out, shining flop.　We all know it, but we don't let on to Old Hammy.　No sense in spoiling another bloke's chances.　He went out travelling with our Mr. Bendick in London and our Mr. Stone in the provinces, and he was just no good at it.　Not the slightest. In fact, worse than awful.　I had it from both Mr. Bendick and Mr. Stone.　They said it was pitiable.　He was obviously terrified of entering a shop lest he should prove a nuisance, and he blushed and stuttered as he produced his samples, and at the first unkind word he apologized and came out again.　Well, I mean to say ! you can't make a Publisher's Representative if you're as thin-skinned as that. You've got to have bounce and push and a hide like a buffalo. Nothing to do but wait till young Michael grows up. Our Mr. Allan Mourne was the complete mutt at it. He's much too much the gentleman.'

' I don't believe a word of it. I'm sure he did it very nicely,' objected Lucy.

' Call me a liar ! '

' I do. Yes, I think I do, dear.'

' Liar ! ' shouted Michael.

' Liar ! ' Sheila echoed. ' Daddy's a liar. Daddy's a fibber.'

' Well ! Upon my soul ! ' Wyn spat upon his palms to prepare them as weapons of punishment.

' Liar ! ' Michael repeated boldly, to provoke this gratifying and joyous castigation.

' But it's all perfectly true, Lucy,' I assured her. ' The one thing I learned from my weeks on the road was that if ever I'm a publisher on my own, in a small way, I shall never be able to travel my own books ; I shall have to pay someone else to do that job. . . . It's not a lie at all ; and your two children mustn't be allowed to say such things ' ; whereupon I, too, spat on my hands and got up to aid Wyn in his paternal task of correcting effrontery and insolence. The subject perished in a disorderly embroilment on the floor.

§

To these two children, Michael and Sheila Fellowes, I owe the founding of the House of Allan Mourne. In this little home, this warm and comfortable womb, my one and only book (if it deserved such a name) was born. Michael and Sheila were its begetters, Wyn its midwife. The children always called me ' Tam ' or ' Tammy,' from the initials of Theodore Allan Mourne, and they came to regard me as an entertainer whose talent was even larger than Wyn's and immeasurably superior to Lucy's. My method at first was simply to reproduce all the jests and tricks of my father, but after a while I contrived an ' act ' of my own, which proved a success above all others and was in constant and imperious demand. Soon it was an established custom that before either of the children would go to bed, Tammy must ' do them a Tale.' And I, after many protests, which were part of the fun, would sigh and sit down at the table with a pencil and some paper, and a child on either side of me, uncomfortably close ; while Wyn took to a fireside chair with his paper, *The People*, and Lucy sat opposite him with some sewing or darning. This domestic scene was always in the little dining-room, because the parlour was kept for ' company,' and I was not ' company ' but ' one of the family.' And slowly, and very deliberately, the pitiless children urging me on, I would tell them a tale of three uncivil children, two boys and a girl, of whom the worst, and therefore the most interesting, was the hot-tempered girl, Nancy Tantrum ; and, as I spoke, I sketched line by line an illustration, which was never completed till the last word was said, and the tale told. My tales were ordinary enough, many of them being no more than heightened versions of old escapades with Gentle and Con ; but the illustrations, I cannot deny, had merit. There were two topics, I soon learned, which particularly stirred and delighted these children. One was the Police, and my portrait of a new and important character—the character, you might say, who ' played opposite ' Nancy Tantrum—a certain Police Constable A. Restem, had much animation and verve. Nay, since I haven't much else to be proud of, I will say it was inspired. Always just before the end of the tale, P.C. A. Restem rushed in—on foot, on a cycle, on a horse, or with a Black Maria ; and once with a wheeled stretcher to gather up the remains of a child whom Nancy Tantrum had damaged. The other topic was Corporal Punishment, but, in chivalry, my pencilled studies of this business showed only the boys in receipt of it, while Nancy looked on. I don't know why—and I don't know that I want to know why—but these studies were the most popular of all.

The children would scream with laughter as tale and picture developed, and, when all was over, Lucy would drop her sewing and clap, and the children would copy her (for the sake of making a noise) and Wyn would get up, paper in hand, and, examining the pictures, declare that they were quite good and he couldn't imagine why I'd become a publisher's hack if I could draw like that.

This reception of my work was so gratifying that, just before Christmas, I bought a stout sketch book and assembled in it, with Indian and coloured inks, a collection of these illustrated tales. I gave the volume a highly decorated title page, ' The Tantrum Tales, by Theodore Allan Mourne, Illustrated by " Tam " ' ; and the publisher's imprint on this page was ' The House of Allan Mourne, London, New York, Toronto, and Melbourne.' There was also a Dedication : ' To the Onlie Begetters of these Insuing Tales, Sheila and Michael Fellowes, No Critics, but the Best Audience in the World.' And when on Christmas Eve I took this booklet, together with far handsomer gifts, to the children's parents, Lucy of course exclaimed, 'Oh, but it's lovely ! Look, Wyn. He ought to publish it.'

'Nonsense,' I demurred. 'It's only a little Xmas card for the kids.'

Wyn glanced through it and said, 'I don't know, old boy ; I think there's something in what she says. Not much, perhaps ; but something. This sort of thing is quite saleable.'

'Rats !' I scoffed. 'It's silly, cheap stuff.'

'That doesn't matter,' he said ; and I'm not sure that I was pleased with his ready assent. 'That doesn't matter if it's stuff that'll sell. You should see some of our juveniles. They're too awful—much worse than this. And, anyhow, it's the illustrations that sell them. All that the mothers and the aunties consider in the bookshops is the illustrations—and the book's bulk. So pile on the illustrations, and add some more yarns to give it bulk, and then put it up to Old Hammy, eh ?'

'Don't be an ass, Wyn. Is it likely he'd look at anything so frivolous ?'

'He'll look at anything if he thinks there's money in it. And I happen to know he wants to improve our juvenile list—as well he might. If a children's book catches on, it goes on selling Christmas after Christmas ; it's a small gold-mine. And look, old cock, you've no artist to pay. My God, my lad, if it caught on, you'd be sitting pretty !'

§

Whether he believed all this, or whether he was merely warming up with arguments to justify a pleasant fancy, I can't say ; but I was secretly excited by his words and in the next weeks compiled a fuller collection of the stories and generously illustrated them. It was no great task because the tales had been already told, and the pictures flowed so easily from my pen that they were a delight to draw. But not a word said I to anyone of the occupation that was filling my evenings ; I closed my bedroom door on it as I'd closed the door on my work at Oxford. In a month the new volume was finished, and one morning I carried it, with a vacillating heart and a damp, exuding brow, up to Old Hammy in his famous front room.

My interview was by appointment, and he greeted me in the friendliest way, thrusting back his desk chair and lowering his tiny spectacles like a flag, as I came in. 'Ah, yes. Theo. You were going to show me some manuscript or other, weren't you ? Sit down, sit down, my dear boy.' And, smiling, he ran up the spectacles to half-mast, as it were, and peered at me over them. 'Now what exactly is it, Theo?'

Never had I been so contemptuous and ashamed of my manuscript as in that moment. I wished that Wyn had kept his mouth shut and not encouraged me to make a fool of myself like this. I wished those idiot drawings had never been drawn. Nancy Tantrum, indeed! And P.C. A. Restem. This to Old Hammy! Absurd, ludicrous, to bring so trivial and foolish an offering into a room which had received for consideration the manuscripts of Wilberforce and Cobden and Coleridge. *Coleridge!* Coleridge and Nancy Tantrum. I wished I could sink Nancy and the police constable deep beneath the bowels of Gower Street; but alas, this was no longer possible, and I must go on in my shame. I sat down opposite Old Hammy's huge desk, and handed him the book.

'I don't know that it's any good,' I warned him hastily, as he opened it. 'It's only a juvenile.'

He pushed back his thin-rimmed glasses to study it. 'Oh, it's *your* work, is it?' asked he, scratching one grey whisker. 'I'd forgotten that.'

'Yes,' I admitted, from my pit of guilt. 'Yes . . . it's mine.'

'Really?'

'Yes.'

'Is that so? Yours?'

He turned page after page while my heart shook like a stranded jellyfish, and I had to knock the continuing sweat from my brow. He never once smiled. Not a smile for Nancy. Not a glimmer of a grin for the constable. On the contrary, he took a pinch of snuff, as if to refresh himself on a wearisome trek. Watching him, I soon realized that he'd never be able to believe in a book which was the work of one of his underlings. 'H'mm,' he said, and 'H'mm' again as he turned the pages over. 'I didn't know you could draw.'

'I'm afraid I'm only an amateur,' I said unwisely.

'H'mm. . . . H'mm, well, Theo.' He put on his saddest face as he laid the book aside and removed the spectacles. 'The market for juveniles is a treacherous thing. They're very costly to produce with all their illustrations; you can't sell them at more than three and six or five shillings; and in view of the fact that the big buyers *will* order an assortment of juveniles instead of a large quantity of a single title, it's almost impossible to get your money back, let alone see a profit. A heart-breaking business, juveniles. I don't know a worse. There's nothing in them, as a rule, nothing at all . . . or hardly anything. Just occasionally. . . .' But this occasion was apparently so rare as to be unworthy of further words. He raised despairing fingers from his desk instead, and lowered them again.

' I see,' said I.

' Still, I'll have your little book read in the usual way.' I didn't quite like the way he said ' little.' ' I'll send it to Merryman and Mrs. Holt, both excellent judges of juveniles. We won't let them know it's by one of the firm, and we'll just see what they say.'

' Thank you. Thank you very much.'

Less than a fortnight later he summoned me to his room again and said, ' I'm sorry, Theo, but neither of these reports on your little book is very favourable. Mrs. Holt liked parts of it, but Merryman was very critical.'

Instantly I believed in my book as never before and determined that it should be published at any cost.

' Neither of them recommend publication, I'm afraid.'

' No. I quite understand.'

' A pity. I'm sorry. I'm really sorry, Theo.' And with a most kindly smile he handed the book back to me. ' I'd have liked to publish a little book of yours.'

My disappointment was heavy, because I'd been allowing myself to dream of a huge, unexpected success, an inrush of money, a new standing with the firm, and the attractive modesty with which I would carry my triumph. My disappointment, I say, was great, but my indignation was greater. A little grooming and feeding of this indignation, and it became a power in the field. Old Hammy had turned my book down : all right ; I would give it to another house, and he should learn what he had missed. That same morning, using Old Hammy's paper, string and stationery, I sent it off to Mr. Grant Stevens, whom I believed to be a publisher of more imagination and enterprise. And I waited again.

Well, my little book repeated the story of every unknown author's manuscript : it came back unwanted from Mr. Grant Stevens, and from all the other publishers to whom I offered it. And with each rejection my belief in it grew and my indignation swelled—swelled like a poisoned arm, till at length I was determined to teach the whole tribe of them a lesson. God damn them all. I would adventure on a great gamble. I would ask Hammy to publish the thing for me on commission terms, or, in other words, to take a lump-sum for production and promotion and a commission on all sales. For the last three years, so hard was my ambition riding me, so sharp its spur, that I had put aside in secret the whole of my father's allowance and, by dint of living as frugally as possible with Mother and Con, had saved a substantial part of my salary, with the result that I now had nearly five hundred pounds in the bank. I would stake as much of this as was necessary. All if necessary. I put the idea before Wyn, and he, on the whole, was against it, but allowed, ' Of course if it came off, you'd be in No. 1, Happy Street, just taking the cash as they brought it in, but . . .' and he shrugged as a man with little hope. ' In any case, it'd be some time before you saw your outlay back . . . if you ever did. . . .' ' I don't mind that,' said I, ' so long as it comes back one day ' ; and I instanced famous authors who'd paid for their own books, Browning and Samuel Butler and even Dickens on one occasion.

' Yes, and wished he hadn't afterwards,' said Wyn.

But I was not to be reasoned with. The idea was a ferment within me. Walking the streets with bent head, I would calculate and calculate : say fifty pounds for printing a first impression of two thousand copies ; thirty for making two sets of three-colour plates and paper ; forty for binding, thirty—no fifty—for advertising and promotion ; ten per cent. commission to Hammy, something for warehouse charges . . . certainly warehouse charges, if Old Hammy did it. . . . Oh, God . . . my gloom gathered as I reckoned that I should have to sell all the two thousand copies before I broke even and three thousand before I began to make a profit. Three thousand ! Who would buy three thousand ? But even as I had refused to allow argument to mount my back and rein me round, so I unseated gloom and found reasons for going on. Old Hammy's travellers, who liked me, and liked me all the better, I thought, because I'd been such a failure in the job they did so well, would push my book for all they were worth. Jolly Sam Bendick would work hard for me ; so would Jack Stone. Yes, I was going on. I'd risk it. I'd risk all.

I asked for another interview with Hammy and went up to him with my proposal. As I expounded it, seated nervously on my side of his desk, he shook his head many times, but not so much in a flat rejection of the idea as in a distressing attack of doubt and pessimism. Once he smiled at me kindly but very pityingly ; and more than once he comforted his despondency with snuff. I had brought the manuscript with me, and he turned its pages as I spoke. He continued turning them after my voice had ceased ; then closed the book.

' No, Theo,' he said, removing his glasses and wiping them. ' I most strongly advise you against it. I do really, my dear boy. It's a hazardous business, paying for the publication of your own book ; hazardous in the extreme. I don't want you to throw away your money.'

' I'm prepared to risk it,' I said.

' Yes, but do you know the usual history of such a book ? We of course should try to do better for something of yours, but this is what usually happens to a book published on commission terms. The publisher binds up only a few copies at first, because he doesn't really believe in the book or he'd have acquired the rights himself, and he suspects that none but the author's friends will buy any copies and that the remainder market will be precious little interested in his surplus stock. And he's generally right in this : he sells perhaps fifty copies, and after that—what ? ' He spread before me two fat hands, empty of hope.

' Well, what ? ' I asked, trying to smile and appear amused.

' After that, my boy, the unbound sheets of your masterpiece are used to bind up the successful works of other men. A depressing business, don't you think ? '

' It certainly sounds so,' I agreed, turning my smile into something humorously grim.

' I can't see you beginning to get your money back till you've sold two thousand copies, and who do you imagine is going to buy two thousand copies ? '

I felt like replying, ' Two thousand people,' but decided it would be impolitic, so only answered, sorrowfully, ' I suppose it *is* asking a lot.'

' And don't imagine there's anything in it for the publisher,' he hastily enjoined. ' Dear me, no. Generally speaking, nothing at all. Less than nothing. It may seem that if he's carrying no risk, he must stand to lose nothing and possibly to gain. But it is not so. I assure you, Theo, it is not so. Some small vanity publishers—yes—they may make a pound or two out of the author's folly ; but not a firm like ours. Oh, no. And shall I tell you why ? It's because in a large and properly run business, the overheads are at least twenty per cent. of the turnover, and we can't—or we don't—ask more than ten or fifteen per cent. commission from the author. So where are we ? Down. Definitely down. Five, ten per cent. down. Of course, if the book were a success there would be certain compensating advantages, but the fact would remain that we were selling our services to the author at less than cost price. Do you see ? '

' Yes,' I sighed ; and could think of no more to say.

' The few books I've published on a commission basis—and I've done a few, I admit—I published chiefly for the purposes of prestige—and prestige is about all I've ever got out of them. Now you would hardly claim that your little book had any prestige value—or would you ? ' And he smiled at me, as if with a deep understanding of the vanity of authors.

' No, I suppose not,' I agreed, sighing again. ' No, but I thought there was just a chance it might be a good seller. And as a seller I thought . . . I imagined . . . it might be a useful title in anyone's list.'

He looked at me sitting there in my disappointment ; and after a little he smiled. It was the kindest and most fatherly smile he'd given me yet. ' But of course, Theo, if you really want us to do your little book for you, on these terms, we'll do it. For whom else should we do it, if not for you, my dear boy ? And I need hardly say that we'll do our very best for it, as it's yours. I've told you the worst. There's always a chance that it might have some sale. Do you still want to take the chance ? '

' Yes,' I said.

' All right. Then we'll do it. In time for the Christmas trade.' And he tossed the book to the side of his great desk, among other manuscripts that were awaiting publication.

I went out shivering. What had I done ? I had said the word, and all my money was at the hazard. Thank God, nobody at home knew the tricks I was up to, and nobody would ever know, should the die turn against me. All that day at my desk my hand quivered like the hand of a drunkard.

§

This was in June, and the next three months I lived and walked with anxiety, and at night lay down with it. I had no one to share it with, except Wyn, who of course behaved splendidly, telling our publicity department and our travellers that they'd *got* to put their shoulders behind the book because it was Young Theodore's. Together with the hopes and fears of a young author for his book my anxiety included the trepidations of an ambitious young schemer lest he lost the whole of his savings. Not a day in that three months but I was harbouring wild hopes and at the same time training myself to expect no more than that my money would be safe. I did sums in my head as I walked to my bus in the mornings, and began them again as I left the office in the evening. If the book were a success, I told myself, strolling slowly, head bent, down Gower Street, I might make as much as forty per cent. of its receipts. Say, one and six on each copy. Seventy-five pounds on a thousand copies ; three hundred and seventy-five on five thousand ;

seven hundred and fifty on ten thousand—and so on into New Oxford Street.

The travellers were subscribing the book, and I awaited their reports with a heart that drummed ever and again a funeral rataplan in my breast. The reports came, and it was Wyn who got hold of them and rushed into me with the news.

The first impression of two thousand copies was over-subscribed, and Hammy had consented to a second of fifteen hundred.

Two impressions before publication.

' What does that really mean, d'you think ? ' I asked as the drum-beat at my heart changed sharply from a corpse's to a conqueror's tattoo.

' It means the book's quite a nice little success, and may become a big one. It's the illustrations that have done it.'

' The letterpress wasn't so bad,' I suggested.

In the event the book was rather the nice little success than the big one. It was no ' sensation ' in the shops, but it was a wonderfully steady seller. Repeat orders came in soon after publication, and a third impression of two thousand was put in hand. The book received quite a few press notices, but always in a column where it was herded with several other ' Books for the Children.' I was soon in a position to know that I should make a profit but not a fortune.

§

A week or two after publication day, the book being now well established in the shops, I judged with some excitement that the time had come to tell the family. From the office I posted a copy to Father, ' with the compliments of the author, Theodore Allan Mourne,' and hurried home the same evening with a copy each for Mother, Con, Uncle Humphrey, and Lettice.

The reactions of the family as I dealt out the books—' This is a little book of mine that I've just published. It's nothing much, but it's going rather well '—were almost as gratifying as on that occasion when I announced to them the result of my Finals. Con who had so completely changed towards me since I'd become a man, and now, because her life was enclosed and narrow, chose to be proud of her tall brother and boast of his achievements—Con, I say, as she opened the book, screamed in a pleasure-laden surprise, ' Doric ! ' And he's never told us a thing about it ! Oh, isn't that just like him ? One day he'll come home and tell us he's married.   Oh Doric, but how lovely, how wonderful ! '   Good enough.

Mother's response was even more satisfactory.   As she grew older, a lonely fat woman with no husband to ridicule and correct her sentimentalities, Mother had become excessively emotional and had seemingly lost all mastery of her lachrymal glands.   I have never met anyone else who so easily abandoned herself to a sweet leakage of tears.   At anything the least sentimental or admirable her eyes were awash, her lips unsteady, and her nose calling to be blown.   She was, so to speak, perpetually at a stage-play which was full of moments that hit the heart.   And now she took my little book, looked through it, turned back to the author's name, and lost the power to speak.   How could she speak when her lips had begun to vibrate and twist, her eyes were blinking and wet, and her fingers were fumbling for the handkerchief in her waistband ?   She blew her nose so vigorously that it sounded a trumpet call ; and I shall always account that fine brazen song the proclamation of my second triumph over Mother.   The relief to her nose enabled her to speak, and she began, ' My children are doing so well——' and would have developed this thesis, only the words so moved her that she had to struggle with her tears again.   Splendid.   I could have asked nothing better.

Uncle Humphrey took his copy and said, ' Well, I do congratulate you, Doric,' and it was immediately obvious to me that this necessary congratulation covered an increasingly painful jealousy.   Disgust perhaps would not be too strong a word for his dismay that I should have become the family's author, despite his membership of the Authors' Society and the Authors' Club. ' It's really selling, is it, Doric ?   In its third impression ?   Well, I do felicitate you ; I do, really.   Of course it's light stuff—and it's light stuff that pays every time.   I *am* glad.   I could never have written a popular book myself.'   At first I was made angry by this wrapped-up derogation, but then, since the triumph was mine, my anger gave place to pity ; and pity for the less successful is not, one regrets to say, empty of pleasure.

Pleasant, then, though these first reactions of the family were, I was not wholly satisfied in the next weeks that they fully appreciated the success of my book.   There were things that pricked and chafed me.   One day Con came running in to cry, ' Doric, Doric !   There's a copy of the book at Smith's in the High Street ' ; and I felt like asking, ' Why not ?   Is there anything surprising in that ?   I should have thought that the surprise would be if it were not there ' ; but I refrained, in part because I didn't want to disappoint her when she was

trying to please me, and in part because I must hide my vanity.
Instead I went out to look at the book. At another time
Mother greeted me, ' Oh Doric, what do you think I heard
to-day ? Mrs. Haydn told me that they're actually reading
your book to the junior children at Queensgrove School. Isn't
that an honour ? ' and I wanted to answer, ' I don't see why.
I think it's very nice for the children,' but as in fact I was pleased
with the report, I said only, ' Dear me ! What an extraordinary thing to do. But I hope it's a habit that spreads.'

From Father I received no immediate acknowledgment of
the book ; and I couldn't understand why. I should have
liked to visit him on some pretext and so hear his surprise and
praises, but as usual my pride wouldn't let me. I had no
doubts of him, however ; as sure as Uncle Humphrey's attitude
to the book was one of private dismay and hidden sorrow, so
surely would Father's be one of high excitement and public joy.

Father was seventy-three now, but as strong and lean and
active as he'd ever been. Physically he was in admirable
shape ; mentally he was a martyr to boredom. His romance
with the lady he had brought from India, that last romance of
his life, had long ago faded into a smiling friendship ; and
now he was nearly always alone. Except for an occasional
board meeting, which he welcomed as a man with an aching
sprain welcomes a cold compress, he had little to do, and his
ennui was like a garment that burdened and fretted him. Weary
of reading in his comfortable chambers, weary of his club and
the papers and books on its tables, weary unto death of *Punch*
and the *Sporting and Dramatic* and the *Stage*, and of *Who's Who*
and the Army List, he would resume his top hat and his wash-
leather gloves and cane and wander out into the grey London
streets, to seek some new interest for his eyes or some faint
amusement that would kill the tedious hours. In the mocking
summer days he would take a seat in St. James' Park and watch
the water birds on the lake or the pretty women strolling by
or the lovers embracing on the grass. Or he would turn into
Lords and, seating himself in the pavilion by some old grey
acquaintance, study the cricket of his favourites, Plum Warner,
Gilbert Jessop, the Jam Sahib, and Charles Fry. On Sundays,
if the sun was about, he never failed to take his seat in
Hyde Park for the Church Parade and to pass in review the
dresses, and doubtless the figures, of the fashionable ladies
who promenaded up and down. On a wet weekday he turned
into an art gallery or a museum or the Sweated Industries
Exhibition at the Queen's Hall and, stalking slowly among the
exhibits, swinging his cane between his fingers, was not amused.

Sometimes in the evening, utterly at a loss for anything to do, his old eyes tired and damped by reading, he would stroll into a theatre, sit alone in a stall, and admire Isabel Jay, Ellaline Terris, or Gertie Millar, who were the queens of the musical comedy stage in those days. Or he would repair to the old Empire, take his seat there, and love Adeline Genée and several of the members of her corps de ballet and wish he was young again. 'One can love them all without desire,' he once said to me.

About this time, the Bioscope, 'The Wonder of the Age,' appeared in London, generally in some unrented shop, and I am grateful to those first picture theatres because, with their scratched and flickering episodes of comics stunning each other with croquet mallets and sooner or later sliding on to their bottoms on a greased pavement, gave many a loud haw-haw to Father in his back seat on an otherwise empty and arid afteroon. But it was always a melancholy moment when he came out from this brief divertissement into a London evening crowded with hurrying people but empty of friends for him. He wandered homeward among the people, swinging his stick. There were two lean solitaries mooning along the streets of London at that time, one as a rule in the north and the other in the fashionable west; a young one in a stiff white collar, three inches high, dreaming of his lover in the past and his fame in the future, and an old one in a top hat and yellow gloves, who, I suppose, had little but the past to dwell upon.

As these unlively and unlovely days went trailing by, like so many faded, indigent, and melancholy ladies, Father would lament, ' Oh my God, *'credieu, 'credieu,* I wish something pleasant would happen '; and he would affirm to some play-fellow of his own age and humour, ' Clearly the time has come to us, old boy, when the grasshopper is a burden, and desire shall fail, and the mourners go about the streets.'

So you can imagine that he was delighted when my book in its parcel burst upon him like a little bomb, and something pleasant could really be said to have happened. He walked out with the book to his club and talked about it to everybody there; he sat down and wrote to friends, contriving to mention it before his letter ended; he left it face upward in his room for his servant and the charwoman to see; he put a copy into the book rack on a club table so that idle and browsing members, hitherto uninformed about it, might notice the name, Theodore Allan Mourne, and ask him to enlighten them; he passed no bookshop without going in to see whether the management was doing its duty by it; and if he found it in some inconspicuous place, he re-arranged the counter, or the shelf, that it might stand out in greater prominence.

There were many, far too many shops, where he couldn't find it at all ; and in them he created, with perfect courtesy, a little focus of trouble. On the Saturday after publication day I was free of the office and spent the morning sauntering past one bookshop after another to see if by any chance my book was in the window and, if not (as was always the case), to enter the shop furtively and look for it inside. Every book-shop in Charing Cross Road had a visit that day from an innocent-seeming young man who sidled in from the pavement, browsed along the counter and shelves, and slipped quietly out again, either greatly uplifted or heavily cast down. This surreptitious and guilty search brought me by Coventry Street and Piccadilly to the bourne where I most desired to be, the famous bookshop of Pymm's in Bond Street. Not among the books in this window, of course ; one could not expect to see a juvenile in so select a gathering ; and I lit a cigarette to strengthen my nerves for the reconnaissance patrol inside. No sooner had I wandered uncomfortably in than my eye fell upon the tall, shapely back of a man in a top hat who had three brown-paper parcels of equal size—the size of my book—under his arm. One glance at his malacca cane with its gold band assured me who he was. He did not see me because he was conducting a gentle, well-mannered controversy with a young shop-assistant almost as well-tailored as he.

'You haven't got it ! ' he was saying. 'But that's extra-ordinary, isn't it ? It's a most talked-of book, and I've seen it reviewed myself in glowing terms. Dear me . . . and I was going to buy several copies for various nephews and nieces. Extraordinary. It's the first time I've ever known Messrs. Pymm's fail me. It's inconceivable to me that you can't have had it in stock. I suppose you had it, and have sold out ? '

'I don't think so, sir. I don't remember the title.'

'Extraordinary. Most extraordinary.'

'What was the author's name, again, sir ? '

'Allan Mourne. Yes, Allan Mourne, as far as I remember.'

'No, sir, I don't recall the book.'

'Well, I can't understand it. I just can't understand it. It's a book for which there's obviously going to be a big demand this Christmas. One review that I read said it was a children's book that had come to stay, because it was so original, and so different from anything else in that line. And I saw some-where that the publishers—Sands and Hume, I think—ha sold several editions before publication.'

' Is that so, sir ? '

' Yes ; and, unless I'm mistaken I read somewhere that it was having quite a vogue in America, too.   But perhaps I'm imagining that.'

The well-dressed young man, his defences now seriously shaken and his young, inexperienced heart invaded by self-distrust, said humbly, ' Well, I may be wrong, sir.   It may be that it just hasn't come my way.   I'll see if there are some copies in the stock room.'

' No, please don't do that,' said Father rather quickly, re-arranging the three copies under his arm.   ' I beg you not to put yourself to any trouble.   I can easily get it somewhere else.'

' No trouble at all, sir, if you wouldn't mind waiting a few minutes.'

' I can't wait long.   No, I don't think I can wait.   I have to——'

' Only one minute, sir.'

' Oh, very well.'   He bowed slightly.   ' I am greatly obliged to you.'

The young man bowed in reply and disappeared most surprisingly through the wall.

I touched Father's arm.   He swung round.   ' Good God. Damnation, Doric.   What are you doing—how did you get— for mercy's sake don't let him know who you are.   Better not know me, I think.   The young man's a fool, but—do they know you by sight here ? '

' Of course not.'

' Well . . . that's good . . . perhaps I'm exaggerating the danger.   Thank God they don't know me either.   I get all my books at the Army and Navy Stores.   The young man's gone to look for your book.'

' I know.   I was listening.'

' I pray God that he doesn't find any copies.   I really can't afford any more, Doric ; I am but a poor man.   Here are three infernal copies that I've been landed with this morning in shops that had it in stock.   And they nearly all have, Doric ; they nearly all have.   It's splendid.   Are you making a lot of money ? '

' Only a little.   But do you like it yourself, Father ?   You didn't even write to say you'd received it.'

' My dear chap, I haven't had time.   I only got it two evenings ago and since then I've been, as you might say, travelling the book all over London.   I went into about twelve shops yesterday, and this must be the sixth I've been into this morning. I rather enjoy it. Some of the shops I visited yesterday had had it and were sold out, my boy. Sold out ! All the others were quite interested to hear about it.'

' Thank you, Father. A very fine effort.'

' Yes, I think I've done good work for you. I've put it into an exceedingly prominent position in several shops ; and yesterday I bought about six copies—I forget the exact amount. God knows whom I'm going to send them to. Do *you* know any children ? Do *you* want any spare copies ? Hush, here comes the foolish young man. . . . Well, have you found me a copy ? '

' No, sir. We haven't had it in stock yet.'

I alone caught Father's faint sigh of relief. ' You haven't ? Well, it's most extraordinary. I've never known Pymm's fail me before.'

' Can I not order it for you ? '

' No, no, no. Please don't trouble to do that. I can easily get it somewhere else. I thank you very much for all your kindness. Come, Humphrey——' the first name he could think of for me, and he offered it for the young man's hearing— ' come, we'll go ; have you heard of this book—it's by someone called Allan Mourne, a son of old General Allan Mourne, I'm told.'

' Indeed ? And is that so ? ' I said, equally loud, as we approached the door. ' General Allan Mourne ? And who's he ? '

' A distinguished old veteran of the Crimea and other campaigns. But a bit past it now. I meet him occasionally, and he looks very old to me.'

' Does he indeed ? Senile, do you mean ? '

' A little. I fear we shall not have him with us much longer. Still, he's had a good innings——'

But by now we were safely at the door, and passed quickly into the security of Bond Street.

§

And last of all, Gentle. I got a throb of pleasure in the heart of pain whenever I thought of her seeing in some journal an advertisement of the book, and my name. But even if her eye didn't light on one of these she must hear of the book, and of its success, from Con or Henrietta. Would she write me a letter sparkling with congratulations ? I hoped not. Days passed, weeks passed ; she did not ; and I was glad, for what could it mean but that she still loved me and was afraid of her love ?

CHAPTER II

MY OLD friend who for twenty years was my neighbour at No. 11 Henrietta Street, Covent Garden, and the best of men and publishers (peace to his shade) used to say, ' When young men ask me how they can make a career in journalism or publishing, I always exhort them to write a book and get their name upon a title page. It is extraordinary what faith an editor or publisher seems to put in the judgment of someone other than himself. The editor will read your article and receive you in a cloud of hesitation ; and after many minutes surcharged with doubt and indecision will inquire, " Have you ever had anything published ? " You reply with fitting decorum that Messrs. Macmillan recently reprinted the second edition of your *British Butterflies,* and a light from within suddenly illumines his features. " Ah, yes," he says, " I like your article very much. Perhaps you would care to review this book, *The Exegesis of St. Paul* by Hermann Weiss." It's the same with a publisher. His opinion of a young man—I've experienced the phenomenon in myself—undergoes a profound change if the young man publishes a book on any subject on earth. All publishers, you see, are modest, timid, self-distrustful souls.'

This was certainly true of my experience with Old Hammy. *The Tantrum Tales* was the only book I ever published, and a very small one at that ; the inspiration that produced it was a trickle and no more ; my real and strong inspiration pulsed elsewhere in my heart. But Hammy was impressed—not with the book but with its success—and discreetly improved my salary and my position in the firm. He reminded me one day that I could have a small financial interest in any book I introduced to the firm ; and, much attracted by this bait, I did find him a couple of books that he was pleased to publish. One of these was only an indifferent success ; the other proved an acquisition in terms both of profit and prestige. It was by Norman Webster, a history don and friend of mine at Oxford. Entitled *Ordeal at Hand,* it argued without heat but without mercy, its style as cold and clear as mountain water, that the struggle for the future of the world between the vast iron and steel empires was already in being and must be decided by battle, not within a generation but within the next ten years. Germany would march when she was ready, her pretext for the great sortie being of small import ; and since the world was now an economic whole, a single pattern, the war must race along the economic fuses and fire the whole earth.

To me this grim work, since it brought me some credit with the firm and a little money to my bank was a source of nothing but pleasure. Even if I'd ever taken seriously its cold words of alarm, I quickly forgot them, because another book which we published at this time suddenly diverted the slowly swelling stream of my life into fatter meadows and handsomer parklands than any it had visited before. This book was Lord Cranmere's *Evening Memories*.

§

Lord Cranmere, whose London house was just round the corner from Gower Street in Bedford Square, was a little mischievous twinkling man with a face so broad and shallow that it reminded one of a beaming cat. His peerage at this date was only eight years old, and the world still thought of him as Sir Ayrton Sanctuary. Born in 1834, the son of middle class parents, he was educated at Bedford and Trinity, Cambridge ; rose rapidly at the Bar ; took silk in 1870 ; and entered Parliament in 1874. Both at the Bar and in the House he was a twinkling focus of electric storms, so that the name of Ayrton Sanctuary was pleasantly familiar to all who read the newspapers. If the headline was not ' Judge rebukes Mr. Ayrton Sanctuary ' or ' Sharp Clash between Judge and Counsel,' it was ' Scene in the House. Mr. Ayrton Sanctuary Walks Out,' or ' The Speaker Defied. Mr. Ayrton Sanctuary Suspended.' Any revolt or mutiny in the Conservative and Unionist ranks was sure to have Ayrton Sanctuary as one of its leaders ; and his own party were as often vexed by him as the Liberals seated opposite. All the same he was one of the most popular members in the House, because the House will always take kindly to anyone whose capers amuse it. Between 1886 and 1905 he was in and out of office, and in 1883, being out of office then and temporarily out of the limelight, he married the ' much discussed Society beauty,' Lady Mary Manley, nearly thirty years younger than himself, and so drew the limes upon his figure again. His party, returning to power in 1886, tried to sweeten him with a knighthood ; but the sweetening effect dissolved rather quickly ; his devilments started up as actively as heretofore ; and in 1900 they put him away as a peer.

It was with the typed record of this lively and eventful history that he came round the corner of Bedford Square to our door in Gower Street and (unlike General Allan Mourne who had no such titles to fame) was shown up at once to Old Hammy's front room.   There, so he told me afterwards, for he was neither discreet nor scrupulous, Old Hammy had said to him, ' I've got exactly the right lad to look after this book of yours.   A brilliant lad ;   a real Live Wire.   He took a First at Oxford and is by way of being an author himself.   He's got a real flair for books that'll sell ;   and I don't mind telling you, in the strictest confidence, that I've got my eye on him for Manager of our General Books Department one day.'

The typescript of *Evening Memories* by Lord Cranmere, came up to me in my office, and I was much titillated as I scanned it, for it was as impish as the career it recorded.   His political career finished, his book written, his time on his hands, and his house round the corner, this restless little lord would come blowing into my office, twice a week and more, with new schemes for the book's format, illustration, decoration, appendices, or publicity—especially publicity ;   and one morning, my shyness warmed out of me by such a merry little brazier, I submitted to him that the title, *Evening Memories*, was ' not really good enough.'

' What's wrong with it ? ' he flashed.   ' It's a beautiful title. Absolutely right.   It's evening now, and I'm tired.   I have nothing but memories to comfort me.   It's the perfect title, young man.'

' But isn't it a little ordinary ? ' I dared to ask.   ' A little commonplace ? '

' Is it ? '

' Well—I mean—it has been done before.'

' Has it ? '   He saw the light at once.   ' Of course it has.   A damned silly title.'

' It won't sell a copy for you,' I said.   ' Your name'll sell a lot, but there's no reason why the title shouldn't help as well.'

' None at all.   And it's *got* to help.   We must certainly have a title that'll help.   My God, that was a filthy title.   But can you think of a better, young man ? '

' Well, sir, as a matter of fact, I have thought of one.'

' You have, have you ?   Damn your impudence.   Well, let's hear it.'

I prepared the ground for my suggestion.   ' What I feel, sir, is that people will always think of you as Sir Ayrton Sanctuary. That is so, is it not ? '

' That is so, surely.'

' They no more think of you as Lord Cranmere than they think of Disraeli as Beaconsfield ? '

' I appreciate the comparison, young man.'

' And—er—if you will allow me to say so, the career of Sir Ayrton Sanctuary has been a trifle stormy at times——'

' Shockingly stormy. And now at last I'm at peace.'

' Exactly. And the title I had in mind—it's only an idea, sir. You understand it's only an idea ? '

' Most assuredly it's only an idea.'

' Just a suggestion, sir.'

' Just a suggestion. No more.'

' You can say if you don't like it.'

' I have every intention of doing so.'

' Well, it's—it seems to fit the—may I say—impish mood of your book——'

' *Impish*, young man ? '

' Well, shall we say the somewhat irreverent, slightly disrespectful style——'

' Irreverent, yes. I accept irreverent. Continue. What is your title ? '

' It's—er—it's *Quiet in the Sanctuary.*'

He considered this for five seconds ; stood up ; and thrust forth a hand. ' Superb. An absolute stroke of genius, young man. I shall tell old Scotch Whiskers downstairs so. *Quiet in the Sanctuary* : it'll sell another million. I must go and tell my missus. Thank you, indeed. You must come and meet my family sometime. I've two boys much of your age, and a girl.'

This I took to be no more than a verbal discharge with no hard core of truth in it, a mere blank cartridge ; but sure enough one day in June he came blowing up our stairs with an invitation to a week-end house party at Cranmere Place in Berkshire. And on the Saturday afternoon I arrived at the little Cranmere station, to find a chauffeur and a long car waiting for me. The car swept me through the lanes, through an ornamental gateway, through a timbered park and into the courtyard of a modern house as large as a hydropathic hotel.

A manservant led me across a wide and pillared entrance hall, like a roofed atrium, into a large south room. The sunlight from the park, trespassing in the big room, showed me that it was oblong and panelled in new oak, with a refectory table as long as a shop's counter standing by the east wall, and doors and windows opening on to a white-paved terrace. Lord and Lady Cranmere, who had been sitting on the terrace came in to welcome me. Lady Cranmere, once the ' much discussed Lady Mary Manley,' was still beautiful in her late forties, slender, erect, and grey-haired. Lord Cranmere, some inches shorter than she, presented me. ' Here you are, my dear : this is my young collaborator. Any success my book may have will be entirely due to him. He's corrected all my English and removed all the bad language. A very severe young man indeed : wouldn't let me keep anything the least bit libellous. He's probably saved me thousands of pounds in damages—but I was sorry to lose that bit about Baxter Plowden ; I owed old Bax one. What did you say your Christian name was ? We can't go on Allan Mourning you all the time. Theodore ? Oh, yes. Well, Theo, the children are out playing tennis. Go and get into some flannels and come down here to tea. Edmonds will look after you.'

A manservant—a younger man than the one who'd opened the door to me—led me up a wide staircase to a larger bedroom than any I'd slept in outside a hotel. It faced south, and I went to one of the high windows and looked out. And at once the idea came to me that this green prospect was very like the view from the Chapter Mill, except that in every detail it was more imposing. The difference was between a nobleman's park and a country gentleman's garden. The home gardens sloped down, not to a mill stream but to a broad river ; instead of a single tennis lawn there were three side by side ; instead of rough meadows around the garden there was an undulating park ; and instead of copses and spinneys on the far side of the valley, there were massed and billowing woods.

Remembering our flat in Addismore Mansions I was a little awed by the grandeur and harried with doubts about my hand-bag, hair brushes, and pyjamas . . . and at the same time wished that Gentle could see me here. Leaving this handsome chamber, I felt financially several sizes too small in the long corridors and on the grand staircase, as I went down to tea.

In the oak room below I found all the rest of the party assembled and waiting for tea. Three young men and four young girls stood talking to Lord and Lady Cranmere. These young people were quickly identified to me as Iris Sanctuary and three of her friends, and the two Sanctuary boys, Roger and Stane, and a friend of Roger's from Oxford. I made the fourth of the young men.

Lord Cranmere presented me to his daughter in much the same terms as he had used to his wife. ' Iris, young woman, this is Theo who's kindly rewritten my book for me in the Queen's English, I mean the King's, God Bless him. You always wanted to meet an author ; well, here's one. He writes books that sell in thousands. And, Roger, he's a lesson to you, too. He got a First in something or other at Oxford. You'd better get together with him some time and find out how it's done. My daughter, I should tell you, has recently come of age. I never had much control of her, and now I have none.'

He and the others drifted off, but Iris lingered deliberately at my side.

One may be done with love, as I was ; one may have lost the power to love again ; but a beautiful girl, and the scent about her, can still shake the blood in one's veins. Iris was as tall and slight as the long sword-leaf of the iris flower ; her skin had the colour and texture of a snow-drop beneath her black hair, and her eyes—well, a flatterer might have found a further justification for her name in the purple iris of those dark eyes. But even as I was shaken by the closeness of her beauty—a beauty as of black and white ivory—I found myself saying, ' Gentle . . . Gentle . . . My dear. . . . '

' Well now come along all to tea,' said Lady Cranmere, and we went to the chairs about the refectory table. Iris deliberately took the chair beside me.

During tea she talked only to me ; and most of her talk was questions ; she, the daughter of this great house, seemed to think of me as a person of some distinction and of much interesting experience. She asked me about books and authors and our famous house in Gower Street ; and said very little herself. Often between her questions she went into long silences ; and behind her silence, behind her reserve and the unfinished smile which she allowed herself but rarely, I seemed to feel a kind of imprisoned vitality, something impatient but impenetrable. Twice she spoke with an excited fluency : once when I mentioned a new book on the Irish Literary Revival which we had both read, and once when Roger Sanctuary jeered at the militant suffragists, calling them ' wild, wild women,' and she defended them with a suppressed fury, as if ice should glow with submerged fire.

Did I compare her with Gentle, as we talked together ? Of course I did : all the time. They were proud young creatures both, I thought, but whereas Gentle would spray you with liquid fire if you touched her self-esteem, Iris would be too proud to answer you. Gentle, if she decided after immense thought that she'd behaved badly, would fling her arms around you, gaze up at you from the depths of her funded love, and plead, ' I'm being good now ; ' Iris would admit an error but be too proud to weep or plead.

After tea we went out to tennis and here at least I was not only equal but superior to all these gilded children. Tennis was the one game in which I excelled.

At dinner, since I was the oldest of the young men, Lady

Cranmere placed me on her right, and again Iris sat herself next to me. She tried to talk about books as before ; and this again was fortunate for me because on this subject, as on the tennis courts, I played a more expert bat than any of them.

Next day was less kind since they all went riding and I had to admit that I'd never learned to ride. I could only stand with the grooms and watch the cavalcade ride out of the courtyard. Iris sitting her horse well in her long, draped, side-saddle skirt, was plainly disappointed that I was not of their number, but in her silent fashion, she said nothing.

Well, Iris and I paired off that brief week-end by some mutual understanding and without a word said. She preferred my talk and my tales to the talk of her brothers and her girl friends. These boys and girls paired off, too, in the way of young people at a house-party. On the Sunday evening she took me for a walk through the park and the woods. The warm balmy air drew confidences from each of us as it drew scent from the soil and song from the birds, and soon Iris was bewailing to me the dullness and futility of her existence. She was talking fluently now, and I was the listener. We passed from the sunlight on the lawns into the shadowed coolness of a woodland ride ; and here the deep scented quiet, spiced with leaf-mould and resin, seemed to lay its own silence upon her and bend down her head ; and it was I who had to speak.

' I should have thought you had a rather wonderful life,' I said.

' Me ? *Me ?* But just how ? It's not too bad in the season ; I quite enjoy balls and parties and the theatres and the opera and all that ; but it isn't enough. And what about the rest of the year ? What about the winter ? I entirely refuse to go hunting——'

' You refuse to go hunting ? '

' Of course I do.'

' Why ? '

' Because I think it's cruel and wicked, and nothing'll ever make me think anything else. Daddy says that's not my real reason ; he says it's just that I want to be clever, and different from everybody else ; and I daresay that's partly true ; but it's not the whole truth, honestly it's not—I *do* think hunting and shooting are abominably wicked. I think that in three hundred years or so we shall be as surprised that we were capable of such brutalities as we are surprised now that once we could torture human beings and burn them alive.'

' I'm so glad you think that. I agree, I agree absolutely.'

' Yes, I rather thought you would.'

' What made you think so ? '

' Oh, I don't know. I suppose because you look slightly more intelligent than the boys about here. Tell me also that you think it's wicked that women can't do anything really interesting with their lives.'

' If it's so, I quite agree.'

' Of course it's so. You know it's so. And I'm just *going* to do something. I've quite a lot of money that Grandma settled on me, and I'm going to start up in something really interesting.'

' Such as what ? '

' Oh, I don't know. I wish I did. P'raps I shall start a fashionable dress shop like my friend Dahlia Groome, but I don't really care for the people who've no other interest but dress, though I like lovely clothes as well as anyone. Sometimes I think it'll be a picture shop. Darling Mother's horrified when I suggest this. She thinks it's still 1860.'

' Why not an antiquarian bookshop, dealing with rare and beautiful second-hand editions ? Like Quaritch's in Piccadilly. It might become one of the literary shrines of London.'

She stood still for a second on the path ; then walked on. ' Oh *what* an idea ! Honestly, that rang a bell inside me. In fact it rang bells all over the house. Crumbs, I must dwell more on that.' The ' Crumbs ' showed how recently she'd been a schoolgirl.

' But would your parents let you ? '

' They'd have to,' she said.

I asked her if she didn't want to marry, and she said, ' Oh yes, but not to be *only* married ; ' and then I told her all about my particular and resplendent dream, as volubly as she'd told me about hers, and she said, Oh, it was wonderful, and why couldn't *she* do something like that. And so, brushed at times, I remember, by the strong scent of azaleas, we walked on between the great pines and the green walls of hazel, our feet breaking the fallen twigs and the crisp old leaves, and our lips building insubstantial palaces with a mass of words, and all the way Gentle's ghost walked beside me, hanging with both hands upon my arm.

§

When on the Monday morning I had to return, all the party came out to see me off. Their laughter and jokes surrounded me, as I stepped into the car ; and only Iris was silent. I think the only word she said was good-bye ; and from the sadness in her face it was plain as the morning's sunlight that she didn't want me to go.   And just before the end an odd little incident happened : when the chauffeur had spread a rug over my knees and was picking up my bag to place it beside him, it was Iris who shut the car door with a sudden, sharp slam, as if she were accepting defiantly that all pleasant things must end.

I waved to them all as I went, and she waved back to me a little longer than the others.

And as I sat in the car, remembering that sorrowful slam of the door and that sustained waving of her hand, I saw nothing of the passing hedgerows because a temptation had descended upon me, and entered me, like a sudden corrupting spirit.   Strange how it was shaking me : it shook my body to the finger tips even as a spun web is shaken in every thread when the spider slips in from the leaf.   I could not love Iris ; I could never give her the love which her proud young eagerness and her delicate beauty deserved ; but I could desire her—desire her so that I trembled at the thought of possessing her.   She was beautiful above many ;   yesterday in the wood she had worn a dress of deep royal blue which had brought out the blue in her black hair and in her dark eyes and in the veins of her arm ;   and she had seemed to me to have a beauty as of some unnamed blue-and-white iris flower.   Seeing her now, instead of the passing hedgerows, I could desire her with all the hunger of a lad who for three years—ever since Gentle went to another—had starved himself of a woman's touch.   Iris as a wife. . . .   Of what was I being reminded as I brooded upon this picture and upon my knowledge that it would be wrong to take her ?   Of myself walking up and down by the Steward's Room before I took two silver coins.

Iris would be beautiful to possess ;   she would bring money and power to my dream ;   she would feed my pride in every room and every assembly into which I led her ;   she would give me a new position in the world ;   above all, the noise of my marriage to Iris Sanctuary, who had beauty and distinction and wealth, would be the most incredible triumph of all over Mother and Henrietta—and Gentle.   Gentle, I must always believe had married to punish and hurt me ;   now it was my turn ;   and I would administer a discipline sharper than hers.   Inevitably I found myself saying, ' You tried to chastise me with whips, Gentle; I will chastise you with scorpions.'

Like drops of shining quicksilver the desires ran together into one temptation, and the most powerful desire of all was the hunger to teach Gentle.

CHAPTER III

ONE DAY that week I was walking down Bloomsbury Street to take a meagre lunch in Holborn (for I was still saving every penny) ; my hands were lightly clasped behind my back, and my head was bowed with thought, when I felt a finger's touch upon my elbow, and heard a soft contralto voice say, ' Hallo, Lonely.'

' Iris ! ' I cried ; and a trembling promise seemed to come from the deeps of her to me, like the thrill along an angler's line.

' Yes, it's Iris,' she said, and smiled, and tossed her head because of a sudden undisciplined blush.

' And how nice to think it's Iris. But I thought you were still at Cranmere.'

' Good Heavens, no ! We came back two days ago. And now I'm only round the corner from you. Where are you off to, you grave and solitary man ? '

' I was off to eat a roll and butter somewhere. But I say ! I suppose you couldn't come and have lunch with me ? I'd give you something better than that. I know a very savoury little Greek restaurant in Percy Street.'

' Oh, I'm sorry—I can't—I'd have loved to—but I'm just going to meet Daddy and have lunch with him.'

' And which way are you going ? '

' To the Haymarket and the Carlton.'

' Then I'll come with you, part of the way.'

' That'll be very nice. Thank you.'

' And some other day you really will have lunch with me ? To-morrow ? No, that's asking too much.'

' To-morrow, of course. I'd love to. And don't forget— *please* don't—that you promised to show me your house and the room where all the famous people have been.'

' Come any day you like. Just come, my dear. The walls will fall before you.'

' But what about old Mr. Hamilton Hume ? He won't want a stray young female floating around.'

' He'll receive you with the utmost gallantry. And if I know him, he'll want to do all the honours himself.'

' Oh, I'd much rather you did that. I should be frightened of him. And you *will* show me the room where you work ? '

' It's not a room. It's a—a bit. It's like a dressmaker's cubicle—or a horse-box. And there's nothing to see there except a desk and piles of dog-eared manuscripts.'

' Never mind.   You're doing something for the world there.'

' Are we ?   Sometimes perhaps.   More often we're just making money.'

' But when you have your own firm—oh, it'll be wonderful. It'll be doing something, something, *something* !   I'm almost as excited about it as you are.   I want it to be the most terrific success.   Can't you take me on as your secretary or something ? I'm sure I should be quite magnificently useful, because I'd be as keen about everything as you.   I'd only want a quite minor rôle.'

' Talk sense, Iris dear.   Can you see your parents letting you do anything like that ? '

' I shouldn't ask them.'   For a second the defiance in her face stripped it of beauty, but it passed like a momentary darkness, and she said serenely, ' I intend to lead my own life, Theo dear.'

That was the first time she'd added ' dear ' to my name, and though it was only an echo of my ' Iris dear,' it gave me a moment of sharp pleasure.   I dropped into silence, while I wondered whether I'd ask her to call me Doric or keep that name for Gentle.   We were walking now through St. Martin's Lane and Seven Dials, places as unsightly, and as stained with human crime, as the wood last Sunday had been lovely with nature's innocence ;   but here we were—walking side by side in the unfragrant street, just as we had among the rhododendrons and the pines.   And while I was strengthening myself to take the name Doric from Gentle and give it to her, I became aware that she was looking up at me.   I kept my eyes ahead, pretending to be unconscious of her look.   And after a little, in that low contralto voice which was as sensuously seductive as her skin or the scent about her, she asked me, ' Why do you always look so sad ? '

' *What ?* ' I feigned a fine indignation.   ' I do nothing of the sort.'

' Yes, you do.   Oh, you can laugh and be amusing and all that, but as soon as you've done laughing, your face turns so sad.'

' It's a lie.   I'm a jovial type.   Anyone'll tell you so.   And the more I think of it, the more I decide that I'm exceedingly sanguine and confident.   I always believe that the best is going to happen one day, and that all my plans will succeed.   And on the whole they have ;   they did at Oxford ;   they did with that silly little book ;   and——'

' And they're going to with your publishing house.   I know they are.   And I think it's a shame you won't let me have a hand in it.   I should be extremely useful.'

'Iris, you're very sweet,' I said.

She flushed from throat to brow, and said, ' Oh, nonsense,' softly, with her eyes swerved away ; and we fell into another long silence.

In Coventry Street, at the corner of the Haymarket, we stood for a minute while she reaffirmed her promise to lunch with me to-morrow, laying her head on one side as she did so, and putting a grateful gleam into her eyes. Then we parted ; and I watched her as she walked down the street. She walked with grace among the shuttling people. Once she turned her head, saw me watching, and swung her eyes away ; and I could not but see, in that quick and shamefast movement, the shyness of a proud girl in love. I continued watching, certain that she would not turn again. Her steps, and the light swaying of her erect body, were pleasing as her low voice or her proud, pale face. My heart beat like an exhausted wrestler's, as I fought the knowledge that it would be a crime to take her when I had no love to give.

§

But of course I took what was spread before me. She visited the Gower Street house, and her passage raised a fine dust of chaff for me in the vicinity of Wyn Fellowes. She came many times to lunch with me, and one day in late July, when the season was at an end, and a long separation before us, I arranged a very special lunch at Wynter's in Piccadilly. And, waiting on the pavement before the restaurant, I did not see her approach, because my eyes were on the ground ; I only felt her fingers on my arm and heard her voice, ' Hallo, Thoughtful.'

I started ; looked at her in some fear, as at something I was disposed, against conscience, to steal ; and stuttered, ' Hallo, Iris dear.'

' Miles and miles away as usual,' she laughed. ' Why are you always in a dream ? What were you thinking about then ? '

' Perhaps I'll tell you before the day's out,' I said. ' Now come in and eat.'

The lunch I ordered was an expensive one, and she rebuked me for spending my money on her. She wanted me to keep all my money for the publishing house, she explained.

When the meal was over, and our coffee drunk, she sighed, ' And now I suppose you'll have to go back to your old office,' and I demanded, ' What are you doing this afternoon, young woman ? '

' Nothing,' she replied, lifting her eyebrows as if to query my meaning, just as Gentle used to do.

' Then let's go for a walk.'

' Oh, I'd love to ! ' she said with eyes looking into mine ; and I knew I could lead her anywhere.

Picking up her hand, I said ' Come,' and led her out into the sun-splashed afternoon.

Where to ? Not to the park—the park was full of memories of Gentle—not there. Take her far from there. But let it be some lovely place.

Piccadilly leads straight to Kew. It becomes the Great West Road and goes on and on to Kew. The buses, running heedlessly past us, had their faces to the West and Kew.

' Do you ever ride on a bus ? ' I asked.

' Of course I do. What do you think I am ? '

' I read the other day that the Queen had never been in the Underground, so I wondered if you'd ever been on a bus.'

' Don't be quite ridiculous, Doric.'

Yes, I was Doric to her now. I had told her to call me Doric in a moment when I was thinking of Gentle and the way she had jilted me. I had handed the name to her in a passion of resentment.

On the tops of two buses we got to Kew. And we wandered in the gardens, now filled with the shadows of summer. And after we had roamed between the paraded flowers—red dahlias, pink begonias, and old red roses—we turned on to the grass beneath the great trees. And when we were far away from all other people we lay down under a sycamore, heavy with early fruit. I did not speak because a fear of what I wanted to say was breaking up the beat of my heart ; and Iris did not speak for a while, because the varied beauty of the many-vista'd garden, like the continuing music of a great orchestra, was filling her with dreams. I know this because she suddenly begged, ' Tell me more about the publishing house. I love to hear about it. Will you be able to start it fairly soon ? '

' Not till I've saved a lot more money, my sweet.'

' But couldn't you take a partner with money ? '

' If I did that, he'd be the boss. And I want to be my own master. And I'm most horribly vain : I want the house to have my name only, the House of Allan Mourne.'

' Well then, I'll be your partner. Wouldn't that be rather nice ? And I'll promise to be a very junior one so that you can have the final word about everything. And you needn't worry about the name of the house. It need never be anything but the House of Allan Mourne.'

Was I wrong in thinking that she was encouraging me, helping me on my way towards her, making my path straight ?

I turned my head and looked at her lying there. She was now leaning on one arm and picking up the winged seeds of the sycamore that lay about the grass. And I told myself that I could love her. I could love her in a way. I could love her with all the love I had left. I loved her love of me ; I admired her fine, unsatisfied longings and her taut control of them ; I was attracted by her rare but sure smile, so much smaller and more reserved than Gentle's ; and—most of all, I suppose—I wanted her pale beauty.

' Iris,' I began ; and I laid my hand upon hers.

' Yes ? ' Her hand under mine trembled.

' Oh God, Iris, I wish you were a lot less than you are.'

' Less ? What on earth—I don't know what you mean.'

' I want to ask you something, and I don't know that it's right to.'

Her eyes were staring into mine now, and she was speechless, because the question was coming.

' I want to ask you to marry me, but I've so little to offer you. Look, dear—perhaps it's only a dream—but supposing I did well and made money, would you marry me ? '

The fright faded from her eyes, and the faint, rare smile moved her lips.

' Well ? ' I requested. And it comes back to me now that even in this moment I half hoped—or should I say, quarter hoped ?—that she would discourage me and save me from sin. ' Well, dear ? '

She picked up a sycamore seed and looked at its twin spread wings, so as to keep her eyes from mine. She broke the seed with her two hands. The seed of the sycamore breaks very easily at the heart.

' Please ask me differently,' she said. ' I don't want an awful lot. Say " Iris, will you marry me as I am ? " '

' Iris ! . . . *will* you ? '

' Oh, my dear, of course I will.'

' But . . . ? ' The ' buts ' seemed so many and so large that I could only pack them together in that one bewildered syllable.

' There are no " buts " for me, Doric dear.' It was the very sentence I had used to Gentle. ' I'd marry you if you had nothing at all. Don't you see that I—— ? '

' That you love me ? '

' Yes. Of course I do.'

I picked up her hand and kissed it reverently. 'And I love you with all my heart,' I lied, since she must not doubt and be hurt.

'Oh, you're so sweet ; so beautifully courteous ! I love it. I love everything about you.' She encased my hand in both of hers, almost passionately. 'And you're going to let me help in everything ? You're going to let me really be your partner ? I can't imagine anything I'd rather do or be. Oh, but it'll be too wonderful ! '

'My God—Iris, my dear—I hope I never fail you.'

'I'm not afraid of that. I know it's going to be marvellous. I'm happy—I'm really happy for the first time for years.'

'But Iris—precious one—we've got to be sensible. What will your parents say ? '

'What should they say ? '

'They won't think I'm anything like good enough for you.'

'But that's nonsense. We're nothing very much. We're terribly *new*. I can't get used to being the Honourable Iris, and all that—it's so stupid—it means nothing.'

'But your mother ? '

'Yes, she's ancient, and may be rather difficult. But I've got Daddy in my pocket, and he'll soon manage Mummy. And even if he can't——'

'Do you mean that if your parents wouldn't consent, you'd marry me just the same ? '

'Why, naturally.' And again she lifted protesting eyebrows in the way that reminded me so of Gentle. 'You *are* being silly.'

'Then we are engaged now—this moment—whatever happens ? '

'Whatever happens.'

I slipped an arm behind her and drew her against me, as I'd longed to do for many days ; her lips parted in anticipation ; and while I kissed them, and because her kisses were sweet, my heart broke with love for Gentle.

§

On the whole it would be true to say that the 'buts,' the road-blocks across our path, were conquered and subdued by Father. He it was who overcame—or sufficiently overcame— the doubts of Lord Cranmere and the more-than-doubts of Lady Cranmere. After leaving Iris at her door that day I ran with my news, like an urgent and laden messenger, to Father's chambers in Pall Mall. Breaking in on him in his sitting room, I found him seated by the empty fireplace, a book splayed upon the floor at his side, as if it had fallen from his fingers while he slept. Very tired and lonely he seemed to me in my hour of excitement and hope. When I'd told him all, and answered all his questions, he rose and, walking to the window, looked out upon the traffic of St. James's Park and the Mall.

' I'm happy if you are,' he said. ' Very happy. I've met Cranmere more than once—a funny little man—but I've never seen his girl. If she's anything like her mother, she must be beautiful.'

' She is,' I assured him. ' *You'll* love her, I know.'

He did not answer at once, but turned his eyes to the roadway below. I knew he wanted to say something and was shy of saying it. When he spoke he kept his back half-turned to me, to avoid my eyes.

' Doric, I'm the last person to preach, I know, but I do want you to be happy in life—or as happy as anyone can be in this not-very-satisfactory world—so may I say just this ? There's only one way to be happy . . . only one way. . . .' His brow was pleated and cleft above the ' absent ' eyes, as he tried to see a truth and find language in which to enshrine it. ' You must try to love her always . . . her, and no one else. I'm telling you this because it's what I failed to do, as you know, and I've learned my lesson. I don't want you to fail. One day you'll be seventy-four like me, and at that age one can be very lonely if one's forfeited one's companion. . . . One needs a companion at seventy-four. . . . So listen, my boy ; this is wisdom ; keep the love of one woman who'll be with you at the end. . . . Yes, that is wisdom ; you know it at the end.'

The words drove straight at the guilt in me, and the doubt, but I buried my thoughts and said, ' I'll try, Father.'

' Do, my boy. It's never easy, but do try. I so want you to be happy.'

How greatly moved he was by my sudden news I learned the next morning—the very next morning when an envelope arrived for me containing his gift. This was much too soon for a wedding gift, but I understood why he had sent it within an hour or two of my leaving him. It was because his emotion wouldn't let him wait ; because he wanted to be first with his offering ; because he wanted to strengthen my position with the Cranmeres ; and lastly because he was feeling old and in melancholy moments had a fancy that anything might happen to him any day now. With the gift there was nothing but a card on which he had written in a tremulous hand, ' My little offering to you and dear Iris. A small contribution to the publishing house.' The gift was a cheque for two thousand pounds.

Great as was my gratitude, it could not silence the little thought that he had more money than he'd ever admitted to us.

Next he put on his best garments and went round to see Lord and Lady Cranmere in the house in Bedford Square. And he looked so stately in their drawing-room (Iris told me) holding his silk hat, cane and gloves, and towering above her little father like a handsome Quixote above a smiling Sancho Panza, that Lady Cranmere was much comforted and the pallisade she had erected began to crack. Between Iris and him it was, as I had foretold, love at first sight. His courtesy, and his obvious heartfelt affection for someone young and eager and vulnerable, won her adoration as surely as they'd won Gentle's.

I have to confess that, in my snobbery or my fear, I was glad he went to Bedford Square before Mother and Con, because they were both so terrified of Lady Cranmere and her drawing-room that they talked much too loud in a brave effort to appear at ease ; and I'm pretty sure that after their departure some of Lady Cranmere's doubts came marching home again.

But neither of her parents could have broken down the determination of Iris ; and so we were married, Roberta, on a June day in a village church, just as your mother was. Indeed our wedding reminded me all the time of your mother's ; it seemed the same thing on a greater scale. The church in Cranmere is much smaller than the one in Holm St. Martin, but Cranmere Place, as I've told you, is much larger than the Chapter Mill ; and its grounds, while resembling the Mill garden in configuration, are grander in every contour and feature. There was a great gathering of guests in the church, and all the village stood about its doors, waiting to see the daughter of the Big House come out in her pearl-white satin and lace veil, and to cheer her and her husband on their way. The pressmen and photographers were at the gate. All my family and friends were there, on the groom's side of the church—all save one : Father and Mother ; Uncle Humphrey and Con and Lettice ; Brian and Henrietta and Max Drury ; Old Hammy ; Wyn and Lucy Fellowes ; and old Mr. Fellowes from our Trade Counter, together with some of our travellers who'd served my little book so well. I'd insisted that these last were my real friends and must be there among the wealth and fashion ; and Iris had enthusiastically agreed.

So all whom I loved were there—except Gentle. Max came bringing the news that she was ' not very well,' and my heart leapt at the lie. Why had she stayed away ? I knew, I knew :

it was because she loved me still and had shrunk from my wedding at the last minute, though I had borne the burden of hers. This knowledge was my sweetest thought all that day.

I know not how to set down the truth of my wedding, Roberta. How is it possible to be at the same time happy and unhappy ; exulting and disconsolate ; triumphant, acclaimed, delighted— and a little forlorn ? And yet that was how it was. All my ambition, vanity, and proud desire to chastise Gentle were regaled that day ; my body too was lit with anticipation ; but all that was honourable in me, and all that was Gentle's, were hurt and buffeted and confused. I never loved Gentle with such poignance as I did throughout the ceremonies and festivities of that day ; and yet I was pleased to think of her seated alone in the Rent House of Holm St. Martin and receiving my lash on her back. My pride, laying its hand on its old, unhealed and throbbing wound, taunted her, ' If you wouldn't have me, Gentle, there was another that would. And she is very beautiful—more beautiful than you, my dear. She loved me enough to give everything to me.' Through and through my mind raced these thoughts as I stood at the altar with that brilliant congregation behind me and this lovely, proud, and fine-wrought creature at my side. And yet, as the priest bade me say after him, ' I, Theodore, take thee, Iris, to have and to hold from this day forward . . . to love and to cherish, till death us do part,' I spoke the words loud enough for all the congregation to hear, and in my heart I said, ' I love you only, Gentle . . . you only, my sweet, my beloved . . . till death us do part.'

§

After the breakfast in the Great Drawing Room of Cranmere Place the guests rambled about the gardens or sat in the ample stretches of sunlight and shade. Seated in one place I saw Henrietta and Brian and Mother and Con, all a little lost in these green preserves of the *haute monde*, and keeping together for mutual support. In quite another part I saw Father and Uncle Humphrey seated side by side. Father after a few courtly and constrained exchanges with his wife and daughter, and with Henrietta and Brian, had escaped from a quarter in which he felt neither loved nor admired and sat himself beside a beech tree which at least was empty of criticism and hostility. And after a time Uncle Humphrey, equally lonely, had strolled across the garden and joined him ; and now these two old brothers were seated together in the shade.

I both saw and heard Max. He'd been uncompanioned and silent at first, but now, after drinking well at the breakfast and the buffet, he was very cheerful, and his loud laugh rang often over the heads of the company. He had found a friend of his own age, and these two and some other young men had got among a pack of girls and were having sport, persuading them to drink as the waiters came round with the trays. If a tray was not in sight, Max went and found one, either bringing it himself like a trophy or leading a waiter like a prisoner behind him.

Max was fuller in body and more florid and veined in face than when I'd last seen him four years ago at his own wedding ; but he was still a fine, square-shouldered, powerful figure as he neared his forties. The old sparkle still sprang in his dark eyes ; the loud laugh waited ever behind his lips. A laugh can carry much character, and not a little of Max's life at Holm St. Martin seemed to come ringing towards me whenever he threw back his head and released that great cachinnation. It sang of his popularity in sick roms and hospital wards, of his lively cricket on village greens, and of his geniality and jocularity in bar parlours and by the tavern doors at closing time. I didn't doubt that he was not only a plentiful drinker in the taverns, but a generous treater too. He might have many of the faults of a self-indulgent man—inconsiderateness, irascibility and moodiness—but meanness was not among them.

So much I suspected from his laugh ; what else might lie in that handsome dark head, what passions, secrets, and shames, I had no means of divining.

Till now I had avoided him, but I must speak to him once before the end of the day (lest Gentle thought me jealous of him), and when the young men had fallen apart from the girls and coalesced in some kind of young-masculine congress, I walked up to join them. Buzzing over an argument, like wasps over a broken fruit, they didn't notice my approach ; and I heard one of them, Max's friend, say, ' It's coming. It's coming all right. It's no longer a question of " whether," but " when " ! '

' Well, when ? ' demanded Max, an untroubled smile in his moist eyes. His voice was wet and thick, and he had to clear a way for it.

' In five years' time ; or maybe sooner.'

' B——s ! ' Max scoffed ; and others echoed him with less violent syllables, ' Bosh ! ' and ' Rats ! ' and ' Poppycock ! '

' It isn't poppycock. I read an amazing book the other day —you ought to read it—it showed that war is just about as certain as that it'll rain to-morrow or the day after.'

'Why?' demanded Max.

'Why, Tony?' asked another, less aggressively.

'Oh, I can't give you the whole bally book—there's five hundred pages of it—but briefly, it dealt first with the economic roots of this absolutely certain war; then explained why these roots would flower above ground in Germany as a denial of Christianity and a religious exaltation of Power; and then showed that this was exactly what was happening. You've old Nietzsche proclaiming that the only morality is for the strong to exploit the weak; and another boorish old bore, called Treitschke, a professor in Berlin, teaching his ugly little German lads that their first business is to overthrow the British Empire which alone stands in the way of an empire of their own——'

'The horrible old stinker!'

'Yes; and the book shows—it's an extraordinary book, documented at every point; you must get it—it shows that Germany's not only prepared spiritually for war but will soon, and *very* soon, have all her material preparations complete. The naval force she's assembling at Kiel and Wilhelmshaven has no relation whatever to her peace-time needs—her trade doesn't require it, and her coast line doesn't require it—so what's it for? *Us!* The book calculates that she'll have everything ready by about 1913, and any time after that she'll strike.'

'*Will* she?' Max rubbed his hands together. 'I just hope she does. She'll get all she deserves. And I shall be there to knock sweet hell out of her.'

'Oh, no, you won't,' jeered one of the youngest of them. 'I shall be there, but you won't. You'll be too old.'

'Too old?'

'Yes. There's four years to go before 1913, and you'll be forty then.'

'My dear young lad!' Max's nostrils opened in a large but tolerant contempt. 'Are you aware what my profession is? I'm the only one here who's absolutely certain to go. You'll probably be rejected for flat feet or disorderly heart or chronic alcoholism, but not me. I shall be an M.O. They'll want every doctor they can get. See, ma' wee laddie?'

'All right. But doctors can't fight. They're forbidden to by the Geneva Convention.'

'I strongly supsect that this M.O. can, little boy, Geneva or no Geneva.'

'Never mind all the fine things old Drury's going to do,' put in another of them. 'What's this charming book called?'

'*Ordeal at Hand.*'

'I published it,' said I grandly.

'Ah, the hero, the young hero of the hour ! ' Max greeted me ; and when I'd boasted how I'd discovered the book and induced our house to publish it, he went on, impatient at the interruption, ' By my gosh, but that's a nice little piece you've chosen, old horse. She's lovely. I like them dark myself. A lucky old sinner, isn't he, Tony ? I'd give something to be in your place in an hour or two . . .' and, compressing his lips in a tight smile, he nodded and gave me a knowing look. Then, thinking of the privileges which he enjoyed, he said, ' I'm sorry Gentle couldn't come.'

' What exactly was the matter ? '

' Don't ask me. I haven't the faintest idea. She seemed quite all right last night and to be looking forward to the drive. You haven't seen my latest car, have you ?—the prettiest little thing ever. A four-seater tourer ; and runs as sweetly as an electric brougham, though ten times as fast. I brought Pa and Ma Greaves along in it, and they had some bad moments when she touched seventy. No fault of mine that Gentle wasn't with us. I badgered her to come. I said it was sure to be a good show with plenty of phiz ; and by God, it has been. It's her loss.'

From the impateince of his tone I knew that he was often exasperated by her and quarrelsome with her ; and I was glad.

' A pity she couldn't come,' I said.

' Don't know that I'm so sorry now. I'm quite enjoying being a grass widower for a day. Have another drink.' A servant had appeared with a tray. ' You'll need it. You've all your troubles to come. We old married men know, don't we, Tony ? '

I could play this game of badinage well enough with another, but never with Max ; and I answered weakly, ' I'm not expecting much trouble.'

' You wait. Women are damned difficult things to manage, and the most loving are often the worst. They play up in the most extraordinary way. It's wearisome at times. The only thing to do is to let them know at the beginning who's boss, and how much you're going to stand. Is that right, Tony ? '

' That's right, Maxy.'

' See ? He knows. So drink deep, old hoss, and always have plenty in the house. As your doctor I prescribe it. Here's to you. And to Mrs. Iris Allan Mourne.'

Later, when Iris was receiving the flattery of a dozen women, and I was standing apart, I gazed about to see what Max was doing, and saw him walking with one of the prettiest girls, Sibyl Waynewright, along the flower beds. Neither was looking at the flowers ; and from the inclination of his head I suspected that he was offering gallantries and she was liking them. The sight fascinated me and I kept my eyes on them. Very slowly, laughing together, she looking up and he looking down, they drifted across the sloping lawn to the wood by the river. A small plank bridge led over a dry ditch into the wood. Unabashed, Max hooked one of his fingers into one of hers and led her over the planks into the loneliness of the wood. They did not emerge again, and I, thinking, ' I must know. I have a right to know,' though I could specify no right, lit a cigarette, tossed the match away, and sauntered towards the skirts of the wood. The ditch kept to these skirts, and I strolled along on this side of it, pretending to smoke and keep my eyes on the ground, but really sending sidelong glances through the tall fringe of undergrowth, while the heavy grass muted my steps. The girl had a blue frock, and soon I discovered her like a cloud of wood-smoke behind the hazels and the elders. Why so still ? Why so silent ? As, long ago, I used to listen at doors to things of great import to me, so now I stopped and peeped through the ragged branches. Max was tilting up her face and dropping kisses on her mouth.

I came away, glad that he was failing Gentle. The cigarette, only half consumed, I threw into the ditch, like something which had served its purpose. And then suddenly, as I ascended the slope again, my pleasure changed into an outrush of love and pity for Gentle. Was she unhappy ? She must not be. ' Oh, Gentle, no.' Within me the words said themselves. ' Gentle, my beloved, if ever you want me, I will come. You are mine. I love only you.'

I felt happy because these words had proved that I loved her still with an aching and all-giving love, and it is so much sweeter to love than to resent. I went back smiling to the people on the lawns and to Iris, my bride.

CHAPTER IV

WE MADE our home in Queensberry Place, in a white-painted house that was similar to, but smaller than, the old home in Coburg Square. Like that house it had a basement, four stories and a pillared portico and stood in the Royal Borough of Kensington. We could furnish it but sparsely at first, leaving the upper rooms empty ; and it must have seemed bare and small to Iris after Cranmere Place ; but she was as pleased with it as a child with a new possession, and would walk about it, in our first weeks there, to gaze at and rearrange the rooms.   I, too : my pride and pleasure were no less than Father's in his first days at Coburg Square ; only my expenditure was much less than his.   One by one, however, we bought pieces of furniture and pictures and ornaments, and gradually furnished the empty rooms.

But the charm of this first ' home of my own ' was soon transcended by another house : a high, lean, ugly house, of pepper-black brick and grimy windows, which rose, with its neighbours shouldering it, above a racket of market carts and a reek of vegetables.   I was walking along the brief chasm of Henrietta Street, Covent Garden, weaving my way among the carts and the porters towards the Market, when I saw it standing there empty and blind, with a notice-board projecting above its shop-window, ' Lease to Let.'

A lease in Covent Garden !   There are three places in London where publishers most do congregate ; along the walls of the British Museum, at the entrances to Covent Garden Market, and beneath the north shadow of St. Paul's in Paternoster Row. That the producers of scholarly books should have flown to the precincts of the Museum, as to a bird sanctuary, we can well understand ; and that the producers of holy books and good Sunday reading should have set up their booths in the flank of the cathedral ; but why such publishers, and others like them, went to the brims of Covent Garden Market who can say ? That the theatrical costumiers and wig-makers should sit among the wholesale potato merchants, the fruit salesmen, and the nurserymen is intelligible enough, since here are London's two greatest theatres, Covent Garden and Drury Lane ; but why the staid publishers ?   Why did they dress their shop-windows along these uncleanly gutters, littered with cabbage stalks, straw and horse dung ?   Why did they staff their offices and counting houses in rooms where you can hardly hear yourself count for the clangour of horse-hooves and iron-shod wheels on granite setts ; and where all day long, outside your windows there's a rattle of drays, vans, pony shays and hand-barrows, a drumming of tumbled crates, boxes, baskets, and sacks, and a dissonant chorus of porters, carters, hucksters, and flower-women, squabbling, cursing, singing, whistling and laughing ? Why have a house which you can hardly get into for sacks of cabbages and cauliflowers piled on the footway ; and why sit for ever in a smell of apples, earth, flowers and dung ?

Was it the old ghosts who drew them there ?   The ghosts of the old actors, say, who lived and made merry for so long in and about the piazzas of 'The Garden,' and now sleep, so many of them, under the pavements of its church and churchyard? When the bustle ceases at the end of the day, and the street sweepers with their long brooms have swept up the refuse and the dung, and the streets for a Sabbatical hour or two are quiet and fairly clean, you do not need much imagination to see again these fine old troupers, gentlemen and ladies, strolling or strutting along with mannered gait or mincing steps, to their lodgings, their coffee houses, or the boards of Covent Garden and Drury Lane.   I assure you I have seen them often from my window in Henrietta Street : Garrick and Macklin, Peg Woffington and Kitty Clive, Mrs. Bracegirdle and Mrs. Siddons and Nell Gwyn herself, a mighty pretty creature.

Or the old writers and bookmen who either lived here or passed their time here when, in Dick Steele's words, Covent Garden was ' the Heart of the Town,' or in Lamb's words, it was ' dearer to him than any garden of Alcinous '—these perhaps explain the pious arrival of the publishers.   I must not boast, but I cannot lie, and I declare that I have often looked into Henrietta Street and seen Johnson lumbering along the cobbles towards Mr. Sheridan's house and touching every stone post that he passed ; and Jane Austen coming along a little demurely to her brother, the banker's, at No. 10 ; and Charles Dickens turning into Offley's tavern over the road where he always found ' a fine collection of old boys ' and where the coffee-room upstairs 'had double windows lest the convivial singing of an evening awoke the dead in the churchyard below.   And in Maiden Lane, when my premises spread and I had back windows looking down into it, have I not seen Andrew Marvell coming home to his ' poor set of second-floor rooms ' there and, greatest of all, Voltaire bringing his skinny and bright-eyed face to his lodging at the White Peruke ?   And here come Swift and Pope and Congreve to visit him——

But I go on too long, because I so loved my ugly house in Henrietta Street, the House of Allan Mourne.   I cannot speak of the old artists, Sir Peter Lely who painted the great and famous, and Zoffany who painted the old actors, and Hogarth who painted all the world ; save only to mention that when I think of Hogarth, I remember that the subject-matter of literature and therefore of the publisher's wares, is the whole human scene, so why shouldn't I, at my publisher's window, people the street below and the market-place beyond with fops and wits and footpads, with gamesters and strumpets and bawds, and, as the night falls, with chairmen and link-boys and watchmen, with rowdies and bruisers and pick-purses, and with the beggarly children of Dickens lying under the market arches, homeless and ragged and wan ?

Certainly it was this old dead population which had made me hope from the beginning that when I hung out my sign it would be in this noisy but haunted quarter rather than in the academic quiet of the Museum or in one of the alleys that lie under the wing of and feel the discipline of St. Paul's.

You may imagine that my heart gave a bound when I saw the sign ' To Let ' above a shop-front in Henrietta Street.

§

' Stop me if I'm about to do something silly,' I begged of Iris, when I had rushed home to tell her of that notice-board. ' But think of it : a lease in Henrietta Street—yes, in Aunt Henrietta Street, and that's an excellent name for it, because all the houses are tall and narrow and Victorian and ugly.'

She was as excited as I, and we went over the house the very next day. ' Here's the Trade Counter, and here's Reception and Enquiries, and here's the Waiting Room,' I said as we looked in at the dusty ground-floor rooms. ' And this is *my* room,' I announced after we'd climbed the dark stairs and entered the large front room on the first floor. ' The Boss's room—and one day, long after I'm dead, it'll be as famous as Old Hammy's. The Managing-Director's room, my dear ; the Board Room,' and she squeezed my arm. We allocated other rooms to Production, Editorial, Art and Design, Advertising, and Sales ; and then, drawn by my dream, went back to *my* room, the first-floor front. I threw up a window, letting in at once the hubbub of market vehicles and porters' voices, and the smell of earth and green things. Leaning out over all this fuss and ado, I looked up and down the street at the homes of my brother publishers. Pulling Iris to my side, I showed her Trollope and Matthew Arnold entering the doorway of No. 11, and Herbert Spencer coming out of No. 14, and Tennyson, Patmore, Kingsley, Maurice and Huxley crossing the mouth of our road as they came from their publishers in Bedford Street. Ever must I stare at steps and doorways which had known the feet of the famous.

Next morning I was in Hammy's front-room, telling him of my desire. He was very gloomy about it. He shook his head frequently. He spread fat hands empty of encouragement.

Of the new publishers who'd lately come into the field, said he, not one in ten had lasted for more than a few years. Not one in ten. 'How can they in the present competition ? Just think : you can only have a small list of books to start with, and they have to carry all your working expenses. Some of them are bound to be failures and involve you in loss ; and the expenses and losses together will soon drain away all your capital, unless it is inexhaustible.'

'It certainly isn't that,' I said.

'Exactly,' he agreed ; and seemed pleased with this piece of bad news, since it proved his point. 'And that means that you'll have to rely largely on such credit as printers and binders will give you ; and you can only get second-best service that way. It stands to reason they're going to give their best and promptest service to publishers whose payment is immediate and certain—but I don't want to discourage you. Don't let me discourage you.'

'Oh, that's all right,' I said, as one does to a dentist when he expresses a hope that he will not hurt.

'And then you're so young. What are you ? Twenty-eight. Heavens, that's nothing. Young men always think they've nothing to learn, but, believe me, successful publishing needs immense knowledge.'

'I've been at it six years, and in one of the best houses,' I reminded him with a smile.

'It's not learnt in six years,' he averred sadly, shaking his head with much conviction. 'Nor in ten ; nor in twenty. I've been at it nearly fifty years, and never a day passes but I realize that I've something still to learn.'

I listened, agreeing with much of his heavy counsel, but persuaded, irrationally persuaded, that I was different ; that I had a store of new ideas larger than anyone else's—not to say, genius ; and, above all, that I'd had a summons to this work and would be sustained in it.

And Hammy, perceiving that I was not to be shaken, ended his homily by saying kindly, 'Well, I don't want to stand in a young man's way. Go in and win if you can.' And he rose and put his fat hand on my shoulder. 'I shall watch this adventure of yours with great interest—greater than any I've ever felt before, I think. And maybe I can put some good business in your way ; maybe I can send you some good authors ; who knows ? If I can I will. And if at any time you want an old veteran's advice, come here and get it. It's here for you at any time, my dear boy.'

I was always a young fool, unable to support kindness or

tenderness without a risk of tears ; and I had to press my lips tight to hold back the emotion, as he patted me on the shoulder and smiled benevolently upon my withdrawal.

§

At first we could lease only the ground floor and the first floor ; but what happy days we had, Iris and I, furnishing and equipping these few rooms. We furnished them handsomely, judging the money well spent since our House must appear prosperous, even if it was not. Meanwhile I had engaged two secretaries and advertised for an experienced Sales Manager who should look after Paper, Orders, Deliveries, Travellers, Trade Counter, Stock and Accounts ; while I was Editorial, Production, Art and Design, and Publicity—and Iris all these things, too. What fun it was, discussing and designing our Emblem—the emblem for our title pages and our book spines. To understand our final choice, which earned for me much merciless chaff from Wyn Fellowes, you must remember my original inspiration—the inspiration which came to me at Oxford when I was studying the *philosophes*—the ancient inspiration which seemed so new and bright to me that day. It was merely the old belief of all the sages, and all the ages, that the evil in Man is largely ignorance and incompleteness ; that Enlightenment can drive back the empire of cruelty, easy hatred and violent vengeance, and establish, however slowly, a New Order of love, understanding, forgiveness, patience and peace. My task as a publisher was to scatter this light about the world. Books were the vehicle of the light, and as many as possible of my books should carry it. But mine should not be solemn or heavy books ; by giving their central light a radiance of gusto or fun they should charm the people and win their allegiance. And so it was that I arrived at my emblem : a many-pointed sun rising upon the face of the waters, with *Fiat Lux* below and the letters A. and M., one on either side. Wyn roared with laughter when he saw it, called me God's junior partner, and asked whether A. M. stood for Allan Mourne or *ante meridiem* ; but I stuck to my design, declaring that it exactly expressed my aim, that A. M. could stand for either or both if the fool liked, and that, anyhow, in this business one had to be God's junior partner.

'Even so ? ' he grinned.

'Even so,' I mocked him. 'And in five years' time that imprint will be as famous as any in England. You'll see.'

§

We inaugurated the House with a fine party in Henrietta
Street, to which I invited every author, agent, publisher and
critic I knew.   The goodwill of everyone was enormous.   Towards the end of the evening its vocal expression was riotous
enough to wake the old ghosts in their churchyard over the
road.   At one time, not very appropriately, we were singing
Rule Britannia, and surely Dr. Arne, who lies over there, stirred
in his sleep to hear his tune at midnight.   Especially remarkable
was the kindliness and goodwill of the publishers.   Probably
they thought I should die soon.

My programme was to publish at first about twenty books a
year : ten in the spring and ten in the autumn.   I calculated
that even if some of these were failures, as they certainly would
be, we might yet make a profit of a hundred or two on the first
year's working.   That was all I looked for at first.   But if—*if*,
sooner or later, one of my books became a big seller, then the
profit would be entered in four figures instead of three, and we
would salt it all down for the future.

I shall not easily forget the fear and the happiness of those
first days in Henrietta Street.   The apprehensive—and at times
awestruck—gamble that it was !   Its touch and go !   The
sudden hope of gain ;   the all-too-frequent threat of loss.   My
dread of failure, and of being thrown back beaten to the starting-
point again, in the face of Henrietta and Mother, and now
Lady Cranmere . . . and always Gentle !   Many times my heart
stood in my mouth, but it could never stay there long.   I seemed
unable to believe in disaster.   Beneath my fear I felt a strange,
secret, surging confidence, a belief, almost religious, that I had
begun on the work which some Power or other had commanded
me to do, and that I should not be allowed to fail in it.

The happiness at all times was greater than the fear.   Each
morning I ran up the steep, dark staircase with joy at my elbow,
and, entering my handsome ' Manager's Room,' sat down with
pride at my side.   I was a publisher.   I was a ' Chief ' like
Old Hammy.   I had a secretary.   My imprint and my name,
to a small extent, was in the booksellers and the libraries and on
the tables of the people.   No one need know how small a house
we were, as yet.   Sometimes when my telephone rang, and
there was no secretary to answer it, I lifted the receiver myself
and to the question, ' Could I speak to Mr. Allan Mourne ? '
replied in a disguised voice, ' I'll just see if he's in his office.
Will you kindly hold the line ? '

Our first year showed a loss : only a slight one, but it sunk my heart very low—for three days. The second year showed a profit of between £200 and £300, thanks to a novel which had a very fair sale, and my hopes soared as buoyantly as last year they had dismally sunk. And at this stage I resolved to hazard all on a series that had my heart. And because it was my own conception and engrossing hobby, the ideas leapt up around it. First the title, *The Great Humanes*, because it was to be a series of popular biographies of all those seers and saints and sages who had seen the single vision, which, if one word could hold it, was Humanity or Humaneness : Buddha, Lao Tse, Socrates, Marcus Aurelius, St. Francis, and more modern figures like Lincoln and Pasteur and Father Damien. These expository biographies were to be as interesting and appealing as any novel, and to capture their readers as the life-story of Condorcet had once captured me. Then an idea for their advertising and promotion : every parson in the country, condemned to the fearful business of preaching week in, week out, sought diligently, and maybe with tears, for new matter for his sermons ; and here was abundant stuff for him ; every parson in his pulpit, mentioning my books, would be an unpaid publicity agent for the House of Allan Mourne ; so I would send a prospectus of *The Great Humanes* to every clerical collar in Britain. I set about this task, and was shocked to learn how many parsons, priests and ministers there were in our midst ; Gracious Powers, how was it that with all these good men to exhort us we were still so bad ? The expense would be terrific, so I concentrated first on the Nonconformists, as the fellows who did most of the preaching : then on the Anglicans ; and in the end left the R.C.'s to their altars, deciding that they would not believe too easily that pagan seers had seen the essential Christian vision. Then I worked down the 'published price' till there'd be hardly a halfpenny profit on each copy ; and this (between ourselves) reduced the author's royalty. So merciless is a man when Righteousness assails him.

Twelve, fourteen, and sixteen hours a day I worked on that series. Often there was a light in the windows of my Henrietta Street room till midnight or after. It was the pattern of my life at Oxford over again : grim resolve, and slavish service of that resolve, alone, and behind a closed door, while other men played or slept. It was the pattern of my *Tantrum Tales* over again : I flung all my money into the hazard and shivered at what I had done. And in the outcome the same truth was brought home to me : *what you want to do enough in this world you will succeed in doing*. This series was my first big success.

To win popularity for the series I put out first the ' lives ' that made the most picturesque or dramatic reading : Socrates, Buddha, St. Francis, Lincoln, and Marcus Aurelius—and at the name, Marcus Aurelius, an idea rushed into my head. The name recalled a conversation with Uncle Humphrey—one which I could never forget, because it ended with the announcement of Gentle's engagement—and I heard him saying, ' My descent is through the Stoics, Seneca, Epictetus, Marcus Aurelius. . . .' I would give the book on Marcus Aurelius to Uncle Humphrey to do ! Uncle Humphrey should really publish a book before he died ! My series was doing well enough to carry a book by him, though it had but poor success, and even if it were a failure. I could stand a small loss for his sake. The idea appealed to both sides of me, the altruistic and the egotistic : it sprang partly from a desire to please him, partly from youthful mischief, and partly from a joy in the exercise and display of power ; but I can honestly say that the desire to please him, and to fulfil his lifelong dream, was the strongest motive.

§

Few pleasures equal the carrying of a gift ; and I could not stop till I was at the flat and in his room. When I broke in upon him he had just returned from an afternoon walk and was sitting on the nearest chair to recover from this exercise. He was breathing as if fatigued, and his black overcoat was thrown open, and his blue shawl thrown back. Shawl ?—why, yes : more than ever, as he grew older, Uncle Humphrey had joined those who, because they have failed to express their genius in any published work, express it in their clothes and their hair. Did the weather offer him the least encouragement he put on his overcoat and draped this picturesque shawl over his shoulders. His black hat, crowning the picture, had a wider brim than any worn by the unphilosophical. His beard, once black and cut square, now grey and untrimmed, grew down to his waistcoat and splayed outward from his slack, rubbery cheeks, as it might be the beard of Karl Marx, or of the prophet, or of the Bon Dieu Himself. He wore also, in his wistful dog-like eyes, a kind and tolerant smile for all he met—a smile as of an infinite under-standing, like God's. In all the streets along which he walked, in the busy Kensington and Hammersmith Roads, and in the parts about Olympia, he was reputed to be ' a very famous philosopher '—Lord knows why, unless the reputation sprang from the brim of the hat, the shawl, and the beard.

Once, years before, when Father still lived with us, and was little more than sixty, I remember him looking into the mirror of the overmantel and, greatly chagrined by the wrinkled and crumpled image that faced him there, exclaiming, ' Devil take it, Humphrey, we're getting old. Old and damned unsightly. God, what a face ! '*Cré nom d'un nom d'un nom*, what are we to do about it, Humphrey, old son ? There's only one thing to do, as far as I can see, and it's this : if we can't look handsome we can at least look rugged. I shall set about looking picturesque like you.'

' D'you think I look picturesque ? ' asked Uncle Humphrey, well pleased with the suggestion.

' Why, of course ! Aren't you ? Isn't that your idea ? ' He turned towards Uncle Humphrey as if surprised that his suggestion should need any confirmation. ' I mean : the beard ? The tie ? The hat ? The expression ? Oh, yes, picturesque, my dear Humphrey ; and I wish I were too.'

' Well, you're tall,' said Uncle Humphrey, meaning to comfort him. ' We can't have everything.'

But Father wasn't at all comforted by this ready agreement with his modest disclaimer of picturesqueness. ' Dammit, I'm as picturesque as you are,' he snapped ; and quickly turned back to the mirror to make sure of it. ' Me unpicturesque, compared with you ! Death and the devil, Humphrey, I believe you're right.'

In the house, pursuing the picturesqueness, Uncle Humphrey wore a black skull cap and a frogged purple smoking jacket ; and to-day, as soon as I'd hailed him, ' Hallo, Uncle, I want your help,' he rose, sloughed off the shawl and coat, and indued this jacket and cap. Always pleased to be approached for help, he panted, ' Certainly, Doric. Put a match to the fire, and draw up a chair.'

I lit the gas-fire, which piped and whistled in its sound ; and we sat down on either side of it, he in his easy chair, leaning forward and spreading his hands for warmth, I on a hard one, my elbows on my knees and my hands clasped.

' Well, what is it ? ' he inquired.

I temporized. ' The *magnum opus*—how's it going ? '

' Oh, so-so. Only so-so. I suppose it'll be finished one day— if I live long enough.' Up to a point he could laugh at himself. ' But *magnum opus* is the word. I gave myself too tremendous a task, Doric. Twenty years I've been messing about with it. Still, that's me : I'd rather not write at all than write quickly and carelessly. It's not designed to be a light and popular book, you see. I couldn't write a popular book if you asked me to.'

' No ? ' I queried.

' No. No, definitely not. You were able to, and I'm glad. You showed it in that little book of yours.'

' Oh, that was nothing,' said I, very modest. ' Just a lucky fluke. And I've never been able to do it again.'

' Still, you had a success—quite a little success '—something forced him instantly to modify the success—' and that must have been pleasant. I've never expected to get any recognition while I was alive. I like to think that perhaps after I'm dead——'

' Oh, before that, I hope, Uncle. Long before that.'

' No. I'm not one of your popular writers. I fully recognize the fact.' So does pride veil itself in modesty, and the skeleton show through. He sank back into the chair. ' I couldn't write a popular book if I tried. What was the help you wanted ? '

' Oddly enough, it was on the subject of popular books. You know my *Great Humanes* series ? '

' Yes.'

' Well, what do you really think of them ? '

He brought the tips of his fingers together, and beat them together three times as he mused on his answer. ' Well, Doric, if I'm to be frank, I must say that it's very difficult for a scholar to believe that anything really profound can be said in a two-shilling book. I don't think—speaking quite truthfully—that wisdom can be potted down and made easy like that. I'm afraid I distrust all popularizations.'

' Even my little *Humanes* ? '

He shrugged, unwilling to say the word that would hurt me.

' They're having quite a success, Uncle.'

' I don't doubt it, and I'm very glad for your sake. But what sort of success is it ? A success in making people complacent about their knowledge ? '

' Oh, but that's hardly fair, Uncle. Don't you think that these books may stir up *some* people's enthusiasm somewhere and whet their appetite for deeper study ? '

' I doubt it. I doubt it extremely. I can't believe that any lasting impression is ever made unless the brain is taxed and extended. It's always a case of " easy come, easy go." '

' Then you wouldn't be prepared to write one for me ? '

' What ? ' His eyes shot to my face and stayed resting there.

' I was going to ask you to write one for me. On Marcus Aurelius. It was to be a commissioned book with immediate publication guaranteed. I wanted to give it heaps of publicity.

I was going to send a notice of it to every parson in the land and a free copy to all the most prominent. I'd have had them quoting from it in all their pulpits.'

' Marcus Aurelius ? '

' Yes. And, great God, what a story to tell ! Marcus Aurelius in his war camps, fresh from the battles, noting down sorrowfully—wistfully—day after day, his ideas for the true way of life ! Marcus Aurelius, Emperor of the World, and yet so lonely in his tent as he writes down—Listen, Uncle '—I could quote my Marcus Aurelius as readily as Father could quote his Bunyan, and I spouted, not without pleasure in my low voice and stirring intonation—' " In anger let the thought be always present that indignation is no form of courage, but that humility and gentleness are not only more human but also more manly and it is he who possesses these who has strength." Why, it is the very essence of everything I want to say ! God, Uncle, what you could do with it . . .'

' Well . . .' he began ; and I knew the word for the first quick crack in his proud fortress.

' I know Marcus Aurelius is one of your masters——'

' " Masters " is hardly the word, Doric. I don't think I'm any man's disciple. But go on. I certainly admire him, and I think I may claim to know a lot about him.'

' Just so. And that's why you could do a brief popular life of him wonderfully. And you'd combine with it a simple but most moving exposition of the *Meditations*.'

' Well, it's an entirely new idea to me, Doric, but——'

' Mind you, I don't want you to do it, if it'd go against the grain.'

' Oh, no—no—it wouldn't do that. I don't think it would go against the grain. In the case of Marcus Aurelius, no, certainly not.'

' I was going to say that I believe Dr. Reeves, of Oriel, would do it for me if you felt it would go against the grain.'

' But I don't feel that, Doric. Not in the case of Marcus Aurelius. No.'

' Reeves is a great authority——'

' Yes, yes, but I don't want to boast'—which words are always a certain sign that one does want to boast : I know this whenever I use them myself, which I do rather frequently—' I don't want to boast, Doric, but I can't think he knows more about Marcus Aurelius than I do.'

' Well, then, is there some hope that you would do it for me ? '

' Well, yes, Doric. I certainly feel I could do it for you in the case of Marcus Aurelius.'

' But there are just one or two stipulations, Uncle. First, it's got to be absolutely simple.'

' Yes, I quite see. Simple. And easy. And lucid.'

' And clean,' I was about to add, but decided not to spoil his happy moment with chaff. ' I want the wonderful tale told as simply and clearly as if you were telling it to intelligent children.'

' Well, I can do that. I think that by this time I know how to write. I've been studying the craft for forty years.'

' Good. Then I want all the dramatic and pathetic values brought out to the full. And indeed the humour.'

' I think I'm as humorous as most.'

' I'm sure you are. But listen, Uncle : the chief object of this series—and very certainly in the case of Marcus Aurelius—is to emphasize that the Christ-like vision has been the wisdom of the wisest in every age and clime. I want it shown that just because Marcus was one of the wisest of men, he was also one of the most humane. D'you remember ? '—and again I began to spout— ' " I have contemplated the nature of the sinner and seen that it is kindred to my own. . . . How can I be angered with my kith and kin, or cherish hatred towards them ? " That kind of thing. Now I know that you claim to be a pessimist and a sceptic, and to doubt all things, including the Christian ethic ; and I wouldn't have you compromise with your conscience.'

' But I wouldn't be compromising with my conscience.'

' You wouldn't ? '

' No. Not in the case of Marcus Aurelius. I've been chang- ing a lot myself, of late, you see. I've changed my views a lot.' I was pretty sure he'd only changed them that minute, to be in time for publication. ' I feel in complete agreement with him on that point.'

' On which point ? '

' On—well, on most points. On—what was it you said ?— something about the sinner being the same as us all and it being fatal to cherish hatred towards him. Yes, I think I may say I'm in fairly complete agreement with Marcus Aurelius.'

' That's fine. Then there's only one other point. There's a time-limit, Uncle. And you always say you can never work fast.'

' Yes . . . yes . . . but in the case of Marcus Aurelius——'

' ——you might manage it. Fine. Can you deliver the copy to me in six months ? '

' Why, of course, of course. I have all the matter here ; I have all the matter at my fingers' ends. I'll start on it straight- away.'

§

And start on it he did, there and then. He abandoned
instantly the Great Work, on which he'd been labouring for
twenty years. He was a real author at last. Few things have
given me more satisfaction than that I was able to turn my
Uncle Humphrey, after fifteen minutes of abracadabra, into
a real author. His life was justified at last by a small fruit.
And not only was he a real author, but for six months he was the
epitome, the very distillation and quintessence, of all authors ;
he was, so to say, the archetype and Platonic idea of an Author.
He manifested all the pride and all the agonies of this febrile and
difficult species. Proudly he spoke to his friends at the Author's
Club of ' my publishers ' and explained, when possible, that his
was a ' commissioned book.' Proudly he declined invitations
because he had to complete his book and ' deliver the copy '—
how he loved the trade jargon—within six months. If someone
asked him if the book was a novel, what pain he endured. ' No,
not a novel,' he said. ' I couldn't write a novel. It's a work on
philosophy.' Once someone inquired if it was a thriller, and
the wound was deep indeed. The writing of the book in his
little room was *penible*. ' You see, I can't bear to have a word
wrong,' he told everybody, as if in this he was different from most
other authors. Con typed his chapters for him, and she told me
that his distress was extreme if she put in a comma where no
comma should be, or typed ' military orders ' as ' military
ordure ', or mis-spelt ' began ' and ' because ' as ' begna ' and
' becuase '. Deep and frequent was his distress over begna and
becuase. And when the galley-proofs came, did they bring
him more pride or anguish ? He took the long slips to his club
that his fellow-members might see him correcting them, but he
was seized with alarm and anxiety when the print slanted or
' fainted ', he groaned like a dying man when reader or com-
positor had added an interjection mark to point one of his sly
jokes, and he stamped in a fury if they'd cut up and rebuilt his
paragraphs. ' Do they think they know better than I do ? '
he demanded ; and since the answer to this was all too obviously
' Yes,' he chafed and burned till his marginal comments should
reach them and convict them of an impertinence.

And when at length the book was a made thing in his hand,
printed and bound and jacketed, he stared at it, back and sides,
and close to and far away ; he smoothed and felt it ; he studied
a page here and a page there ; and then, longing to see it in the
shops, he went quickly into the streets—without a shawl and

without a hint of weakness or weariness. I showed a copy of it to Father when next he came wandering into Henrietta Street (as he often did), and he said, ' Oh my God, have I got to go the rounds and ask for Old Humphrey's book now ? ' and I answered, ' Most assuredly. It's the least you can do for your brother ; and he sighed, ' Oh, well, I suppose I must. Yes, we must see the old boy through.' And, having nothing else to do, he went off to do his duty by Uncle Humphrey's book, as he had once done it by mine—but on this occasion he wearied rather quickly.

And what manner of book was it, when it was finished ; was it, in fact, good or bad ? The best that I can say of it is that it was much better than I had feared. When he brought the copy to me himself (not trusting the post) I was very nervous lest it proved pompous and dull, but quite ready to do my best with it for his sake. I took it home and read it and was most agreeably surprised. The old man had taken immense pains with it and, remembering my conjurations, had told the fine tale as simply, lucidly and thrillingly as he could. There was no doubt that in forty years he had learned something about writing. Nor could I doubt that, after years of constipated labour and straining, he had really produced a nice, interesting little book. I was so relieved, and so anxious to please him, that I rushed round to the flat and told him, ' It's exactly what I wanted, Uncle. It just couldn't be better. I think you've done it wonderfully ' ; which was unwise, because it gave him hopes and dreams which couldn't be fulfilled.

Thanks to the popularity of the series, Uncle Humphrey's book got a fair meed of reviews, and Uncle Humphrey got a deal of suffering out of them. Always their praise, being less than he'd hoped for, engulfed him in despondency. One reviewer described the book as ' worth reading ' and sank him in misery. Another spoke of it as ' a readable little book,' and again he went to the murky bottom, to remain there for a long time, sunk without trace. A third criticized his prose, and this was a knock-out blow on his heart, so that he went forth into the streets, there to walk up and down with all the long sadness of humanity in his eyes.

Nor did he collect much happiness when, day after day, he went spying in the bookshops, from which he was quite unable to keep away. If there were two copies of his books there, he decided that it ' wasn't selling ' and turned unhappily into the street. If there was but one to be seen, he muttered inwardly that the shop ought to be ashamed of itself for not having more in stock, and came away, uncomforted. And if, as was too often the case, he could see no sign of the book anywhere—no, not though he sought it for half an hour, on counter and shelf—he went slowly from the shop, with nothing but his manhood to save him from tears.

Furthermore the book nearly cost him all his friends, since there was none who praised it in adequate terms, and he found it hard to forgive those who said, ' I quite liked it,' and those who shouted with a foolish laugh ' That was a jolly little effort of yours, Allan Mourne ' ; and quite impossible to forgive the few who adversely criticized it.

The book was not a failure, but equally not a success ; I lost a few pounds on it. For many months he clung to his hope of a large sale and a loud *réclame*, but when six, seven, and eight months had gone by, and the book, after the fashion of all books save a very few, had receded into a silence like the silence of the interstellar spaces, he let his hopes die, and found his comfort in saying to himself, and to his friends (as do all authors, of whom he was the portrait and parable), ' I always feel that it would have been more successful if it had been produced very differently ; ' in other words, if the publisher had known his business.

CHAPTER V

SLOWLY I consolidated and enlarged the position of the House of Allan Mourne. My plan had always been to advance as cautiously as a commander who secures at every stage his flank and rear and reinforcements ; and in the main I succeeded in doing this. Some of my books failed, others merely broke even, but the rest were successful enough to deposit a small profit ; and most of this profit I poured back to meet losses and sustain slow starters. By such means I made the walls of my little house stouter and stouter and threw out a wing here and a wing there.

And in 1912 I did a most excellent piece of business. I secured George Byng as my partner. George brought in few new reserves, for his capital was small, but he strengthened the foundations and the walls by adding a ' business toughness ' which I did not possess. He'd been twenty years in the Business Department of Craven and Hills and knew how to handle agents and buyers with a charming smile and an obduracy equal to theirs. Ten years older than I ; forty ; and as round and plump and ripe in appearance as I was long and slight and youthful-looking,

he presented a new, massive bastion to the world at the point
where our walls had been weakest.   This gravely weak place
had been created, of course, by a weakness in me, a malady most
hapless in a business man.   I had an impelling desire to be liked
by all visiting authors, agents, printers, binders, and buyers.
Thus I was always in danger of concluding an uneconomic
bargain with them rather than that they should speak unkindly
of me or call me Jew.   It was not at all that I was over-generous
but simply that I longed to be liked.   The risk I took with Uncle
Humphrey's book was an illustration of this weakness at work.
Sometimes a big author, who'd learned his way around, or an
astute agent, who'd descried this crack in the wall, would dine
and wine me nobly in a gilded salon till, after the liqueur or the
whisky-and-soda I offered him the earth ; and in the morning I
would wake up and tell myself in some dejection that a good
publisher's spoken word was as binding as a written agreement
and must certainly stand.

There was no such nonsense about George Byng.   George
had big, soft cheeks as round and white as the fat of a York
ham ; festooned over these ample spaces he had two long, soft,
blond moustaches, as gold as the chain festooned over his
waistcoat ; beneath the moustaches, as likely as not, the softest
and friendliest of smiles creased the porky jowl ; but never did
anything belie its wearer more than the softness in George's
cheeks, moustaches, and smile.   His head was as hard, and his
hide as thick, as that of any customer who sat opposite him ; nor
could the oldest liqueur brandy, or the sixth whisky, soften his
business brain or render his skin sensitive.   Neither became the
least porous.   He gave nothing away at the dinner table or in his
office, except the smiles and perhaps a cigar.   I vow that sometimes I had to plead with him for my authors, and even for their
agents.   But it was seldom, if ever, that I got through to his
excellent but strictly ex-business heart.   ' Bunk,' he would say,
pulling one of the silky moustaches, ' Don't be soft, laddie.
Business is business.   *Laze affairs sor laze affairs* ' (for his pronun-
ciation of French was shocking) ; and before an author entered
my room for an interview, he would beg, ' For God's sake, and
my sake too, don't discuss terms with him ' or, overcome with
doubt of me, he would attend the audience and sit there as fat
and round and still, as silent and contemplative, as the great
Kamakura Buddha but ready to come to earth and speak, if I
showed signs of giving anything away for nothing.   I soon nicknamed him ' Bung ' and ' Bunco '—' Bung ' because he instantly
stopped up any hole in the cask where there was danger of a leak,
and ' Bunco ' because this tough morsel of current slang meant a

trick whereby any simple fellow was taken aside and swindled. Not that he wasn't a scrupulously honest business man : he was perfectly fair with everybody, but only just so.

I used to explain to my visitors, in George's presence, that he exemplified all the vulgar, money-grubbing, materialist values against which a fine mind must struggle if it were not to be strangled by them. I might even point out that, sitting there grinning, with his great fat belly, he could pose very well for the God Mammon ; or that, in simple fact, and without knowing it, poor fellow, he was the agent of Satan, Baal, and Antichrist. And to all this cheerful reprobation he would retort, still grinning, that it was by the activities of such money-grubbers as he that we poor visionaries were able to live and try out our dreams ; and I would allow to the visitors that he had some small value as ballast ; and so we would all proceed happily to business.

Quickly perceiving that he was the perfect counter-balance to me ; I handed over the business side to him. I called myself the Literary Director and him the Business Director ; and in these two spheres we were both happy, and good friends.

Have I ever been happier than in these days of fair success and steady building ? Perhaps not. I was happy because I was fully extended by my work, wholly consumed by it. Never did I lose the pleasant sensation of mounting the steep and narrow staircase to ' Mr. Theodore's Room,' greeting my secretary, Edith Peers, and dictating to her the morning's correspondence amid the cries of the porters of Covent Garden. At some time in the morning, letters done, I would visit all the departments to greet my staff and hear their queries and comments. These were my people, my ever-increasing family, and I could but know that they liked me and were happy to work for me. At one o'clock George and I, good companions, would walk fifty paces round the corner to the Garrick Club for lunch. For George's enthusiastic driving power, which few could resist, I had invented the verb, ' to george ' ; so you will understand me when I say that George had recently georged himself into the Garrick, that cosy and carpeted hive of celebrities, where he could make acquaintance with authors, judges, K.C.'s and actors, many of whom had marketable books in them ; and that now with the aid of these friends, he georged me into it too. So there in its famous coffee room which had heard the laughter of Dickens and Trollope and Lever and Irving, we would take our lunch together, beneath the huge framed pictures of the old actors of Covent Garden and Drury Lane. In the afternoon I would welcome the authors who wished to discuss their books with me—authors coming to *me* who'd once been led out of Harlen's Lecture Hall, thrashed and disgraced. Or there would be a staff meeting attended by all the 'heads of departments'—some of which heads, since our house was still small, were the torsoes, limbs, and feet of their departments as well. Or I would give these quiet hours, the Vegetable Market being stilled at last, and only steps, steps, coming along the street, to reading the sheaves of some manuscript which had been favourably reviewed by our readers—reading in hope, and sometimes in excitement if the manuscript was a striking one. Then in the evening signing all letters, and so home through the dusk in some content, taking, as a publisher should, my manuscripts with me.

§

One such evening, rising above ground into the arcade of South Kensington Underground Station, I passed a little grey man in a tired black suit, down-at-heel shoes, and clerical collar ; and a pang of recognition swung my head round to him. It was he. Beyond question it was he. He had no bristling black moustache now, and his black toothbrush eyebrows were grey and torn ; but I must have known that face anywhere. In the old days he had never worn a clerical collar on a week-day, and now his collar was as deliberately clerical as it could be : it was as tall and upright and white as a jam jar. It was cracked, to be sure, in places, faintly yellow along the rim, and obviously made of celluloid ; but it proclaimed his priestly character to all who might look his way. Yes, by all that was incredible, it was he—but so shabby, so old, and so surprisingly small ! Fifteen years had transformed him from a little black, confident, authoritative man into a little grey, self-assertive, insecure one ; they had shrunk the air of authority into one of timid jauntiness whose root lay surely in some buried shame. A walking stick hung on his forearm, and he carried gloves in his hand ; and the gloves, I'd no doubt, were a folded flag to tell the world he was a gentleman. I turned and watched him as he stepped down the stairs to the trains. He had not noticed me, but I had recognized him : Harlen.

Curiosity seized me like thirst : why was he so grey now, so seedy and indigent, so old for his years ? I ached to know the answer but he had gone down the stairs and, more likely than not, I should never see him in this world again.

But some days later Father was lunching with me at the Garrick where I often invited him because he was so lonely in his chambers and I was proud of him and proud of my new club. And as we sat at our guest table by a window I mentioned this brief glimpse of Harlen. Instantly a light sprang up in his old eyes ; a light as of a lamp well primed ; I think the Eddystone Light springs alive like that, in the dusk.

' That fellow ! ' he said. ' Oh, I've known all about him for a long time.'

' Known what ? ' I inquired, concealing my eagerness.

' My dear boy, thank God you've asked me at last. I've been burning to tell you for a year or more, but—I don't know— I decided that perhaps the less said to you about that particular little man the better. My dear chap, I've kept it bottled up inside me for a year—ever since I heard it from old Archdeacon Bletchley or Fletchley or Something in the Athenæum. It's been, I don't mind telling you, something of a strain.'

Once again I saw how Father's tenderness to me could lift him above his natural weaknesses and give him a nobility. I had a vision of him running to me with the scandal, directly it'd been given him and then turning round in love and going home again, disappointed.

' Well, unbottle it now,' I said.

' Thank you. " For this relief much thanks." Well, I met this padre fellow, Archdeacon Bletchley or Fletchley or Catchpole or Something, in the Athenæum after dinner one night. He was a big, burly, bragging fellow, full of good wine—as I knew whenever he breathed over me—and he went out of his way to tell me that he was one of the governors of Draycote. Just to show that I knew what he was talking about I asked if Harlen was still the Head, and immediately I saw that I'd touched oil, and that the oil would gush with a very little probing. I saw that he was bursting to tell me a scandal, and, between you and me, I was eager to hear it, so I helped him gently to get on with it, for his happiness and mine. He didn't need much help. A word—two words—that was all. The more unsavoury a scandal, Doric, the more savoury it is on the tongue ; and this curious fact, it seems, is as true of archdeacons as of any of the rest of us. These padres are not much better than you and me, you know : I suppose you've discovered that. I don't blame him for wanting to tell me—*nom d'un nom*, I'm longing to tell you now—but I blame him because, being a professional padre, he wrapped up his betrayal (which was what it really was) in heavy sanctimonious terms. He began, " It's always sad when one of our brethren goes to pieces "— " *sad*," he said ; and the man was delighted ! Delighted because it'd given him a good story to tell. I wonder when

they'll realize that we can see through them, these padres ?
I remember one in India——'
  ' Yes, yes ; but what was the story ? '
  ' You can imagine it. I wasn't at all surprised to hear it
of a bachelor master who so plainly enjoyed beating his boys.
He developed a grand passion for one of the older lads and took
him with him on a holiday. You can guess the rest. The
father reported him to the governors, and the governors to his
bishop ; and from further inquiries it appeared that this wasn't
an isolated incident. They behaved very decently to him. The
old archdeacon, with that delight in legal terms which affects
simple minds, explained that if he'd denied it all, the bishop
would have had to try him in his Consistory Court and, on
conviction, depose him, but instead he promised the poor fellow
that, if he'd confess the whole truth he'd take no steps against
him beyond declining to licence him any further. He said that,
if he'd withdraw from all attempts to exercise his ministry he'd
do his best to find him some 'different employment, and help
him to build a new life. . . . Is that the wine steward ? What
about another glass of this ? If you want a good long tale, you
must keep me in good form. . . . Harlen accepted this generous
offer at once, leaving the school in the middle of the term. It
was all rather pathetic, Doric. He asked to be allowed to say
goodbye to his boys, and he went into every classroom and said,
" I want to say goodbye to you all. I have to go to some
different work. Mr. So-and-so will be looking after you. Be
good lads. Try to do honour to your school " ; and he shook
hands with every boy there, and went from each classroom
unable to speak and '—but Father's voice tripped over a large
sob and his eyes filmed with tears. ' He really loved them, you
see ; he really loved them. Thank you, waiter.' Pulling out
the cream silk handkerchief, he blew his nose vigorously, wiped
both eyes and a cheekbone, and dragged himself with an effort
out of this morass ; while I looked down at the table-cloth.
' They found him a small clerking job in the headquarters of
the Church Army, at a pound or two a week, and out of that,
as I understand, he has his old mother to keep . . . in an
institution . . . an institution.' Here Father was in some peril
of tears again, but survived. ' The old Bishop stipulated that
he must live for a year or two at a Church Army hostel where
they could keep an eye on him ; and now he lives somewhere
by himself, doing all his own work. Pretty pitiable for one who
a year or so ago was lord of his little heritage ; he's fallen the
whole way, Doric. When I asked the archdeacon if he'd ever
be able to get back, the old turkey shook his head and expounded

in his best sanctimonious style—he was having a delightful evening—that the bishop, as Chief Pastor, has to consider, not only mercy to the sinner, but the safety of his flock and the good name of the Church.'

' Well, well,' I commented, as the waiter brought the sweet. ' What a tale ! '

' Yes, but that was the least interesting part of it to me ; and I should think to——' He was about to say ' to you,' but stopped himself. ' There's more to come. Not much, but it's illuminating—oddly illuminating. You remember he acted as his own bursar—well, after he'd gone the new bursar reported to the new headmaster that there were certain transactions entered in the books which ought to be explained in more detail. It was not that there were any palpable defalcations, of course, but that some of the round sums he'd entered up as " expenses " were very difficult to justify. It's wonderful the round sums you can put down as " postages " and " entertaining " and " travelling " if you're your own treasurer—I wouldn't say but that I'd done a little in that line myself, *vis à vis* the Inland Revenue—but some of old Harlen's sums were so round that, bless my soul, the new bursar's eyes became round too. No doubt he'd contrived to satisfy his conscience that they were fair ; but what interests me, Doric, is that in his view it was utterly unpardonable and a matter for public execration to lift a half-crown from the Steward's shelf, and a more or less natural business to write down every pound he spent as thirty shillings, when he was doing his accounts.'

I could not speak about this, but looked away ; and Father added, ' The governors pursued the matter no further, both for the sake of the school and because the man was kicked out already. That's all. That's the whole story. Was I right in thinking you offered me a glass of port ? If so, I accept. The last port I had here was an excellent wine.'

§

My first emotion, as I listened to this tale, had been a primitive sharp pleasure, a keen satisfaction that the man who'd cast me out should himself be cast out. And I have to confess that the pleasure stayed with me for some hours, in my office in Henrietta Street, in my study at home, and in my bed as I waited for sleep.

But then, suddenly, an enemy of this vindictiveness sprang into my mind, and offered it battle. This armed challenger was the old vision, the creed which I really believed and loved, the faith for whose propagation my publishing house was built. Perhaps it was Harlen himself who had placed me for ever at the side of the ' man in the dock,' whether murderer, thief, or coward, so that I must plead with his judges for understanding and clemency. The old vision was bound to win, even though Harlen was the candidate for understanding and pity, because I so loved it. Pity ? Why, yes ; how could one do other than pity him who'd exchanged a headmaster's throne for a drudge's stool and sat there week after week, addressing envelopes for the Church Army and remembering his days of position and power, and wondering if Draycote ever was real.

So complete was the vision's conquest that I was soon possessed, and most happily possessed, by a plan to help and lift him up again. Look : I could help him as few others could. He was a scholar ; he knew much about books and especially about school books ; he had written two small books on education himself ; George and I wanted to enlarge our Educational List, because school books were among the best of steady-selling, ' bread and butter lines ' ; presumably he knew something about theology, and we hoped to start a Theological Department soon ; I could offer him a job as an outside reader with an *ad hoc* fee for every manuscript he reviewed and a retaining fee if his advice proved valuable. One day I might even commission him to edit a school text, and if he could introduce to us any good books, he could have a small financial interest in them, as I had had at Sands and Hume's.

Wholly won by this idea now, I hastened into George Byng's room next morning and said, ' Bung, you great barrel, I want to talk. Put those papers down and listen.' It was necessary to tread delicately with him, lest he should think I was giving something away for nothing, so I emphasized, and—yes— exaggerated, Harlen's scholastic attainments, but there was no hoodwinking so shrewd an eye as George's, and when I mentioned my expulsion from Harlen's school ' for pinching something,' and Harlen's present disgrace and distress, and my belief in understanding and compassion, he lifted up his voice and cried, ' Oh my God, Theo, what are you up to now ? Here, give me a pen while I write my resignation. I thought I was joining a business house, not a charitable institution.'

I told him not to be a fat fool ; that this was no charity, but good business ; that he ought to be grateful to me for getting him a famous headmaster cheap, and a superb theologian for next to nothing ; that it was no more than an experiment which could be stopped if it failed ; and that he could leave my house as soon as he liked and go next door to Chapman and Hall's or Williams and Norgate's, but I hoped we could remain friends and lunch sometimes together at the Garrick Club.

He shrugged and smoothed his long, blond, Viking moustaches. ' Well, if it's only an experiment. . . .'

' Certainly it's only an experiment. . . .'

' All right then,' he conceded, but as despondently as a man who is told that the only thing to do about an income-tax demand is to pay it.

The next question was how to approach Mr. Harlen. We could write to him ' c/o Church Army,' but on what paper ? Not on our firm's paper with its heading ' The House of Allan Mourne ' because that name might stir a memory and hurt him. Better that he should not know at first who was approaching him. It was here that George who, having entered upon a task, however unwillingly, couldn't do other than give his keen wits to it, suggested in cheerless tones, ' It's quite simple. I go across to the Garrick, and on its most impressive notepaper write to the old fool saying that I'm a partner in a publishing house which wants to extend its School and Theological Lists and to that end desires some outside readers who will report and advise on manuscripts submitted. I mention the *ad hoc* fee but certainly no retaining fee——'

' You certainly mention the retaining fee.'

' Oh, well then—hell !—the retaining fee, and if he's disposed to consider the idea, will he come and meet my partner and I in a little lunch at the Garrick——'

' He certainly won't come if you write " meet my partner and I." Publishers of school books should appear to be literate.'

' Why, what's wrong with " my partner and I " ? ' he demanded ; and there was a short intermission while I explained. Next I pointed out that Harlen couldn't possibly come to lunch since he would only have an hour off from his Church Army stool, far away in the Edgware Road.

' O.K., then—will he come one evening at some hour suitable to himself when my partner and I—no, my partner and me, or —oh, hell—whatever you say it is—will be pleased to discuss the matter with him. That's it, isn't it ? ' And George thrust his hands in his pockets and his legs out before him.

' That, I think, is it,' I said.

' All right ; I can put that letter together for you this afternoon, I suppose. I'll send it off to him from the Garrick. And he'll come like a shot from a gun—that's the devil of it—he'll come.'

The letter went from the Garrick that afternoon ; and the

reply was there the next afternoon, delivered by hand. Harlen must have hurried with it to the club doors in his luncheon hour. It was penned in his most careful hand and couched in his handsomest phrases. He was most grateful for Mr. Byng's suggestion, he wrote, and believed, without immodesty, that the work proposed was such as he could discharge with satisfaction to us after his long experience of the scholastic world. He would greatly like to meet Mr. Byng and his partner at the Garrick Club, but unfortunately his present work at the Church Army Headquarters precluded him from coming except after six in the evening or on a Saturday afternoon.

'Oh my Lord,' sighed George, reading the letter, 'have we got to stand him a dinner?'

'No,' I said. 'Don't worry. He'll be happier at tea time on a Saturday afternoon, I suspect, and the club will be quiet then.'

§

The club was indeed quiet on the Saturday afternoon. A few members were taking tea in the Smoking Room, and a few more in the 'Lounge,' which is the comfortable screened area that lies in the embrace of the great staircase. The Morning Room, that fine chamber on the first floor, was empty, its pictures, statues, and treasures unvisited. George and I sat in the Lounge, waiting for Harlen to appear. Punctually, as the clock on the wall said four, we saw the porter leading him towards the cloak room. His time-worn black suit was well brushed, his high celluloid collar well cleaned, and he carried his stick and his gloves as a gentleman should in the halls of the wealthy. George went to the staircase foot to welcome him. I stayed in the screened Lounge, where no stranger may be introduced.

George greeted him and led him up the staircase to the Morning Room, saying, 'My partner will be with us in a minute.'

In the shadows of the Lounge, under the staircase, I could watch them ascending the wide carpeted treads and hear every word they uttered.

'And the name of your firm?' Harlen was asking politely.

'Mourne,' said George; and I could see that the name meant nothing to our visitor. Rather was he concealing by his silence the fact that he'd never heard of it—as one does with a strange author when he tells one the name of his best-known book. Gazing up at the great canvases which decorated the walls

from floor to roof, he said rather loudly as people do who want
to seem at ease, ' These are all theatrical pictures, aren't they ? '

' Yes,' said George.   ' The most famous collection of theatrical
pictures in the world.   There's Nell—pretty, witty Nell.'

' Is that so ?   I've often been to the Athenæum—and the
Reform—but never here.   I've never found it worth my while
to have a London club because until recently I lived in the
country.   All your members are celebrities in literature and the
arts, are they not ? '

' Oh, by no means.   I, for one, am completely undistinguished.
Just a commonplace tradesman.'

' Well it's certainly a beautiful and imposing place.'

' Yes, quite a decent pub,' said George.

They and their voices passed.   A waiter went up to the
Morning Room in response to George's ring.   After two minutes
I rose for the strange encounter, my heart shaking.   Going
slowly up the wide staircase, treading the soft carpet, I remembered that evening, fifteen years before, when in the hands of
my captors I went in terror to his study.   The two ill-matched
horses that throughout my life drew my chariot along were in
their traces now, the egotistic animal glad that my headmaster
and I should meet again in this fine and famous place, the
better beast (which I can honestly say was pulling the stronger)
painfully anxious that an unhappy man should not be further
hurt.

The Morning Room is the largest and most palatial in the
Garrick.   As in the Coffee Room and the Entrance Hall, so too
here : on its lofty walls the old dead actors posture and pose
in their gilded frames, for the Garrick is the Valhalla to which
they have fled, and there in their bright costumes they act
again their scenes of tragedy, comedy, and happy or terrible
recognition.   Their cold busts stand about the great room ;
and in the show-cases against its walls lie the swords and chains
and snuff-boxes which once they vaunted before their public in
Old Drury and Covent Garden.

Entering quietly, I saw George and Harlen seated in two
deep leather chairs by the marble chimneypiece.   I heard George
saying in most gracious voice, ' In an educational publishers an
immense part is played by outside readers—ah, here we are :
here is my partner—not to say, my Chief.'

He did not rise, but Harlen did, as nervously as a schoolboy
at the entrance of the Head.   As I walked towards him with a
smile I observed that his white collar and black stock were new-
bought for this visit, but that his shirt-cuffs were old and cracked.
Conscious of this, he thrust one of them nervously back up his

sleeve. Was this little man my late Headmaster, who had been black haired, thick-set and ruddy ? With his hair and stubble eyebrows so grey, his cheeks so colourless, his body so spare, he seemed washed-out, shrunken, limp.

' Dear me, you are very young,' he said, affecting a perfect ease, and not recognizing me at all. ' The publisher who published two little books of mine was a man of—well—very mature years.'

' Yes, I'm afraid our firm is a rather young one, sir, but Mr. Byng here provides it with stability. Have you ordered tea, Bung ? '

' Yes, Chief. It's on the way.'

Harlen spoke again promptly, rather than appear ill-at-ease. ' A wonderful place you have here, Mr.—I don't think Mr. Byng told me your name.'

' Mourne,' said George—quickly, and rather low.

' Oh yes ; Mourne.' The name, so ordinary, stirred no deeps. ' Remarkable pictures, these, Mr. Mourne. They remind me of Charles Lamb's essay *On Some of the Old Actors*. I trust you are a devotee of the inimitable Elia. I confess I dote on him—dote on him immoderately.' Just as his clothes were the best he could produce from his cupboard, so were the language and the topics with which he was decking his person. ' Elia, I always say, sits with Montaigne and Addison, Goldsmith and Steele. Of course he does.' He advanced this claim with a preacher's sweep of his hand, and instantly pushed back the cuff. And having said it, he sat down and dragged his shoes under his chair, conscious of their cracks.

' My partner has explained our idea to you ? ' I asked, sitting too.

' To a certain extent, yes, Mr. Mourne.'

' And does it interest you at all, sir ? '

' Very much. It is work that I should greatly like to do. And I think I may say, without undue vanity, that it is work I could do tolerably well.' He turned towards George. ' May I ask who gave you my name as a likely reader ? '

' Eh ? ' George threw a glance like an angler's line at me, fishing for the best reply. ' The Chief will explain that.'

I looked down guiltily. ' We are asking a number of schoolmasters—and clergymen—to help us, and I suddenly thought of you. I'm afraid we do not know as many clergymen as we should. Mr. Byng here was no help at all. He couldn't think of one. He remembered one in his childhood, but that's rather a long time ago. Thank you, waiter. . . . Do help yourself, sir.'

' I see. I understand. Well, it should be most interesting work, I'm sure. And may I ask—if you'll forgive the sordid question—what would be the—er—the emoluments ? '

George coughed an unnatural cough, and I saw his eyes sternly trained on me like two warning pistol-mouths.

Turning from this threat with a grin, I said to Harlen, ' We should suggest, sir, a retaining fee of fifty pounds and a guinea or two for every book read, according to the labour involved. It's not much, I fear——'

George's chair creaked. He swung round in it and looked out of the window. The action was meant to tell me that he was withdrawing from any further part in these proceedings. He began to stroke one of the blond moustaches and curl its end, with a very definite suggestion that this was all he could now do to employ his wasted time.

' It's little enough for expert work,' I said firmly, ' but it's the usual fee.'

' A trifle more than the usual,' said George to the window.

' Yes, as a matter of fact, it is,' I agreed. ' But, even so, little enough for such scholarly work.'

Knowing my George, I heard his ' 'Tsst ' within his teeth, but Harlen didn't. Harlen only said eagerly, ' All the same, it's most interesting work. Most interesting, most congenial, to an old scholar like me, if I may call myself so.'

' I think it should be interesting, sir. And that isn't quite all we could offer——'

George's chair creaked again, impatiently.

' That isn't quite all we could offer, Mr. Harlen. If, by any chance, you could introduce to us a profitable book we would gladly give you a small financial interest in its sales.'

What George did with his old leather chair that afternoon was quite wonderful : he made it mutter and protest and cry out and groan. At this point it said quite plainly, ' Whoever heard such nonsense. Is it likely that the old fool will ever be able to find us a good book ? ' And when I turned towards it to acknowledge its comment, it added, ' Promising him guineas and retaining fees and financial shares just because he's down and out ! For God's sake keep your head.' I bowed slightly to it, and I'll swear it grumbled out, ' Business is business— good God ! ' I smiled in agreement, and it insisted as he slithered on it, ' *Laze affairs sor laze affairs.*'

' Certainly,' I said to the air—or to George and his chair— and turning to Harlen, affirmed, ' That is the usual custom.'

' Sometimes,' George muttered ; and the chair muttered it too.

Courteously, Harlen turned to George, to keep him in the conversation. 'And what, may I ask, would I be called . . . in this—er—character?' He asked it like a schoolboy, eager to boast of a new title to his friends.

'One of our readers,' George suggested.

'Let us say rather,' I amended, 'since Mr. Harlen is going to help us with his advice, one of our Literary Advisers.'

Plain that with these words I had offered our visitor a mouthful much to his taste. 'That sounds very fine. I hope I may prove worthy of that title. But, Mr. Mourne, you still haven't explained why you suddenly thought of me.'

I smiled to make it easy for him. 'You don't remember me, Mr. Harlen?'

He considered my features. 'I don't think so. Have we met before?'

'Yes.'

'When was that?'

'Some time ago.'

'I think your face is familiar. Yes, of course it is. Where was it? At some Guards' Dinner?' This he asked, laughing, because I was so tall.

'I was once a peculiarly unsatisfactory pupil of yours. Only for a few months. That was all you could stand of me.'

'I find it hard to believe that. . . . Mourne? . . . Mourne? . . .' Suddenly a light of recognition swept over his countenance, overthrowing doubt but bringing dismay. His stubbly eyebrows, which had been knitted, parted ; his lips, which had been compressed, opened. 'You are——?'

'Theodore Allan Mourne, whom you had to remove for a nasty little piece of shoplifting.'

'You are Allan Mourne?'

'Yes, I'm afraid so, sir, but don't bring it up against me.'

'Allan Mourne . . . Allan Mourne. . . . Yes, I see it now. . . .'

George's chair creaked no more ; nor was he any longer turned towards the window ; he sat there, very still, staring at us.

'Allan Mourne,' Harlen repeated, his voice scarcely audible. 'And you—bear me no malice?'

'After fifteen years, sir? Hardly.'

'But I was too severe with you. I remember your father said so. Much too severe.'

'Oh, I don't know, sir. I deserved punishment.'

He shook his head and said, 'Not what I thought fit to give you. It's always a mistake to be too harsh with anyone . . .

always. One learns it later . . . as one gets older.' Then he fell silent. Perhaps he was seeing the Lecture Hall again and the scene which had taken place there, and after that the long corridors and playing fields of Draycote, which he had loved, and from which he had been cast forth. ' Forgive me, but what did you do after you left Draycote ? '

' I went up to Oxford in due course. I was at Magdalen.'

' Oxford . . . I was at Merton,' he said sadly, and drew in his cracked shoes. ' I was there with the present Attorney General and—however, what school did you read ? '

' Only History I'm afraid.'

' And you took your degree ? '

' Yes.'

' A good one ? '

' I managed to pull off a First by a fluke.'

' *Did* you ? A First ? Really ? That was good. That was excellent. I am very glad, Allan Mourne ; very glad. Yes, I'm glad of that . . . I got a First in Mods and a Second in Greats. . . . Not bad. . . .'

' Yes, and you were always a real scholar, sir. That was why we—may we consider you'll do this work for us ? '

But he was still staring at me—probing, probing my eyes, face, and lips for the real meaning of this surprise invitation, and this interview in a noble room. ' You heard that I resigned the headmastership ? ' he asked.

' I imagined you must have done, since I heard you were now working for—that you were now giving your services to the Church Army.'

' I had a difference with the Governors. It was sad, very sad to go after twenty-four years.'

' I'm sure it was, sir.'

' Do you know anything about the work of the Church Army ? '

' Nothing at all, I'm ashamed to say. I imagine they do magnificent work.'

But it was no good. He knew. Still staring at me, he knew all. He knew that I knew everything and was trying to help him. And he knew that it was to be a tacit pretence between us all that none of us knew anything. He let his eyes fall to the ground and did not speak ; only he thrust back a falling cuff. To lighten the uncomfortable silence I asked, ' Won't you have some more tea, sir ? Let me order you another slice of cake.'

He lifted his face and fixed me with his eyes : those eyes, beneath bristling brows, which had looked at me so furiously fifteen years before, and were so sad and emptied now. He attempted a smile. ' I'd like to say this, Allan Mourne. I think it's exceedingly nice of you to have remembered your old head-master—and remembered him kindly—in spite of all.'

' Not at all, sir,' I demurred. ' We wanted your help.'

' And you shall have it. The best I can give—the very best. Be sure of that.'

§

When he was gone, George asked me, ' Would you just step across the road to Henrietta Street so that I can sign my resigna-tion ? It was my intention to join a publishing house, not a public assistance board ; ' and I said I would willingly go, but what was wrong with writing it here in the Smoking Room, where there were perfectly good writing tables and pens, ink, and paper ? I submitted, however, that in calmer moments he would regret his action because, unless I was mistaken, I had just done a fine bit of work for the house of Allan Mourne.

And in this I was right. On the Monday I sent Harlen some manuscripts that had come from agents and one of them re-turned from him in two days with a long and elaborate essay attached. The handwriting and the phrasing showed that he had given laborious hours to it. It was phrased in magnilo-quent periods such as Gibbon would have approved, and while commenting on the author's views, it missed no chance of dis-playing his own scholarship. It dealt severely with any collo-quial or slip-shod expressions and subjoined a list of grammatical errors. Strange irony that my headmaster should now be send-ing up a neat and laboured essay in an effort to impress me.

It was only at first that his reports were solemn and pompous like this ; later, when he felt confident and secure with us, they were often witty and gay ; and it was good to read in them his new happiness and ease. He had little feeling at first for the commercial chances of a book, but George and I had talks with him on this aspect of things, and he listened with eyes concen-trated on us and many nods, straining to learn. So resolute a pupil soon acquired some of the necessary flair. His school-master's eye for grammatical mistakes was so keen that our Chief Editor showed him how to edit books and prepare them for press, and he would take manuscripts home with him and do the work with scrupulous care.

Soon he made a habit of coming to Henrietta Street every Wednesday afternoon to collect the manuscripts that stood wait-ing for him in the Enquiries office ; as many as eight or ten of them, perhaps, since we were now well satisfied with him.

Always on these occasions he came dressed as a Literary Adviser should be, in his new dark suit, a sternly clerical collar and a somewhat literary black hat, soft in the crown and broad in the brim ; and for the carriage of the manuscripts he brought a black bag which had once held his robes and his sermon. He was now a familiar and popular figure with all our staff, because he was so courteous and shy with them, though capable of sly jests. When he knew that he was liked the shyness fell away but never the courtesy. It might be that he would ask to see ' Mr. Theodore ' or ' Mr. Byng ' but always apologetically : ' Not if he's busy, *please*. I wouldn't wish to disturb him. But if he can afford me one minute. . . .' Busy or not, I never had the heart to exclude him, and he would come up to my front room with a new idea for a book, because he gave much of his time to thinking out new ideas that would further justify him in our sight. Some of these ideas were quite good and then he would be much pleased with my interest ; but he was always on the edge of his chair, and anxious to remove himself quickly lest he were ' being an encumbrance.' Sometimes I would send down a courteous message, ' Would Mr. Harlen do me the favour of coming to my room ? ' and, upon my soul, I think he was always pleased by this and counted it an honour. But in fact he was of real use to me now : he was of use in the three series that I most delighted in—*The Great Humanes, Western Sages and Eastern Seers*, and the new-fashioned school books that were to be full of fun and excitement for the children. Sometimes I would mischievously give him a manuscript that set out to liberate its readers from the stranglehold of Orthodoxy (like the *philosophes* of old) and after reading it, he would remember his clerical collar and say : ' You cannot expect me to agree with this, but well, well, the Church isn't afraid of a little controversy ; ' or, remembering his collar but forgetting my knowledge of his past, he would say, ' For my part, my only fear is lest the undermining of people's faith should lead to a slackening in their morals.'

His visit over, he would leave us with a smile and a jest and depart along Henrietta Street, carrying the black bag between the vegetable crates with one black arm extended as a counterpoise to the weight of the manuscripts. No longer employed by the Church Army, because he was taking some three or four hundred a year from us, he had a comfortable little home in Wandsworth, and many friends, to whom (as we came to hear) he would describe himself as ' Literary Adviser to Allan Mourne's ' and their ' Principal Reader '. ' I advise them on Theological and Educational books,' he would say. ' It's anxious and responsible work because in a sense the good repute of the house is in my keeping.' Pleased to humour him in this little conceit I would often suggest to our authors that they should ' come and discuss the matter with " our Reader " ' and then he would sit with one of them in our small back room and converse very seriously and expertly, using all the jargon of the trade—' I'll have it cast off for you. . . . You'll get your galley slips in a week or two. . . . I can't express an opinion upon that : we have to consider the ratio of publicity costs to total turnover. I'll discuss it with Mr. Theodore.'

Yes, it was pleasant to think of him there, a contented, confident, industrious man, using fine abilities to the full and to a fair purpose.

CHAPTER VI

SUCH WAS my house in Henrietta Street : a healthy youngster, ever astir with the fervours and energy of youth, and putting on muscle every day. What of my house in Queensberry Place, my home ? Was the heart of that as sound ?

Iris and I had been married about three years, and our son, Hugh, was about fifteen months old—a little dark boy with full promise of his mother's Mexican black hair—when she surprised the truth. These had been happy enough years for her, and not unhappy for me. I was fond of her, proud of her, and grateful to her ; I shared with her our love for Hugh, and all my plans and dreams, though she had ceased to work in Henrietta Street soon after Hugh was born. Particularly I shared with her my jokes. We were partners, and laughing partners too ; but I could not give her love. I could not say—or only with an effort—the adoring words that a woman craves, even though she's as reticent and self-controlled as Iris. I couldn't caress her in the daylight : something held my hand and chilled my lips. Only at night when we lay together did desire empower me to speak insincere words and fondle her passionately ; but even as I held her in my arms and kissed her closed eyes and her uncovered breasts, my heart said, ' Gentle . . . Gentle . . . ' and when I turned from her, passion spent, I said to my pillow, ' Gentle . . . I haven't forgotten you, my beloved.'

I had told her once about my ' boyish love ' for Gentle but when she asked me, as even the proudest woman will, ' Did you love me as much as Gentle ? ' I lied immediately, saying, ' Why, of course, my dear ! That's an old dead story,' both so as not to hurt her and so as to hide my offence.   Never again, unless the subject could not be evaded, did I speak of Gentle—and this was a mistake, because my very silence made her wonder.   But since when I was not pouring forth my plans to her, or playing the buffoon, I was a quiet husband, silent about many things, she did not let the wonder grow ; she just strangled it and left it for dead.   Proud as I, far more reticent than Gentle, she did not ask that womanly question again—at least, not till she stumbled upon the truth and had to speak.

I think that my superabundance of high spirits and jocosity in these years—was not business booming in Henrietta Street ? —served to blind her to the truth as with a veil of shimmering light.   I was moody and silent sometimes, like Father, and she was patient with me then, but far more often I was boisterous, and then, too, she had need to be patient for, when the high spirits effervesced, I could only ease their pressure by acting like a clown.   Iris, sitting at home was the first target for my jokes, good or bad, and the only target if they were peculiarly bad.   Truth can often disguise itself in the motley and bells ; was it significant, perhaps, that so many of my jokes played around the idea of myself as a husband who was failing badly in his rôle and who deserved to lose the love of his wife ?   Returning from the office, I would run up the stairs to her favourite room, the little ' Indian room ' on the first half-landing (so called because it housed most of the treasures, in silver, ivory, brass, and silk, which Father had brought from India) and, seeing her seated there with her book or her needle, I would declare, ' There's a strange air of melancholy in the house.   Is it me ? ' And if she did not answer, but only smiled, I would stand before her, hands in pockets, eyes on her face, and insist, ' Young woman, please tell me.   Am I the cause of it ?   I can stand the truth.   I realize that I am most damnably difficult to live with. Pray understand that I fully appreciate that.'   She would answer perhaps that she'd had a slight headache all day, and promptly I demanded, ' Am I the headache ?   Yes, of course I am.   I'm the suppressed disappointment of your life, and it comes out in the form of a headache.   I do apologize.   You can't imagine how profoundly I apologize.'   And on her enjoining me ' not to be such a perfect ass,' I would argue with a show of great reasonableness, ' But you're depressed, my dear.   You're obviously depressed.   What can it be but me ?   I mean, you quite like the little boy.'

Or the high spirits at the end of the day would shoot me up two flights of stairs to Hugh in his nursery—not having seen him for nine hours—and after I'd watched him playing and slobbering

on his floor, and heaved him up to the ceiling two or three
times, and tickled him in suitable parts, I would walk down to
Iris in her Indian room, enter, and proclaim, ' I produce a very
fine type of child. That at least you must admit. I take it
that you are grateful to me for providing you with a thoroughly
nice little boy. Ponder on it sometimes. I protest, it's greatly
to my credit.'

Or, if I'd had fine news at the office, I might race up the
stairs, seize her by both hands and dance her round, ring-o'-
roses fashion, while I bawled a song of that year :

> Every evening hear them sing—
> It's the cutest little thing—
> Itchy-koo, itchy-koo, itchy-koo. . . .

Yes, it was fair weather for Iris in those years, with only a little
cloud, and many a burst of sunshine. And then in the autumn
of 1912 I went on my first visit to America to sell them my
' Humanes' and ' Seers', thinking that they needed this instruction
and illumination quite as much as we did. I was secretly very
proud of this journey and anxious that Mother and Con, and the
distant Gentle, should know all about it, for, though thirty now,
I still felt like the schoolboy of sixteen. In the States I not only
sold the rights of some of my books, and editions of others in
sheets, and picked up the English rights of some of their books,
but I picked up also the bacilli of typhoid fever. I had not been
back a week before I sickened. For days I tried to go on with
my work, but the fever grappled with me and flung me on my
bed. And thence it bore me through grey and awful lands of
dissolving phantasmagoria to an airless, breathless Limbo only a
few steps this side of the cliff and the black abyss. Iris and the
nurses held me back from that abyss.

And how was Iris rewarded for this ? Ever ready to relieve a
nurse for an hour, she would come into the darkened room where
I lay clawing at the bedclothes and muttering in delirium. I
see her coming now, a white figure among the grey phantasmagoria, and I feel again my eyes staring at her white gown and
at her familiar eyes above the white mask. The nurse tip-toes
out, and Iris comes nearer and looks down upon me lying there,
long and thin as a midnight spectre. She sits and picks up my
burning hand as if to keep me. And I gaze at her with my fever-
lit eyes and try to draw the hand away. And, still staring at her,
frowning at her, as if in bewilderment or recoil, I say, now in a
weak whisper, now almost shouting, ' Gentle, Gentle, I love you
only . . . I love you only till death us do part. In sickness
and in—I am dying, Gentle. The church is all dark—what

fools these people are to think I love her—a white bride—they call me the "happy man". Die too, my darling, and come with me.'

Which suffers the more in the darkened room : the patient tossed and ridden with dissolving horrors or the wife bending low, perforce, to catch the gibbered words ? I am racked, but she is put to a torment too : she is racked by a question that only I can answer, and that I may not live to answer.

I stare and stare at her with puckered brow, and after a time I say, 'Gentle Greaves . . . Gentle Mary Greaves . . . you didn't spare me, and I hope I punished you. Yes, lady : you went out of your way to hurt me when you married him. Max, *Max !* Ha !—Let me out ! Let me out ! I can't get out, I can't breathe—oh, why can't I die . . . die . . . ? You started the game, but I think I returned your ball harder than—I—I——' Iris stoops low, with her ear turned to my gabbling lips : 'You what, dear ? ' and I answer, 'She is lovely, Gentle ; lovelier than you, dear child . . . and better too—a nobler person in every way—and I want *you*, my beloved, my darling. We are one.'

Tenderly Iris puts back and smooths the tumbled sheet, and whispers, 'Do you think you could sleep ? Try to sleep, my dear. Try to sleep.' And she repeats as if she would hypnotise me, 'Try to sleep . . . sleep . . . sleep.'

But I, never taking my eyes off hers, continue the wild dis-ordered rambling. 'You shall send for me first, Gentle : I plead to no one : I am no one's suppliant. If you wait for me to make a move, Madam Proud, you'll wait a long time. I shall do the waiting. I can wait. I can wait . . . while you—no, don't take him, Gentle. Don't let him—oh no, no ; I can't bear it !—you are mine—your sweet body is mine only. *No !*——'

Here I start up, or try to, weakly shouting, and she lays a hand on my white, emaciated fingers as they pick and scratch at the sheets and whispers, 'It's all right, my dear. Lie down. There there. . . .' And with a sigh she moistens my caked lips, and eases my parched throat, with a sip of lemon and water ; and I, still staring at her, say, 'All right, take him—and I will take a lovelier than you, whether I love her or not. She loves me, sweetheart ; she gave me everything you wouldn't give ; and we are happy. Ha, yes, I suppose so. We have Hugh ; and you have no children. Thank God for that. No children . . . no children. . . . The children of Gentle call Bartrum father —no, thank God—bear him no child, my dear. Only to me . . . only to me . . . Gentle . . . my wife.'

§

Three weeks, and my temperature began to fall.   It continued falling for eight days.   And now, though weak and thin, I was fully alive and joking again.   I joked with the nurses and with Iris, unaware that in my sickness, when the tormentors racked me, I had torn down the curtain from my secret place.   When I was completely well, I returned to Iris's bed ; and then it was my turn to wake and wonder, while Iris slept.   One night, after I'd made some play at love and we'd turned apart to sleep, I dozed for a moment, only to be awakened by a slight tremor of the bed—such a tremor as might come if a door slammed or a dead weight fell.   I did not move ; and the bed quivered again. This time I knew its cause : Iris was sobbing, but with sobs as soundless as her pride demanded.   I stirred, and instantly she stopped the sobs—stopped them as one stops with one's hand the clapper of a bell.   She lay quite still, in her pride and in her desire not to hurt me.   I said nothing, because I did not want that pride to suffer ; but I could not sleep for wondering.   She slept ; and her sleep, like my delirium, unloosed the proud control, and I heard her moaning to herself, ' Oh, God, God. . . .'

In the morning, having decided that there was nothing unusual in a troubled sleep, I rallied her for this weeping and groaning. I joked in the old fashion, saying, ' Golly, I knew I was bad, but I didn't know I was as bad as that,' and she only smiled rather sadly, and said she must have been having a nightmare.

Nothing more did she say till I was plainly strong enough to bear it.   And then one night, when we were sitting together in the Indian room, I on my usual chair with some sheaves of dog-eared manuscript, she on the white Indian rug with her legs drawn under her and her knitting in her hands, she let the work fall to her knees and gazed into the fire.   There was no other light in the room except the reading lamp behind my head and the flames of this restless and breaking fire.   The November night was cold, and the closed windows and the drawn curtains shut out all sounds of traffic from the Harrington and Cromwell Roads.   The servants were in the basement, and Hugh in his nursery above, and we seemed isolated from the world in that little shut room.   Far out in the silent distances were Mother, Con, Father, the Greaves, and Max with Gentle.

Gazing into the fire, Iris said, ' Are you very busy ?   May I ask you something ? '

' Anything you like, dear,' said I, dropping a sheaf to my lap. ' Go ahead.'

But she did not put her question at once ; and I encouraged her, ' What is it ? '

Not taking her eyes from the flames, she asked, ' How much did you love Gentle ? '

' Very much.' I had said this with deep feeling, but it was hardly uttered before the sentimental and cruel part of me was feeling proud of my old love for Gentle, and glad that Iris should know of it.

' How much do you love her now ? '

Ashamed of that moment of pride and cruelty, I said at once, ' That's all past, my dear. We called an end to that years ago.'

' Are you sure ? ' And she told me all my ravings in delirium, giving the actual words I had cried out ; and I was greatly alarmed and troubled.

' One can say anything in delirium,' I parried. ' I suppose I was living in the past.'

' But, Doric, that isn't all. I did a very dreadful thing while you were lying there. I'm terribly ashamed of it—I've never done anything like it before—at least, not since I was a child— but when one is suffering a terrible suspense or suspicion, one is just driven—one has to *know*. I felt mad ; I felt quite unlike my usual self ; and Doric, I . . . '

' Don't mind telling me. I've done lots of wrong things in my life.'

' I—I looked in your desk for letters from Gentle. I looked in all your drawers. I hated myself while I was doing it, but——'

I picked up her hand to help her. ' I understand perfectly, my dear. I've done that sort of thing myself . . . quite often . . . all too often.' And indeed I was glad that she could sin too and be my companion in weakness.

' But there's worse . . . one drawer was locked, and I took the keys from your bedroom while you were lying there so ill and opened it. . . . I *had* to . . . and there I found all the letters from Gentle and her photograph tied round with a ribbon.'

' They are very old letters. Did you read them ? '

' Only one . . . and then I was ashamed and stopped and put them back again. Why did you keep them ? '

' Does one ever destroy such things ? '

' Do you read them sometimes now ? '

' Never. I haven't read them for years. I daren't.'

Oh, how was it I made that mistake : was it carelessness, or compassion or cruelty, or a blend of the three, that let me reveal all in those two syllables, ' I daren't. ' ?

Iris cried ' Oh !' and dragged her hand away and buried her face in both palms.

I put my hand on her shoulder, pretending I'd said nothing of any significance. ' What is the matter ? What is it, my sweet ? '

' You love her, and her only, and you always will.'

Again I was seized with pride in this and did not speak. Dimly, as I waited, I heard the traffic of the world outside.

Iris lowered her hands from her face. ' Will you tell me one thing ? '

' I will try to.'

' Did you love me when you married me ? '

' Of course.'

' Was I first—just then ? '

' First ? ' She was too fine for lies ; and I would not, could not, deny Gentle ; and I was tired of sinning. Defeated, I did not answer.

She bit on her mouth to master and hide a spasm of pain. ' I see.'

' I hadn't forgotten Gentle,' I said, countering weakly. ' One never really forgets——'

' Oh, why did you marry me ? ' she cried, her hands clenching into fists and quivering, down at her knees. ' Why did you take me ? You married me only to hurt her. You said so.'

' I loved you in my way, as I always shall.'

' I had but one life. . . .'

' I loved you too,' I said feebly.

But she was not listening ; she leapt to her feet and stood with her fists pressed together at her breast. ' Oh, God, my God. . . . I had but one life. . . . I wanted someone who loved me. I wanted someone who loved me only. . . . Is that Hugh crying ? . . . No. . . . I wanted someone who loved me.'

My pity and remorse were such that I must rise and take her in my arms. She had too much dignity to rebuff me crudely or violently, and she remained in my embrace, but cold and rigid as a corpse. I tried to kiss her brow, but she shook her head.

' Please,' I begged.

Gently she unlaced my arms and pushed me away. ' Who will give me back my best years ? Listen.' She sank to the floor again, picked up the fallen knitting, and held it down there at her knees. ' I had a dream : I was going to be the perfect wife, just as others want to be the perfect artist, or you wanted to be a wonderful publisher. There was never going to be anyone like me. I told no one about this—not even Father or Mother—but I used to live with it as my dream.'

' You *have* been wonderful.'

' Oh, no ; one can only be the perfect wife to a husband who loves one ; and you love Gentle. I shall never be it now. I don't believe that in your heart you ever think of anyone else. . . . Oh, well, it can't be helped . . . but . . . I should have liked to be loved once like that.'

' Iris, dear——'

' It's too late now. One loves where one loves.'

Having no fit words, I gathered up her hand again ; and she said—it was her only cry for help, ' Don't let me feel quite alone.'

' I have told you that I love you too.'

Her head shook in an unspoken No ; and then she looked up at me and tried to smile. ' Well, we must make the best of it, my dear. Promise that you won't tell anyone else, and I shan't speak of it to anyone—certainly not to Mother or Father or my brothers. I don't want anyone to pity me.'

§

It may have been two days later that I set forth on a tour of all the big booksellers in the North. I believe I was one of the first publishers to decide that it would be good business to make personal friends of all those booksellers who were carrying my books and to listen respectfully to their comments and their counsel. In this I stole a march on nearly all my competitors. As the head of a new but up-and-coming house, and the originator of two most successful series, I no longer suffered from that shuddering shyness, that sick dread of a rebuff, that used to hamper me when I tried to sell, as their representative, the books of Sands and Hume. I knew that I was sure of the friendliest welcome because I had come, not to get, but to give what every man longs to receive : a hearing for his difficulties, his grievances, and all his latest ideas.

I was away five weeks ; and on the night of my return I went to Iris's bed and by my touch showed my desire to be a lover. Instinctively she turned from me, there in the darkness, and a ' No ! ' escaped her like a gasp of pain.

To one of my exaggerated sensitiveness that repulse was like an unforeseen stab that reached the heart. And it was a hurt that could never heal. Never again, in my withdrawn and frozen pride, could I offer myself to Iris unless she were first to approach me ; and that would be impossible to her, a proud creature with a nobler wound than mine. That moment an iron portcullis of pride and pain dropped down between us.

§

Thus was our wedding undone, that merry, crowded and ' fashionable ' wedding in the little Cranmere church three and a half years before. The marriage was made in the sunlight before the world ; it was undone in the darkness of our room. I had no wife any more. I had a friend and helper in the home, an audience for my dreams and my jokes ; a good mother for Hugh (on whom she centred all her love) ; a skilled house-keeper and a handsome hostess for my friends. She was all these things to me, and I was grateful for them, but I could seldom look at her face, at our table among our friends, or in her chair when we were alone, because it hurt to do so.

And the odd thing was that this was not too unhappy a relationship. I felt no resentment against her, because I accepted my exile as just. And, pitying her, I was filled by a bewildered, trammelled, but truly tremendous desire to give when I could to her who had once come to me, bringing her all, as a wife. I used to think then, with pain and shame, what a wonderful word was ' wife.' All that I could give her I gave ; and I do not know that she needed greatly the thing which I could never give, or she receive, again. There was always that in the proud and self-enclosed Iris which could turn her cold. Nor did I need very much that which was no longer mine to take. Nearly all my creative force spent itself in the building of my publishing house ; what was left unused ran in dreams to Gentle. And if, outside my home, I was now something of a broody and moonsick solitary again, wearing at times a mask of fun, well, that was what I was always ready to be. It was in my nature, as it was in my father's.

I tended to take my holidays alone now, having discovered a new happiness in wandering by myself on the craggy traverses or the rock-strewn tops of Swiss and English mountains. Our excuse for these, my lonely flights from home, was that Iris had no head for heights, but the truth was that I preferred to walk the barren silences alone. Brooding along a dangerous edge where the rocks fell steeply to a valley below, I would sometimes see a parable in this place, and wonder if Iris and I, despite our friendliness and laughter, were walking near the edge of —what ?

§

Her loyalty was there for me, ever ready as usual, when we
came to a happy agreement about Father.

Father was only two years short of eighty now. The years,
while bending his tall figure hardly at all, had creased and
cracked his large-featured face, turned the black curls that
fringed his bald and shining sconce a tarnished silver, and
bleached the long, yard-arm moustaches into a swan's white.
His clothes hung rather more loosely than of old on this lofty
framework, but they were the best clothes—the very best the
Army and Navy Stores could make him. When light-hued
they had a pleasant roughness, when dark a handsome sheen,
and always a distinction and *ton*. As yet there were no signs of
frailty in his walk, in his big brown hands that held the cane
and gloves, or around the crinkling rims of his deep-set mischievous eyes. It may be that I have always looked at him
through too kindly a glass, but at least Iris endorsed my view
that he was as splendid an old man as we had ever seen.

Still, seventy-eight was a great age, as he would frequently
deplore to us, and a very serious matter indeed. ' I count my
years forwards, and I count them backwards, but I cannot
make them less than seventy-eight. If anyone asks me my age
I say seventy-two, but it is not so. It is not true, Doric.' He
had recently resigned all his directorates, and was very proud
of this honourable action and of the ' extreme poverty ' which
ensued. ' I am not only lonely now but poor,' he said to me
one day when he'd come to visit us, as he so often did, having
all time on his hands and so few friendly doors to knock at.
' I have been rich and now am poor, yet never saw I the righteous
man . . . but leave that. I know I did the right thing in going
when I did. A director of eighty is an odious spectacle and
enough to depress the shareholders and the shares of the soundest
business. I did not wait for them to hint at my departure, but
went. Rather than outstay my welcome, I walked out into a
financial blizzard.' The story of Scott's last days in the
Antarctic, and of Captain Oates, the ' very gallant gentleman,'
who, ill and disabled, resolved to be no burden to his comrades
and walked out into the blizzard to die, had just rung through
England, shaking all hearts, and Father, who'd been shaken
into tears by it, was not slow to see a resemblance between his
action and the Captain's. ' " He went out into the blizzard
and we have not seen him since," ' he would quote with much
feeling and a tremble in his voice. ' I do not put my action

quite on a level with his, but I did go out into an economic
blizzard for my brethren and companions' sake. It was the
act of a very gallant gentleman.'

I said, ' It certainly was, Father ' ; but took leave to doubt
if the poverty was as extreme as he implied.

' The poverty I can stand,' he admitted, as if my thought, in
passing, had touched him with its wing. ' I do not need much.
A little soup and bread . . . a room to sleep in . . . a wall on
which to hang my old, rusty sword . . . but the solitude and the
boredom I find hard to bear. That's why I'm inflicting myself
on you now when you have important work to do, improving
mankind. But, Doric, I'm glad that you, at any rate, have
taken my counsel and given your love to one woman only, and
so secured her as a companion for life. One should grow into
a habit for one person at least. I have no one to whom I'm a
habit. Old Humphrey's really much happier than I am, since
he went off with my wife.'

I laughed. ' I wonder if he thinks so,' I said.

' Probably not. The man was always rather an old woman
who could think of nothing but his pains. But he'd know it if
he walked in my shoes. It's sad, very sad, Doric, to approach
the Shades alone. One should have an arm to lean on. . . .
So hold on to what you've got in Iris, my dear fellow. A life-
long companion is a treasure to be worked for and won ; it's
something to sacrifice quite a lot for. One sees this at seventy-
eight. Indeed, I perceived it at seventy-four, but it was too
late, too late. " The soul's dark cottage, battered and decayed,
Lets in new light through chinks that time has made." Yes,
I am filling with light now.'

' Good,' I said, since this seemed as sensible as anything else
to say.

' The loneliness is not too bad in the daylight,' continued
Father, casting his glance through the window. ' One can walk
in the sun. But it's an oppression, a deathly oppression, when
evening comes down. Have you ever thought, Doric, of the
awful blindness and dumbness of a front door where there's
nothing but silence behind ? And of the emptiness of the room
upstairs ? I tell you : one hour of that emptiness, and I feel
suicidal. . . . No, of course you haven't ; when you come home
to your door there's a dear little wife behind it. Me—I have
nothing to do but climb the stairs and sit in an empty room
and meditate on a wasted life.'

' Rubbish ! ' I expostulated. ' I doubt if anyone ever wasted
his life less.'

' Oh, but it's true, Doric ; only too true.' Father was not to be denied this count in his self-indictment : it provided too fine a text for pathetic and eloquent speech. 'One may have done a few useful things here and there, but if you've failed to create one lasting love, you've wasted your grand opportunity. You're given seventy years to do it in. I've had my ration of years now—though for some reason which I don't understand, a few more years are being thrown in *gratis*. But there's no doing anything with them now. Nothing like that will ever happen now. No, no, "My name is Might-have-been ; I am also called No-more, Too-late, Farewell." '

He spoke in jest, but the words hid their core of truth ; and that evening they brought forth in me an idea which I laid with some diffidence before Iris. She leapt at it, embraced it, and adopted it at once ; and for the rest of the evening we were occupied with happy and exciting plans. 'You must go to him to-morrow,' she said ; and I : 'Nothing of the sort. It's you alone who'll be able to persuade him.' So the next evening, after office hours, we went off together to his chambers in Pall Mall, pleased as two children carrying a gift. The street door was open, and we ran up the stairs. I tapped on his sitting-room door, received no answer, and opened it. He lay back in his easy chair, clad in a long silk dressing-gown and dozing with his mouth partly open.

The boards creaked beneath our feet, and he started up.

'Doric ! *Mon dieu*, I trust I didn't look too awful. And our Iris, our dear Iris ! ' At the sight of a lady in his room he immediately rose. ' Tell me she didn't see me like that. A most repulsive spectacle. Iris as well as Doric ! Sit down, my dear. This is the most comfortable chair, I think. A cushion ? Upon my soul, this is a visitation which brings the sunlight into my room.' Father showed courtesy to any woman (except, in forgetful moments to his wife or mistress) ; to a woman who was young and beautiful he showed something more than courtesy —a tenderness ; and to Iris, because she was my wife, the greatest tenderness of all. 'That's right. Are you sure you're quite comfortable ? Good. And you will forgive Doric and me if we smoke ? I thank you. Here you are, Doric, old man.'

I did not at first give the slightest attention to the silver cigarette-box which he was proffering. 'General,' I said, standing opposite him. 'General Allan Mourne, sir. We have come for you.'

'You have come for me ? I don't quite understand.'

'Iris and I have decided that you're going to live with us.' And at this point, since, bewildered, he was still holding out the box of cigarettes, I took one.

'Yes,' said Iris, 'it's decided. It's absolutely and finally decided. And we're thrilled about it.'

'But this is absurd,' he protested, turning from one to the other. 'This is ludicrous; I'm undone.'

'It is not at all ludicrous,' I declared over my match-flame. 'We've made up our minds. Aren't you having a cigarette yourself?' And I sat myself down on the arm of a chair. 'How soon can you come?'

'I'm not coming at all. I never heard such nonsense.'

'It's not nonsense,' said Iris. 'And we haven't come here to argue. We've merely come to let you know.'

'Now, now, my dear, it's very kind—very kind and touching of you—not to say, staggering. But I'm certainly not going to encumber you with a horrible old grandfather. Good gracious, no. Some almshouse, where I can hang my rusty sword . . . some hostel, some institution, where they take old men who refuse to die.'

'Exactly,' agreed Iris. 'And the institution is 39, Queensberry Place.'

'No, no, my child. You are young. You want young people about you. You don't want a horrible old man in a state of increasing disintegration. I want you to be happy. I like all people to be happy, especially the young.'

'Oh dear, oh dear, Doric, he's going to be difficult. Talk to him. Make him understand that he'll disappoint us most horribly if he refuses. He has some pity. Appeal to that.'

'No, dear child, it is sweet and charming of you, but . . .' He shook his head many times. 'You see, Iris dear, it's like this: I may be a fool, but I've a strong desire to be loved, and I've learned, with many tears, that I'm easier to love at a distance. I want you to like me—you particularly—and—it's a foolish idea—but I want to be remembered after death with some small pleasure, not with an acute distaste.'

'Doric, tell him not to be so silly and tiresome. As if it wouldn't be much easier to love him in Queensberry Place than in Pall Mall, where nobody ever sees him.'

'Oh no, dear.' Father spoke with conviction. 'That's where you're wrong. That's where you're grievously wrong. Listen—Doric needn't listen to this: it's just between you and me—there used to be some idealization of me by young Doric when he was a small boy. It was quite undeserved, but it was pleasant. It's no doubt gravely impaired now, but I don't want it entirely destroyed.' He turned to me. 'Your excellent mother sees me all too clearly; and so, I fear, does Tricks, with some assistance from her mother—and from her ridiculous

auntie.   You've met Henrietta Greaves, haven't you, Iris dear ?
—well, you'll grasp what I mean.   An extraordinarily foolish
woman, but I suppose she can't help herself——   No, Doric, it
was a great grief to me when Tricks no longer thought me
perfect—or even really approved of me.   You seem to have
retained a certain blindness.   Keep it.   Keep it a year or two
longer—only a year or two—and then the kindly haze of
death——'
    'Oh, heavens !' interrupted Iris.   'Where have we got to
now ?   Who's talking about the kindly haze of death ?   Make
him understand we really want him.'
    'Father,' I said.   'Will you listen to me instead of doing all
the talking——'
    'I ?   Talking ?'
    'Yes, and talking a lot of gaff.   Now listen : with all my
heart and soul I want you to come.   This is true.   The idea
no sooner came to me than I knew I wanted it more than
anything else.'
    Iris rose and went up to him and put both hands on his
shoulders.   'Me, too.   Please . . . please will you come and
make us happy ?'
    His lips pressed together ;   his mouth beneath the white
moustaches moved up and down and sideways, exactly like
Mother's when she was keeping a grip on her tears ;   his hand
dived into his breast pocket for the silk handkerchief and for
its first-aid ;   but it remained there, for he'd managed—though
only just—to draw back the tears without any too shameful
secretions.   When it was safe to unlock his lips, he took one of
her hands from his shoulder, bent over it, and kissed it.   'My
dear little lady, you speak with all the generous hopefulness of
youth ;   but you must look at this seriously.   You must always
examine every inch of the enemy's ground before you embark
upon a campaign.   Now consider.   Take it that I sink into
second childhood—God, may I die first !—take it that I lose all
control of my tongue and become garrulous, like that peculiarly
blasted old bore, Lord Ravenhope, at the club.   I've suspected
traces of this in myself of late and been greatly distressed by
them.   I have noticed—or it may be my imagination—that
whenever I start expounding a topic in the club, someone
immediately hands round cigarettes.   Take it that I begin to
make gross and unpleasant noises.   You should hear old Colonel
Betlingham when he's coughing and sneezing and hawking—he
makes the welkin ring.   You don't want that in your nice home.
And wasn't there some revolting old man whose eyes purged
thick amber and plum-tree gum ?   Polonius, I think.   My

memory isn't what it was. Or take it that I fall about the house, and up and down the stairs. I did once many years ago and have been in terror of doing it again every day of my life since. Oh no, rather than that, the blizzard every time. You cannot imagine how intense is my desire not to become a burden. Why can I not walk out into the blizzard, like Captain Oates, before I'm a burden on anyone ? '

' Well, you can't, because there's no blizzard to walk into,' explained Iris. ' So when can you come ? '

' When can I come ? '

' Yes. I've got to begin getting your room ready.'

' My room ? No, no. . . . No, certainly not. . . . I—I could pay you well, I suppose——'

' Doric, he's yielding ! Take over quick. We've got him on the run.'

' Nothing of the sort. I never run. The whole thing's impossible. A very attractive idea, but impossible. It would certainly be very pleasant to come home once again to a door behind which there was something more than silence—to turn one's latchkey and hear the voices of . . . yes, one's children. I don't know. . . .' With his fingers he beat a meditative tattoo on the mantelshelf. ' I don't know . . . perhaps I could be completely shut off somewhere at the top of the house.'

' Yes, certainly,' said Iris.

' Is there a part with a door ? '

' We'll put up all the doors you like. Two—three—if you like.'

' No, not too many. I shall like to hear your voices. And my little grandson's. There's no sound so pleasant as the happy prattle of children——'

' Then it's settled ? ' cried Iris, jumping up and down. ' Settled, settled, settled ! '

' I shouldn't need much. A little soup and bread. Or a bowl of gruel, perhaps.'

' Yes, and we can undertake to provide all that. I'll make the gruel myself.'

' I imagine it would not be for long.'

' It'll be for years yet. You're looking splendid. Doric and I were saying we'd never seen you look better.'

' An antique patina, my dear. You see it on all furniture a hundred years old.'

' Then is it settled ? *Yes !* Oh, Doric, isn't this lovely ? Isn't this wonderful ? '

' Yes,' said I.

But Father shook a dubious head. ' It's a very great risk. I'm risking all. It's all I've got, Doric's wounded but still living loyalty, and your affection, such as it is. This is touch-and-go. I am very grateful, and very much afraid.'

She kissed him. 'There's nothing to be afraid of. Nothing.'

'I must try to behave well,' he said.

§

The day that he was to come to us has always seemed remarkable for a strange elation that sprang up from somewhere deep down in me. It was the love of the boy Doric speaking again. More than twenty years fell from me that day, and I was once again that little boy in the old Coburg Square house, wandering restlessly about and longing for his return.

Like two children Iris and I had begged him to stay in town till the evening so that we might have his furniture and chattels arranged and his room all set for display. And fully an hour before he was expected the room was ready ; a fire dancing in the grate, flowers standing on the dressing table, a box of his favourite cigars on his desk, his clothes neatly stowed in cupboards and drawers, a reading lamp by his bed—and Uncle Humphrey's book on the bed-side table.

Now there was nothing to do but wait, and I wandered about the house, glancing at clocks, listening to sounds in the street, just like the boy Doric. A long day was nearly done, and he was coming home from the City in the evening.

The taxi jarred by the kerb ; feet grated on our hearthstoned steps ; and before the bell could sound below I flung open the door.

'Come in, General.'

'It's a great risk,' he said, slightly shaking his head as he stepped in.

'General Allan Mourne, Iris dear.'

'Welcome,' said Iris and rose on her toes to kiss him, while Deakin, our butler, paid off and dismissed the taxi.

We led him up to his room, proud of our work on it. He looked round upon everything. 'You are good children,' he said. 'It is excellent—more than excellent. But what ? ' He was looking out on to the landing. 'No door? No door to shut me off? '

'No, no door,' said Iris, 'but '—and she pointed to a large blank space on the wall—'there's the place for the rusty sword.'

He bowed. If anyone was satirical with Father he invariably replied in the same key, pretending to accept the words as the simplest statement of fact. 'It should hang there very well,' he said, without a smile.

So Father was now upstairs in our house, and it was obvious, as the days went by, that he was trying to behave very well. Never now did he shout in enormous voice down the stairs, as he used to, once upon a time, in this house where I am writing now. Never did he say a rude or unkind word to anyone. We could feel that he wanted to keep our affection and that he lived in some fear of being an incubus. He would slip from the drawing-room after dinner if he thought that we two ' young lovers ' wanted to be alone ; he would make some effort at tidying his bedroom in the morning so as to help the servants ; he would bring home little presents for Iris at frequent intervals, to consolidate her affection, and far too many, far too expensive, ones for Hugh—we had to stop these at last, because the small boy was beginning to look for one whenever his grandfather came through the front door and even to prosecute inquiries if a gift was not produced. It was always a curious, even a mysterious, experience for me to watch little Hugh re-enacting, with hardly a movement changed, a twenty-year-old drama, as he raced to the door at the sound of my father's key.

His courtesy to our butler and maids was nothing unusual, for he had always (or nearly always) spoken to servants as if they were dukes and duchesses ; but this courtesy now was manifestly inspired by his desire that they should like him.

At our dinner parties he laboured to be a useful guest instead of a vexation ; he mixed the gin and angostura for us before the guests arrived ; if the guests took sherry before the meal he poured it out at a side-table and carried it among the ladies like a footman ; during the meal he would sometimes sit very quiet, and I knew that he was either determining not to be a garrulous old man, or avoiding topics in which the young people were deeply interested but in which he was out of his depth ; after dinner if we had a Reception with tea and light refreshments, once again he was among us as a servant waiting on all with his trays and his persuasive words and his little courtly bowings.

Our monthly dinners and Receptions at Queensberry Place in the years 1912 and '13 were becoming quite a feature of the literary life of London. It had always been my aim, since first the dream of being a publisher seized hold of my life, to have such parties and to make them as famous as the parties of the second John Murray in his house at Albemarle Street. One day they should be celebrated in the biographies of the famous. And this ambition, like so many of my other ambitions, I was half way to creating in 1913. To my dinners and soirées came authors, critics, editors, and even judges, bishops, and statesmen whose memoirs George Byng and I were publishing. It gave me pleasure that these parties should give such gratification to Iris who'd always wanted to entertain ' famous and interesting people.' I might have failed to give her the one thing needful, but at least I had given her this.

I would get old Uncle Humphrey along to some of these parties because I knew he would love it so. And he certainly did, wandering among the celebrities, cottoning up to one after another, and establishing his right to be accounted one of them by the statement, ' Yes, my young nephew published for me a book of mine.' You'd have thought from his tone that it was one of twenty books which he'd published, and that I was lucky to get it.

I wanted Mother and Con to come too, but Mother wouldn't for fear of meeting Father and because she now felt some resentment against me for having taken him into my home. Con, on the other hand, came at a run, eager to meet, or at any rate to see, all the famous people. Unaccustomed to such circles in the neighbourhood of Addismore Mansions, she once begged Father to tell her how to comport herself; and, according to her story, this is the gist of what he replied. ' It's all very simple, Tricks dear. What are you worrying about? You laugh at every silly witticism which any man unloads on you, but you do not roar or shriek. At the table you refrain from discussing with your neighbours the food on your plates, or anybody's illnesses, or surgical operations of any kind. Dress as nicely as you can, but wear only a *soupçon* of jewellery : too much locket or bangle marks the difference between a lady and a barmaid. And remember above all that if in the drawing-room things begin to hang fire, and if you can play or sing, or do anything else to fill up the time, it's the truest kindness not to do so.'

When Con came to a party I always tried to put on the best possible show both in the *dramatis personæ* and in the furnishings of the scene ; and this not only to impress a sister but that she might one day tell Gentle all about it. I wanted Gentle, who, if all the tales were true, was far from happy and often left alone in her black-and-white house at Holm St. Martin, to hear of my dinner parties, and of Iris's splendid table, and of the celebrities to be met there ; for Gentle as well as Iris used to number among her ambitions a longing to meet and entertain the famous. She must hear of what she had missed. I foraged to find out what newspapers Max Drury ordered for the Rent House, and learning without surprise that the *Morning Post* was one, I contrived, working like an underground mole in the brain of my friend, the editor, to get a description of one of our finest *soirées* into its society columns. I could not be sure that Gentle would read it in the morning, but I could hope so. And I did not really discourage, but rather encouraged with a pretence of modest doubt, the Editor of *Town and Home* when she asked to do a feature article entitled *An Evening at the Allan Mournes*. Gentle I knew read *Town and Home*, its every feature and every advertisement (especially the latter) ; and it was like a wave of pleasure, troubled by an undertow of shame, to see the article with its pictures of myself and Iris and Hugh and our drawing rooms, and to read, and think of Gentle reading its exaggerated and garish description.

' In the old days (it said) some of the heads of our greatest publish-ing houses used to make it their business to play the host on the most generous scale, and at regular intervals, to their authors and to the great and distinguished of their day. This tradition is being most worthily maintained by Mr. Theodore Allan Mourne, of the House of Allan Mourne which, though young in years, grows daily in strength and repute, and by Mrs. Allan Mourne his beautiful and attractive wife, daughter of Lord Cranmere, and as gracious and gifted a hostess as you will find in the length and breadth of London. Their monthly " even-ings " during the Season at their residence in Queensberry Place are acquiring a celebrity that is by no means limited to the *gens de lettres*. Queensberry Place is not, perhaps, Mayfair, but there on a Thursday Evening, when the month is new, you may see more than one of the Mayfair " four hundred " in animated and, let us hope, scintillating conversation with writers, artists, veteran warriors, and luminaries of the law. The rooms in Queensberry Place are inevitably smaller than those of Charles Street or Belgrave Square, but it is probable that at No. 39 on a First Thursday you will see more famous faces to the cubic inch between ten o'clock and midnight than you will detect in vast assemblies further east. Towards midnight the actors may come. . . .'

Sometimes I tried to be true to my vision and to feel only forgiveness for Gentle, but my heart would not hold it for long. It was only my intelligence that could cast out the vindictive-ness and the desire to hurt her ; my blood kept them, and it is the blood that primes the heart. Harlen I could forgive, and do all in my power to help, but I must continue to punish Gentle.

And the evenings and the mornings, the months and the days, were the year 1913.

CHAPTER VII

SO 1914 BROKE, and for six months the name 1914 was no different from 1910, '11, or '12 ; it was still but a unit in a uniform procession. The German scare was no worse ; indeed its impact had lost potency, because it had been with us so long, and our skins were now becoming indurated to it and callous. Comfortable thinkers all, we chose to believe that each new German ' crisis ' would slip into the past as the German gun-boat *Panther* in 1911 had slipped out of Agadir, rather than lay the flambeau to the fuse. We enjoyed the rumours which buzzed like bluebottles in club rooms and drawing rooms— that Sir Claude Fürstemberg was building concrete gun-plat-forms in his Surrey park for the bombardment of London ; that mysterious men had been taking photographs or making sketch-maps of our east-coast countryside—though why they didn't buy picture postcards and Ordnance maps at the stationer's and save themselves the trouble I never quite understood ; that unidentified aircraft had been seen flying over Sheerness or Dover ; that a German spy or an English brigadier had been shot in the Tower—we enjoyed them all, and got on with our port or our business.

All those who have figured in this tale were among the com-fortable thinkers. 1914 broke over Queensberry Place and found Iris and Father and me living together without perfect happiness, but in some content. It broke over Addismore Mansions to find Mother and Con chiefly interested in the affairs of their church, and Uncle Humphrey chiefly interested in himself. It broke over Holm St. Martin, and over the grave of Brian Greaves who had died in the autumn. In Holm St. Martin it saw the widowed Henrietta sitting in her long crape and beads in the Chapter Mill ; and Dr. and Mrs. Max Drury living the life that habit had ordained for them in their black-and-white house, both seeking their own ends, and both in-different to the state of the world ; it saw the people of the village and of the fast-growing factory area far more interested in rumours of discord in the doctor's house, and in a certain new whisper about the doctor's wife, than in any rumours about the house of Europe and the likelihood of discord there. It broke over Covent Garden Market and found that wide lap still filled with all the fruits and flowers of the world, and there in the midst of the green produce our tall, ugly Henrietta Street house with George and myself in our offices, well satisfied with last year's success and busy outlining the future. Here before me, faded and stained, is our List for that long dead Spring ; and under the heading ' General ' I see the titles of two books which I had commissioned in pursuit of my dominant purpose, *Beyond Cruelty, Peace* and *The Adulthood of Man*. The last page is headed *For Publication in the Autumn*. . . . I who eight years before had secured the publication of Norman Webster's *Ordeal at Hand* had never really believed in its cold, grim argument, because I didn't want to.

To us old men, Roberta, the war of 1914, that first of the new religious wars, may be flickering and growing dim in memory, but the manner of its coming is not forgotten.   Indeed I remember the days of its approach more vividly and in sharper detail than those days, twenty five years later, when the second round began.   It was *my* war, the war of us who are bald and grey now, and ready quite soon to dismiss.   To you who were born in its first year it is, I imagine, but a vague and ill-comprehended tale.   The word 1914 does not sound in your heart, as it still does in mine, like a distant tocsin ; the name Serajevo, if known to you at all, is but a name, not a first pistol shot in the peaceful sunlight of June.

Let me tell you a few things.   The murder of the Archduke in Serajevo on the 28th of June startled us but faintly, and its echoes quickly died away in the peace of a perfect summer. For three weeks we comfortable thinkers forgot it.   In Britain we were interested in a flaming quarrel between Ulster and the Irish Nationalists ; in France they were watching the trial of Mme. Caillaux, the wife of the late prime minister, for the murder of a journalist ; in Russia they were troubled by rumbles of revolution which could be felt from the Baltic to the Caucasus. Britain, France and Russia forgot the Archduke.   But not Germany.   I picture Germany as an iron warrior with his horse at the gate.   He is watching our preoccupations with a compressed smile and drawing on the last of his armour, the steel glove.   At his side stands Austria, his leal squire.

On June 24th Iris, Father and I, sitting at breakfast, read that Austria had sent an ultimatum to Serbia tabling impossible terms of self-punishment for the Archduke's murder and demanding an answer in forty eight hours.

' God above, what does this mean ? ' I asked of Father.   ' You are a general ; you ought to know.'

' War,' said Father.

' War ? '

' Yes.   No nation could accept such terms.   And they don't want her to.'

' War between Austria and Serbia, you mean ? '

' No, war between Austria and Germany on the one hand, and Britain, France, Russia and Serbia on the other.'

' I don't believe it.   You said just the same at the time of Agadir.   You were going to get out your old uniform then.'

' And the rusty sword,' said Iris.

' Ah, I was only seventy-six then, and could have done good work. I am seventy-nine now, and they may think that too old.'

' But why in the world have *we* got to fight ? ' pursued Iris.

' Because,' I explained proudly (though I had just said the opposite), ' Russia is bound to go to the help of her blood brother, Serbia ; France is pledged to support Russia ; and we can't let France be overrun and the channel ports occupied.'

' But what'll it mean to us personally, to the nice, peaceful Allan Mournes ? '

' The end of everything,' I announced, with that pleasure one always feels in stating the worst. ' All my books will be out-dated and unsaleable, and in any case nobody'll want to buy books, and there won't be any paper to print them on even if any-body wanted to read them. So we'd all better get ready to starve.'

That was what I said, rising from the table because it was late ; but I hardly believed a word of it. Austria would mitigate sentence—Serbia would bow to the whip—our Foreign Minister, an admirable man, would save the situation—he would place Britain at the side of France—and the *Panther* would once again steam out of Agadir. I kissed and tickled Hugh as jovially as ever, waved goodbye to Iris and Father, and stepped out into the street. I have often thought since how little I knew, as I went down my steps into the welcoming sunlight of that morning, what I was walking to—not to any of the disasters I had so cheer-fully proclaimed, for it was yet some days before the Continent cracked open—but to the deep fissure which split my life in two.

I arrived in Henrietta Street and made my way through the market carts and barrows, the aproned porters and shouting carmen, to my publishing house door. I ran happily up the narrow stairs to my room on the first floor, found Edith Peers, my secretary, sorting out my letters, glanced at one or two which she deemed urgent, and sat down at my large mahogany desk to dictate replies, feeling very like Old Hammy. It was not yet twenty past nine, and I was only half-way through the second letter when the door-handle turned as if touched by uncertain fingers, the door came open a little way, and Con looked in, her face pale and troubled. Con ! She had not been announced or shown up to me ; she must have found the house door open and hurried up the dark stairs to my room.

' Con ! ' I exclaimed. ' You're early abroad.'

' Yes. Can I speak to you ? '

' Certainly. Why not ? What is it ? '

She looked at Edith Peers, doubtingly ; and that capable and careful, if unbeautiful, woman immediately rose with her notebook and a letter and saying, ' I'll be getting on with this,' went from the room.

' Well, Con,' I asked when we were alone, ' you look worried. Is it Austria and Serbia ? '

' Is it what ? '

I explained, or began to explain, and she interrupted, ' Oh, I know nothing about that. I'm not interested in that. I haven't looked at the paper. Doric . . . Gentle's disappeared.'

' Gentle . . . what do you mean ? '

' She's disappeared, and no one knows where she is. She's been gone for days. Henrietta arrived this morning in despair —she left Holm St. Martin at seven o'clock and came to us, having no one else to turn to ; and I've come straight to you. I couldn't think of anything else to do. Nor could Mummy.'

' Disappeared ? '

' Yes, and we don't even know . . .' Con paused, not without an unconscious relish in the dreadfulness of her words ' . . . we don't even know if she's alive. Oh, Doric ! . . .'

I sprang up from my chair. ' Don't say such things ! Of course she's alive.'

' But Doric . . . she's been in the hands of the police, and——'

' The *police* ? What are you talking about ? Has she escaped from them ? '

' No, no. They let her go, and she . . . disappeared. You see : Max is in hospital. She . . . she hurt him. She struck him, and . . .'

I stood immobilized, while she told me all she knew. She told me a story that shivered my heart with its heavy shock and in one detail tore at it with jealousy.

' He's going to get all right, but they weren't sure at first, and the police were called in and she had to go with them for a little. Then there was an ugly scene in the village where he was so popular, and she ran from the place—in terror, I suppose. She must have been nearly mad because she left the house as it stood.'

' How long has she been gone ? '

' More than two weeks.'

' But why haven't we heard of it before ? '

' Max didn't tell Henrietta or anyone about it, and he wouldn't let his old mother, who's there with him now, tell anyone—he said there'd been sensation enough—and the poor old lady was too afraid of him to disobey—at first. He's very bitter, Doric. He'd had a letter of four words from Gentle saying, " I shall not return," and he swore he wasn't the sort to beg anyone to come back to him, or to go and look for them if they chose to

go away.   He said she'd come back soon enough of her own
accord, because she'd hardly any money with her, and hardly
any clothes ; and then it'd be a question if he'd have her back.
But she hasn't come back, Doric.   Henrietta had a brief note
after a time, saying, " Don't worry, Mum, I'm all right," but
since then there's been nothing.   And now the whole village is
talking about it, and what with all the gossip and the hinting and
the gloomy suggestions, poor Auntie Henrietta is beside herself.
She's carrying on like a mad woman.'

' Has she told the police about the disappearance ? '

' No, she says she was too afraid of Gentle to do that, and too
afraid of the police because there'd been all this trouble with
them already.   She just came to us distraught.   She's almost
hysterical.   She keeps saying, " She's done away with herself.
My Gentle's done away with herself." '

' Oh no, no ! . . .'

' Yes, but you know what she is.   She keeps moaning, " Oh,
if only they'd had a little baby !   It'd have made such a difference.   If only they'd had a little one !   I always wanted to see
my Gentle with a baby at her breast."   She keeps saying things
like that.'

' Gentle's alive,' I cried, my voice on the summit of a sob.
' She's alive.'   I repeated it in a repressed anguish, and my
heart within me cried out, ' Gentle, Gentle, where are you ?
I am coming.'

And as these words said themselves, I walked to the door ;
unable to stand here talking, unable to stay within four walls,
unable to remain inactive one minute more.   ' Bung !   Bung ! '
I shouted to George ; and while waiting for him to come said
to Con, my palm pressed against my addled forehead, ' All
right, Con . . . please go . . . I shall find her . . . somehow
. . . I know I shall find her.'

' But how ? '

' Christ, I don't know.   But when I've found her, I'll let you
know.   Tell Henrietta not to worry.   Gentle is safe somewhere.'

' Doric . . . do you really think she's all right ? '

' All right?   Of course.   Haven't I said I will find her ?   Oh,
George, I've had bad news.   I must go at once. · Take over
everything.   I don't quite know when I shall be back.   You
can expect me when you see me.'

' But look,' began the atonished George.   ' About those——? '

' No, dammit, take *carte blanche*—decide everything for yourself—I don't care what you do.'

' But what about that book, *Kinship or Identity* ? '   This was
a long and learned manuscript which had come into our hands

because we were known to publish such works. It set forth, if
somewhat heavily, the very thesis of my heart : that the mystics
of every colour, clime, and church had all in their hours of
illumination seen the same single truth. I longed to publish
it even at a loss. George was hotly against me in this ; and not
merely, as he was careful to say, because in his view it was a mass
of windy words, but mainly because they were not words he
could sell. ' What about old *Kinship* ? '

' Oh, do what you like about that,' I said. ' Decide against
it if you want to. I don't care. I couldn't care less.'

' *Good !* ' he muttered. ' Then *that* book's a goner.'

' Tell him enough to make him understand, Con. She will
tell you, George. Please, please don't keep me now. I tell
you I must go.'

And I went. Just as Gentle left her house as it stood, I left
my publishing house. I ran down the stairs into Henrietta
Street ; and straightway all the interwoven noises of the market
place, which had been cancelled while Con spoke with me, beat
upon my ears again : the clatter of pony shays, the ringing of
iron-tyred wheels on granite setts, the champing of horses, and
the shouting of draymen and salesmen. I tore impatiently
through this besieging army. The world with its barter and
quarrelling meant nothing to me any more. At the corner of
Bedford Street an old newsvendor stood with his papers tucked
under his arm and a newsbill hanging like an apron before his
knees. It said, ' Austria—Servia. Is it War ? ' And I cared
nothing for the question. The words reminded me for a moment
of our discussion at the breakfast table, and of Iris and Hugh.
And Iris and Hugh, my wife and my child, had hardly any
existence for me now. Nothing seemed to have substance or
value except a breathless statement in my heart, ' Gentle . . .
Gentle, I am coming.'

BOOK V

GENTLE

CHAPTER I

CON STAYED with Gentle in the August after my wedding
and, unaware that there'd been more than a silly flirtation
between us, years before, prattled on about the fashionable folk
in Cranmere Church, the grandeur of Cranmere Place and park,
and the beauty of Iris. And some time after the subject had
fallen by the wayside Gentle made herself an opportunity of
saying, ' I am happily married.'

When I heard this from Con I wondered, and was well content
to wonder. Henrietta when she came up to town used to clack
by the hour with Mother about her ' little girl's ' happiness.
' It's so nice to see them so happy together. Everyone says she's
so cheerful and witty at tennis parties and dances, the very picture of a happy little wife. And Max is absolutely loved,
especially by all the workers in the new factories, to whom he's
Kindness Itself. I think my Gentle is a very lucky little girl '—
but I had no faith in Henrietta's capacity to see anything beneath
the surface or behind a screen. I, too, had laughed and made
fun before the world. When Uncle Humphrey's book was
published, Gentle sent him a warm-hearted letter of congratulations and good wishes which he showed me ; and I thought I
read in it a nostalgia for the old days. ' Do you remember,
Uncle dear, when you saved me from a horrible death at the
window-sill of darling Uncle Kingsley's room ? I often think
of those days and what awful children we were, but rather nice.
Oh, I do hope your book is the most *colossal* success.' There
was so much affection in it that I could only suppose that this
new tenderness for Uncle Humphrey, to whom she'd never
written before, was an overspill of her love for the past—and
for me ?

' I am happily married.' Yes, present your gay façade to the
world, my dear, and especially to one whom you sent angrily
away and who married a woman more beautiful than you.
But the time came, in those eleven strange, exalted days we

spent together, when Gentle, with many a vivid and cascading narrative, showed me the dark things that lived behind the façade. Max, as I had always guessed, combined a natural heartiness with a temper like a Mills grenade. And that is to say that he was usually on the most blithe and genial terms with everybody except the one with whom he had to live. Domineering, he had only to be thwarted or irked in his home for the bomb to burst. Add to this the taste for castigation which springs from the lust of a sensual man. Max would boast to his pals, ' From the first I put my little wife through a course of training. Nothing like training 'em early on, old boy. I came home to meals when I thought fit and stayed away when I thought fit ; and no questions answered, unless I chose to.' Not a doubt but he enjoyed hurting her : never with blows but with words or when he had her in his arms as a lover. Many a time, after beating her with words till the tears came, he would hug and force himself upon her, and then his kisses were almost a punishment and his embrace at once a savage, hurting and impassioned love. (When Gentle told me this, I told her I could understand. I told her how I, too, used to long to hug her after I'd scourged her with words ; how once my heart had leapt when she asked me merrily why I didn't shake or beat her.) She painted well for me the contrast between Max the loud pal in the pub and Max the husband in the home. In her bed she would hear him at the door of the Teamster's Arms, rather drunk, and shouting good night to his pals and sending his loud laugh to the stars. On such a night he came into her and wanted to make love ; and when in distaste she turned away and denied him, as Iris had denied me, he stood by the bed and shouted, ' You are the complete wash-out as a wife, spiritually, mentally, emotionally, and now physically.' He tried to seize her for his purposes, and she fought him. ' You know my temper, Doric. If there'd been anything at hand I'd have struck him.' And he, defeated by her fury said, ' O.K., my precious. I'll go elsewhere. Don't have any doubt about that. I can have those whom I like. There are others who love me.'

It is easy to ask, Roberta dear, why your mother, Gentle, the haughty, the defiant, the sometimes violent, didn't walk out of that house ? The habit of the years held her ; an unconquerable recoil from Henrietta's pity stayed her from a flight to her parents ; she had lied to them about her happiness, and did not care to shatter the lie ; the obstacles to any other flight were like mountains closing her in—she had no money of her own or any profession wherewith to earn it—and so she postponed and postponed any desperate act, and the months passed, and twelve months make a year. 'I used to hope that something would happen of itself to cut the knot. Shall I make a ghastly confession, Doric ?—don't think too awfully of me. I used to dream of his being drunk in his car and crashing—but then I would see him lying dead on the road, and feel an agony of pity. Poor, poor Max ; he has his right to live. Max who was always so bursting with life ! My feelings for him are so mixed. They are not hate. Sometimes after he thinks he's been cruel he apologizes and even cries, and it goes to my heart, and I almost love him. Oh, it's all so mad.'

Lastly came the strongest reason of all : she was too proud and obstinate to show failure to me who was happy with Iris.

§

For a time she tried another method than anger and thoughts of flight. She had read one of my books ; it was the one on Gautama Buddha in the *Great Humanes* series, and it set forth the Master's vision that the only way to overcome pain is to be done with selfish desires ; to exchange egocentric cravings for service to your fellows ; in a word, to end disappointment by beginning to be good. Gentle promptly tried it. She tried to be good, away there in Holm St. Martin. She set about being good in order that she could bear. And, being Gentle, she set about it with vehemence. 'I saw that I could either be noble or loathsome, and decided to be noble. And for a long time I *was* noble. I was Sweetness Personified. And I enjoyed it. I sang about the house. It's quite extraordinary the happiness that comes when you start being unselfish. It's the Peace of the Saints.' And just as I did, after I'd seen the same vision by the river on her bridal night, she made efforts—violent efforts—to sacrifice herself at every opportunity ; to give things away when she didn't want to ; to say nothing against anyone, even though she knew thrilling things to tell ; and least of all to reveal the truth about Max though Henrietta's praise of him grated upon her, and his unqualified popularity with the people seemed so blinkered and unfair.

Much of the praise given him was just : he had no snobbery with the factory hands—every one of them was ' old chap ' to him or ' Mother ' or ' My dear ' ; he rejoiced in being generous to them when they were ill, and a quiet support in their cottages when death sat in an upper room ; they called him ' the best doctor anywhere about ' and this was true enough of him as a

mental healer because he entered their sick rooms like a health-
giving breeze, but quite untrue if it meant that he troubled to
acquire the latest knowledge ; only once or twice had he been
drunk in the daytime and they forgave him this with a smile
and even liked him the better for it ; and at night time when he
drank with them in their locals there were few so friendly in
their cups and none whose laugh so rocked the saloon. Only
Gentle knew that he could be one thing in bar-parlours and
cottages, and another thing in the home.

It was a fine, sustained effort of Gentle's, a tower struggling to
the skies, but it was mainly a creation of her brain ; it had no
steel framework of religion, for which she felt a repugnance,
having had too much of it from Henrietta ; and when it over-
toppled, the collapse was complete. There was nothing left
but a dust in the air.

She had tried hard to support it when it was palpably cracking,
but one night, as she sat alone and somewhat fretfully in her
drawing-room, Max having wandered from the house directly
after dinner with the rather shamefaced words, ' I think I'll
stagger along to the Teamsters' and see the boys for a bit,' there
came a single knock on the front door and a quick ring of its bell
in the kitchen. It was late for such a ring. Max had been away
above two hours, and Gentle had been hearing in her room,
whose windows abutted on the pavement, the singing in the bar
of the Teamsters' Arms whenever its doors opened and voices
shouted good-night. Curious to see who was on her threshold
at this hour, she rose and looked into the hall and saw Joe
Fawcett, the butcher's assistant, talking to Evans, their old parlour maid.

Joe Fawcett was a little, middle-aged fellow with a thick-set
body but with legs so brief and bandy that he looked almost a
dwarf. As often in very little, waddling men his face was usually
a-twinkle with merriment, and you could almost see the same
smile and twinkle in his short, curved, hurrying legs ; so naturally he was one of those whom Gentle called ' an adorable little
man,' ' a pet ', and ' unbearably pathetic.' But there was
no grin on Joe's face to-night ; only white strain and alarm ;
and Gentle, who knew from Max that his wife was ill, asked
immediately, ' What is it, Joe ? '

' I'm sorry to disturb you, m'm,' he stammered, ' but Mrs.
Fawcett's in great pain ; she's moaning and groaning and
begging me to get the doctor to her. I don't really like to get
the doctor out as late as this, but he's always very kind, and if
you think he wouldn't take it amiss——'

His doubtful and apologetic words, matching so ill with the

dog-like appeal in his eyes, touched Gentle in the very quick of her pity, and she answered, ' He's out at the moment, Joe. I think he's at the—no, listen : you go straight back to your wife, and I'll go and find him for you. I know he'll come at once.'

' It's very kind of you, m'm. If you would. Mrs. Fawcett's real poorly to-night. I don't like the look of her at all. She says she's kind'a got pains all over, and at times they're something chronic. If you really could get the doctor to her——'

' Of course I will. You hurry home to her, and I'll find him. He's no distance away.'

And there and then she slipped on a coat and ran hatless along the pavement to the Teamsters' Arms. One part of her was pleased with a message which seemed to rebuke his long stay in the tavern. She pushed through its doors and found herself in the grasp of a fog of tobacco fumes, and on the fringe of a thick crowd of standing and chanting men, who might have been a noble army of martyrs singing triumphantly in the smoke of the furnace that burned them. Against the wall, a young man with a velour hat on the back of his head sat cross-legged, thrashing out an accompaniment on his mandoline ; some of those around him conducted their own performance with their tankards and glasses ; others just stood with their elbows at their sides, their eyes upturned to heaven, and all their molten souls in the cadences they were sending aloft.

> Sing me to sleep, the shadows fall ;
> Let me forget the world and all. . . .

Nowhere could Gentle see Max's dark head, though he was as tall as any here and taller than most. The nearest chorister to her, a heavy, grey, wrinkled man, who was old enough to be behaving better, turned towards her, discerned through the smoke that her face was a woman's, and addressed the rest of his song to her. ' Sing me to sleep, your hand in mine. . . . Love, I am lonely, Years are so long. . . .' She smiled uncomfortably and asked, ' Excuse me ; is my husband here ? There's a call for him ; ' and the chorister, when at length her identity, and the dramatic value of her words, penetrated the aqueous vapours behind his eyes, yelled out, ' Hi, boys ! Shut your disgusting row. Has old Dr. Drury been here ? Here's his missus wanting him. And quick. Anyone seen the old doc ? " Meat, meat, meat. Puss, puss, puss. Anyone seen our doc ? " '

Mr. Buck Marsden, the landlord, swung his face from his beer-pulls, saw Gentle, and said, ' He's not been here to-night, Mrs. Drury.'

And the grey chorister, having this impressive authority for the statement, endorsed it. 'No, he's not been here to-night, dear madam. Sorry. Can't oblige.'

'Oh,' said Gentle, halting undecided. 'I thought he said he was coming here.'

The landlord reaffirmed his statement. 'No, not to-night, Mrs. Drury. He's given us the go-by to-night.'

And the old chorister assured her with a benevolent smile that it was so. 'No, he's not here to-night—no. There's been many in to-night, madam, but not the doctor. No.' He was more than ever convinced of it, and more than ever courteous. 'I am sorry, but not the doctor. No, madam.'

'Oh, thank you. . . .'

'Not the doctor. Oh no, no, no, dear lady. Dear me, no.'

'I see. I wonder where. . . .'

A lonely greybeard in a bowler hat, seated near the door and taking no part in the songs or the chatter, but dreaming in silence over his pint, spoke up. 'I see him in London Lane earlier to-night, Mrs. Drury. But that was a couple'a hours ago. Yes, I see him then.'

'London Lane. Oh, I see. Thank you. I see.'

And yes, Gentle saw; she saw London Lane and knew where Max was. London Lane did not, as you might imagine, lead to London but to an old windmill; it was but a rough road on the border of the village, climbing a slope for some two hundred yards and growing greener underfoot all the way till at last, changing its mind entirely, it became a round green waste where two weak-knee'd gates opened on to a meadow; and there stood the mill. Small new bungalows squatted on both sides of the road, and in one of the latest of these lived Bruce and Pam Innersley, two young, smocked artists who were either married or not. Pam Innersley was a flaxen and massy young woman in whom woman's richest glories had not only built themselves apace but now obtruded themselves upon your notice by their loose and lively oscillations under her artist's smock. It was public small-change in the town that she seldom wore stays. Max used to speak of her as 'a really succulent blanc-mange;' and Gentle, while supporting a friendship with her, had little doubt that she was an exceedingly ripe plum which others than Bruce Innersley might nibble. And Bruce, she now remembered was away in town for a week.

'Oh, I see.' To hide her thoughts she added, 'Yes, he might be there. I think he has a patient there. Thank you so much.'

The grey chorister, though he had not provided the information, smiled his personal acknowledgment of this gratitude, and after getting a firmer grasp upon the intellectual position, and upon a slight windiness in his gullet, besought her, ' Have a quick one. Yes, have a nice little quick one now. One for the road. Buck, you old devil, here ! A lady. Ladies first.'

' No, thank you so much.' Quickly Gentle stopped him. ' I must go. There's someone ill.'

' Someone ill.' He dwelt upon this. ' Someone ill.' Its significance came into focus. ' Then 'op it, lady. I quite understand. Another time you'll have a little quick one—I mean a quittle lick one—with me, but to-night '—he waved the pleasant prospect aside and shook his head—' no.'

Gentle hurried through the dark and empty streets to London Lane, not sorry to have an excuse for going there and learning if Max was alone with Pam.

The Innersley's bungalow was the only one that showed a light behind its curtains. She stood outside it, listening. No sound filtered out with the light. She crept nearer the orange-bright window, unbreathing, like a spy. Her ears grew keener, straining to hear what she did not want to hear. And she heard it : Pam's smothered laugh, Max's low voice, a kiss.

She walked noisily to the porch and pressed the spring bell in the centre of the door. It rang alarmingly in the little wooden house, enforcing an instant silence there.

A pause, quick slithering steps, and Pam opened the door. She was straightening her blonde hair as she peered out, and fingering the top button of her blouse.

' Oh, Pam, I'm sorry to trouble you at this time of night, but is Max here by any chance ? '

' Gentle ! My God, fancy it being you ! . . . Max ? . . . yes . . . yes, he's here. . . . Yes, that's right.'

' There's an urgent call for him.'

Pam had recovered herself. ' I say, do come in.'

' No, I won't come in. There really isn't time. Tell him it's Mrs. Fawcett.'

' Max. It's Gentle. Someone's ill and wants you.'

Max appeared in the living-room doorway. His tie was awry and his dark hair was sprung upward, as if fingers had run through it or played with it. But a man cannot see his hair or his tie, so Max was able to affect a perfect ease. ' Hallo, Gentle ducky, what's the sudden alarm ? '

' It's Mrs. Fawcett. Joe begged me to get you.'

' Oh, to hell ! Will they never leave me in peace ? Who'd be a doctor ? '

' Joe says she's in pain.'

'Well, can't you come in? She won't die if you come in a minute.'

'Oh yes, *come* in Gentle ; *there's* a sport. Come and have a tiny tot.' Pam was also well at ease now that her hair and blouse were in order.

'No,' snapped Gentle. 'I'm not coming in. It's twenty minutes since Joe called and I promised him Max'd come at once.'

'Oh God to hell! I suppose I must go, Pam dear. Joe's a decent little devil and Mrs. F. is an old pal of mine. We dearly love each other. So long, my sweet.' Deliberately he kissed her brow as if his kisses were bonhomie and no more. 'Thanks for the drink.' He waved a second kiss with his fingers, and together Gentle and he walked homeward. Their silence matched the darkness and emptiness of the lane.

Max spoke first. 'When did Joe come?'

'I told you : about twenty minutes ago.'

'Why didn't you say I'd come directly I got back?'

'I thought it might be urgent.'

'Couldn't you have got old Thurkle?'

'I saw no sense in doing that if you were to be found.'

'You weren't spying on me, were you?'

Gentle halted one second in anger ; then walked on. 'What do you mean? I don't spy on people.'

'Oh . . . well, I'm glad. I hate being followed around.'

'I don't follow people around. If you're going to adopt that tone, I'll walk home alone. I'm not going to be bullied because I tried to help one of your patients.'

'How the hell did you know I was at Pam Innersley's?'

'They told me so at the pub.'

'At the pub, did they? How the devil could they know? All that happened at the pub was that I saw Pam there with another bloke, and she asked me to come round and have a drink. I said I would, but I didn't follow her till a long time afterwards. I stayed in the pub. Too many of my pals there.'

'They told me you hadn't been there to-night.'

'They said what?' This was a parry, a recoil, while he recovered his stance.

'They said you hadn't been there to-night. The landlord said so.'

'What pub are you speaking of?'

'The Teamsters'.'

'Oh, well! . . . hell . . . I'm talking of the Keeper and Dog. I went there for a change.'

'You said you were going to the Teamsters'.'

'Oh, Jesus, don't keep *getting* at me ! What are you hinting at ? I'm not lying. I do loathe being hinted at. I started off to go to the Teamsters' and went to the Keeper and Dog instead. Is that clear ? '

'It's perfectly clear, thank you.'

'Fine. Now we know where we are—but wait : how the blasted hell did anyone at the Teamsters' know that I was at the Innersley's ? '

'Someone saw you going there two hours ago.'

'Two hours ? ' Gentle's blow had shot past his guard again. 'But that's bilge,' he said, a little dazed. 'I haven't been there more than half an hour. Three-quarters perhaps. They're all drunk.'

They said not another word. They reached the Rent House : Max went in silently ; found his bag, and went out silently again.

Gentle waited till his steps were lost in the distance ; then walked to the closed door. She hesitated this side of it for twenty seconds ; then went quickly out into the night, driven by the awful need to know, the same need which would drive me to door-cracks and had sent even Iris to my locked desk and Gentle's letters. She went straight to the Keeper and Dog. 'Is my husband here ? ' 'No, he's not been here to-night, Mrs. Drury. He's probably at the Teamsters'.' 'Thank you. I'll see. There's a call for him.'

She came slowly home. Impossible to charge Max with his lies because she'd have to confess that she'd spied on him. She went to bed, turned her face from the door, and there in the darkness overthrew, with one glorious thrust, her high, unstable tower of goodness. I say there was nothing left of it now but a dust in the air. And in the morning, in the sunlight, she arose to an immense sense of freedom ; a sense as of chains undone, prison doors wide and a vast and varied country before her. She was free—free to indulge all her desires, to feel hate and bitterness, to speak the truth of Max, to have done with the strain of forgiveness, and to dream of another lover who was sometimes a nameless shadow, but was usually me. 'I shall do everything I want. What he does I can do. I shall seek my own ends and be happy.' And all that day she sang about the house because of her freedom.

§

She served this new god of freedom as vehemently as yesterday she served the god of goodness. Did she want to smoke, she helped herself promptly to one of Max's cigarettes—and soon she had given herself up to limitless, will-less smoking. And in those days, though some women had begun to smoke in London it was still considered ' fast ' in the country. Did she feel bored in the house, she left it to look after itself and went off alone to London to see the shops or a play, and nearly always on such occasions she wandered off to the Brompton and Earls Court streets and looked for quite a while, unwilling to come away, at the old house and the square garden and the pavements where we used to play. Did she decide that she wasn't feeling as happy and as hearty as she'd a right to feel, well, then she didn't hesitate to sip liberally of the spirits in the house—and of these there was usually a good supply in the sideboard, for Max was a ready and convivial host.

One morning, instead of her usual ample ' tot,' she drank angrily of half a tumbler. They had quarrelled the previous night ; Max had driven off after breakfast without a word, a contempt in his silence and in his going. And contempt in Max woke defiance in Gentle. She sat alone in her work-room, declining to work, and thinking all the time of me and of days we had spent together in the Park, in Oxford, and in the Holm St. Martin lanes. Out of the smoke of her cigarettes she built a dream of herself as my wife. Her head ached, and with an angry hand she poured out for herself this half-tumbler of whisky. ' What he does I shall do. Here's to a little happiness. There are not so many pleasures in the world. What's happening to me I don't know and I don't care. Here's to some life.' And she paced her carpet, sipping the drink and smoking. She sipped till the glass was empty. Often before had she felt the stimulus and well-being that are the gift of such ardent waters, but never as now. All depression, all doubt, went away in a vapour ; she was happy and vigorous and free ; she was ready for anything and equal to anything. Somewhere beyond a circumnambient haze lurked the fear that so splendid a release —like the bliss of a drug after pain—would teach her to seek it again, but she felt too alive and well to trouble about that now.

Perhaps it was six months after this—anyhow, it was a winter day—when the people of Holm St. Martin saw her walking along their streets a little wildly as it seemed : hatless, the wind in her blonde-tawny hair where the grey was peeping ; her coat collar turned up against the frosty wind, and her hands in her coat pockets. It was early afternoon and those on the margin of the town watched her walking with rapid, resolute, but still graceful steps towards the open country, and sometimes tossing back her head as a blade of the wind touched her. Later some

of them, motoring home, saw her sitting sideways on a field-
gate, many miles from the village, her hands folded on her lap,
her feet crossed over and swinging, just as the child Gentle used
to sit on the nearest window-sill when her turn with the ball
was over. One man who walked by spoke afterwards of the
sadness in her face. They did not know, any of them, that she
was weighing the idea of suicide, nor did they remark that the
railway ran on the far side of the field. How should they know
that whenever a train went by she knew she could do nothing
about it because she wanted, no matter how unhappy she might
be, to stay in the same world with me? Nor could they know
that now and again she played with the idea of rushing to me
for one day of love and help, but perceived that though she
was ready to do anything else she liked, she couldn't in her pride
do this.

In the evening those in a lonely wayside inn, a good mile
from Holm St. Martin, saw her sitting in its bar, sipping from
a glass, and staring before her in a reverie. It was a tavern,
though she did not know this, where Max was well known, for
he would often call in there for a drink and a joke on his way
home, and where, accordingly, Max's wife was easily recognized.
It was dark when a few persons saw her walking home through
the village, in the middle of the road, a little unsteadily, and
with her lips moving as if she talked to herself. They turned
to look after her, and she, as though conscious of their inquisitive
glances, turned to look back at them and seemed not to care.

It was then that the whispers began to run about the town.
They visited in time every house and cottage, every shop counter
and factory bench. One house only they avoided, the Chapter
Mill, where lived Henrietta, widow of the late Brian Greaves, J.P.

And so the months and the days completed the year 1913.

CHAPTER II

GENTLE KNEW of the whispers but continued defiantly on
her course. ' There are not so many pleasures,' she would say,
as she lit her twentieth cigarette and tossed the match like a
scruple aside. Or ' Here's to some life,' she would think as she
dashed off to London to have a lonely lunch somewhere and see
a film or a play. Sometimes, in the mad mood of ' What he
does I shall do,' she would turn into the Teamsters' Arms,
her sideboard being empty, and order herself a drink, careless
of the bar-loungers' glances.

At first the whispers were pitying. 'Dreadful in a young woman,' the people would lament, and they would recall to one another what she had been : the liveliest, if not the loveliest, girl in Holm St. Martin. 'Terrible, terrible.' 'I saw her the other day on the station, and she'd quite obviously taken too much. I didn't know this, of course, and I went up and spoke to her, and she smiled and laughed and chatted, but, my dear her breath . . . and it was quite plain to me that half the time she hardly knew what she was saying. What does her husband think ? He must know. It must be a tragedy for him. Of course he drinks a lot himself, but it's different in a man. Poor dear Doctor Drury—and she was one of the loveliest brides I've ever seen ! '

But then the whispers changed. They changed from pity to a hard hostility, because they had a new content. It was this new content which had clawed at my heart with jealousy when Con told me of it. I spoke of it with Gentle, too, when I was with her, but though she answered me frankly enough, or tried to, it was only with averted eyes, and sad, impatient tossings of her head. I heard most of it in after years from Dame Bridget Crewse, a beautiful and kindly old lady in Holm St. Martin, who, being completely civilized, spoke of it only with compassion. And how often have we spoken of it, she and I, for she loved Gentle, and Max too. Do not think, Roberta dear, that the wound in me when Con outlined the story was more than jealousy's sharp laceration. There was no condemnation in it. How could I who had once, when a hungry and unhappy boy, snatched at those silver coins condemn Gentle when, hungry at heart, she snatched something very different in kind, but equally wrong to take ? She was thirty-two then, but was she less of a lost child ?

In the High Street of Holm St. Martin there was a large provision store, Applins. It had grown with the population of the town. Fifty years earlier it had been a small village shop, selling everything from bread to bull's-eyes, with the name ' Fred Applin ' above its crowded and often fly-blown window ; now the name ' Applins ' stood above three fine contiguous shops : above the Grocery and Provisions, the Wines and Spirits, the Confectionery and Cakes. Old Fred Applin, its founder, still alive at eighty-seven, would walk the street before his fine creation, admiring it, loving it, or he would wander in and about the departments and be something of a nuisance to all hands : a little tottering man with a valance of grey beard and a suit of old black holiday broadcloth—for his life was a perpetual holiday now. His enormous son, Matthew Applin, as much bigger than he, in height and frontage, as the new store was bigger than the old, managed his business in his stead. Matthew Applin's generous frontage, beneath his grey alpaca managerial coat, seemed to cover a cellar well stocked with his own provisions, and especially perhaps with those from the Wines and Spirits. If it is true, as it certainly appears to be, that good shopkeepers grow like the wares they sell—the butcher like his steaks, the fishmonger like his cods—then we may say with some fitness that Arthur Applin's face, at fifty-six, was as round as one of his Dutch cheeses, and as soft and pink as the soapiest of them, except in moments of provocation, when it was as hard and shiny as the stalest. Then its tint was that of his claret, and its mouth would shut tight and shoot forward, leaving, so to say, its lips behind.

He was assisted in the shops by his two elder sons, lads as tall as he, though very much slighter—but these we may leave behind their counters because they play no part in the coming scene. The third and youngest son, Gerald Applin, was nine-seen at this time and took no interest in the shop, nor in any business of buying and selling. The artist's fire, which bloweth where it listeth and alights where it will, had illumined the head and kindled the brain of this grocer's son, and he was now at a Municipal Art School with a scholarship, studying (since he must make some sort of living) commercial art. Had the father girded at him for his defection, we should have here an old familiar pattern, but Matthew Applin did nothing of the sort : on the contrary, he was rather proud of his son's talents, and very proud of his own tolerance. 'I don't understand anything about art meself,' he would declaim, 'but the boy must go his own road, and if his old dad can help him at all, he will. They say he's very promising—very promising indeed—and I shouldn't be surprised if he made a bit of a name for hisself, before he's through.' Gerald, at nineteen, was slim, over-tall and pale, but he clothed and carried himself well, and there was nothing in his speech, accent, or manners to distinguish him from the product of a university. He reminded Gentle of me in my first term at Oxford.

In the spring of 1914 he had an accident. Glazing a cucumber frame in his father's garden, he slipped on some wet leaves and, throwing out a hand to break his fall, drove it through a cracked pane with such force that the shattered glass severed the radial and ulnar nerves in his wrist. Max, summoned at once, sent him to the Cottage Hospital and returned home with the tale, very ready to stress its drama. 'It's damned serious for the boy,' he pointed out. 'It's his right hand, you see. I only

hope it'll mend all right, but there's always a danger of paralysis.
And if his right hand goes, where is he ? I imagine it'll about
finish him as an artist. We'll do our damnedest for him, you bet ;
old Matt Applin's one of my best pals. So's his old man Freddie.'

Now Gentle's bitterness may have overthrown the most of
her self-command, but it hadn't unseated her pity : it had
probably increased it ; and she was still in the habit, after hearing a piteous tale from Max, of hurrying with comforts to the
home of her husband's patient, especially if the sufferer was
poor or old or a child. She could never resist the appeal of a
suffering child. She had early discovered that there is no pleasure like giving, and I've little doubt that this pleasure was even
sharper now that she herself was suffering. Gerald Applin
was not a child, but to Gentle at thirty-two he seemed very
young and appealing and 'pathetic.' She hastened to the
hospital with a bunch of flowers and a selection of books on
art. He begged her to come again and she readily consented.
She visited his bedside several times ; and after three weeks he
came out of the hospital with an assurance that his hand could
be saved (and what was of profounder interest to him) a
passionate love for Gentle.

He could not keep away from her. First he came nervously
to her house to say his thank-you for all she'd done ; then he
took to lingering in the High Street for a sight of her as she came
out to shop ; more than once he followed her from afar off
when she was strolling alone in the country ; and at last, when
both were far from the town, he came abreast of her and asked
if he might keep her company. She welcomed him ; they
walked on, speaking of casual things ; a silence fell ; and then,
with stammering lips and his eyes on distant hills, he told her
of his love. ' I only want to worship you,' he said and, moved
by his own words, let the tears wash over his eyes. Of course
she remonstrated with him, but she was touched, and later,
when he asked, ' Might I kiss you ? ' she allowed him to do so.
He tried to hold the kiss a long time, and she had to end it with
a smile, saying, ' That must do.' But she let him kiss her again
before they parted.

Gentle found his worship and his kisses sweet, and she began
to long for the comfort of that young and ardent embrace.
She took to accepting it. If you have no longer the will to
deny yourself a cigarette or a whisky, how shall you resist
a young man's kisses? 'What Max does I can do.' Without overt encouragement, she let Gerald meet her on her
walks in the warm days of early summer ; they sauntered
together along the lanes as once she had sauntered with

me, and into the woods among the shreds and sheddings
of the trees ; and there in the woods she let him kiss her, after
which, sitting in a green and chequered twilight, her self-
command further loosened by his love and her own relaxed
behaviour, she would tell him about her unhappiness at home
and about her first love for me.   Not without self-dramatization,
she would shake her head and tell him sadly that she had no
love to give to anyone but me.   And he would say that he
understood and that at least he was glad she didn't love Max ;
and so they would sit in their sheltered silence talking of themselves and indifferent like all the rest of us to what was happening
in the world and what was coming.

Once or twice she let him for a little into her home when it
was empty, so that she might have again the sweetness of his kiss.

They were seen walking in the lanes and sitting on a hill-
slope.   He was seen entering the Rent House when the doctor
was away.   And the whispers, which had been pitying, blazed
up into a brisk, angry and joyous scandal.   The flames of anger
burned up the pity, at all events in the women.   Some of the
phrases they used were ' A dreadful woman. . . .   Lost to all
sense of decency. . . .   Carrying on with a shopkeeper's son. . . .
I can remember when Applins was a tiny little all-sorts shop.
. . . It's a crying scandal ; it is really : the doctor ought to be
told ; and her mother, too.   Betraying him like that while he's
going about doing good ! . . .'   The men's phrases, on the
face of them, were as brutal, but their substance was softened
by laughter.   ' That's a nice little bit of baby-snatching, isn't
it ? . . .   Poor old Doc, doesn't he know that she's going to
another shop now ?   Gawd's love, she's as fast as a public-house
clock, that little piece. . . .   Can't be he's not doing his duty by
her—not our Doc.   No, it's just that the goods in the new shop
are a little fresher.   They often like a change at thirty. . . .
Never thought to see our Doc being played for a sucker.   Suppose
he's too darned well satisfied with himself to suspect anything
like that.   Some day someone's going to put him wise.'

The day came ; an evening ; and Matthew Applin, rejoicing,
triumphing, in his task, stood outside the Cottage Hospital.
where Max's car, the latest Rover model, new and shining,
showed that he was within.   Max came out, laughing and
waving and throwing a kiss to the Matron at the door ; he
came happily to his car ; and there stood Matthew Applin,
in the sunlight, waiting.

' Half a minute, Doc—could you spare me half a minute ? '

' Why, yes, Matt ; fully three-quarters, if you like.   Finished
for to-day, I *hope* ! '

' Well, look here, Doc : we're good friends, and you won't take badly what I'm going to say. I've nothing against you, you understand ; we all think the world of you, as you know.'

' God, Matt, you old hearse, what's worrying you now ? '

' It's not going to be easy, Doc. If it'd been the other way round, I mean if Gerald had been me daughter instead of me son and—well I'd pretty soon have settled the matter myself, and no one much the wiser. I'd have settled it with this here stick. I may be fifty and more, but I reckon I could take the hide of any young man who'd been mucking around with a daughter of mine—I seldom see a lad these days that you and I couldn't make a meal off, and still have sixpence over—but when it's the other way round, when it's a lady and your friend's missus, you see, it seems to us it's a matter for her husband to deal with, see ? '

' In the name of God, Matt, what are you talking about ? '

' Well, to put it frankly, it's about your good lady and my boy.'

§

Max came glorying to punishment. Once he had left Matt Applin, the fire in him was free to burn, and he flung fuel on it as he drove the car fast into the ' Stag Inn ' stable, where it lodged ; left it there with the stable doors unshut ; and strode like a storm-wind into the house, across the wide hall, and into his surgery. The surgery was on the left of the hall ; once it had been a small front room, but Max, as his position and prosperity increased, had extended it into the room behind, so that it was now a long trough of a room with his desk set obliquely under the arch in the centre. A long red and blue carpet of the pattern often seen in London clubs stretched from street window to garden window ; and, what with the handsome new furnishings and up-to-date equipment which Max was for ever buying, it was a brown, business-like, masculine room and one in which his heart delighted. Spread about the desk this evening, on and beside his blotting-pad, were some of the instruments he had used during his surgery hour in the morning : a sphygmomanometer, a hæmoglobinometer, a syringe, a binawral stethoscope and an ophthalmoscope. Of the ophthalmoscope he was particularly proud. It was one of the first of the self-luminous ones, with an electric battery in its cylindrical steel handle to feed its own little lamp. Max, who must always possess the latest tool or gadget, had just acquired it and felt fine as he used it on an ignorant patient.

Having thrown down his bag on his examining couch, and

his hat after it, he came to the room door and called, ' Gentle.'
In such a tone does a father, apprised of a child's disobedience,
summon him to the cane.

Waiting for her to come, he went back to the desk and stood
there, drumming his knuckles upon it. Of the measuring instruments on that table there was none that would determine which
pulsed the stronger in his present ferment—his pleasure or his pain.

Gentle came ; and learned from one glance at his face that
his whip was ready for her. ' What is it ? '

' What is it ? ' he echoed, scoffing. ' It's the end so far as
you and I are concerned.' What matter how reckless the words
so long as they hurt ? ' One or other of us is going.'

' What on earth is the matter ? '

' For God's sake shut that door. You and I have got to have
something out. Shut that door.'

His tone whipped up the old childish temper in Gentle. ' I
am not your servant. What are you talking to me like this for ?
Shut it yourself.'

He strode to the door, swung it so that it banged, and returned
to the table.

' I've just seen Gerald Applin's father. He was waiting for
me outside the hospital, like a policeman. I never knew I'd
live to know a moment like that. He told me all about you
and his wretched weed of a son, and, if you please, requested
that it should stop. He says, " You don't mind what I'm going
to say, do you ? " Oh, no, one doesn't mind when a father
comes and politely asks one to teach one's wife how to behave.
Oh, dear me, no. It's nothing. It's just a little thing that
might happen any day of the week. He says to me, " My dear
fellow, you're the only person for five miles around who doesn't
know all about it." He said *that* to me. To *me* ! And he
was right—that's the bloody thing ; he was bloody well right ;
it was something that had never entered my head. I trusted
you—I didn't doubt you for a moment—mug that I was.'

' Will you please tell me what he said about me and his son ? '

' Oh, I'll tell you. I'll tell it all. He told me that the sawny
fool was for ever in your pocket, and that you encouraged him
to make love to you. Just that. Nothing really serious. He
further explained that you walked in the sweet woods together,
and that he came to this house when I was out. *My* house !
He's been in my house with you alone, and I've little doubt that
he's also been in my bed.'

' You believe that ? '

' Of course I do——'

' You would.'

' Let me speak ; let me go on.' He was determined to say all the violent and dagger-sharp things that had come to him in the car, before a denial could blunt them. ' That's what the whole town thinks. That's what all the women are saying, bless their little hearts. And they're sorry for me. D'you think I'm going to let myself be pitied ? I used to be loved by all the people once ; now I'm only pitied—or laughed at. That's what my wife's done for me. You've made me the bawdy joke in the village—— '

' Quiet, *please* ! The servants will hear.'

' I don't care who hears me. D'you think it's pleasant to have a father ask me in the street, " Will I kindly keep my wife away from his son because he doesn't want the boy contaminated ? " And that father the local grocer, still smelling of his ham and his lard—— '

' Perhaps in a minute you'll allow me to say something ? '

' All right ; say it ; and we'll see how much I believe. Is he in love with you ? '

' Yes. Yes he is.'

' Indeed ! How nice ! He has said so, I imagine.'

' Yes.'

'And you haven't told him to clear out of your sight and keep out?'

' No.'

' No. I see. We haven't done that.'

' Perhaps I should have done, but I didn't.'

' Perhaps you should have done, but you didn't. I see. You've let him kiss you ? '

' Yes.'

' My God ; and you can stand there and tell me that ? '

' I no more stopped him kissing me than you stopped Pam Innersley—and many others, for all I know.'

' All right ; let that go : he kisses you, and how much more ? '

' Nothing more.'

' And I don't believe you. Why should I ? I call you a liar.'

Gentle gave him one look and turned to walk away.

But he was not to be deprived of his punishment. Half the wounding sentences which he'd sharpened in his car had yet to be said. Knives one has sharpened must be tried. He seized her by the shoulders and swung her round to face him, holding her there by both her arms. She could feel in his clinching fingers the pleasure that he always got from man-handling her ; she could see that lust in his eyes. ' Oh, no. You're not going like that. You're going to hear a few things I've got to say. You're a little slut—do you see—a common little slut. Yes, how do you like that ? You're a filthy little rotter, a cheap little

tart ; you're any man's free-for-all—Oh, no, you don't—you're
not getting away yet—you've made me a laughing-stock, and
you're going to pay for it.   You're going to feel something.   It'd
have been better if I'd done this long ago.'   And he slapped her
cheek.

'You dare—— ! ' she cried, struggling to free herself.

'Oh yes, I dare. *And* like that.'   He slapped her again.

Gentle, maddened, ablaze, snatched blindly at a weapon on
the table and swung it towards his face somewhat as a policeman
swings a truncheon.   It was the ophthalmoscope ; and in her
blinded and blazing fury she swung it too viciously.   It must
have been something she had long wanted to do.   The heavier
half impacted on his jaw and without a murmur he fell from her
as a felled horse drops beneath the slaughterer's hammer.   He
lay on the carpet, one arm falling over his breast, one arm feebly
extended, and one knee lying on the other—unconscious, unmoving.

Gentle, unmoving too, gaped at him there.   His face, which a
second ago had been red and mottled with wrath, was now white,
except—except for a blue bruise which had already formed at
the site of the blow.   Sweat shone his brow, and his eyes, half-
closed, half-open, seemed to be looking at her.   The line of his
mouth had shot to one side so that his look was sullen.   Gentle,
staring down, could not be sure that he was breathing through
that still, distorted mouth.

'Max, Max ! '   Kneeling at his side, she lifted his hand.
The arm was as limp as the arm of a doll.   'Max ! '   But yes—
yes !—his breast was lifting and falling weakly ; he was breathing as a sick sleeper breathes.   He was alive.   'Max, Max.'
She tried to insert an arm beneath his broad, heavy shoulders,
but paused—had she not read that one might do more harm than
good by moving an injured person? 'Oh, Max, what am I to do?'

Rising, she ran to the telephone on the wall.   She stuttered
into it the number of Max's partner, old Dr. Thurkle.   Panting,
complaining, she awaited the answer.   The distant telephone
clicked.   'Is Dr. Thurkle there?'   'Dr. Thurkle is away for the
night.'   'Oh, no !'   'Yes. He's not at home, madam. Could you
leave a message for him?'   'Oh, no . . . thank you. . . .'

Who then ?

The nearest to the Rent House was Dr. Gayne on the Green.
But—Dr. Gayne ? Gayne was an austere, middle-aged doctor,
long established in Holm St. Martin, whose relations with his
brother physician, the younger Max, were no more than correct.
He had never approved of Dr. Thurkle's boisterous young
partner, holding, and often stating, that he ' lacked all sense of

professional dignity .' Max's frequenting of the village inns, and his hilarity among the customers there, he called ' popularity mongering ' ; and wise eyes had little doubt that he was jealous of Max's immense popularity among the villagers and factory hands. And now he disapproved of Max's wife, who was reputed to be ' drinking ' ; and he would suggest to his friends, ' It seems to me that Drury and his wife are a pair.' For months his manner had been cold to her—was she to summon *him* ? Still, he was the nearest—and what did *she* matter ? All that mattered was to get help to Max. In a quiver of alarm, remorse, and self-punishment she rang and gave Dr. Gayne's number.

' Is that Dr. Gayne ? Oh, look ; can you come at once ? Mrs. Drury speaking. My husband has had an accident. He . . . fell, and his head is hurt. He's unconscious. He's lying unconscious. I don't know what to do. . . . What ? Oh, don't ask me to explain now. I'll tell you everything when you come. I'll explain everything then. Oh, doctor, please come quickly. I'm frightened. . . . Oh, thank you ; thank you so much.'

She hung the receiver on its bracket again and turned and looked at the terrifying figure on the carpet. She stepped nervously towards it and stood at its feet. Oh God, there was now a trickle of blood from his mouth. The bruise seemed to have darkened, and a faint blue tinge to have flushed the pallid skin. The half-opened eyes still glistened at her ; the mouth maintained its sidelong and contemptuous grimace.

' Oh, live, live ! ' Her teeth chattered as she said it. Kneeling again, she gently felt his pulse. It seemed faint and fluttering, and the touch of his wrist was cold ; and her eyes sought again that terrible red fruit at his mouth. ' Oh, Max ! Is he going to die ? What did I do ? I never meant to do this. If he dies. . . .'

She rose to her feet to deal with this thought. ' If he dies.' Brows knit, hands clasped together—hands almost as cold as Max's—she looked at it. And then she was not seeing the walls of the surgery but the walls of a cell, the walls of a court, and a red judge on his bench. She saw her mother and, more awful still, Max's mother. She saw my father and mother, and Con and me. She saw me as I had been in the days when I used to hold her in my arms and look down into her eyes—and, remembering me thus, she cried, ' Doric. Oh, *Doric !* ' I wonder that this suppressed cry didn't come to me in my room, but when in later years I used often to work out what I was doing at that exact moment, I knew that I had heard nothing and felt nothing. And yet I ought to have done, for I was alone in my room in

Henrietta Street, working late upon a manuscript; George Byng and all my staff had gone home ; and the market without was as quiet as the neighbouring church garden, or as the convent garden which it once was, and which gave it its name.

Gentle, alone with her terror, unheard by me in my distant room, became conscious of the voices and the wheels in the High Street. Someone had laughed at the door of the Teamsters' Arms. Someone was shouting, ' Good-bye, you old —— I'm sick of you. Besides, my old woman wants her tea. If I don't go back now I shall get the rolling pin.' And she envied the easy happiness of these people, the care-free content which could shout its quips in the street and—suddenly she saw it—make jokes about a rolling pin.

' Only a few minutes ago I was happy. I imagined I was desperate but, compared with this, I was at ease and happy. I was an ordinary person. I was the same as anyone else in the street. I was the same as the person whose steps these are. They're a woman's steps, and she has no fear of arrest and exposure and imprisonment, and perhaps *that*. . . .' and she was still the same Gentle ; she felt little different from what she had felt as a child—the child who played and fought with us in Coburg Square. ' Oh to be back where I was a few minutes ago. Free. Oh, that this thing which has happened could be undone. That it could be as if it had never been. I know now I'd never do anything like this again.' She shut her eyes, as if to open them and find it had never been real.

And the door-bell rang loudly, lifting her heart from its seat. In a mad moment she wondered if the police had come. Then she remembered Dr. Gayne. She ran to the door to open it before the maid could do so. Evans, the old parlour-maid, the only other person in the house, was coming through the kitchen door on the other side of the wide hall. ' It's all right. The master's had an accident. It's the doctor.'

' An accident, ma'am ? '

' Yes . . . yes, please go.'

' Can I do anything to help ? '

' No, no . . . please. . . . Please don't come. It's terrible.'

Evans, thin and grey, who always looked so much older in her cap and apron and black dress, because it was the natural uniform of a young woman, stood there for a moment, but when her mistress looked at her despairingly and motioned to her to keep away, she retreated into the kitchen. But she did not quite close the door.

Gentle opened the hall door. Dr. Gayne was on the threshold. He was a tall, narrow man with a slightly rounded back, grey hair, and pinched, aristocratic face. His clothes proclaimed his sense of the dignity of his calling and (one guessed) of the dignity of his appearance. The black coat, striped trousers, and swelling cravat, half as big as a cabbage, seemed his daily rebuke to the loose lounge suits and looser behaviour of young Dr. Drury. The starched wing collar and starched white cuffs were like a statement of his stern probity. In manner and voice he affected the sustained quiet of the family physician, and it is probable that his speech grew quieter and quieter as Max's laugh grew louder and louder. None of Max's ' my dear's ' came from Dr. Gayne as the women opened their doors to him ; none of Max's reassuring pats on the back. He was their doctor, he would say, not their uncle.

As Gentle opened to him, he said not a word but stepped in with his bag.

' Oh, doctor,' said Gentle, ' thank you for coming so quickly. What can have happened to him ? '

He maintained his unexcited pose, though he must have remarked her blanched face and lips. ' Don't worry. It may be only concussion. If so, he'll soon be all right. Where is he ? ' They were comforting words, but coldly said.

' He's in here.' Gentle's voice was muted with guilt.

' He fell, you say, and hurt his head ? ' asked the doctor, as he walked with her across the hall. And Gentle saw what he was imagining and was not displeased to imagine : that Max had been drunk.

' No, not quite that, doctor. I will tell you.' They passed into the surgery, and he shut the door.

Dr. Gayne was looking at the recumbent figure, with its bruised cheek, skewed lips, and ooze of blood.

He said nothing, and Gentle had to speak. ' Doctor, we had a quarrel, and he lost his temper and struck me. It has never happened before, and I went mad for a moment, and struck him back. With—with this.'

She picked up the ophthalmoscope, and he looked at it as if he'd never before seen one with its own lamp. It appeared to interest him more as a new model than as a weapon.

Since it was his pose to show no surprise or emotion of any kind, he asked in the same untroubled voice, ' How exactly did you strike him ? '

' Like this. I didn't know what I was doing. I was blind with rage.'

' I understand.'

' Oh, doctor. . . .'

' We will see if the damage is serious.'

His movements were quiet, purposive, and unexcited, as of a man who dealt with accident cases every day. He knelt by the supine and silent body, lifted an arm and let it flap back lifelessly on the carpet ; he drew a torch from his pencil pocket and, lifting the eyelids, flashed it on each dilated pupil ; he murmured, ' Yes. . . .' and ran his thin, skilled fingers over the site of the injury ; he pressed very gently as if feeling, or listening, for something ; then lifted the upper lip and looked into the mouth ; he called, ' Drury ' and louder, ' Drury. Do you hear me, Drury ? You've had a nasty blow, haven't you ? ' but there came no answer and, as though the silence were his answer, he said ' No,' and rose to his lean height, shaking down his trousers and replacing the torch in his pocket.

His mien as inscrutable as ever, his manner to all appearances completely composed, he said only, ' Well, Mrs. Drury, his jaw is fractured ; there is no doubt about that. Whether there is any more serious injury I can't say as yet.'

' What more serious injury ? ' Gentle stared into his face, trying to read his thoughts but apprehending only a hostility to her and a condemnation.

' There may be a fracture at the base of the skull, but I sincerely hope not. There's always a danger of it with this kind of fracture.' He had said this abruptly, almost unsparingly, and Gentle knew at once that he had said it for her punishment. Then, as if ashamed of his harshness, he modified it. ' A danger ; that is all.'

Gentle summoned up all her will-power to ask, ' He'll be all right, won't he ? '

' If this is just concussion, he should be all right. Where is the telephone ? '

Why did he ask that ? What was he going to do ?

' It's over there. . . . But, doctor, why was he so cold ? '

' There's no need to get alarmed about that.' Again she perceived the conflict between his decent desire to say a comforting thing, and his long-nurtured and now justified prejudice against her. ' It's just that his blood pressure has fallen so.'

' Is that why he's so pale ? '

' Yes.'

' Doctor . . . he won't die, will he ? Say he won't die.'

But he did not answer, either deliberately because of his mingled emotions towards her or unconsciously, because he was now at the telephone with the receiver against his ear. Having given the number of the Cottage Hospital, he turned to Gentle, saw her walking towards Max, and said sharply, ' Don't touch him. Don't do anything at all. . . . Dr. Gayne speaking.

Who's the house surgeon on duty, nurse ? Dr. Selwyn ? Yes, I want to speak to him at once. Thank you.' He played a finger tune on the telephone desk. ' Is that you, Selwyn ? Gayne speaking. I've got Drury here, seriously wounded. Yes, Dr. Drury. With you an hour ago, was he ? Well, he's sustained a serious injury, a fracture of the jaw, the result of a— a blow. In his home. . . . What? . . . Yes, I'm afraid I do mean that. A quarrel, but I'll explain it all later. . . . Naturally, naturally. . . . Well, who can say ? '

Gentle standing at Max's feet and gazing at the doctor's back, knew that she and the whole of the surgery had been temporarily annihilated for him, and that he was seeing only the young house surgeon and the hospital telephone which he knew so well. Her hands helpless at her sides, she stood there watching a colloquy which had become private.

' Of course, of course . . . it may be a desperately serious case.' No more than another, however impassive his mask, no more than Max or Gentle herself, was he above feeling a pleasure in making his story as dramatic as possible. ' Yes, perhaps ; it's on the cards certainly. . . . What does one do in that case ? I don't know. I'm wondering. To tell the truth, I've been wondering about that for the last few minutes. . . . There seems to be a possible duty to do so, doesn't there ? . . . Of course, of course ; I fully appreciate that, but then, *he* is our patient—no one else—and it seems possible that our duty to him coincides with the other duty. . . . Exactly, exactly, that's what I feel. It may indeed be desperately serious. . . . Perhaps you might warn them—no more—for your own protection. Yes, I think you might do that ; then if it's a case of a dying deposition—as it may be—you'll have safeguarded yourself. . . . Perhaps it's better not to run any risk. Yes, all things considered, I think perhaps I should. . . . All right, then, while you ring them up, I'll get the ambulance.'

And Gentle, standing there, knew what he had done. In a case of conscience, because of his hostility to her and his jealousy of Max, he had argued himself into the view that his duty to his patient and his duty to Society were the same. Or perhaps behind his still, poker face, he hadn't even troubled to argue with himself. None could know better than she that doctors, like judges and priests beneath their professional robes of probity and incorruptible rectitude, had hearts as subject as other men to hypocrisy, malignance, and the meaner sins. He had played upon the ignorance and timidity of a young house surgeon to secure her questioning by the police. He had betrayed her on her telephone, and while she watched—wrapping up the

betrayal in a cloud of high-principled phrases. He had gratified an old dislike and called it duty.

As he hung back the receiver the surgery built itself round
him again, and he turned and saw her. She was asking, ' What
were you saying to him ? '

' What ? '

' Were you telling him to inform the police ? '

His manner was now a little less unmoved, a little less un-
shaken, because he was capable of shame. He had to collect
himself before replying, ' I left it to his discretion.'

' You did not. You told him to. Was that necessary ? '

' I imagine it was, if I decided to do so. There are aspects of
our calling, Mrs. Drury, which you can't be expected to understand. I suggested a notification—nothing more. And there
may be nothing in it. If this is not too serious, if there's no deep
injury to the brain, and no chance of a fatal termination, there'll
be nothing to worry about. If on the other hand things take a
serious turn, then the truth will have to come out. It's best to
be frank from the first. For *all* our sakes, Mrs. Drury.'

' It was not necessary. I shall never believe it was necessary.
I am a doctor's wife and know it was not necessary. I know why
you did it——'

' It was very necessary.' He was angry now, and anger
filled him with self-justification. It poured forth the exculpa-
tion that his guilt demanded ; it bade him, having hit once, and
doubtfully, to hit again, and harder, for his own peace. ' Do
you not realize that your husband may die ? Do you think that
it's a little thing that has happened ? One cannot strike as one
pleases at others and expect no uncomfortable consequences.
There is such a thing as the Offences against the Person Act, and
it would be a good thing if more people realized it. I don't want
to exaggerate what has happened, or what may happen, but——'
but at this point he hardly knew what he was saying.

' You could have waited a little longer. Surely you could
have waited a little longer. Oh, why do all you men delight in
cruelty ? '

' I don't delight in cruelty. On the contrary I have given
my life to the relief of pain.'

' You did it because you hate my husband and you hate me.'

' I did it because I thought it best and right. It is the sort of
thing you must trust us to decide. We can only act, each of us
according to the light that is in us.'

' Ha—Good God ! ' Gentle laughed scornfully. ' And you
really think that that sort of talk deceives *me*, Dr. Gayne ? I
dare say you manage to deceive yourself with it, but I'm afraid

you don't deceive me. I've lived long enough to know what men are behind all their fine talk.' She was almost as ready to strike at him with the first words that leapt as she had been to strike at Max with the first instrument to hand. ' I wonder when men will realize that we can see through them. It was spite—spite against us—just spite and nothing else——'

But the ambulance bell rang in the road and Gentle's eyes became wild. It clanged nearer the house ; wheels slurred up to the kerb ; voices sounded in the road. ' What do I do now ? Do I go with him or stay here and wait for the police ? You know what I do ; I don't. These are your arrangements. Do I wait for the police ? Do they come for me ? Do they come with a van ? '

The door-bell rang in the kitchen.

' Now don't get excited. Calm yourself—calm yourself— that's the first thing to do. You'd better just stay here. If I were you, I'd just stay here until we know a little more. The hospital will let you know just as soon as possible how he gets on. I very much hope that they will have encouraging news for you.' And with that he went to the front door and admitted the two ambulance men with their double-poled stretcher. Gentle at the door of the surgery saw Evans at the door of the kitchen, peeping. Evans retreated as the men came into the room, shep-herded by the doctor. Very little was said by them or the doctor. They placed the stretcher at Max's head in a straight line with his body and opened up the blankets. Dr. Gayne folded Max's hands over his chest. The two bearers knelt at Max's left side, Dr. Gayne at his right ; and all three slid their arms beneath him and lifted him a little way.

' Now, Mrs. Drury, if you will just slip the stretcher under him.'

She did so, and the three men lowered him on to it.

' All right. I'll follow you,' said Dr. Gayne.

They bore him forth to the street door and the ambulance. Gentle did not follow them. She feared to. That ambulance bell must have drawn faces to the windows, and a small crowd to the door : and she dared not show herself to the street. Standing at the surgery door, she said to the doctor as he went, ' Thank you. Thank you for all you've done ; ' and then shrank into the protection of the empty room. And there, as the ambu-lance belled and sighed itself away, and the voices outside diminished and ceased, she stood quite still, her hands clasping and unclasping, her head stunned as if kicked by a horse, her breathing deranged : the loneliest and most frightened creature in Holm St. Martin.

CHAPTER III

THE POLICE must have heard by now. What would happen?
Gentle in the surgery, now standing, now pacing, saw the police
station on its triangular site at the forking of two roads : a new
building of red brick and white stone, erected since the town
enlarged ; a not uncomely building with a central pediment
and the courtroom on one side and the police office on the other.
What was in train for her there ? If you cared to glance through
a gate at the courtyard behind you could see a row of small
windows high and barred : the windows of the cells. She had
often glanced at them, fascinated. Would she be put behind
one of those windows ? ' I, Gentle ? . . . I, Gentle, who still
feel like a child . . . ? '

Now and then, as she remembered Max, her pity leapt into
life, and her remorse with it ; but for the most part her terror
for herself thrust all thought for others to the edges of her mind ;
and even as her pity cried aloud, ' Oh Max, I'm sorry,' her fear
was asking, ' What will they do ? What are they doing now ?
Will they come and take me away ? Those bars ! Oh I should
go mad, shut in there. Listen : footsteps on the pavement. Is
it them ? '

She lit herself a cigarette with blundering fingers ; she walked
up and down with it ; she fetched the whisky decanter and
syphon from Max's cupboard and with clumsy hands mixed
herself a drink ; but it had no effect ; it had no more effect on
her pain than it would have had on an aching tooth ; she
learned, as I had learned years before on her bridal night, that
if your pain is intense enough you can take whisky after whisky,
and they will not touch your power to suffer.

Had someone knocked softly on her door? A sickening
bound of her heart, for the knock had come again—very gently.

' Come in.'

Evans. ' Can I be of any help, ma'am ? Is it very serious ? '
Evans standing there : driven to the door by a real desire to
help and a great desire to know.

' I don't know, Evans. The master fell. He fell heavily and
injured—he is injured.'

' Oh dear, ma'am ! Unconscious, wasn't he ? '

' Yes. Yes, it was concussion, the doctor said.'

' Good gracious ! However did he manage to fall as heavily
as that ? '

' I don't know. Please don't worry me now. Concussion
may not be as serious as it looks. Please . . . I am very worried.'

' Can I bring you anything ? '

' No . . . nothing, nothing. . . . I am only waiting to hear
from the hospital. I just have to wait.'

' Would you like me to keep your dinner back ? '

' I shan't want any dinner. Please leave me alone.'

' Are you sure there's nothing I can do ? '

' Nothing, nothing. Please go.'

Forty minutes—forty four actually—since he telephoned to
the hospital. The police must have known at once : forty
minutes ago. ' Oh, come, if you're coming. Let me know, let
me *know* what you're going to do to me.'

Open a door—let me escape from this narrow cell of fear—
I pace it and pace it—come . . . *come.*

The bell ! Suddenly, commandingly, the bell jarred in the
kitchen. And, strangely, her fear, though cold as marble, and
as black, was veined with relief.

She stepped quickly across the hall to get to the door before
Evans could—and to know. But her pride halted her for one
moment on her side of the door. Before her fingers touched the
handle she amassed all her courage. She threw back her
shoulders, and lifted up her head and her breast. Then opened.

Two men before the door. One a man of about forty with a
round pleasant face under a round bowler hat ; his figure
roundly expansive so that in its loose blue suit it looked even
bigger at the hips than at the shoulders. The other, a younger
man, much taller, and with a waist ; thirty perhaps ; in a
brown hat, grey suit, and heavy black boots. The first looked
like a friendly publican, all the way round ; the second looked,
every inch of him, like a policeman in disguise.

' Yes ? ' inquired Gentle with courtesy, as of the lady of the
house, but making it sound as if she expected no one.

' Mrs. Drury, isn't it ? ' The older man smiled pleasantly.

' Yes. I am Mrs. Drury.'

' You don't know me by sight, do you ? '

' No, I don't think so.' And Gentle smiled back, pretending
to be amused.

' No, but I know you very well—*and* the doctor. We know
our Doctor Drury, don't we, Bill ? Yes, he's been quite often
round at the station on one job or another, and he's very well
liked by the boys.' It was kindly meant, his cordiality, but to
Gentle it seemed, like himself, a trifle too rotund ; that is to say,
it was of the right stuff, but there was a little too much of it ;
an over-eagerness not to alarm had resulted in this excess fat.

'Sorry to disturb you at this time of the evening—it must be just on your supper-time, isn't it?—but could we speak to you a minute or two? I am Detective Inspector Place, and this is Detective Sergeant Hursley.'

The police-titles shook her heart; but thank God one's heart, that convulsive thing, could not be seen. 'Yes?' She said it beneath raised eyebrows, as if she couldn't imagine what they wanted.

'We've heard that the doctor is in hospital with a fractured jaw, and that there's some fear there may be deeper injuries. I'm so sorry. There's not a nicer chap—gentleman—anywhere. I do hope he's going to be all right. It seems it was caused by a blow, and we should just like to make a few inquiries as to how it came about, Mrs. Drury. We appreciate that you must be very upset, but could you help us?'

'I will do all I can. Will you come in?'

'Well—thank you—yes, for a minute or two.' Though the evening was dry and fine, he wiped his boots on the hall mat, respectfully. 'You see, the Station Officer has been in touch with the hospital—come on, Bill—but they still can't tell him anything very much.'

'I am waiting for news myself. This way.'

'He's still unconscious, they say, and they doubt if we can see him before the morning. So we came along to you to know what you could tell us. This way, is it? Thank you. These are just routine inquiries.'

'Naturally I will tell you everything.'

They were crossing the hall as they spoke, Gentle leading like a hostess. The sunlight in the kitchen was brighter than the dusk of the hall and she was able to see, through the gaping kitchen door, that Evans stood there, peering. Did Evans, who was an old inhabitant of Holm St. Martin, know the Inspector by sight? Or the Sergeant?

'You'd better come in here: my husband's surgery. It was here that it happened.'

Both men entered and took chairs. The Inspector sat with plump hands splayed over parted knees; the Sergeant with his long legs crossed and his long fingers interlaced round them; and the attitude of both implied that they were not staying long.

'Would you care for a drink, Inspector?' The decanter from which she'd mixed herself a drink was still on Max's desk, and she laid hold of it by the neck. She gripped it tight to stop the trembling of her hand. They must not know that her heart was dying within her.

' No, nothing, thank you, Mrs. Drury.'

' Sure ? '

' Quite sure.'

' You, Sergeant ? '

' No, thank you, ma'am.'

The Inspector drew a cigarette case from his vest pocket.
' Do you mind if I smoke ? '

' Of course not. But please don't smoke your own. Have
one of my husband's.' Her voice was in danger of trembling
as she said ' my husband.' She got tight hold of it. ' Have
one of these. My husband's favourite brand.'

' No, I won't have one of yours, if you don't mind. I'm used
to these here. A fag, Bill ? '

' Ta, sir.' Bill helped himself from the Inspector's case.

It was only later that she perceived a significance in these
polite refusals : they must not take favours from a suspect.

The cigarettes lit, the Inspector thrust his case back in his
pocket. ' Now, Mrs. Drury, will you tell us what you can—
quite simply. Won't you sit down too ? '

But she remained standing, having hardly heard him. ' You
realize that it was I who struck him ? '

' We didn't at first, but that is what we've since been given
to understand.'

' We had a quarrel—he lost his temper and slapped me rather
violently—and I didn't know what I was doing.' She saw his
quick, trained glance at her cheek and his unwitting nod : was
the mark of Max's hand still there ? ' I seized something—it
was this—and struck him with it. Oh, my God ! ' She plunged
her face into her hands. The pride had broken down ; she
could act no more. ' Oh, God . . . God. . . .'

' Now, don't get too distressed, Mrs. Drury. Things may
not be as bad as you fear. Do sit down now——'

But, wiping her eyes, she shook her head, as though she had
no right to sit down. ' I didn't know what I was doing. It
seemed to do itself. It did itself before I knew what——'

' Just a minute, Mrs. Drury. I think we shall like to take
down what you say in writing. Would you consent to that ?
You're not obliged to say anything if you don't want to, you
know. I sincerely hope that this won't result in any crim—
any charge being preferred against you ; but just in case it
does I have to warn you that any statement you care to make
could be used as evidence.'

Gentle caught her breath. Those familiar words ! The
caution before a charge, and spoken to *her* ! To her who felt
so little different from the child who'd once played with us—

and played too at ' Police ' and ' Detectives ' and being marched away to prison.

' What would the charge be ?   I didn't mean to do anything.'

' I imagine it would be a charge of causing grievous bodily harm.'

' Oh, well.'   She tossed her head despairingly.   ' I can only tell the truth.'

' It'll be better.   Then can I take it you will make a statement which we may write down ? '

She pressed the base of her palm against her temple.   ' I don't know . . . yes, I suppose so.   Yes, I must, I suppose.'

The Inspector produced a notebook from his jacket and a pencil from his waistcoat.   Gentle stared at pencil and book. Would these two things, between them, weave the rope that would bind her—and perhaps the rope that would—but *this* thought could not even be glanced at.

The Inspector played the pencil on the book like a drumstick on a side-drum, and then put the book away again.

Hope sprang in Gentle, a wild illogical hope.

But the Inspector said only, ' Do you know, Mrs. Drury, I think it would be best in every way if you came round with us to the station.   It's no distance, and we can do the thing properly there.   It'll be a fairly long business.'

' The station ?   Oh, the police station, you mean.'   The hope had lifted her a little way, only to drop her into a chasm more frightening than before.   ' Oh, must I ?   I want to hear about my husband.   I am waiting to hear.'

' We will keep in touch with the hospital at the station.   Yes, you come along with us, Mrs. Drury.   You will be quite comfortable and easy at the station.'

' You can't do it here ? '

' Not properly.   I haven't the right papers.'

' Oh, well . . .'

' Yes, you run up and put on something.   May I use the doctor's telephone ? '

' It's there. . . . Oh, well. . . .'   Despair was an analgesic, producing at last insensibility to pain.   She went slowly up the stairs, and in her room, putting on a light coat, she heard his voice speaking into the telephone, ' Ask the Matron to come round ' and then, as the telephone clicked home, addressing the Sergeant : ' Poor lady, she's properly scared, isn't she ?   Scared out of her ten senses.   But I thought it best to have her at hand when the news comes through.   We may have to ask further questions when we know more.   Dammit, old boy ; don't forget ; I may have a dead man on my plate.'

A dead man ! And then . . . Those barred windows. Those cells. An iron door.

She went down to them. ' I am ready.'

' Good,' said the Inspector ; and the three of them passed across the hall into the street, Evans at her kitchen door, watching.

It was merely manners that the Inspector walked on one side of her along the pavement, and the Sergeant on the other, but a verse flung itself into her memory as she walked between them—a verse often spouted by my father for the entertainment of us children, from his favourite Tom Hood :

> Two stern-faced men set out from Lynn,
>   Through the cold and heavy mist,
> And Eugene Aram walked between,
>   With gyves upon his wrist.

And this childhood memory led her to another : Con and me on either side of her marching her, in the character of Captain Dreyfus, after her degradation before her assembled comrades, to her life-long prison in the coal-cellar. Those happy, careless days.

§

It was a sunny evening, and they passed many people : lovers hand-in-hand, city men trudging homeward from the railway station, a policeman strolling past the shuttered shops, three men and one woman standing outside the 'Teamsters' Arms.' She passed them with her shoulders back and her head high ; talking and laughing with the Inspector that they might suspect nothing. But she knew that eyes had turned to follow her ; those, perhaps, which had seen the ambulance at her door.

Here was the new red-and-white police station on its triangular site where two roads converged upon the Railway Approach. Fascinated, unable to stop herself, as they passed a side gate, she glanced into the courtyard at those high, barred windows. They turned her sick, but she walked with a fine stride up the gravel to the central doorway, wearing her shame and her fear like invisible robes. Her breath stopped, momently stifled, as they passed out of the sunlight into the half-light of a lobby.

' Come up into my office,' invited the Inspector. ' It'll be nice and quiet there. You too, Bill, please. I'll lead the way, shall I ? '

A massive policeman in shirt sleeves, reading a notice on the wall, did not trouble to turn round as they went by. Just before they stepped on to a stone staircase between white-tiled walls Gentle snatched a quick glimpse of the large bare Charge Room with the Detention Room opening off it and, next to this door, an iron grating closing the passage to the cells.

The Detective Inspector's office was a narrow but bright little room on the first floor. His desk with its documents, files and telephone stood against the wall by the side of the window ; his swivel chair before it. The only other furniture was a hard chair at the nearer end of the desk, two similar chairs on either side of the fireplace, a hide-covered easy chair in a corner, and a map, a chart, and some framed photographs on the wall. The photographs included one of a police football team and one of a social gathering of C.I.D. officers in a hotel garden. Extraordinary the comfort of those two very ' human ' pictures : on that bleak official wall they were like two gleams of normal, everyday sunlight flung from the free world outside.

But then Gentle, waiting bewildered, turned and saw on a row of hooks a woman's dirty dressing-gown, a soiled white petticoat with a torn lace flounce, and a stained, discoloured petticoat-bodice ; and, bundled on the floor beneath these, a frayed rug, a faded cushion, two black stockings and a pair of down-trodden buttoned boots. Her brain, always quick but never so quick as now, guessed what they were : exhibits in some squalid case of violence—or murder. *Violence.* Murder perhaps. For a moment the hanging dressing-gown looked like a woman on a scaffold.

As their feet sounded in the room a door opened on the far side of the fireplace, releasing the dead clatter and quick tinging of typewriters, and a wide, comfortable woman in a blue overall entered and smiled a predetermined smile at Gentle, while closing the door behind her. A wardress ?

' This is our matron, Mrs. Annie MacNeil,' the Inspector explained. ' Her husband was one of the best officers we ever had. A Scotty, of course ; he kept Holm St. Martin in order, but with his heart in the Highlands all the time—eh, Matron ? She kept him in order, and now she does the same kindness for us. That so, Bill ? This is Mrs. Drury, Matron. Maybe you know her.'

' How do you do, dear ? ' said the Matron. ' Now you sit here and be comfortable.'

And she pulled forward the chair by the Inspector's desk, smiled again as Gentle obediently sat in it, and then went to a chair against the wall and sat in it very upright, her hands in her lap.

' You needn't mind Matron,' said the Inspector. ' She's used to this kind of thing.'

' I'm here to help you all I can, dear,' said the Matron. And smiled again.

' Thank you . . .' acknowledged Gentle, in a voice hardly audible.

' There's nothing to be afraid of, you know, my dear.'

' *I'm* not afraid,' declared Gentle.

' That's right, honey. Just take it quite easily. We don't want to worry you too much ; you must be ever so anxious about your poor husband. We quite understand that. Just take it easy.'

Meanwhile the Sergeant had sat himself on the other upright chair, between the fireplace and those sad, captured, huddled exhibits.

Seated before his desk the Inspector drew from a drawer some sheets of foolscap with ruled lines and something printed on top. He dipped an empty fountain pen into an inkpot and began to write. ' Hólm St. Martin Station . . . July . . . 1914. What is your first name, Mrs. Drury ? '

' Gentle.'

' What ? How much ? '

Gentle repeated the name.

' Indeed ? " Gentle "—it's a pretty name. Never come across it before except as a surname. " Gentle "—yes—well now ! Any other name ? '

' Mary.'

' Gentle Mary . . . Drury . . . The Rent House . . . Married Woman. . . . Now tell it to us from the beginning. The doctor came home about six o'clock. . . .'

Two hours it took ; two hours of patient, courteous questioning ; two hours of unhurried encouragement and discreet pauses, with eyes turned away from a caught and terrified creature who might be acting a proud self-possession but was really trembling like an animal in a cage. And all the time the Matron sat upright in her chair with her hands on her lap and a smile ready for Gentle whenever she glanced her way ; and the Sergeant sat in his chair with his legs crossed, now this way, now that, and his lower lip ready to languish when he became bored with a too-familiar performance.

Only once did the Inspector pause in his questioning and writing ; and this was to say to the Sergeant, ' Go and see if Ginger's back yet, Bill, and if he's got any news.'

The Sergeant rose and walked into that inner room of voices and clattering and tinging typewriters—presumably the C.I.D.

office—and after a few minutes came back. During those few minutes Gentle heard again the voices and wheels in the roads outside and on the Railway Approach, and the rumble and whistling of trains carrying free people to London or the sea.

' No. He's not back yet, sir.'

' Okay. Then we'll just go on. We were saying, Mrs. Drury. . . .'

When the long task was done, he said quite cheerfully, ' Well, there it is, Mrs. Drury. Would you like to read it through, or shall I read it to you ? I read it ? Okay.' And he read it to her, before the Matron and the Sergeant ; and sentence after sentence was like a poniard's stab. ' You're satisfied with it ? Okay. Then I'll just add, " I have read this statement, and it is true and correct " . . . There. Now will you just initial those few corrections and sign each page—here, please—and Bill—Sergeant Hursley, I mean—will witness your signature. That's right.'

Her fingers quivering like an octogenarian's, she signed each page, wondering as she did so if she was signing away her freedom—or even her life. The Inspector pinned the sheets together, and then—silence. An uncomfortable, unbroken silence.

' Do I—do I go now ? ' asked Gentle.

' I'm afraid we shall have to wait a little longer. Just a little longer.'

' Why ? Why is that ? '

' We must wait till we hear the extent of your husband's injuries. I don't think it'll be much longer.'

' And if they prove to be serious, do you——'

He held up a hand to stop her. ' We must just wait and see.' And as a dentist will talk of general subjects while he waits for the anæsthetic to take effect, he began, resting his arm on his desk : ' You must have seen many changes in Holm St. Martin, Mrs. Drury. You've been in the neighbourhood a long time, haven't you ? Twelve years ? Why, you must have come as a child ! I've only been here four years, and it's nearly doubled its population in my time. A pity, in some ways. . . . Would you like a cup of tea ? Matron can get it for you in no time. No ? Sure ? All right then. Yes, it's a pity in some ways to see a pretty little village becoming an industrial town and a dormitory area for London. It changes its character ; but I suppose the shopkeepers like it. It's good business for them. There's Applin's : they tell me Applins began from almost nothing at all——'

A knock on the inner door. ' Come in. Well, Ginger, what's the position ? ' This to a tall young man with thick red hair and a thin red moustache, whose hat was in his hand. ' What's the news ? '

' It's not so bad as they feared at first, sir. They're satisfied that it's no more than a fractured jaw.'

' Splendid ! D'you hear that, Mrs. Drury ? If that's all, we shan't need to detain you. We know all about fractured jaws—eh, Bill—we meet quite a few of 'em in our time, and more than ever now that there are some rough customers in the town. So sorry to have had to put you through all this.'

He had risen ; so Gentle rose too. ' Does this mean you're not going to charge me with anything ? ' The relief, the lessening pain, the falling away of fear !

' I mustn't be quite as definite as that yet, but I think so, I think that's the position. Yes, I think you can hope that.'

' Oh dear, oh dear, but how soon can I *know* ? How long is this going on for ? '

' I think it's going to be all right, my dear.' He laid a hand upon her back and patted it thrice : it might have been Max comforting a worried wife or mother. ' I feel pretty sure that I'll be able to tell you that quite definitely tomorrow. And in the meantime you won't go away, will you ? You do understand that we don't want to make trouble for you if we can possibly avoid it. We've quite enough trouble on our plates without looking round for more. Isn't that so, Sergeant ? '

' It sure is, sir.'

' Now you go home and get some sleep, dear,' said the Matron touching her shoulder. ' And I hope to-morrow'll bring you good news.'

' Yes, and then you'll be able to forget that you've ever seen my fat, ugly face,' jollied the Inspector, ' and Sergeant Hursley's too, which is even uglier. Let me show you the way out.'

' Thank you. Thank you.'

Out to the free air again, and the boundless sky ; out into the golden fall of a summer evening and the happy, zestful syllables of gathering birds ; alone, unescorted, free, with her great hope—but a hope so fickle, so harrying, that it seemed the half-sister of fear.

§

Returning into her home, she felt readmitted to life—but was it so, was it sure ? All night the question tossed her ; she dozed with it, woke to it, looked at it, argued it. ' Oh for the morning and movement ! ' Her brain kettle-drummed the Inspector's words : ' Tell you definitely to-morrow ' ; and at last, sleep wholly lost, she lay watching that morrow brightening behind the blinds.

Morning. Dressing despite the blinding headache. Telephoning as soon as reasonable to the hospital. Hearing in suspense her call clicked through from main switch to ward ; and the ward answering : ' This is Sister Maitland speaking. Dr. Drury has had a fairly good night and is doing as well as can be expected. . . . No, I think it would be better if you came later. Say, after twelve o'clock.' Cold ? Antagonistic ? Or had she imagined it ?

All the morning to wait. Unable to work, to read ; the far-away irrelevance of everything in the newspaper, its sentences building up no sense ; unable to do anything but pace the closed dining-room, or stand still and sigh. Evans and the cook talking, talking, in the kitchen : of what else but last night ? The fret of the door-bell ringing again and again, during Max's surgery hour, and of Evans' excited and delighted answer to the patient at the door : ' The doctor's in hospital.'

The bell again, and this time Evans was not sending anyone away but bringing people into the house. Men's feet were crossing the hall to the drawing-room ; Evans was coming to her. ' Two gentlemen to see you, ma'am.' ' To see *me* ? Who is it ? ' ' The gentlemen who came last night. The police gentlemen.' Then she *did* know who they were. ' All right, Evans.' She called up her courage again. Oh, the weariness of forever calling up courage from an exhausted heart ! And yet she was not displeased to go to them, because she was thinking, ' In a minute I shall know.' The Inspector and the Sergeant stood in the drawing-room, two heavy, incongruous figures in that elegant and delicate room, and in that bright morning hour. And the Inspector began at once, happy to be the bearer of good news, ' Well, I've good news for you, Mrs. Drury. Everything's going to be all right.' The sweet, healing draught of it ! The relief, the release, more wonderful than any wine ; like a gift of new life ! He and the Sergeant had seen Max in hospital, he said, and learned from the house surgeon that they had no fear at all now of any deeper injury. Dr. Drury was all bandaged up round his head and his chin but he'd managed to mumble his answers. ' And shall I tell you just what he said, Mrs. Drury—you know what the doctor is sometimes : a bit free with his language. He said—and in front of the nurse too—" It was all my b. fault, old boy. I asked for it." And, being the doctor, he had to bait us a little ; he calls me an old busybody and says it's got nothing to do with the cops. And he asks the nurse to tell us that it'd be thoroughly bad for him if we went about making trouble ; it might finish him off—you know what the doctor is. Always must joke, even if his face is all bound up and he's hardly able to speak. I felt quite justified in telling him at once that he needn't worry but just lie back and get well ; as we shouldn't prefer any charge. He was pleased, I could see, but he just said—if you'll excuse my quoting his exact words again—he said—and before the nurse : " For Christ's sake keep your large mouth shut about it," and you can be sure, Mrs. Drury, I promised him I would.'

Peace. The exquisite peace that comes when a haunting fear is removed, and in this instance a double-headed fear, the fear for herself and the fear for Max. Peace, but not happiness. She must go to the hospital ; she must face the porters and the nurses; she must face Max. Courage again. But this time her courage was suddenly helped by her pity. Now that she need fear no more for herself, she had a free open space for her pity, and it came rushing in like a tide ; it swept over her like the Severn bore in its estuary. Poor, poor Max, with his face all bound up, and his attempts at some jokes in spite of his pain. The strong pity drove her along the gauntlet of the streets to the hospital and past the gaping nurses to the small private room where Max lay. She expected to find him also in a softened mood, but no : when she touched his hand in contrition, he drew it sharply away, and she shivered with humiliation. She saw at once that he had been brooding since he came back from unconsciousness : brooding over the boy, Gerald ; over his father, Matt Applin, and that encounter at the hospital gate ; over the police at his bedside and his need to admit his own offence ; over the certainty that the news would reach every house in the little town and damage his bright reputation therein—he the innocent party ! He was very bitter against her and determined that she should see it. To the police he might pretend that it was a quarrel best forgotten ; not to her. So far as he could speak at all through the swathed bandages he was going to strike again ; this time with words. ' I've stopped all action,' he muttered proudly, through lips that hardly moved, ' but you can thank your stars that the Inspector was an old pal of mine. I took the blame upon myself. I told him I had provoked you. I said nothing about *my* provocation.'

And as at the touch of a rod her pity was transformed into anger ; and she struck back. ' You saved yourself something by stopping all proceedings.'

' I don't admit it. If ever a slap was deserved, that one was ; and most men would say so.'

' No doubt they would, since most men are bullies. Evidently you don't want to be friends again.'

' I don't know what I want. I'm not sure that you can't go

back to your grocer's boy. I'm not particularly interested in another man's leavings. And I'm not the forgiving type. I never was.'

'I can go away, if you want me to.'

'I don't know that there's any need for you to go away. For my part I'm going to get well and leave this place for ever.'

'That's just talking nonsense. Could we talk sense? Do you wish me to come and see you again?'

'We must keep up appearances, I suppose—if there are any left to keep up. My mother is coming.'

'*What?*'

'I have written to her this morning.' He indicated a writing-block on his bedside table. 'And if I know anything about the old lady, she'll be here to-morrow.'

Gentle walked away to the window. 'Oh, very well.'

And gazing through the window, she saw, not the hospital grounds, but the reasons why Max had written so promptly to his mother : his wound was a distinction that must be published to those at home ; the solicitude of a woman was a desirable thing even at the cost of much distress to that woman, and since his bitterness excluded Gentle from this part, the next to be cast for it was obviously his mother ; he wanted a bedside listener before whom he could unpack his bitterness and parade his magnanimity ; and, finally, guessing that Gentle would dread his mother's visit, he inflicted it upon her as a punishment.

Best not to show that the knout had fallen. 'All right then, Max. I'll go and make ready for her. Good-bye.'

But by reason of his surly attitude and this sudden announcement she wandered home from the hospital, feeling as if her head had been split open by a succession of blows.

§

The police had withdrawn, but they were not the only people interested in this extraordinary affair. Through many conduits the story with all its details (and with some that didn't belong to it at all) came pouring into the village streets and over the surrounding country. Evans and the cook spoke of the arrival of the doctor and the police to all who would listen (and that was all whom they met). Dwellers in the High Street were full of information about the ambulance at the Rent House door and about someone carried out on a stretcher. The young nurses at the hospital, excited by the advent of one of their doctors on a stretcher, though they were forbidden to discuss

their patients outside the environs of the hospital, nevertheless
chatted their little heads off in the streets. Mr. Applin, Mrs.
Applin and Grandfather Applin had splendid information to
offer in low, sad, deprecating voices that bore no relation whatever to the glow of importance in their hearts.   The Clerk to the
Justices, to whom the police on the first alarm had suggested
that they might need a Justice of the Peace to ' convene a court '
at the hospital and take a deposition, had not been so strong as to
withold from his wife a matter of such immense local interest ;
nor she so scrupulous as to deny it to her confidantes.   And Sir
Thomas Guy Barron, who seemed the only justice accessible
that night, a stupid old man, had been as excited as the youngest
of the nurses by the Clerk's story and chattered about it in his
home, at a house where he was dining, and in the Conservative
Club in the morning.   ' I am standing by in case the worst happens,' he expounded to all with considerable self-satisfaction.
   The story gathered picturesque additions as it flooded and
eddied over a grasping and thirsty soil.   ' It's touch-and-go
whether he'll live.   That's a fact.'   ' The cops were at his bedside all night ; waiting to take a statement.'   ' She nearly killed
him : it's a fact.'   ' It must'a been one helluva blow.   Some
of the nurses thought he was dead when he was carried in from
the ambulance.'   ' She nearly killed him : just think of it !
Poor old Doc.   What a shame ! '   ' They arrested her ; they
took her away that night ; it's a fact.'   ' Well, I never !   Young
Mrs. Drury !   You can hardly believe it.   She was in my shop
only the other day.   What'll she get ? '   ' Something pretty
stiff, I should think, though it seems the old doc. socked her one
first.'   ' Well, from all one hears, she deserved it.   Carrying on
like she done with that young Jerry Applin.'   ' If he dies, she's
for it.   Properly *for* it.   Manslaughter at least, if not murder.'
' Yes, and manslaughter means anything up to ten or fifteen
years.'   ' Fifteen years !   And she was in my shop only the
other day ! '
   And then, hard after these glittering ' facts ', came the word,
' *They've let her off.*'
   At once the happy comments change into discontented
murmurings.   ' God she's lucky ! ',   ' Bloody influence, that's
what does it.'   ' Yes, the old doc.'s going to be all right—I know
—but that's not the point : she nearly killed him ; they say
it'll be weeks before he's out of hospital.'   ' Yes, just let her go.
That's what comes of being a lady and having a father a magis-
trate.   It'd have been very different, if she'd been a simple
working woman.'
   In the afternoon, obliged to do some shopping against the

arrival of Max's mother, Gentle called up the courage once more, set her head high, and went out into the streets.   And as well as possible, though her heart was a sick and sinking thing, she endured the turning heads, the following eyes, the whispering voices, and the embarrassment or coldness in the shops.   From these darts and barbs, this cold but ineluctable pursuit, she hurried back into her home, as glad to get behind its walls as a fox who has escaped the hounds and crouches shivering in his earth.

In the evening, when work in Holm St. Martin was mostly done for the day, she was seated in the dining-room, striving, though her head pounded and her breast shuddered, to make a shopping list for to-morrow, when she became aware, alarmingly aware, of voices on the other side of the window.   She jumped up and from a safe distance bent her head and peered through the curtains.   A few persons, and three idle children stood on pavement or roadway, looking at the front of her house, its curtained windows, its tight-shut, black-painted door, and its brass plate by the side of the door : ' Dr. Robert M. Drury.'   And as she watched them, this scatter of people multiplied, since a few persons, if they will but stand in the street and stare at something, quickly become a small inquisitive crowd.   It was the hour when men and women in some numbers were returning home along the High Street from factory, yard, shop and station ; and it is not in human nature, no, not in the best of us, to come up with a crowd without stopping for a while and adding our persons to it.   All the children within sight, and they were many in this playtime hour, came posting up—on bicycles, on foot, with their hoops or their bats.   They came like precipitated elements in a chemist's solution depositing themselves as a sediment.   And so the crowd multiplied drawing larger accretions as it grew larger.

It was at no time a really large crowd, but you cannot have fifty gathered together without ten of them (and more likely forty of them) being righteous men : that is to say men who are righteous in the presence of other sins than their own.   And in this little crowd that assembled long ago there was a generous sprinkling of such persons, ready to be vocal in their righteousness and, by infecting others with their enthusiasm, to bring public obloquy to bear upon a sinner.   Was not Dr. Drury their well-liked doctor, and had he not been struck down and nearly murdered ?   Let us show, if we can, that we are good men and righteously indignant.   The rest were either quieter creatures, ready to enjoy a common indignation but not to lift their voices in a public place, or simple and decent folk who yet wanted to see all that was happening and would happen.

And Gentle, standing back, terror-gripped and shivering, heard the low gossiping of that crowd, and the actual words of those livelier agitators who were inspired to speak loudly for the incitement—or the amusement—of the crowd. ' How much did she pay the police ? ' ' She's in there, I sor'er. I saw someone moving. Reckon she's afraid to show 'erself.' ' Don't wonder. Plug a stone through the blasted window.' ' No '—a saner voice—' don't do that. There's no sense in that.' ' All right, cock, I didn't really mean it.' ' Think she was tight when she done it ? They say she knows how to put the stuff away.' ' Was it money she gave the cops, or something else, eh, mate ? ' Someone, in joyous mood, let loose a cat-call. Another started a low *boo*, and immediately the bolder lads, ready to follow any lead, jeered in unison. Faces appeared at windows on the other side of the street ; doors opened, and families stood on their steps, watching.

' Oh, go, *go !* Why don't they go ? ' Gentle stood gripping the top of a chair, her shoulders hunched up to her ears—feeling she must shriek or beat her fists on her brows, if they didn't go. ' God, take them away. Please—please—take them away. I didn't mean to hurt Max like that. I didn't mean to do it.'

Rat-ta-tat-*tat.* Someone had rattled the knocker as an inspired musical rendering of his indignation, or of his high spirits. Evans was crossing the hall from the back parts.

' No, don't go, Evans. Oh, don't open the door.'

' Why, whatever is it, ma'am ? '

' I—I don't know. I don't know what's happening.'

' Happening ? '

' Yes, yes, don't open the door. There are people there.'

' People, ma'am ? '

' Yes. They're—they're saying things. Shouting things. They're upset about the master. Oh——' and unable to bear Evans' bewildered and startled eyes she hastened back into the room and to the chair which she gripped again, as if it were the sanity she must control.

' Nice mistress you've got.' Evans must be at the hall window, looking out. ' What did she give the police to let her go ? ' ' Yes, go and arst'er what she give the cops ? '

Someone fell against the door, so that it shook. A loud laugh, and the knocker rattled again. Cheers for the loud rattle of the knocker.

' Oh, God . . . God help me. . . . Go, go—will they never go ? Oh God, be merciful. I didn't mean to do it. I am sorry. I am sorry.'

Children, excited, screamed with delight ; the wheels of cars and carts slowed as their drivers tried to catch a glimpse of what was afoot ; the clock in the hall stupidly, incuriously, caring only for its own affairs, struck the half-hour—and ticked on monotonously, doing the work for which it was paid, and no more. Cook was now in the hall with Evans, watching the scene and deploring it in a small, shocked voice. But now a voice in the street cried, ' Look out : a cop ! ' and the children panicked and stampeded, the gentler watchers walked away slowly with an effort at dignity, while the toughs loafed off in clusters and couples, glancing back and grinning at a policeman who was strolling towards the house. Faces retreated from windows ; doors closed ; pedestrians went by without a glance at her windows ; and the street was as it had been a few minutes—or an epoch— ago.

§

Max's mother arrived next day in a passion of anxiety and incipient despair. An imposing woman of sixty-five with a pile of curled, white hair and large black eyes, this Maurya Mac- Shennan Drury was a Mediterranean type such as can often be encountered in Ireland, and she could stage (if an audience was available) a Mediterranean drama of tragedy, horror, and lamentation, syphoning up the tears and anguish from the vast reservoir in her capacious and well-frilled bosom. Gentle had long known her for a handsome and foolish woman who'd always given far more thought to the improvement and adornment of her voluminous body than to the improvement and furnishing of her mind ; to the tempering of her emotions she'd never given any thought at all. ' What is it, what is it ? ' she demanded, flinging herself on to the first chair in the dining-room, and throwing wide her feather boa so that her chest could heave. ' Is it serious ? Is he making light of it, so as to deceive me ? I feel sure he is. How did it happen ? '

' It was my fault. He will tell you all about it. Please don't ask me. I can't bear to speak of it.'

' Your fault ? But how can that be ? The poor boy says his jaw's fractured. Oh, will he be disfigured for life ? Was it a fall ? '

' Yes, yes—no, no.' Gentle drummed her foot on the carpet. ' Oh, please leave me alone. I am nearly mad with it.'

' But I must know. He is my son. I'm all in the dark. I've worried myself nearly sick with worrying. Oh, where is he ; where is this hospital ? I must go to him.'

' He's getting better—he's going to be all right. I can't tell you any more. Ask *him*, ask *him*.'

And madly she ran from the room—careless of courtesy—anywhere—up to her bedroom where she shut herself in.

Max's mother went to the hospital and in an hour returned with all the story stowed away in her roomy bosom, and, wrapping it round, a harsher hostility to Gentle than she'd ever nursed before. (And this is saying much, for of late years she'd been highly critical of her son's wife because Max had confided his criticisms to her and she'd promptly and with much relief and pleasure made them her own.) She accorded Gentle only a dreadful politeness that evening ; she punished her, at dinner and in the drawing-room by surrounding her, so to say, with a siege-train of loaded silences. Gentle clenched her fists in her lap, pressed her teeth together, and tried to bear it, though something in her cried out, ' I can stand it no more.'

But she tried to stand it : in the morning she went out into the streets again and let the heads turn and the eyes follow and the voices whisper. She struggled to the hospital and went through a painful half-hour with Max, whom she found more surly and querulous than ever because his mother had confirmed him in his dark resentments. He bludgeoned her with more talk about leaving Holm St. Martin for ever and going to South Africa or Australia or Canada—alone. She came sadly home, and, entering the house, heard Mrs. Drury at chatter with the servants in the kitchen.

And an idea that had smouldered within her for years began to flame into a resolve. Some time on the following day it became more than a resolve ; it burst into action. Even as her violent blow on Max's face had been the bursting of something long pent within her, so her sudden wild movements were now an old hidden dream bursting all walls and issuing as action. Go out into those streets again ? No. Enter that hospital again ? No. Spend more nights seated in a cross-fire between old Mrs. Drury's bombardment by silence and the servants' unceasing enfilade by means of fascinated stares, inquisitive questions, and perpetual low commentary in the kitchen ? No. And now Henrietta, who'd been away in Harrogate with Brian's sister, was coming back. She'd be back in two days. To be near when those two old ladies, Mrs. Drury and her mother, discussed her in her own home or in the Chapter Mill—the thought was not to be endured. No, no. Henrietta was the last gramme in the mixture which set off the explosion.

She poured herself many whiskys, and they fed the flame. Her brain began to work with an incandescent clearness. Money ? She had a little ; enough ; enough to support her till she could find means of making more. And there must be ways, many ways, by which she (who, like most of us, had an exaggerated idea of her talents and her value in the competitive market) could earn money and keep herself. Passionately she fingered the swell of several gold sovereigns in her purse, and the feel of them, between finger and thumb, filled her, as did the gold in her glass, with a sense of power and wings. Wings for the flight. Clothes? She'd take only as many as she could wear or carry. If the rest had to be abandoned, well, it was part of her mad self-martyrdom to sacrifice them. 'I am never coming back. No one shall know where I am '—so she might say, but probably she suspected that they could one day be got to her. The immediate act was to go, to go as suddenly as a quenched light, to disappear without leaving a clue behind, and so to teach them all a lesson. The exact nature of this lesson she left somewhere in a fog. If the furies that drove Gentle to her packing that night, while Mrs. Drury and the servants slept, were three in number, then one was shame, one was dread of more pain, and only the third was pride—but she called them all pride. Her lips were not less clenched than the lock when she closed her heavy bag.

She slept a little ; got up early ; wrote a letter to Mrs. Drury : ' I shall not return, Gentle ' ; took up the bag ; put two coats over her arm ; and went out into the clean, empty morning. She struggled with the bag to the station, saw the police station standing opposite it, and was glad to go. ' I am never coming back,' she said as the train bore her away into the green, unpeopled landscapes, out of sight of Holm St. Martin.

CHAPTER IV

WHEN I turned aside to tell you of these events I had left myself, you will remember, among the market carts after I'd run from Henrietta Street almost as wildly as Gentle fled from Holm St. Martin. To the romantic in me it has always been a disappointment that when Gentle, in her agony by the body of Max, cried ' Oh, Doric . . . ' I heard and felt nothing ; but equally I have always been happy to remember how, after hearing of her disappearance, my brain worked with a heightened understanding, a kind of supernormal sympathy that was almost telepathic, till at last it carried me to where she was.

A superheated pressure of love and anxiety put speed into my feet and power into my brain. I had a confidence as complete as it was irrational that I would find her—or was it

Irrational, was it not a confidence that such a pace of brain-
work must sooner or later complete its task? In her blind,
undirected flight she would go first, I told myself, to the parts
she knew well, the parts which in her childhood had been the
centre of the world. Always when she came to town she had
done this; she had gone to the same private hotel in Redcliffe
Square, near her first home in Redcliffe Street, and her second
in Coburg Square. On the first lap of her flight she would go
to this hotel. The postmark on her letter to Henrietta, 'I am
safe,' was 'S.W.'—so Con had told me—but from this I deduced
no more than that she was in London. 'S.W.' covered a great
area north and south of the river, and, anyhow, if Gentle wanted
to conceal her hiding-place she could well have walked to a
different part of London to post her letter. It was faith only
that drove me towards the scenes of our childhood.

'Redcliffe Square,' I said to a taxi-driver in Cranbourn
Street, and, sitting in the cab, leaned forward as if I would go
faster than its wheels.

Piccadilly, Knightsbridge, Brompton Road—the car sped
along these highways; I gazed out; and in the high July sunlight the glistening shops, the strolling people and the lively
bus-riders seemed undisturbed by that Austrian ultimatum,
unafraid that it would invest their city with war, and certainly
unaware that it would bring one long phase of human history
to an end. Who knew that in a few days the roar of monster
cannon at Liége would advertise the new æon?

Had any such awareness been apparent, it would have meant
nothing at this moment to me. Only Gentle meant anything.
We passed within a few yards of Queensberry Place—within a
few yards, that is, of Iris and Hugh—and I cast them from my
thoughts into a wilderness; not without pain, but even as
Abraham, at a word from Sarah, cast forth Hagar the Egyptian
and Ishmael her child.

My excitement, as we raced on, had to wrestle with two
anxieties: the one a jealousy of that young man, Applin (remember, I had no details of this story as yet), and the other a
fear, a dread amounting to a terror, lest when I came upon
a Gentle who looked older and trouble-worn and perhaps
raddled, *I should not love her.* Can you understand this terror?
My love of Gentle was my life's centre and it was as if in going
to her now I were flying from that centre, as if I were leaving
the safety of a dream for the harshness of reality—yes, as if I
were safer away from Gentle because then I had all my love.
'When I love thee not, chaos is come again.' Had Óthello
known the fear that sat with me in that cab?

I was exactly right in my first guess. At the hotel they told me she had been there for a single night about two weeks ago. My confidence soared at this initial success and I could not begin to fear when they told me she'd left no address. ' I shall find her. I know I shall.'

Back in the street, walking slowly, head down, I asked, ' What did she do next ? ' Her first wild step behind her, and still in a moidered state, she would dread being found by any of her people, and so would take some cheap lodging and set about looking for work. Now came the first cold touch of fear—the immensity of London !—but I brushed it away : ' I *know* I shall find her.' Possessed by the faith that she would keep somewhere close to the locations of her childhood, I walked the few steps to Coburg Square as if inspiration were waiting for me there ; and I looked up at the old house which was somewhat broken in fortune now and down in the world ; gazing particularly at the playroom window and thinking, ' If only the young Doric and the young Gentle could have looked out from that window into the future and seen me standing below as I am now.'

If she was somewhere in this decaying neighbourhood, then she must go occasionally to the food shops, and from them I could learn the address to which her orders were sent. Straightway I went among them—did I not know them all ?— in Old Brompton, Earls Court and Lillie Roads. Dairies, grocers, butchers, pastrycooks, I visited them all and came away with nothing.

It was now mid-day and the lunch hour, and I went into every café, teashop, and restaurant, looked around, and walked out again. The July heat, smiting upward from pavement and tarred road, drew forth the question, ' Would she, if free, repeat the habit of childhood and saunter in Kensington Gardens ? ' To the Gardens I hurried, visiting at speed all our favoured places, not omitting, of course, the flower-boarded walk where she'd slipped her hand into mine after my disgrace. All the time I half expected to see her figure in the next avenue, and often I ran after figures that were a little like hers, but always encountered a disappointment.

Now I was staving off the fear of defeat. Fighting it—' I *know* I shall find her '—I went back to the old neighbourhood, for thither something stronger than reason seemed always to draw me.

By the side of a newspaper and toy shop I saw a framed case of ' Wanted ' advertisements, all written in different hands on cards or sheets of notepaper : ' Married couple required. . . . Experienced Housekeeper available. . . . Daily Sewing Woman. . . .

Small gas fire for sale '; and these lit up in me a new, exciting, tumultuous idea. Now surely I might track her. What employment would she seek ? A secretarial job in an office ? But she had no training. Governess or Mother's Help ? My mind would not say ' Yes ' to these. Teacher ? She had no paper qualifications, but that never seemed to matter in a private school. Possibly a teacher, but, if so, she could not start work till next term, in September.

Still seeing no certain light, I went to every employment agency I could find. And to their lady registrars I lied as fluently and skilfully as ever my father did : I was Mrs. Drury's ·brother, I said, just back from abroad and had heard that she had come to this part to find employment ; I was a solicitor with important news for her ; I was the executor of a will under which she was a considerable beneficiary—this last never failed to make them open their registers and give me the address of another agency when they could find nothing. It was late evening when I had worked them all, and I was still as empty as at the beginning of the day.

All the rest of that evening I tramped those streets, hoping to see her. I visited every restaurant again : they must have wondered what sort of local idiot I was, drifting in at meal-times and looking round among the diners, and straying sadly out again.

Baulked, nonplussed, all energy spent, I could only slink back, in the body if not in the spirit, to Queensberry Place, hiding my story, my shame, and my knowledge that I should fly from them again in the morning. All night, my brain revolving and revolving like a motor engine, I lay awake, tossed about this way and that by a hundred visiting questions. And in some small hour a new idea sprang me wider awake than ever. It seemed a good chance, but its hope of success rested on my immovable intuition that she was somewhere in the parts she knew so well. If this was an illusion, then I must fail.

In the morning I went from the house as though to South Kensington Station and Henrietta Street, but once out of sight I turned towards Old Brompton Road. I ran to the Public Library and Reading Room by Cranley Gardens. If Gentle advertised in a local paper, it would be the one she had known as a child. I went to the stand which held the *Brompton and Earls Court Press* and swept my eye down its ' Situations Wanted.' No help here, unless I were to write to every Box Number reference that seemed at all likely. I wrote down a few of these numbers unhopefully. Then it occurred to me that this was only yesterday, Friday's, paper ; I ran to the office of the Press

and asked to see the issue of two weeks ago.   No, nothing there.
But she would hardly have had time to get it into that issue.
' The back file of one week ago, please.'   This was given me,
and with a pounding heart, I turned to the only column that
interested me.   Here, for an instant hope stirred as I alighted
upon ' Lady, 32, good cook, offers services daily to family or
school '—Gentle was thirty-two—and while I was thinking this
I saw, without at first taking it in, ' Educated woman, 30, seeks
post, literary nature, London preferred. Greaves, 4A Luton
Grove, S.W.'

' Greaves ' !   If this was she, and I was wildly sure it was,
then I knew why I had met with no success at the employment
bureaux : in a passionate resentment against Max she'd thrown
off his name and resumed her own.   ' 30 ' ?   Well, near enough.
' Educated woman ' !   I could have wept with pity for Gentle,
who had but the usual uncoordinated smatterings from High
School and Finishing School.   ' Literary nature ' !   The pitiable
vagueness and naïvety of it.   This was the old Gentle who had
longed to entertain literary celebrities.   ' Luton Grove.'   It
was on the far side of Fulham Road, not in, but on the very
edge of our childhood's domain.   My one strong intuition had
been right all the time.

My head alight with pride, I ran into the street.

§

To Luton Grove, then, as fast as the fastest walk could take
me.   Luton Grove was a long, grey road, ending in a mist and
a tall steeple : its grey houses were smaller than those on the
other side of the Fulham Road, and even more tired, outmoded,
and down in the world.   But they were pompous, too, in their
smaller way, with their cement facing, their piered gates, and
their lift of eight steps to their porticoed doors.   Their bright
day, however, was done, and they were for the dark : grime
had blackened their porticoes, time had veined their plaster
with cracks, or swollen it into blisters, or sloughed large parts
of it away.   No. 4A—here it was, almost at the mouth of the
street, on its western side.   Obscuring its narrow and shallow
area were a few privets, some tall weeds, and one conscientious
but uninspired tree.   There it was, 4A, with Gentle, perhaps,
behind its few inches of brick wall.

The fear of what I was going to find, and that my love might
take its mortal wound, sharpened in me and shook my heart
as I went up the steps.   Not at once, but after a fear-filled pause,

I drew out the old-fashioned bell-pull, and a bell ding-donged and died in the basement.

As steps came up from below, further disturbing my heart, I looked down into the area pit and saw, without quite realizing what I saw, two dust-bins, a perambulator, and two milk-cans.

The door opened to show me a little skimped woman in her work-worn thirties, with peaked features, lank hair, and face and shoulders both tapering towards her neck ; but clean and neat withal, and wiping her hands on her apron. Behind was a clean little passage, covered with oilcloth and strips of worn carpet. She looked at me doubtfully.

'You have a Miss Gentle Greaves staying here ? ' I inquired, slurring the ' Miss ' so that it might sound like ' Mrs.' in case that was what she would expect.

'Miss Greaves ? Yes. Yes, that's right.' Her eyes groped over my face.

'Miss *Gentle* Greaves ? '

'Yes. That's right.'

God ! I could hardly stay my lips from stuttering as I asked, ' Could I see her ? '

' Is she expecting you ? '

' Well, no . . .' and I smiled. ' She may be surprised to see me, but glad, I think.'

My manner satisfied her ; moreover she was curious to know who I was ; so she said, ' I'll just see if she's in. I'll just nip up and see. Will you step in a minute ? And as I stepped in she nipped—a good word for her quick little steps—up the staircase treads, both hands holding her skirt out of the way of her toes.

My whole body shivering, I stepped forward to see which floor she visited, which door she knocked at. The first floor. The front room. ' Miss Greaves ? ' No answer. ' Miss Greaves ? ' again ; and still no answer. The door opening ; shutting ; and the little landlady coming down again.

' No, she's out. I thought, being as early as this, she'd be in. But she's gen'lly out most of the day. Breakfast is the only meal she ever——'

' Is she at her place of work ? '

' Pardon ? '

' I understood she was working somewhere.'

' Working ? I don't think so. She never told me nothing about it, if she is. I don't think she can be because she doesn't go out early enough for that. She gen'lly leaves——'

' Would she be back soon, do you think ? This afternoon perhaps ? '

'Well, that I can't say. Sometimes she doesn't come in till quite late, but she might 'sarfternoon, being Saturday. Yes, she might.' She thrust five parted fingers into the disordered coils of her hair, and kept them there, musing. 'Mr. Mills and I won't be here—still, she could let you in herself, couldn't she? Mr. Mills and I are going to see his sister in Wandsworth, whose husband's poorly, and he likes Mr. Mills and I to come round for a chat of an afternoon. I thought I'd come back soon after they'd had their tea because they'll only be talking politics together : you know what men are.' The fingers came down from the hair, and she pressed two of them against her cheek. 'Isn't it awful, all this talk about a war? I don't think there'll be one, do you?'

'I'm sure I couldn't say, Mrs. Mills.'

'Oh, no—I mean, not with England. I mean, what's it to do with us? Let 'em get on with it theirselves, *I* say. But Mr. Mills says he's shore there'll be one and that the Germans'll try and land at Southend and Tilbury, but he's always one to fear the worst, I say. D'you think there'll be one?'

'I doubt it. There's always trouble in the Balkans——'

'Yes, I'll have to get back to give Mr. Wiltshire his supper. He's a commercial and comes back this evening. He's my only other lodger at present. I had my top floor let up to a week ago : a young railway clerk and his wife, just married, as nice a young couple as you could want. But they've gawn now and no one's come in their place yet. Things are always quiet in the summer what with holidays——'

'Thank you, Mrs. Mills. I'll come back later then.'

'I'd arst you to wait, but there don't seem much sense in that. You could wait in the parlour if you like, but I can't say at all when she'll be back and I expect you've a lot of other things to do. Who shall I say called if she comes back before I've gawn?'

'What? Oh, yes . . . say it was her brother. Her brother, Theodore.'

'Her *brother*? Oh, why didn't you say so before? Yes, you favour her, I think.'

'I—what did you say?'

'You favour her. You're like her. Now that you tell me you're her brother, I can see it.'

'I never thought we were very much alike.'

'People of the same family can never see if they're like each other, I always say. Anyone could see you were her brother. We like your sister ever so much, Mr. Greaves. I often say to Mr. Mills, I wish they were all like her, hardly any trouble at all. As a rule I don't care for having single ladies, they're ten times as much nuisance as men, but I took to her at once and so did Mr. Mills—she must 'a bin ever so pretty once——'

'I'm so glad you feel like that about her, but I must really be going——'

'Yes, you'd hardly know she was in the house. But, if I may say so, Mr. Greaves, I'm glad you come, being as you're her brother '—she followed me down the steps and as far as the pavement—'because Mr. Mills and I're a little bit worried about her ; she looks kind 'a worn out to me. Of course it's no business of mine and I don't want to interfere, but, between you and me, I began to suspect she was getting a bit hard-up and was too proud, like, to say so. She doesn't look to me as if she was eating enough.'

'If that's so, Mrs. Mills, we'll soon put it right. Good-bye.'

'Well, I'm glad—good morning—I'm glad indeed you come. And I'll tell her if I see her before we go out. Good-bye.'

But I didn't intend that this little woman should see Gentle before I did, so I lingered at the corners of that road like a bailiff's man, watching the house all that morning and afternoon and trying to avoid the eyes of gossiping women and of the children at their Saturday games. I saw Mr. Mills return, and Mrs. Mills, all dressed up for a call, leave the house with him an hour later, their faces set towards Wandsworth. The afternoon sank into evening, and still Gentle had not appeared. I kept my watch till an utter weariness in legs and back and a dry thirst, if not a hunger, drove me into the ' Luton Arms ' at the Fulham Road corner, where I had a stiff whisky and a sandwich from the counter. So bone-weary was I in back, feet and legs that I sat at my saloon table for the best part of an hour, resigned, if so it must be, to let Mrs. Mills catch Gentle before I could.

But when, on the clock striking seven, I came out again and made towards the house, wondering if Gentle had returned, I saw Mrs. Mills coming from the opposite direction at a quick step, as if she'd stayed gossiping too long in Wandsworth. No hope now of entering her house before she could, so I went towards her, smiling. ' We seem to have come back at the same time,' I said.

' She hadn't come home before I left, Mr. Greaves, but I'm pretty shore she must be back now. I'll nip in and see. I'm later than I thought : we got talking, you know how you do.'

Unlocking the door, she tripped up her stairs, knocked on Gentle's door, opened it, and came softly down again.

' She's sitting there fast asleep. I hadn't the heart to wake her. What d'you think : would you like me to tell her you're here ? '

' I'll go up myself, and wait there till she wakes.'

Mrs. Mills nodded and smiled her assent.

§

Surely, though the door was still unlatched, Mrs. Mills having forborne to close it, Gentle must hear the battering of my heart as I stole in. But she did not : she lay there in an old deep, easy chair, by the fire-place, one of her arms resting along its soft arm, her head couched in her elbow's crook, and her feet drawn to the chair's foot, as if she would have curled them under her. It was not a beautiful posture, but rather one that would have been beautiful if she could have completed it. As it was, and since her tarnished-gold hair was a little tumbled, it might have been posed for a picture, ' Weariness at the End of the Day.'

An oval table stood under the window, with a cane chair before it. I tip-toed, quite soundlessly, to this chair and sat in it beside her, leaning both elbows on my knees.

I looked at her, seeking from her face and figure the answer to my terrible fear. There were threads of grey in the hair ; the line of her cheek, which was all I could see, had caved in a little ; her hands, hanging relaxed, one over the chair's arm and one between her knees, were thinner than they used to be ; and the shoes on her drawn-up feet were worn down and split.

And my answer came at once : an outrush of love so full, so swelling, that it was like a great pain. She wrecked my heart with the old love. How could I have doubted ? It was the old love and more, for at this moment I seemed to want nothing for myself and all for her. I knew I could never doubt again, however I might fall back into selfishness ; and the knowledge spent me with joy.

Down below I heard voices : Mr. Wiltshire perhaps had come home for his supper. Out in the street I heard voices : the cries of children at play and of mothers loudly adjuring them. And nobody in house or street knew that I was sitting here, as still as the furniture in the room, but overcharged with that extreme of happiness which is the gift of self-annihilating love.

I looked round the room : it was clean and polished like everything else in Mrs. Mills' home, but very cheaply furnished. Designed as a bed-sitting room for a married couple, it had an

Iron-and-brass bedstead, a chest, washstand and sideboard, a sofa that smelt of its horsehair and a gas-fire with a slot meter. Some of Gentle's garments bestrode the bed-rail, and others crowded into hiding behind a curtain in a corner.

My chair creaked ; Gentle stirred ; she woke ; saw me smiling there ; spread wide her eyes, and—well, there was a brief, a moment's, halt in Time while we sat gazing at each other, I smiling, she confused.

Then she gasped, ' Doric ! '

I picked up her hand and enclosed it in both of mine.

' Oh, *Doric*—what—where've you come from ? How did you get here ? '

I didn't answer, but drew her to her feet and into my arms. She cried, ' Oh, my darling,' and clasped me, sobbing. I couldn't say anything or I should have sobbed, too. I only passed my hand over her hair.

She flung back her head. ' But I've been thinking of you all day ; I was thinking of you as I dropped off to sleep : it's quite clearly a miracle ; there's no doubt about it—it's a miracle.' And she hugged the miracle to her. ' Oh, gosh ! A hundred times gosh ! '

' You were thinking of me ? '

' My lamb—my sweet—I never think of anyone else now, I'm so silly ! '

Forcing her against me that we might seem one body, I held up her face by her chin. There was a blue darkness round her eyes, and the cheeks were sunken, but this hollowness only revealed the beautiful structure of her bones and chin. About her lips there was the old, controlled smile, like the private smile of a Leonardo's St. Anne. I pressed my lips on that smile. ' Thank you, Gentle.'

' It *is* you, isn't it—and I'm not gone crazy ? It isn't that I've not been eating enough, and am now a little mad ? ' And she passed her hand down my back and along my arm, which, deciding that it was solid, material stuff, she clutched fiercely. ' Yes, it *is* him ; I think it is. But it can't be a miracle ; miracles just don't happen. Explain it. Go on. Tell me.'

But I only smiled down at her, to tease her with my silence.

' Oh, why doesn't the man say something ? *Say* something.'

' Is it a miracle that someone should love you and find you ? '

' Yes. Yes, of course it is.'

' I found you in less than two days.' (I was very proud of this.)

' But why did you trouble to ? Why have you come ? '

'Because nothing in the world means anything to me but you.'

'You mustn't say that, my angel, but it's lovely to hear you say it. Say it again.'

I said it again and added, 'You are mine now, and no one's going to hurt you any more—unless it's me, who'll probably do it sometimes, but I'm going to try never to. You are mine, my dear.'

'That can never be—how can it?—besides, you can't really love me as you did. I'm a Disgraced Woman—did you know it?—I'm a case for the Police, I've been In their Hands, and, what's worse, I'm getting old and ugly.'

'You lie ; you lie very grievously, woman.'

'But it's so. I'm going grey. Look here at these awful——'

'Child, I was looking at you just now and I knew I loved you more perfectly than I'd ever done. It almost killed me, the love I felt for you. I can never, never forget what I felt then.'

'Are you meaning this ? '

'I mean it.'

'Good heavens ! . . .'

'I mean it as I've never meant anything before.'

'Good heavens. . . . God is good. . . .'

'God is good indeed.'

'But, darling heart, you're a great and famous man now— you're getting so famous I hardly ever open a paper without reading something about you—you're a Distinguished Man——'

'I am not.'

'You've the world at your feet——'

'I care nothing for the world ; only for you.'

'—while I'm no longer respectable. I'm—darling, in Holm St. Martin '—her eyes opened wide, in a kind of humorous despair—' I'm looked upon as a strumpet.'

'Did you love that boy ? '

She laid her hand on my breast, fingers upward. 'Ought I to say the truth ? '

'Yes.'

'But not to you ? '

'Most certainly to me.'

'No, I don't think I should.'

'Say it instantly.'

'I've never had any love to give anyone but you. Never, never. I think I pretended he was you.'

I pressed her hand closer. 'My child, you look so terribly tired. What have you been doing ? Tell me all about it.'

'I have hardly known what to do. I've been nearly mad with despair the last few days. I'm never going back to Holm St. Martin and I've been wandering around reading advertisements till I loathe the sight of them, writing tedious letters, and calling on awful people, but there was nothing I really wanted to do, even if anybody engaged me. There seems to be nothing but barely paid, living-in, mother's-help jobs for people like me. Oh, I don't know why anyone's a woman. My money began to go, and I left a nicer room I had for this one which is cheaper—oh, I shall get something some day, but in the meantime I've stopped eating. It costs money, you see. I put an advertisement in the paper, but no one has answered it.'

'Yes, someone has.'

'Who ? Where ?'

'Here. I answered it.'

And I told her that story, and pointed out that she was thirty-two, not thirty.

'Yes, isn't it awful ? It horrifies me. . . . Please say it again, what you said just now.'

'What was that ?'

'Something about " nothing matters "——'

'Nothing matters to me in the whole wide world but you.'

'Darling !' The old upward gaze was upon me, as if she were sunk deep in her immense fund of love and looking up from its depths. 'But what are we going to *do* ? What's going to happen ?'

'We're going to stay together always.'

She shook her head. 'That just isn't possible.'

'Nothing else is possible now. You're never going back ?'

'No, no.'

'Then I'm never leaving you. That's what's going to happen. Nothing else.' And I added what may have been my lifelong illusion—but to this hour I do not know, Roberta ; nor perhaps shall I ever know. 'We are one, and this was always meant to be.'

'Oh, you mustn't say or even feel like that—but it makes me so happy . . . you must go back . . . you must go . . . oh, what fools we all are !'

The house was silent. I suppose Mr. Wiltshire was in his room somewhere and Mrs. Mills far below ; and neither knew that a long story was coming to its climax in a neighbouring room : a long wave rising to its crest and breaking.

'We are one.' I passed my hand over her body and limbs. 'I want you so.'

She whispered, 'No, no' ; but without strength.

' My body aches for you.' And I asked, longing for the answer that would make the ecstasy unbearable, ' You too ? '

But she only gazed up.

' You too ? ' I begged.

She raised her eyebrows as one ashamed but helpless, fingered my coat button, and· gave me in answer more than I asked. ' It always has.'

' My *wife*. You are my wife. I have no wife at home now.'

At this she glanced up, startled.

' It is so, Gentle. I've had none for nearly two years, since Iris discovered that I still loved you. She has been a friend and companion to me since then, but cannot bear to be anything more. I have no wife.'

Straightway she undid my arms and led me to her bed. She prepared herself for me and took me to her. And not with tenderness only, but also, and even more, with an almost savage and rejoicing cruelty, I poured my life into her, and she craved it all. This was Gentle, this was I—at last. The giving and receiving of it were like the infinite healing of death, and we lay thereafter in each other's arms like two who had died together.

CHAPTER V

WHAT NOW ? Blind to my ultimate aims, blind also to the shadows which this hour in history was throwing across the path of all, I took Gentle away from that grey street to a small white hotel on the north side of the Park, and there we lived together. I sent no word to Iris of what I was doing because I did not know what I was doing. If for an instant I tried to look into the future, my sight went from me.

Even now I cannot discern how far my actions were selfish and how far self-forgetting. I know that the larger part of my love *seemed* to be all for Gentle : something pouring out of me to wrap her round. I convinced myself that she needed me to restore and rebuild her and that nothing else mattered in the world.

And she for the present was blinded, too. She might shake her head and say, ' No, it cannot be,' when I declared that I was going to stay with her for ever, but she said no more and did no more to stop me. She only gazed up, defeated. We knew in our depths, I suppose, that cold facts were waiting for

us, somewhere on the other side of a mist, but we contrived to
veil every glimpse of them.

Eleven days we had together and four of them were thus
insulated in the mist. Very happy, for the most part, were all
those days. I can remember a few shocks of disappointment
when her language or her looks differed from my dream of her,
and that dread lest I lost my love grabbed at my heart, but
always an outrush of pitying love, like that which I had felt in
her grey lodging, poured out to drown the dread. I don't
think that she, less introspective and self-worrying than I, was
visited by such moments. Her love was demonstrative, and
I could see no speck of doubt in it. When I had her in my
nightly embrace I had the perfect thing at last, and my heart
so melted my head that I could only utter absurd things—the
absurder the better—and express my love by its opposite. ' You
little wretch, how I hate you ! ' I would grit at her through
closed teeth. ' You're the plague of my life. . . . You little
devil, you've bedevilled my life ever since you first touched
my hand, and I hate you. Why were you ever born ? You're
a pain, I tell you, a very terrible pain, and I can't bear you.'

' Nor I you.' She hardly breathed it from under my lips.
' It's so wonderful. . . .'

Yes, for a little we both had what all the world longs for.

For those first four days we moved in a timeless paradise,
though the Time which we had deserted was more pregnant,
more laden with significance (as I think now) than any in a
thousand years. All who are old enough to remember those
last days of the ancient world will remember that in their outward seeming they were quite lovely, their skies swept clean and
shining and their air steeped in the heat of high summer. The
Park beneath our windows was full of the sun, and we strolled
and idled in it, she hanging on my arm with both her hands
linked over it, in the old way. Or we hooked our fingers
together and swung them between us as we walked. Sometimes
we even sang softly and danced along for a few steps. On the
Sunday, when the rampageous orchestras of Bayswater Road
and Park Lane were muted, we lay in a clump of chestnuts,
whose shadow made an island of darkness in the sea of sunlight,
and listened to the church bells clashing over our Royal Borough
of Kensington, while we gazed between the trees at the children
playing, the dogs gambolling, the other lovers strolling inter-
twined, and the sleepers lying about like casualties on a battlefield. It was still only Sunday, the 25th July ; and we remained
shut within ourselves, with no window open upon the continents
where the first of the armies were gathering.

Not till the hot, calm evening of Wednesday did we really open those windows to catch the sounds of the outer world. That evening we were lying beneath a lime-tree near the Bird Sanctuary, and I became well aware that a man, seated on a green chair two yards away, was watching me with an eye like the Ancient Mariner's because he'd got a story to tell. And when he decided that this particular wedding guest had done with trifling and was ready for the story, he fixed me with his glittering eye and began, ' The first shots' a been fired, mate.'

I had been resting on an elbow, and now sat up, both to hear this news and to give him the happiness of telling it.

' Yepp.' His lips closed firmly on the fact. ' The Austrians are bombarding Belgrade. They're firing acrost the Danube. That's their answer to that little pistol shot at Serra Jeevo.'

' A pretty violent riposte,' I suggested.

' A what, mate ? '

' A pretty severe reply.'

' Oh, I dunno. I reckon the Serbs arst for it. *Yurse.*'

He was a long, wiry man dressed in a labourer's clothes, with a muffler round his neck and straps round his corduroy trousers under his knees. His hair was grizzled and his eager face crumpled, but all this seemed the weathering of the wind rather than the print of age. I do not think he was forty. Anyhow, it was not in his imagination that the war, before it was over, would trap *him* in its meshes, and I'm sure that, delighting in this drama across the Danube, he would not have wished the hour to be other than it was.

' This'll bring us all in,' he said, nodding. ' Bah'nd to.'

I argued that we could limit the war to the Balkans, ' where there was always trouble,' but he wouldn't agree, because he didn't want to.

' *Nah!* Don't you believe it, guv'nor. The bloody Russians —beg pardon, lady—the Russians are mobilizing and the British Fleet's standin' ready at its war bases. I got a mate who's served his time in the Navy, and whose boy's on a battleship now ; and he knows all about it. He was tellin' me. Now listen. The Grand Fleet—four hundred perishin' vessels— assembled at Spithead ten days ago—didn't they ? And what for, may I ask ? '

' For a review. A grand review by the King.'

' Ah, that's what they tell us. That's what they tell you and me. But why was they fully provisioned and armed ? You don't need to be fully provisioned and armed for a review. No, the Navy knew a fortnight ago what was coming. It's their business to. The Navy can't take no risks. And what

happened as soon as the royal inspection was over. Eh? Tell
me that.'

' I can't tell you because I don't know. What happened ? '

' I'll tell you. They just disappeared. They disappeared
into the mist. And would you like to know where they are ?
They're at Scaper Flow and Crommerty Firth, waiting for the
Germans to come out. The Germans only got two sally ports,
the Kiel Canal and the Skaggerak, and we shan't let anything
come out or go in, neither naval vessels nor merchant vessels.'

' Good for us ! Up the British ! Rule, Britannia ! '

' Yurse, we got 'em by the throat there. It'll finish the
blood—pardon, lady—the ruddy war in three months.'

' So ? Well, that'll be fine.'

Gentle was now sitting up too and leaning forward to listen,
but leaving it to the men to be wise about politics.

' There are no dreadnoughts like ours,' said this labouring
man, their part-owner on his twenty shillings a week, very
proudly. ' That was a smart bit o' work, getting 'em all to their
war stations ten days before the Austrians fired a shot. Yah,
you don't catch our Navy on the wrong foot, not in a 'undred
years. They been at the game too long. Gum, I'd 'a liked
to've seen 'em sailin' away into the mist.'

The warm evening seemed quite still, but the blue tracery of
our lime-tree's shadow was waving lightly over the sun-flushed
grass, and the fruit of the lime was falling softly about us, as if
an idling wind troubled the tops of the trees. The warmth
seemed to muffle the circling traffic, and the only sound we
really heard was the children's careless voices, as constant and
as scattered as birdsong. White butterflies drifted over a width
of bearded grass which the horse-mower had yet to shave ; and
they and the faltering thistledown seemed the very spirits of the
summer peace.

I looked before me at the pleasant scene, and tossed the lime
fruit towards it as one tosses pebbles on a beach ; but in my
mind I was seeing those huge grey weighted ships, in line ahead,
heaving through silent seas.

' Well, so long, mate,' said the man.

' So long.' I lifted a hand to him. ' Happy days.'

' D'you believe he was right ? ' asked Gentle, when he was
gone. ' D'you really think that war is inevitable now ? '

' It may be, but I'm not the least convinced by anything *he*
said. He just *wanted* to state the worst. We all do. Alarm's
such a much better line than hope. *I* still hope.'

' Oh, and I, too.'

She sank into silence then, and I knew she was musing upon

the part that war must play in our story. I refused to consider
this yet, not daring to do so, and went on tossing the lime fruit
before me. And while we sat there, unspeaking, one bugle and
another sounded in the hazy distances. They were blown,
perhaps, in Wellington Barracks and in some camps in the
parks, and I suppose we'd heard them on other days. But
to-day we really listened and took note of them, as they sang
in the pleasant sundown and behind this happy scene ; and
I've often thought of them since as symbols of the one sure fact,
that life is invested by death ; beauty, whether of leaf or love,
by destruction ; and the ecstasy of union by an everlasting
loneliness.

§

Still hoping, we ran next day to the Serpentine, for an hour
on the water like those we used to enjoy as children. I bought
two papers on the way, but did not dare to open them at once.
We hired a boat at the boathouse and I rowed Gentle under
the bridge to the Long Water and as far as the willow by which
we had stayed our boat on that afternoon, sixteen years before.
Then two grey geese had followed us to the willow ; this morning two swans swam up to look at us and swam away again.
It was yet early in a hot July day, and there was a hush upon
the water as if the birds drowsed. The trees stood still as pictured
trees. Far away the rumour and sighing of traffic rounded
the silence like a frame, and only the occasional cry of a water-
fowl shivered the stillness within the frame. The influence of
the tranquil water lulled us into dreaming, and it was a long
spell before at length, and in fear, I opened a paper.
   The Times addressed me in a normal headline. ' The Arming
of Europe. A Situation of Extreme Gravity.' The other paper,
a halfpenny one, blared forth its statement in a full-page
' streamer ' headline—the first I'd ever seen—' Belgrade Burning.
The Fuse is Fired.'
   Closing and letting fall this paper, I said to Gentle, not with
a relish in the drama like our friend of yesterday, but with a
bitter savour of dismay : ' It's here, my dear.'
   She looked up from the water. It was the very water from
which, sixteen years before, she'd looked up to tell us her dreams
of a happy life. ' What is here ? '
   ' The War.'
   ' *No ?* '
   ' Yes ; it's on us now.'
   ' But why ? You said yesterday they could limit it to Austria
and Serbia.'

'I didn't really believe it.' And I explained, as I had to
Iris, but with only a faint pride to-day in my political wisdom :
' It's impossible that Russia shouldn't go to the help of Serbia.
In a few days all Europe will be alight. Belgrade isn't in
China ; it's a European capital, and it's burning.'

Her eyes lit with alarm ; she turned them from me and looked
down again into the water. And suddenly she shuddered as if
a thought had pricked her, and tossed her head as though to
toss the thought from her. And she mumbled angrily, ' *No !* '

' What are you thinking of ? ' I asked.

' Oh, my dear, I'm awful, awful. Why'm I so awful ? '

' You're not.'

' I am. D'you remember how I told you that I used to
think of Max being killed in his car, so that I could be free
again ? Well, some years ago, when there was all that talk of
war, I used to hope for a moment that the war would come—
because he'd certainly go, he's always said he would—and
perhaps—oh, it's awful—perhaps he'd be killed, and I should
be free, and still young—I was only twenty-nine then. But
I didn't let myself think this for more than a second : it was
too wicked. It was like being a murderer ; I saw him lying
dead—poor, poor Max ! He had his right to live as well as
me. And now it has come—and for a second I had the same
wicked thought just now.'

' One can't help these thoughts,' I comforted her. ' We all
have them. Come, we must go back now. Take the tiller lines
again.'

' Poor Max—and what good would it have done ? There's
still Iris, and I've never, never had such a wicked thought about
her. You *do* believe that, don't you ? '

' Of course, my sweet.'

' I'm not as bad as that. I'm not really. I don't want
people to die.'

I dipped my oar and rowed away from the mockery of that
tranquil scene. Disembarking at the boat-house, I left Gentle
on a seat by the waterside (she smiled very sadly at me as I
went) and hurried to the office to talk business with George
Byng. I had visited him once or twice in the past few days,
on the understanding that he wasn't to ask where I was staying
or what I was doing. He discussed several questions with me
and then said, ' Oh, by the way, there's a letter come addressed
" care of " you. Where is it ? Oh, here you are ' ; and he
handed it to me.

It was in Max's hand, and addressed ' Mrs. Drury, c/o
T. Allan Mourne, Esq., House of Allan Mourne, Henrietta Street.'

In the six days we'd been together he'd learned the truth. Easy to see how this had come about. It was not in Con to keep silence about our interview—after all, *I* had disappeared too now—and she'd talked to Mother ; nor was it in Mother to keep silence about anything, and she'd talked to Henrietta, and Henrietta to Max. The letter was thick ; only a passionate letter would demand so many pages ; and I immediately suspected what had happened. After his first fury with me all Max's love and desire for his wife had flamed up afresh now that she'd been approached by another man. This was a fervid appeal to her to return.

The temptation sprang upon me to destroy the letter. All the old schoolboy deceitfulness, which used to lead me to eavesdrop and spy and secrete, rose up from its underground prison to confirm the temptation. It may be that in some other hour of our country's story I should have yielded, but a strange nobility was abroad just then beneath our English sky, and it touched me, and I carried the letter to Gentle.

She looked at it, stammered, ' Oh no ! ' and desperately thrust it from her ; but she opened it at last when I told her this was best.

I stood with my arm about her shoulder where she sat, and we read it together.

> ' Darling Gentle, please, please forgive me and come back to me. I love you so. I know I'm not worthy of you—who could be ?—I know I've been a brute sometimes, I know I've deserved all I've got, but, my dearest, my darling, I've had my lesson, I'm almost glad of what's happened, almost glad that you went, because I've recovered the tremendous joy of loving you, adoring you, again. This joy almost outweighs the terrible pain, the agony, of thinking of you with someone else. I'm no longer angry with him, or I'm trying not to be, because I can understand why anyone must love you, but I want you so, you are my wife, my own darling wife. Come back to me, come soon. There may not be much time to be together again, I shall be needed for this war, and I'm going of course. They say I shall be out of hospital in a week or so and perfectly fit in another month, and then I shall go. And I mean to get to the very front of the battle with the infantry, not in any damned casualty clearing station or base hospital. Anything may happen to me, Gentle, so this may be our last chance to be together, our last ever. Come back, my dear and darling wife. . . .'

Page after page of it, and when Gentle had finished, she laid it down and said, ' Poor sweet.'

And I exclaimed, ' *What* ? I think it's a damned unfair letter. He could have left the war and his possible death out of it.'

' But that's just Max. He's so crude and touching.'

' I may go to the war too.'

' You ? Oh, no ! ' She leapt up and flung both arms about my neck, hanging them there as an Indian hangs a garland round the neck of his guest of honour. And she looked up into my eyes in that way she had, as if her love were too deep for speech and you were all that mattered in the world. ' Don't go to the war. I want you in the world, even if——'

' Even if what ? '

' Oh, don't let's talk about it yet. It's not time to decide anything yet, is it ? Let's be happy just a little longer. Would that be very wrong ? '

' I'm ready to decide something now : to keep you for ever.'

' No . . . please. . . . Don't say that.'

' After all I've had of you now, how can I bear to go ; how can I let *you* go ? I can't ; it's not possible ; I'm no longer strong enough.'

' We mustn't be selfish.'

'How can I hand you back to someone else after——'

' You wouldn't be handing me back. Not in that way. Oh, but please may we not talk of it just now ? If we've got to do something dreadful, I must get used to the idea gradually : I'm such a coward. . . . Poor Max, poor pet. . . .'

And she unclasped the circle of her arms and, letting them fall, turned from me with a sigh.

Poor Max. Inevitably her pity for her husband raised a kindred thought in me, but I closed the door on it sharply. In that closed oom was Iris, rand Hugh with her : Iris, silent, too proud to plead like Max, her face white but her head erect ; Iris Sanctuary who had come to help me, and whom I had married ; and Hugh, whom I had got out of her, Hugh, but four years old. A coward too, I kept away from that room, and turned my eyes from it, as children avoid a death-chamber, running quickly past it down the stairs.

§

For three more days we ran together from reality, refusing to greet it and take it by the hand. And now it was Sunday, the second day of August and our second Sunday together. In the

morning papers we learned that France had declared war on
Germany, and that the German army, a hundred thousand
strong, was marching into Luxemburg.   We walked out into the
streets where the heat was shimmering up from the roadways
and glittering on the pavements.   We found a different Sunday
in the streets from any we had known : the shops were shuttered
as usual, but the roads, instead of being empty, clean, and quiet,
were full of people : some in loose, free garments, crowding on
to the buses with bags and baskets, for it was the eve of Bank
Holiday ; others, in serious clothes—and there were amazingly
many of these—walking with prayer books towards the churches.
The church bells clanged overhead, and their note was new ;
they seemed to have shed the peaceful music of last Sunday and
to have borrowed a strange urgency.   For old time's sake we
were walking along the Kensington and Earls Court Roads, and
we saw a congregation streaming into St. Mary Abbots Church
and a long, patient queue waiting outside the church which
used to be the pro-cathedral of the Catholics.   We both felt a
desire to go with these worshippers into their hushed and comforting aisles ; but we could not, because we were sinners.

In Soldan Road we came upon a Drill Hall where a throng
of young men, some in mufti, some in khaki, were coming and
going through the wide-open doors.   Inside, near the doors, we
saw a heavy sergeant, with a pair of South African ribbons and
a moustache like a South African assegai, seated at a trestle
table with a corporal clerk at his side and a posse of young men
before him.   The Territorials were embodying, and their feet
and voices echoed in the large bare hall.

In the afternoon we sat in the park again ; and to-day the
voices and the feet and the rumble of wheels were many times
multiplied because of the coming Bank Holiday.   Innumerable
families were spread about the grass before us, the men with
coats off and shirts undone.   The lovers lay beneath the trees
and among the drifts of yellow leaves which had died too soon.
I don't know how it was, this being both Sunday and a special
holiday, but a man was hosing a flower-bed of purple and white
petunias and its sister bed of salmon-red and lemon-yellow
dahlias.   The children ran with a shrill clamour into the edges
of his spray, and sometimes for fun he swung this splendid and
glistening parabola towards them, whereupon they screamed in
rapture and alarm.

And a great question was over them all—these people of
England who had not known a world war for a hundred years.

We all talked to each other without ceremony.   The man
nearest to you, whether working man or well-dressed gentleman,

was your brother of England and interested in your news and views. Rumours passed from lip to lip, and from chair to chair. The Germans were invading France ; they had reached the capital of Luxemburg ; five nations were at war now, Austria, Serbia, Russia, Germany and France ; the Germans were demanding a right of way through Belgium, and you know what that was for : to get to the channel ports and attempt an invasion of England.

France, Luxemburg, Belgium : as I sat in the evening sunlight—the sky above me a bowl of blue just stained with milky cloudlets and brightening down from zenith to horizon in an ever-increasing glow—I had a vision of those drilled, blue-grey, helmeted armies, in battle line extended to a width of a hundred miles, coming over the fields and getting nearer England.

As I thought of this I felt, like a great pressure in my heart, another love than my love for Gentle. It was that love of England which had sprung up in me one morning in the Magdalen water-meadows, and again on a beech-crowned hill-top the following day, when I sat with Gentle among the fallen leaves, and England's kind and homely landscape lay spread beneath our feet.

We talked of this love this evening, as we had on the hill-top, and Gentle allowed enthusiastically that it was in her too ; but I suspected from the nature of her words, dutiful rather than deeply felt, that it was less strong in her than in me. Perhaps it is never as strong in a woman whose world is so much smaller than a man's.

While we were talking a report like a cannon shook the southern sky. We never learned what it was—perhaps a grenade mishandled in some armoury where young men were arming, so that before its echoes had rolled away the first English dead lay stretched upon the ground—but it sounded like the single gun which in some cities proclaims the hour of twelve and the end of the forenoon ; or like the maroon which in later days was to command a two-minutes' silence in memory of the dead.

Certainly it commanded a silence of some seconds in the park that evening. Gentle's hand shot into mine and closed upon it, in a sudden terror. But almost at once the silence was obliterated by loud laughs, shouted jests, and the shrill mimicries of children. A humorist somewhere behind me yelled, ' Christ, they've come ! '

§

On the Monday night we walked along Whitehall, since it was the street of Government and Britain's G.H.Q., to see what might be happening there. A full moon blanched the sky above the street's long canyon and paled the stars. Nearly every window, in the Admiralty, War Office, and Treasury, was an oblong of light, and many of them were open in the heavy warmth, so that in the lower rooms we were able to see men in shirtsleeves hammering on typewriters or moving about with documents in their hands. It was the eve of the Ultimatum, and no doubt they would continue working till late in the night. As we drew near Parliament Street we saw the people in front of us running towards Bridge Street and New Palace Yard. Suddenly excited, we ran too, hand in hand, and reaching the corner, saw what was drawing them.

An infantry battalion was turning out of Broad Sanctuary to march over Westminster Bridge. They were marching at ease and rather slowly, with rifles slung, caps pushed back, and collars open ; because their officers had been merciful to them in a heat which damped their uniforms with sweat under their loaded equipment. Was it Waterloo Station to which they were going—but how could that be, since their horses clattered and clinked with them, the colonel and adjutant riding ahead, and the company commanders in front of their companies, and a baggage train following behind. These were the horses and hooves of the old war, Roberta, very different from the rattle and clatter of mechanized vehicles which you were to hear. The Houses of Parliament watched and listened in the moon-light as they passed over the bridge, singing rather wearily a ribald version of *John Brown's Body* :

> John Brown's baby's got a pimple on his *'mmm.* . . .
>   But his soul goes marching on.
> Glory, glory, Hallelujah. . . .

Men watching the procession shouted out encouraging words : the women kept silence, but paid their tribute with tear-glistening eyes and twitching mouths.
    ' Take care of yourselves.'
    ' Give 'em hell if they try to come 'ere.'
    ' Come back safe and sound, lads.'
    ' God bless yer.'
    ' Good luck, good luck.'
    ' Keep smiling.'

I felt Gentle's hand shivering in mine and knew that her body was taut with unshed tears.

As their feet and jingling harness dwindled into the darkness on the far side of the river, we turned and walked home silently. And both of us knew that in this hour of the exaltation of the nations the pressure of that other love was strong indeed ; but I at least would not listen to what it was saying. Oh no—no— it was too hard a saying : who could bear it ? I shut my ears to it, and tried to think of other things.

In our room at the hotel, a large front room, Gentle sat her-self on the bed and, drawing her feet under her, sank her head in thought. I could see her in the mirror of the dressing table before which I was undoing my tie. I can see her still, and the room around her. Nothing had been altered in that room for twenty years : neither its corpulent walnut suite nor its curtains of faded red rep, nor its antimacassars over the red-plush elbow chairs ; we might have beeen moving in a room of our childhood.

Gentle lifted her head and began, ' Darling.'

' Yes, sweet ? '

' There *is* going to be war, is there ? '

' I'm afraid so. England's bound to declare war. And I think I want her to now. I don't want her to fail.'

' Well then, listen, my treasure, my angel : we must go back.'

' No ! ' I swung round, and her eyes met mine.

' You must go back to Iris and little Hugh.'

' I'm *not* going back. I'm never leaving you again.'

' Yes, you are, my darling. You know I'm right. Iris is good to you—oh, I wish she'd been beastly to you ! But obvi-ously you must be with them now, when God alone knows what's going to happen. And I must go and look after Max and help him pack. I can't just let him do everything alone and go off to the war and p'raps be killed. Besides, I hurt him very cruelly, and I owe him something.'

' You mean you'd live with him again ? '

' Only for a little while, and not as his wife. I promise you that. Just as Iris does with you, trying to be good to you.'

' No, Gentle, heart——' I stuttered, but had no more words.

' And you won't give yourself to—yes, you will if she wants you to. Yes, of course you will. I want you to. Remember I—I said that.'

' My darling——' I began to protest.

' Dearest, it's no use. I can't see poor Max doing everything in that house alone. Someone must help the poor sweet pack, and look after the clothes he leaves behind, and shut up the house after he's gone.'

' There's his foul old mother.'

' Will she be there ? She has her own home to look after.'

' You're not going back. What d'you mean : " going back " ? D'you mean we never see each other again ? '

' Yes, as far as I can see, it means that.' And she fixed her sad eyes on mine. ' We must do it properly.'

' Well, we aren't going to do it, and it's not going to happen —do you hear me ? I won't have it.'

' I hear you.' She pulled the pins from her hair and let it fall ; then shook and tossed her head to throw the amber mass behind her neck. And when it rested down her back she smiled at me. ' I heard you, and, oh my dear, it sounded so like Max when he starts to bully. Gosh, I do think people are awful, the way they bully people. Don't make it more difficult for me, darling heart. It's rather like death, as it is.'

' You mean you're going back to that place where they've all been swines to you ? '

' I've got to. I'm terribly frightened at the idea, but I must go through with it. They'll all stare in the streets, and how in the name of Mercy I'm going to face the servants on the door-step I don't know. And his mother if she's there. She's dire.'

I sat at her side, drew her head on to my shoulder, and rested my hand on her hair—then played with it. ' Darling, if I've known anything in these last few days, when I've had you in my arms, it is that we're bound up together for ever. That's a bigger fact than anything else, and I want to be loyal to it, in spite of all the wars under the sun.'

She rested a hand on my thigh and stroked it as if indeed it were a part of herself. ' I think I feel something like that too, but one must follow the only truth one can see.'

' Why can't you go and look after him and come back to me ? '

' Because there's still Iris and Hugh. Oh, you know you can see it really.'

I could see it, of course, and the more I saw it, the more I strove not to, the more I searched for excuses. ' I wanted to complete something. I wanted to make a perfect whole of our life together. We're incomplete without each other ; that's something all the gods can see.'

' Yes . . . and no. Oh, don't look so sad, my precious— no, don't—I can't look at you without wanting to cry. My precious, my own sweet, I'm not half as clever as you——'

' And that's rubbish.'

' —but I've learned a lot from you and all the marvellous

books you've published, and—am I being a fool ?—but it seemed
to come to me, when I saw all those men marching to Heaven-
knows-what, and singing so quietly as they went to it, that no
one's incomplete who's ready to sacrifice himself for others.
Isn't that so ?   Wouldn't you say that ? '

Probably it was this fine sentence that conquered me, who,
like so many others, had a heart cast for such appeals though
with only a feeble will to follow them.   But I would not admit
the conquest, and, rising almost sulkily, went to the open window,
pulled up the blind and looked out.

London was very quiet beneath the lulling warmth.   The
quiet seemed to heighten the scintillation of the stars.   Stars
and lamps were like gems and golden beads on a blue velvet
cloth flood-lit by the moon.   I could hear no voices : only the
patter of horses, the pounding of lorries, and the low bassooning
of distant cars.   It was not yet the carnival night ;   only its
vigil;   and the many who need not make decisions had
gone home, like us, to bed.   To-morrow we would bring in the
war with shouting and crowding and jubilee.

' How extraordinarily quiet it is.   What is the time ? '

' Long past midnight.'

' Is it ? . . . ' said I despairingly.   ' Well, I'm tired, terribly
tired.   Let's sleep.'

Gentle came and, turning me towards her with encircling
arms, pressed her cheek against mine.   ' We've both had something in these last few days, and it's been terribly wonderful.
How far it was wrong I shall never know ;   but I know it's made
me feel I want to be good again.   You've done that, darling.
I suppose it's just that I've had what I wanted and don't feel
rebellious any more.   Tell me : would it have been like this,
would we have loved like this, if we'd come together at first—
or if we stayed together now : *I* don't know.'

' We should have quarrelled, of course.   I can be a beast
sometimes.'

' And I too.   I was thinking only yesterday that there was
nothing really very nice about me.'

' Then you were thinking nonsense.   You've hardly any
faults worth speaking of.'

' Of course I have : tons.   Oh, please be good and help me,
instead of being difficult.'   She led me back to the bed, gathered
both my hands in both of hers, and smiled at me through tears.
' Your task's going to be easy compared with mine.   I've got
to go back to a place where I'm looked upon—I really *am*, my
dear—I'm looked upon as a Hussy !   And it's going to be more
difficult than ever now that I've created a new sensation by

running away. It's going to be too awful, creeping back like a girl who's sorry she's been naughty and is going to be good in future. The very thought of it—oh dear, oh dear, be still, my stomach !—how am I going to survive it ? But I will, I will.'

' And where will you go, after you've seen your dear husband off to the wars ? '

' Oh, I don't know. I shall run away somewhere. I am Disgraced for Ever and must find somewhere to hide.'

' That's ridiculous. The war will have swept away all memory of that.'

' Will it ? Oh, well, that's nice of it.'

I looked down upon her, thinking I must lose all sight of her soon, and in desperation asked, ' Oh, why didn't you marry me ; why did you go and marry him ? '

' Why ever did I ? I no longer know. Does anyone know at thirty-two why they did something at twenty ? Do *you* know why you didn't marry me ? '

' No,' I said ; for she was right : I no longer knew. ' Because I was mad—mad. Oh beloved, if by any chance there's no war, will you stay with me ? '

She didn't answer at once ; then shook her head. ' In that case I shouldn't go back to Max—but, oh dear, oh dear, there'd still be Iris and poor little Hugh. No, I'm not as bad as that, my precious. And, anyway, why ask that question ? There's going to be war, and you must go back to them.'

So she pronounced her judgment, and the only possible sentence. And I could nothing but accept it. One day more perhaps, and then good-bye again. We both knew her words were just and incommutable, and, having consented to them, we clung together all that night.

§

Jubilee in the streets. All roads led to Buckingham Palace. West London, in the hot summer night, was a catchment area draining its people into the great ornamental reservoir before the palace—yes, and even into the actual water-basins of its Queen Victoria Memorial, where the more enterprising spirits paddled and clambered to get a better view of the royal windows. The people were pouring towards the palace along the Mall, down Constitution Hill, along Buckingham Palace Road and over the grass and the geranium beds from Birdcage Walk. They had learned this evening that Britain had sent an

ultimatum to Germany in the name of four hundred million people,
promising war at midnight unless she halted the armies which
had crossed the Belgian frontier. And now that it was approaching midnight, and no answer had come, nor would come, London,
the capital of Britain, and still in those days the capital of the
world, was hurrying to salute the King, just as if this were the
hour of his coronation.

Those who did not care to leave their houses, and those who
could not, stood watching the broken streams of people : the
masters and mistresses on their balconies or at their brightly
lit windows ; the parlour maids and cooks and under-butlers
at the tops of their area steps, exchanging quips with unknown
passers-by. ' Get a move on, or you'll be late.' ' Keep moving
now ; keep moving.' Passengers stood on the tops of the
labouring and frustrated buses to see the excitement ; public
houses emptied their patrons on to the pavements where they
raised their glasses, and their voices, to any who would look their
way. ' Cheerioh, mate—here's to it, miss. Don't know where
you're going, but hope it keeps fine for you.' ' So long, chum :
won't detain you if you're pushed for time.' ' Come and tell us
what there is to see.' ' Don't overstrain yourself, cock ; the
Germans aren't here yet.'

Bowler hats, straw hats, felt hats, opera hats, women's hats,
women's uncovered coiffures (just out of the theatre) went bob-
bing along the Mall, that Jubilee road, between its grave plane
trees and lofty lamps ; and among them were my brown trilby
and Gentle's wide-brimmed brown straw. For the present a
great swelling of pride in my country was forcing aside all thought
of our parting to-morrow. Now and then that memory got close
to my heart, but always in the company of another which helped
me a little to bear it : war was upon us, no longer an ' if ' but a
' yes ' ; and that house in Queensberry Place was pulling,
pulling me . . . calling me. Gentle seemed to know when I
was thinking this ; I felt the knowledge in her fingers which were
lightly playing with and pressing mine.

In the space before the palace we found the people as closely
packed as grass blades on a lawn. The Victoria Memorial
towered up from the midst of them : proud monument to an
age that was passing that night. We no sooner reached this
dense multitude than we were fused with it by a press of people
behind. I had to keep an arm about Gentle lest she were forced
away.

From the surface of this sea of heads a din of voices drove
towards the front of the palace like a wind—a cheering and
singing and cat-calling, and a shouting in unison of ' *We want*

the King. We want the King.' It must have been about eleven
o'clock when, to a great roar a window opened between the
Corinthian columns of the façade, and the King, the Queen,
and the Prince of Wales stepped on to the balcony.   Instantly
that dark acre of hats and heads became a field of waving hands
and handkerchiefs, and of straw hats ablow on the tops of sticks ;
as if a crop of market flowers should spring up at a breath.   And
the voices rose, too, gathering in volume till they were one great
unanimous song :

> Send him victorious,
> Happy and glorious,
> Long to reign over us,
>   God save the King. . . .

He raised his hand in greeting, and the Queen after waving
her handkerchief, touched with it the side of her eye.

> For he's a jolly good fellow . . .

They stood there, hearing this song through, to its last great
final cheer ;   then turned with a last salute into their home.
The crowd loosened, many having scuttled off to Piccadilly
Circus, that other and more frivolous heart of the British world.
But it was still a vast, eddying throng before the palace, a multitude whose sense of fitness seemed to be telling that that this was
the only place to hear, in all their terrible significance, the chimes
at midnight.   There was some question among the wise and
knowing as to whether, because of the difference in Central
Europe's time, the Ultimatum would expire, and the State of
War be with us, at eleven, twelve or one.   But for the great,
unthinking majority our English midnight was the hour.
    Gentle and I hung about with the others here, because we,
least of all, were feeling frivolous, even though the infectious
excitement was holding our darkest thought at bay.
    Someone was singing : a man's voice as strong and beautiful
in the night as some gondolier's beneath the Venetian sky ; and
we hurried along with others towards it, glad of something to fill
our minds and shut out the dark memory.   On the east base of
the Memorial, under the very eyes of Queen Victoria herself
(who appeared to be turning her face away) a short, rounded
tub of a man had climbed on to the pedestal of one of her groups
of statuary—a gigantic bronze female figure stepping bravely
forward with a lion for companion—and with his right hand in
a trouser pocket and his left on the lion's mane was throwing
back his head and singing with all the pride and power of his

lungs, while a crowd listened in silence, so fine his voice, so apt his words :

> If the Dons sight Devon, I'll quit the port o' Heaven
> And drum them up the Channel as we drummed them long ago.

A roar of cheers greeted his last note, and the little man, obviously a professional and delighted both to display his voice and to give it free to-night in his country's service, burst again into :

> Here's a health unto His Majesty,
> With a fa-la-la, lalla-la-la.

Of what was I thinking as I gazed at him, perched up there, his swaying head just level with the huge bronze lady's navel, and his right hand ' conducting ' himself in his fa-la-la, lalla-la-la ? What was coming back to me out of the dying past ? Gotley—little Felix Gotley whom I'd loved—standing on a bed in the dormitory at Draycote and singing to his grinning school-fellows. The boys that night had joined him in his ' folderolol,' and now all this company was singing softly, falteringly, because not sure of the words :

> And he that will not drink this health
> I wish him neither wit nor wealth,
> Nor yet a rope to hang himself,
> With a fa-la-la, lalla-la-la.

Another voice—somewhere under the plane trees behind us— a very different voice, high-pitched, hoarse, sometimes even screaming—drew us and others away from the singer ; and we came upon an enormous negro, almost as big and quite as metal-black as the bronze statues about the Memorial, who was standing upon a seat under the ranked plane trees and haranguing a large and increasing crowd. Sweat moved down his shining brow like damp condensing on the ebony newel of a stair-rail. The whites of his eyes shone yellow as he swung them to left and right over the upturned faces of his listeners.

' Yes, ma white friends,' he was hoarsely screeching as Gentle and I added ourselves to his swelling congregation, ' dat is so— never mind if it's only poor black man who says it ; de good Lord can sho' use de black man for his mighty purposes as well as de white folks ; and let me tell you dis, brudders : way back in ma African home de dear Lord Jesus is a black man like me——'

' Aw, stow it, mate,' interrupted a mocker on the fringe of the crowd. ' Jesus Christ wasn't no darky.'

' Nah ! ' called another. ' He was a yid.'

' Yes, sah! ' reaffirmed the negro, a light lather forming at his pale lips, ' for me and ma people He's a black man with thick

lips and white teeth and fuzzy hair like dis yere ; an' why?
' Cause He's ma brudder as well as yours. And fo' ma little
brudders and sisters in China he's a little yellah man—yes, sah !
—an' very small like dem with long, narra' eyes——'

' And a pig-tail, chum ? '

' Yeah ! Oh, yeah : a pig-tail too, if it brings Him nearer
dem. He's Son o' Man, ain't He, not only Son o' White Man
but Son o' Black Man and Son o' Yellah Man too ; an' Ah tell
you dis : when Ah kneel and look up to de Throne o' Grace
it's a big coal-black nigger Ah see settin' on de right han' o' God
de Fah'der Awmighty ; and it's a poor crucified darky that'll
sho' come one day to judge de world. And it's dat same darky
as is settin' 'ere right now in dis poor simple black man's heart
and tellin' me to say dis to you—as sho' as God's in His Heaven,
He's *shoutin'* to me to say to you, " Listen poor white folks, mebbe
dis is His hour . . . !" You laff—you grin at poor black man,
but mebbe it is. You know not at what hour de Son o' Man
cometh ; de day of de Lord cometh as a thief in de night ; and
mebbe He's comin' now—right now——'

' Crikey ! '

' 'Ere, 'ere.'

' *Somet'in's* comin', how'ebber much you mock like dem dat
mocked at His resurrection ; *some'tin's* comin' ; and comin'
tonight. If it's not de Lord in His power, it's His judgment on
us all. Comin' for sho'. Comin' in a few minutes. Be ready
fo' de stroke o' midnight, my brudders and sisters in Jesus. It
was at midnight dat de cry went up, " Behold de Bridegroom
cometh." He's comin' ! He's comin' ! Ah tell you——'

' " I'm coming, I'm coming," ', sang the mockers, ' " for my
head is bending low——" '

' Aye, you look up at me and don't believe, and laff, but He's
comin' in one form or anudder—comin' wid' a great judgment
on de nations of de world, and if your lamps ain't alight, where
are you ? '

' In the dark, mate.'

' That's right. In the bleedin' dark, Rosebud.'

' Dat's so : in de darkness of your sins. Den make haste, poor
chillun ; remember what de Book says : ' Stablish your hearts,
for de comin' of de Lord draweth nigh when de wicked shall be
turned into hell——'

' Christ ! I must go back and pack me bag.'

' ——and all de nations dat forget God——'

' That's right : the bleedin' Germans. They got it coming.'

' ——but, oh ma dears, Ah tell you now, before it's too late,
de good Lord knoweth how to deliver de godly outa' temptation

and to reserve de unjust unto de day o' judgment. If you wanna flee from de wrath to come, dare's only one way, and de dear Lord Jesus is callin' to you—callin' to you outa' His seat in dis poor black man's heart—and sayin' " Ah am de Way. No man cometh to de Fah'der but bah Me. Repent—repent while dare's yet time and be converted dat yo' sins may be blotted out, 'cause except ye repent ye shall all likewise perish. Believe on de Lord Jesus Christ, and cleave unto Him, and thou shalt be saved, thou and thy House." Hallelujah ! '

' 'Ere, 'ere ! '

' Jesus. Jesus.' He screamed the name, and the spittle shot from his mouth. ' Dare is none udder name under Heaven whereby we must be saved. Whoso despiseth dis Word shall be destroyed——'

Gentle pulled at my arm. ' Come away. He's mad.' And we left this poor black Baptist and Forerunner, left him there, God-inspired, apocalyptic, a voice in the night. Faintly— ever more faintly—we heard him shouting, as we strolled back to the crowds before the palace, ' Watch—watch and pray, ma dears, dat ye may be counted worthy to escape all dese tings dat shall come to pass and to stand before de Son o' Man. All we like sheep have gone astray——'

' It's a strange form of madness,' said Gentle. ' I can never understand how people get like that. . . . What are you thinking of ? Why don't you answer ? '

' He may or may not be mad,' I said. ' He's certainly very naïve, with a mind like the mind of a six-year-old child. But all he says happens to be true.'

' True ? '

' Yes.'

' Doric, what do you mean ? '

' If by "de Lord Jesus" you choose to understand, not the individual man, but rather the best of our human vision, the vision of all the wisest who've ever lived—which has practically always been the same, and could well be called the Christ principle—then I say he's just about right : there *is* no other name whereby we may be saved. And he couldn't have chosen a better moment to say it.'

So I said to Gentle, trying to be clever perhaps, as we tarried, hand in hand, among the waiting people ; but it seems to me now, after the last eight years, with their second and more fright-ful war and all the sickening vengeances and inhumanities that have followed it, that my words were even truer than I knew. That old vision, or mankind faints and falls in its march.

Gentle, pleating her brow in an effort to understand, said at last that she saw what I meant ; and then dropped into silence ; and I know she was considering its heavy indorsement of our task to-morrow, because I was considering it too.

The crowd was now becoming a great crush again, as the time drew near to midnight.   They were waiting for the clocks to strike as they wait on the last day of the old year for the new year to come in.   They fell quiet as the hands of their watches entered upon the last minute, lest they missed the chimes over London. And now the clocks struck, and the loudest chime came from the tower of the Houses of Parliament, over the trees of St. James's Park.   Those heavy, dominant, palpitating notes, if I feel the pulse of History aright, were the most signal chime it ever played ; and it will hardly play another quite like it, unless it is still standing when a new era comes in with an upward change in the nature of Man.

The multitude greeted the booming notes with a great cheer ; then broke, one and all, into *Rule Britannia*.   I remember still the unbearable appeal of the young girls' voices and the young men's, singing beneath the bright lamps to welcome their tragedy. Where are they now, those young men ?   *Où sont-ils, Vierge souveraine. . . . Où est le preux Charlemagne ?*   Men like our fat friend on the statue's pedestal led them in song after song : some relevant and irrelevant, jocular songs and serious songs.   ' In the shade of the old apple tree . . . '   ' Who were you with last night, Out in the pale moonlight . . . '   ' Yo-ho, little girls, yo-ho . . . '   The jocular songs clashed with hymns which were being sung in another part of the crowd.   ' Come on and hear, come on and hear Alexander's rag-time band . . .   I fear no foe with Thee at hand to bless . . .   Steadily, shoulder to shoulder, Steadily blade by blade . . .   Our shelter from the stormy blast, and our eternal home.'

' Hurray !   Hurray !   Hurray ! '

§

In the clean August morning we walked to the station through the park.   Drive there we could not, because the cab would have gone too quickly ; so I sent Gentle's bag and coats by a messenger, and we set out on this last walk, unencumbered.   We entered the park in the wake of a column of soldiers which was also heading for the station, and for much of our way we walked with them, they on the camber of the road, we on the path under the trees.   At first our pace was quicker than theirs so that we came abreast of the middle of the column ; then for a time the

tramp of their boots kept us in step with them. Gentle was putting
out a brave show of gaiety, hanging on my arm with both hands
and swinging her stride with mine. One of my palms lay upon
her clasped fingers and patted them ; and to the soldiers, who
were interested we must have looked like two lovers on holiday
in the first days of their love.

They called out ''Oi's' and 'What ho's' to Gentle, and
'Hallo, Gorgeous.' The word 'gorgeous' pierced me like an
arrow, as I thought that her beauty was to be no longer mine ;
and at the same time I felt a pride that I had possessed it to the
uttermost for eleven days of my life.

One man called out, ' 'Morning, miss. How're you to-day ? '
and another, somewhere behind, commented loudly, ' How'd
you like that for supper ? '   A dozen or so answered him, ' Not
'alf ! ' and I inquired of Gentle, trying to be merry, if men were
in the habit of calling out to her as she went by. With a little
skip of pretended pleasure she answered, ' Oh, yes, often.'

' Good gracious ! ' I protested, pretending to be shocked.

' But they only do it when I'm alone, as a rule ; not when
I'm handsomely protected like this.'

' Well, blast their impudence ! And what do you do ? '

' Oh, blush and walk on and pretend I haven't heard anything.'

' Isn't it rather embarrassing ? '

' Yes, I suppose so ; but I shouldn't like it if they didn't.'

Again I made a show of being shocked. ' My *God* ! '

' It'll be awful when they stop. And they will soon. All too
soon. Heighho, I'm getting old.'

Silence for a few seconds. Silence was dogging us like an
invisible companion ; I must not let him step in between us ;
so, looking at the soldiers marching to their war stations, as we
to ours, I suggested ' This old war's like the Pied Piper ; it's
drawing all the world after its miserable pipe ; ' and she,
squeezing my arm in appreciation, exclaimed, ' Gosh, I'm witty,
but I should never have thought of that.' Then, speaking of
any subjects but the parting which was so close, I talked of my
publishing ideas and achievements, bragging a little of those
which had succeeded ; and she said, ' Oh, I'm so glad ! ' and
when, self-pityingly, I asserted that the war would kill them all,
she said, ' Oh, no, it mustn't ; it just mustn't.'

' Well,' said I, ' even if it doesn't mean my bankruptcy, it
means the bankruptcy of all the ideas that I wanted to propagate.
It's nothing less than that ; ' and she thought awhile and,
squeezing my arm, said, ' I don't think so. It just means there
never was a time when it was so necessary to keep them alive '—

a sentence which was to stay with me and help me in the next days.

I dared not speak of Iris, but I told many a comic story of Hugh as we walked along, and always she exclaimed, ' The pet ! ' and ' Bless him ! ' and squeezed the arm a little as if to show her pleasure that I'd got such a child.

Grosvenor Place ; and Victoria Station there at the bottom of it. I should have liked to slow my step, but somehow one had to keep pace with the soldiers, and we did so, walking under the wall of the King's garden, and speculating on what must be happening in the Palace this morning. The soldiers were held up by the traffic at Lower Grosvenor Place, and we went on without them. A sigh escaped me as we entered the station yard, and, rather than go too quickly into the station itself, I made her wait to see the soldiers come in. They came, singing and cheering and jeering, and passed under the arch into the South Eastern and Chatham side ; when the last of them was gone we turned and went into the Brighton and South Coast station.

Here the circulating area was full of other soldiers, in ranks or in broken formation, their equipment on their backs, their rifles slung, their kit bags at their feet. Women stood about, waiting and watching them and smiling bravely when their own men caught their eyes. Beneath the wide leap of the roof a hundred imprisoned noises jostled among themselves : voices, hurrying feet, drumming wheels, colliding buffers, and the fussy whistling or sudden quick snores of engines anxious to be gone. This vast, impersonal din, stertorous, strident, continual, seemed like the War itself just arrived at our great main station and busy already upon its trade with us all.

' Right. March ! '

Even as we glanced at the noisy scene an officer shouted this order, and a platoon of soldiers marched away towards a waiting train, while some women, two of whom were leading children by the hand, threaded through the crowding civilians to keep near to them.

The indicator showed that a train was leaving for Holm St. Martin in twelve minutes, and our eyes, swinging to platform fifteen, saw its long coaches standing there.

Best not delay. Let the axe fall. We did not say this but, silently thinking it, passed through the barrier and secured for her a window seat ; after which I found her baggage and stowed it on the rack above.

Thank God, only eight minutes more. I don't know what we talked about in seven of those minutes, but when the last of them had us in its power, and passengers were shutting their doors, we held each other very tightly, and I begged of her, ' Don't tremble so. Oh, what can I do for you ? '

She looked up and tried to smile encouragingly. ' Only go on loving me. It won't be wrong to feel you're loving me, if I keep away from you, will it ? Can I feel I belong to you somehow—would that be very wrong ? '

' Whether you feel it or not, whether it's right or wrong, it's true.'

' Bless you, oh bless you.'

' May I not see you sometimes ? '

' No.' The bravery in that crowded and clamouring station, under its arched and echoing roof, strengthened her to shake her head and say no, even as she drew me yet tighter to her breast so that I shouldn't suffer too much. ' I want you to love me, and it wouldn't be fair to let you love me and see me. I'm going to behave properly after to-day.'

' But can't I write ? '

' No, my dream. No, please not. Let's be fair.'

' All right, darling, if that's what you—but oh, Gentle, don't tremble like that ! I can't stand it.' The engine had just whistled, and the coaches had clanged together and faltered and stopped. ' Are you afraid ? '

' I'm a little afraid of Holm St. Martin, but I must conquer it. And I'm a little afraid of the future . . . no, I shall be all right ; I'm going to be fine. Don't trouble about me. I want you to be happy. And I want Iris to be happy.'

' I love you.'

' That's all that matters. I shall be all right as long as I remember that.'

' Oh, my heart, my life, why did we lose each other ? '

' I must go, dear. Bless you always. Be good to Iris.'

' No, don't go.'

' Good-bye, my sweet.'

' *Gentle, my beloved !* '

But she was in the compartment now because the train was moving ; and as it drew out she made her lips smile at me through her corner window, whatever her eyes were doing. She did not lean out and wave, and I could only watch the train curving away till it was out of sight.

So be it. I turned and walked towards the area where the soldiers were now lifting their kit-bags on to their shoulders or under their arm-pits, ready to entrain. Good-bye, lads ; good luck ; keep safe if you can. And keep smiling. It's war, and we must all leave our little lives behind us, I suppose, and lose ourselves in some larger history.

BOOK VI

THE LARGER HISTORY

CHAPTER I

'CREEP HOME and take your place there.' How father used to love to spout the little poem to us children, his right hand conducting his performance like the fat man on the statue's pedestal, and his voice falling and lifting as he gave full expression to their pathos. Usually he quoted them with reference to his great age, for he was then in his fifties. 'When all the world is old, lad, and all the trees are brown . . . Creep home and take your place there. . . .' And how they ran in my head, these last words, as I crept home to Queensberry Place that evening, guilty and afraid of my reception. I had telephoned from the office that I would be back in the evening, and I was walking home—walking all the way, both because it was easier to walk with an anxiety than to sit in a train with it, and because I wanted to postpone the painful meeting with Iris and with Father.

The streets wore a strange face that August evening. People stood about in clusters, as if they'd come out in search of company. If a figure went by in khaki they stopped their parleys to look at him ; if a grey army vehicle rattled between the buses they stared at it till it was out of sight. The closed banks and some closed shops contrasted oddly with the provision stores which seemed to be filled with women buying tinned foods in a sudden fear of famine. The news-bills of the paper boys shouted at us from their street corners, 'Government Taking Over the Railways,' and 'Turkey Joins Germany.' One said simply, 'England Expects. . . .'

As I nervously opened my front door I heard our servants exchanging loud chatter in their basement parts, and I wondered if they knew why the master'd been away. Father's cough came down the stairs from the little Indian Room ; which was curious, for as a rule he never sat in that room, leaving it and its two easy chairs to Iris and me.

'Anyone at home ? ' I tried to shout the words gaily, but

at my voice the house went silent, as if Death had entered, or
an evil enchantment struck it like the palace of the Sleeping
Beauty. The servants stopped all talk, and I knew that they
knew.

'Daddy!' Hugh was the only one whom the enchantment
could not touch. He came racing down the stairs to me, just
as I used to run to Father. 'Hallo, Daddy. I've got a farm.'

'Where's your mother?'

'Upstairs with Grandad. Come and see my farm. It's a
bigger one than Robbie's; it's the biggest you've ever seen.'

'Is it now? Well, that's fine.' I kissed him, and walked up
behind his impatient feet, my heart trembling, my throat
gulping.

In the room, seated in the two easy chairs, were Iris and
Father; Father with his spectacles on his nose and my old
school atlas on his knees, open at a 'physical' map of the
Low Countries; Iris sewing, her face very pale; and my
sharpened eyes saw that she was mending a shirt of mine whose
cuffs had frayed. Hugh had a huge toy farm, with its animals
and trees spread about the carpet.

Irish looked up with sad eyes and said nothing. Father, to
help us all, made an effort at naturalness. 'Hallo, Doric, old
man. Here—this is your chair.'

'No, that's all right, Father. You keep it.'

'Well, I shall be going in a minute in any case. I was just
sitting with Iris. . . . Well. . . .' He hesitated, embarrassed.
'What do you think of it all? War. Really war.'

'I don't know what to think. It's too big. Can we win it?'

'We've got to. *Nom de Dieu*, we've got to! In the name of
God why didn't this happen ten years ago? I was only seventy
then, and could have said I was fifty-five.'

'You'll have to leave it to us now.'

'You?' He looked startled. 'Don't be absurd. You're
thirty-two. The recruiting ages are from eighteen to thirty,
aren't they? You're out of it.'

'I'm twenty-nine exactly.'

'And that's a lie. You must never tell lies.'

'Where've you been, Daddy? Mummy said she didn't know
if you were ever coming back.'

'I did *not*, Hugh.' Iris denied it with emphasis; her first
words.

'Yes, you did. You said, I don't know if Daddy's ever coming
back; you said it when you was angry.' Now I knew why
the kitchen knew; Hugh had carried this prattle down the
basement stairs. 'Are you going to stay with us, Daddy?'

' Of course he's going to stay with you,' said Father. ' Don't worry him now. He wants to talk to your mother.'

' Look what Grandad's given me. It's a farm. Robbie says it must'a cost pounds.'

' It's a marvellous farm, darling. What are *you* doing, Father ? Studying geography ? '

' I'm deciding where we can stop the brutes. If only we can contain them along the Belgian frontier, while the Russians come up behind. . . . They've got to carry Liége and Namur, which are mighty fortresses, especially Namur, and if they reduce Liége and Namur they've got to force the Sambre, and then there's still Lille and Maubeuge. It's going to be no walk-over.' His thick, barbed eyebrows sank beneath the rims of his spectacles as he bent his eyes on the cheap little map. A soldier and a general officer, he was proud of his strategic knowledge and pleased to display it. ' After Lille I can see nothing but the heights of the Pas de Calais, but we can't stand there and leave them to sit in Dunkerque and Calais. Not in a thousand years ! We shall have to hold them on the flats. What the French are doing, mucking about in Alsace and Lorraine, when every man'll be wanted up here, I don't know, though it warms the heart to think of them entering those lost provinces which they've mourned for forty years. The French will leap to arms at the words " Alsace and Lorraine." ' Then he remembered Iris and me and shut the atlas smartly. ' But it's impossible to settle to anything. I'm going for a stroll in the sun. Mr. Hugh, did you hear that ? I'm going for a stroll, and nobody need come with me who'd rather not. But I seem to recollect there's a certain excellent sweet-shop in the Old Brompton Road where one can buy certain confections : and even, I conceive, an ice. But nobody need come who's not interested.'

Hugh had jumped up from his farm. ' Can I come, can I come ? '

' You must ask your kind mother. You must never do anything against the wishes of your kind mother. Always remember that.'

' Of course he can go,' said Iris, ' but don't make him ill.'

' You hear that, Mr. Hugh ? You can come if you like. But you don't really want to take a walk with a tedious old grandfather. You *do* ? Goodness gracious. Well, run to the excellent Mabel who's so good to you, and ask her to put on your hat. We may see some soldiers going off to the war.'

' One minute, darling.' Iris called back the excited child, brushed the hair from his eyes, and dusted his sailor blouse. ' There, run along, my sweet.'

Oh, how that ' my sweet ' sounded like Gentle.

Father followed the boy, shutting the door very quietly on us both. Iris dropped her eyes on her needle. Still standing there before her, I said only, ' I am sorry.'

' It can't be helped.' She glanced up with her beautiful, pale face. ' One loves where one loves.'

' My dear, I love you, too.'

' One loves only once like that.' She shook her head to herself as she resumed the sewing. I looked down upon her black, parted hair and her lithe, slight, graceful figure, and thought that if ever a young creature deserved something better than a second-best love, it was that Iris Sanctuary whom I'd found in the first ripeness of her youthful beauty, and in a noble home.

' Are you very angry with her ? ' I asked.

She dropped the sewing to her lap. ' I was a little bitter at first—no, I was terribly bitter—but I suppose I've learned something from our long talks together—I remembered you and Mr. Harlen—and I know you're really right : one's happier when one tries to understand and forgive. After I'd conquered my bitterness I thought I would like to help her.'

' She's all right now. She's gone back to him.'

' I'm glad if she's happy again.'

' She told me I must come back to you and Hugh.'

' Did you not want to come back ? '

Even then I couldn't say the words that would deny my love for Gentle, so I avoided a direct answer. ' I want to do what's best. And you ? You want me to come back ? '

' I'm glad for Hugh's sake. It's no time to break up a home.' She picked up the sewing again. ' God knows what's coming to us all.'

I bent and kissed her brow. It was cold, and she did not lift it.

' We must make the best of things,' she said. ' I haven't spoken to anyone about it—not even to your father, though of course he knows.'

' Has he said anything ? '

' Oh, need we go into it all ? '

' Not if you'd rather not, my dear.'

But, remembering that she didn't want to be bitter, she decided to tell me. Plying the needle, she began, ' He was very sweet. He came in here one evening and said, " Do you mind a very old man speaking to you ? " I didn't answer because I guessed what he wanted to speak about ; and he picked up my hand and said, " Keep a brave heart, my little one." ' Iris touched her eyes with the ball of handkerchief that lay on her lap. ' He patted my hand and said, " Try and be good to him. We're all weak, and he is better than many of us." And he said, " Remember we get better as we get older, and Doric's by no means the worst." He—he said he was sure you would come back, and that he'd been out all day trying to find you for me.'

' And what—what did you say ? '

' I couldn't say a word. And he just kissed my hand in his stately way and went out and came back with some flowers. She glanced up from her work for a second. ' Those are they.'

I looked round and saw roses, dahlias and delphiniums on table, chimney-piece and bureau. ' He is a dear,' continued Iris, sewing again, ' and he seemed to think he could help me by bringing presents for Hugh. He's been bringing in something new almost every evening. Perhaps he thought it'd stop the little boy asking where his father was. And he's come here and sat with me every night, always asking first if he'd be in the way. He's just sat there saying nothing, but trying to make me feel, I suppose, that he was at my side.'

I could stand no more of it, and I lifted her up and took her in my arms. For a moment her pride broke, and she cried on my shoulder and, wiping her nose, said, ' Don't let me feel too terribly alone.'

But that was the only time she let a cry escape her. Thereafter her pride and her silence were not less than mine when Gentle jilted me.

After that appeal, ' Don't let me feel too terribly alone,' I got out of the room, for the torment was too much. I went up to my bedroom. It was at the back of the house, and I could hear Father's voice in the small garden below. ' Well thrown, sir. Oh, exceedingly well thrown.' He had returned from the sweet-shop and was playing ball with Hugh, so that Iris and I might have our reconciliation alone. ' Very fine, Mr. Hugh. Now what about this one ? Not quite ? Never mind, it was a shocking throw, a really disreputable throw on my part. Back again, sir, if you please. Oh, I say ! Butter-fingers, General, butter-fingers ! This won't do. He's too skilful for you. His throwing is truly remarkable.' And I could hear Hugh's shrieks as he danced with delight every time his grandfather muffed the ball. For a minute I stood by the bed where, in this house, I slept alone. It was my first night without Gentle ; Iris was here, but she was a sealed tomb to me. Gentle. I fell on my knees by the bed and, with my head on my arms, let the tears have their way.

§

So Iris and I took up our life again and, as the days passed, discussed the excitements of the war and even managed to joke as we used to do. But I could feel that her wound was beyond mending. Those eleven days that I had spent with Gentle marched always with us and, as it were, lay between us like a cold, hard area which could never be crossed. We made the best of things, but it was a sorry business, living with someone who was always hiding a pain behind commonplace talk. This was an unstable compromise, I felt, and it could not last. But what could happen to ease or change it was beyond my sight. I could only wait on events and try meanwhile to smile and joke.

I was not suffering from the loss of Gentle as much as I had foreseen or—if I may put it so—as much as I had hoped. Life is so much wider than love, and it was never more so than now, in these first months of war. My love was temporarily diminished to below its real size, like something seen through war binoculars turned the wrong way round. That 'other love,' the love of England, filling so much of my heart, enabled me to bear the loss of Gentle. I had my memory of those eleven days and my knowledge that she was mine and would never give her body again to Max. And always I nursed an irrational and unjustified hope that I would find her again. Yes, it was bearable ; disappointingly bearable ; and made more so by the business worries which poured in to claim my thoughts.

In these first months the war hit my young firm like a blast from the east. It so shook and lambasted it that I feared for its fall. Was I going to lose both Gentle and the House of Allan Mourne ?

There was an instant drop in all my book sales. Some of the books, not in their first youth, fell dead. Others, and these some of the best books of a fine autumn list, books on which I had built high hopes and spent much money, fell still-born on the market-place. The foremost literary critic of the day, in a literary review, solemnly announced that ' book-lovers must face the situation frankly and realize that, during the next few years, there will be positively no imaginative literature published throughout the Continent of Europe.'

Troubles marched up my narrow stairs, one treading the heels of another. The Shortage family came first ; six tart virgins : shortage of paper, shortage of cloth, of boards, of leather, of labour, and of transport. Then the Rise family, a grasping, greedy crowd : rises in the cost of paper, of printing, of binding,

of wages and working expenses, and of transport. Next came
the Government, a most unwelcome and clumsy visitor, like a
bull in a china shop, or an elephant among those gossamer
threads called Spiritual Values. Books of fine intellectual
quality, and books of real spiritual power, which I had imported
from America I could not clear from the docks, nor could
I import any new ones like them, because the Government,
after the fashion of all governments, had quickly decided that
Culture could well be a first casualty of the war. Then my
staff began to waste away, one by one of the young men going
down those stairs and out of my doorway to a recruiting office
—with my blessing and good wishes and sighs. Then the booksellers, instead of suggesting a lower discount to help me in my
grievous case, demanded a larger one. To meet all these new
costs I might have increased the price of my books, but I feared
to do this lest the few that were selling lay down and died with
the rest.

It was extraordinary, that autumn, to look back upon the
previous spring as a golden age now dead, an age which we had
not appreciated when it was with us, an age of ease, when
production costs were low, and advertising cheap, and a publisher's working expenses not above 20 per cent. of his turnover,
and a six-shilling novel showed a profit on a sale of a thousand
copies.

I had loved my house, which seemed to be growing yearly
in strength and favour, as a painter loves his almost-completed
canvas, or an author his almost completed book, and I can only
liken my feelings now to the wracking and sleepless anxiety of
an artist who fears that his beloved creation, the labour of years,
has been lost or damaged beyond repair. I swore that I would
save my house and all the fine dreams which it had enshrined.
I remembered Gentle's words that last morning, ' There never
was a time when it was so necessary to keep your ideas alive ' ;
I told myself that my duty, my best service to the world in such
an hour, was to fight for my ideals. But——

But after a very few weeks another question lodged in my
mind and loitered there, let me say, with intent to rob my house
of something I deemed indispensable to it—and week after
week I just remanded it in custody, not wishing to hear a word
in its defence. No, I must stay where I was ; I must not go ;
who but myself could save my firm in this sudden squall ; who
but its creator would watch over it and, sacrificing himself,
slave for it night and day ; who else would find the paper and
the labour and the books ; who else would inspire the staff,
persuade the printers, plead with the binders, visit and ingratiate

the booksellers, who else would be animated by sheer parental love to fight for it, and for its chief purpose, at every point ? George Byng would do his best ; he might save it as a commercial concern, but he had never been interested in its more altruistic aims—'quixotic' he called them and 'sentimental'— and these would be the first he would jettison from the aeroplane now that the fuel was low. And I was not going to give them up. I, and I alone, could hold on to them and somehow keep my little firm airborne. But——

'Lord Kitchener Wants *You*' : the eyes of the War Secretary stared at me from every hoarding, and his finger pointed straight at me. 'They want more men' ; a despatch-rider, his motor-cycle halted, looked at me from the post while his arm pointed to a flaming battle-field. 'Surely you will fight for your King and Country.' This poster showed only the king's tired face and the map of England. 'Once more we hear the word That sickened earth of old : What stands if Freedom fall ? Who dies if England live ? ' These lines hung blazoned across the face of a building in Summers Street. 'What stands if Freedom fall '—i.e. to what purpose save your house if England fall ?

Ever drawn on my way by those two ill-matched steeds, the young horse, Service, and that old but powerful beast, Self, I was at their mercy now ; and the inferior animal was pulling on the traces quite as strongly as his mate. All the men of my own age were going, and many much older ; and I'd no mind to be contrasted unfavourably with them. There was Max. I soon learned from the gossiping Con and Mother that Max had been passed by a medical board and ordered to an R.A.M.C. unit on Salisbury Plain. Gentle had helped him buy his uniform and equipment, and packed his valise for him, and seen him off ; but they were now finally separated, Gentle having denied herself to him. 'I am not coming back,' he had said more sadly than angrily. 'I cannot offer myself to be rejected.' There was no deed of separation, because there'd been no time for legal formalities ; they had just parted, Gentle promising, however, to act as his agent and do all that was necessary for him while he was away or abroad. She had sold the Rent House, which her father had given them, and with the money accruing from this, which Max agreed she should keep, she had left Holm St. Martin for London, where she had joined a Voluntary Aid Detachment and been sent to work in an officers' hospital. Max had gone to the war, and he was over forty. Was Gentle admiring him for this ? Did she contrast him with me ? I remembered her shivering admiration of the men who had marched over Westminster Bridge. Would Max win distinction and popular acclaim, while I . . . ?   Say he won the ultimate distinction of a bullet in his breast—oh, no, that must not be ; it would set Gentle free to marry again ; Max, as long as he lived, held her untouched by another man, and kept her mine.   I dreamed of earning distinction on the field before Max could achieve it, and of Gentle reading about my gallantry in the newspapers ; I even dreamed of my death in a military hospital and of Gentle there at my bedside weeping and holding my hand before I passed into the dark.

'Khaki is the only wear,' people were saying, and I longed to put on an officer's uniform with its Sam Browne belt and show myself in it to Mother and Con, who would be so proud in their simple way, and to my friends in the Garrick Club and to my staff in Henrietta Street.   I remembered Iris's parents, Lord and Lady Cranmere ; what were they thinking about me.   Her two brothers were already in the army, Roger in the Artists' Rifles ; Stane in the Guards.   I craved, too, the adventure, the violent experience, the escape from quiet city routines, and the strong-savoured cups of danger that the reverberating battle-front seemed to offer.   Was I missing something, something huge and high-seasoned, which other men were tasting ?   Was History passing me by ?   Lastly, I was in a mood to fly from the pain at home.   Let Iris try as she might to hide her hurt, I felt it always ; I suffered it with her and my shame as well ; and I hated these feelings, as Father used to hate them. I would be glad, on that score, to go.

§

'They are coming closer.'   Daily we said this, in home and office and street.   'They're getting most damnably close.' They had swept over Belgium, splintering the fortresses of Liége and Namur like acorns under foot.   They had entered Brussels and forced the Sambre and carried Charleroi.   They had burned Louvain.   They were driving the British from Mons.   Lille fell, and Maubeuge ; and they were far on the soil of France. Rumour whispered that they were in Dunkerque, Calais and Boulogne.   On Sunday, August 30th, in a special edition, *The Times* published its 'Amiens' despatch.   Who that lived through it will forget that Sunday ?   'Broken British Regiments' ran the headline, and the story, sent home by a special correspondent of great experience and discretion, told of a British Army broken and retreating in disorder, with its right flank cut off from the French and exposed to encirclement ; and it ended with an appeal for ' reinforcements, reinforcements, and more reinforcements.'

The morning after the Amiens despatch Father, who was within five days of his eightieth birthday, rose somewhat earlier than usual and spent a careful half-hour shaving very close so that no glimmer of grey stubble should shine in the sun. He smoothed back the long, wiry moustache and pressed down again and again, with no success, the thick, springy eyebrows. He studied the shaven jowl from several angles in the hope of discerning in it a fairly youthful look. He put on and straightened a youthful bow-tie, and a suit of square-cut grey tweed which, having a country look, suggested vigour, toughness and athletic agility. He said little to us at breakfast and, when that rather silent meal was done, went out into the hall, felt his cheeks again, braced back his shoulders, and went forth into the street.

I knew what he was up to. Father had broken his battle-ensign at the masthead and was sailing out of Queensberry Place to deal with the foe.

' I went straight to the War Office,' he told us in the evening, as he sank his over-fatigued body into an easy chair, letting the arms fall limp, ' and there I was made to sit against a wall in the corridor till some young cockchafer could see me. I sat there for a solid two hours, Iris, my dear, with my stick between my knees, and my hat on my stick, and the Germans coming closer all the time. There were a lot of other men sitting there, all of them old soldiers, I was pretty sure, and all on the same game as me ; and I was distressed to see that some of them looked a trifle old. Some of them must have been seventy at least, and I kept my eyes from them, because there were a rather discouraging sight ; they seemed, if I may say so, a bit far gone. One or two went to sleep and made a very sorry show. One of them was a peculiarly unlovely sight. Even rather nauseating, I found him. Some wretched little Boy Scouts, hurrying past with messages, looked at us all and grinned, and I had a horrible feeling that they included me as a feature in the comic spectacle——'

' Oh, no,' I objected. ' No, no, Father ; that's not possible.'

' I'm not so sure, old chap. I'm not at all confident about it. Anyhow, I protest I felt like an out-patient in an Institute for Old Men. I nearly got up to go, because I do not stomach humiliation easily, but at last a young sawney in a staff officer's uniform—some A.D.C. or other who looked as though he'd been in the Upper Fifth a year ago—invited me with great courtesy (they have manners, these children) to " come with him," and he led me up interminable stairs to a large room, where he presented me to a Brigadier-General Lord Troutbeck, or some such name, a young fellow of about fifty. And this imbecile, if you'll believe it, said, ' Well, General, what can I do for you ? ' with the Huns at the gate ! I submitted that it was a question of what I could do for him in his desperate circumstances. And he had no idea.'

' You don't say so ? ' I pretended amazement. ' Shocking. Deplorable.'

And Iris declared loyally that he ought to have been ashamed of himself.

' Precisely,' said Father. ' The man was a brigadier and a fool. So I suggested a few things. I said I didn't mind how humble the job was, so long as it helped. Could I not be a Town Major in some village in France, thereby setting a younger man free for the trenches ? Why not a Camp Commandant at the Base ? Why not an Assistant Provost Marshal behind the lines ? Why not O.C. Troops on a channel transport, or an R.T.O. at some wayside station ?'

' Why not ? ' I interposed, as he paused for breath. ' You'd make a splendid R.T.O.'

' I think so. Yes. Or why not such a job as he was doing—with such signal incompetence ? I tell you, children, I submitted a dozen such ideas to him, not one of which had entered his head before, and all of which produced the unmistakable symptoms of sudden illumination. You know—the kind of illumination which leaves you bewildered. But they were not for me. I'm not a fool, Doric——'

' You are not, Father.'

' You concede that ? Good. Very well, I quickly saw——'

' He's not a fool, is he, Iris ? '

' Certainly not.'

' Certainly not, my dear ; and I say I quickly saw that, however polite he might be, and whatever promises he might make, he thought me—how shall I put it ?—a shade on the old side. I couldn't lie to any adequate extent about my age, because, confound it, this was the War Office, and they could find out the truth about me in a twinkling. They're digging out a lot of old retired officers, but they haven't dug quite as deep as me yet. I saw I hadn't a chance with a lot of young striplings of seventy in the field against me. I could see he thought I should be more nuisance than I was worth and would probably want to fight the Crimea all over again. I knew I shouldn't hear anything from this institution for months and months, if at all ; so I thanked him for his courtesy and his promises, and bowed and went out, and now I'm a special constable.'

' You're *what* ? '

' A special constable.'   Quite recovered now, Father selected from the table at his side a cigar for the new constable, and lit it for him, tossing the match into the grate.   ' Oh yes.   I went straight to the police station and told them I was—er—sixty-eight and a half—I thought the " half " lent an air of veracity to the information, and it was dark in their office ; and they accepted me at once.   Why not :   they've plenty of old men in the Special Constabulary.   I know of one who's seventy-two. I report for duty to-morrow evening.   It's not much, but it's something.'

' It's fine,' I said.   ' And you'll make a most imposing cop. Only think of that now : P.C. Allan Mourne.   I protest, you're a great credit to me.'

§

He was given a blue-and-white armlet with a metal badge ' Special Constable 52 ', and a wooden truncheon, and, later, a policeman's peaked hat.   Wearing always his best blue suit, to increase his constabular appearance, and the armlet above his wrist, and the smart blue hat on his head, he looked fine indeed, if every bit of his sixty-eight years ; and one evening as he fared forth in this kit, with his truncheon under his arm to preserve the peace, some men on a scaffolding across the road gave him a cheer.   He took it in good part, raising his truncheon in acknowledgment before concealing it in a trouser pocket.   He did most of his duty at night, three nights a week, from ten o'clock till two, guarding depôts and power stations, or strolling about the dark streets.   At first he was given a young regular policeman for a bear-leader, and it was characteristic of Father that he never once embarrassed his youthful mate, young enough to be his grandson, by mentioning that he was a general.   He told him that he was a stockbroker.   And, on another occasion, having forgotten the stockbroker, that he was a publisher.   One evening, at his invitation, I watched him being lined up with twenty other specials before the Christian Men's Club (which was their commandeered headquarters) and inspected by a young officer of about twenty-five who'd been given command of this heterogeneous muster.   As they were going on night duty they'd been provided with borrowed police overcoats, and in this long blue garment Father looked quite the handsomest, as he was certainly the tallest and the oldest.   The young officer, pleased with his brief authority, moved along the ranks of his men, examining their buttons and caps and lapels, including

Father's. Father looked very grim as the boy patted down the lapel of his coat, but he bore it for his country's sake.

He suffered many such strains with no more than a lifting of his eyebrows and a tight setting of his lips. There was a fear of Zeppelin raids at this time, and the specials had instructions to see that motor drivers extinguished their headlamps and shopkeepers screened their more brilliant lights. Father, now promoted to walking his dark beat alone, would invite their co-operation with his usual courtesy, and be a little shaken when the motor driver said, ' All right, cock ' ; or the shopkeeper murmured against the officiousness of the Law, but allowed, ' It's not your fault, chum. There's nothing a mere peeler like you can do. You and I are just nobodies. We're there to be kicked around.' One rude greengrocer, greatly vexed, suggested that Britain must be in a bad way if she had to rely on old codgers like Father, with one foot in the grave ; and Father exercised a restraint in the best traditions of his new service, in not hitting him on his apex with the truncheon, to show that he was sufficiently alive.

§

Max . . . Father . . . Roger and Stane . . . all my friends, one by one . . . and all those patient volunteers crowding against the walls of the recruiting stations or marching to some barracks behind a tin-pot band . . . I was ashamed to walk past these recruits : men of all types, all sizes, and all ages : ragged and well-dressed, in mufflers and high, stiff collars, van boys and graduates, plough boys from the country and play-boys from the West End. The health and vigour in my body cried their reproach at me ; memories of Oxford added their rebuke. ' Young Men of Good Education Wanted as Officers.' With my degree I could be gazetted to-morrow. The conflict harried my mind in trains, in buses, in my Henrietta Street room, and by the fire at home. ' Keep your head. You're not the sort to be swayed by the mob. Think it out. Never mind your own glory or what people will say ; forget that, for God's sake. All that matters is, what's your real duty. Decide what it is, and do it. The war is a just war—' yes, so I believed then, and after thirty years, Roberta, though I can see deeper into the causes of that war and assign some guilt to all nations, I still do not see what else we could have done. A treaty is a treaty ; we had covenanted to defend Belgium ; and covenants must be honoured if all the strands of civilization are not to break. It seemed as simple as that ; and it does still.

' And, being in the war, we must win.' Of that no question. England defeated by a bullying foe ? I had only to say ' England defeated ' for my blood to shiver at the words and my lips to mutter aloud, ' *No !* ' Fight for my not-very-important little house, or fight for England ? As I have said, some of the better parts of me as well as many of the worse parts were battling in my mind on the side of ' England ' ; and I think I may add with truth that the better parts were only helped, and the weaker parts untroubled, since they longed for danger and distinction, by the stories which Father was bringing home from his United Services Club. Nightly he reported the sayings of Generals and staff officers who should know what they were talking about. ' It's hell over there.' ' The casualties are far heavier than any-one knows.' ' This war's going to cost us a million lives before we've done with it.' ' Their H.E. is something unbelievable.' ' They say the life of a junior subaltern at the Front is about fourteen days.'

My battle ended quite suddenly. Walking homeward one evening, I saw a motley batch of newly-joined recruits marching to their barracks behind a band and cheering and singing and waving good-bye, and my battle ended in a sudden blind resolve of the heart—as sudden and blind as my rush, against all argument, from Henrietta Street to Gentle's side. ' If it has to go, it has to go,' I said of my house, and I felt, not without some self-esteem, a little like Abraham offering up his first-born, Isaac. The decision made, all the lower motives joined my heart, cheering it.

Father, Iris and Hugh were in the Breakfast Room on the ground floor. Our butler had gone ; we were economizing in labour and money ; and the Breakfast Room was now the general living-room and the heart of the house. On the wall a huge map of the war area, pierced with tiny flags along the battle line, showed the preoccupation of our days. Father reclined in one deep chair, reading the *Westminster Gazette* ; Iris sat on the brink of the other, knitting a Balaclava helmet for a Ladies Working Party ; Hugh sprawled on the carpet with his toy soldiers, shouting ' Bang ! Bang ! ' and ' Fire ! Fire ! '

I said, ' Look, people : I've come to a decision.'

Father glanced up and removed his spectacles. Iris lowered the knitting. I walked up and down, with my hands in my pockets.

' I must go,' I said, in a would-be merry tone.

' To the war ? ' asked Iris.

' Yes.'

Father said not a word. For once he had no fine phrases, no

ready quotations, no suitable lie.   He would not say anything to stop me, and he would not say he was glad.   He just sat and listened to Iris and me, sometimes bringing his thick eyebrows together.

'What's Daddy saying, Mummy?' demanded Hugh.

'Quiet, dear.   He's saying he may have to go away again for a while.'

'Bang!   Bang!'   The child was already uninterested.

'I've known for some time you were going to say this,' said Iris, looking into the fire.   'I've been waiting for it.'

'Have you?   Well, there it is.'   Walking back and forth, I wondered what her thoughts were and wished there were nothing dividing us in this hour.   'You think I'm right, don't you?'

'I think you're right, if you think you are.   Yes, of course you must do it if you feel it's right.   How soon would you go?'

'At once, I suppose.   You said, Father, that Colonel Ewen could get me a commission at any time?'

Father spoke his first words.   'He said so.'

'Well, will you write to him?'

'Hadn't you—hadn't you better sleep on it?'

'My dear Father, I've slept on it for weeks.'

'Have you discussed it with your mother?'

'No, I'm afraid I haven't.   I'm afraid I never thought of that.   But—*you* think I'm right, don't you?'

He did not answer directly; when he did speak, it was in a monosyllable.   'Yes.'

'Good.   Then will you write to Colonel Ewen?'

'To-night?'

'Yes, I suppose so.   Why not?   Will you?'

'If you wish.'   And he turned and looked at the fire.

'But what does " at once " mean?' asked Iris.   'How much longer will it be before they—before you go?'

'I don't know.   Never been a soldier before.   How long, Father?'

'A matter of days only.   You'll have a few days to get your equipment and then be gazetted.'

'Is that so?   Smart work!'

'And what happens to the House of Allan Mourne?' continued Iris.

'It goes down the drain I should think,' said I; and then, shamed of this cheap piece of melodrama, altered it to 'George Byng'll carry on as best he can.   He'll keep it afloat if it's possible.   And I can do a little to help, reading manuscripts and advising, as long as I'm quartered in this country.   But I don't really know that it can survive.'

' Nonsense. Of course it can survive. It's going to survive.'

' Easier said than done, my dear. Publishing's a very delicate and personal business, especially with a young house like ours. Lop its head off, and it's apt to lie down and die. An old established business may be able to run about like a chicken with its head off, but I can't see Allan Mourne's doing it.'

' There's George.'

' Yes, but . . . I love old George dearly, but, if I know him at all, he'll only save it by changing its character. He'll george it along on his own lines. There's no one but myself who could have kept it on its original lines and still have saved it. I believe I could have done this because my whole heart would have been behind it, and, as I've always said, what you want enough in this world, you do. Once I'm gone, there'll be nobody in the firm to fight for its original inspiration.'

' There might be.'

' No.' Striding up and down, I shook my head at the carpet. ' I could get no one with the necessary enthusiasm for my peculiar and rather unreasonable ideas.'

' You could.'

' No, I couldn't. And even if I found someone with the necessary vision, I couldn't give him enough authority to argue the toss with George.'

' Oh, yes, you could.'

' Well, who, pray ? '

' Me.'

I swung round and stared at her, void of words ; and she went on : ' Yes. I've had this idea in my head for days. Do you remember how I used to say I wanted to run a business ? ' Her eyes turned sad, because she used to imagine in those days that we were perfectly happy together. ' And I did run it with you for a little time, didn't I ? And I don't know what you thought, but I always thought I managed rather nicely. All right : I'll go back and be your deputy and fight old George at any point you want me to. I'm not afraid of George.'

' God ! ' I said. ' This is a rather wonderful idea.'

' Of course it is. And so simple ! '

' I believe you could do a lot, if we kept carefully in touch.'

' What's Mummy going to do ? ' cried the voice from the floor.

' Put you to bed,' answered Iris. ' It's half-past six. You ought to have been in bed long ago.'

' No, not yet, Mummy. No—please. Just a tiny bit more.'

' Gosh, I feel rather happy about this,' said I, not listening to the child but striding the carpet faster. ' I'm happier than I've been for days. Yes, we'll fight old Bung, you and I.' Gratitude for her loyalty and admiration for her fine-tempered quality rose up in such strength that my heart began to fight them and to cry out within me, ' No, Gentle, you only. I love you only. Nothing shall take my love from you. You are the inmost heart of me.'

' Come,' said Iris to Hugh. ' Bed.'

During dinner we discussed the matter at length and excitedly, Iris and I only, for Father's thoughts were not with the publishing house.

After dinner, back in the Breakfast Room, he was standing before the war-map, with his spectacles on his nose and hands clutching behind him, when I said, ' Well, what about it, General? Will you write this darned letter ? ' and he came away from the wall, pushed the spectacles nearer his eyes and went to the desk. I stood nearby as he took paper and wrote, and I noticed how the pen shook in his large brown, grey-haired hand. When he'd written it he handed it to me with a smile, and I said, ' Well, here goes,' and went out into the dark and posted it.

§

The rest of the evening was very quiet. I fell to reading a Manuscript I'd brought home with me : a last task. Neither Iris nor Father spoke. Her knitting needles clicked as rhythmically as the timepiece on the mantelshelf, save when she paused to count her stitches ; the fire chattered and shifted at our feet. Father searched his paper for more news ; then laid it aside and, fingering his cigar, gazed into the fire. Once he said, ' It's rather cold, isn't it ? ' and leaned forward and stirred the embers. He placed two logs on it, poked them home and, lying back in his chair, watched the flames leap up and lap at them like friendly dogs. Ever and again his eyebrows came together as if his eyes were aching.

Because of my life-long unity with him I believe I knew well enough the pictures he was seeing above the glow of the fire and beneath the smoke of his cigar. The pageant of his life, eighty years long, was moving before him. He saw the Crimea, and India, and my mother, the beautiful Una Crawford, and his brief love for her, and the birth of Con and me in the little house at Walham Green, and the half-happy days in the one house he'd really loved, our handsome mansion in Coburg Square, where a little boy would come tearing down the stairs to meet him. He saw Gentle and me together in that house ; and I think that, as he remembered me and Gentle, he saw the women he had loved and lain with—where were they now ? They were gone from him, Una and Con were gone from him, and now I was going, never perhaps—no, say rather, never in all probability to return ; and he would be quite alone at the end.

The cigar went out ; the logs warmed the room ; and his eyes closed. His head nodded. Iris and I talked softly so as not to disturb him. With his lips parting, and one hand drooping helplessly over the chair's arm, the other resting upwards on his knee, he lay asleep in the comfort of the fire ; too tired to consider the mystery of life any more.

CHAPTER II

GAZETTED A second lieutenant, I was given a brief fortnight in a training camp and then went to join a new battalion of Kitchener's Army in a south-coast town. It was too late in the year for camp life ; the town had no barracks ; and I found the battalion, officers and men, billeted on householders, three, four, and six to a house. The officers were an odd miscellany of Indian Army veterans, old rankers with South African ribbons, and young public-school boys just commissioned from their O.T.C.'s. The N.C.O.'s were largely time-expired men who'd returned to the service. The men were a fine stew of those heterogeneous elements which yesterday I'd seen crowding into the recruiting stations. Officers and N.C.O.'s wore the proper khaki uniforms, but the privates, owing to the shortage of khaki, had only cheap, dull uniforms of dark blue, which made them look like the attendants of an asylum.

The extemporized character of Kitchener's Army or, as the men called it, Fred Karno's Army, was admirably illustrated by the fact that we paraded as a rule on a large waste-ground, or unfenced building site, between two blocks of small, grey, genteel houses. On this poor substitute for a barrack square, all pits and hummocks, coarse grass and tamarisk, we did our squad drill, company drill, musketry and bayonet practice, to the barked or snarled commands of our old-time sergeants and officers ; and neither the small boys leaving the houses for school nor the women cleaning their steps or gossiping on the pavement bothered any more to watch us, so familiar and indeed wearisome a spectacle were these our daily evolutions.

If one impression of this strange winter lingers with me more

than another it is one of abounding health. We were young ;
our training aimed at a perfect fitness ; and soon our bodies were
in such a state of well-being that we would wonder, those of us
who'd escaped from office chairs, and were not now corroding
our guts with whiskys and gins, whether we'd ever known,
since childhood, what real health could be. The morning runs
along the metalled roads, the ' physical jerks ' in the frosty air, the
football matches in a high, breezy hollow, the wet route marches
into the wide country, and through the sea-salt wind, put a fresh
colour on to our cheeks, a new lustihood into our sinews and a
joie de vivre into our hearts. I found that I just could not worry :
whether about my business in Henrietta Street, or the war and the
suffering not a hundred miles away, or the dark question-mark
that waited for me on the other side of that wide, grey sea. I
observed also in myself a heightened percipience as if some
childish vision had been restored to my eyes. I loved the frost on
the waste ground which made the grass grey as ashes and the
earth brittle as piecrust, and, turning the dew into crystals, hung
every branch and cobweb with the spangles of the hoar. On
such a day of winter and sun a route march was a joy ; all things
were beautiful : the hoar-frost lying like snow on the roofs and
on the faces of the hills ; the bare woods patching with their
browns and mauves the green of plain or slope ; the firs standing
sentinel on a brow against an horizon tinted with rose ; and the
trees and the cows throwing long shadows at three in the afternoon. Not a man among us, not the simplest, but was inspired
by the stillness, and the soft pastel tints, and the invigorating air ;
so that we marched back into our town singing in chorus, ' Here
we are, here we are, here we are again. There's Pat and Mac
and Tommy and Jack and Joe. When there's trouble brewing.
When there's something doing, Are we downhearted ? *NO !*
Let 'em *all* come ! ' And all the way back to our waste ground
we greeted every girl, pretty or otherwise, with a whistle or a
word or a song, ' 'Ello, 'ello, 'ello ! It's a different girl again,'
just as that column in the Park had greeted Gentle on the first
morning of the war.

§

I chanced to see Gentle once in these months. It was soon
after I was gazetted and had a new uniform to display. Chanced ?
No, that is less than the truth. Purpose and chance together
begot the meeting. I was up in town one week-end and had to
return to my regiment on the Sunday evening. I knew Gentle's
war hospital in Spen Gardens, off Trafalgar Square, and on the

Sunday afternoon, against my promise not to see her, I walked past the large white house quickly, guiltily, and then dawdled in the vicinity, hoping to meet her ' by accident ', and unable to drag myself away.   I felt just as guilty dandering there as ever I used to, standing in the dark passage and listening at Mother's door.   Truly that eavesdropping child was the father of this man in khaki.

I had no success.   Does a watched house or a watched street ever yield up the person you want ?

It grew dark and I came away, walking back towards Victoria Station along Whitehall and remembering our night walk there together, on the eve of war.   Half-way down Victoria Street I saw her—though in the dark we almost passed each other without recognition.   She was in uniform too : the blue uniform of the V.A.D.'s : double-breasted coat with a brass name and number on its shoulders ; cap with turned-up flap at sides and back, and the Red Cross in front ; black stockings and shoes. I stopped ; she stopped ; her eyes lit up, amazed, and she cried, ' Doric !   Is it—oh, but you look exquisite in khaki—a dream ! ' and holding both my hands in hers, she travelled her eyes over my uniform.

' My *darling !* ' I exclaimed and tried to draw her to me, but she said, ' Hush.   Now be good.   But you do look so adorable in that uniform.   Only—do take care of yourself.'

' You look very beautiful too.'

' *Too !*   Very beautiful *too !*   Listen to the man !   I didn't say you looked very beautiful.   But that just shows that you really think you do.   Gosh, the conceit of men !   Talk about women ! '

' Be quiet, you little beast.   One may kiss, may one not ? '

' No . . . please.'   A momentary terror dimmed the pleasure in her eyes.   ' No—no, Doric—you shouldn't have met me like this at all.   What are you doing in Victoria Street, anyway ? '

' Never mind that, sweet child.   Maybe I have national business in these parts, of which you know nothing.   Where are *you* going ? '

' I'm hurrying back to duty, and I think I'm going to be late.'

' I'm going with you.'

' Are you ?—oh, well, I suppose that's all right.'

' I don't care a damn whether it's right or not.'

' Yes, but you must care.   No, not like that '—she removed my arm from her shoulder—' if you're going to walk with me you must walk respectably.'

So we walked back along Victoria Street and Whitehall like two mere acquaintances, not even linking our fingers as we

used to do. But I looked at her all the way, and my heart
held her close. Gentle : this was Gentle ; here beside me once
more. A love like that which poured from me when I found
her asleep in her grey lodging went out and surrounded her
again—surrounded her all the way up Victoria Street and Broad
Sanctuary and Parliament Street and Whitehall. As we walked,
she told me all about her tasks in the hospital ; and menial tasks
they were : sweeping and scrubbing floors, washing crockery,
pushing trolleys, carrying trays, emptying b.p.'s——

'B.p.'s ? '

'Bed-pans,' she explained.

'Oh . . . dear me . . . isn't it all rather awful ? '

'Yes, I hate heaps of it—and yet in a way I don't think I've
ever been quite so happy.' She looked up at me with eyebrows
lifted half in amusement, half abashed by her words. 'It's the
first time in my life I'm not thinking of myself—at least, not too
much—but trying all the time to help other people. The officers
are all adorable—or nearly all—especially the older ones, and
so sweet to me.'

'Damn them.'

'And the young ones are rather lambs in their way. So
conceited often—rather like you. But not quite as intelligent,
I don't think. Still, they're rather heart-breaking, in their
bandages and splints. They show me the pictures of their girls.
Some of them seem to think I'm forty.'

'You're not in love with any of them, I trust.'

'Don't be ridiculous. You know I—but, really, Doric, it *is*
rather wonderful, being a good girl, all unselfish and helpful,
for a change. I'm enormously surprised at myself. I never
used to think I was very nice—but now, gosh, Doric, I sometimes
get quite worried about being so good. It doesn't seem natural.
I did try it once before, as I think I told you, but it was the most
frightful flop then. I'm succeeding quite well now, and enjoying
it enormously. I've always really *wanted* to be nice. Have you
tried it ? It's marvellous : one really begins to be happy. I
think I'm going to be a saint.'

'I don't want you to be *too* happy without me.'

'Please don't talk of that. Please—or I shall wish we hadn't
met. Do you think I shall be able to keep this nobility up ?
I do hope so. Somehow the old war seems to help.'

So she talked, and told me most things, as we walked along,
but nothing of the secret which she must then have known. I
wonder that I did not see it in her eyes, as they looked up at
me. Sometimes I wonder why she did not tell me that day,
and I conclude, first, that her heroic mood persuaded her to

keep silence for Iris' sake and mine, and secondly that, ever emotional rather than rational, she was telling herself, ' It's not time yet, and anything may happen.'

Once I said to her, after gazing down upon her face, ' Am I right, child ?   Do you look a little sad ? '

' No ! ' she cried, turning up a deliberately radiant face. ' Of course not ! '

' Well, shall I say a little more serious than you used to ? '

' Oh, well, perhaps a little——' and then she instantly corrected herself and declared, ' But no ; I'm a beaming character really.'

We parted at the door of her hospital, holding both hands, but allowing ourselves no more—unless we said a great deal more with our eyes.   Her last words to me, spoken with a half-smile and her head laid appealingly to one side, were ' Please take care of yourself.   Doric, you *will* be careful, won't you ? '

§

That was what she said ; and in the first ripeness of spring—but no, there are things I must tell you first.

In the spring we of the 21st North Surreys found ourselves on Firbright Common, on the borders of Hampshire.   Our camp was but one cantonment in a world of sand and heath, where innumerable huts of wood or corrugated iron—guard rooms, mess rooms, men's huts, dressing stations, and recreation rooms—stood among the pines and silver birches, with their skirts lifted, so to say, out of the paddled sand.   The whole population, apart from the birds, seemed to be soldiers in fatigue dress or smart walking-out kit ; and the aristocrats of this vast male society in the sand were the field-rank officers, strolling about and swinging their swagger canes, and the regimental sergeant-majors strutting along the Lines, like full-breasted turkey-cocks with their canes tucked under their arms.   All day long the rifle shots from the many ranges cracked and echoed in the scented air ; and at intervals, monotonously, the blended song of the bugles broke into this continual music of bird notes and rifle percussion.   Far and near, from hill-tops and hollows, the threads of the bugle-calls wove a ragged chorus over (as it seemed) the half of Hampshire and Surrey.   From Reveille to the calls of Quarter Dress, Parade, Cookhouse and Officers' Mess, and so to the lovely Retreat at sundown and the Last Post at night.

My days were a chain of platoon drill, company drill, musketry courses, lectures, concerts, night marches, and ever-recurrin rumours that next week it would be my turn to go in a draft of officers, or to take a draft of men, to some massacred battalion at the Front. Neuve Chapelle had happened ; and a battle which at first we had believed to be a glorious victory, and perhaps the beginning of the end for the Huns, was now whispered to have been a mad and murderous affair, as costly as it was sterile. It was known now—our colonel admitted it—that we had sacrificed five hundred officers and twelve thousand men to gain a parcel of ground little bigger than a peasant's croft. In the eight months of war our battalions had lost, all told, as much as two hundred and fifty per cent. of their original number ; and that meant that the shells, machine guns, and sickness were thinning the regiments faster than our drafts could reinforce them.

Any day now, I imagined, I should get my orders to go, though after but five months in the army I was still a pretty raw subaltern. I was eager to go ; eager for the excitement, the danger, the historic experience, and the chance of some heroic and well published deed, which secretly I longed to perform. The self-centred part of me wanted Gentle to hear that I was going and to be anxious about me and so to love me even more poignantly. I tried to crush this desire down, but it was there, and not easily suppressed. In body and heart, as I have told, I was so extraordinarily hale that, try as I might, I just *could* not feel enough about other people's pain, in these days of bereavement and fear, nor about the odds-on chance that out there in the smoke and din I might encounter physical agony or death.

And one bright-eyed April morning, when the world was full of a new health too, and the sun had an August warmth, and the scent from the pines seemed one with the warm breeze, and a chaffinch was shouting for joy somewhere, over and over again, I sauntered forth, parades done, to quaff like him the fragrance of the woods and to enjoy the soft springing of the turf and the crackling of twigs beneath my feet. Everywhere around me the noon sunlight, split into a thousand Jack-a-lanterns, hid among the dark pines and the pale piebald birches. Through all my senses I drank deep of the woody wine, blended of sun-gleams, shade, fragrance, warmth and song.

And while in my solitary fashion I was wandering deep into the woods, and listening to a chiffchaff or watching the pied wagtails run and flirt their tails on the moss-plumped rides, a telegraph boy cycled up to our gate ; the sentry, after challenging him, passed him inside to the Officers' Mess ; a mess waiter, taking the telegram, shouted to the mess sergeant, ' Telegram for Lieutenant Allan Mourne ; ' the sergeant telephoned to my company office to inquire where I was, and, learning that ' they hadn't the ghost of an idea,' detailed a mess orderly to find my batman and give the telegram to him.   My batman, properly excited, as all people are, by the buff envelope and eager for the pleasure of showing it to me, hurried with it in his hand along the woodland aisle which he'd seem me enter thirty minutes before.   He met me coming back to mess, happily slashing, as I came, at tall shrubs and pendent branches with my swagger cane, or tossing it up into the air and catching it.

'A telegram for you, sir.'

'What ? An army telegram ? '   One tiny quiver of the heart : was this some order to ' proceed forthwith . . . ' ?

'No, sir. Civilian.'

'Oh.'   A faint, unexpected relief, I think ; as of reprieve. I could imagine nothing to fear in a civilian telegram.

I took it, tore the envelope, and read : ' Gentle dangerously ill Hospital of Our Lady of Mercy and Good Counsel please come Max.'

CHAPTER III

IT WAS not till nearly five o'clock that I, made mad by difficulties with cars, trains, and taxi-cab, arrived at the hospital gate.   As I stepped out of the taxi and saw the familiar grey mansion among its ancient elms, twenty years melted away like a shadow-show and I saw again the twelve-year-old Gentle running up those white steps and giggling as she led Con and me on the somewhat hysterical ' adventure,' a secret visit to Father in hospital.   How she had longed to see the nuns and the statues and Father in his hospital room with a picture of the Sacred Heart !   And how like Gentle to seek this hospital which she'd known as a child, now that she was ill and in danger, perhaps, of death.   It seemed larger now than it had been twenty years ago, with a third red-brick and white-stone wing, so that the original grey-brick and pillared mansion looked like a small, incongruous annexe, the relic of a dead past.

Yes, it looked a great hospital and splendidly, mechanically efficient.   ' Oh God, grant that they can save her.   Forgive me my sins.   I know I deserve nothing, but oh God, save her, and I will try to be better.'   Even so, twenty years ago, the small boy of twelve had promised God that he would be righteous if only his prayer for his father could be heard.   ' Dangerously ill.' What could it mean? Had she caught some illness in the accursed hospital where she worked? But she was only thirty-two. She would recover. . . . Yet why send for me?

To a young, clean-shaven porter, very different from the burly, big-moustached porter who had looked so dubiously at the giggling Gentle, I said 'Mrs. Drury?'—a name which it always hurt me to pronounce—and he said, 'Yes. Private Maternity. Two floors up. Along to the right.'

Maternity!

The old painted statues looked down upon me as I ascended the stairs : the Good Shepherd with His finger pointing upward and the legend above His head, 'In this Hospital I reign'; and on the first landing the crowned Madonna with her baby in her arms. It was spring now as it had been then, and a vase of narcissi and tulips touched the hem of the Madonna's robe.

Maternity !

I went up past the corridor where Father's room had been to the corridor above. It was a duplicate of the one below : an avenue of big windows and closed doors, with nothing in its long vista except the sunlight, the trolleys against the wall, the clean disinfectant smell, and the echoing of my steps.

A very young nurse, maybe a probationer, hurrying my way on some errand, saw me, stopped, and asked, 'Can I do anything for you?'

'I've come to see Mrs. Drury,' I said.

'Are you a relation?'

'Well . . . yes . . . I'm a cousin.'

'Oh.' Plainly this was an unimpressive relationship, and she added, 'Oh well, I'll see Sister,' and, turning in her tracks, went knocking at door after door and peeping in to see if the sister was there. She found her behind the fifth door and sent her out to me : a nursing nun in a voluminous white overall and wide-winged cap, or cornette, like an enormous white butterfly. She was a much smaller and older woman than the Sister Mary Evangelist who had beamed on us children so long ago—where was Sister Mary Evangelist now? I never learned this little old sister's name, having other things to think of.

When I explained myself she nodded, but seemed doubtful of admitting me to Gentle's room. Who was I that I should be admitted? 'Yes, Dr. Drury told me about you,' was all she said.

'How is Mrs. Drury?'

Looking into my face, she answered, 'I don't know how much Dr. Drury has told you.'

' In his telegram he only said she was dangerously Ill. Sister, what does that mean ! Is she—is she dying ? '

After hesitating she said, ' We never give up hope. With God's grace . . .'

' Sister, I said she was my cousin. But we are more like brother and sister. We were brought up together. She means a very great deal to me.'

' I am sure she does. She is a dear creature, and we are all very fond of her here. We—we're all praying that Our Lady will intercede for her.'

' Thank you, thank you.'

' I'll get Dr. Drury for you. If he says you can go in to her, that'll be all right, I'm sure.'

' He will. He sent for me.'

She bowed and, leaving me, went to a room three doors away. She entered it and in a few moments Max came out of it. He had a high-collared white gown tied loosely over his uniform, the khaki puttees and brown boots looking odd beneath it. With his height and girth, his black massy hair and camp-tanned skin he looked a handsomer and more heavily masculine figure than I had remembered.

His eyes, looking straight into mine, were obviously embarrassed, but he held them fixed there. It was as if he found it difficult indeed to blend his look with mine, but was determined not to move his eyes away. And in a low but completely level tone he said, ' Good. I'm glad you've come.'

' Thank you for sending for me.'

' What else could I do, my dear chap ? She asked for you. That was enough.'

' She asked for *me* ? '

' Yes. Yes, naturally.'

' Then——'

' The child is yours. That's what I'm saying.'

' I see.' Blind, complacent, unimaginative, self-centred fool that a man can be, not till the porter had said the word ' Maternity ' had I once considered this possibility—simply because Gentle had said no word to me about it. The knowledge seemed to smash my thinking to fragments. ' I knew nothing of this.'

' I know you didn't. She told me you didn't. Well, there it is, old chap : a little girl. And naturally they all think it's mine. It's along there somewhere, and they call it " Baby Drury." " Baby Drury "—ha ! The brat's all right, but——'

' Gentle ? '

' Puerperal infection ; and she's dying.' He said it dramatically,

after his habit, and brutally.   Not that he was feeling
much malice ; he was both too shaken for that, and too proud
to be doing the decent thing by his wife and me ; but he felt
that I should be hurt.

' Dying !   *No !* '

' Yes.'   He sighed and, being a doctor, fell into the correct
medical terms, perhaps even proud of them.   ' Puerperal infection as a result of prolonged and difficult labour, followed by
instrumental delivery and laceration.   I know what that means.'

' *Dying !* '   Gentle dying of my child.   Then I had killed her.
I was her murderer.   When she gave herself so readily to me,
after I'd said ' I have no wife now,' she had given herself to
death.   This was the price of the joy I had snatched.   I saw
again that grey room in Luton Grove, and the little white hotel
by the Park.   That was the seed ; this the fruit.   And a fruit
that was about to fall.   Gentle a wind-fall in the orchard !
Why, oh, why ?   ' No sparrow shall fall on the ground without
your Father——'   In this moment I could have cursed God,
but I dared not, lest it undid my prayer ; lest He punished me
by killing Gentle as he punished David and Bathsheba long ago.

' The nurse said there was hope, Max.'

' There isn't.   There's none.   I should be lying if I said anything else.   Her strength is going.   She knows it.'

' Oh, God.'

' Don't worry too much, old chap.   This is Life.'

' It was good of you to send for me.'

' I'm a doctor, old boy.   I know this sort of thing backwards.
At a time like this they crave the father—and that's you.'

It was impossible to answer this ; and he went on, bragging
a little.   ' I'll do my job as a doctor properly—even to my wife.
But I won't have her old mother here.   Not on any account.
I assured the nurses she'd only distress her—you know what
the woman is.   It's a mercy I'm a doctor : they do anything
I tell 'em.   Well, come in—wait, I'll get you a gown.   You'd
better have one.'   He went back into Gentle's room and came
back with a gown like his.   This he put about me, over my
uniform, buttoning its collar and tying its tapes behind, almost
in the manner of an affectionate parent.   When the tapes were
tied, he said imperiously, like an officer giving an order, ' Come
on, then.'

I followed him into the room.   It was exactly similar to the
one Father had had on the floor below, except that the bed
extended into the midst of the room from the left wall, and, over
the fireplace, instead of the picture of the Sacred Heart, the
gentle face of Mother Mary Catherine McAuley looked down

upon her patient. The windows were open to the warm April air, but the blinds were drawn, and the light dim.

Gentle lay in semi-recumbent position, the pillows arranged around her, and her brass-brown hair parted on one side and braided into two long plaits, so that it might be out of her way on the pillow. That the nuns had braided it for her I saw from the two neat bows which were made from a white bandage. Instantly the past lived again and I saw Father welcoming the child Gentle into this hospital with his ' Good day to you, Two Yellow Bows.'

The little old sister was still with Gentle, and as we came in she asked, ' Well, are you feeling all right, my dear ? '

' Quite all right,' said Gentle.

' Good, dear ; then I'll go. Ring if you want me.' And with a parting smile at the door, she went.

Gentle smiled up at me as if ashamed to be here. ' Hallo, Doric.' It was the most tired voice I had ever heard.

' Hallo, my dear.'

' Isn't this stupid ? Why've I been and gone and done this ? '

' Yes, why ? ' I was now on the far side of the bed, and I picked up her thin hand. It was all I could do, with Max standing there. ' What have you been doing ? '

' Gosh, I'm ashamed of myself.'

' There's nothing to be ashamed of.'

' D'you remember darling Uncle Kingsley in this hospital and how we came to see him ? '

' Do I not ! '

' I'm so glad I'm here. The sisters are so sweet.'

Suddenly Max spoke. ' You can kiss her if you want to. Give her a kiss.' And he turned away.

' Max has been so sweet,' she said after I'd kissed her brow.

' I know.'

' He brought those wallflowers. He looked so huge and pathetic with his little bunch of wallflowers, I could have cried.'

Max said, ' Shall I go ? ' and, though I shook my head, he continued, ' Yes, I'll go for a little. I'll be out there in the passage.' And he went out rather sheepishly, like one unwanted, quietly shutting the door upon us.

' Gosh, he's behaving well, poor darling Max,' said Gentle.

' He is.'

' It was awful, telling him. I asked him to hold my hand while I told him, and he held it all the time.'

' Don't talk too much.'

' When I'd finished, he just got up and walked away, as he did then, but he turned round and saw my eyes following him and he said, " Shall I get him for you ? " It was his idea. He said it first.'

' Don't talk too much. You mustn't tire yourself.'

' Then he told the nurses—you know how splendidly he can lie—that you and I were brought up together and that you were his best friend and mine and that he must have you here.'

' That was love, wasn't it ? He loves you, in his way.'

' Yes, I think he always has : in a way, and all he can. Darling.' She looked straight at me, her eyebrows slightly lifted. ' I believe I'm going to die.'

' No, my beloved.' Obeying something other than my will, I fell on my knees at her side and gathered up her hand in both of mine. ' Don't say such a thing, or even think it. You're *not*, you're *not*.'

' Yes, my sweet, I'm afraid so. I can see it in all their faces that they think so.'

' No, no. No, no.'

' I did so want to see you, in case. . . . Oh, I'm glad you're here. I wanted to tell you that I didn't regret anything. Just that, see ? And that you're never to regret anything. Promise ? '

' You're not going to die. You belong to me. You're going to live—and live with me—always—you and me and the little girl. What shall we call her ? '

' It would have been rather wonderful.'

' Oh, don't talk like that ! ' I plunged my face in my hands and sobbed. I felt her hand pass over my hair, and heard her say, ' Don't mind, my beloved.'

Mastering myself, I raised my head and picked up her hand again. ' You're not going to die. If you do, I'm coming too, I'm coming with you, I'm not staying in the world without you.'

' No, that is only talk——'

' It is not, it is not ! '

' —but I like to hear you say it. Perhaps I shall be able to be near you. Do you think, darling—tell me—you're cleverer than I am—is there any sort of after-life where we can be together again—one day ? '

' There must be. There is. There's no sense in anything else.'

And oh, I don't know, but in that moment, looking upon her, I seemed to know that love at its strongest is not subject to mortality and that somehow, somewhere, and some day, its meaning will be explained to us. It has been difficult in later years to recover that moment of conviction, but I remember it ; I hold on to it. I hold on to it in hope—but it's only a very little hope.

' I wonder,' murmured Gentle.   ' I hope so.'

' I am sure.   I am sure.'

' It's funny—it's funny—but shall I change, shall I be different somehow—oh, I hope not——'

' There's no need to talk of such things.'

' I shan't forget you all, shall I ?   They won't let me forget you—oh, no ! '

' No,' I said.

' Kiss me.'

I left my lips upon her brow.

The door handle turned once, and stayed turned.   Deliberately Max had turned it, and waited, that I might be warned of his coming.   I raised my face, and he came back into the room, saying, ' I'm sorry—may I come in ?—but I don't think I ought to let her talk much more.   We mustn't tire her.'

Hot and restless with her fever Gentle had pushed the bedclothes down from her breast, and he put them back for her and, sliding his arm under her shoulders, raised her a little way, turned the top pillow over, that she might have its cool side.

' Thank you, dear,' she said ;   and patted his hand.

I saw then that he was crying.

' Shall I go for a bit ? ' I asked.

' No, oh no,' begged Gentle.   ' I want you.   I want you both to be here.'

' No, you stay,' Max allowed.   ' I'll make it all right with Sister.   They all do what I tell 'em here.   They just eat out of my hand.   But, Gentle, dear, you're not to talk and get excited.   If you do, I shall take him away.'

' All right,' smiled Gentle.   ' I'll be good.'

We drew up chairs and sat on either side of the bed, our faces towards her.   Max held one of her hands.   I was afraid to do this too, in front of him, and kept my fingers linked on my lap.

We spoke hardly at all for a long time.   If anyone spoke, it was Gentle, and we just answered with a few words or a smile.   She sighed often, and was restless ;   and often Max rearranged her clothes or her pillow for her.

After a while she seemed easier—or at any rate, more still.   In her plain white hospital nightgown, with its square yoke bare of all trimming ;   with her arms flowing from her pink bed-jacket on to the sheet like water sculptured in marble, she looked almost statuesque ;   and if ever I have worshipped anyone or any thing, Roberta, I was worshipping that still figure then.   Behind my closed lips and my gazing eyes I was saying always, ' Gentle . . .   Gentle . . .'

Once she caught my gaze and, smiling wanly, said ' I was

thinking I've done nothing good with my life—done nothing, and the chance has gone now. Except just at the end. I tried to be useful then.'

To this I did not know what to answer ; and it was Max who said, after dwelling upon her words, ' The child is beautiful.'

She turned towards him to acknowledge this with a smile, and after a further minute of thought he asked, ' Would you like me to get it for you ? '

So difficult for her to say yes, since it was not his child ; and she only looked at him, discomfited.

' My dear,' he said, ' I'm here to serve you.'

And he rose slowly and went out.

In a minute or two he came back with the little old sister, who was carrying the child. Instinctively I rose to greet them both. My heart pulsed more in nervousness than excitement as I looked at the child, Gentle's and mine. Five days old, it was a little scruffy thing with a good colour and straight but ruffed fair hair. The Sister placed it in the crook of Gentle's arm, Max helping her.

I saw Gentle try to press it to her breast; and then the Sister said with an affectionate smile for the child, ' Come, Baby Drury. Back to beddy-byes. Mustn't tire Mummy any more to-night ' ; and, lifting it away, carried it out again.

Gentle watched it go from her, saying only, ' The pet ! ' and ' Bless her ! '

I to death, you to life, said Socrates to his judges, and which is better, God alone knows.

Perhaps because it was the hour for some nourishment, or perhaps to take Gentle's mind from the child, the Sister came back bringing a fruit-drink on a tray. She laid the tray on the bedside table and, slipping her arm under the top pillow and gradually bringing forward Gentle's head, she held the invalid cup to her lips. But Gentle had hardly sipped from it when the chapel bell rang in the garden. It was six o'clock, and the hour of the Angelus. Promptly the Sister straightened up her back, bundled (it is the only word) the invalid cup into my hands, who was standing opposite her, clasped her own hands and bent her head. She let me give the drink to Gentle while her own lips moved over the unheard words, ' *Angelus Domini. . . . Ecce ancilla Domini. Fiat mihi secundum verbum tuum. . . .*'

As the last of the bells sounded, she made the sign of the Cross, and taking back the cup from me, completed her task. Carrying the tray away, she signalled to Max to accompany her ; and out in the corridor she asked him if he didn't think ' two people in there' were too much for her, and shouldn't 'his friend' come away. But Max said, ' No. I'll see that everything's all right. She's very fond of him, and he stays'; and, being a doctor, he had his way.

And we continued to sit with her for I know not how long. Once the obstetrician came to see her, and the Resident Medical Officer once or twice. The R.M.O. told Max that his Chief had said as he went, ' I can do no more.' The room grew darker, and a nurse came in and lit the bedside lamp, throwing a square of green material over its opaline shade. This flushed the twilit room with a green glow.

Gentle's eyes were often closed now, and Max, watching, would show by significant glances or shakings of his head that he feared she was slipping into unconsciousness. He rose and picked up her right hand. I rose, too. She opened her eyes at his touch, smiled weakly and said, ' It seems so funny because I still feel a child. . . . I feel so little different, Doric, from what I did when we came to this hospital before. . . . Do you remember ? ' Max's lips came tightly together and trembled, and when he could speak, he said, ' Gentle, forgive me if ever I've hurt you '; and she nodded, because she could hardly speak.

' I too,' I said. I had ruined her life. I had killed her.

' Nothing—nothing to forgive . . .' and about her lips was all that was left of the old half-hidden smile.

' Yes, yes.' I had killed her, Gentle, the lively, the gay.

' Nothing,' repeated Gentle, and laid her other hand over mine.

After this light caress she lifted the hand away and left it on the counterpane ; and Max, looking at me, who had no right to hold a hand of hers as he was doing, suddenly leaned over the bed and placed her fingers in mine. And we both sat down again, each holding one of her hands. She had little power to press our hands, but for some time I felt her finger moving up and down my palm as if she would say all she could in this way.

She watched with piteous eyes as she went from me, and I tried to smile all the time she could see my face. Once she turned her eyes from me to Max and back again, and whispered, ' Help each other,' then closed the eyes very wearily.

The movement of her finger slackened and ceased.

Max, satisfying himself that she was now unconscious, let go her hand ; but I did not ; I could not. He walked out into the corridor once or twice ; but not I. The Sister came in and out, many times, as they do when a patient is dying. I no longer cared whether she wondered at my holding of her hand, or what she was thinking. I only wished to God she would go away and keep away.

It was quite dark outside now, and I remember that at one time I heard a jingle of bits and a rattle of iron wheels and an excitement of many voices and hurrying feet, out there in the Fulham Road.   I imagine it was a long chain of limbers and guns going by.   A young nurse whom I'd not seen before came in and, according to rule, removed the flowers from the room, just as though this day were the same as any other day for Gentle.   I never once let go of her hand—I could not—and at some time I felt, with a sick terror, that it was cold.   I did not dare say so to Max for fear of what he would tell me ; but he came in from the corridor, looked at her, and sighed.   With a shrug, and shake of his head, he went through his doctor's business, feeling her pulse and slipping his hand on to her heart. He placed back the bed-clothes very gently and said, ' I'm afraid that's all, old chap.'

CHAPTER IV

BACK IN the deep of lost time, thirty years back, among the scenes that are fading and the outlines that are blurred, I seem to hear two men talking.   They sit with their coffee and cigars —was ·it not so ?—on a leather settee in a corner of my club ; and they are Max and I, both in uniform : Capt. Robert Drury, R.A.M.C., and 2nd Lieut. Allan Mourne, 21st North Surreys. And Max, in his crude but kindly way, relishing both the rough, slangy, would-be humorous words and his own decency, is saying as he blows out the smoke from his cigar ' This is your bastard, old son, not mine.   I won't queer the little blighter's pitch—she looks a decent little thing—but to hell with any legal obligations.   You see that, don't you ?   Legally, I suppose the child is mine, since we were still nominally living together and could have—well—but, as I say, to hell with all that.   If that's the law, they can have it, as far as I'm concerned, for twopence. I can't tell old Henrietta the truth—she'd perish everlastingly. Of course, if she wasn't such a perfect fool, she'd jump to it, but I'll take my oath that the old hen never believed anything she didn't want to.   She's snuffling and gurgling and goo-ing about how wonderful it is that Gentle and I should have had a little child after all, and in spite of everything, and what a consolation it must be to me, and how it was only the thought of that poor little helpless thing which saved her from utter despair, and how we must all bear up for its sake. Oh, well, she means well, and she's going to be useful. She's got hold of an idea that we ought to call it Roberta after me ; she gets immensely gushing and weepy about this. I'm not the fool that she is, and I strongly suspect, old boy, that she wants it called Roberta because she isn't really quite sure that the little lamb is Robert's handiwork at all.'

' Let her be called Roberta,' I answer. ' If you consent, I am willing.'

' Me ? So far's I'm concerned, you can call her what you like. Call her MacSweeny, if it pleases you. Henrietta'll look after her all right ; she says she's going to give up her " few remaining years " to the little darling as a " sacred duty." O.K., that's fine, but the kid's got to be paid for, naturally ; so this is my idea, and I think it's a good one : you cough up a lot, and I settle it all on her. You can trust me to keep my mouth shut, for all our sakes. Like hell, yes ! And what d'you say to this : you're its godfather ? You're the obvious person to be one of its god-parents, and then you can give it all you like for the rest of your life. And, what's more, if anything happens to Henrietta—and she never looks too good to me—you can take it into your own home. I don't think I'm at all a bad agent for unofficial fathers and misplaced children. I meet a lot of that sort of thing in my profession. They always call them " love children." Have you told your wife ? '

' Told her what ? '

' The truth.'

' Yes. Can I get you some more coffee ? '

' The truth—oh. No, no more coffee, thanks. Oh, well, perhaps that wouldn't work. Perhaps you can't have it in your home. Let's hope Henrietta goes on for a long time yet. Dammit, she's only sixty-three, and I daresay she's really a tough old scarecrow. Most of these long, scraggy women go on for ever. You can't kill 'em. As a matter of fact, I should think her expectation of life's a good deal better than yours or mine just now. But if she does peg out, what then ? '

' There's my mother and sister.'

' Do they know ? '

' No. Nothing. Nothing for certain. But they loved Gentle, and they'd take the child beyond all question. I'm sure Con would take it now—and probably love to—if Henrietta hadn't the stronger claim.'

' Right, then ; everything's going to be fine. We'll establish the kid in the world all right, for Gentle's sake. She's rather a dear little thing, though I say so myself.'

' Thank you, Max.'

So it was settled, Roberta. You went to the Chapter Mill and were baptized in the village church where your mother was married, Con and I standing as godparents both (though I, back in camp, was there by proxy), and Henrietta and Mother watching and weeping, and Max standing by, for your sake. Nearly five years you lived in the Chapter Mill and played in its gardens and down by the mill-stream, while the world tore itself in pieces from the Atlantic to the China Sea. They were happy years for you, I think ; the last of them are years which you remember.

§

Soon after this Iris left me. Quite suddenly, Iris, my brief visitor, went back into the distance and the otherness from which she came ; and Hugh went with her. You will have observed that I tend to see parables in things, and it has always seemed a parable to me that she went back at first to Cranmere Place, to her great house and park and the noble names, from which I had taken her.

She had worked for some months with George Byng in Henrietta Street, but now this generous attempt to help me was no longer necessary. All my fears and prognostications had been proved wrong : the one thing that was not a casualty of the war, the one thing I didn't lose, was the House of Allan Mourne. Sometime late in '15 it became clear that the book trade, instead of tottering into a decline, was going to recover from a temporary debility and stand up in the stoutest health. It began to put on this unexpected weight, and this bright, merry eye, not very long after the departure of our larger armies for France, Egypt, Gallipoli and Mesopotamia. Suddenly we found that almost every book we printed we sold. They were printed on poor paper, which must have turned yellow by now and perished at the edges, but if any purchasers noticed this, they realized that it was the only paper we could get, and *à la guerre comme à la guerre* : the books sold. They were bought for the boys ' over there ' ; for the wounded and sick in the base hospitals ; for the prisoners of war in the hands of the enemy ; and for the hundred thousand sailors on the seas. They were bought by the Canadians, Australians and New Zealanders ' over here,' who had plenty of money and were lavish with it. They were bought by people in munition works and government jobs who were making, most of them, better money than ever before and had fewer amusements to spend it on. The whole of Britain, it appeared, was reading. Some read to escape into realms of fancy from the awful reality of this present world ; some to study with a new seriousness the desperate human situation. It was by no means only light fiction and easy memoirs that we sold. Even George Byng perceived, with a gleam in his eyes, that there was a considerable public now for the kind of stuff I'd always wanted to publish ; and if he was little interested in the ' message ' such books carried, he was greatly interested in the money they brought, and he printed and published them as fast as Iris or I could wish. In those days you might have seen him scratching around, in his clubs and among the agents, for ' books of a high idealistic quality.' Good poetry was selling as never before —and never since ; and it was no infrequent thing to see George buttonholing his pals in the Garrick and asking if they knew any ' war poets.'

Never perhaps had there been such an opening for me and my first Oxford dream, but, alas, I was only half-hearted about it now. Half-hearted indeed : one-half of me lingered with that old love ; the other half, the self-centred half, was listening to a very different drum. This part was even less interested in the human lot and its amendment than George used to be ; it was hearkening to the drum-fire along the front and dreaming carelessly of a charge in the waste of No-Man's-Land and a bullet that would send me to wherever Gentle might be—into some brighter day, or some wan grey light, or into the everlasting dark. *Ex umbris . . . in veritatem.*

Not that I was unbearably wretched after Gentle's death, for, once again, though walking always with a sadness, I was not quite as unhappy as I imagined I should be, or as I hoped to be. Her death, you see, had cut all knots and ended all threats ; dead, she was out of the body : no man could touch her any more ; jealousy and fear need start no more ; she was mine only now. She was cloistered for me in death, and the shameful dregs of selfishness in me were glad to have it so.

Only the intermittent, spasmodic thought, ' I killed her, Gentle, the lively, the gay,' was something not to be borne. Forget that. Forget . . . .

§

Yes, I was finding life sufficiently bearable among the heath and pines of Firbright Common, where we were still encamped and awaiting orders. And then, one evening in late summer

—it came in the evening, so I imagine Iris had been writing till late in the night—I received the letter from her.

It began affectionately, maybe guiltily, 'My dear,' and told me that she was in love with a Colonel Milder and believed she could be happy with him.

This Lieut.-Colonel Milder had done brilliantly at the Front and was now one of the youngest colonels in the Army. The War Office had just begun to learn that it'd lose the war if it didn't give plenty of command to the younger men ; and Geoffrey Milder was only twenty-seven—six years younger than me : how that hurt ! He had been wounded in the trenches a week after Neuve Chappelle, invalided to an Officers' Hospital in London (was it, by any chance, Gentle's hospital ?) and was now doing a staff job at the War Office. Iris had met him first, coming from my office in Henrietta Street ; she had seen much of him in the last few months ; they loved each other, and if it was possible, would like, in these menacing times, to marry as soon as the Law allowed.

I went with the letter into the woods. I wandered deep into the woods till I was lost among glades of birch and pine, or on some open tableland of heath, bilberry, wild rosebay, and tall, bearded waybent. I never to-day smell the resin of the pines, or see the loose mauve willow-herb among the wild grasses without remembering that late summer evening among the woods in 'fifteen.

I had to counter at first a certain indignation, especially against the colonel, and a silly, leaping self-pity which kept murmuring to the grey-lichened tree-boles, 'I have no one now ' ; but gradually I rallied myself to sense and to sympathy. I made myself understand. It was not logical perhaps, but natural that the birth of Gentle's child and mine should have been more than the proud Iris could bear. It was natural that she, who had once said to me that she ' used to dream of being a perfect wife,' should go towards her dream ; I had learned from my own life that one goes slowly but surely, over every obstacle, towards one's master-dream. And it was natural that, however she might try not to be bitter, she should have a desire, buried perhaps, to ' teach ' me as I to teach Gentle, and Gentle to teach me. She had waited till my grief should be a little assuaged and then determined to go—if possible with dignity and friendliness. Only a year or two ago such a step might have been more difficult for her, a child of Victorian parents, but she'd always been something of a proud rebel, and now it was 1915 and all the old morals were changing. The New Age was with us : one year old. Henrietta and

Mother, closeted together, might entertain each other with their shocks and despairs ; they might lay their fingers on each other's laps and say, ' Oh, my dear, I think it's so terrible. What is the world coming to ? There was Doric, but he is his father's son, and history repeated itself there—but Iris ! Iris, with her upbringing ! Iris, Lord Cranmere's daughter ! Are there to be no moral standards at all ? '—but they were left behind. For good or ill History, with its guns on its shoulder, was stepping out faster than they.

The thought of Henrietta and Mother, and my ever-present desire to take the opposite line from theirs helped me to be generous to Iris and her colonel. Soon the resentments were driven from the field by a longing (of the same family as Max's) to be as magnanimous as possible ; and I hurried back to my hut and wrote a letter beginning ' My dear, I quite understand and will arrange everything.'

§

It was not difficult to arrange, and when, some months later the case was heard, hardly any publicity attended it. The eyes of Britain were fixed on larger things than a monotonous procession of young soldiers through the divorce court, one of whom was a Captain Allan Mourne.

My colonel, when I told him something of Iris's letter, willingly secured me a special leave pass ' for urgent family reasons,' and I went home to undo—not my marriage, which had been undone *à huis clos* two years before—but a companionship and a partnership which had been very fair, and not without its pleasures, but now must end. Our major steps, those by which we should take our different paths, were simple enough ; the most worrying question was the care of the house and Father. I at once suggested to him that Con should come and keep house for him ; but would she, could she, leave Mother and Uncle Humphrey, to say nothing of Lettice, who was still with them and over seventy ? I must ask her to ; but if she could not, who else ?

§

It was after Father had left me for a little, and as I sat alone, that a most warm and living idea came and stood before me. I looked at it, and it so pleased me that I determined, there and then, bringing a fist like a gavel on to the table, to bring it about.

It gratified everything in me : my old love for Father, my new and kindlier feeling in this war-shadowed scene and in my sorrow-chastened heart for all the family, my poor limping worship of the sages' wisdom, and my sense of mischief, which, however sad I might be, was always up to its games in my heart.   I jumped from my chair, went from the house, and sped as fast as cab could carry me through a scourging rain to Addismore Mansions.   The family knew that Iris and I had parted, and that I had come home to marshal my affairs, so they would not be surprised to see me.   Con, Mother, and Lettice were all in the flat, and I fetched Con into the little dining-room, sat her on a chair, and, walking up and down before her, propounded the plan.

They were all coming to live in Queensberry Place.   They were all going to be together again.   Father was eighty-one, Uncle Humphrey seventy-eight, Lettice seventy-three, and Mother nearly sixty—surely they could all be friends now, at the end of the day.   Surely the war cancelled all little family feuds whose roots were twenty years in the past.   Father and Uncle Humphrey had been boys together seventy years ago : let them be chums again at the other end of their lives.   Father, Mother, and Con could be husband, wife and child again—or as near as made no difference.   All forgiven all round.   Lettice too : Lettice who still complained, and perhaps more than of old, that she was but yewman, and that there was a limit to what yewman flesh and blood could do : Lettice could be something of a lady, with my young servants to help and look after her. And when I came home on leave (though, as I said this, I wondered if I would ever come home on leave) the whole Family, which, all said and done, had been fairly happy in Coburg Square, would be a natural unit again, in another tall white house in Queensberry Place.   All would be as it had been, save that (we neither of us mentioned this) there would be no merry visits from Gentle.

Con was delighted with the idea ; she was eager to come at once ; and off we went to the drawing-room to persuade Mother. Mother was not so easily conquered, and right at the beginning I made a gross tactical error by advancing my fine phrase, ' All forgiven all round.'   Mother immediately asseverated that *she'd* done nothing that needed forgiveness, and I hastily abandoned this approach.   I pointed out that, such being the case, all the pleasure and honour of forgiveness would be hers, and that Father was much changed now and could be described a kindly, considerate and really delightful old gentleman, and that the house was exceedingly comfortable, and that the servants adored him, and liked Con, and were not without some affection for me. She said she'd think about it, and perhaps pray about it, and I said there was no time to think or pray, as I wanted, before my leave expired, to see them all together, and as pretty as a picture ; and she at length, though still breathless and agitated, conceded that perhaps it was her duty, and accepted the invitation ' if your father agrees,' and stated that at bottom I was a good boy.

Lettice was a fortress I felt confident I could carry single-handed. To her in the kitchen I went, and she looked at me over her small steel spectacles as I came in. At rest for a while in her rocking chair she continued to stare at me over the spectacles as I expounded the great idea. Thereafter she defended the fortress for twenty minutes, stating that she doubted she could get on with them young girls and that it was late in her life to be chopping and changing about; but I silenced these batteries with some powerful flattery, declaring that the Family wouldn't be the Family without Lettice, and I wanted the Family complete ; and she wept a little and wiped the spectacles and said that, as for her personally, she'd always liked me, Master Doric, and always found my father a perfect gentleman.

Uncle Humphrey was out. He was strolling the Hammer-smith Road in his large, black, wide-awake hat, with his blue shawl round his shoulders and his white beard on his breast, manifestly a most distinguished philosopher. A philosopher dwelling in too high and rare an atmosphere for any commerce with the unleavened multitude—though not in the case of Marcus Aurelius.

His absence in the Hammersmith Road, however, or in the clouds, didn't matter ; we didn't need to discuss the business with him ; he would follow along behind Mother when the time came.

So back through the rain to Father with the consent of all, except Uncle Humphrey, in my pocket. I burst upon him in the breakfast room where he sat poised upright on his easy chair, a cheroot at his lips, his spectacles on his nose and a war map draped over one hand. The Battle of Loos had begun in the rain, and he was seeking with his gold pencil the La Bassée Canal, the Hulluch Road, and the villages of Haisnes, Douvrin, and Coté St. Elie. His cigar smoke seasoned the room, but at the moment his cheroot had gone out, so deep his strategic interests. He dropped the map, however, and unshipped the spectacles, as I entered.

' General,' I commanded, ' kindly listen. Do you know whom I'm getting to keep house for you ? '

' Don't worry about me,' he said. ' You're not to. You've

other things to think about. I can go anywhere. Some
hovel . . . some insanitary hutment . . . some charitable
institution for the old——'

' No need to go to any hovel—or to any insanitary hutment
either. And there's no need to allude to your rusty sword ; it
can hang where it is. I've arranged everything splendidly.'

' You have, have you ? And who, pray, is coming ? '

' Just Con, and Lettice . . . and Mother.'

' Your mother, did you say ? '

' Yes. Of course. Con and Lettice and Mother. They're
enthusiastic about it.'

' Did you say your mother was enthusiastic about it ? '

' Certainly. Why not ? '

' Well . . . I thought perhaps . . . well, there's some ill-will
towards me in that quarter, isn't there ? '

' Certainly not. Not a trace. Not a shade. Why should
there be ? '

' Well . . . there were reasons . . .'

' Were there now ? Fancy that ! But reasons can't go on
for ever, and I'm not letting them. I'm in command of this
operation. I'm gathering the Clan together. Clans always
gather together in time of war. Like any other pack in a storm.
Like Barbary sheep.'

' Like what ? '

' Barbary sheep—they do it, don't they ? '

' I haven't any idea. Do they ? '

' I should imagine so. Surely. All sheep do, don't they ? '

' I don't know.'

' Well, let's hope so. The Allan Mourne's are going to,
anyhow.'

' Con and your mother, and Lettice ! Con. Yes, it would be
pleasant to have Tricks about again. Have one of these cheroots.
They're Army and Navy.'

' Ta.'

' No, no ; please, please ; I beg of you ; not " Ta." I
protest I cannot stand "Ta." Con would be all right. I like
to have young people about. I shall miss greatly—yes, Con
would be a comfort to me in my declining years. There's a case
for your sister coming, perhaps, but——'

' They're all coming. Everyone of them. Make no mistake
about it.'

' But think, Doric : when you come home, when this infernal
war is over and you come home—you are still young——' He
stopped. He tried to light his cheroot again, but abandoned
it to the ash tray and took another from the box ; and I knew

he was hesitating thus, because he didn't want to mention Iris. 'You may want to marry again, and then you will want your nice house, and your little wife will want it too.'

'I shall not marry again. But if I did I should just move the Clan to some other place, round the corner. Please don't *look* for difficulties. I'm terribly keen on this. I want to think of you all together again while I'm at the Front.'

'It's an extraordinary idea.'

'It's a perfectly obvious idea. Everybody loving everybody again ; everyone coming home at last ; I take it that you see it in all its beauty.'

'I take it that I don't quite see it yet, but that I may shortly. It's a generous thought of yours.'

'Not at all. It's merely a matter of convenience. And economy too.'

'I wouldn't wish to be a nuisance, or a burden on anyone. As an old soldier I can always——'

'——as an old soldier you can always find some booth or shanty in which to doss down for the last few nights of your life. Quite. I know all about that. I fully realize it. But this happens to be your shanty for the rest of your life. Kindly understand that.'

'Yes—but talking of bodily disintegration, which we weren't, is Uncle Humphrey coming too ? '

'Certainly. Can't leave him behind.'

'Good God ! '

'Let brotherly love continue. Behold how joyful a thing it is to dwell together in unity.'

Partly because he could never resist a quotation, and partly to show that he was well away with this one, Father continued it for me. ' It is like the precious ointment that ran down into Aaron's beard. Well, old Humphrey's always amusing. And of course where my wife goes, he goes too. I've never really known if she was my wife or his, since he ran off with her. And Lettice, did you say ? '

'Naturally. Can't do without Lettice.'

'Well, I always liked Lettice.'

'And she loves you.'

'But tell me : you're not thinking of bringing Henrietta along?'

'Heavens, no.'

'I'm glad of that. I don't think I could have borne that. A singularly foolish woman. I've had but small joy listening to her, at certain stages of my life. When does this invasion take place ? '

'Just as soon as possible. I want to see them all aboard before I go back. I've set my heart on it.'

' Well, in that case, I suppose——'

' Exactly,' I said.

And nearly three weeks later, only two days before I must return to camp, Father and I were in the breakfast-room, I standing at the window with my hands behind my back, and looking to see if they were coming, and Father sitting in his chair and trying to read the afternoon paper, but palpably nervous. ' Here it is : here's the taxi,' I announced at last. And there it was : weighted above and below with their baggage. But— how was this ?—it stopped three doors away. The driver must have got my number wrong. None the less the whole family, in a nervousness akin to Father's, stepped out on to the pavement : first Lettice, then Con, then Mother, and lastly, with some difficulty and care, Uncle Humphrey : Uncle Humphrey in his wide-awake hat and blue shawl. A voice at my ear, for Father had risen to see the sight, exclaimed ' *Gott in Himmel !* look at old Humphrey ! What's he got on ? Is it a shawl ? *Nom d'un nom*, we can't have him going about like that. This isn't a mental hospital. Why, the man looks a fool. And we shall have to get some shears to that beard of his, Doric : it makes him look like God the Father. *Caramba*, he looks a hundred : do I look as old as that ? '

' You forget. He's one of our Major Prophets,' I said, and ran out to bring them in. ' Come along, people,' I commanded them. ' May as well come to the right house. They don't want you in there.'

And along to my door they all came, in single file : Con, Lettice, Mother, and Uncle Humphrey following sadly behind ; and the taxi, repentant, bringing up the rear like a baggage train.

Father was now standing on the top step, framed in the portico like a tall statue in a niche. Long ago he had stood in the same way on the steps in Coburg Square, to receive us all into his proud new home, and the only differences in that tall statue this after-noon were the deep imprint of twenty-five more years on his face, the overcoat with the lamb-skin collar which he'd slipped on because he was nervous of the autumn cold, and the long new cigar which he'd just lit up as a sedative, because he was nervous of Mother.

Lettice, in the general embarrassment, was first up the steps, and Father's great hand came forward to greet her. ' Well Lettice ; this is good. This is like old times. It must be eighteen years since we've shaken each other's hands, isn't it ? And I declare you look exactly the same.'

' It's good to see *you* looking so well, sir.'

' Me ? ' Father spread his hands despairingly, as though he, for most practical purposes, were already dead. 'I hope you're going to be very comfortable here, Lettice. You've an exceedingly nice room. This, Mabel, is Lettice, my most excellent friend. And this is Mabel who will, I am sure, do everything for your comfort.' My young parlourmaid, Mabel, had just appeared in the passage, having gathered from the traffic of feet and voices upstairs that the master's family was come. 'The excellent Mabel will show you everything, Lettice. Be so good as to look after her, Mabel. A friend of thirty years.' Father, being nervous, was armoured in his stateliest manner. 'Be you so good as to—thank you, Mabel ; I thank you.' And he handed Lettice over to the parlourmaid as one hands a fire-bucket to the next in the human chain. 'And Con ! My Tricks, as ever was ! Well, well, well !' He removed the cigar well away on to his port beam while he kissed her. 'It is kind of you to come and look after your old father, just until he goes hence, and his place knows him no more. I think I shall not detain you very long.'

'Oh, it's going to be lovely. We're going to be so happy.' She gave him an affectionate hug, and on release he wiped his eyes, both of them, with his voluminous silk handkerchief.

When he was fit to speak again, and when the cigar was replaced, which of necessity had been held aside while he attended to these few tears, he said, 'Go you in my dear. Go you and make yourself at home '—and then perceived that Mother stood immediately before him. There she was, standing there and looking at him and saying nothing. Very awkward. For once Father could meet a situation only with silence. He bowed from his waist as one does to the Queen.

And it was she who said, 'How are you, Kingsley ? '

'Me ? ' Again he spread his hands as if they were but waiting now the advent of death. 'I drag along ; I drag along, somewhat hampered by my terrible weight of years. And you—, how er—how are you ? All right ? ' He stuttered over it because as a question it seemed a bit overdue and a trifle inadequate. So late and inappropriate, in fact, that he did not wait for an answer. 'This is all very kind. It's an excellent arrangement of young Doric's. We must—er—ah, Humphrey ! Well, well, well ! I haven't seen you for a dozen years. Where do you hide yourself ? How are the various pains ? I'm so glad you were able to come along, too. You look more distinguished than ever. One of these days I must really grow a beard. And I vow he doesn't look a day older, does he, Una ? '

At this point his Reception on my steps was necessarily at an end, and he turned indoors to lead all these guests over the house.

'Come along, all, and you shall see over the house. Tricks is the only one who's ever been here, I think. It's a nice house.' He was talking hastily, abundantly, lest Mother talked and embarrassed him. 'And you shall see your rooms. You should be quite comfortable in them, I imagine. Young Doric and I and the excellent maids have given some pains to making them tolerably attractive. Doric even put a few flowers in the Ladies' rooms and a small box of cigars in his Uncle Humphrey's.'

'And that's a lie, Mother,' I said. 'He put them there himself. He went out without a word to anyone and got them this morning. And he spent about twenty minutes adorning all the rooms, including Lettice's. Lettice's most of all, I think.'

'What? What's that? *I* got them? Nonsense, nonsense; *allons donc*; and what does it matter who got them? This is the breakfast room, where we've been inclined to live, of late, now that our staff is somewhat depleted. In time of war——'

'General Allan Mourne. Could I say something?'

'Why, yes, my boy. What was it you wanted to say? Fire ahead.'

'I wanted to tell Mother that we thought the little Indian room could very well be hers and Con's, and this a kind of smoking room for you and Uncle Humphrey—if that suits everybody.'

'That'll be very nice,' began Mother.

But Father quickly prevented further speech from her. 'Yes —quite—that was our idea. You'll see the Indian room in a minute. I can promise you, Humphrey, that that's an exceedingly comfortable chair. I hope you'll occupy it sometimes, if you can be induced to leave your chamber upstairs. Now come into the dining-room. Is the man bringing in the baggage? This way. *Par ici.* This is—yes, that's the *Toilette.*'

'The what-did-you say?' asked Con, as yet unfamiliar with this continental word.

'The *cabinet d'aisance*, my dear. Very convenient. There is, of course, another upstairs, Una, and one, I am told, for the kitchen staff below. We're subject to this mortification at all social levels. There you are : the dining-room. A princely room, as you see : you will be able to preside there with much grace, Una.'

'It's very——'

'And now upstairs. Follow me. Yes, lay the luggage there, my man. Have you paid him his fare, Humphrey? No? Well, you meant to, I'm sure. Perhaps you'll deal with him, Doric. This way. *Par ici.* Permit me to go first and lead the way.' And he led the procession up the stairs, proudly : Mother, Uncle Humphrey, Con—and me, last of all.

' This is the Indian room. It is used to—the Indian room which, as Doric told you, we propose to set apart for the ladies. I think you can be happy here. I sincerely hope so. This drawing-room we do not use much now, though young Doric's had some fine assemblies here in the past. This is no time for entertaining ; though of course, Con, if you want to have your little friends sometimes . . . young people must have their fun. And you, Una ; you may like to have an At Home here occasionally. There's a fire here now, because Doric thought you should all take your tea in glory here, your first night. Now come along ; we'll—but I don't know why I'm doing the honours. This is Doric's house, and I'm the least person in it. Than me there is nothing lower.'

' Continue, General. You're doing fine.'

' Right. Now this way, Una. There's a little room here which we use as a guest room. See ? Pleasant and sunny. You can put anyone you like in here—so long as it isn't Henrietta. That's about all on this floor. Up again. *Allons*. Upward and onward.'

And up again we went : Father, Con, Mother, Uncle Humphrey—and I.

' There, Una, that'll be your room, the best in the house. And Con is just beside you. Humphrey and I are upstairs, two old boys together.'

' Stairs, stairs,' sighed Uncle Humprey ; and there was a note of disapproval, or disappointment, in his voice, which Father didn't quite like.

'Yes, stairs. A succession of treads one after the other, and out of the horizontal, so as to attain to a higher level. That's the only method of ascension we have in this house. If you don't like that somewhat primitive method——'

' Yes, yes, Father,' I intervened—though amused by this early hint that the future would be by no means one of flawless peace between Father and Uncle Humphrey. ' Now then, you two chaps : no bickering. If Uncle Humphrey finds the stairs too much, he can have the little guest room downstairs.'

' Absurd. He's only seventy-eight ; I'm eighty-nine——'

' Eighty-one, Father.'

' Eighty-one then. If I can do it, he can. He's a mere youth.' Father was now leading the way up the next flight, followed by Uncle Humphrey ; with Mother and Con behind, and lastly me. ' But still, this is Doric's house, and I am the least person in it. Doric is the proprietor, and if anyone is dissatisfied with the hotel——'

' I only said stairs,' objected Uncle Humphrey. ' I suppose

I can say stairs if I want to. I don't like the way he speaks to me sometimes, Una. I confess I don't. I don't like it at all.'

' Tush ! ' said Father, or some such syllable, to the staircase treads ahead of him.

' Is mine a fairly large room ? ' snapped Uncle Humphrey, maintaining his right to submit reasonable questions. ' I shall be bringing my desk and bookshelves.'

' About half as large as a swimming bath,' announced Father without turning round.

' And not too cold, I hope ? ' continued Uncle Humphrey, still asserting his rights.

' Exceedingly cold, I should say.   But much can be done with a fireplace, some coals and wood, and an old number of *The Times.*'

' Now then, you two chaps ! '

Uncle Humphrey turned his head right round to address me far in the rear. ' Don't think I'm not grateful to you, Doric. It's just that I'm not the type that takes very kindly to palpable snubs.'

' Snubs ? Who's snubbing anyone ? ' demanded Father, his humour recovered. ' I never snub people. I'm a fundamentally gentle type. I thought I was merely making certain statements of fact in response to certain inquiries from you. If they sounded discourteous, I am greatly distressed. There, Humphrey : this is your room and I hope you—I mean, we all hope you'll be very happy there.'

' That's right,' I called encouragingly, from my place far behind. ' Let brotherly love continue.'

Half an hour later, when all were settled in, and washed and tidied, I enjoyed a silent but very deep and warm satisfaction to see them all seated in my drawing-room : Mother filling the tea-cups on the low rosewood table, Con curled up on the sofa, Uncle Humphrey divested of his shawl and at ease in a corpulent arm-chair, Lettice, who I insisted must be there, sitting perched uncomfortably with her plate in her hand on a high-backed chair, and Father sitting very erect on my Aubusson tapestry fauteuil, with his knees apart and his hands on his knees, and talking far too much because he was still under the impression that he alone could give the necessary ease and liveliness to this reunion. Like a good general, he assumed full responsibility for the progress of the action. Con laughed often at his chatter ; even Mother laughed once or twice ; Lettice smiled in duty always ; and Uncle Humphrey sat watching them as usual, from the heart of his private dreamland. The fire in my hearth warmed them all, Father, Mother, Con, Uncle Humphrey and

Lettice, and its unsteady light flickered over their faces, playfully and affectionately, in the darkening room.

§

I left them there, left them sitting as they used to sit in the old house ; and I went out into the darkened streets, shutting my front door very quietly. For some time I'd been impatient to leave them and be by myself because of something Con had told as we sat over tea. She had told me that, far away in Scotland, Max had married again. Married a very young girl, and Henrietta of course was professing a great shock. ' Not six months since my beloved Gentle died ! And he has a beautiful little daughter who will need him and his love when I die. Not once has he come to see her. That is unavoidable, perhaps, in these dreadful days, but to have married again so soon—so dreadfully soon ! I do not understand it.' I understood it. Oh, yes : the softening influence of death had been lifted from his shoulders, and with the days a natural and increasing resentment against Gentle and me had disburdened him of all desire for the customary seemliness, so that he had not only felt free to marry again, but had been quick to marry again. Besides, his opportunity was brief. He, like me, must proceed at any hour to the front and to the great question which awaited us all over there.

And oh, I was pleased—pleased that he had married again. That was why I had felt in the mood to be alone in the darkened streets. I knew where I was going, and I walked slowly along the Old Brompton Road till, looming up before me, heavy and grey, I saw the parade of massive arches and the monumental Roman gateway which were the front wall and entrance of Brompton Cemetery. The gates were closed now and I could only look through the railings under the arches to the far distance, where among the many thousand tombs and statues Gentle lay. They are no longer there, those railings through which I stood gazing that night. Like the railings round the garden in the square beneath my window, they were hacked down, by saw and flame, some five years since, and taken to the foundries to make our guns. I stood looking through them while, like wraiths and shadows in the mothy darkness, the pedestrians and the hurrying vehicles passed me by : nameless, fleeting images that meant nothing. The night-sounds of a restless city were behind me ; and a world of silence before me, in the darkness beyond those iron bars, like the silence of an inland

sea. Standing quite still, I tried to send my words towards
Gentle through the bars and across that mute and lightless
anchorage of the dead. ' He has left you now for ever, my
dear, and you are mine only, mine as never before. Forgive
me if I killed you and laid you there ; I didn't mean to. This
is as close as I can get to you to-night, but soon, very soon,
I shall be going into the battle, and there, if only God is good
to me, I shall be killed, too, and come to you. You are mine ;
and if I can, I am coming.'

CHAPTER V

IT IS an evening in April, and my battalion, in column of
fours, is marching along the straight road between the poplars.
The men in their greatcoats are burdened like pack-mules, with
full equipment and rifles slung. All of us are wearing steel
helmets : it is the first time for centuries (so the Quartermaster
told us, when he was issuing yesterday the singular things) that
the British Army has put on armour for a battle. We have
been marching since early afternoon when, with the suddenness
of a *minenwerfer*, the order to proceed to the battle fell upon our
peaceful camp and scattered it like an anthill overturned. The
men are weary. But the evening is gentle and courteous ; the
level green lands on either side of the pavé lie graciously beneath
a setting sun ; and the men sing, not with gusto, as when we
sallied forth, but with a softness that matches the evening air.
 ' We're here Because we're here Because we're here. . . .'
They chant this rhythmic but monotonous refrain because, like
a drove of sheep or oxen, they do not know why they're here,
nor where they are, nor whither they are going—except that it
is up to the line where a battle opened two days ago. ' Probably
we're losing it,' they opine to one another, ' or they'd never
'ave sent for us,' who are but Kitchener's rag-time army.

> We are Fred Karno's Army,
> What ruddy use are we ?

 In the evening stillness they hear ever and again—far beyond
the green horizon, somewhere under the sunset, the beat and
pulse of the battle ; and they mutter ' Crimes ! ' and ' Holy
Jesus ! ' and one of the wits leads them in ' Oh, my, I don't
want to die, I want to go 'ome.' The word ' home,' an appealing word, conducts a number of them into a sweet melodious

alr, sung very softly or lightly hummed, ' Rolling home, Rolling home, By the light of the silvery moon.'

They share their songs, but not their thoughts.

I march at the head of my company, alone. I walk with greater ease than they because only my pack hangs from my British Warm overcoat, and in my hand I carry only my ash-plant walking stick and my gloves. With this stick and gloves I feel sometimes a little like Father walking from his club up the Haymarket to Piccadilly. At other times I remember a battalion night-marching over Westminster Bridge on the eve of war, and Gentle watching them at my side, her body shaking with tight-held tears.

But how comes it that I march at the head of a company ? It's but four months since I was drafted out here and posted to ' C ' Company of this battalion ; and now I march in command of it. These I conceive to be the reasons : we had much winter sickness and many chance casualties in our trenches before Hébuterne, down by the Somme ; my seniority dated back to 1914 ; and, for the rest, my Colonel had confidence in me because I was thirty-four and grey, because I was a very silent person, because I was the head of a business house and reputed a man of wealth, because I had married a peer's daughter, and because my father was General Allan Mourne.

I have no such confidence in myself. On the contrary, though I hide it well, I have a very great diffidence. Consider the operation before us now. The Colonel defined and explained it to us company commanders in Battalion Headquarters four hours ago, and I understood it but dimly then, and what I did manage to understand I am now forgetting.

' It's this damned Mound,' he said—he is a big, dark, swearing fellow, yet with a heart behind his oaths, and he reminds me sometimes of Max. ' This Mound.' Then, seeing that our four faces were still blank, he explained further, ' The Mound of St. Just—the Mound of St. Just, boys, in old Fritz's line just north of Loos. Here it is. Here, see ? It's only a pimple, a foot or so higher than Allan Mourne there, but it's been annoy-ing the old General for months. The Hun's artillery observers can see a great deal too much from it, and it's got to be bitten off. Just that. Well, apparently it can't be carried by a frontal attack, so the only thing to do is to get round it. The show started the day before yesterday, and our chaps got nicely round on the right flank and consolidated there, but they were driven back on the left with a shocking, incredible, absolutely crippling number of casualties. And that's galled the old General more than a little because, as you all know, he likes to have his way.

These trenches on the left have got to be taken by to-morrow night, or the old bird won't enjoy his dinner ; and we and the West Kent Fusiliers and the D.L.I.'s have got to bloody well do it. So that's that. And do it we will. Yes. Because, in point of fact, gentlemen, the job is important—and I mustn't make fun of the old General : he just happens on this occasion to be right. The straightening of the line here has some bearing on events that are to take place down—well, never mind that. Forget that. But unless we're all mistaken this—these forth-coming events are going to be a turning-point of the war, and our preliminary job up here is very well worth doing. I want you to think that, gentlemen, and to go at it like hell and do your damnedest. I know you will, because it'll be a contri-bution to—well, everything—humanity, decency and all that muck. I know you will, whatever it costs us. Thank you. Now look here, carefully.' And he ran his explanatory pencil over a very sketchy map of a British and German trench system. ' Understand, all ? '

The other company commanders said, ' Yes, sir,' crisply ; and he turned to me, silent as usual.

' You, Theo ? '

I nodded, denying a confusion which was only a little better than a fog, that I might seem worthy of my new command.

§

We marched on the right of the road. Left of us, rattling, clattering, lumbering, clamouring, went a stream of horse, mule, and motor traffic, up towards the line : G.S. wagons, A.S.C. lorries, old London buses turned into troopers and painted green, despatch riders, grey staff cars with high officers at ease in them, a long ration train, and, more interesting than these, a string of cavalry, clip-clopping and jingling, with a hairy dog, ever the friend of man, even as far as the battle, following at their side and occasionally looking up at them like an officer in command.

' Cavalry ! ' cried the men up and down the column. ' Caw ! We musta' won the war. We've broken through. Can we go 'ome, please, Sergeant ? '

Beyond this strong-flowing stream, travelling in the opposite direction, came a much slighter, slower, and wearier one : ambulances coming down from the Casualty Clearing Stations ; ammunition limbers and ration carts returning empty ; a file of walking wounded with blood-soaked bandages ; a battalion not much more than a hundred strong, straggling to their rest billets—battle-torn, mud-caked, empty of laughter and songs, though one of them wore a full-dress German helmet, spiked and splendid with its brass eagle, above his grimed and grinning face. And now a bag of Boche prisoners, all big and fair and young, being marched like tamed wild beasts to their cage in the circus field.

Sometimes I left my place at the head of the company and walked up and down the platoons, ordering them, ' Close up now ; close up, men. Keep closed up behind. That's better.' And whenever I did this my Company Sergeant-Major appeared from somewhere and promptly exceeded me in a demonstration of efficiency, because he'd been recently promoted like me. ' Close up at the rear, close Up, can't you ? And get into step now. Christ, you look like a Sunday school outing, after their supper. Come along now. By the *right* ! Think out which is your right, Number Eleven. *Left*, right ! Left, right ! Left. . . . left. . . .'

§

And yet they were not marching badly. That was not my reason for leaving my place and strolling sometimes to the rear. My Sergeant-Major knew nothing of certain thoughts in the mind of his tall, grey, silent commander ; and much ashamed would I have been if he or any of my two hundred men could have perceived them. Marching alone at my company's head, along this crowded and jostling *route militaire*, I was as much a solitary as ever I had been in the streets of London ; and my thoughts for most of the time were with Gentle, Iris, Father, and the past—but sometimes they were with one other. The truth about this ' one other ' I will not be ashamed to set down now, after thirty years.

There had come a junior officer to the Company, Ronnie Francis, a schoolboy from Radley, who must have been nineteen years old in the official records, since no lad under that age was now allowed at the Front, but in actual fact was almost certainly eighteen, if indeed seventeen wasn't the true figure. His face was the face of an impudent boy, the cheeks still smooth, the nose still unformed, the brown eyes as fine and flippant as those, say, of Gentle in her most mischievous mood ; I had lost Gentle, I had lost Iris and Hugh, I didn't expect to see them or any of my family ever again ; and I suppose the simple truth is that I wanted someone for whom I could feel a little love ; and when Ronnie Francis first walked into my company office, a cellar in Hébuterne, he won almost immediately a part of my heart, because of his youth, his beauty as of a child, and his gaiety. This love, for it was little less, I kept immured within myself; I even avoided much talk with Ronnie because I was self-conscious in his company; but I enjoyed watching him from a distance and dreaming dreams, like a schoolboy, in which he lay wounded in No-Man's-Land, and I dashed through the whipping bullets to carry him back to safety. To be in the Army is a little like being at school again, and I had slid a little way back into the moods of that angular and lonely schoolboy who had felt so sharp a love for the child, Felix Gotley. Ronnie gave to my grey hairs and lined face all the respect which he gave to his senior masters at Radley, and some of the impudence, too; he liked and admired me because affection, even though unspoken, will always get through to its object and awaken a response; and I would wonder, as I sat with a pipe in my dug-out, what he would think if he knew that his grave senior officer had been expelled from school for stealing, had been guilty of much furtiveness, some cruelties, and many a secret weakness as his youth went by, and was even now capable of walking up and down the length of his company, not only to see that the men were marching properly, but also to see Ronnie himself marching at the head of his platoon and perhaps to exchange a word or a smile with him.

§

Now we were among the heavy guns. There across the fields we could see a huge howitzer skulking under the leaves of an oak spinney, and another, its sister, crouched in the high undergrowth of a hazel copse. Their teams were serving and firing them, and we watched the action through the poplars as we marched. 'Fire!' A flame among the leaves; a lifting smoke; a furious recoil of the gun's stout barrel back towards the men who'd taken such a liberty with it; a report that stunned the ear-drums; and look, look there!—one could see the shell like a small canister travelling along its high trajectory towards the enemy over the horizon.

Our men, as the reverberations died away, burst into an apposite song, 'We are the boys who fear no noise——' but the rest may not be set down; for it was an indecent song, as one of the wits conceded by starting up:

> It's a hell of a song that we've just sung.
> *Skibboo, skibboo.*
> And the blighter that wrote it oughta' be hung
> **Skibboo, skibboo.**

But now, gripped by a great interest, I was marching through the first of the villages upon which Father had pondered that night when he was studying in his big war-map the Battle of Loos. From now on I should march through names which he'd dotted with his gold pencil as he tried to re-create the battle in the smoke of his cigar. Here were the real places. This one was still partly inhabited even though the guns hid in the fields around it. See, there is an estaminet from which indeed the heart has gone out, but it is still alive with its syrops and sweets in the window. And there is a pâtisserie with its few sad cakes displayed. Most of the shutters are tight closed over the white façades, like eyelids on the faces of the dead ; but here and there a weary house has its mattresses up-ended in its ground-floor windows, showing that a tenacious proprietor still keeps his home there in hope and fear.

Yes, but this must be the last of the living villages. Now we are well within the ' effective beaten zone ' of the enemy's guns ; and the Colonel halts us on the quiet road ; and orders come down from voice to voice that we are to march in smaller groups.

' Fifty yards between platoons.'

' Fifty yards,' echoes my Company Sergeant-Major in a voice louder than any other. He has materialized out of the dusk, an enthusiastic apparition, and is barking up and down the column in support of the officer class. ' No, wait for it ! Wait for it ! Right. By the right.'

On again through the last of the light. I wait to see that my platoons are keeping their distances and then go back to my lonely place, now more completely isolated than ever, in front of No. 9 Platoon. The landscape is even flatter now, with a far-stretching view like a prairie : damp, reedy marches with sparse greenwood and a few lone trees. And yet we come upon a red-roofed farmhouse which is a hospital or C.C.S., and at its gate, waiting, shoulder to shoulder on their stretchers, lie three human shapes sewn up in blankets with labels above their breasts. They are awaiting conveyance in G.S. wagon or ambulance to their last rest billet. Shall we to-morrow be as they, cloaked for travel, and waiting ? And this be all ? ' Come, my coach ; good night, sweet ladies.' A man in the ranks ahead, his attention drawn to them, tries to amuse us with the lament, ' What did I join the Army for ? ' but his song is not a success ; it is, in fact, a chilling failure, and he lets it dwindle into a silence broken only by the metronome beat, beat, beat of our army boots.

§

Dark now, and the front comes brilliantly alive before us along the hem of the night.   As a drawn bow bends at the point of the shaft, so the front sweeps in an arc round the end of our long, straight road : an arc of flashes and flares, of sullen thunder and muttering small-arm fire.   There it is, scintillating, quarrelling, moaning ; and this must mean we are near the end of our march and can rest soon.   As the darkness thickens the Verey lights curve up from the arc and hang and sink ; and their pallid and transient glare appears to silhouette a dark and tossed skyline which we conceive to be the foremost rampart of the enemy.

'Halt ! Spread out farther.   A hundred yards between each platoon.   And no talking.   No talking anywhere.'

'Shush !   Things are getting dangerous.'

'Silence, I said ! ' roars the Company Sergeant-Major.   'Shut your traps, all of you.   J'ear what I said?   Not another word.'

A command little needed ; most of the men fell silent long since ; I, too, marching mechanically in my solitary place with my stick and gloves.   The thoughts that drag down my head in unmilitary fashion (but who shall see me in the dark ?) are oddly conflicting, as always in my life.   First among them is the query, ' Finished for ever one year ago ?   It cannot be.   We must be going to find each other again.   It must have meant something, that love.   She exists somewhere—somewhere on the other side of those flames and guns.   I am coming, Gentle. To-morrow, perhaps.   Be there, oh, please be there.'   But— but do I believe we shall meet again ?   I don't know.   I don't think I do.   Love is a trick, I suspect, and if so, well, let's die, too, for life is an insult.   Dreams of childhood, and of the old house, and of spring-time in Oxford, play themselves out against the incidental music of the guns and the ceaseless patter of our boots ; phantoms march at my side.   I think how my men account me fearless in the trenches or on a raid, and admire me for it ; but it is only that I am indifferent to death ; it is only that I stroll with my stick in No-Man's-Land, detached from fear, because in my mind is a hope, like an ecstasy, that Gentle may be on the other side of death.   And, marching on through the dark towards the coruscating battle-line, I tell myself, with some complacency, that I have provided for all my family and can honourably go, if only I can find a flying bullet—but—*but* is not this the same self-seeking love that snatches things to which it has no right : silver coins once, then

Iris, then Gentle, and now the sweetness of a bullet? Have
I any more right to death in No-Man's Land than to Gentle in
that grey lodging-house room? I hear Henrietta quoting old
Omar's monody, ' " And if the Wine you drink, the Lip you
press End in the Nothing all things end in . . ." ' and I answer
Yes. Yes, I agree with him; I accept his philosophy : take
your pleasure while you may, and when it has no savour for
you any more, why, then, care not in this clay carcase to abide.
But do I really believe that the universe in which we find ourselves is empty of all purpose and meaning, and that all our
human hopes are but a mirage in the dust of a desert? Aye,
I do ! Since I have been out here discharging my part in this
utter animal silliness and ferocity of war I have cast away all
my hopes of human growth. Our human kind are hopeless
because unteachable. Sages and saints have wasted their
breath in vain. ' With them the Seed of Wisdom did I sow,
And with my own hand laboured it to grow : And this was
all the Harvest that I reaped. . . .' Yes, Omar said the only
words for me, and Henrietta simpered as she quoted them, not
caring what they meant. As I said to Gentle (and, remembering it, I take pride in the phrase), ' This war is the bankruptcy
of all my dreams.' But wait—hold—does not the old surging
something leap up in me to deny it? To bid me hope ever?
Do I not feel Gentle hanging on my arm with both hands, and
hear her saying, ' I don't agree. It only means that there never
was such a time when it was so necessary to keep them alive.'
But, away with that memory and that thought. I don't want
to think it. I don't want to believe her right. I cannot go
back again to that heavy, intractable, unrewarding task. No ;
I look instead at that flashing and drumming arc and give
myself up to the thought—the thought which fills me with a warm
sweet glow—that to-morrow, perhaps—the wonder of it !—I shall
find Gentle again. Gentle whom I had killed. Is it possible that
she can see me walking through the dark towards her ?

§

' Halt.'
The leading company is turning off the road into what seems
an orchard or little wood. There are huts among the trees.
Then this is where we rest for the night—or for the first part of
it. Good ; good indeed ; for we are very tired.
' Forward. Lead on, men.'
Now our company is turning on to a track of clinkers and
rubble between the trees, and an old grey officer with a lantern

directs it to our assignment of huts. My men toss off their
equipment and throw themselves wearily down on the hard
boards.   I see them disposed as comfortably as may be, look to
their meal, and then walk to the single hut in which all the
company officers are housed.   Finding that my batman has
made a bed for me on the floor, I step out again into the dark
and look through the pillars of the trees at the shimmer and
fulguration of the Front.   And as I stand there watching the
nervous star-shells I feel a figure approaching.   It is Ronnie
Francis.   By the light fanning out from the hut door I see that
he has brushed and straightened his uniform after the march,
and damped and parted his abundant and springy boyish hair.
He is smiling at me with a smile half grim, half impudent.
   ' What's the latest, sir ? '
   ' Nothing new, Ronnie.'
   ' When's it to be ? '
   ' It ? '
   ' Yes, sir.'   He grins again.
   ' To-morrow, I think, Ronnie.'
   ' And the time ? '
   ' Dawn.'
   ' Fine !   Hurray !   I'm looking forward to it.'
   A throe of pity for him grips at my heart.   That such a
splendour of young promise, such a surge of new, eager life,
should be perhaps annulled to-morrow seems so base and idiotic
a thing that for the moment I feel I am ready to fall instead
if it will save him : ' I've had my thirty-four years.   God preserve him.   It is not right.   It is not right.'   And this upswell
of affection for him, there in the covering dark, swings my
thoughts between opposite poles : at one moment I am more
hopeless than ever about our human progress and decline any
more to lay my shoulder to it ; at another I feel such a love
for an invisible multitude who are duplicates of Ronnie that
I have a mind to survive and get home and fight for them all
from my little headquarters in Henrietta Street.   And there are
moments when the second of these thoughts seems the stronger.
   This much did 2nd Lieut. Francis put into my hand to take
with me into the battle.
   I grin down at him : he is not so tall as I.   ' Looking forward
to it, are you ?   Quite sure ? '
   ' Yes, rather !   Yes, I think so.   I've never been over the top
before.   Have you ? '
   ' Only on wiring parties and raids.   And not so many of them.'
   ' The men say you're wonderful on a raid.   They say you
direct operations with your walking stick as if you were showing

your gardeners where the tennis lawn would be, and where you'd like the herbaceous border. They say you never turn a hair.'

'Which is balderdash.' Actually I use a stronger word. 'The men are romantics, one and all, and talk only in superlatives, bad or good. I can be just as frightened as anybody.'

'I've never been on a raid. Been out wiring and patrolling, that's all.'

'I know you haven't. I've seen to that.' It is pleasant to hint like this at an affection that must not be spoken. 'Raids at your time of life? Rubbish.'

'But why? If I may say so, sir, if it's not a remark prejudicial to good order and discipline, I don't think you ought to have stopped me.'

'Don't you now? Is that so?' I feel a little like General Allan Mourne quizzing his young son, Doric. 'Well, look here, Ronnie: when this war's over, you're going to tell me your real age.'

'I'll tell you now. It's nineteen and a half.' But his mouth, closing over the words, quivers. 'Nineteen and six months, sir. Honest to God.'

'When anyone begins saying, "Honest to God," I suspect he's lying.'

'Do you, sir?'

'Yes. Nineteen and a half—just old enough to be out here: that's what you say, is it?'

'Certainly, sir. That's what I say.'

'I've been a bit of a liar myself, Ronnie, in my time.'

'Have you, sir? I can't imagine *you* telling lies.'

'Shows that you're still very callow. I too have been young, you know.'

'Yes, sir, but—hell!—excuse me, sir—you won't stop me going over to-morrow?'

'I would if I could, like a shot. But I've no choice, old man.'

'And thank God for that. I wouldn't miss this for anything. I think it'll be fun. Frightful fun.'

How far is he pretending eagerness to comfort and encourage himself?

'I don't think it'll be too bad,' I say, to add to the comfort. 'There'll be a barrage in front of us all the way. And covering fire from the left. The bombardment should smash up the old Hun's machine-gun nests, and the covering fire keep his head down. Hallo, Sergeant-Major. Quiet enough, isn't it? Men comfortable?'

' Not too bad, sir.　A bit footsore, some of them.'

' They sound happy enough, singing and whistling.　Is that a band they've got ? '

' Kind of percussion band, sir.　A petrol can and some tins.'

' Well, get your own grub now, Sergeant-Major.'

' Yes, sir.　Good night, sir.'

' Good-night.'

' Good-night, Sergeant-Major,' says Ronnie, copying me, and as if he were the sergeant's senior in years as well as rank.

' Good-night to you, sir.'

' Yes, we have more guns than he has now, Ronnie—so the Colonel says.　He's had his *der Tag*, and it didn't quite come off ; now our *der Tag* begins.'

' But I thought all the guns were massing down south ? '

' Down South ? '

' Yes, sir.　For the Big Push there ? '

' Second Lieutenant Francis, in the name of Sanity, what are you talking about ? '

He doesn't answer, but gazes at me very knowingly.

' I know nothing about any show down south.'

' Then you must be the only person who doesn't, sir.　The Somme, sir.　In about three months' time——'

' Shut up, you little fool.'

' Sorry, sir.'

' I've a good mind to crime you for such talk.'　And as I say this, I feel a faint, very faint, reproduction of the pleasure that used to be mine when I pictured myself punishing Gentle. ' Consider yourself under close arrest.'

' Very good, sir.'

' No, I'll let you off this time.　But do remember, you little idiot : *Méfiez-vous !　Les oreilles enemies vous écoutent.*'

' Precisely, sir.　Every time.'

' O.K.　Well, let's go in and see if there's any grub.　I hope the mess sergeant has put up something good.'

He has indeed ; and when a remarkable meal of tinned salmon, bully rissoles, stewed figs and custard is over, I step out again to be alone for a little in the night air.　In the nearest hut the men are singing softly :

> Far, far from Ypres I long to be,
> Where German snipers can't snipe at me.
> Damp is my dug-out,
> Cold are my feet,
> Waiting for whizz-bangs
> To send me to sleep.

The tune is the tune of ' Sing me to sleep ' which Gentle and I used to sing in unison as we strolled arm in arm along the lanes. I look once more at the nervous front line : it keeps lighting up uneasily, as if lifting its eyebrows to glance at our camp. Two fidgety searchlights have sprung from its base and are fingering the sky and brushing the stars above our heads. I watch for a while ; then turn into our hut for a few hours of rest.

§

Single file ; and no noise ; no clink, if possible, from equipment or helmet or rifle. Whispered commands only ; and tread softly. The men obey willingly enough, for that arc of lights is very close now—too close—just at the end of our road ; and, except for the crack of a questing rifle or the prophylactic stammer of a machine-gun the night is so still that the shuffle of our boots is disturbingly audible. ' If he begins to shell take instant cover in this ditch at the side of the road.' But he does not shell : it is an hour before dawn, the quietest hour of the night. Our road, like a bridge, crosses a trench that has men in its firebays : a sentry with fixed bayonet and a man from a carrying party burdened with a case of something— ammunition, maybe, or rations, or bombs ; we have passed before we know. Very safe they seem down there, below the table of the earth, while we move along up here like a string of targets at a fair. Was that trench our firing line ? Are we then in No-Man's Land ? As far as we can see there are no communication trenches in the wet and battered wastes beside us ; nor a bush nor a tree ; only a grey undulation and a few water-filled shell-holes reflecting the sky like dew-ponds. ' Halt.'
' Captain Mourne, sir ? '
' That's me.'
' This way, please. I'm your guide.'
' Oh, I see. Right you are. Follow me, lads. See that they understand, Sergeant-Major. O.K., Guide.'
' Ready, sir ? '
' Sure.'
And this untroubled youth, a junior subaltern, not much older than Ronnie, leads us diagonally across a wilderness of mud and spongy grass to a shattered trench which was once, I suppose, a forward or cover trench but is now no more than a chain of ditches and cavities with a bedraggled parapet before them. In these troughs and fosses I hide my men, whispering the order, ' Fix bayonets—quietly, for Christ's sake ' ; and

adding for their comfort, ' It won't be long now '—if that is any comfort. Out of a past almost as dim as the night comes Father's voice, telling me what to do when the odds are against me : ' Fix bayonets and charge.' I select a place for myself in the centre where there is a broken fire-step from which I can leap when the moment comes. My officers know what to do when my whistle blows. But since an hour must slowly drain away before I sound that blast, I clamber out of my shallow dike and wander in the open, up and down my line, partly to hear and answer all queries, partly to see Ronnie and give him a last encouraging word, and partly to savour the haunted air and pore over the macabre furnishings of an old battlefield ; because these dead acres, as I remember, were on the north of Father's map, and bloodily contested in the Battle of Loos seven months ago.

It fascinates me, this reservoir of bygone emotions ; and I wander away from my line, in and out of the shell-holes, scanning its face by courtesy of the enemy's punctual star-shells and his inconstant and moody searchlights. Every piece of litter arrests my steps and speaks to me : a scrap of grey uniform, a rusty cartridge clip, a pink telegraph form, this drunken screw-stake, and the mad dancing wire that strays and loops across the field like the pencilled scrawl of an infant ; a scatter of one man's bones—white bones so soon ? and odd domestic things like a cracked enamel mug, a letter in German script, and a sodden sheet of the *Berliner Tageblatt* whose date is September 12th, ten days before the Battle of Loos. On an idling wind come a reek of lyddite and stray mortuary whiffs of rotting food or rotting men. One peculiarly brilliant star-shell forces me to stand as still as a tree-stump till it has sunk and died, and in the same brief time illuminates for me the whole malevolent landscape, gouged up and pocked and interspersed with silent tarns, like some grey-green sector on the lifeless moon.

Back to my place ; is not the darkness faintly thinning ? In the German lines, as always before the dawn stand-to, there is a new nervousness, a restlessness as of a sleeper awake. Stand-ing in my trench and looking eastward over the kneaded mud of No-Man's Land I see bullets pattering softly to earth like the first rain drops before a storm. I swerve from one that whines past my ear : an evil insect whose sting had been death. The machine-guns chatter to each other : when one jabbers like a parrot, another responds, and another ; till it sounds at times like a general causerie. A distant German gun is firing our way with no manifest aim ; its splinters sizz into the mud or kick a spark from the fragmented and mashed pavé, which was once

a peaceful fairway for the adventures of men. It is the continuation of the road we took yesterday and this morning, and
is as good a picture as the next of the shattered and sunken end
into which Man's road has run.

The grey along the east brightens ; the small-arm fire increases
like the crackle of thorns under a pot ; is the Hun standing-to
behind his parapet ? Has he a premonition of what is coming
to him ? Far behind his trench system I hear a rumble on the
roads and, once, the whinnying of a horse.

Before I can answer this question a single British shell deton-
ates with a flash in the very centre of our objective—like the
prick of a pencil—and like the tap of a conductor's baton too,
for now the bombardment opens. The bombardment is ahead
of the dawn. Our shells rip the grey air as though it were a
linen sheet ; and the linen shrieks as it is rent ; detonations
dance along the German line in a ballet of black clouds and
tan clouds which join hands and become a grey pall. And,
even as this monstrous ballet proceeds, the watery mists of dawn,
heedless of these alien and noisy trespassers, slowly and quietly
unwind their coils over the stretches of No-Man's Land, which,
after all, is their own home field. There is no relation, no
intercourse, only, as it were, a colour-bar, between these white
native mists and those dark contemptible intruders ; the mists
roll on with their backs to the invasion, deaf to it all ; nor do
they halt their quiet movement when a skeleton tree in the heart
of them bows to the earth with a crack that beats the guns.

What can live beneath such punishment ? Surely our guns,
making a threshing floor of the German's trench system, must be
beating their bodies from their souls like chaff. Maddened
lights are leaping along the German arc ; and there, and there
again, a thread of flame lets fall two green drifting jewels : it is
the Hun's S O S, and my men, momentarily exalted by the
spectacle and the drumming of the guns, cry out—cry out like
children with delight—' *Old Jerry's got the wind up ! He's fairly
got the breeze up !* '

' *Poor old Fritzy !* '

' *Keep your head down, Jerry, while we turn on the tap.*'

' *We're fairly on top of you now, I reckon. You got it coming to
you, chum, but you arst for it.*'

' Their machine guns can't live in this,' I shout to the men,
eager to strengthen them. ' It won't be too bad.'

So I say, but the blood races through my heart and there is
a creeping of my scalp as, with one foot on the fire-step, I watch
the dawn blow open like a rose in the sun's eye, behind those
black earth-spouts—spouts which, instead of white spray, send

their clouds of grey and yellow smoke sidling down the wind. The excitement and exaltation of my first battle are at war with my fear and doubt and self-distrust ; the pumping of my heart seems to have emptied all of my body below the diaphragm. I swallow my spittle ; I cough and clear my throat. I feel again and again for my revolver as a nervous speaker for his notes ; and my hand, fingering its butt, trembles. The watch on my wrist I consult unnecessarily often ; and sometimes, as I do so, the wrist convulsively quivers.

With the daylight and its meaning for them, the men have become very quiet too : each is alone with his doubts and his one hope. They grasp their rifles and look up at me with white faces, far too often, as I at my watch. My whistle is between my lips ; day is on their bayonets. Slowly, too slow for sight, the long hand of the watch shifts towards zero hour. Over to our right among the German trenches, the ground is humped a little behind the smoke : a low swelling or tumour ; no more. It is the Mound of St. Just. . . . 'Gentle, any minute now. What is a moment of agony if it's the door through which I get to you ? But do I really believe we shall meet ? I don't know, but I am coming to see. This fire-step is my first step on the way to you. And now the minute hand '—it is but one minute away—thirty seconds—fifteen—it is there. It touches the hour.

'Ready, boys ? '

'Yessir ! '

'O.K. Time, gentlemen, please.'

My whistle shrills.

'Wait.' With my stick extended I hold back the centre of my company while the first wave goes over on my right, Jack Ormerod leading. Good lads ! The second wave sweeps forward on my left, shouting and cheering ; Bill Clarke and Ronnie Francis in front, the latter leaping excitedly and waving his revolver above his head. Good lads—good lads again.

'Now. Come.'

With a leap from the fire-step I scramble up the parapet to be ahead of them. 'Spread out. Extend. Keep your distances.' Our guns have stopped ; perhaps to lengthen ranges for the lift. But not the German guns : their raging retaliation still pounds and pulps the earth behind us. God, if they shorten range ! All are thinking this, and we run the faster for the thought. 'Come on, come on ! ' I shout, as I sweep them forward with my stick. The viscid mud grapples at our boots, or it slides beneath our soles and nearly throws us. Bullets flay the sickly surface : his machine guns are traversing our extended line. Machine guns, and many of them. Then those wretched guns didn't perish in the bombardment. He must have sunk them deep while our shells beat upon his parapets, and now he has raised them again. Competent brute ; one who seldom makes mistakes and never smiles. He has everything spread for our entertainment now : bullets, bullets, bombs and shells. Men pitch forward and crumple up like punctured balloons— so abruptly is life's fine candle quenched. Oh God, if Thou art there, and if this is the end, forgive me all my many sins. Help Thou mine unbelief. ' Don't bunch. For the love of Allah, don't bunch.' Some of them are following me like scared sheep. Barbary sheep, Father ; a gathering of the Clan. ' Extend into line. Open out, but keep touch.' What is Father doing now ? And Iris and Hugh. The little boy is asleep in his bed, I know not where ; Iris lies in another's arms. ' Keep opened out. Keep level.' Mother, Con, and old Uncle Humphrey, I see them still asleep in the rooms I made for them. I look to my left-front. Ronnie still leads his platoon, waving his revolver like a flag and yelling and laughing. I look up : a lark is still there, hovering in his home sky, heedless of this monstrous episode below him.

We seem to be in the middle of No-Man's Land now, for here is wet, green grass : this is the ribbon which the guns of both sides have left in peace. The going is easier—but look out ! splinters delve and gash the green pelt. ' Get on, get on, for dear life's sake ; they've got the range of us now. Oh, leave him. Leave him, you fool. What are stretcher-bearers for ? We can't stop for everyone that's hit.' Mud again : we're getting near him. Wire—wire in the smoke but all smashed down—good work, gunners—wire ! then we've reached his first line. Over or through it somehow. Its barbed tendrils grab at and hold on to our clothes like the fingers of a recumbent beggar at a church door ; I feel my breeches and my tunic rip. To get through it at an easier place Ronnie and some of his men run nearer to me.

' Don't bunch, lads. Keep them spread out, Ronnie.'

' Yes, sir. Gosh, this is fun, isn't it ? '

The trench ! Ronnie shouts ' Hurray ! ' and leaps into it, heels together, like a boy into the deep end of a swimming bath.

' Into it, lads,' I shout, waving them on with my stick and gloves.

The fire-bay before me is a crumpled pudding and I leap over it like a greyhound. There were dead men in it, and one live one with hands upraised, begging mercy. I keep my eyes from bloody work, but hear the scream. Meanwhile, left and right, the trench is carried, as far as eye can see. ' On to the next line.

The next is our objective, boys. On and hold it. This is fine.'
Ronnie's voice echoes mine. ' On to the next, boys '—' boys '
from *him !*—' Hurray ! ' And like a keen centre-forward he
races in front of me and in front of his wings.

Mud—or rather mucilage—again, and a much broader stretch
to cross this time—hundreds of yards of it. And rapid fire from
the distant trench. More, they are firing at us from the flank.
Are A and B Companies held ? Are we—is my company in
the air ? No, the torn but advancing line extends on my right
as far as I can see. Good old A and B—though the weak vain
part of me would have liked C Company to be in front even if
its unsupported advance meant the loss of the battle. Bullets
whistle towards us from the rear. It's some machine gun
they've left unsilenced in a redoubt. God send some bombers
to deal with it. Meanwhile eyes front ; that's where our real
business lies. Only get there and do our work, and we shall
lie safe. We shall rest. Only a minute, a few seconds, more of
this and we can—a stifled scream on my left : Ronnie has
pitched on to his face like a diver whose foothold slipped. He
rolls on to his back in an agony.

At once I leave my place and run towards him, remembering
in the same instant a passionate rush from my duties in Henrietta
Street when I heard dark news of Gentle. ' Ronnie, are you
badly hurt ? Can I help you ? ' I arrive at his side and throw
myself down, for the bullets are flying. The blood gushes from
a hole in his throat.

' Ronnie, are you——'

' I've stopped one,' he splutters, with terror in his eyes. ' I've
stopped mine. Oh God . . . God . . . It does hurt so.' And
he tries to lift a hand to his throat, but lets it fall again. ' This
has finished me. . . . This is my packet. . . . Never mind.'

' Wait.' I feel for the field-dressing in the flap of my tunic.

' No—no—go on, sir—go on—I'm done for, I think. It can't
be helped. I—I don't mind.'

And with that word he closed his eyes on life and began to die.
I spoke again, I called his name, but he did not hear. His face
with its pallor and its blood was the face of a dying child.

I could feel nothing but despair. Lying there dying in the
beauty and grace of his youth, he seemed the picture of Man's
self-slaughter, a miracle wilfully undone, and therefore a last
lethal answer to all my faith and ideals. Faith and hope drained
away with the blood from his throat.

Oh, well, leave him. What are stretcher-bearers for ? I
suppose I must get on with my duty. I believed in this war
once. Can't remember why, but perhaps I was right then.

There were three loves then : Gentle, and my dream of Man's amendment, and England. The last remains. I care for England still ; and she is not going under to any howling Hun if I can help it. And there are my men ; I care for them, my company of grumbling, faithful men ; aye, that I do. My place is in front of them. I run to take it again ; I reach it ; I urge them onward with my stick, and in the same second strike the oven-blast and stinking breath of a shell-burst. Something white-hot scorches my right thigh with a kick that fells me flat. An agony rolls me over on to my back like Ronnie, while the stick and the gloves fly. And then I dare not move for pain.

A man is bending over me. ' Hurt, sir ? '

' Oh no,' I laugh, ' I'm loving it. Keep on. Keep going, you fool. What do I matter ? Get it, and hang on. Do you want to get killed too ? This is war, not a—tell them to get it and hold on and fortify.'

My head begins to swim ; the battlefield rotates ; and as I shut my eyes I know that I'm going to faint or die. Will Gentle be there ?—I wanted it before this pain. Is it possible we shall meet ? To think this is to light up, even in the heart of this pain, a faint glimmer of the old ecstasy. Somewhere a grim, jesting voice says, ' Napoo. Fini. *Capout* ' ; and I know he is speaking of me ; and another yells, ' The Captain's copped it. The O.C.'s hit. Any stretcher-bearers yet ? '

I open my eyes for the last time. ' To hell with stretcher-bearers. Are you mad ? Get on, all of you. Hold and fortify. Get it and consolidate . . . consolidate. . . .'

Which they did that day—good stubborn, trustworthy men of England's hewing—but I saw none of it. The rotating battlefield became a wheeling aureole of blue-green darkness— ' Gentle, is this It ? Shall I find you any moment now, oh my dear ? Have I made my way to you ? '—but the wheeling darkness roared ever louder and louder ; it enlarged ever faster and faster—' Oh, God, forgive me all '—then faded into the nothing that all things end in here.

CHAPTER VI

AND THAT is really all, I think, Roberta. My wound that day wrote ' Fini,' not to my life, as the jesting voice said, but to my service in the Line. The femur of my right leg was shattered by the splinter, and I have limped very slightly ever since.

They made me the Adjutant of a training battalion in England, and in this office I remained till the Armistice discharged me. But if our small preamble to the Battle of the Somme only disabled me, the great three-months battle itself extinguished for ever the lively, if often explosive, heart of Captain Robert MacShennan Drury, your 'father'. He was killed by another splinter in the third month while attending his wounded with laughter and a high heart in his Advanced Dressing Station behind the Thiepval Ridge. I make no doubt that, despite an occasional explosiveness, he was as popular with his men in their trenches and dug-outs as ever he was in the cottages and bar-parlours of Holm St. Martin, and that he died bravely, and their praises followed him.

All the rest is within your memory. You tell me that you remember the day, though you were but five years old at the time, when good Mrs. Bradford and I fetched you from the Chapter Mill, where your grandmother lay dying in the care of Mother and Con. Yes, you may just remember it, but you cannot know what it meant to me to gaze at you there in the train and to think that you were Gentle's flesh and were coming to me as my adopted child. You stared out of the window, longing to see London, whose chief interest and distinction for you just then lay in my reminder that it was ' the place where you were born : ' You asked if you could see from the train the Hospital of Our Lady of Good Counsel and any of the nuns ; I stared at you, telling myself many times with a triumph that was perhaps unworthy, ' She was mine once, and she and I alone produced this little child in whom we endure together.'

You may not remember how your grandfather welcomed you at the door in Queensberry Place with a most stately bow and, after his manner, escorted you to your room on the second floor, exhorting the maids, ' You will do everything, I know, for the comfort and happiness of Miss Drury. She is now the most important person in the house. I am nothing ; I am less than the least of you all ' ; but you will recall how, while he was still with us, he would play with you and tease you, and you, in your impudence, copying me, would call him, ' General.'

My old ideals and aims I found to be somewhat lamed and limping like myself, after the war ; but I put them to their tasks again, and we drove on. When they seemed a bit broken-winded I used one whip to hustle them on, and it was Gentle's, ' I don't agree. I think there never was such a time for them.' Thus, you see, I managed to add the old pressure of my love for your mother to the old pressure of my love for the dream and my love for England and an increasing love and pity for young people, as I grew older ; and with this blended force to drive my will, I was able in time to build up into a considerable establishment the first little House of Allan Mourne.

The hidden foundation of the House of Allan Mourne is a belief in the possibility of human progress. The times are not good for such a belief. It is very difficult to save that base from cracking. No, things are not made easy for us. It was not easy to give Hugh, who when he was old enough became my fine young partner and very good friend, to *his* war and to a death in the battlefield that was a little like the death of Ronnie Francis. But I try to maintain my belief as my first hero, Condorcet did, even when he was hiding from those who would execute him. Even then he wrote his essay on the progress of the human spirit. No, belief is too stout a word ; let me rather say, an obstinate trust. I surmise that things are not meant to be easy. We are required to know that evil is real and of great power ; and, before God, these last few years have shown this to us ! We are required to look the evil full in the face and endure a death of the spirit that we may rise again with our manhood remade ; else is our trust but an easy evasion, empty of truth. For some people the contrast between our human aspirations and the world in which we find ourselves is so searing a thing that they cite it in condemnation of the universe. It is not so for me. For me Man's obstinate aspiration is not the condemnation of the universe but its justification.

One last word. You have told me often, have you not, that I ought to marry again. *Tais toi, tais toi,* my child, *on n'aime qu'une fois* ; and since the events which are here set down for you, I have stayed within the serenity of tempered loves. Sometimes I am appalled that I can work and be happy for months together without one thought of Gentle, and that when I do think of her there is barely a trace of pain. And that at times I can hardly recall her face any more. But there is one thing which tells me the love only sleeps, and it is this : whenever I think of death (which one does rather too often as the marked year of seventy hurries towards one) the prospect or, if you will, the faint chance, of seeing her again fills me with an excitement, a hope, a kind of ecstasy which is no less now than on that delicate and misty morning, thirty-one years ago, when the guns were affronting the dawn, and I stood with one foot on the fire-step, very ready in my heart to go to her.

EX UMBRIS

ROBERTA, STANDING in the empty room, after doctor and nurse had gone, gazed down upon her dead father's face and lived through all these strange and hitherto unimagined scenes again. Because of her intense personal interest in them, and the avid attention she had given them, they were invested for her with a dreamlike vividness and a magic of romance, above anything that she'd read in words before. The face of her father was the face of Sir Theodore Allan Mourne, a quiet man of distinguished presence, highly regarded in his own province, the world of letters ; the manner which he had presented to her and to the world was one of a shy, sad, smiling gaiety ; and she meditated, poring over the fine countenance, now still and becalmed, upon the contrast between that reserved, studious, humorous manner and the dark shadows of muddle, sin, and anguish which he had hidden always on ' the far side of the moon.'

Most of all she remembered the scenes of childhood and early youth which had played themselves out within these very walls. And, thinking always of those two children, her father and her mother, she went from the room and wandered slowly about the house, now so hollow and silent. She walked contemplatively down the stairs on which they had played ; she stood in the hall where Doric would run to meet the General at the end of day ; she turned and looked at that garden door which still kept the red and orange panes of fifty years ago ; she ascended the stairs again and looked into her father's study, once the famous playroom ; and then went up to her own room which had once been Uncle Humphrey's and then her mother's, and where Gentle and Doric had lain so happily and guiltily together.

And so down again to that quiet face on the pillow and its mystery. Strange was the thought, very strange and happy, and not yet fully to be grasped : ' I am the fruit of it all ; I am all that is left of their love.'

And suddenly, thinking thus, she came upon an idea which eased, gladdened, and excited her heart. Oh, was it possible ; could it be done ? He had told her, when they were talking together last night, that she would find in a drawer of his desk, and attached to his will, a statement of his wishes regarding his burial. ' But don't look at it yet,' he had said with a rather

shamefaced smile. ' Wait till the time comes.' Was there anything in that statement to defeat her happy idea ? She hastened
down again to his study, unlocked the drawer, and found the will
in a sealed envelope with the statement clipped to it. It was but
a brief statement, quickly read. So ? Even when saying good-
bye at the door of death, he had been too shy, too ashamed, to
tell her of something he had done, thirty years since, in 1916,
when he came back from the war. The same idea which was
hers now had been his then ; he had anticipated it by thirty
years. When, all too seldom, she had visited her mother's
grave, she had always noticed that the plot on its left was still
unoccupied ; and her sudden idea had been to acquire that plot,
if possible, and lay him there ; and now she knew that it had
always been untenanted because he had bought it all those years
ago.

And she was glad that the thought should have come so strongly
into her mind before she'd seen it written on this paper—almost
as if it had come from him lying dead. She remembered how
last night he had spoken of a ' frail hope ' that he might find her
mother again after his death, and had asked her what she believed.
She had answered, ' My dear, I can only say the same as you ;
I cannot say I believe, only that I hope.' And he had answered,
smiling, ' Well, I suppose I shall know very soon now.' Still
holding the paper unawares, she went back to where he lay and,
looking down upon him again, thought with a small shake of the
head, ' Perhaps you know the answer now, my dear, and perhaps
you don't and never will, because there is none : I do not know
what I believe ; but at least you and my mother, whom I too
could have loved so well, shall lie side by side now, and the same
earth clasp you both.'